By What Authority?

By Robert Hugh Benson

PANTIANOS
CLASSICS

Published by Pantianos Classics

ISBN-13: 978-1979917278

First published in 1904

Contents

Part One

Chapter One - The Situation

To the casual Londoner who lounged, intolerant and impatient, at the blacksmith's door while a horse was shod, or a cracked spoke mended, Great Keynes seemed but a poor backwater of a place, compared with the rush of the Brighton road eight miles to the east from which he had turned off, or the whirling cauldron of London City, twenty miles to the north, towards which he was travelling.

The triangular green, with its stocks and horse-pond, overlooked by the grey benignant church-tower, seemed a tame exchange for seething Cheapside and the crowded ways about the Temple or Whitehall; and it was strange to think that the solemn-faced rustics who stared respectfully at the gorgeous stranger were of the same human race as the quick-eyed, voluble townsmen who chattered and laughed and grimaced over the news that came up daily from the Continent or the North, and was tossed to and fro, embroidered and discredited alternately, all day long.

And yet the great waves and movements that, rising in the hearts of kings and politicians, or in the sudden strokes of Divine Providence, swept over Europe and England, eventually always rippled up into this placid country village; and the lives of Master Musgrave, who had retired upon his earnings, and of old Martin, who cobbled the ploughmen's shoes, were definitely affected and changed by the plans of far-away Scottish gentlemen, and the hopes and fears of the inhabitants of South Europe. Through all the earlier part of Elizabeth's reign, the menace of the Spanish Empire brooded low on the southern horizon, and a responsive mutter of storm sounded now and again from the north, where Mary Stuart reigned over men's hearts, if not their homes; and lovers of secular England shook their heads and were silent as they thought of their tiny country, so rent with internal strife, and ringed with danger.

For Great Keynes, however, as for most English villages and towns at this time, secular affairs were so deeply and intricately interwoven with ecclesiastical matters that none dared decide on the one question without considering its relation to the other; and ecclesiastical affairs, too, touched them more personally than any other, since every religious change scored a record of itself presently within the church that was as familiar to them as their own cottages.

On none had the religious changes fallen with more severity than on the Maxwell family that lived in the Hall, at the upper and southern end of the green. Old Sir Nicholas, though his convictions had survived the tempest of unrest and trouble that had swept over England, and he had remained a convinced and a stubborn Catholic, yet his spiritual system was sore and inflamed within him. To his simple and obstinate soul it was an irritating puzzle as to how any man could pass from the old to a new faith, and he had been known to lay his whip across the back of a servant who had professed a desire to try the new religion.

His wife, a stately lady, a few years younger than himself, did what she could to keep her lord quiet, and to save him from incurring by his indiscretion any further penalties beyond the enforced journeys before the Commission, and the fines inflicted on all who refused to attend their parish church. So the old man devoted himself to his estates and the further improvement of the house and gardens, and to the inculcation of sound religious principles into the minds of his two sons who were living at home with their parents; and strove to hold his tongue, and his hand, in public.

The elder of these two, Mr. James as he was commonly called, was rather a mysterious personage to the village, and to such neighbours as they had. He was often in town, and when at home, although extremely pleasant and courteous, never talked about himself and seemed to be only very moderately interested in the estate and the country-life generally. This, coupled with the fact that he would presumably succeed his father, gave rise to a good deal of gossip, and even some suspicion.

His younger brother Hubert was very different; passionately attached to sport and to outdoor occupations, a fearless rider, and in every way a kindly, frank lad of about eighteen years old. The fifth member of the family, Lady Maxwell's sister, Mistress Margaret Torridon, was a quiet-faced old lady, seldom seen abroad, and round whom, as round her eldest nephew, hung a certain air of mystery.

5

The difficulties of this Catholic family were considerable. Sir Nicholas' religious sympathies were, of course, wholly with the spiritual side of Spain, and all that that involved, while his intense love of England gave him a horror of the Southern Empire that the sturdiest patriot might have envied. And so with his attitude towards Mary Stuart and her French background. While his whole soul rose in loathing against the crime of Darnley's murder, to which many of her enemies proclaimed her accessory, it was kindled at the thought that in her or her child lately crowned as James VI. of Scotland, lay the hope of a future Catholic succession; and this religious sympathy was impassioned by the memory of an interview a few years ago, when he had kissed that gracious white hand, and looked into those alluring eyes, and, kneeling, stammered out in broken French his loyalty and his hopes. Whether it was by her devilish craft as her enemies said, or her serene and limpid innocence as her friends said, or by a maddening compound of the two, as later students have said—at least she had made the heart and confidence of old Sir Nicholas her own. But there were troubles more practical than these mental struggles; it was a misery, beyond describing, to this old man and his wife to see the church, where once they had worshipped and received the sacraments, given over to what was, in their opinion, a novel heresy, and the charge of a schismatic minister. There, in the Maxwell chapel within, lay the bones of their Catholic ancestors; and there they had knelt to adore and receive their Saviour; and now for them all was gone, and the light was gone out in the temple of the Lord. In the days of the previous Rector matters were not so desperate; it had been their custom to receive from his hands at the altar-rail of the Church hosts previously consecrated at the Rectory; for the incumbent had been an old Marian priest who had not scrupled so to relieve his Catholic sheep of the burden of recusancy, while he fed his Protestant charges with bread and wine from the Communion table. But now all that was past, and the entire family was compelled year by year to slip off into Hampshire shortly before Easter for their annual duties, and the parish church that their forefathers had built, endowed and decorated, knew them no more.

But the present Rector, the Reverend George Dent, was far from a bigot; and the Papists were more fortunate than perhaps, in their bitterness, they recognised; for the minister was one of the rising Anglican school, then strange and unfamiliar, but which has now established itself as the main representative section of the Church of England. He welcomed the effect but not the rise of the Reformation, and rejoiced that the incrustations of error had been removed from the lantern of the faith. But he no less sincerely deplored the fanaticism of the Puritan and Genevan faction. He exulted to see England with a church truly her own at last, adapted to her character, and freed from the avarice and tyranny of a foreign despot who had assumed prerogatives to which he had no right. But he reverenced the Episcopate, he wore the prescribed dress, he used the thick singing-cakes for the Communion, and he longed for the time when nation and Church should again be one; when the nation should worship through a Church of her own shaping, and the Church share the glory and influence of her lusty partner and patron.

But Mrs. Dent had little sympathy with her husband's views; she had assimilated the fiery doctrines of the Genevan refugees, and to her mind her husband was balancing himself to the loss of all dignity and consistency in an untenable position between the Popish priesthood on the one side and the Gospel ministry on the other. It was an unbearable thought to her that through her husband's weak disposition and principles his chief parishioners should continue to live within a stone's throw of the Rectory in an assured position of honour, and in personal friendliness to a minister whose ecclesiastical status and claims they disregarded. The Rector's position then was difficult and trying, no less in his own house than elsewhere.

The third main family in the village was that of the Norrises, who lived in the Dower House, that stood in its own grounds and gardens a few hundred yards to the north-west of the village green. The house had originally been part of the Hall estate; but it had been sold some fifty years before. The present owner, Mr. Henry Norris, a widower, lived there with his two children, Isabel and Anthony, and did his best to bring them up in his own religious principles. He was a devout and cultivated Puritan, who had been affected by the New Learning in his youth, and had conformed joyfully to the religious changes that took place in Edward's reign. He had suffered both anxiety and hardships in Mary's reign, when he had travelled abroad in the Protestant countries, and made the acquaintance of many of the foreign reformers—Beza, Calvin, and even the great Melancthon himself. It was at this time, too, that he had lost his wife. It had been a great joy to him to hear of the accession of Elizabeth, and the re-establishment of a religion that was sincerely his own; and he had returned immediately to England with his two little children, and settled down once more at the Dower House. Here his whole time that he could spare from his children was divided between prayer and the writing of a book on the Eucharist; and as his children grew up he more and more retired into himself and silence and communing with God, and devoted himself to his book. It was beginning to be a great happiness to him to find that his daughter Isabel, now about seventeen years old, was growing up into active sympathy with his principles, and that the passion of her soul, as of his, was a tender deep-lying faith towards God, which could exist independently of outward symbols and ceremonies. But unlike others of his school he was happy too to notice and encourage friendly relations between Lady Maxwell and his daughter, since he recognised the sincere and loving spirit of the old lady beneath her superstitions, and knew very well that her friendship would do for the girl what his own love could not.

The other passion of Isabel's life at present lay in her brother Anthony, who was about three years younger than herself, and who was just now more interested in his falcons and pony than in all the religious systems and human relationships in the world, except perhaps in his friendship for Hubert, who besides being three or four years older than himself, cared for the same things.

And so relations between the Hall and the Dower House were all that they should be, and the path that ran through the gardens of the one and the yew hedge and orchard of the other was almost as well trodden as if all still formed one estate.

As for the village itself, it was exceedingly difficult to gauge accurately the theological atmosphere. The Rector despaired of doing so. It was true that at Easter the entire population, except the Maxwells and their dependents, received communion in the parish church, or at least professed their willingness and intention to do so unless prevented by some accident of the preceding week; but it was impossible to be blind to the fact that many of the old beliefs lingered on, and that there was little enthusiasm for the new system. Rumours broke out now and again that the Catholics were rising in the north; that Elizabeth contemplated a Spanish or French marriage with a return to the old religion; that Mary Stuart would yet come to the throne; and with each such report there came occasionally a burst of joy in unsuspected quarters. Old Martin, for example, had been overheard, so a zealous neighbour reported, blessing Our Lady aloud for her mercies when a passing traveller had insisted that a religious league was in progress of formation between France and Spain, and that it was only a question of months as to when mass should be said again in every village church; but then on the following Sunday the cobbler's voice had been louder than all in the metrical psalm, and on the Monday he had paid a morning visit to the Rectory to satisfy himself on the doctrine of Justification, and had gone again, praising God and not Our Lady, for the godly advice received.

But again, three years back, just before Mr. Dent had come to the place, there had been a solemn burning on the village-green of all such muniments of superstition as had not been previously hidden by the priest and Sir Nicholas; and in the rejoicings that accompanied this return to pure religion practically the whole agricultural population had joined. Some Justices had ridden over from East Grinsted to direct this rustic reformation, and had reported favourably to the new Rector on his arrival of the zeal of his flock. The great Rood, they told him, with SS. Mary and John, four great massy angels, the statue of St. Christopher, the Vernacle, a brocade set of mass vestments and a purple cope, had perished in the flames, and there had been no lack of hands to carry faggots; and now the Rector found it difficult to reconcile the zeal of his parishioners (which indeed he privately regretted) with the sudden and unexpected lapses into superstition, such as was Mr. Martin's gratitude to Our Lady, and others of which he had had experience.

As regards the secular politics of the outside world, Great Keynes took but little interest. It was far more a matter of concern whether mass or morning prayer was performed on Sunday, than whether a German bridegroom could be found for Elizabeth, or whether she would marry the Duke of Anjou; and more important than either were the infinitesimal details of domestic life. Whether Mary was guilty or not, whether her supporters were rising, whether the shadow of Spain chilled the hearts of men in London whose affair it was to look after such things; yet the cows must be milked, and the children washed, and the falcons fed; and it was these things that formed the foreground of life, whether the sky were stormy or sunlit.

And so, as the autumn of '69 crept over the woods in flame and russet, and the sound of the sickle was in folks' ears, the life at Great Keynes was far more tranquil than we should fancy who look back on those stirring days. The village, lying as it did out of the direct route between any larger towns, was not so much affected by the gallop of the couriers, or the slow creeping rumours from the Continent, as villages that lay on lines of frequent communication. So the simple life went on, and Isabel went about her business in Mrs. Carroll's still-room, and Anthony rode out with the harriers, and Sir Nicholas told his beads in his room—all with nearly as much serenity as if Scotland were fairyland and Spain a dream.

Chapter Two - The Hall and The House

Anthony Norris, who was now about fourteen, went up to King's College, Cambridge, in October. He was closeted long with his father the night before he left, and received from him much sound religious advice and exhortation; and in the morning, after an almost broken-hearted good-bye from Isabel, he rode out with his servant following on another horse and leading a packhorse on the saddle of which the falcons swayed and staggered, and up the curving drive that led round into the village green. He was a good-hearted and wholesome-minded boy, and left a real ache behind him in the Dower House.

Isabel indeed ran up to his room, after she had seen his feathered cap disappear at a trot through the gate, leaving her father in the hall; and after shutting and latching the door, threw herself on his bed, and sobbed her heart out. They had never been long separated before. For the last three years he had gone over to the Rectory morning by morning to be instructed by Mr. Dent; but now, although he would never make a great scholar, his father thought it well to send him up to Cambridge for two or three years, that he might learn to find his own level in the world. Anthony himself was eager to go. If the truth must be told, he fretted a little against the restraints of even such a moderate Puritan household as that of his father's. It was a considerable weariness to Anthony to kneel in the hall on a fresh morning while his father read, even though with fervour and sincerity, long extracts from "Christian Prayers and Holy Meditations," collected by the Reverend Henry Bull, when the real world, as Anthony knew it, laughed and rippled and twinkled outside in the humming summer air of the lawn and orchard; or to have to listen to godly discourses, however edifying to elder persons, just at the time when the ghost-moth was beginning to glimmer in the dusk, and the heavy trout to suck down his supper in the glooming pool in the meadow below the house.

His very sports, too, which his father definitely encouraged, were obviously displeasing to the grave divines who haunted the house so often from Saturday to Monday, and spoke of high doctrinal matters at meal-times, when, so Anthony thought, lighter subjects should prevail. They were not interested in his horse, and Anthony never felt quite the same again towards one good minister who in a moment of severity called Eliza, the glorious peregrine that sat on the boy's wrist and shook her bells, a "vanity." And so Anthony trotted off happy enough on his way to Cambridge, of which he had heard much from Mr. Dent; and where, although there too were divines and theology, there were boys as well who acted plays, hunted with the hounds, and did not call high-bred hawks "vanities."

Isabel was very different. While Anthony was cheerful and active like his mother who had died in giving him life, she, on the other hand, was quiet and deep like her father. She was growing up, if not into actual beauty, at least into grace and dignity: but there were some who thought her beautiful. She was pale with dark hair, and the great grey eyes of her father; and she loved and lived in Anthony from the very difference between them. She frankly could not understand the attraction of sport, and the things that pleased her brother; she was afraid of the hawks, and liked to stroke a horse and kiss his soft nose better than to ride him. But, after all, Anthony liked to watch the towering bird, and to hear and indeed increase the thunder of the hoofs across the meadows behind the stomping hawk; and so she did her best to like them too; and she was often torn two ways by her sympathy for the partridge on the one hand, as it sped low and swift across the standing corn with that dread shadow following, and her desire, on the other hand, that Anthony should not be disappointed.

But in the deeper things of the spirit, too, there was a wide difference between them. As Anthony fidgeted and sighed through his chair-back morning and evening, Isabel's soul soared up to God on the wings of those sounding phrases. She had inherited all her father's tender piety, and lived, like him, on the most intimate terms with the spiritual world. And though, of course, by training she was Puritan, by character she was Puritan too. As a girl of fourteen she had gone with Anthony to see the cleansing of the village temple. They had stood together at the west end of the church a little timid at the sight of that noisy crowd in the quiet house of prayer; but she had felt no disapproval at that fierce vindication of truth. Her father had taught her of course that the purest worship was that which was only spiritual; and while since childhood she had seen Sunday by Sunday the Great Rood overhead, she had never paid it any but artistic attention. The men had the ropes round it now, and it was swaying violently to and fro; and then, even as the children watched, a tie had given, and the great cross with its pathetic wide-armed figure had toppled forward towards the nave, and then crashed down on the pavement. A fanatic ran out and furiously kicked the thorn-crowned head twice, splintering the hair and the features, and cried out on it as an idol; and yet Isabel, with all her tenderness, felt nothing more than a vague regret that a piece of carving so ancient and so delicate should be broken.

But when the work was over, and the crowd and Anthony with them had stamped out, directed by the justices, dragging the figures and the old vestments with them to the green, she had seen something which touched her heart much more. She passed up alone under the screen, which they had spared, to see what had been done in the chancel; and as she went she heard a sobbing from the corner near the priest's door; and there, crouched forward on his face, crying and moaning quietly, was the old priest who had been rector of the church for nearly twenty years. He had somehow held on in Edward's time in spite of difficulties; had thanked God and the Court of Heaven with a full heart for the accession of Mary; had prayed and deprecated the divine wrath at the return of the Protestant religion with Elizabeth; but yet had somehow managed to keep the old faith alight for eight years more, sometimes evading, sometimes resisting, and sometimes conforming to the march of events, in hopes of better days. But now the blow had fallen, and the old man, too ill-instructed to hear the accents of new truth in the shouting of that noisy crowd and the crash of his images, was on his knees before the altar where he had daily offered the holy sacrifice through all those troublous years, faithful to what he believed to be God's truth, now bewailing and moaning the horrors of that day, and, it is to be feared, unchristianly calling down the vengeance of God upon his faithless flock. This shocked and touched Isabel far more than the destruction of the images; and she went forward timidly and said something; but the old man turned on her a face of such misery and anger that she had run straight out of the church, and joined Anthony as he danced on the green.

On the following Sunday the old priest was not there, and a fervent young minister from London had taken his place, and preached a stirring sermon on the life and times of Josiah; and Isabel had thanked God on her knees after the sermon for that He had once more vindicated His awful Name and cleansed His House for a pure worship.

But the very centre of Isabel's religion was the love of the Saviour. The Puritans of those early days were very far from holding a negative or colourless faith. Not only was their belief delicately dogmatic to excess; but it all centred round the Person of the Lord Jesus Christ. And Isabel had drunk in this faith from her father's lips, and from devotional books which he gave her, as far back as she could remember anything. Her love for the Saviour was even romantic and passionate. It seemed to her that He was as much a part of her life, and of her actual experience, as Anthony or her father. Certain places in the lanes about, and certain spots in the garden, were sacred and fragrant to her because her Lord had met her there. It was indeed a trouble to her sometimes that she loved Anthony so much; and to her mind it was a less worthy kind of love altogether; it was kindled and quickened by such little external details, by the sight of his boyish hand brown with the sun, and scarred by small sporting accidents, such as the stroke of his bird's beak or talons, or by the very outline of the pillow where his curly head had rested only an hour or two ago. Whereas her love for Christ was a deep and solemn passion that seemed to well not out of His comeliness or even His marred Face or pierced Hands, but out of His wide encompassing love that sustained and clasped her at every moment of her conscious attention to Him, and that woke her soul to ecstasy at moments of high communion. These two loves, then, one so earthly, one so heavenly, but both so sweet, every now and then seemed to her to be in slight conflict in her heart. And lately a third seemed to be rising up out of the plane of sober and quiet affections such as she felt for her father, and still further complicating the apparently encountering claims of love to God and man.

Isabel grew quieter in a few minutes and lay still, following Anthony with her imagination along the lane that led to the London road, and then presently she heard her father calling, and went to the door to listen.

"Isabel," he said, "come down. Hubert is in the hall."

She called out that she would be down in a moment; and then going across to her own room she washed her face and came downstairs. There was a tall, pleasant-faced lad of about her own age standing near the open door that led into the garden; and he came forward nervously as she entered.

"I came back last night, Mistress Isabel," he said, "and heard that Anthony was going this morning: but I am afraid I am too late."

She told him that Anthony had just gone.

"Yes," he said, "I came to say good-bye; but I came by the orchard, and so we missed one another."

Isabel asked a word or two about his visit to the North, and they talked for a few minutes about a rumour that Hubert had heard of a rising on behalf of Mary: but Hubert was shy and constrained, and Isabel was still a little tremulous. At last he said he must be going, and then suddenly remembered a message from his mother.

"Ah!" he said, "I was forgetting. My mother wants you to come up this evening, if you have time. Father is away, and my aunt is unwell and is upstairs."

Isabel promised she would come.

"Father is at Chichester," went on Hubert, "before the Commission, but we do not expect him back till to-morrow."

A shadow passed across Isabel's face. "I am sorry," she said.

The fact was that Sir Nicholas had again been summoned for recusancy. It was an expensive matter to refuse to attend church, and Sir Nicholas probably paid not less than £200 or £300 a year for the privilege of worshipping as his conscience bade.

In the evening Isabel asked her father's leave to be absent after supper, and then drawing on her hood, walked across in the dusk to the Hall. Hubert was waiting for her at the boundary door between the two properties.

"Father has come back," he said, "but my mother wants you still." They went on together, passed round the cloister wing to the south of the house: the bell turret over the inner hall and the crowded roofs stood up against the stars, as they came up the curving flight of shallow steps from the garden to the tall doorway that led into the hall.

It was a pleasant, wide, high room, panelled with fresh oak, and hung with a little old tapestry here and there, and a few portraits. A staircase rose out of it to the upper story. It had a fret-ceiling, with flower-de-luce and rose pendants, and on the walls between the tapestries hung a few antlers and pieces of armour, morions and breast-plates, with a pair of pikes or halberds here and there. A fire had been lighted in the great hearth as the evenings were chilly; and Sir Nicholas was standing before it, still in his riding-dress, pouring out resentment and fury to his wife, who sat in a tall chair at her embroidery. She turned silently and held out a hand to Isabel, who came and stood beside her, while Hubert went and sat down near his father. Sir Nicholas scarcely seemed to notice their entrance, beyond glancing up for a moment under his fierce white eyebrows; but went on growling out his wrath. He was a fine rosy man, with grey moustache and pointed beard, and a thick head of hair, and he held in his hand his flat riding cap, and his whip with which from time to time he cut at his boot.

"It was monstrous, I told the fellow, that a man should be haled from his home like this to pay a price for his conscience. The religion of my father and his father and all our fathers was good enough for me; and why in God's name should the Catholic have to pay who had never changed his faith, while every heretic went free? And then to that some stripling of a clerk told me that a religion that was good enough for the Queen's Grace should be good enough for her loyal subjects too; but my Lord silenced him quickly. And then I went at them again; and all my Lord would do was to nod his head and smile at me as if I were a child; and then he told me that it was a special Commission all for my sake, and Sir Arthur's, who was there too, my dear.... Well, well, the end was that I had to pay for their cursed religion."

"Sweetheart, sweetheart," said Lady Maxwell, glancing at Isabel.

"Well, I paid," went on Sir Nicholas, "but I showed them, thank God, what I was: for as we came out, Sir Arthur and I together, what should we see but another party coming in, pursuivant and all; and in the mid of them that priest who was with us last July.—Well, well, we'll leave his name alone—him that said he was a priest before them all in September; and I went down on my knees, thank God, and Sir Arthur went down on his, and we asked his blessing before them all, and he gave it us: and oh! my Lord was red and white with passion."

"That was not wise, sweetheart," said Lady Maxwell tranquilly, "the priest will have suffered for it afterwards."

"Well, well," grumbled Sir Nicholas, "a man cannot always think, but we showed them that Catholics were not ashamed of their religion—yes, and we got the blessing too."

"Well, but here is supper waiting," said my lady, "and Isabel, too, whom you have not spoken to yet."

Sir Nicholas paid no attention.

"Ah! but that was not all," he went on, savagely striking his boot again, "at the end of all who should I see but that—that—damned rogue—whom God reward!"—and he turned and spat into the fire—"Topcliffe. There he was, bowing to my Lord and the Commissioners. When I think of that man," he said, "when I think of that man—" and Sir Nicholas' kindly old passionate face grew pale and lowering with fury, and his eyebrows bent themselves forward, and his lower lip pushed itself out, and his hand closed tremblingly on his whip.

His wife laid down her embroidery and came to him.

"There, sweetheart," she said, taking his cap and whip. "Now sit down and have supper, and leave that man to God."

Sir Nicholas grew quiet again; and after a saying a word or two of apology to Isabel, left the room to wash before he sat down to supper.

"Mistress Isabel does not know who Topcliffe is," said Hubert.

"Hush, my son," said his mother, "your father does not like his name to be spoken."

Presently Sir Nicholas returned, and sat down to supper. Gradually his good nature returned, and he told them what he had seen in Chichester, and the talk he had heard. How it was reported to his lordship the Bishop that the old religion was still the religion of the people's hearts—how, for example, at Lindfield they had all the images and the altar furniture hidden underground, and at Battle, too; and that the mass could be set up again at a few hours' notice: and that the chalices had not been melted down into communion cups according to the orders issued, and so on. And that at West Grinsted, moreover, the Blessed Sacrament was there still—praise God—yes, and was going to remain there. He spoke freely before Isabel, and yet he remembered his courtesy too, and did not abuse the new-fangled religion, as he thought it, in her presence; or seek in any way to trouble her mind. If ever in an excess of anger he was carried away in his talk, his wife would always check him gently; and he would always respond and apologise to Isabel if he had transgressed good manners. In fact, he was just a fiery old man who could not change his religion even at the bidding of his monarch, and could not understand how what was right twenty years ago was wrong now.

Isabel herself listened with patience and tenderness, and awe too; because she loved and honoured this old man in spite of the darkness in which he still walked. He also told them in lower tones of a rumour that was persistent at Chichester that the Duke of Norfolk had been imprisoned by the Queen's orders, and was to be charged with treason; and that he was at present at Burnham, in Mr. Wentworth's house, under the guard of Sir Henry Neville. If this was true, as indeed it turned out to be later, it was another blow to the Catholic cause in England; but Sir Nicholas was of a sanguine mind, and pooh-poohed the whole affair even while he related it.

And so the evening passed in talk. When Sir Nicholas had finished supper, they all went upstairs to my lady's withdrawing-room on the first floor. This was always a strange and beautiful room to Isabel. It was panelled like the room below, but was more delicately furnished, and a tall harp stood near the window to which my lady sang sometimes in a sweet tremulous old voice, while Sir Nicholas nodded at the fire. Isabel, too, had had some lessons here from the old lady; but even this mild vanity troubled her puritan conscience a little sometimes. Then the room, too, had curious and attractive things in it. A high niche in the oak over the fireplace held a slender image of Mary and her Holy Child, and from the Child's fingers hung a pair of beads. Isabel had a strange sense sometimes as if this holy couple had taken refuge in that niche when they were driven from the church; but it seemed to her in her steadier moods that this was a superstitious fancy, and had the nature of sin.

This evening the old lady went to her harp, while Isabel sat down near her in the wide window seat and looked out over the dark lawn, where the white dial glimmered like a phantom, and thought of Anthony again. Sir Nicholas went and stretched himself before the fire, and closed his eyes, for he was old, and tired with his long ride; and Hubert sat down in a dark corner near him whence he could watch Isabel. After a few rippling chords my lady began to sing a song by Sir Thomas Wyatt, whom she and Sir Nicholas had known in their youth; and which she had caused to be set to music by some foreign chapel master. It was a sorrowful little song, with the title, "He seeketh comfort in patience," and possibly she chose it on purpose for this evening.

"Patience! for I have wrong,
And dare not shew wherein;
Patience shall be my song;
Since truth can nothing win.
Patience then for this fit;
Hereafter comes not yet."

While she sang, she thought no doubt of the foolish brave courtier who lacked patience in spite of his singing, and lost his head for it; her voice shook once or twice: and old Sir Nicholas shook his drowsy head when she had finished, and said "God rest him," and then fell fast asleep.

Then he presently awoke as the others talked in whispers, and joined in too: and they talked of Anthony, and what he would find at Cambridge; and of Alderman Marrett, and his house off Cheapside, where Anthony would lie that night; and of such small and tranquil topics, and left fiercer questions alone. And so the evening came to an end; and Isabel said good-night, and went downstairs with Hubert, and out into the garden again.

"I am sorry that Sir Nicholas has been so troubled," she said to Hubert, as they turned the corner of the house together. "Why cannot we leave one another alone, and each worship God as we think fit?"

Hubert smiled in the darkness to himself.

"I am afraid Queen Mary did not think it could be done, either," he said. "But then, Mistress Isabel," he went on, "I am glad that you feel that religion should not divide people."

"Surely not," she said, "so long as they love God."

"Then you think—" began Hubert, and then stopped. Isabel turned to him.

"Yes?" she asked.

"Nothing," said Hubert.

They had reached the door in the boundary wall by now, and Isabel would not let him come further with her and bade him good-night. But Hubert still stood, with his hand on the door, and watched the white figure fade into the dusk, and listened to the faint rustle of her skirt over the dry leaves; and then, when he heard at last the door of the Dower House open and close, he sighed to himself and went home.

Isabel heard her father call from his room as she passed through the hall; and went in to him as he sat at his table in his furred gown, with his books about him, to bid him good-night and receive his blessing. He lifted his hand for a moment to finish the sentence he was writing, and she stood watching the quill move and pause and move again over the paper, in the candlelight, until he laid the pen down, and rose and stood with his back to the fire, smiling down at her. He was a tall, slender man, surprisingly upright for his age, with a delicate, bearded, scholar's face; the little plain ruff round his neck helped to emphasise the fine sensitiveness of his features; and the hands which he stretched out to his daughter were thin and veined.

"Well, my daughter," he said, looking down at her with his kindly grey eyes so like her own, and holding her hands.

"Have you had a good evening, sir?" she asked.

He nodded briskly.

"And you, child?" he asked.

"Yes, sir," she said, smiling up at him.

"And was Sir Nicholas there?"

She told him what had passed, and how Sir Nicholas had been fined again for his recusancy; and how Lady Maxwell had sung one of Sir Thomas Wyatt's songs.

"And was no one else there?" he asked.

"Yes, father, Hubert."

"Ah! And did Hubert come home with you?"

"Only as far as the gate, father. I would not let him come further."

Her father said nothing, but still looked steadily down into her eyes for a moment, and then turned and looked away from her into the fire.

"You must take care," he said gently. "Remember he is a Papist, born and bred; and that he has a heart to be broken too."

She felt herself steadily flushing; and as he turned again towards her, dropped her eyes.

"You will be prudent and tender, I know," he added. "I trust you wholly, Isabel."

Then he kissed her on the forehead and laid his hand on her head, and looked up, as the Puritan manner was.

"May the God of grace bless you, my daughter; and make you faithful to the end." And then he looked into her eyes again, smiled and nodded; and she went out, leaving him standing there.

Mr. Norris had begun to fear that the boy loved Isabel, but as yet he did not know whether Isabel understood it or even was aware of it. The marriage difficulties of Catholics and Protestants were scarcely yet existing; and certainly there was no formulated rule of dealing with them. Changes of religion were so frequent in those days that difficulties, when they did arise, easily adjusted themselves. It was considered, for example, by politicians quite possible at one time that the Duke of Anjou should conform to the Church of England for the sake of marrying the Queen: or that he should attend public services with her, and at the same time have mass and the sacraments in his own private chapel. Or again, it was open to question whether England as a whole would not return to the old religion, and Catholicism be the only tolerated faith.

But to really religious minds such solutions would not do. It would have been an intolerable thought to this sincere Puritan, with all his tolerance, that his daughter should marry a Catholic; such an arrangement would mean either that she was indifferent to vital religion, or that she was married to a man whose creed she was bound to abhor and anathematise: and however willing Mr. Norris might be to meet Papists on terms of social friendliness, and however much he might respect their personal characters, yet the thought that the life of any one dear to him should be irretrievably bound up with all that the Catholic creed involved, was simply an impossible one.

Besides all this he had no great opinion of Hubert. He thought he detected in him a carelessness and want of principle that would make him hesitate to trust his daughter to him, even if the insuperable barrier of religion were surmounted. Mr. Norris liked a man to be consistent and zealous for his creed, even if that creed were dark and superstitious—and this zeal seemed to him lamentably lacking in Hubert. More than once he had heard the boy speak of his father with an air of easy indulgence, that his own opinion interpreted as contempt.

"I believe my father thinks," he had once said, "that every penny he pays in fines goes to swell the accidental glory of God."

And Hubert had been considerably startled and distressed when the elder man had told him to hold his tongue unless he could speak respectfully of one to whom he owed nothing but love and honour. This had happened, however, more than a year ago; and Hubert had forgotten it, no doubt, even if Mr. Norris had not.

And as for Isabel.

It is exceedingly difficult to say quite what place Hubert occupied in her mind. She certainly did not know herself much more than that she liked the boy to be near her; to hear his footsteps coming along the path from the Hall. This morning when her father had called up to her that Hubert was come, it was not so hard to dry her tears for Anthony's departure. The clouds had parted a little when she came and found this tall lad smiling shyly at her in the hall. As she had sat in the window seat, too, during Lady Maxwell's singing, she was far from unconscious that Hubert's face was looking at her from the dark corner. And as they walked back together her simplicity was not quite so transparent as the boy himself thought.

Again when her father had begun to speak of him just now, although she was able to meet his eyes steadily and smilingly, yet it was just an effort. She had not mentioned Hubert herself, until her father had named him; and in fact it is probably safe to say that during Hubert's visit to the north, which had lasted three or four months, he had made greater progress towards his goal, and had begun to loom larger than ever in the heart of this serene grey-eyed girl, whom he longed for so irresistibly.

And now, as Isabel sat on her bed before kneeling to say her prayers, Hubert was in her mind even more than Anthony. She tried to wonder what her father meant, and yet only too well she knew that she knew. She had forgotten to look into Anthony's room where she had cried so bitterly this morning, and now she sat wide-eyed, and self-questioning as to whether her heavenly love were as lucid and single as it had been; and when at last she went down on her knees she entreated the King of Love to bless not only her father, and her brother Anthony who lay under the Alderman's roof in far-away London; but Sir Nicholas and Lady Maxwell, and Mistress Margaret Hallam, and—and—

Hubert—and James Maxwell, his brother; and to bring them out of the darkness of Papistry into the glorious liberty of the children of the Gospel.

Chapter Three - London Town

Isabel's visit to London, which had been arranged to take place the Christmas after Anthony's departure to Cambridge, was full of bewildering experiences to her. Mr. Norris from time to time had references to look up in London, and divines to consult as to difficult points in his book on the Eucharist; and this was a favourable opportunity to see Mr. Dering, the St. Paul's lecturer; so the two took the opportunity, and with a couple of servants drove up to the City one day early in December to the house of Alderman Marrett, the wool merchant, and a friend of Mr. Norris' father; and for several days both before and after Anthony's arrival from Cambridge went every afternoon to see the sights. The maze of narrow streets of high black and white houses with their iron-work signs, leaning forward as if to whisper to one another, leaving strips of sky overhead; the strange play of lights and shades after nightfall; the fantastic groups; the incessant roar and rumble of the crowded alleys—all the commonplace life of London was like an enchanted picture to her, opening a glimpse into an existence of which she had known nothing.

To live, too, in the whirl of news that poured in day after day borne by splashed riders and panting horses;—this was very different to the slow round of country life, with rumours and tales floating in, mellowed by doubt and lapse of time, like pensive echoes from another world. For example, morning by morning, as she came downstairs to dinner, there was the ruddy-faced Alderman with his fresh budget of news of the north;—Lords Northumberland and Westmoreland with a Catholic force of several thousands, among which were two cousins of Mrs. Marrett herself— and the old lady nodded her head dolorously in corroboration—had marched southwards under the Banner of the Five Wounds, and tramped through Durham City welcomed by hundreds of the citizens; the Cathedral had been entered, old Richard Norton with the banner leading; the new Communion table had been cast out of doors, the English Bible and Prayer-book torn to shreds, the old altar reverently carried in from the rubbish heap, the tapers rekindled, and amid hysterical enthusiasm Mass had been said once more in the old sanctuary.

Then they had moved south; Lord Sussex was powerless in York; the Queen, terrified and irresolute, alternately storming and crying; Spain was about to send ships to Hartlepool to help the rebels; Mary Stuart would certainly be rescued from her prison at Tutbury. Then Mary had been moved to Coventry; then came a last flare of frightening tales: York had fallen; Mary had escaped; Elizabeth was preparing to flee.

And then one morning the Alderman's face was brighter: it was all a lie, he said. The revolt had crumbled away; my Lord Sussex was impregnably fortified in York with guns from Hull; Lord Pembroke was gathering forces at Windsor; Lords Clinton, Hereford and Warwick were converging towards York to relieve the siege. And as if to show Isabel it was not a mere romance, she could see the actual train-bands go by up Cheapside with the gleam of steel caps and pike-heads, and the mighty tramp of disciplined feet, and the welcoming roar of the swarming crowds.

Then as men's hearts grew lighter the tale of chastisement began to be told, and was not finished till long after Isabel was home again. Green after green of the windy northern villages was made hideous by the hanging bodies of the natives, and children hid their faces and ran by lest they should see what her Grace had done to their father.

In spite of the Holy Sacrifice, and the piteous banner, and the call to fight for the faith, the Catholics had hung back and hesitated, and the catastrophe was complete.

The religion of London, too, was a revelation to this country girl. She went one Sunday to St. Paul's Cathedral, pausing with her father before they went in to see the new restorations and the truncated steeple struck by lightning eight years before, which in spite of the Queen's angry urging the citizens had never been able to replace.

There was a good congregation at the early morning prayer; and the organs and the singing were to Isabel as the harps and choirs of heaven. The canticles were sung to Shephard's setting by the men and children of St. Paul's all in surplices: and the dignitaries wore besides their grey fur almuces, which had not yet been abolished. The grace and dignity of the whole service, though to older people who remembered the unreformed worship a bare and miserable affair, and to Mr. Norris, with his sincere simplicity and spirituality, a somewhat elaborate and sensuous mode of honouring God, yet to Isabel was a first glimpse of what the mystery of worship meant. The dim towering arches, through which the dusty richly-stained sunbeams poured, the far-away murmurous melodies that floated down from the glimmering choir, the high thin pealing organ, all combined to give her a sense of the unfathomable depths of the Divine Majesty—an element that was lacking in the clear-cut personal Puritan creed, in spite of the tender associations that made it fragrant for her, and the love of the Saviour that enlightened and warmed it. The sight of the crowds outside, too, in the frosty sunlight, gathered round the grey stone pulpit on the north-east of the Cathedral, and streaming down every alley and lane, the packed galleries, the gesticulating black figure of the preacher—this impressed on her an idea of the power of corporate religion, that hours at her own prayer-desk, or solitary twilight walks under the Hall pines, or the uneventful divisions of the Rector's village sermons, had failed to give.

It was this Sunday in London that awakened her quiet soul from the lonely companionship of God, to the knowledge of that vast spiritual world of men of which she was but one tiny cell. Her father observed her quietly and interestedly as they went home together, but said nothing beyond an indifferent word or two. He was beginning to realise the serious reality of her spiritual life, and to dread anything that would even approximate to coming between her soul and her Saviour. The father and daughter understood one another, and were content to be silent together.

Her talks with Mrs. Marrett, too, left their traces on her mind. The Alderman's wife, for the first time in her life, found her views and reminiscences listened to as if they were oracles, and she needed little encouragement to pour them out in profusion. She was especially generous with her tales of portents and warnings; and the girl was more than once considerably alarmed by what she heard while the ladies were alone in the dim firelit parlour on the winter afternoons before the candles were brought in.

"When you were a little child, my dear," began the old lady one day, "there was a great burning made everywhere of all the popish images and vestments; all but the copes and the altar-cloths that they made into dresses for the ministers' new wives, and bed-quilts to cover them; and there were books and banners and sepulchres and even relics. I went out to see the burning at Paul's, and though I knew it was proper that the old papistry should go, yet I was uneasy at the way it was done.

"Well," went on the old lady, glancing about her, "I was sitting in this very room only a few days after, and the air began to grow dark and heavy, and all became still. There had been two or three cocks crowing and answering one another down by the river, and others at a distance; and they all ceased: and there had been birds chirping in the roof, and they ceased. And it grew so dark that I laid down my needle and went to the window, and there at the end of the street over the houses there was coming a great cloud, with wings like a hawk, I thought; but some said afterwards that, when they saw it, it had fingers like a man's hand, and others said it was like a great tower, with battlements. However that may be, it grew nearer and larger, and it was blue and dark like that curtain there; and there was no wind to stir it, for the windows had ceased rattling, and the dust was quiet in the streets; and still it came on quickly, growing as it came; and then there came a far-away sound, like a heavy waggon, or, some said, like a deep voice complaining. And I turned away from the window afraid; and there was the cat, that had been on a chair, down in the corner, with her back up, staring at the cloud: and then she began to run round the room like a mad thing, and presently whisked out of the door when I opened it. And I went to find Mr. Marrett, and he had not come in, and all the yard was quiet. I could only hear a horse stamp once or twice in the stable. And then as I saw calling out for some one to come, the storm broke, and the sky was all one dark cloud from side to side. For three hours it went on, rolling and clapping, and the lightning came in through the window that I had darkened and through the clothes over my head; for I had gone to my bed and rolled myself round under the clothes. And so it went on—and, my dear—" and Mrs. Marrett put her head close to Isabel's—"I prayed to our Lady and the saints, which I had not done since I was married; and asked them to pray God to keep me safe. And then at the end came a clap of thunder and a flash of lightning more fearful than all that had gone before; and at that very moment, so Mr. Marrett told me when he came in, two of the doors in St. Denys' Church in Fanshawe Street were broken in pieces by something that crushed them in, and the stone steeple of Allhallow Church in Bread Street was broken off short, and a part of it killed a dog that was beneath, and overthrew a man that played with the dog."

Isabel could hardly restrain a shiver and a glance round the dark old room, so awful were Mrs. Marrett's face and gestures and loud whispering tone, as she told this.

"Ah! but, my dear," she went on, "there was worse happened to poor King Hal, God rest him—him who began to reform the Church, as they say, and destroyed the monasteries. All the money that he left for masses for his soul was carried off with the rest at the change of religion; and that was bad enough, but this is worse. This is a tale, my dear, that I have heard my father tell many a time; and I was a young woman myself when it happened. The King's Grace was threatened by a friar, I think of Greenwich, that if he laid hands on the monasteries he should be as Ahab whose blood was licked by dogs in the very place which he took from a man. Well, the friar was hanged for his pains, and the King lived. And then at last he died, and was put in a great coffin, and carried through London; and they put the coffin in an open space in Sion Abbey, which the King had taken. And in the night there came one to view the coffin, and to see that all was well. And he came round the corner, and there stood the great coffin—(for his Grace was a great stout man, my dear)—on trestles in the moonlight, and beneath it a great black dog that lapped something: and the dog turned as the man came, and some say, but not my father, that the dog's eyes were red as coals, and that his mouth and nostrils smoked, and that he cast no shadow; but (however that may be) the dog turned and looked and then ran; and the man followed him into a yard, but when he reached there, there was no dog. And the man went back to the coffin afraid; and he found the coffin was burst open, and—and—"

Mrs. Marrett stopped abruptly. Isabel was white and trembling.

"There, there, my dear. I am a foolish old woman; and I'll tell you no more."

Isabel was really terrified, and entreated Mrs. Marrett to tell her something pleasant to make her forget these horrors; and so she told her old tales of her youth, and the sights of the city, and the great doings in Mary's reign; and so the time passed pleasantly till the gentlemen came home.

At other times she told her of Elizabeth and the great nobles, and Isabel's heart beat high at it, and at the promise that before she left she herself should see the Queen, even if she had to go to Greenwich or Nonsuch for it.

"God bless her," said Mrs. Marrett loyally, "she's a woman like ourselves for all her majesty. And she likes the show and the music too, like us all. I declare when I see them all a-going down the water to Greenwich, or to the Tower for a bear-baiting, with the horns blowing and the guns firing and the banners and the barges and the music, I declare sometimes I think that heaven itself can be no better, God forgive me! Ah! but I wish her Grace 'd take a husband; there are many that want her; and then we could laugh at them all. There's so many against her Grace now who'd be for her if she had a son of her own. There's Duke Charles whose picture hangs in her bedroom, they say; and Lord Robert Dudley—there's a handsome spark, my dear, in his gay coat and his feathers and his ruff, and his hand on his hip, and his horse and all. I wish she'd take him and have done with it. And then we'd hear no more of the nasty Spaniards. There's Don de Silva, for all the world like a monkey with his brown face and mincing ways and his grand clothes. I declare when Captain Hawkins came home, just four years ago last Michaelmas, and came up to London with his men, all laughing and rolling along with the people cheering them, I could have kissed the man—to think how he had made the brown men dance and curse and show their white teeth! and to think that the Don had to ask him to dinner, and grin and chatter as if nought had happened."

And Mrs. Marrett's good-humoured face broke into mirth at the thought of the Ambassador's impotence and duplicity.

Anthony's arrival in London a few days before Christmas removed the one obstacle to Isabel's satisfaction—that he was not there to share it with her. The two went about together most of the day under their father's care, when he was not busy at his book, and saw all that was to be seen.

One afternoon as they were just leaving the courtyard of the Tower, which they had been visiting with a special order, a slight reddish-haired man, who came suddenly out of a doorway of the White Tower, stopped a moment irresolutely, and then came towards them, bare-headed and bowing. He had sloping shoulders and a serious-looking mouth, with a reddish beard and moustache, and had an air of strangely mingled submissiveness and capability. His voice too, as he spoke, was at once deferential and decided.

"I ask your pardon, Mr. Norris," he said. "Perhaps you do not remember me."

"I have seen you before," said the other, puzzled for a moment.

"Yes, sir," said the man, "down at Great Keynes; I was in service at the Hall, sir."

"Yes, yes," said Mr. Norris, "I remember you perfectly. Lackington, is it not?"

The man bowed again.

"I left about eight years ago, sir; and by the blessing of God, have gained a little post under the Government. But I wished to tell you, sir, that I have been happily led to change my religion. I was a Papist, sir, you know."

Mr. Norris congratulated him.

"I thank you, sir," said Lackington.

The two children were looking at him; and he turned to them and bowed again.

"Mistress Isabel and Master Anthony, sir, is it not?"

"I remember you," said Isabel a little shyly, "at least, I think so."

Lackington bowed again as if gratified; and turned to their father.

"If you are leaving, Mr. Norris, would you allow me to walk with you a few steps? I have much I would like to ask you of my old master and mistress."

The four passed out together; the two children in front; and as they went Lackington asked most eagerly after the household at the Hall, and especially after Mr. James, for whom he seemed to have a special affection.

"It is rumoured," said Mr. Norris, "that he is going abroad."

"Indeed, sir," said the servant, with a look of great interest, "I had heard it too, sir; but did not know whether to believe it."

Lackington also gave many messages of affection to others of the household, to Piers the bailiff, and a couple of the foresters: and finished by entreating Mr. Norris to use him as he would, telling him how anxious he was to be of service to his friends, and asking to be entrusted with any little errands or commissions in London that the country gentleman might wish performed.

"I shall count it, sir, a privilege," said the servant, "and you shall find me prompt and discreet."

One curious incident took place just as Lackington was taking his leave at the turning down into Wharf Street; a man hurrying eastwards almost ran against them, and seemed on the point of apologising, but his face changed suddenly, and he spat furiously on the ground, mumbling something, and hurried on. Lackington seemed to see nothing.

"Why did he do that?" interrupted Mr. Norris, astonished.

"I ask your pardon, sir?" said Lackington interrogatively.

"That fellow! did you not see him spit at me?"

"I did not observe it, sir," said the servant; and presently took his leave.

"Why did that man spit at you, father?" asked Isabel, when they had come indoors.

"I cannot think, my dear; I have never seen him in my life."

"I think Lackington knew," said Anthony, with a shrewd air.

"Lackington! Why, Lackington did not even see him."

"That was just it," said Anthony.

Anthony's talk about Cambridge during these first evenings in London was fascinating to Isabel, if not to their father, too. It concerned of course himself and his immediate friends, and dealt with such subjects as cock-fighting a good deal; but he spoke also of the public disputations and the theological champions who crowed and pecked, not unlike cocks themselves, while the theatre rang with applause and hooting. The sport was one of the most popular at the universities at this time. But above all his tales of the Queen's visit a few years before attracted the girl, for was she not to see the Queen with her own eyes?

"Oh! father," said the lad, "I would I had been there five years ago when she came. Master Taylor told me of it. They acted the Aulularia, you know, in King's Chapel on the Sunday evening. Master Taylor took a part, I forget what; and he told me how she laughed and clapped. And then there was a great disputation before her, one day, in St. Mary's Church, and the doctors argued, I forget what about, but Master Taylor says that of course the Genevans had the best of it; and the Queen spoke, too, in Latin, though she did not wish to, but my lord of Ely persuaded her to it; so you see she could not have learned it by heart, as some said. And she said she would give some great gift to the University; but Master Taylor says they are still waiting for it; but it must come soon, you see, because it is the Queen's Grace who has promised it; but Master Taylor says he hopes she has forgotten it, but he laughs when I ask him what he means, and says it again."

"Who is this Master Taylor?" asked his father.

"Oh! he is a Fellow of King's," said Anthony, "and he told me about the Provost too. The Provost is half a Papist, they say: he is very old now, and he has buried all the vessels and the vestments of the Chapel, they say, somewhere where no one knows; and he hopes the old religion will come back again some day; and then he will dig them up. But that is Papistry, and no one wants that at Cambridge. And others say that he is a Papist altogether, and has a priest in his house sometimes. But I do not think he can be a Papist, because he was there when the Queen was there, bowing and smiling, says Master Taylor; and looking on the Queen so earnestly, as if he worshipped her, says Master Taylor, all the time the Chancellor was talking to her before they went into the chapel for the Te Deum. But they wished they had kept some of the things, like the Provost, says Master Taylor, because they were much put to it when her Grace came down for stuffs to cover the communion-tables and for surplices, for Cecil said she would be displeased if all was bare and poor. Is it true, father," asked Anthony, breaking off, "that the Queen likes popish things, and has a crucifix and tapers on the table in her chapel?"

"Ah! my son," said Mr. Norris, smiling, "you must ask one who knows. And what else happened?"

"Well," said Anthony, "the best is to come. They had plays, you know, the Dido, and one called Ezechias, before the Queen. Oh! and she sent for one of the boys, they say, and—and kissed him, they say; but I think that cannot be true."

"Well, my son, go on!"

"Oh! and some of them thought they would have one more play before she went; but she had to go a long journey and left Cambridge before they could do it, and they went after her to—to Audley End, I think, where she was to sleep, and a room was made ready, and when all was prepared, though her Grace was tired, she came in to see the play. Master Taylor was not there; he said he would rather not act in that one; but he had the story from one who acted, but no one knew, he said, who wrote the play. Well, when the Queen's Grace was seated, the actors came on, dressed, father, dressed"—and Anthony's eyes began to shine with amusement—"as the Catholic Bishops in the Tower. There was Bonner in his popish vestments—some they had from St. Benet's—with a staff and his tall mitre, and a lamb in his arms; and he stared at it and gnashed his teeth at it as he tramped in; and then came the others, all like bishops, all in mass-vestments or cloth cut to look like them; and then at the end came a dog that belonged to one of them, well-trained, with the Popish Host in his mouth, made large and white, so that all could see what it was. Well, they thought the Queen would laugh as she was a Protestant, but no one laughed; some one said something in the room, and a lady cried out; and then the Queen stood up and scolded the actors, and trounced them well with her tongue, she did, and said she was displeased; and then out she went with all her ladies and gentlemen after her, except one or two servants who put out the lights at once without waiting, and broke Bonner's staff, and took away the Host, and kicked the dog, and told them to be off, for the Queen's Grace was angered with them; and so they had to get back to Cambridge in the dark as well as they might."

"Oh! the poor boys!" said Mrs. Marrett, "and they did it all to please her Grace, too."

"Yes," said the Alderman, "but the Queen thought it enough, I dare say, to put the Bishops in prison, without allowing boys to make a mock of them and their faith before her."

"Yes," said Anthony, "I thought that was it."

When the Alderman came in a day or two later with the news that Elizabeth was to come up from Nonsuch the next day, and to pass down Cheapside on her way to Greenwich, the excitement of Isabel and Anthony was indescribable. Cheapside was joyous to see, as the two, with their father behind them talking to a minister whose acquaintance he had made, sat at a first-floor window soon after mid-day, waiting to see the Queen go by. Many of the people had hung carpets or tapestries, some of taffetas and cloth-of-gold, out of their balconies and windows, and the very signs themselves,—fantastic ironwork, with here and there a grotesque beast rampant, or a bright painting, or an escutcheon;—with the gay, good-tempered crowds beneath and the strip of frosty blue sky, crossed by streamers from side to side, shining above the towering eaves and gables of the houses, all combined to make a scene so astonishing that it seemed scarcely real to these country children.

It was yet some time before she was expected; but there came a sudden stir from the upper end of Cheapside, and then a burst of cheering and laughter and hoots. Anthony leaned out to see what was coming, but could make out nothing beyond the head of a horse, and a man driving it from the seat of a cart, coming slowly down the centre of the road. The laughter and noise grew louder as the crowds swayed this way and that to make room. Presently it was seen that behind the cart a little space was kept, and Anthony made out the grey head of a man at the tail of the cart, and the face of another a little way behind; then at last, as the cart jolted past, the two children saw a man stripped to the waist, his hands tied before him to the cart, his back one red wound; while a hangman walked behind whirling his thonged whip about his head and bringing it down now and again on the old man's back. At each lash the prisoner shrank away, and turned his piteous face, drawn with pain, from side to side, while the crowd yelled and laughed.

"What's it for, what's it for?" inquired Anthony, eager and interested.

A boy leaning from the next window answered him.

"He said Jesus Christ was not in heaven."

At that moment a humorist near the cart began to cry out:

"Way for the King's Grace! Way for the King's Grace!" and the crowd took the idea instantly: a few men walking with the cart formed lines like gentlemen ushers, uncovering their heads and all crying out the same words; and one eager player tried to walk backwards until he was tripped up. And so the dismal pageant of this red-robed king of anguish went by; and the hoots and shouts of his heralds died away. Anthony turned to Isabel, exultant and interested.

"Why, Isabel," he said, "you look all white. What is it? You know he's a blasphemer."

"I know, I know," said Isabel.

Then suddenly, far away, came the sound of trumpets, and gusts of distant cheering, like the sound of the wind in thick foliage. Anthony leaned out again, and an excited murmur broke out once more, as all faces turned westwards. A moment more, and Anthony caught a flash of colour from the corner near St. Paul's Churchyard; then the shrill trumpets sounded nearer, and the cheering broke out at the end, and ran down the street like a wave of noise. From every window faces leaned out; even on the roofs and between the high chimney pots were swaying figures.

Masses of colour now began to emerge, with the glitter of steel, round the bend of the street, where the winter sunshine fell; and the crowds began to surge back, and against the houses. At first Anthony could make out little but two moving rippling lines of light, coming parallel, pressing the people back; and it was not until they had come opposite the window that he could make out the steel caps and pikeheads of men in half-armour, who, marching two and two with a space between them, led the procession and kept the crowds back. There they went, with immovable disciplined faces, grounding their pike-butts sharply now and again, caring nothing for the yelp of pain that sometimes followed. Immediately behind them came the aldermen in scarlet, on black horses that tossed their jingling heads as they walked. Anthony watched the solemn faces of the old gentlemen with a good deal of awe, and presently made out his friend, Mr. Marrett, who rode near the end, but who was too much engrossed in the management of his horse to notice the two children who cried out to him and waved. The serjeants-of-arms followed, and then two lines again of gentlemen-pensioners walking, bare-headed, carrying wands, in short cloaks and elaborate ruffs. But the lad saw little of them, for the splendour of the lords and knights that followed eclipsed them altogether. The knights came first, in steel armour with raised vizors, the horses too in armour, moving sedately with a splendid clash of steel, and twinkling fiercely in the sunshine; and then, after them (and Anthony drew his breath swiftly) came a blaze of colour and jewels as the great lords in their cloaks and feathered caps, metal-clasped and gemmed, came on their splendid long-maned horses; the crowd yelled and cheered, and great names were tossed to and fro, as the owners passed on, each talking to his fellow as if unconscious of the tumult and even of the presence of these shouting thousands. The cry of the trumpets rang out again high and shattering, as the trumpeters and heralds in rich coat-armour came next; and Anthony looked a moment, fascinated by the lions and lilies, and the brightness of the eloquent horns, before he turned his head to see the Lord Mayor himself, mounted on a great stately white horse, that needed no management, while his rider bore on a cushion the sceptre. Ah! she was coming near now. The two saw nothing of the next rider who carried aloft the glittering Sword of State, for their eyes were fixed on the six plumed heads of the horses, with grooms and footmen in cassock-coats and venetian hose, and the great gilt open carriage behind that swayed and jolted over the cobbles. She was here; she was here; and the loyal crowds yelled and surged to and fro, and cloths and handkerchiefs flapped and waved, and caps tossed up and down, as at last the great creaking carriage came under the window.

This is what they saw in it.

A figure of extraordinary dignity, sitting upright and stiff like a pagan idol, dressed in a magnificent and fantastic purple robe, with a great double ruff, like a huge collar, behind her head; a long taper waist, voluminous skirts spread all over the cushions, embroidered with curious figures and creatures. Over her shoulders, but opened in front so as to show the ropes of pearls and the blaze of jewels on the stomacher, was a purple velvet mantle lined with ermine, with pearls sewn into it here and there. Set far back on her head, over a pile of reddish-yellow hair drawn tightly back from the forehead, was a hat with curled brims, elaborately embroidered, with the jewelled outline of a little crown in front, and a high feather topping all.

And her face—a long oval, pale and transparent in complexion, with a sharp chin, and a high forehead; high arched eyebrows, auburn, but a little darker than her hair; her mouth was small, rising at the corners, with thin curved lips tightly shut; and her eyes, which were clear in colour, looked incessantly about her with great liveliness and good-humour.

There was something overpowering to these two children who looked, too awed to cheer, in this formidable figure in the barbaric dress, the gorgeous climax of a gorgeous pageant. Apart from the physical splendour, this solitary glittering creature represented so much—it was the incarnate genius of the laughing, brutal, wanton English nation, that sat here in the gilded carriage and smiled and glanced with tight lips and clear eyes. She was like some emblematic giant, moving in a processional car, as fantastic as itself, dominant and serene above the heads of the maddened crowds, on to some mysterious destiny. A sovereign, however personally inglorious, has such a dignity in some measure; and Elizabeth added to this an exceptional majesty of her own. Henry would not have been ashamed for this daughter of his. What wonder then that these crowds were delirious with love and loyalty and an exultant fear, as this overwhelming personality went by:—this pale-faced tranquil virgin Queen, passionate, wanton, outspoken and absolutely fearless; with a sufficient reserve of will to be fickle without weakness; and sufficient grasp of her aims to be indifferent to her policy; untouched by vital religion; financially shrewd; inordinately vain. And when this strange dominant creature, royal by character as by birth, as strong as her father and as wanton as her mother, sat in ermine and velvet and pearls in a royal carriage, with shrewd-faced wits, and bright-eyed lovers, and solemn statesmen, and great nobles, vacuous and gallant, glittering and jingling before her; and troops of tall ladies in ruff and crimson mantle riding on white horses behind; and when the fanfares went shattering down the street, vibrating through the continuous roar of the crowd and the shrill cries of children and the mellow thunder of church-bells rocking overhead, and the endless tramp of a thousand feet below; and when the whole was framed in this fantastic twisted street, blazing with tapestries and arched with gables and banners, all bathed in glory by the clear frosty sunshine—it is little wonder that for a few minutes at least this country boy felt that here at last was the incarnation of his dreams; and that his heart should exult, with an enthusiasm he could not interpret, for the cause of a people who could produce such a queen, and of a queen who could rule such a people; and that his imagination should be fired with a sudden sense that these were causes for which the sacrifice of a life would be counted cheap, if they might thereby be furthered.

Yet, in this very moment, by one of those mysterious suggestions that rise from the depth of a soul, the image sprang into his mind, and poised itself there for an instant, of the grey-haired man who had passed half an hour ago, sobbing and shrinking at the cart's tail.

Chapter Four - Mary Corbet

The spring that followed the visit to London passed uneventfully at Great Keynes to all outward appearances; and yet for Isabel they were significant months. In spite of herself and of the word of warning from her father, her relations with Hubert continued to draw closer. For one thing, he had been the first to awaken in her the consciousness that she was lovable in herself, and the mirror that first tells that to a soul always has something of the glow of the discovery resting upon it.

Then again his deference and his chivalrous air had a strange charm. When Isabel rode out alone with Anthony, she often had to catch the swinging gate as he rode through after opening it, and do such little things for herself; but when Hubert was with them there was nothing of that kind.

And, once more, he appealed to her pity; and this was the most subtle element of all. There was no doubt that Hubert's relations with his fiery old father became strained sometimes, and it was extraordinarily sweet to Isabel to be made a confidant. And yet Hubert never went beyond a certain point; his wooing was very skilful: and he seemed to be conscious of her uneasiness almost before she was conscious of it herself, and to relapse in a moment into frank and brotherly relations again.

He came in one night after supper, flushed and bright-eyed, and found her alone in the hall: and broke out immediately, striding up and down as she sat and watched him.

"I cannot bear it; there is Mr. Bailey who has been with us all Lent; he is always interfering in my affairs. And he has no charity. I know I am a Catholic and that; but when he and my father talk against the Protestants, Mistress Isabel, I cannot bear it. They were abusing the Queen to-night—at least," he added, for he had no intention to exaggerate, "they were saying she was a true daughter of her father; and sneers of that kind. And I am an Englishman, and her subject; and I said so; and Mr. Bailey snapped out, 'And you are also a Catholic, my son,' and then—and then I lost my temper, and said that the Catholic religion seemed no better than any other for the good it did people; and that the Rector and Mr. Norris seemed to me as good men as any one; and of course I meant him and he knew it; and then he told me, before the servants, that I was speaking against the faith; and then I said I would sooner speak against the faith than against good Christians; and then he flamed up scarlet, and I saw I had touched him; and then my father got scarlet too, and my mother looked at me, and my father told me to leave the table for an insolent puppy; and I knocked over my chair and stamped out—and oh! Mistress Isabel, I came straight here."

And he flung down astride of a chair with his arms on the back, and dropped his head on to them.

It would have been difficult for Hubert, even if he had been very clever indeed, to have made any speech which would have touched Isabel more than this. There was the subtle suggestion that he had defended the Protestants for her sake; and there was the open defence of her father, and defiance of the priests whom she feared and distrusted; there was a warm generosity and frankness running through it all; and lastly, there was the sweet flattering implication that he had come to her to be understood and quieted and comforted.

Then, when she tried to show her disapproval of his quick temper, and had succeeded in showing a poorly disguised sympathy instead, he had flung away again, saying that she had brought him to his senses as usual, and that he would ask the priest's pardon for his insolence at once; and Isabel was left standing and looking at the fire, fearing that she was being wooed, and yet not certain, though she loved it. And then, too, there was the secret hope that it might be through her that he might escape from his superstitions, and—and then—and she closed her eyes and bit her lip for joy and terror.

She did not know that a few weeks later Hubert had an interview with his father, of which she was the occasion. Lady Maxwell had gone to her husband after a good deal of thought and anxiety, and told him what she feared; asking him to say a word to Hubert. Sir Nicholas had been startled and furious. It was all the lad's conceit, he said; he had no real heart at all; he only flattered his vanity in making love; he had no love for his parents or his faith, and so on. She took his old hand in her own and held it while she spoke.

"Sweetheart," she said, "how old were you when you used to come riding to Overfield? I forget." And there came peace into his angry, puzzled old eyes, and a gleam of humour.

"Mistress," he said, "you have not forgotten." For he had been just eighteen, too. And he took her face in his hands delicately, and kissed her on the lips.

"Well, well," he said, "it is hard on the boy; but it must not go on. Send him to me. Oh! I will be easy with him."

But the interview was not as simple as he hoped; for Hubert was irritable and shamefaced; and spoke lightly of the Religion again.

"After all," he burst out, "there are plenty of good men who have left the faith. It brings nothing but misery."

Sir Nicholas' hands began to shake, and his fingers to clench themselves; but he remembered the lad was in love.

"My son," he said, "you do not know what you say."

"I know well enough," said Hubert, with his foot tapping sharply. "I say that the Catholic religion is a religion of misery and death everywhere. Look at the Low Countries, sir."

"I cannot speak of that," said his father; and his son sneered visibly; "you and I are but laymen; but this I know, and have a right to say, that to threaten me like that is the act of a—is not worthy of my son. My dear boy," he said, coming nearer, "you are angry; and, God forgive me! so am I; but I promised your mother," and again he broke off, "and we cannot go on with this now. Come again this evening."

Hubert stood turned away, with his head against the high oak mantelpiece; and there was silence.

"Father," he said at last, turning round, "I ask your pardon."

Sir Nicholas stepped nearer, his eyes suddenly bright with tears, and his mouth twitching, and held out his hand, which Hubert took.

"And I was a coward to speak like that—but, but—I will try," went on the boy. "And I promise to say nothing to her yet, at any rate. Will that do? And I will go away for a while."

The father threw his arms round him.

As the summer drew on and began to fill the gardens and meadows with wealth, the little Italian garden to the south-west of the Hall was where my lady spent most of the day. Here she would cause chairs to be brought out for Mistress Margaret and herself, and a small selection of devotional books, an orange leather volume powdered all over with pierced hearts, filled with extracts in a clear brown ink, another book called Le Chappellet de Jésus, while from her girdle beside her pocket-mirror there always hung an olive-coloured "Hours of the Blessed Virgin," fastened by a long strip of leather prolonged from the binding. Here the two old sisters would sit, in the shadow of the yew hedge, taking it by turns to read and embroider, or talking a little now and then in quiet voices, with long silences broken only by the hum of insects in the hot air, or the quick flight of a bird in the tall trees behind the hedge. Here too Isabel often came, also bringing her embroidery; and sat and talked and watched the wrinkled tranquil faces of the two old ladies, and envied their peace. Hubert had gone, as he had promised his father, on a long visit, and was not expected home until at least the autumn.

"James will be here to-morrow," said Lady Maxwell, suddenly, one hot afternoon. Isabel looked up in surprise; he had not been at home for so long; but the thought of his coming was very pleasant to her.

"And Mary Corbet, too," went on the old lady, "will be here to-morrow or the day after."

Isabel asked who this was.

"She is one of the Queen's ladies, my dear; and a great talker."

"She is very amusing sometimes," said Mistress Margaret's clear little voice.

"And Mr. James will be here to-morrow?" said Isabel.

"Yes, my child. They always suit one another; and we have known Mary for years."

"And is Miss Corbet a Catholic?"

"Yes, my dear; her Grace seems to like them about her."

When Isabel went up again to the Hall in the evening, a couple of days later, she found Mr. James sitting with his mother and aunt in the same part of the garden. Mr. James, who rose as she came through the yew archway, and stood waiting to greet her, was a tall, pleasant, brown-faced man. Isabel noticed as she came up his strong friendly face, that had something of Hubert's look in it, and felt an immediate sense of relief from her timidity at meeting this man, whose name, it was said, was beginning to be known among the poets, and about whom the still more formidable fact was being repeated, that he was a rising man at Court and had attracted the Queen's favour.

As they sat down again together, she noticed, too, his strong delicate hand in its snowy ruff, for he was always perfectly dressed, as it lay on his knee; and again thought of Hubert's browner and squarer hand.

"We were talking, Mistress Isabel, about the play, and the new theatres. I was at the Blackfriars' only last week. Ah! and I met Buxton there," he went on, turning to his mother.

"Dear Henry," said Lady Maxwell. "He told me when I last saw him that he could never go to London again; his religion was too expensive, he said."

Mr. James' white teeth glimmered in a smile.

"He told me he was going to prison next time, instead of paying the fine. It would be cheaper, he thought."

"I hear her Grace loves the play," said Mistress Margaret.

"Indeed she does. I saw her at Whitehall the other day, when the children of the Chapel Royal were acting; she clapped and called out with delight. But Mistress Corbet can tell you more than I can—Ah! here she is."

Isabel looked up, and saw a wonderful figure coming briskly along the terrace and down the steps that led from the house. Miss Corbet was dressed with what she herself would have said was a milkmaid's plainness; but Isabel looked in astonishment at the elaborate ruff and wings of muslin and lace, the shining peacock gown, the high-piled coils of black hair, and the twinkling buckled feet. She had a lively bright face, a little pale, with a high forehead, and black arched brows and dancing eyes, and a little scarlet mouth that twitched humorously now and then after speaking. She rustled up, flicking her handkerchief, and exclaiming against the heat. Isabel was presented to her; she sat down on a settle Mr. James drew forward for her, with the handkerchief still whisking at the flies.

"I am ashamed to come out like this," she began. "Mistress Plesse would break her heart at my lace. You country ladies have far more sense. I am the slave of my habits. What were you talking of, that you look so gravely at me?"

Mr. James told her.

"Oh, her Grace!" said Miss Corbet. "Indeed, I think sometimes she is never off the stage herself. Ah! and what art and passion she shows too!"

"We are all loyal subjects here," said Mr. James; "tell us what you mean."

"I mean what I say," she said. "Never was there one who loved play-acting more and to occupy the centre of the stage, too. And the throne too, if there be one," she added.

Miss Corbet talked always at her audience; she hardly ever looked directly at any one, but up or down, or even shut her eyes and tilted her face forward while she talked; and all the while she kept an incessant movement of her lips or handkerchief, or tapped her foot, or shifted her position a little. Isabel thought she had never seen any one so restless.

Then she went on to tell them of the Queen. She was so startlingly frank that Lady Maxwell again and again looked up as if to interrupt; but she always came off the thin ice in time. It was abominable gossip; but she talked with such a genial air of loyal good humour, that it was very difficult to find fault. Miss Corbet was plainly accustomed to act as Court Circular, or even as lecturer and show-woman on the most popular subject in England.

"But her Grace surpassed herself in acting the tyrant last January; you would have sworn her really angry. This was how it fell out. I was in the anteroom one day, waiting for her Grace, when I thought I heard her call. So I tapped; I got no clear answer, but I heard her voice within, so I entered. And there was her Majesty, sitting a little apart in a chair by herself, with the Secretary—poor rat—white-faced at the table, writing what she bade him, and looking at her, quick and side-ways, like a child at a lifted rod; and there was her Grace: she had kicked her stool over, and one shoe had fallen; and she was striking the arm of her chair as she spoke, and her rings rapped as loud as a drunken watchman. And her face was all white, and her eyes glaring"—and Mary began to glare and raise her voice too—"and she was crying out, 'By God's Son, sir, I will have them hanged. Tell the—' (but I dare not say what she called my Lord Sussex, but few would have recognised him from what she said)—'tell him that I will have my will done. These—' (and she called the rebels a name I dare not tell you)—'these men have risen against me these two months; and yet they are not hanged. Hang them in their own villages, that their children may see what treason brings.' All this while I was standing at the open door, thinking she had called me; but she was as if she saw nought but the gallows and hell-fire beyond; and I spoke softly to her, asking what she wished; and she sprang up and ran at me, and struck me—yes; again and again across the face with her open hand, rings and all—and I ran out in tears. Yes," went on Miss Corbet in a moment, dropping her voice, and pensively looking up at nothing, "yes; you would have said she was really angry, so quick and natural were her movements and so loud her voice."

Mr. James' face wrinkled up silently in amusement; and Lady Maxwell seemed on the point of speaking; but Miss Corbet began again:

"And to see her Grace act the lover. It was a miracle. You would have said that our Artemis repented of her coldness; if you had not known it was but play-acting; or let us say perhaps a rehearsal—if you had seen what I once saw at Nonsuch. It was on a summer evening; and we were all on the bowling green, and her Grace was within doors, not to be disturbed. My Lord Leicester was to come, but we thought had not arrived. Then I had occasion to go to my room to get a little book I had promised to show to Caroline; and, thinking no harm, I ran through into the court, and there stood a horse, his legs apart, all steaming and blowing. Some courier, said I to myself, and never thought to look at the trappings; and so I ran upstairs to go to the gallery, across which lay my chamber; and I came up, and just began to push open the door, when I heard her Grace's voice beyond, and, by the mercy of God, I stopped; and dared not close the door again nor go downstairs for fear I should be heard. And there were two walking within the gallery, her Grace and my lord, and my lord was all disordered with hard riding, and nearly as spent as his poor beast below. And her Grace had her arm round his neck, for I saw them through the chink; and she fondled and pinched his ear, and said over and over again, 'Robin, my sweet Robin,' and then crooned and moaned at him; and he, whenever he could fetch a breath—and oh! I promise you he did blow—murmured back, calling her his queen, which indeed she was, and his sweetheart and his moon and his star—which she was not: but 'twas all in the play. Well, again by the favour of God, they did not see how the door was open and I couched behind it, for the sun was shining level through the west window in their eyes; but why they did not hear me as I ran upstairs and opened the door, He only knows—unless my lord was too sorely out of breath and her Grace too intent upon her play-acting. Well, I promise you, the acting was so good—he so spent and she so tender—that I nearly cried out Brava as I saw them; but that I remembered in time 'twas meant to be a private rehearsal. But I have seen her Grace act near as passionate a part before the whole company sometimes."

The two old ladies seemed not greatly pleased with all this talk; and as for Isabel she sat silent and overwhelmed. Mary Corbet glanced quickly at their faces when she had done, and turned a little in her seat.

"Ah! look at that peacock," she cried out, as a stately bird stepped delicately out of the shrubbery on to the low wall a little way off, and stood balancing himself. "He is loyal too, and has come to hear news of his Queen."

"He has come to see his cousin from town," said Mr. James, looking at Miss Corbet's glowing dress, "and to learn of the London fashions."

Mary got up and curtseyed to the astonished bird, who looked at her with his head lowered, as he took a high step or two, and then paused again, with his burnished breast swaying a little from side to side.

"He invites you to a dance," went on Mr. James gravely, "a pavane."

Miss Corbet sat down again.

"I dare not dance a pavane," she said, "with a real peacock."

"Surely," said Mr. James, with a courtier's air, "you are too pitiful for him, and too pitiless for us."

"I dare not," she said again, "for he never ceases to practise."

"In hopes," said Mr. James, "that one day you will dance it with him."

And then the two went off into the splendid fantastic nonsense that the wits loved to talk; that grotesque, exaggerated phrasing made fashionable by Lyly. It was like a kind of impromptu sword-exercise in an assault of arms, where the rhythm and the flash and the graceful turns are of more importance than the actual thrusts received. The two old ladies embroidered on in silence, but their eyes twinkled, and little wrinkles flickered about the corners of their lips. But poor Isabel sat bewildered. It was so elaborate, so empty; she had almost said, so wicked to take the solemn gift of speech and make it dance this wild fandango; and as absurdity climbed and capered in a shower of sparks and gleams on the shoulders of absurdity, and was itself surmounted; and the names of heathen gods and nymphs and demi-gods and loose-living classical women whisked across the stage, and were tossed higher and higher, until the whole mad erection blazed up and went out in a shower of stars and gems of allusions and phrases, like a flight of rockets, bright and bewildering at the moment, but leaving a barren darkness and dazzled eyes behind—the poor little Puritan country child almost cried with perplexity and annoyance. If the two talkers had looked at one another and burst into laughter at the end, she would have understood it to be a joke, though, to her mind, but a poor one. But when they had ended, and Mary Corbet had risen and then swept down to the ground in a great silent curtsey, and Mr. James, the grave, sensible gentleman, had solemnly bowed with his hand on his heart, and his heels together like a Monsieur, and then she had rustled off in her peacock dress to the house, with her muslin wings bulging behind her; and no one had laughed or reproved or explained; it was almost too much, and she looked across to Lady Maxwell with an appeal in her eyes.

Mr. James saw it and his face relaxed.

"You must not take us too seriously, Mistress Isabel," he said in his kindly way. "It is all part of the game."

"The game?" she said piteously.

"Yes," said Mistress Margaret, intent on her embroidery, "the game of playing at kings and queens and courtiers and ruffs and high-stepping."

Mr. James' face again broke into his silent laugh.

"You are acid, dear aunt," he said.

"But—" began Isabel again.

"But it is wrong, you think," he interrupted, "to talk such nonsense. Well, Mistress Isabel, I am not sure you are not right." And the dancing light in his eyes went out.

"No, no, no," she cried, distressed. "I did not mean that. Only I did not understand."

"I know, I know; and please God you never will." And he looked at her with such a tender gravity that her eyes fell.

"Isabel is right," went on Mistress Margaret, in her singularly sweet old voice; "and you know it, my nephew. It is very well as a pastime, but some folks make it their business; and that is nothing less than fooling with the gifts of the good God."

"Well, aunt Margaret," said James softly, "I shall not have much more of it. You need not fear for me."

Lady Maxwell looked quickly at her son for a moment, and down again. He made an almost imperceptible movement with his head, Mistress Margaret looked across at him with her tender eyes beaming love and sorrow; and there fell a little eloquent silence; while Isabel glanced shyly from one to the other, and wondered what it was all about.

Miss Mary Corbet stayed a few weeks, as the custom was when travelling meant so much; but Isabel was scarcely nearer understanding her. She accepted her, as simple clean souls so often have to accept riddles in this world, as a mystery that no doubt had a significance, though she could not recognise it. So she did not exactly dislike or distrust her, but regarded her silently out of her own candid soul, as one would say a small fearless bird in a nest must regard the man who thrusts his strange hot face into her green pleasant world, and tries to make endearing sounds. For Isabel was very fascinating to Mary Corbet. She had scarcely ever before been thrown so close to any one so serenely pure. She would come down to the Dower House again and again at all hours of the day, rustling along in her silk, and seize upon Isabel in the little upstairs parlour, or her bedroom, and question her minutely about her ways and ideas; and she would look at her silently for a minute or two together; and then suddenly laugh and kiss her— Isabel's transparency was almost as great a riddle to her as her own obscurity to Isabel. And sometimes she would throw herself on Isabel's bed, and lie there with her arms behind her head, to the deplorable ruin of her ruff; with her buckled feet twitching and tapping; and go on and on talking like a running stream in the sun that runs for the sheer glitter and tinkle of it, and accomplishes nothing. But she was more respectful to Isabel's simplicity than at first, and avoided dangerous edges and treacherous ground in a manner that surprised herself, telling her of the pageants at Court and fair exterior of it all, and little about the poisonous conversations and jests and the corrupt souls that engaged in them.

She was immensely interested in Isabel's religion.

"Tell me, child," she said one day, "I cannot understand such a religion. It is not like the Protestant religion at Court at all. All that the Protestants do there is to hear sermons—it is all so dismal and noisy. But here, with you, you have a proper soul. It seems to me that you are like a little herb-garden, very prim and plain, but living and wholesome and pleasant to walk in at sunset. And these Protestants that I know are more like a paved court at noon—all hot and hard and glaring. They give me the headache. Tell me all about it."

Of course Isabel could not, though she tried again and again. Her definitions were as barren as any others.

"I see," said Mary Corbet one day, sitting up straight and looking at Isabel. "It is not your religion but you; your religion is as dull as all the rest. But your soul is sweet, my dear, and the wilderness blossoms where you set your feet. There is nothing to blush about. It's no credit to you, but to God."

Isabel hated this sort of thing. It seemed to her as if her soul was being dragged out of a cool thicket from the green shadow and the flowers, and set, stripped, in the high road.

Another time Miss Corbet spoke yet more plainly.

"You are a Catholic at heart, my dear; or you would be if you knew what the Religion was. But your father, good man, has never understood it himself; and so you don't know it either. What you think about us, my dear, is as much like the truth as—as—I am like a saint, or you like a sinner. I'll be bound now that you think us all idolaters!"

Isabel had to confess that she did think something of the sort.

"There, now, what did I say? Why haven't either of those two old nuns at the Hall taught you any better?"

"They—they don't talk to me about religion."

"Ah! I see; or the Puritan father would withdraw his lamb from the wolves. But if they are wolves, my dear, you must confess that they have the decency to wear sheep's clothing, and that the disguise is excellent."

And so it gradually came about that Isabel began to learn an immense deal about what the Catholics really believed—far more than she had ever learnt in all her life before from the ladies at the Hall, who were unwilling to teach her, and her father, who was unable.

About half-way through Miss Corbet's visit, Anthony came home. At first he pronounced against her inexorably, dismissing her as nonsense, and as a fine lady—terms to him interchangeable. Then his condemnation began to falter, then ceased; then acquittal, and at last commendation succeeded. For Miss Corbet asked his advice about the dogs, and how to get that wonderful gloss on their coats that his had; and she asked his help, too, once or twice and praised his skill, and once asked to feel his muscle.

And then she was so gallant in ways that appealed to him. She was not in the least afraid of Eliza. She kissed that ferocious head in spite of the glare of that steady yellow eye; and yet all with an air of trusting to Anthony's protection. She tore her silk stocking across the instep in a bramble and scratched her foot, without even drawing attention to it, as she followed him along one of his short cuts through the copse; and it was only by chance that he saw it. And then this gallant girl, so simple and ignorant as she seemed out of doors, was like a splendid queen indoors, and was able to hold her own, or rather to soar above all these elders who were so apt to look over Anthony's head on grave occasions; and they all had to listen while she talked. In fact, the first time he saw her at the Hall in all her splendour, he could hardly realise it was the same girl, till she laughed up at him, and nodded, and said how much she had enjoyed the afternoon's stroll, and how much she would have to tell when she got back to Court. In short, so incessant were her poses and so skilful her manner and tone, and so foolish this poor boy, that in a very few days, after he had pronounced her to be nonsense, Anthony was at her feet, hopelessly fascinated by the combination of the glitter and friendliness of this fine Court lady. To do her justice, she would have behaved exactly the same to a statue, or even to nothing at all, as a peacock dances and postures and vibrates his plumes to a kitten; and had no more deliberate intention of giving pain to anybody than a nightshade has of poisoning a silly sheep.

The sublime conceit of a boy of fifteen made him of course think that she had detected in him a nobility that others overlooked, and so Anthony began a gorgeous course of day-dreaming, in which he moved as a kind of king, worshipped and reverenced by this splendid creature, who after a disillusionment from the empty vanities of a Court life and a Queen's favour, found at last the lord of her heart in a simple manly young countryman. These dreams, however, he had the grace and modesty to keep wholly to himself.

Mary came down one day and found the two in the garden together.

"Come, my child," she said, "and you too, Master Anthony, if you can spare time to escort us; and take me to the church. I want to see it."

"The church!" said Isabel, "that is locked: we must go to the Rectory."

"Locked!" exclaimed Mary, "and is that part of the blessed Reformation? Well, come, at any rate."

They all went across to the village and down the green towards the Rectory, whose garden adjoined the churchyard on the south side of the church. Anthony walked with something of an air in front of the two ladies. Isabel told her as they went about the Rector and his views. Mary nodded and smiled and seemed to understand.

"We will tap at the window," said Anthony, "it is the quickest way."

They came up towards the study window that looked on to the drive; when Anthony, who was in front, suddenly recoiled and then laughed.

"They are at it again," he said.

The next moment Mary was looking through the window too. The Rector was sitting in his chair opposite, a small dark, clean-shaven man, but his face was set with a look of distressed determination, and his lower lip was sucked in; his eyes were fixed firmly on a tall, slender woman whose back was turned to the window and who seemed to be declaiming, with outstretched hand. The Rector suddenly saw the faces at the window.

"We seem to be interrupting," said Mary coolly, as she turned away.

Chapter Five - A Rider from London

"We will walk on, Master Anthony," said Mistress Corbet. "Will you bring the keys when the Rector and his lady have done?"

She spoke with a vehement bitterness that made Isabel look at her in amazement, as the two walked on by the private path to the churchyard gate. Mary's face was set in a kind of fury, and she went forward with her chin thrust disdainfully out, biting her lip. Isabel said nothing.

As they reached the gate they heard steps behind them; and turning saw the minister and Anthony hastening together. Mr. Dent was in his cassock and gown and square cap, and carried the keys. His little scholarly face, with a sharp curved nose like a beak, and dark eyes set rather too close together, was not unlike a bird's; and a way he had of sudden sharp movements of his head increased the likeness. Mary looked at him with scarcely veiled contempt. He glanced at her sharply and uneasily.

"Mistress Mary Corbet?" he said, interrogatively.

Mary bowed to him.

"May we see the church, sir; your church, I should say perhaps; that is, if we are not disturbing you."

Mr. Dent made a polite inclination, and opened the gate for them to go through. Then Mary changed her tactics; and a genial, good-humoured look came over her face; but Isabel, who glanced at her now and again as they went round to the porch at the west-end, still felt uneasy.

As the Rector was unlocking the porch door, Mary surveyed him with a pleased smile.

"Why, you look quite like a priest," she said. "Do your bishops, or whatever you call them, allow that dress? I thought you had done away with it all."

Mr. Dent looked at her, but seeing nothing but geniality and interest in her face, explained elaborately in the porch that he was a Catholic priest, practically; though the word minister was more commonly used; and that it was the old Church still, only cleansed from superstitions. Mary shook her head at him cheerfully, smiling like a happy, puzzled child.

"It is all too difficult for me," she said. "It cannot be the same Church, or why should we poor Catholics be so much abused and persecuted? Besides, what of the Pope?"

Mr. Dent explained that the Pope was one of the superstitions in question.

"Ah! I see you are too sharp for me," said Mary, beaming at him.

Then they entered the church; and Mary began immediately on a running comment.

"How sad that little niche looks," she said. "I suppose Our Lady is in pieces somewhere on a dunghill. Surely, father— I beg your pardon, Mr. Dent—it cannot be the same religion if you have knocked Our Lady to pieces. But then I suppose you would say that she was a superstition, too. And where is the old altar? Is that broken, too? And is that a superstition, too? What a number there must have been! And the holy water, too, I see. But that looks a very nice table up there you have instead. Ah! And I see you read the new prayers from a new desk outside the screen, and not from the priest's stall. Was that a superstition too? And the mass vestments? Has your wife had any of them made up to be useful? The stoles are no good, I fear; but you could make charming stomachers out of the chasubles."

They were walking slowly up the centre aisle now. Mr. Dent had to explain that the vestments had been burnt on the green.

"Ah! yes; I see," she said, "and do you wear a surplice, or do you not like them? I see the chancel roof is all broken— were there angels there once? I suppose so. But how strange to break them all! Unless they are superstitions, too? I thought Protestants believed in them; but I see I was wrong. What do you believe in, Mr. Dent?" she asked, turning large, bright, perplexed eyes upon him for a moment: but she gave him no time to answer.

"Ah!" she cried suddenly, and her voice rang with pain, "there is the altar-stone." And she went down on her knees at the chancel entrance, bending down, it seemed, in an agony of devout sorrow and shame; and kissed with a gentle, lingering reverence the great slab with its five crosses, set in the ground at the destruction of the altar to show there was no sanctity attached to it.

She knelt there a moment or two, her lips moving, and her black eyes cast up at the great east window, cracked and flawed with stones and poles. The Puritan boy and girl looked at her with astonishment; they had not seen this side of her before.

When she rose from her knees, her eyes seemed bright with tears, and her voice was tender.

"Forgive me, Mr. Dent," she said, with a kind of pathetic dignity, putting out a slender be-ringed hand to him, "but— but you know—for I think perhaps you have some sympathy for us poor Catholics—you know what all this means to me."

She went up into the chancel and looked about her in silence.

"This was the piscina, Mistress Corbet," said the Rector.

She nodded her head regretfully, as at some relic of a dead friend; but said nothing. They came out again presently, and turned through the old iron gates into what had been the Maxwell chapel. The centre was occupied by an altar-tomb with Sir Nicholas' parents lying in black stone upon it. Old Sir James held his right gauntlet in his left hand, and with his right hand held the right hand of his wife, which was crossed over to meet it; and the two steady faces gazed upon the disfigured roof. The altar, where a weekly requiem had been said for them, was gone, and the footpace and piscina alone showed where it had stood.

"This was a chantry, of course?" said Mistress Corbet.

The Rector confessed that it had been so.

"Ah!" she said mournfully, "the altar is cast out and the priest gone; but—but—forgive me, sir, the money is here still? But then," she added, "I suppose the money is not a superstition."

When they reached the west entrance again she turned and looked up the aisle again.

"And the Rood!" she said. "Even Christ crucified is gone. Then, in God's name what is left?" And her eyes turned fiercely for a moment on the Rector.

"At least courtesy and Christian kindness is left, madam," he said sternly.

She dropped her eyes and went out; and Isabel and Anthony followed, startled and ashamed. But Mary had recovered herself as she came on to the head of the stone stairs, beside which the stump of the churchyard cross stood; standing there was the same tall, slender woman whose back they had seen through the window, and who now stood eyeing Mary with half-dropped lids. Her face was very white, with hard lines from nose to mouth, and thin, tightly compressed lips. Mary swept her with one look, and then passed on and down the steps, followed by Isabel and Anthony, as the Rector came out, locking the church door again behind him.

As they went up the green, a shrill thin voice began to scold from over the churchyard wall, and they heard the lower, determined voice of the minister answering.

"They are at it again," said Anthony, once more.

"And what do you mean by that, Master Anthony?" said Mistress Corbet, who seemed herself again now.

"She is just a scold," said the lad, "the village-folk hate her."

"You seem not to love her," said Mary, smiling.

"Oh! Mistress Corbet, do you know what she said—" and then he broke off, crimson-faced.

"She is no friend to Catholics, I suppose," said Mary, seeming to notice nothing.

"She is always making mischief," he went on eagerly. "The Rector would be well enough but for her. He is a good fellow, really."

"There, there," said Mary, "and you think me a scold, too, I daresay. Well, you know I cannot bear to see these old churches—well, perhaps I was—" and then she broke off again, and was silent.

The brother and sister presently turned back to the Dower House; and Mary went on, and through the Hall straight into the Italian garden where Mistress Margaret was sitting alone at her embroidery.

"My sister has been called away by the housekeeper," she explained, "but she will be back presently."

Mary sat down and took up the little tawny book that lay by Lady Maxwell's chair, and began to turn it over idly while she talked. The old lady by her seemed to invite confidences.

"I have been to see the church," said Mary. "The Rector showed it to me. What a beautiful place it must have been."

"Ah!" said Mistress Margaret "I only came to live here a few years ago; so I have never known or loved it like my sister or her husband. They can hardly bear to enter it now. You know that Sir Nicholas' father and grandfather are buried in the Maxwell chapel; and it was his father who gave the furniture of the sanctuary, and the images of Our Lady and Saint Christopher that they burned on the green."

"It is terrible," said Mary, a little absently, as she turned the pages of the book.

Mistress Margaret looked up.

"Ah! you have one of my books there," she said. "It is a little collection I made."

Miss Corbet turned to the beginning, but only found a seal with an inscription.

"But this belonged to a nunnery," she said.

"Yes," said Mistress Margaret, tranquilly, "and I am a nun."

Mary looked at her in astonishment.

"But, but," she began.

"Yes, Mistress Corbet; we were dispersed in '38; some entered the other nunneries; and some went to France; but, at last, under circumstances that I need not trouble you with, I came here under spiritual direction, and have observed my obligations ever since."

"And have you always said your offices?" Mary asked astonished.

"Yes, my dear; by the mercy of God I have never failed yet. I tell you this of course because you are one of us, and because you have a faithful heart." Mistress Margaret lifted her great eyes and looked at Mary tenderly and penetratingly.

"And this is one of your books?" she asked.

"Yes, my dear. I was allowed at least to take it away with me. My sister here is very fond of it."

Mary opened it again, and began to turn the pages.

"Is it all in your handwriting, Mistress Torridon?"

"Yes, my child; I continued writing in it ever since I first entered religion in 1534; so you see the handwriting changes a little," and she smiled to herself.

"Oh, but this is charming," cried Mary, intent on the book.

"Read it, my dear, aloud."

Mary read:

"Let me not rest, O Lord, nor have quiet,
But fill my soul with spiritual travail,
To sing and say, O mercy, Jesu sweet;
Thou my protection art in the battail.
Set thou aside all other apparail;
Let me in thee feel all my affiance.
Treasure of treasures, thou dost most avail.
Grant ere I die shrift, pardon, repentance."
Her voice trembled a little and ceased.

"That is from some verses of Dan John Lydgate, I think," said Mistress Margaret.

"Here is another," said Mary in a moment or two.

"Jesu, at thy will, I pray that I may be, All my heart fulfil with perfect love to thee:

That I have done ill, Jesu forgive thou me:

And suffer me never to spill, Jesu for thy pity."

"The nuns of Hampole gave me that," said Mistress Margaret. "It is by Richard Rolle, the hermit."

"Tell me a little," said Mary Corbet, suddenly laying down the book, "about the nunnery."

"Oh, my dear, that is too much to ask; but how happy we were. All was so still; it used to seem sometimes as if earth were just a dream; and that we walked in Paradise. Sometimes in the Greater Silence, when we had spoken no word nor heard one except in God's praise, it used to seem that if we could but be silent a little longer, and a little more deeply, in our hearts as well, we should hear them talking in heaven, and the harps; and the Saviour's soft footsteps. But it was not always like that."

"You mean," said Mary softly, "that, that—" and she stopped.

"Oh, it was hard sometimes; but not often. God is so good. But He used to allow such trouble and darkness and noise to be in our hearts sometimes—at least in mine. But then of course I was always very wicked. But sitting in the nymph-hay sometimes on a day like this, as we were allowed to do; with just tall thin trees like poplars and cypresses round us: and the stream running through the long grass; and the birds, and the soft sky and the little breeze; and then peace in our hearts; and the love of the Saviour round us—it seemed, it seemed as if God had nothing more to give; or, I should say, as if our hearts had no more space."

Mary was strangely subdued and quiet. Her little restless movements were still for once; and her quick, vivacious face was tranquil and a little awed.

"Oh, Mistress Margaret, I love to hear you talk like that. Tell me more."

"Well, my dear, we thought too much about ourselves, I think; and too little about God and His poor children who were not so happy as we were; so then the troubles began; and they got nearer and nearer; and at last the Visitor came. He—he was my brother, my dear, which made it harder; but he made a good end. I will tell you his story another time. He took away our great crucifix and our jewelled cope that old Mr. Wickham used to wear on the Great Festivals; and left us. He turned me out, too; and another who asked to go, but I went back for a while. And then, my dear, although we offered everything; our cows and our orchard and our hens, and all we had, you know how it ended; and one morning in May old Mr. Wickham said mass for us quite early, before the sun was risen, for the last time; and,—and he cried, my dear, at the elevation; and—and we were all crying too I think, and we all received communion together for the last time—and,—and, then we all went away, leaving just old Dame Agnes to keep the house until the Commissioner came. And oh, my dear, I don't think the house ever looked so dear as it did that morning, just as the sun rose over the roofs, and we were passing out through the meadow door where we had sat so often, to where the horses were waiting to take us away."

Miss Corbet's own eyes were full of tears as the old lady finished: and she put out her white slender hand, which Mistress Torridon took and stroked for a moment.

"Well," she said, "I haven't talked like this for a long while; but I knew you would understand. My dear, I have watched you while you have been here this time."

Mary Corbet smiled a little uneasily.

"And you have found me out?" she answered smiling.

"No, no; but I think our Saviour has found you out—or at least He is drawing very near."

A slight discomfort made itself felt in Mary's heart. This nun then was like all the rest, always trying to turn the whole world into monks and nuns by hints and pretended intuitions into the unseen.

"And you think I should be a nun too?" she asked, with just a shade of coolness in her tone.

"I should suppose not," said Mistress Margaret, tranquilly. "You do not seem to have a vocation for that, but I should think that our Lord means you to serve Him where you are. Who knows what you may not accomplish?"

This was a little disconcerting to Mary Corbet; it was not at all what she had expected. She did not know what to say; and took up the leather book again and began to turn over the pages. Mistress Margaret went on serenely with her embroidery, which she had neglected during the last sentence or two; and there was silence.

"Tell me a little more about the nunnery," said Mary in a minute or two, leaning back in her chair, with the book on her knees.

"Well, my dear, I scarcely know what to say. It is all far off now like a childhood. We talked very little; not at all until recreation; except by signs, and we used to spend a good deal of our time in embroidery. That is where I learnt this," and she held out her work to Mary for a moment. It was an exquisite piece of needlework, representing a stag running open-mouthed through thickets of green twining branches that wrapped themselves about his horns and feet. Mary had never seen anything quite like it before.

"What does it mean?" she asked, looking at it curiously.

"Quemadmodum cervus,"—began Mistress Margaret; "as the hart brayeth after the waterbrooks,"—and she took the embroidery and began to go on with it.—"It is the soul, you see, desiring and fleeing to God, while the things of the world hold her back. Well, you see, it is difficult to talk about it; for it is the inner life that is the real history of a convent; the outer things are all plain and simple like all else."

"Well," said Mary, "is it really true that you were happy?"

The old lady stopped working a moment and looked up at her.

"My dear, there is no happiness in the world like it," she said simply. "I dream sometimes that we are all back there together, and I wake crying for joy. The other night I dreamed that we were all in the chapel again, and that it was a spring morning, with the dawn beginning to show the painted windows, and that all the tapers were burning; and that mass was beginning. Not one stall was empty; not even old Dame Gertrude, who died when I was a novice, was lacking, and Mr. Wickham made us a sermon after the creed, and showed us the crucifix back in its place again; and told us that we were all good children, and that Our Lord had only sent us away to see if we would be patient; and that He was now pleased with us, and had let us come home again; and that we should never have to go away again; not even when we died; and then I understood that we were in heaven, and that it was all over; and I burst out into tears in my stall for happiness; and then I awoke and found myself in bed; but my cheeks were really wet.—Well, well, perhaps, by the mercy of God it may all come true some day."

She spoke so simply that Mary Corbet was amazed; she had always fancied that the Religious Life was a bitter struggle, worth, indeed, living for those who could bear it, for the sake of the eternal reward; but it had scarcely even occurred to her that it was so full of joy in itself; and she looked up under her brows at the old lady, whose needle had stopped for a moment.

A moment after and Lady Maxwell appeared coming down the steps into the garden; and at her side Anthony, who was dressed ready for riding.

Old Mistress Margaret had, as she said, been watching Mary Corbet those last few weeks; and had determined to speak to her plainly. Her instinct had told her that beneath this flippancy and glitter there was something that would respond; and she was anxious to leave nothing undone by which Mary might be awakened to the inner world that was in such danger of extinction in her soul. It cost the old lady a great effort to break through her ordinary reserve, but she judged that Mary could only be reached on her human side, and that there were not many of her friends whose human sympathy would draw her in the right direction. It is strange, sometimes, to find that some silent old lady has a power for sounding human character, which far shrewder persons lack; and this quiet old nun, so ignorant, one would have said, of the world and of the motives from which ordinary people act, had managed somehow to touch springs in this girl's heart that had never been reached before.

And now as Miss Corbet and Lady Maxwell talked, and Anthony lolled embarrassed beside them, attempting now and then to join in the conversation, Mistress Margaret, as she sat a little apart and worked away at the panting stag dreamed away, smiling quietly to herself, of all the old scenes that her own conversation had called up into clearer consciousness; of the pleasant little meadow of the Sussex priory, with the old apple-trees and the straight box-lined path called the nun's walk from time immemorial; all lighted with the pleasant afternoon glow, as it streamed from the west, throwing the slender poplar shadows across the grass; and of the quiet chatter of the brook as it overflowed from the fish ponds at the end of the field and ran through the meadows beyond the hedge. The cooing of the pigeons as they sunned themselves round the dial in the centre of this Italian garden and on the roof of the hall helped on her reminiscences, for there had been a dovecote at the priory. Where were all her sisters now, those who had sat with her in the same sombre habits in the garth, with the same sunshine in their hearts? Some she knew, and thanked God for it, were safe in glory; others were old like her, but still safe in Holy Religion in France where as yet there was peace and sanctuary for the servants of the Most High; one or two—and for these she lifted up her heart in petition as she sat—one or two had gone back to the world, relinquished everything, and died to grace. Then the old faces one by one passed before her; old Dame Agnes with her mumbling lips and her rosy cheeks like wrinkled apples, looking so fresh and wholesome in the white linen about her face; and then the others one by one—that white-faced, large-eyed sister who had shown such passionate devotion at first that they all thought that God was going to raise up a saint amongst them—ah! God help her—she had sunk back at the dissolution, from those heights of sanctity towards whose summits she had set her face, down into the muddy torrent of the world that went roaring down to the abyss—and who was responsible? There was Dame Avice, the Sacristan, with her businesslike movements going about the garden, gathering flowers for the altar, with her queer pursed lips as she arranged them in her hands with her head a little on one side; how annoying she used to be sometimes; but how good and tender at heart—God rest her soul! And there was Mr. Wickham, the old priest who had been their chaplain for so many years, and who lived in the village parsonage, waited upon by Tom Downe, that served at the altar too—he who had got the horses ready when the nuns had to go at last on that far-off May morning, and had stood there, holding the bridles and trying to hide his wet face behind the horses; where was Tom now? And Mr. Wickham too—he had gone to France with some of the nuns; but he had never settled down there—he couldn't bear the French ways—and besides he had left his heart behind him buried in the little Sussex priory among the meadows.

And so the old lady sat, musing; while the light and shadow of reminiscence moved across her face; and her lips quivered or her eyes wrinkled up with humour, at the thought of all those old folks with their faces and their movements and their ways of doing and speaking. Ah! well, please God, some day her dream would really come true; and they shall all be gathered again from France and England with their broken hearts mended and their tears wiped away, and Mr. Wickham himself shall minister to them and make them sermons, and Tom Downe too shall be there to minister to him—all in one of the many mansions of which the Saviour spoke.

And so she heard nothing of the talk of the others; though her sister looked at her tenderly once or twice; and Mary Corbet chattered and twitched her buckles in the sun, and Anthony sat embarrassed in the midst of Paradise; and she knew nothing of where she was nor of what was happening round her, until Mary Corbet said that it was time for the horses to be round, and that she must go and get ready and not keep Mr. James and Mr. Anthony waiting. Then, as she and Anthony went towards the house, the old lady looked up from the braying stag and found herself alone with her sister.

Mistress Margaret waited until the other two disappeared up the steps, and then spoke.

"I have told her all, sister," she said, "she can be trusted."

Lady Maxwell nodded gently.

"She has a good heart," went on the other, "and our Lord no doubt will find some work for her to do at Court."

There was silence again; broken by the gentle little sound of the silk being drawn through the stuff.

"You know best, Margaret," said Lady Maxwell.

Even as she spoke there was the sound of a door thrown violently open and old Sir Nicholas appeared on the top of the steps, hatless and plainly in a state of great agitation; beside him stood a courier, covered with the dust of the white roads, and his face crimson with hard riding. Sir Nicholas stood there as if dazed, and Lady Maxwell sprang up quickly to go to him. But a moment after there appeared behind him a little group, his son James, Miss Corbet and a servant or two; while Anthony hung back; and Mr. James came up quickly, and took his father by the arm; and together the little company came down the steps into the still and sunny garden.

"What is it?" cried Lady Maxwell, trying to keep her voice under control; while Mistress Margaret laid her work quietly down, and stood up too.

"Tell my lady," said Sir Nicholas to the courier, who stood a little apart.

"If you please, my lady," he said, as if repeating a lesson, "a Bull of the Holy Father has been found nailed to the door of the Bishop of London's palace, deposing Elizabeth and releasing all her subjects from their allegiance."

Lady Maxwell went to her husband and took him by the arm gently.

"What does it mean, sweetheart?" she asked.

"It means that Catholics must choose between their sovereign and their God."

"God have mercy," said a servant behind.

Chapter Six - Mr. Stewart

Sir Nicholas' exclamatory sentence was no exaggeration. That terrible choice of which he spoke, with his old eyes shining with the desire to make it, did not indeed come so immediately as he anticipated; but it came none the less. From every point of view the Bull was unfortunate, though it may have been a necessity; for it marked the declaration of war between England and the Catholic Church. A gentle appeal had been tried before; Elizabeth, who, it must be remembered had been crowned during mass with Catholic ceremonial, and had received the Blessed Sacrament, had been entreated by the Pope as his "dear daughter in Christ" to return to the Fold; and now there seemed to him no possibility left but this ultimatum.

It is indeed difficult to see what else, from his point of view, he could have done. To continue to pretend that Elizabeth was his "dear daughter" would have discredited his fatherly authority in the eyes of the whole Christian world. He had patiently made an advance towards his wayward child; and she had repudiated and scorned him. Nothing was left but to recognise and treat her as an enemy of the Faith, an usurper of spiritual prerogatives, and an apostate spoiler of churches; to do this might certainly bring trouble upon others of his less distinguished but more obedient children, who were in her power; but to pretend that the suffering thus brought down upon Catholics was unnecessary, and that the Pope alone was responsible for their persecution, is to be blind to the fact that Elizabeth had already openly defied and repudiated his authority, and had begun to do her utmost to coax and compel his children to be disobedient to their father.

The shock of the Bull to Elizabeth was considerable; she had not expected this extreme measure; and it was commonly reported too that France and Spain were likely now to unite on a religious basis against England; and that at least one of these Powers had sanctioned the issue of the Bull. This of course helped greatly to complicate further the already complicated political position. Steps were taken immediately to strengthen England's position against Scotland with whom it was now, more than ever, to be feared that France would co-operate; and the Channel Fleet was reinforced under Lord Clinton, and placed with respect to France in what was almost a state of war, while it was already in an informal state of war with Spain. There was fierce confusion in the Privy Council. Elizabeth, who at once began to vacillate under the combined threats of La Mothe, the French ambassador, and the arguments of the friend of Catholics, Lord Arundel, was counter-threatened with ruin by Lord Keeper Bacon unless she would throw in her lot finally with the Protestants and continue her hostility and resistance to the Catholic Scotch party. But in spite of Bacon Elizabeth's heart failed her, and if it had not been for the rashness of Mary Stuart's friends, Lord Southampton and the Bishop of Ross, the Queen might have been induced to substitute conciliation for severity towards Mary and the Catholic party generally. Southampton was arrested, and again there followed the further encouragement of the Protestant camp by the rising fortunes of the Huguenots and the temporary reverses to French Catholicism; so the pendulum swung this way and that. Elizabeth's policy changed almost from day to day. She was tormented with temporal fears of a continental crusade against her, and by the spiritual terrors of the Pope's Bull; and her unfathomable fickleness was the despair of her servants.

Meanwhile in the religious world a furious paper war broke out; and volleys from both sides followed the solemn roar and crash of Regnans in Excelsis.

But while the war of words went on, and the theological assaults and charges were given and received, repulsed or avoided, something practical must, it was felt, be done immediately; and search was made high and low for other copies of the Bull. The lawyers in the previous year had fallen under suspicion of religious unsoundness; judges could not be trusted to convict Catholics accused of their religion; and counsel was unwilling to prosecute them; therefore the first inquisition was made in the Inns of Court; and almost immediately a copy of the Bull was found in the room of a student in Lincoln's Inn, who upon the rack in the Tower confessed that he had received it from one John Felton, a Catholic gentleman who lived upon his property in Southwark. Upon Felton's arrest (for he had not attempted to escape) he confessed immediately, without pressure, that he had affixed the Bull to the Bishop of London's gate; but although he was racked repeatedly he would not incriminate a single person besides himself; but at his trial would only assert with a joyous confidence that he was not alone; and that twenty-five peers, six hundred gentlemen, and thirty thousand commoners were ready to die in the Holy Father's quarrel. He behaved with astonishing gallantry throughout, and after his condemnation had been pronounced upon the fourth of August at the Guildhall, on the charge of high-treason, he sent a diamond ring from his own finger, of the value of £400, to the Queen to show that he bore her no personal ill-will. He had been always a steadfast Catholic; his wife had been maid of honour to Mary and a friend of Elizabeth's. On August the eighth he suffered the abominable punishment prescribed; he was drawn on a hurdle to the gate of the Bishop's palace in S. Paul's Churchyard, where he had affixed the Bull, hanged upon a new gallows, cut down before he was unconscious, disembowelled and quartered. His name has since been placed on the roll of the Blessed by the Apostolic See in whose quarrel he so cheerfully laid down his life.

News of these and such events continued of course to be eagerly sought after by the Papists all over the kingdom; and the Maxwells down at Great Keynes kept in as close touch with the heart of affairs as almost any private persons in the kingdom out of town. Sir Nicholas was one of those fiery natures to whom opposition or pressure is as oil to flame. He began at once to organise his forces and prepare for the struggle that was bound to come. He established first a kind of private post to London and to other Catholic houses round; for purposes however of defence rather than offence, so that if any steps were threatened, he and his friends might be aware of the danger in time. There was great sorrow at the news of John Felton's death; and mass was said for his soul almost immediately in the little oratory at Maxwell Court by one of the concealed priests who went chiefly between Hampshire and Sussex ministering to the Catholics of those districts. Mistress Margaret spent longer than ever at her prayers; Lady Maxwell had all she could do to keep her husband from some furious act of fanatical retaliation for John Felton's death—some useless provocation of the authorities; the children at the Dower House began to come to the Hall less often, not because they were less welcomed, but because there was a constraint in the air. All seemed preoccupied; conversations ceased abruptly on their entrance, and fits of abstraction would fall from time to time upon their kindly hosts. In the meanwhile, too, the preparations for James Maxwell's departure, which had already begun to show themselves, were now pushed forward rapidly; and one morning in the late summer, when Isabel came up to the Hall, she found that Lady Maxwell was confined to her room and could not be seen that day; she caught a glimpse of Sir Nicholas' face as he quickly crossed the entrance hall, that made her draw back from daring to intrude on such grief; and on inquiry found that Mr. James had ridden away that morning, and that the servants did not know when to expect him back, nor what was his destination.

In other ways also at this time did Sir Nicholas actively help on his party. Great Keynes was in a convenient position and circumstances for agents who came across from the Continent. It was sufficiently near London, yet not so near to the highroad or to London itself as to make disturbance probable; and its very quietness under the spiritual care of a moderate minister like Mr. Dent, and its serenity, owing to the secret sympathy of many of the villagers and neighbours, as well as from the personal friendship between Sir Nicholas and the master of the Dower House—an undoubted Protestant—all these circumstances combined to make Maxwell Hall a favourite halting-place for priests and agents from the Continent. Strangers on horseback or in carriages, and sometimes even on foot, would arrive there after nightfall, and leave in a day or two for London. Its nearness to London enabled them to enter the city at any hour they thought best after ten or eleven in the forenoon. They came on very various businesses; some priests even stayed there and made the Hall a centre for their spiritual ministrations for miles round; others came with despatches from abroad, some of which were even addressed to great personages at Court and at the Embassies where much was being done by the Ambassadors at this time to aid their comrades in the Faith, and to other leading Catholics; and others again came with pamphlets printed abroad for distribution in England, some of them indeed seditious, but many of them purely controversial and hortatory, and with other devotional articles and books such as it was difficult to obtain in England, and might not be exposed for public sale in booksellers' shops: Agnus Deis, beads, hallowed incense and crosses were being sent in large numbers from abroad, and were eagerly sought after by the Papists in all directions. It was remarkable that while threatening clouds appeared to be gathering on all sides over the Catholic cause, yet the deepening peril was accompanied by a great outburst of religious zeal. It was reported to the Archbishop that "massing" was greatly on the increase in Kent; and was attributed, singularly enough, to the Northern Rebellion, which had ended in disaster for the Papists; but the very fact that such a movement could take place at all probably heartened many secret sympathisers, who had hitherto considered themselves almost alone in a heretic population.

Sir Nicholas came in one day to dinner in a state of great fury. One of his couriers had just arrived with news from London; and the old man came in fuming and resentful.

"What hypocrisy!" he cried out to Lady Maxwell and Mistress Margaret, who were seated at table. "Not content with persecuting Catholics, they will not even allow us to say we are persecuted for the faith. Here is the Lord Keeper declaring in the Star Chamber that no man is to be persecuted for his private faith, but only for his public acts, and that the Queen's Grace desires nothing so little as to meddle with any man's conscience. Then I suppose they would say that hearing mass was a public act and therefore unlawful; but then how if a man's private faith bids him to hear mass? Is not that meddling with his private conscience to forbid him to go to mass? What folly is this? And yet my Lord Keeper and her Grace are no fools! Then are they worse than fools?"

Lady Maxwell tried to quiet the old man, for the servants were not out of the room; and it was terribly rash to speak like that before them; but he would not be still nor sit down, but raged up and down before the hearth, growling and breaking out now and again. What especially he could not get off his mind was that this was the Old Religion that was prescribed. That England for generations had held the Faith, and that then the Faith and all that it involved had been declared unlawful, was to him iniquity unfathomable. He could well understand some new upstart sect being persecuted, but not the old Religion. He kept on returning to this.

"Have they so far forgotten the Old Faith as to think it can be held in a man's private conscience without appearing in his life, like their miserable damnable new fangled Justification by faith without works? Or that a man can believe in the blessed sacrament of the altar and yet not desire to receive it; or in penance and yet not be absolved; or in Peter and yet not say so, nor be reconciled. You may believe, say they, of their clemency, what you like; be justified by that; that is enough! Bah!"

However mere declaiming against the Government was barren work, and Sir Nicholas soon saw that; and instead, threw himself with more vigour than ever into entertaining and forwarding the foreign emissaries.

Mary Corbet had returned to London by the middle of July; and Hubert was not yet returned; so Sir Nicholas and the two ladies had the Hall to themselves. Now it must be confessed that the old man had neither the nature nor the training for the rôle of a conspirator, even of the mildest description. He was so exceedingly impulsive, unsuspicious and passionate that it would have been the height of folly to entrust him with any weighty secret, if it was possible to dispense with him; but the Catholics over the water needed stationary agents so grievously; and Sir Nicholas' name commanded such respect, and his house such conveniences, that they overlooked the risk involved in making him their confidant, again and again; besides it need not be said that his honour and fidelity was beyond reproach; and those qualities after all balance favourably against a good deal of shrewdness and discretion. He, of course, was serenely unable to distinguish between sedition and religion; and entertained political meddlers and ordinary priests with an equal enthusiasm. It was pathetic to Lady Maxwell to see her simple old husband shuffling away his papers, and puzzling over cyphers and perpetually leaving the key of them lying about, and betraying again and again when he least intended it, by his mysterious becks and nods and glances and oracular sayings, that some scheme was afoot. She could have helped him considerably if he had allowed her; but he had an idea that the capacities of ladies in general went no further than their harps, their embroidery and their devotions; and besides, he was chivalrously unwilling that his wife should be in any way privy to business that involved such risks as this.

One sunny morning in August he came into her room early just as she was finishing her prayers, and announced the arrival of an emissary from abroad.

"Sweetheart," he said, "will you prepare the east chamber for a young man whom we will call Mr. Stewart, if you please, who will arrive to-night. He hopes to be with us until after dusk to-morrow when he will leave; and I shall be obliged if you will—No, no, my dear. I will order the horses myself."

The old man then bustled off to the stableyard and ordered a saddle-horse to be taken at once to Cuckfield, accompanied by a groom on another horse. These were to arrive at the inn and await orders from a stranger "whom you will call Mr. Stewart, if you please." Mr. Stewart was to change horses there, and ride on to Maxwell Hall, and Sir Nicholas further ordered the same two horses and the same groom to be ready the following evening at about nine o'clock, and to be at "Mr. Stewart's" orders again as before.

31

This behaviour of Sir Nicholas' was of course most culpably indiscreet. A child could not but have suspected something, and the grooms, who were of course Catholics, winked merrily at one another when the conspirator's back was turned, and he had hastened in a transport of zeal and preoccupation back again to the house to interrupt his wife in her preparations for the guest.

That evening "Mr. Stewart" arrived according to arrangements. He was a slim red-haired man, not above thirty years of age, the kind of man his enemies would call foxy, with a very courteous and deliberate manner, and he spoke with a slight Scotch accent. He had the air of doing everything on purpose. He let his riding-whip fall as he greeted Lady Maxwell in the entrance hall; but picked it up with such a dignified grace that you would have sworn he had let it fall for some wise reason of his own. He had a couple of saddle-bags with him, which he did not let out of his sight for a moment; even keeping his eye upon them as he met the ladies and saluted them. They were carried up to the east chamber directly, their owner following; where supper had been prepared. There was no real reason, since he arrived with such publicity, why he should not have supped downstairs, but Sir Nicholas had been peremptory. It was by his directions also that the arrival had been accomplished in the manner it had.

After he had supped, Sir Nicholas receiving the dishes from the servants' hands at the door of the room with the same air of secrecy and despatch, his host suggested that he should come to Lady Maxwell's drawing-room, as the ladies were anxious to see him. Mr. Stewart asked leave to bring a little valise with him that had travelled in one of the bags, and then followed his host who preceded him with a shaded light along the gallery.

When he entered he bowed again profoundly, with a slightly French air, to the ladies and to the image over the fire; and then seated himself, and asked leave to open his valise. He did so with their permission, and displayed to them the numerous devotional articles and books that it contained. The ladies and Sir Nicholas were delighted, and set aside at once some new books of devotion, and then they fell to talk. The Netherlands, from which Mr. Stewart had arrived two days before, on the east coast, were full at this time of Catholic refugees, under the Duke of Alva's protection. Here they had been living, some of them even from Elizabeth's accession, and Sir Nicholas and his ladies had many inquiries to make about their acquaintances, many of which Mr. Stewart was able to satisfy, for, from his conversation he was plainly one in the confidence of Catholics both at home and abroad. And so the evening passed away quietly. It was thought better by Sir Nicholas that Mr. Stewart should not be present at the evening devotions that he always conducted for the household in the dining-hall, unless indeed a priest were present to take his place; so Mr. Stewart was again conducted with the same secrecy to the East Chamber; and Sir Nicholas promised at his request to look in on him again after prayers. When prayers were over, Sir Nicholas went up to his guest's room, and found him awaiting him in a state of evident excitement, very unlike the quiet vivacity and good humour he had shown when with the ladies.

"Sir Nicholas," he said, standing up, as his host came in, "I have not told you all my news." And when they were both seated he proceeded:

"You spoke a few minutes ago, Sir Nicholas, of Dr. Storey; he has been caught."

The old man exclaimed with dismay. Mr. Stewart went on:

"When I left Antwerp, Sir Nicholas, Dr. Storey was in the town. I saw him myself in the street by the Cathedral only a few hours before I embarked. He is very old, you know, and lame, worn out with good works, and he was hobbling down the street on the arm of a young man. When I arrived at Yarmouth I went out into the streets about a little business I had with a bookseller, before taking horse. I heard a great commotion down near the docks, at the entrance of Bridge Street; and hastened down there; and there I saw pursuivants and seamen and officers all gathered about a carriage, and keeping back the crowd that was pressing and crying out to know who the man was; and presently the carriage drove by me, scattering the crowd, and I could see within; and there sat old Dr. Storey, very white and ill-looking, but steady and cheerful, whom I had seen the very day before in Antwerp. Now this is very grievous for Dr. Storey; and I pray God to deliver him; but surely the Duke and the King of Spain must move now. They cannot leave him in Cecil's hands; and then, Sir Nicholas, we must all be ready, for who knows what may happen."

Sir Nicholas was greatly moved. There was one of the perplexities which so much harassed all the Papists at this time. It seemed certain that Mr. Stewart's prediction must be fulfilled. Dr. Storey was a naturalised subject of King Philip and in the employment of Alva, and he had been carried off forcibly by the English Government. It afterwards came out how it had been done. He had been lured away from Antwerp and enticed on board a trader at Bergen-op-Zoom, by Cecil's agents with the help of a traitor named Parker, on pretext of finding heretical books there arriving from England; and as soon as he had set foot on deck he was hurried below and carried straight off to Yarmouth. Here then was Sir Nicholas' perplexity. To welcome Spain when she intervened and to work actively for her, was treason against his country; to act against Spain was to delay the re-establishment of the Religion—something that appeared to him very like treason against his faith. Was the dreadful choice between his sovereign and his God, he wondered as he paced up and down and questioned Mr. Stewart, even now imminent?

The whole affair, too, was so formidable and so mysterious that the hearts of these Catholics and of others in England when they heard the tale began to fail them. Had the Government then so long an arm and so keen an eye? And if it was able to hale a man from the shadow of the Cathedral at Antwerp and the protection of the Duke of Alva into the hands of pursuivants at Yarmouth within the space of a few hours, who then was safe?

And so the two sat late that night in the East Chamber; and laid schemes and discussed movements and probabilities and the like, until the dawn began to glimmer through the cracks of the shutters and the birds to chirp in the eaves; and Sir Nicholas at last carried to bed with him an anxious and a heavy heart. Mr. Stewart, however, did not seem so greatly disturbed; possibly because on the one side he had not others dearer to him than his own life involved in these complex issues: and partly because he at any rate has not the weight of suspense and indecision that so drew his host two ways at once, for Mr. Stewart was whole-heartedly committed already, and knew well how he would act should the choice present itself between Elizabeth and Philip.

The following morning Sir Nicholas still would not allow his guest to come downstairs, and insisted that all his meals should be served in the East Chamber, while he himself, as before, received the food at the door and set it before Mr. Stewart. Mr. Stewart was greatly impressed and touched by the kindness of the old man, although not by his capacity for conspiracy. He had intended indeed to tell his host far more than he had done of the movements of political and religious events, for he could not but believe, before his arrival, that a Catholic so prominent and influential as Sir Nicholas was becoming by reputation among the refugees abroad, was a proper person to be entrusted even with the highest secrets; but after a very little conversation with him the night before, he had seen how ingenuous the old man was, with his laughable attempts at secrecy and his lamentable lack of discretion; and so he had contented himself with general information and gossip, and had really told Sir Nicholas very little indeed of any importance.

After dinner Sir Nicholas again conducted his guest to the drawing-room, where the ladies were ready to receive him. He had obtained Mr. Stewart's permission the night before to tell his wife and sister-in-law the news about Dr. Storey; and the four sat for several hours together discussing the situation. Mr. Stewart was able to tell them too, in greater detail, the story of Lord Sussex's punitive raid into Scotland in the preceding April. They had heard of course the main outline of the story with the kind of embroideries attached that were usual in those days of inaccurate reporting; but their guest was a Scotchman himself and had had the stories first-hand in some cases from those rendered homeless by the raid, who had fled to the Netherlands where he had met them. Briefly the raid was undertaken on the pretended plea of an invitation from the "King's men" or adherents of the infant James; but in reality to chastise Scotland and reduce it to servility. Sussex and Lord Hunsdon in the east, Lord Scrope on the west, had harried, burnt, and destroyed in the whole countryside about the Borders. Especially had Tiviotdale suffered. Altogether it was calculated that Sussex had burned three hundred villages and blown up fifty castles, and forty more "strong houses," some of these latter, however, being little more than border peels. Mr. Stewart's accounts were the more moving in that he spoke in a quiet delicate tone, and used little picturesque phrases in his speech.

"Twelve years ago," said Mr. Stewart, "I was at Branxholme myself. It was a pleasant house, well furnished and appointed; fortified, too, as all need to be in that country, with sheaves of pikes in all the lower rooms, and Sir Walter Scott gave me a warm welcome, for I was there on a business that pleased him. He showed me the gardens and orchards, all green and sweet, like these of yours, Lady Maxwell. And it seemed to me a home where a man might be content to spend all his days. Well, my Lord Sussex has been a visitor there now; and what he has left of the house would not shelter a cow, nor what is left of the pleasant gardens sustain her. At least, so one of the Scots told me whom I met in the Netherlands in June."

He talked, too, of the extraordinary scenes of romance and chivalry in which Mary Queen of Scots moved during her captivity under Lord Scrope's care at Bolton Castle in the previous year. He had met in his travels in France one of her undistinguished adherents who had managed to get a position in the castle during her detention there.

"The country was alive with her worshippers," said Mr. Stewart. "They swarmed like bees round a hive. In the night voices would be heard crying out to her Grace out of the darkness round the castle; and when the guards rode out they would find no man but maybe hear just a laugh or two. Her men would lie out at night and watch her window (for she would never go to rest till late), and pray towards it as if it were a light before the blessed sacrament. When she rode out a-hunting, with her guards of course about her, and my Lord Scrope or Sir Francis Knollys never far away, a beggar maybe would be sitting out on the road and ask an alms; and cry out 'God save your Grace'; but he would be a beggar who was accustomed to wear silk next his skin except when he went a-begging. Many young gentlemen there were, yes and old ones too, who would thank God for a blow or a curse from some foul English trooper for his meat, if only he might have a look from the Queen's eyes for his grace before meat. Oh! they would plot too, and scheme and lie awake half the night spinning their webs, not to catch her Grace indeed, but to get her away from that old Spider Scrope; and many's the word and the scrap of paper that would go in to her Grace, right under the very noses of my Lord Scrope and Sir Francis themselves, as they sat at their chess in the Queen's chamber. It's a long game of chess that the two Queens are playing; but thank our Lady and the Saints it's not mate yet—not mate yet; and the White Queen will win, please God, before the board's over-turned."

And he told them, too, of the failure of the Northern Rebellion, and the wretchedness of the fugitives.

"They rode over the moors to Liddisdale," he said, "ladies and all, in bitter weather, wind and snow, day after day, with stories of Clinton's troopers all about them, and scarcely time for bite or sup or sleep. My lady Northumberland was so overcome with weariness and sickness that she could ride no more at last, and had to be left at John-of-the-Side's house, where she had a little chamber where the snow came in at one corner, and the rats ran over my lady's face as she lay. My Lords Northumberland and Westmoreland were in worse case, and spent their Christmas with no roof over them but what they could find out in the braes and woods about Harlaw, and no clothes but the foul rags that some beggar had thrown away, and no food but a bird or a rabbit that they could pick up here and there, or what their friends could get to them now and again privately. And then my Lord Northumberland's little daughters whom he was forced to leave behind at Topcliff—a sweet Christmas they had! Their money and food was soon spent; they could have scarcely a fire in that bitter hard season; and God who feeds the ravens alone knows how they were sustained; and for entertainment to make the time pass merrily, all they had was to see the hanging of their own servants in scores about the house, who had served them and their father well; and all their music at night was the howling of the wind in those heavily laden Christmas-trees, and the noise of the chains in which the men were hanged."

Mr. Stewart's narratives were engrossing to the two ladies and Sir Nicholas. They had never come so close to the struggles of the Catholics in the north before; and although the Northern Rebellion had ended so disastrously, yet it was encouraging, although heartbreaking too, to hear that delicate women and children were ready gladly to suffer such miseries if the religious cause that was so dear to them could be thereby helped. Sir Nicholas, as has been said, was in two minds as to the lawfulness of rising against a temporal sovereign in defence of religious liberties. His whole English nature revolted against it, and yet so many spiritual persons seemed to favour it. His simple conscience was perplexed. But none the less he could listen with the most intense interest and sympathy to these tales of these co-religionists of his own, who were so clearly convinced of their right to rebel in defence of their faith.

And so with such stories the August afternoon passed away. It was a thundery day, which it would have been pleasanter to spend in the garden, but that, Sir Nicholas said, under the circumstances was not to be thought of; so they threw the windows wide to catch the least breath of air; and the smell of the flower-garden came sweetly up and flooded the low cool room; and so they sat engrossed until the evening.

Supper was ordered for Mr. Stewart at half-past seven o'clock; and this meal Sir Nicholas had consented should be laid downstairs in his own private room opening out of the hall, and that he and his ladies should sit down to table at the same time. Mr. Stewart went to his room an hour before to dress for riding, and to superintend the packing of his saddle-bags; and at half-past seven he was conducted downstairs by Sir Nicholas who insisted on carrying the saddle-bags with his own hands, and they found the two ladies waiting for them in the panelled study that had one window giving upon the terrace that ran along the south of the house above the garden. When supper had been brought in by Sir Nicholas' own body-servant, Mr. Boyd, they sat down to supper after a grace from Sir Nicholas. The horses were ordered for nine o'clock.

Chapter Seven - The Door in The Garden-Wall

On the morning of the day after Mr. Stewart's secret arrival at Maxwell Hall, the Rector was walking up and down the lawn that adjoined the churchyard.

He had never yet wholly recovered from the sneers of Mistress Corbet; the wounds had healed but had not ceased to smart. How blind these Papists were, he thought! how prejudiced for the old trifling details of worship! how ignorant of the vital principles still retained! The old realities of God and the faith and the Church were with them still, in this village, he reminded himself; it was only the incrustations of error that had been removed. Of course the transition was difficult and hearts were sore; but the Eternal God can be patient. But then, if the discontent of the Papists smouldered on one side, the fanatical and irresponsible zeal of the Puritans flared on the other. How difficult, he thought, to steer the safe middle course! How much cool faith and clearsightedness it needed! He reminded himself of Archbishop Parker who now held the rudder, and comforted himself with the thought of his wise moderation in dealing with excesses, his patient pertinacity among the whirling gusts of passion, that enabled him to wait upon events to push his schemes, and his tender knowledge of human nature.

But in spite of these reassuring facts Mr. Dent was anxious. What could even the Archbishop do when his suffragans were such poor creatures; and when Leicester, the strongest man at Court, was a violent Puritan partisan? The Rector would have been content to bear the troubles of his own flock and household if he had been confident of the larger cause; but the vagaries of the Puritans threatened all with ruin. That morning only he had received a long account from a Fellow of his own college of Corpus Christi, Cambridge, and a man of the same views as himself, of the violent controversy raging there at that time.

"The Professor," wrote his friend, referring to Thomas Cartwright, "is plastering us all with his Genevan ways. We are all Papists, it seems! He would have neither bishop nor priest nor archbishop nor dean nor archdeacon, nor dignitaries at all, but just the plain Godly Minister, as he names it. Or if he has the bishop and the deacon they are to be the Episcopos and the Diaconos of the Scripture, and not the Papish counterfeits! Then it seems that the minister is to be made not by God but by man—that the people are to make him, not the bishop (as if the sheep should make the shepherd). Then it appears we are Papists too for kneeling at the Communion; this he names a 'feeble superstition.' Then he would have all men reside in their benefices or vacate them; and all that do not so, it appears, are no better than thieves or robbers.

"And so he rages on, breathing out this smoky stuff, and all the young men do run after him, as if he were the very Pillar of Fire to lead them to Canaan. One day he says there shall be no bishop—and my Lord of Ely rides through Petty Cury with scarce a man found to doff cap and say 'my lord' save foolish 'Papists' like myself! Another day he will have no distinction of apparel; and the young sparks straight dress like ministers, and the ministers like young sparks. On another he likes not Saint Peter his day, and none will go to church. He would have us all to be little Master Calvins, if he could have his way with us. But the Master of Trinity has sent a complaint to the Council with charges against him, and has preached against him too. But no word hath yet come from the Council; and we fear nought will be done; to the sore injury of Christ His holy Church and the Protestant Religion; and the triumphing of their pestilent heresies."

So the caustic divine wrote, and the Rector of Great Keynes was heavy-hearted as he walked up and down and read. Everywhere it was the same story; the extreme precisians openly flouted the religion of the Church of England; submitted to episcopal ordination as a legal necessity and then mocked at it; refused to wear the prescribed dress, and repudiated all other distinctions too in meats and days as Judaic remnants; denounced all forms of worship except those directly sanctioned by Scripture; in short, they remained in the Church of England and drew her pay while they scouted her orders and derided her claims. Further, they cried out as persecuted martyrs whenever it was proposed to insist that they should observe their obligations. But worse than all, for such conscientious clergymen as Mr. Dent, was the fact that bishops preferred such men to livings, and at the same time were energetic against the Papist party. It was not that there was not an abundance of disciplinary machinery ready at the bishop's disposal or that the Queen was opposed to coercion—rather she was always urging them to insist upon conformity; but it seemed rather to such sober men as the Rector that the principle of authority had been lost with the rejection of the Papacy, and that anarchy rather than liberty had prevailed in the National Church. In darker moments it seemed to him and his friends as if any wild fancy was tolerated, so long as it did not approximate too closely to the Old Religion; and they grew sick at heart.

It was all the more difficult for the Rector, as he had so little sympathy in the place; his wife did all she could to destroy friendly relations between the Hall and the Rectory, and openly derided her husband's prelatical leanings; the Maxwells themselves disregarded his priestly claims, and the villagers thought of him as an official paid to promulgate the new State religion. The only house where he found sympathy and help was the Dower House; and as he paced up and down his garden now, his little perplexed determined face grew brighter as he made up his mind to see Mr. Norris again in the afternoon.

During his meditations he heard, and saw indistinctly, through the shrubbery that fenced the lawn from the drive, a mounted man ride up to the Rectory door. He supposed it was some message, and held himself in readiness to be called into the house, but after a minute or two he heard the man ride off again down the drive into the village. At dinner he mentioned it to his wife, who answered rather shortly that it was a message for her; and he let the matter drop for fear of giving offence; he was terrified at the thought of provoking more quarrels than were absolutely necessary.

Soon after dinner he put on his cap and gown, and to his wife's inquiries told her where he was going, and that after he had seen Mr. Norris he would step on down to Comber's, where was a sick body or two, and that she might expect him back not earlier than five o'clock. She nodded without speaking, and he went out. She watched him down the drive from the dining-room window and then went back to her business with an odd expression.

Mr. Norris, whom he found already seated at his books again after dinner, took him out when he had heard his errand, and the two began to walk up and down together on the raised walk that ran along under a line of pines a little way from the house.

The Rector had seldom found his friend more sympathetic and tender; he knew very well that their intellectual and doctrinal standpoints were different, but he had not come for anything less than spiritual help, and that he found. He told him all his heart, and then waited, while the other, with his thin hands clasped behind his back, and his great grey eyes cast up at the heavy pines and the tender sky beyond, began to comfort the minister.

"You are troubled, my friend," he said, "and I do not wonder at it, by the turbulence of these times. On all sides are fightings and fears. Of course I cannot, as you know, regard these matters you have spoken of—episcopacy, ceremonies at the Communion and the like—in the grave light in which you see them; but I take it, if I understand you rightly, that it is the confusion and lack of any authority or respect for antiquity that is troubling you more. You feel yourself in a sad plight between these raging waves; tossed to and fro, battered upon by both sides, forsaken and despised and disregarded. Now, indeed, although I do not stand quite where you do, yet I see how great the stress must be; but, if I may say so to a minister, it is just what you regard as your shame that I regard as your glory. It is the mark of the cross that is on your life. When our Saviour went to his passion, he went in the same plight as that in which you go; both Jew and Gentile were against him on this side and that; his claims were disallowed, his royalty denied; he was despised and rejected of men. He did not go to his passion as to a splendid triumph, bearing his pain like some solemn and mysterious dignity at which the world wondered and was silent; but he went battered and spat upon, with the sweat and the blood and the spittle running down his face, contemned by the contemptible, hated by the hateful, rejected by the outcast, barked upon by the curs; and it was that that made his passion so bitter. To go to death, however painful, with honour and applause, or at least with the silence of respect, were easy; it is not hard to die upon a throne; but to live on a dunghill with Job, that is bitterness. Now again I must protest that I have no right to speak like this to a minister, but since you have come to me I must needs say what I think; and it is this that some wise man once said, 'Fear honour, for shame is not far off. Covet shame, for honour is surely to follow.' If that be true of the philosopher, how much more true is it of the Christian minister whose profession it is to follow the Saviour and to be made like unto him."

He said much more of the same kind; and his soft balmy faith soothed the minister's wounds, and braced his will. The Rector could not help half envying his friend, living, as it seemed, in this still retreat, apart from wrangles and controversy, with the peaceful music and sweet fragrance of the pines, and the Love of God about him.

When he had finished he asked the Rector to step indoors with him; and there in his own room took down and read to him a few extracts from the German mystics that he thought bore upon his case. Finally, to put him at his ease again, for it seemed an odd reversal that he should be coming for comfort to his parishioners, Mr. Norris told him about his two children, and in his turn asked his advice.

"About Anthony," he said, "I am not at all anxious. I know that the boy fancies himself in love; and goes sighing about when he is at home; but he sleeps and eats heartily, for I have observed him; and I think Mistress Corbet has a good heart and means no harm to him. But about my daughter I am less satisfied, for I have been watching her closely. She is quiet and good, and, above all, she loves the Saviour; but how do I know that her heart is not bleeding within? She has been taught to hold herself in, and not to show her feelings; and that, I think, is as much a drawback sometimes as wearing the heart upon the sleeve."

Mr. Dent suggested sending her away for a visit for a month or two. His host mused a moment and then said that he himself had thought of that; and now that his minister said so too, probably, under God, that was what was needed. The fact that Hubert was expected home soon was an additional reason; and he had friends in Northampton, he said, to whom he could send her. "They hold strongly by the Genevan theology there," he said smiling, "but I think that will do her no harm as a balance to the Popery at Maxwell Hall."

They talked a few minutes more, and when the minister rose to take his leave, Mr. Norris slipped down on his knees as if it was the natural thing to do and as if the minister were expecting it; and asked his guest to engage in prayer. It was the first time he had ever done so; probably because this talk had brought them nearer together spiritually than ever before. The minister was taken aback, and repeated a collect or two from the Prayer-book; then they said the Lord's Prayer together, and then Mr. Norris without any affectation engaged in a short extempore prayer, asking for light in these dark times and peace in the storm; and begging the blessing of God upon the village and "upon their shepherd to whom Thou hast given to drink of the Cup of thy Passion," and upon his own children, and lastly upon himself, "the chief of sinners and the least of thy servants that is not worthy to be called thy friend." It touched Mr. Dent exceedingly, and he was yet more touched and reconciled to the incident when his host said simply, remaining on his knees, with eyes closed and his clear cut tranquil face upturned:

"I ask your blessing, sir."

The Rector's voice trembled a little as he gave it. And then with real gratitude and a good deal of sincere emotion he shook his friend's hand, and rustled out from the cool house into the sunlit garden, greeting Isabel who was walking up and down outside a little pensively, and took the field-path that led towards the hamlet where his sick folk were expecting him.

As he walked back about five o'clock towards the village he noticed there was thunder in the air, and was aware of a physical oppression, but in his heart it was morning and the birds singing. The talk earlier in the afternoon had shown him how, in the midst of the bitterness of the Cup, to find the fragrance where the Saviour's lips had rested and that was joy to him. And again, his true pastor's heart had been gladdened by the way his ministrations had been received that afternoon. A sour old man who had always scowled at him for an upstart, in his foolish old desire to be loyal to the priest who had held the benefice before him, had melted at last and asked his pardon and God's for having treated him so ill; and he had prepared the old man for death with great contentment to them both, and had left him at peace with God and man. On looking back on it all afterwards he was convinced that God had thus strengthened him for the trouble that was awaiting him at home.

He had hardly come into his study when his wife entered with a strange look, breathing quick and short; she closed the door, and stood near it, looking at him apprehensively.

"George," she said, rather sharply and nervously, "you must not be vexed with me, but—"

"Well?" he said heavily, and the warmth died out of his heart. He knew something terrible impended.

"I have done it for the best," she said, and obstinacy and a kind of impatient tenderness strove in her eyes as she looked at him. "You must show yourself a man; it is not fitting that loose ladies of the Court should mock—" He got up; and his eyes were determined too.

"Tell me what you have done, woman," he cried.

She put out her hand as if to hold him still, and her voice rang hard and thin.

"I will say my say," she said. "It is not for that that I have done it. But you are a Gospel-minister, and must be faithful. The Justice is here. I sent for him."

"The Justice?" he said blankly; but his heart was beating heavily in his throat.

"Mr. Frankland from East Grinsted, with a couple of pursuivants and a company of servants. There is a popish agent at the Hall, and they are come to take him."

The Rector swallowed with difficulty once or twice, and then tried to speak, but she went on. "And I have promised that you shall take them in by the side door."

"I will not!" he cried.

She held up her hand again for silence, and glanced round at the door.

"I have given him the key," she said.

This was the private key, possessed by the incumbent for generations past, and Sir Nicholas had not withdrawn it from the Protestant Rector.

"There is no choice," she said. "Oh! George, be a man!" Then she turned and slipped out.

He stood perfectly still for a moment; his pulses were racing; he could not think. He sat down and buried his face in his hands; and gradually his brain cleared and quieted. Then he realised what it meant, and his soul rose in blind furious resentment. This was the last straw; it was the woman's devilish jealousy. But what could he do? The Justice was here. Could he warn his friends? He clenched his fingers into his hair as the situation came out clear and hard before his brain. Dear God, what could he do?

There were footsteps in the flagged hall, and he raised his head as the door opened and a portly gentleman in riding-dress came in, followed by Mrs. Dent. The Rector rose confusedly, but could not speak, and his eyes wandered round to his wife again and again as she took a chair in the shadow and sat down. But the magistrate noticed nothing.

"Aha!" he said, beaming, "You have a wife, sir, that is a jewel. Solomon never spoke a truer word; an ornament to her husband, he said, I think; but you as a minister should know better than I, a mere layman"; and his face creased with mirth.

What did the red-faced fool mean? thought the Rector. If only he would not talk so loud! He must think, he must think. What could he do?

"She was very brisk, sir," the magistrate went on, sitting down, and the Rector followed his example, sitting too with his back to the window and his hand to his head.

Then Mr. Frankland went on with his talk; and the man sat there, still glancing from time to time mechanically towards his wife, who was there in the shadow with steady white face and hands in her lap, watching the two men. The magistrate's voice seemed to the bewildered man to roll on like a wheel over stones; interminable, grinding, stupefying. What was he saying? What was that about his wife? She had sent to him the day before, had she, and told him of the popish agent's coming?—Ah! A dangerous man was he, a spreader of seditious pamphlets? At least they supposed he was the man.—Yes, yes, he understood; these fly-by-nights were threateners of the whole commonwealth; they must be hunted out like vermin—just so; and he as a minister of the Gospel should be the first to assist.—Just so, he agreed with all his heart, as a minister of the Gospel. (Yes, but, dear Lord, what was he to do? This fat man with the face of a butcher must not be allowed to—) Ah! what was that? He had missed that. Would Mr. Frankland be so good as to say it again? Yes, yes, he understood now; the men were posted already. No one suspected anything; they had come by the bridle path.—Every door? Did he understand that every door of the Hall was watched? Ah! that was prudent; there was no chance then of any one sending a warning in? Oh, no, no, he did not dream for a moment that there was any concealed Catholic who would be likely to do such a thing. But he only wondered.—Yes, yes, the magistrate was right; one could not be too careful. Because—ah!—What was that about Sir Nicholas? Yes, yes, indeed he was a good landlord, and very popular in the village.—Ah! just so; it had better be done quietly, at the side door. Yes, that was the one which the key fitted. But, but, he thought perhaps, he had better not come in, because Sir Nicholas was his friend, and there was no use in making bad blood.—Oh! not to the house; very well, then, he would come as far as the yew hedge at—at what time did the magistrate say? At half-past eight; yes, that would be best as Mr. Frankland said, because Sir Nicholas had ordered the horses for nine o'clock; so they would come upon them just at the right time.—How many men, did Mr. Frankland say? Eight? Oh yes, eight and himself, and—he did not quite follow the plan. Ah! through the yew hedge on to the terrace and through the south door into the hall; then if they bolted—they? Surely he had understood the magistrate to say there was only one? Oh! he had not understood that. Sir Nicholas too? But why, why? Good God, as a harbourer of priests?—No, but this fellow was an agent, surely. Well, if the magistrate said so, of course he was right; but he would have thought himself that Sir Nicholas might have been left—ah! Well, he would say no more. He quite saw the magistrate's point now.—No, no, he was no favourer; God forbid! his wife would speak for him as to that; Marion would bear witness.—Well, well, he thanked the magistrate for his compliments, and would he proceed with the plan? By the south door, he was saying, yes, into the hall.—Yes, the East room was Sir Nicholas' study; or of course they might be supping upstairs. But it made no difference; no, the magistrate was right about that. So long as they held the main staircase, and had all the other doors watched, they were safe to have him.—No, no, the cloister wing would not be used; they might leave that out of their calculations. Besides, did not the magistrate say that Marion had seen the lights in the East wing last night? Yes, well, that settled it.—And the signal? Oh, he had not caught that; the church bell, was it to be? But what for? Why did they need a signal? Ah! he understood, for the advance at half-past eight.—Just so, he would send Thomas up to ring it. Would Marion kindly see to that?—Yes, indeed, his wife was a woman to be proud of; such a faithful Protestant; no patience with these seditious rogues at all. Well, was that all? Was there anything else?—Yes, how dark it was getting; it must be close on eight o'clock. Thomas had gone, had he? That was all right.—And had the men everything they wanted?—Well, yes; although the village did go to bed early it would perhaps be better to have no lights; because there was no need to rouse suspicion.—Oh! very well; perhaps it would be better for Mr. Frankland to go and sit with the men and keep them quiet. And his wife would go, too, just to make sure they had all they wanted.—Very well, yes; he would wait here in the dark until he was called. Not more than a quarter of an hour? Thank you, yes.—

Then the door had closed; and the man, left alone, flung himself down in his chair, and buried his face again in his arms.

Ah! what was to be done? Nothing, nothing, nothing. And there they were at the Hall, his neighbours and friends. The kind old Catholic and his ladies! How would he ever dare to meet their eyes again? But what could be done? Nothing! How far away the afternoon seems; that quiet sunny walk beneath the pines. His friend is at his books, no doubt, with the silver candles, and the open pages, and his own neat manuscript growing under his white scholarly fingers. And Isabel; at her needlework before the fire.—How peaceful and harmless and sweet it all is! And down there, not fifty yards away, is the village; every light out by now; and the children and parents, too, asleep.—Ah! what will the news be when they wake to-morrow?—And that strange talk this afternoon, of the Saviour and His Cup of pain, and the squalor and indignity of the Passion! Ah! yes, he could suffer with Jesus on the Cross, so gladly, on that Tree of Life—but not with Judas on the Tree of Death!

And the minister dropped his face lower, over the edge of his desk; and the hot tears of misery and self-reproach and impotence began to run. There was no help, no help anywhere. All were against him—even his wife herself; and his Lord.

Then with a moan he lifted his hot face into the dusk.

"Jesus," he cried in his soul, "Thou knowest all things; Thou knowest that I love Thee."

There came a tapping on the door; and the door opened an inch.

"It is time," whispered his wife's voice.

Chapter Eight - The Taking of Mr. Stewart

They were still sitting over the supper-table at the Hall. The sun had set about the time they had begun, and the twilight had deepened into dark; but they had not cared to close the shutters as they were to move so soon. The four candles shone out through the windows, and there still hung a pale glimmer outside owing to the refraction of light from the white stones of the terrace. Beyond on the left there sloped away a high black wall of impenetrable darkness where the yew hedge stood; over that was the starless sky. Sir Nicholas' study was bright with candlelight, and the lace and jewels of Lady Maxwell (for her sister wore none) added a vague pleasant sense of beauty to Mr. Stewart's mind; for he was one who often fared coarsely and slept hard. He sighed a little to himself as he looked out over this shining supper-table past the genial smiling face of Sir Nicholas to the dark outside; and thought how in less than an hour he would have left the comfort of this house for the grey road and its hardships again. It was extraordinarily sweet to him (for he was a man of taste and a natural inclination to luxury) to stay a day or two now and again at a house like this and mix again with his own equals, instead of with the rough company of the village inn, or the curious foreign conspirators with their absence of educated perception and their doubtful cleanliness. He was a man of domestic instincts and good birth and breeding, and would have been perfectly at his ease as the master of some household such as this; with a chapel and a library and a pleasant garden and estate; spending his days in great leisure and good deeds. And instead of all this, scarcely by his own choice but by what he would have called his vocation, he was partly an exile living from hand to mouth in lodgings and inns, and when he was in his own fatherland, a hunted fugitive lurking about in unattractive disguises. He sighed again once or twice. There was silence a moment or two.

There sounded one note from the church tower a couple of hundred yards away. Lady Maxwell heard it, and looked suddenly up; she scarcely knew why, and caught her sister's eyes glancing at her. There was a shade of uneasiness in them.

"It is thundery to-night," said Sir Nicholas. Mr. Stewart did not speak. Lady Maxwell looked up quickly at him as he sat on her right facing the window; and saw an expression of slight disturbance cross his face. He was staring out on to the quickly darkening terrace, past Sir Nicholas, who with pursed lips and a little frown was stripping off his grapes from the stalk. The look of uneasiness deepened, and the young man half rose from his chair, and sat down again.

"What is it, Mr. Stewart?" said Lady Maxwell, and her voice had a ring of terror in it. Sir Nicholas looked up quickly. "Eh, eh?"—he began.

The young man rose up and recoiled a step, still staring out.

"I beg your pardon," he said, "but I have just seen several men pass the window."

There was a rush of footsteps and a jangle of voices outside in the hall; and as the four rose up from table, looking at one another, there was a rattle at the handle outside, the door flew open, and a ruddy strongly-built man stood there, with a slightly apprehensive air, and holding a loaded cane a little ostentatiously in his hand; the faces of several men looked over his shoulder.

Sir Nicholas' ruddy face had paled, his mouth was half open with dismay, and he stared almost unintelligently at the magistrate. Mr. Stewart's hand closed on the handle of a knife that lay beside his plate.

"In the Queen's name," said Mr. Frankland, and looked from the knife to the young man's white determined face, and down again. A little sobbing broke from Lady Maxwell.

"It is useless, sir," said the magistrate; "Sir Nicholas, persuade your guest not to make a useless resistance; we are ten to one; the house has been watched for hours."

Sir Nicholas took a step forward, his mouth closed and opened again. Lady Maxwell took a swift rustling step from behind the table, and threw her arm round the old man's neck. Still none of them spoke.

"Come in," said the magistrate, turning a little. The men outside filed in, to the number of half a dozen, and two or three more were left in the hall. All were armed. Mistress Margaret who had stood up with the rest, sat down again, and rested her head on her hand; apparently completely at her ease.

"I must beg pardon, Lady Maxwell," he went on, "but my duty leaves me no choice." He turned to the young man, who, on seeing the officers had laid the knife down again, and now stood, with one hand on the table, rather pale, but apparently completely self-controlled, looking a little disdainfully at the magistrate.

Then Sir Nicholas made a great effort; but his face twitched as he spoke, and the hand that he lifted to his wife's arm shook with nervousness, and his voice was cracked and unnatural.

"Sit down, my dear, sit down.—What is all this?—I do not understand.—Mr. Frankland, sir, what do you want of me?—And who are all these gentlemen?—Won't you sit down, Mr. Frankland and take a glass of wine. Let me make Mr. Stewart known to you." And he lifted a shaking hand as if to introduce them.

The magistrate smiled a little on one side of his mouth.

"It is no use, Sir Nicholas," he said, "this gentleman, I fear, is well known to some of us already.—No, no, sir," he cried sharply, "the window is guarded."

Mr. Stewart, who had looked swiftly and sideways across at the window, faced the magistrate again.

"I do not know what you mean, sir," he said. "It was a lad who passed the window."

There was a movement outside in the hall; and the magistrate stepped to the door.

"Who is there?" he cried out sharply.

There was a scuffle, and a cry of a boy's voice; and a man appeared, holding Anthony by the arm.

Mistress Margaret turned round in her seat; and said in a perfectly natural voice, "Why, Anthony, my lad!"

There was a murmur from one or two of the men.

"Silence," called out the magistrate. "We will finish the other affair first," and he made a motion to hold Anthony for a moment.—"Now then, do any of you men know this gentleman?"

A pursuivant stepped out.

"Mr. Frankland, sir; I know him under two names—Mr. Chapman and Mr. Wode. He is a popish agent. I saw him in the company of Dr. Storey in Antwerp, four months ago."

Mr. Stewart blew out his lips sharply and contemptuously.

"Pooh," he said; and then turned to the man and bowed ironically.

"I congratulate you, my man," he said, in a tone of bitter triumph. "In April I was in France. Kindly remember this man's words, Mr. Frankland; they will tell in my favour. For I presume you mean to take me."

"I will remember them," said the magistrate.

Mr. Stewart bowed to him; he had completely regained his composure. Then he turned to Sir Nicholas and Lady Maxwell, who had been watching in a bewildered silence.

"I am exceedingly sorry," he said, "for having brought this annoyance on you, Lady Maxwell; but these men are so sharp that they see nothing but guilt everywhere. I do not know yet what my crime is. But that can wait. Sir Nicholas, we should have parted anyhow in half an hour. We shall only say good-bye here, instead of at the door."

The magistrate smiled again as before; and half put up his hand to hide it.

"I beg your pardon, Mr. Chapman; but you need not part from Sir Nicholas yet. I fear, Sir Nicholas, that I shall have to trouble you to come with us."

Lady Maxwell drew a quick hissing breath; her sister got up swiftly and went to her, as she sat down in Sir Nicholas' chair, still holding the old man's hand.

Sir Nicholas turned to his guest; and his voice broke again and again as he spoke.

"Mr. Stewart," he said, "I am sorry that any guest of mine should be subject to these insults. However, I am glad that I shall have the pleasure of your company after all. I suppose we ride to East Grinsted," he added harshly to the magistrate, who bowed to him.—"Then may I have my servant, sir?"

"Presently," said Mr. Frankland, and then turned to Anthony, who had been staring wild-eyed at the scene, "Now who is this?"

A man answered from the rank.

"That is Master Anthony Norris, sir."

"Ah! and who is Master Anthony Norris? A Papist, too?"

"No, sir," said the man again, "a good Protestant; and the son of Mr. Norris at the Dower House."

"Ah!" said the magistrate again, judicially. "And what might you be wanting here, Master Anthony Norris?"

Anthony explained that he often came up in the evening, and that he wanted nothing. The magistrate eyed him a moment or two.

"Well, I have nothing against you, young gentleman. But I cannot let you go, till I am safely set out. You might rouse the village. Take him out till we start," he added to the man who guarded him.

"Come this way, sir," said the officer; and Anthony presently found himself sitting on the long oak bench that ran across the western end of the hall, at the foot of the stairs, and just opposite the door of Sir Nicholas' room where he had just witnessed that curious startling scene.

The man who had charge of him stood a little distance off, and did not trouble him further, and Anthony watched in silence.

The hall was still dark, except for one candle that had been lighted by the magistrate's party, and it looked sombre and suggestive of tragedy. Floor walls and ceiling were all dark oak, and the corners were full of shadows. A streak of light came out of the slightly opened door opposite, and a murmur of voices. The rest of the house was quiet; it had all been arranged and carried out without disturbance.

Anthony had a very fair idea of what was going forward; he knew of course that the Catholics were always under suspicion, and now understood plainly enough from the conversation he had heard that the reddish-haired young man, standing so alert and cheerful by the table in there, had somehow precipitated matters. Anthony himself had come up on some trifling errand, and had run straight into this affair; and now he sat and wondered resentfully, with his eyes and ears wide open.

There were men at all the inner doors now; they had slipped in from the outer entrances as soon as word had reached them that the prisoners were secured, and only a couple were left outside to prevent the alarm being raised in the village. These inner sentinels stood motionless at the foot of the stairs that rose up into the unlighted lobby overhead, at the door that led to the inner hall and the servants' quarters, and at those that led to the cloister wing and the garden respectively.

The murmur of voices went on in the room opposite; and presently a man slipped out and passed through the sentinels to the door leading to the kitchens and pantry; he carried a pike in his hand, and was armed with a steel cap and breast-piece. In a minute he had returned followed by Mr. Boyd, Sir Nicholas' body-servant; the two passed into the study—and a moment later the dark inner hall was full of moving figures and rustlings and whisperings, as the alarmed servants poured up from downstairs.

Then the study door opened again, and Anthony caught a glimpse of the lighted room; the two ladies with Sir Nicholas and his guest were seated at table; there was the figure of an armed man behind Mr. Stewart's chair, and another behind Lady Maxwell's; then the door closed again as Mr. Boyd with the magistrate and a constable carrying a candle came out.

"This way, sir," said the servant; and the three crossed the hall, and passing close by Anthony, went up the broad oak staircase that led to the upper rooms. Then the minutes passed away; from upstairs came the noise of doors opening and shutting, and footsteps passing overhead; from the inner hall the sound of low talking, and a few sobs now and again from a frightened maid; from Sir Nicholas' room all was quiet except once when Mr. Stewart's laugh, high and natural, rang out. Anthony thought of that strong brisk face he had seen in the candlelight; and wondered how he could laugh, with death so imminent—and worse than death; and a warmth of admiration and respect glowed at the lad's heart. The man by Anthony sighed and shifted his feet.

"What is it for?" whispered the lad at last.

"I mustn't speak to you, sir," said the man.

At last the footsteps overhead came to the top of the stairs. The magistrate's voice called out sharply and impatiently:

"Come along, come along"; and the three, all carrying bags and valises came downstairs again and crossed the hall. Again the door opened as they went in, leaving the luggage on the floor; and Anthony caught another glimpse of the four still seated round the table; but Sir Nicholas' head was bowed upon his hands.

Then again the door closed; and there was silence.

Once more it was flung open, and Anthony saw the interior of the room plainly. The four were standing up, Mr. Stewart was bowing to Lady Maxwell; the magistrate stood close beside him; then a couple of men stepped up to the young man's side as he turned away, and the three came out into the hall and stood waiting by the little heap of luggage. Mr. Frankland came next, with the man-servant close beside him, and the rest of the men behind; and the last closed the door and stood by it. There was a dead silence; Anthony sprang to his feet in uncontrollable excitement. What was happening? Again the door opened, and the men made room as Mistress Margaret came out, and the door shut.

She came swiftly across, with her little air of dignity and confidence, towards Anthony, who was standing forward.

"Why, Master Anthony," she said, "dear lad; I did not know they had kept you," and she took his hand.

"What is it, what is it?" he whispered sharply.

"Hush," she said; and the two stood together in silence.

The moments passed; Anthony could hear the quick thumping beat of his own heart, and the breathing of Mistress Margaret; but the hall was perfectly quiet, where the magistrate with the prisoner and his men stood in an irregular dark group with the candle behind them; and no sound came from the room beyond.

Then the handle turned, and a crack of light showed; but no further sound; then the door opened wide, a flood of light poured out and Sir Nicholas tottered into the hall.

"Margaret, Margaret," he cried. "Where are you? Go to her."

There was a strange moaning sound from the brightly lighted room. The old lady dropped Anthony's hand and moved swiftly and unfalteringly across, and once more the door closed behind her.

There was a sharp word of command from the magistrate, and the sentries from every door left their posts, and joined the group which, with Sir Nicholas and his guest and Mr. Boyd in the centre, now passed out through the garden door.

The magistrate paused as he saw Anthony standing there alone.

"I can trust you, young gentleman," he said, "not to give the alarm till we are gone?"

Anthony nodded, and the magistrate passed briskly out on to the terrace, shutting the door behind him; there was a rush of footsteps and a murmur of voices and the hall was filled with the watching servants.

As the chorus of exclamations and inquiries broke out, Anthony ran straight through the crowd to the garden door, and on to the terrace. They had gone to the left, he supposed, but he hesitated a moment to listen; then he heard the stamp of horses' feet and the jingle of saddlery, and saw the glare of torches through the yew hedge; and he turned quickly and ran along the terrace, past the flood of light that poured out from the supper room, and down the path that led to the side-door opposite the Rectory. It was very dark, and he stumbled once or twice; then he came to the two or three stairs that led down to the door in the wall, and turned off among the bushes, creeping on hands and feet till he reached the wall, low on this side, but deep on the other; and looked over.

The pursuivants with their men had formed a circle round the two prisoners, who were already mounted and who sat looking about them as the luggage was being strapped to their saddles before and behind; the bridles were lifted forward over the horses' heads, and a couple of the guard held each rein. The groom who had brought round the two horses for Mr. Stewart and himself stood white-faced and staring, with his back to the Rectory wall. The magistrate was just mounting at a little distance his own horse, which was held by the Rectory boy. Mr. Boyd, it seemed, was to walk with the men. Two or three torches were burning by now, and every detail was distinct to Anthony, as he crouched among the dry leaves and peered down on to the group just beneath.

Sir Nicholas' face was turned away from him; but his head was sunk on his breast, and he did not stir or lift it as his horse stamped at the strapping on of the valise Mr. Boyd had packed for him. Mr. Stewart sat erect and motionless, and his face as Anthony saw it was confident and fearless.

Then suddenly the door in the Rectory wall opposite was flung open, and a figure in flying black skirts, but hatless, rushed out and through the guard straight up to the old man's knee. There was a shout from the men and a movement to pull him off, but the magistrate who was on his horse and just outside the circle spoke sharply, and the men fell back.

"Oh, Sir Nicholas, Sir Nicholas," sobbed the minister, his face half buried in the saddle. Anthony saw his shoulders shaking, and his hands clutching at the old man's knee. "Forgive me, forgive me."

There was no answer from Sir Nicholas; he still sat unmoved, his chin on his breast, as the Rector sobbed and moaned at his stirrup.

"There, there," said the magistrate decidedly, over the heads of the guard, "that is enough, Mr. Dent"; and he made a motion with his hand.

A couple of men took the minister by the shoulders and drew him, still crying out to Sir Nicholas, outside the group; and he stood there dazed and groping with his hands. There was a word of command; and the guard moved off at a sharp walk, with the horses in the centre, and as they turned, the lad saw in the torchlight the old man's face drawn and wrinkled with sorrow, and great tears running down it.

The Rector leaned against his own wall, with his hands over his face; and Anthony looked at him with growing suspicion and terror as the flare of the torches on the trees faded, and the noise of the troop died away round the corner.

Chapter Nine - Village Justice

The village had never known such an awakening as on the morning that followed Sir Nicholas' arrest. Before seven o'clock every house knew it, and children ran half-dressed to the outlying hamlets to tell the story. Very little work was done that day, for the estate was disorganised; and the men had little heart for work; and there were groups all day on the green, which formed and re-formed and drifted here and there and discussed and sifted the evidence. It was soon known that the Rectory household had had a foremost hand in the affair. The groom, who had been present at the actual departure of the prisoners had told the story of the black figure that ran out of the door, and of what was cried at the old man's knee; and how he had not moved nor spoken in answer; and Thomas, the Rectory boy, was stopped as he went across the green in the evening and threatened and encouraged until he told of the stroke on the church-bell, and the Rectory key, and the little company that had sat all the afternoon in the kitchen over their ale. He told too how a couple of hours ago he had been sent across with a note to Lady Maxwell, and that it had been returned immediately unopened.

So as night fell, indignation had begun to smoulder fiercely against the minister, who had not been seen all day; and after dark had fallen the name "Judas" was cried in at the Rectory door half a dozen times, and a stone or two from the direction of the churchyard had crashed on the tiles of the house.

Mr. Norris had been up all day at the Hall, but he was the only visitor admitted. All day long the gate-house was kept closed, and the same message was given to the few horsemen and carriages that came to inquire after the truth of the report from the Catholic houses round, to the effect that it was true that Sir Nicholas and a friend had been taken off to London by the Justice from East Grinsted; and that Lady Maxwell begged the prayers of her friends for her husband's safe return.

Anthony had ridden off early with a servant, at his father's wish, to follow Sir Nicholas and learn any news of him that was possible, to do him any service he was able, and to return or send a message the next day down to Great Keynes; and early in the afternoon he returned with the information that Sir Nicholas was at the Marshalsea, that he

42

was well and happy, that he sent his wife his dear love, and that she should have a letter from him before nightfall. He rode straight to the Hall with the news, full of chastened delight at his official importance, just pausing to tell a group that was gathered on the green that all was well so far, and was shown up to Lady Maxwell's own parlour, where he found her, very quiet and self-controlled, and extremely grateful for his kindness in riding up to London and back on her account. Anthony explained too that he had been able to get Sir Nicholas one or two comforts that the prison did not provide, a pillow and an extra coverlet and some fruit; and he left her full of gratitude.

His father had been up to see the ladies two or three times, and in spite of the difference in religion had prayed with them, and talked a little; and Lady Maxwell had asked that Isabel might come up to supper and spend the evening. Mr. Norris promised to send her up, and then added:

"I am a little anxious, Lady Maxwell, lest the people may show their anger against the Rector or his wife, about what has happened."

Lady Maxwell looked startled.

"They have been speaking of it all day long," he said, "they know everything; and it seems the Rector is not so much to blame as his wife. It was she who sent for the magistrate and gave him the key and arranged it all; he was only brought into it too late to interfere or refuse."

"Have you seen him?" asked the old lady.

"I have been both days," he said, "but he will not see me; he is in his study, locked in."

"I may have treated him hardly," she said, "I would not open his note; but at least he consented to help them against his friend." And her old eyes filled with tears.

"I fear that is so," said the other sadly.

"But speak to the people," she said, "I think they love my husband, and would do nothing to grieve us; tell them that nothing would pain either of us more than that any should suffer for this. Tell them they must do nothing, but be patient and pray."

There was a group still on the green near the pond as Isabel came up to supper that evening about six o'clock. Her father, who had given Lady Maxwell's message to the people an hour or two before, had asked her to go that way and send down a message to him immediately if there seemed to be any disturbance or threatening of it; but the men were very quiet. Mr. Musgrave was there, she saw, sitting with his pipe, on the stocks, and Piers, the young Irish bailiff, was standing near; they all were silent as the girl came up, and saluted her respectfully as usual; and she saw no signs of any dangerous element. There were one or two older women with the men, and others were standing at their open doors on all sides as she went up. The Rectory gate was locked, and no one was to be seen within.

Supper was laid in Sir Nicholas' room, as it generally was, and as it had been two nights ago; and it was very strange to Isabel to know that it was here that the arrest had taken place; the floor, too, she noticed as she came in, all about the threshold was scratched and dented by rough boots.

Lady Maxwell was very silent and distracted during supper; she made efforts to talk again and again, and her sister did her best to interest her and keep her talking; but she always relapsed after a minute or two into silence again, with long glances round the room, at the Vernacle over the fireplace, the prie-dieu with the shield of the Five Wounds above it, and all the things that spoke so keenly of her husband.

What a strange room it was, too, thought Isabel, with its odd mingling of the two worlds, with the tapestry of the hawking scene and the stiff herons and ladies on horseback on one side, and the little shelf of devotional books on the other; and yet how characteristic of its owner who fingered his cross-bow or the reins of his horse all day, and his beads in the evening; and how strange that an old man like Sir Nicholas, who knew the world, and had as much sense apparently as any one else, should be willing to sacrifice home and property and even life itself, for these so plainly empty superstitious things that could not please a God that was Spirit and Truth! So Isabel thought to herself, with no bitterness or contempt, but just a simple wonder and amazement, as she looked at the painted tokens and trinkets.

It was still daylight when they went upstairs to Lady Maxwell's room about seven, but the clear southern sky over the yew hedges and the tall elms where the rooks were circling, was beginning to be flushed with deep amber and rose. Isabel sat down in the window seat with the sweet air pouring in and looked out on to the garden with its tiled paths and its cool green squares of lawn, and the glowing beds at the sides. Over to her right the cloister court ran out, with its two rows of windows, bedrooms above with galleries beyond, as she knew, and parlours and cloisters below; the pleasant tinkle of the fountain in the court came faintly to her ears across the caw of the rooks about the elms and the low sounds from the stables and the kitchen behind the house. Otherwise the evening was very still; the two old ladies were sitting near the fireplace; Lady Maxwell had taken up her embroidery, and was looking at it listlessly, and Mistress Margaret had one of her devotional books and was turning the pages, pausing here and there as she did so.

Presently she began to read, without a word of introduction, one of the musings of the old monk John Audeley in his sickness, and as the tender lines stepped on, that restless jewelled hand grew still.

"As I lay sick in my languor
In an abbey here by west;
This book I made with great dolour,
When I might not sleep nor rest.
Oft with my prayers my soul I blest,
And said aloud to Heaven's King,
'I know, O Lord, it is the best
Meekly to take thy visiting.
Else well I wot that I were lorn
(High above all lords be he blest!)
All that thou dost is for the best;
By fault of Thee was no man lost,
That is here of woman born.'"

And then she read some of Rolle's verses to Jesus, the "friend of all sick and sorrowful souls," and a meditation of his on the Passion, and the tranquil thoughts and tender fragrant sorrows soothed the torn throbbing soul; and Isabel saw the old wrinkled hand rise to her forehead, and the embroidery, with the needle still in it slipped to the ground; as the holy Name "like ointment poured forth" gradually brought its endless miracle and made all sweet and healthful again.

Outside the daylight was fading; the luminous vault overhead was deepening to a glowing blue as the sunset contracted on the western horizon to a few vivid streaks of glory; the room was growing darker every moment; and Mistress Margaret's voice began to stumble over words.

The great gilt harp in the corner only gleamed here and there now in single lines of clear gold where the dying daylight fell on the strings. The room was full of shadows and the image of the Holy Mother and Child had darkened into obscurity in their niche. The world was silent now too; the rooks were gone home and the stir of the household below had ceased; and in a moment more Mistress Margaret's voice had ceased too, as she laid the book down.

Then, as if the world outside had waited for silence before speaking, there came a murmur of sound from the further side of the house. Isabel started up; surely there was anger in that low roar from the village; was it this that her father had feared? Had she been remiss? Lady Maxwell too sprang up and faced the window with wide large eyes.

"The letter!" she said; and took a quick step towards the door; but Mistress Margaret was with her instantly, with her arm about her.

"Sit down, Mary," she said, "they will bring it at once"; and her sister obeyed; and she sat waiting and looking towards the door, clasping and unclasping her hands as they lay on her lap; and Mistress Margaret stood by her, waiting and watching too. Isabel still stood by the window listening. Had she been mistaken then? The roar had sunk into silence for a moment; and there came back the quick beat of a horse's hoofs outside on the short drive between the gatehouse and the Hall. They were right, then; and even as she thought it, and as the wife that waited for news of her husband drew a quick breath and half rose in her seat at the sound of that shod messenger that bore them, again the roar swelled up louder than ever; and Isabel sprang down from the low step of the window-seat into the dusky room where the two sisters waited.

"What is that? What is that?" she whispered sharply.

There was a sound of opening doors, and of feet that ran in the house below; and Lady Maxwell rose up and put out her hand, as a man-servant dashed in with a letter.

"My lady," he said panting, and giving it to her, "they are attacking the Rectory."

Lady Maxwell, who was half-way to the window now, for light to read her husband's letter, paused at that.

"The Rectory?" she said. "Why—Margaret—" then she stopped, and Isabel close beside her, saw her turn resolutely from the great sealed letter in her hand to the door, and back again.

"Jervis told us, my lady; none saw him as he rode through—they were breaking down the gate."

Then Lady Maxwell, with a quick movement, lifted the letter to her lips and kissed it, and thrust it down somewhere out of sight in the folds of her dress.

"Come, Margaret," she said.

Isabel followed them down the stairs and out through the hall-door; and there, as they came out on to the steps that savage snarling roar swelled up from the green. There was laughter and hooting mixed with that growl of anger; but even the laughter was fierce. The gatehouse stood up black against the glare of torches, and the towers threw great swinging shadows on the ground and the steps of the Hall.

Isabel followed the two grey glimmering figures, and was astonished at the speed with which she had to go. The hoofs of the courier's horse rang on the cobbles of the stable-yard as they came down towards the gatehouse, and the two wings of the door were wide-open through which he had passed just now; but the porter was gone.

Ah! there was the crowd; but not at the Rectory. On the right the Rectory gate lay wide open, and a flood of light poured out from the house-door at the end of the drive. Before them lay the dark turf, swarming with black figures towards the lower end; and a ceaseless roar came from them. There were half a dozen torches down there, tossing to and fro; Isabel saw that the crowd was still moving down towards the stocks and the pond.

Now the two ladies in front of her were just coming up with the skirts of the crowd; and there was an exclamation or two of astonishment as the women and children saw who it was that was coming. Then there came the furious scream of a man, and the crowd parted, as three men came reeling out together, two of them trying with all their power to restrain a fighting, kicking, plunging man in long black skirts, who tore and beat with his hands. The three ladies stopped for a moment, close together; and simultaneously the struggling man broke free and dashed back into the crowd, screaming with anger and misery.

"Marion, Marion—I am coming—O God!"

And Isabel saw with a shock of horror that sent her crouching and clinging close to Mistress Margaret, that it was the Rector. But the two men were after him and caught him by the shoulders as he disappeared; and as they turned they faced Lady Maxwell.

"My lady, my lady," stammered one, "we mean him no harm. We—" But his voice stopped, as there came a sudden silence, rent by a high terrible shriek and a splash; followed in a moment by a yell of laughter and shouting; and Lady Maxwell threw herself into the crowd in front.

There were a few moments of jostling in the dark, with the reek and press of the crowd about her; and Isabel found herself on the brink of the black pond, with Lady Maxwell on one side, and Piers on the other keeping the crowd back, and a dripping figure moaning and sobbing in the trampled mud at Lady Maxwell's feet. There was silence enough now, and the ring of faces opposite stared astonished and open-mouthed at the tall old lady with her grey veiled head upraised, as she stood there in the torchlight and rated them in her fearless indignant voice.

"I am ashamed, ashamed!" cried Lady Maxwell. "I thought you were men. I thought you loved my husband; and—and me." Her voice broke, and then once more she cried again. "I am ashamed, ashamed of my village."

And then she stooped to that heaving figure that had crawled up, and laid hold tenderly of the arms that were writhed about her feet.

"Come home, my dear," Isabel heard her whisper.

It was a strange procession homeward up the trampled turf. The crowd had broken into groups, and the people were awed and silent as they watched the four women go back together. Isabel walked a little behind with her father and Anthony, who had at last been able to come forward through the press and join them; and a couple of the torchbearers escorted them. In front went the three, on one side Lady Maxwell, her lace and silk splashed and spattered with mud, and her white hands black with it, and on the other the old nun, each with an arm thrown round the woman in the centre who staggered and sobbed and leaned against them as she went, with her long hair and her draggled clothes streaming with liquid mud every step she took. Once they stopped, at a group of three men. The Rector was sitting up, in his torn dusty cassock, and Isabel saw that one of his buckled shoes was gone, as he sat on the grass with his feet before him, but quiet now, with his hands before him, and a dazed stupid look in his little black eyes that blinked at the light of the torch that was held over him; he said nothing as he looked at his wife between the two ladies, but his lips moved, and his eyes wandered for a moment to Lady Maxwell's face, and then back to his wife.

"Take him home presently," she said to the men who were with him—and then passed on again.

As they got through the gatehouse, Isabel stepped forward to Mistress Margaret's side.

"Shall I come?" she whispered; and the nun shook her head; so she with her father and brother stood there to watch, with the crowd silent and ashamed behind. The two torchbearers went on and stood by the steps as the three ladies ascended, leaving black footmarks as they went. The door was open and faces of servants peeped out, and hands were thrust out to take the burden from their mistress, but she shook her head, and the three came in together, and the door closed.

As the Norrises went back silently, the Rector passed them, with a little group accompanying him too; he, too, could hardly walk alone, so exhausted was he with his furious struggles to rescue his wife.

"Take your sister home," said Mr. Norris to Anthony; and they saw him slip off and pass his arm through the Rector's, and bend down his handsome kindly face to the minister's staring eyes and moving lips as he too led him homewards.

Even Anthony was hushed and impressed, and hardly spoke a word until he and Isabel turned off down the little dark lane to the Dower House.

"We could do nothing," he said, "father and I—until Lady Maxwell came."

"No," said Isabel softly, "she only could have done it."

Chapter Ten - A Confessor

Sir Nicholas and the party were lodged at East Grinsted the night of their arrest, in the magistrate's house. Although he was allowed privacy in his room, after he had given his word of honour not to attempt an escape, yet he was allowed no conversation with Mr. Stewart or his own servant except in the presence of the magistrate or one of the pursuivants; and Mr. Stewart, since he was personally unknown to the magistrate, and since the charge against him was graver, was not on any account allowed to be alone for a moment, even in the room in which he slept. The following day they all rode on to London, and the two prisoners were lodged in the Marshalsea. This had been for a long while the place where Bishop Bonner was confined; and where Catholic prisoners were often sent immediately after their arrest; and Sir Nicholas at any rate found to his joy that he had several old friends among the prisoners. He was confined in a separate room; but by the kindness of his gaoler whom he bribed profusely as the custom was, through his servant, he had many opportunities of meeting the others; and even of approaching the sacraments and hearing mass now and then.

He began a letter to his wife on the day of his arrival and finished it the next day which was Saturday, and it was taken down immediately by the courier who had heard the news and had called at the prison. In fact, he was allowed a good deal of liberty; although he was watched and his conversation listened to, a good deal more than he was aware. Mr. Stewart, however, as he still called himself, was in a much harder case. The saddle-bags had been opened on his arrival, and incriminating documents found. Besides the "popish trinkets" they were found to contain a number of "seditious pamphlets," printed abroad for distribution in England; for at this time the College at Douai, under its founder Dr. William Allen, late Principal of St. Mary's Hall, Oxford, was active in the production of literature; these were chiefly commentaries on the Bull; as well as exhortations to the Catholics to stand firm and to persevere in recusancy, and to the schismatic Catholics, as they were called, to give over attending the services in the parish churches. There were letters also from Dr. Storey himself, whom the authorities already had in person under lock and key at the Tower. These were quite sufficient to make Mr. Stewart a prize; and he also was very shortly afterwards removed to the Tower.

Sir Nicholas wrote a letter at least once a week to his wife; but writing was something of a labour to him; it was exceedingly doubtful to his mind whether his letters were not opened and read before being handed to the courier, and as his seal was taken from him his wife could not tell either. However they seemed to arrive regularly; plainly therefore the authorities were either satisfied with their contents or else did not think them worth opening or suppressing. He was quite peremptory that his wife should not come up to London; it would only increase his distress, he said; and he liked to think of her at Maxwell Hall; there were other reasons too that he was prudent enough not to commit to paper, and which she was prudent enough to guess at, the principal of which was, of course, that she ought to be there for the entertaining and helping of other agents or priests who might be in need of shelter.

The old man got into good spirits again very soon. It pleased him to think that God had honoured him by imprisonment; and he said as much once or twice in his letters to his wife. He was also pleased with a sense of the part he was playing in the rôle of a conspirator; and he underlined and put signs and exclamation marks all over his letters of which he thought his wife would understand the significance, but no one else; whereas in reality the old lady was sorely puzzled by them, and the authorities who opened the letters generally read them of course like a printed book.

One morning about ten days after his arrival the Governor of the prison looked in with the gaoler, and announced to Sir Nicholas, after greeting him, that he was to appear before the Council that very day. This, of course, was what Sir Nicholas desired, and he thanked the Governor cordially for his good news.

"They will probably keep you at the Tower, Sir Nicholas," said the Governor, "and we shall lose you. However, sir, I hope you will be more comfortable there than we have been able to make you."

The knight thanked the Governor again, and said good-day to him with great warmth; for they had been on the best of terms with one another during his short detention at the Marshalsea.

The following day Sir Nicholas wrote a long letter to his wife describing his examination.

"We are in royal lodgings here at last, sweetheart; Mr. Boyd brought my luggage over yesterday; and I am settled for the present in a room of my own in the White Tower; with a prospect over the Court. I was had before my lords yesterday in the Council-room; we drove hither from the Marshalsea. There was a bay window in the room. I promise you they got little enough from me. There was my namesake, Sir Nicholas Bacon, my lords Leicester and Pembroke, and Mr. Secretary Cecil; Sir James Crofts, the Controller of the Household, and one or two more; but these were the principal. I was set before the table on a chair alone with none to guard me; but with men at the doors I knew very well. My lords were very courteous to me; though they laughed more than was seemly at such grave times. They questioned me much as to my religion. Was I a papist? If they meant by that a Catholic, that I was, and thanked God for it every day—(those nicknames like me not). Was I then a recusant? If by that they meant, Did I go to their Genevan Hotch-Potch? That I did not nor never would. I thought to have said a word here about St. Cyprian his work De Unitate Ecclesiae, as F—r X. told me, but they would not let me speak. Did I know Mr. Chapman? If by that they meant Mr. Stewart, that I did, and for a courteous God-fearing gentleman too. Was he a Papist, or a Catholic if I would have it so? That I would not tell them; let them find that out with their pursuivants and that crew. Did I think Protestants to be fearers of God? That I did not; they feared nought but the Queen's Majesty, so it seemed to me. Then they all laughed at once—I know not why. Then they grew grave; and Mr. Secretary began to ask me questions, sharp and hard; but I would not be put upon, and answered him again as he asked. Did I know ought of Dr. Storey? Nothing, said I, save that he is a good Catholic, and that they had taken him. He is a seditious rogue, said my Lord Pembroke. That he is not, said I. Then they asked me what I thought of the Pope and his Bull, and whether he can depose princes. I said I thought him to be the Vicar of Christ; and as to his power to depose princes, that I supposed he could do, if he said so. Then two or three cried out on me that I had not answered honestly; and at that I got wrath; and then they laughed again, at least I saw Sir James Crofts at it. And Mr. Secretary, looking very hard at me asked whether if Philip sent an armament against Elizabeth to depose her, I would fight for him or her grace. For neither, said I: I am too old. For which then would you pray? said they. For the Queen's Grace, said I, for that she was my sovereign. This seemed to content them; and they talked a little among themselves. They had asked me other questions too as to my way of living; whether I went to mass. They asked me too a little more about Mr. Stewart. Did I know him to be a seditious rascal? That I did not, said I. Then how, asked they, did you come to receive him and his pamphlets? Of his pamphlets, said I, I know nothing; I saw nothing in his bags save beads and a few holy books and such things. (You see, sweetheart, I did him no injury by saying so, because I knew that they had his bags themselves.) And I said I had received him because he was recommended to me by some good friends of mine abroad, and I told them their names too; for they are safe in Flanders now.

"And when they had done their questions they talked again for a while; and I was sent out to the antechamber to refresh myself; and Mr. Secretary sent a man with me to see that I had all I needed; and we talked together a little, and he said the Council were in good humour at the taking of Dr. Storey; and he had never seen them so merry. Then I was had back again presently; and Mr. Secretary said I was to stay in the Tower; and that Mr. Boyd was gone already to bring my things. And so after that I went by water to the Tower, and here I am, sweetheart, well and cheerful, praise God....

"My dearest, I send you my heart's best love. God have you in his holy keeping."

The Council treated the old knight very tenderly. They were shrewd enough to see his character very plainly; and that he was a simple man who knew nothing of sedition, but only had harboured agents thinking them to be as guileless as himself. As a matter of fact, Mr. Stewart was an agent of Dr. Storey's; and was therefore implicated in a number of very grave charges. This of course was a very serious matter; but both in the examination of the Council, and in papers in Mr. Stewart's bags, nothing could be found to implicate Sir Nicholas in any political intrigue at all. The authorities were unwilling too to put such a man to the torture. There was always a possibility of public resentment against the torture of a man for his religion alone; and they were desirous not to arouse this, since they had many prisoners who would be more productive subjects of the rack than a plainly simple and loyal old man whose only crime was his religion. They determined, however, to make an attempt to get a little more out of Sir Nicholas by a device which would excite no resentment if it ever transpired, and one which was more suited to the old man's nature and years.

Sir Nicholas thus described it to his wife.

"Last night, my dearest, I had a great honour and consolation. I was awakened suddenly towards two o'clock in the morning by the door of my room opening and a man coming in. It was somewhat dark, and I could not see the man plainly, but I could see that he limped and walked with a stick, and he breathed hard as he entered. I sat up and demanded of him who he was and what he wanted; and telling me to be still, he said that he was Dr. Storey. You may be sure, sweetheart, that I sprang up at that; but he would not let me rise; and himself sat down beside me. He said that by the kindness of a gaoler he had been allowed to come; and that he must not stay with me long; that he had heard of me from his good friend Mr. Stewart. I asked him how he did, for I heard that he had been racked; and he said yes, it was true; but that by the mercy of God and the prayers of the saints he had held his peace and they knew nothing from him. Then he asked me a great number of questions about the men I had entertained, and where they were now; and he knew many of their names. Some of them were friends of his own, he said; especially the priests. We talked a good while, till the morning light began; and then he said he must be gone or the head gaoler would know of his visit, and so he went. I wish I could have seen his face, sweetheart, for I think him a great servant of God; but it was still too dark when he went, and we dared not have a light for fear it should be seen."

This was as a matter of fact a ruse of the authorities. It was not Dr. Storey at all who was admitted to Sir Nicholas' prison, but Parker, who had betrayed him at Antwerp. It was so successful, for Sir Nicholas told him all that he knew (which was really nothing at all) that it was repeated a few months later with richer results; when the conspirator Baily, hysterical and almost beside himself with the pain of the rack, under similar circumstances gave up a cypher which was necessary to the Council in dealing with the correspondence of Mary Stuart. However, Sir Nicholas never knew the deception, and to the end of his days was proud that he had actually met the famous Dr. Storey, when they were both imprisoned in the Tower together, and told his friends of it with reverent pride when the doctor was hanged a year later.

Hubert, who had been sent for to take charge of the estate, had come to London soon after his father's arrival at the Tower; and was allowed an interview with him in the presence of the Lieutenant. Hubert was greatly affected; though he could not look upon the imprisonment with the same solemn exultation as that which his father had; but it made a real impression upon him to find that he took so patiently this separation from home and family for the sake of religion. Hubert received instructions from Sir Nicholas as to the management of the estate, for it was becoming plain that his father would have to remain in the Tower for the present; not any longer on a really grave charge, but chiefly because he was an obstinate recusant and would promise nothing. The law and its administration at this time were very far apart; the authorities were not very anxious to search out and punish those who were merely recusants or refused to take the oath of supremacy; and so Hubert and Mr. Boyd and other Catholics were able to come and go under the very nose of justice without any real risk to themselves; but it was another matter to let a sturdy recusant go from prison who stoutly refused to give any sort of promise or understanding as to future behaviour.

Sir Nicholas was had down more than once to further examination before the Lords Commissioners in the Lieutenant's house; but it was a very tame and even an amusing affair for all save Sir Nicholas. It was so easy to provoke him; he was so simple and passionate that they could get almost anything they wanted out of him by a little adroit baiting; and more than once his examination formed a welcome and humorous entr'acte between two real tragedies. Sir Nicholas, of course, never suspected for a moment that he was affording any amusement to any one. He thought their weary laughter to be sardonic and ironical, and he looked upon himself as a very desperate fellow indeed; and wrote glowing accounts of it all to his wife, full of apostrophic praises to God and the saints, in a hand that shook with excitement and awe at the thought of the important scenes in which he played so prominent a part.

But there was no atmosphere of humour about Mr. Stewart. He had disappeared from Sir Nicholas' sight on their arrival at the Marshalsea, and they had not set eyes on one another since; nor could all the knight's persuasion and offer of bribes make his gaoler consent to take any message or scrap of paper between them. He would not even answer more than the simplest inquiries about him,—that he was alive and in the Tower, and so forth; and Sir Nicholas prayed often and earnestly for that deliberate and vivacious young man who had so charmed and interested them all down at Great Keynes, and who had been so mysteriously engulfed by the sombre majesty of the law.

"I fear," he wrote to Lady Maxwell, "I fear that our friend must be sick or dying. But I can hear no news of him; when I am allowed sometimes to walk in the court or on the leads he is never there. My attendant Mr. Jakes looks glum and says nothing when I ask him how my friend does. My dearest, do not forget him in your prayers nor your old loving husband either."

One evening late in October Mr. Jakes did not come as usual to bring Sir Nicholas his supper at five o'clock; the time passed and still he did not come. This was very unusual. Presently Mrs. Jakes appeared instead, carrying the food which she set down at the door while she turned the key behind her. Sir Nicholas rallied her on having turned gaoler; but she turned on him a face with red eyes and lined with weeping.

"O Sir Nicholas," she said, for these two were good friends, "what a wicked place this is! God forgive me for saying so; but they've had that young man down there since two o'clock; and Jakes is with them to help; and he told me to come up to you, Sir Nicholas, with your supper, if they weren't done by five; and if the young gentleman hadn't said what they wanted."

Sir Nicholas felt sick.

"Who is it?" he asked.

"Why, who but Mr. Stewart?" she said; and then fell weeping again, and went out forgetting to lock the door behind her in her grief. Sir Nicholas sat still a moment, sick and shaken; he knew what it meant; but it had never come so close to him before. He got up presently and went to the door to listen for he knew not what. But there was no sound but the moan of the wind up the draughty staircase, and the sound of a prisoner singing somewhere above him a snatch of a song. He looked out presently, but there was nothing but the dark well of the staircase disappearing round to the left, and the glimmer of an oil lamp somewhere from the depths below him, with wavering shadows as the light was blown about by the gusts that came up from outside. There was nothing to be done of course; he closed the door, went back and prayed with all his might for the young man who was somewhere in this huge building, in his agony.

Mr. Jakes came up himself within half an hour to see if all was well; but said nothing of his dreadful employment or of Mr. Stewart; and Sir Nicholas did not like to ask for fear of getting Mrs. Jakes into trouble. The gaoler took away the supper things, wished him good-night, went out and locked the door, apparently without noticing it had been left undone before. Possibly his mind was too much occupied with what he had been seeing and doing. And the faithful account of all this went down in due time to Great Keynes.

The arrival of the courier at the Hall on Wednesday and Saturday was a great affair both to the household and to the village. Sir Nicholas sent his letter generally by the Saturday courier, and the other brought a kind of bulletin from Mr. Boyd, with sometimes a message or two from his master. These letters were taken by the ladies first to the study, as if to an oratory, and Lady Maxwell would read them slowly over to her sister. And in the evening, when Isabel generally came up for an hour or two, the girl would be asked to read them slowly all over again to the two ladies who sat over their embroidery on either side of her, and who interrupted for the sheer joy of prolonging it. And they would discuss together the exact significance of all his marks of emphasis and irony; and the girl would have all she could do sometimes not to feel a disloyal amusement at the transparency of the devices and the simplicity of the loving hearts that marvelled at the writer's depth and ingenuity. But she was none the less deeply impressed by his courageous cheerfulness, and by the power of a religion that in spite of its obvious weaknesses and improbabilities yet inspired an old man like Sir Nicholas with so much fortitude.

At first, too, a kind of bulletin was always issued on the Sunday and Thursday mornings, and nailed upon the outside of the gatehouse, so that any who pleased could come there and get first-hand information; and an interpreter stood there sometimes, one of the educated younger sons of Mr. Piers, and read out to the groups from Lady Maxwell's sprawling old handwriting, news of the master.

"Sir Nicholas has been had before the Council," he read out one day in a high complacent voice to the awed listeners, "and has been sent to the Tower of London." This caused consternation in the village, as it was supposed by the country-folk, not without excuse, that the Tower was the antechamber of death; but confidence was restored by the further announcement a few lines down that "he was well and cheerful."

Great interest, too, was aroused by more domestic matters.

"Sir Nicholas," it was proclaimed, "is in a little separate chamber of his own. Mr. Jakes, his gaoler, seems an honest fellow. Sir Nicholas hath a little mattress from a friend that Mr. Boyd fetched for him. He has dinner at eleven and supper at five. Sir Nicholas hopes that all are well in the village."

But other changes had followed the old knight's arrest. The furious indignation in the village against the part that the Rectory had played in the matter, made it impossible for the Dents to remain there. That the minister's wife should have been publicly ducked, and that not by a few blackguards but by the solid fathers and sons with the applause of the wives and daughters, made her husband's position intolerable, and further evidence was forthcoming in the behaviour of the people towards the Rector himself; some boys had guffawed during his sermon on the following Sunday, when he had ventured on a word or two of penitence as to his share in the matter, and he was shouted after on his way home.

Mrs. Dent seemed strangely changed and broken during her stay at the Hall. She had received a terrible shock, and it was not safe to move her back to her own house. For the first two or three nights, she would start from sleep again and again screaming for help and mercy and nothing would quiet her till she was wide awake and saw in the firelight the curtained windows and the bolted door, and the kindly face of an old servant or Mistress Margaret with her beads in her hand. Isabel, who came up to see her two or three times, was both startled and affected by the change in her; and by the extraordinary mood of humility which seemed to have taken possession of the hard self-righteous Puritan.

"I begged pardon," she whispered to the girl one evening, sitting up in bed and staring at her with wide, hard eyes, "I begged pardon of Lady Maxwell, though I am not fit to speak to her. Do you think she can ever forgive me? Do you think she can? It was I, you know, who wrought all the mischief, as I have wrought all the mischief in the village all these years. She said she did, and she kissed me, and said that our Saviour had forgiven her much more. But—but do you think she has forgiven me?" And then again, another night, a day or two before they left the place, she spoke to Isabel again.

"Look after the poor bodies," she said, "teach them a little charity; I have taught them nought but bitterness and malice, so they have but given me my own back again. I have reaped what I have sown."

So the Dents slipped off early one morning before the folk were up; and by the following Sunday, young Mr. Bodder, of whom the Bishop entertained a high opinion, occupied the little desk outside the chancel arch; and Great Keynes once more had to thank God and the diocesan that it possessed a proper minister of its own, and not a mere unordained reader, which was all that many parishes could obtain.

Towards the end of September further hints began to arrive, very much underlined, in the knight's letters, of Mr. Stewart and his sufferings.

"You remember our friend," Isabel read out one Saturday evening, "not Mr. Stewart." (This puzzled the old ladies sorely till Isabel explained their lord's artfulness.) "My dearest, I fear the worst for him. I do not mean apostacy, thank God. But I fear that these wolves have torn him sadly, in their dens." Then followed the story of Mrs. Jakes, with all its horror, all the greater from the obscurity of the details.

Isabel put the paper down trembling, as she sat on the rug before the fire in the parlour upstairs, and thought of the bright-eyed, red-haired man with his steady mouth and low laugh whom Anthony had described to her.

Lady Maxwell posted upon the gatehouse:

"Sir Nicholas fears that a friend is in sore trouble; he hopes he may not yield."

Then, after a few days more, a brief notice with a black-line drawn round it, that ran, in Mr. Bodder's despite:

"Our friend has passed away. Pray for his soul."

Sir Nicholas had written in great agitation to this effect.

"My sweetheart, I have heavy news to-day. There was a great company of folks below my window to-day, in the Inner Ward, where the road runs up below the Bloody Tower. It was about nine of the clock. And there was a horse there whose head I could see; and presently from the Beauchamp Tower came, as I thought, an old man between two warders; and then I could not very well see; the men were in my way; but soon the horse went off, and the men after him; and I could hear the groaning of the crowd that were waiting for them outside. And when Mr. Jakes brought me my dinner at eleven of the clock, he told me it was our friend—(think of it, my dearest—him whom I thought an old man!)—that had been taken off to Tyburn. And now I need say no more, but bid you pray for his soul."

Isabel could hardly finish reading it; for she heard a quick sobbing breath behind her, and felt a wrinkled old hand caressing her hair and cheek as her voice faltered.

Meanwhile Hubert was in town. Sir Nicholas had at first intended him to go down at once and take charge of the estate; but Piers was very competent, and so his father consented that he should remain in London until the beginning of October; and this too better suited Mr. Norris' plans who wished to send Isabel off about the same time to Northampton.

When Hubert at last did arrive, he soon showed himself extremely capable and apt for the work. He was out on the estate from morning till night on his cob, and there was not a man under him from Piers downwards who had anything but praise for his insight and industry.

There was in Hubert, too, as there so often is in country-boys who love and understand the life of the woods and fields, a balancing quality of a deep vein of sentiment; and this was now consecrated to Isabel Norris. He had pleasant dreams as he rode home in the autumn evening, under the sweet keen sky where the harvest moon rose large and yellow over the hills to his left and shed a strange mystical light that blended in a kind of chord with the dying daylight. It was at times like that, when the air was fragrant with the scent of dying leaves, with perhaps a touch of frost in it, and the cottages one by one opened red glowing eyes in the dusk, that the boy began to dream of a home of his own and pleasant domestic joys; of burning logs on the hearth and lighted candles, and a dear slender figure moving about the room. He used to rehearse to himself little meetings and partings; look at the roofs of the Dower House against the primrose sky as he rode up the fields homewards; identify her window, dark now as she was away; and long for Christmas when she would be back again. The only shadow over these delightful pictures was the uncertainty as to the future. Where after all would the home be? For he was a younger son. He thought about James very often. When he came back would he live at home? Would it all be James' at his father's death, these woods and fields and farms and stately house? Would it ever come to him? And, meanwhile where should he and Isabel live, when the religious difficulty had been surmounted, as he had no doubt that it would be sooner or later?

When he thought of his father now, it was with a continually increasing respect. He had been inclined to despise him sometimes before, as one of a simple and uneventful life; but now the red shadow of the Law conferred dignity. To have been imprisoned in the Tower was a patent of nobility, adding distinction and gravity to the commonplace. Something of the glory even rested on Hubert himself as he rode and hawked with other Catholic boys, whose fathers maybe were equally zealous for the Faith, but less distinguished by suffering for it.

Before Anthony went back to Cambridge, he and Hubert went out nearly every day together with or without their hawks. Anthony was about three years the younger, and Hubert's additional responsibility for the estate made the younger boy more in awe of him than the difference in their ages warranted. Besides, Hubert knew quite as much about sport, and had more opportunities for indulging his taste for it. There was no heronry at hand; besides, it was not the breeding time which is the proper season for this particular sport; so they did not trouble to ride out to one; but the partridges and hares and rabbits that abounded in the Maxwell estate gave them plenty of quarreys. They preferred to go out generally without the falconer, a Dutchman, who had been taken into the service of Sir Nicholas thirty years before when things had been more prosperous; it was less embarrassing so; but they would have a lad to carry the "cadge," and a pony following them to carry the game. They added to the excitement of the sport by making it a competition between their birds; and flying them one after another, or sometimes at the same quarry, as in coursing; but this often led to the birds' crabbing.

Anthony's peregrine Eliza was almost unapproachable; and the lad was the more proud of her as he had "made" her himself, as an "eyess" or young falcon captured as a nestling. But, on the other hand, Hubert's goshawk Margaret, a fiery little creature, named inappropriately enough after his tranquil aunt, as a rule did better than Anthony's Isabel, and brought the scores level again.

There was one superb day that survived long in Anthony's memory and conversation; when he had done exceptionally well, when Eliza had surpassed herself, and even Isabel had acquitted herself with credit. It was one of those glorious days of wind and sun that occasionally fall in early October, with a pale turquoise sky overhead, and air that seems to sparkle and intoxicate like wine. They went out together after dinner about noon; their ponies and spaniels danced with the joy of life; Lady Maxwell cried to them from the north terrace to be careful, and pointed out to Mr. Norris who had dined with them what a graceful seat Hubert had; and then added politely, but as an obvious afterthought, that Anthony seemed to manage his pony with great address. The boys turned off through the village, and soon got on to high ground to the west of the village and all among the stubble and mustard, with tracts of rich sunlit country, of meadows and russet woodland below them on every side. Then the sport began. It seemed as if Eliza could not make a mistake. There rose a solitary partridge forty yards away with a whirl of wings; (the coveys were being well broken up by now) Anthony unhooded his bird and "cast off," with the falconer's cry "Hoo-ha, ha, ha, ha," and up soared Eliza with the tinkle of bells, on great strokes of those mighty wings, up, up, behind the partridge that fled low down the wind for his life. The two ponies were put to the gallop as the peregrine began to "stoop"; and then down like a plummet she fell with closed wings, "raked" the quarry with her talons as she passed; recovered herself, and as Anthony came up holding out the tabur-stycke, returned to him and was hooded and leashed again; and sat there on his gloved wrist with wet claws, just shivering slightly from her nerves, like the aristocrat she was; while her master stroked her ashy back and the boy picked up the quarry, admiring the deep rent before he threw it into the pannier.

Then Hubert had the next turn; but his falcon missed his first stoop, and did not strike the quarry till the second attempt, thus scoring one to Anthony's account. Then the peregrines were put back on the cadge as the boys got near to a wide meadow in a hollow where the rabbits used to feed; and the goshawks Margaret and Isabel were taken, each in turn sitting unhooded on her master's wrist, while they all watched the long thin grass for the quick movement that marked the passage of a rabbit;—and then in a moment the bird was cast off. The goshawk would rise just high enough to see the quarry in the grass, then fly straight with arched wings and pounces stretched out as she came over the quarry; then striking him between the shoulders would close with him; and her master would come up and take her off, throw the rabbit to the game-carrier; and the other would have the next attempt.

And so they went on for three or four hours, encouraging their birds, whooping the death of the quarry, watching with all the sportsman's keenness the soaring and stooping of the peregrines, the raking off of the goshawks; listening to the thrilling tinkle of the bells, and taking back their birds to sit triumphant and complacent on their master's wrists, when the quarry had been fairly struck, and furious and sullen when it had eluded them two or three times till their breath left them in the dizzy rushes, and they "canceliered" or even returned disheartened and would fly no more till they had forgotten—till at last the shadows grew long, and the game more wary, and the hawks and ponies tired; and the boys put up the birds on the cadge, and leashed them to it securely; and jogged slowly homewards together up the valley road that led to the village, talking in technical terms of how the merlin's feather must be "imped" to-morrow; and of the relative merits of the "varvels" or little silver rings at the end of the jesses through which the leash ran, and the Dutch swivel that Squire Blackett always used.

As they got nearer home and the red roofs of the Dower House began to glow in the ruddy sunlight above the meadows, Hubert began to shift the conversation round to Isabel, and inquire when she was coming home. Anthony was rather bored at this turn of the talk; but thought she would be back by Christmas at the latest; and said that she was at Northampton—and had Hubert ever seen such courage as Eliza's? But Hubert would not be put off; but led the talk back again to the girl; and at last told Anthony under promise of secrecy that he was fond of Isabel, and wished to make her his wife;—and oh! did Anthony think she cared really for him. Anthony stared and wondered and had no opinion at all on the subject; but presently fell in love with the idea that Hubert should be his brother-in-law and go hawking with him every day; and he added a private romance of his own in which he and Mary Corbet should be at the Dower House, with Hubert and Isabel at the Hall; while the elders, his own father, Sir Nicholas, Mr. James, Lady Maxwell, and Mistress Torridon had all taken up submissive and complacent attitudes in the middle distance.

He was so pensive that evening that his father asked him at supper whether he had not had a good day; which diverted his thoughts from Mistress Corbet, and led him away from sentiment on a stream of his own talk with long backwaters of description of this and that stoop, and of exactly the points in which he thought the Maxwells' falconer had failed in the training of Hubert's Jane.

Hubert found a long letter waiting from his father which Lady Maxwell gave him to read, with messages to himself in it about the estate, which brought him down again from the treading of rosy cloud-castles with a phantom Isabel whither his hawks and the shouting wind and the happy day had wafted him, down to questions of barns and farm-servants and the sober realities of harvest.

Chapter Eleven - Master Calvin

Isabel reached Northampton a day or two before Hubert came back to Great Keynes. She travelled down with two combined parties going to Leicester and Nottingham, sleeping at Leighton Buzzard on the way; and on the evening of the second day reached the house of her father's friend Dr. Carrington, that stood in the Market Square.

Her father's intention in sending her to this particular town and household was to show her how Puritanism, when carried to its extreme, was as orderly and disciplined a system, and was able to control the lives of its adherents, as well as the Catholicism whose influence on her character he found himself beginning to fear. But he wished also that she should be repelled to some extent by the merciless rigidity she would find at Northampton, and thus, after an oscillation or two come to rest in the quiet eclecticism of that middle position which he occupied himself.

The town indeed was at this time a miniature Geneva. There was something in the temper of its inhabitants that made it especially susceptible to the wave of Puritanism that was sweeping over England. Lollardy had flourished among them so far back as the reign of Richard II; when the mayor, as folks told one another with pride, had plucked a mass-priest by the vestment on the way to the altar in All Saints' Church, and had made him give over his mummery till the preacher had finished his sermon.

Dr. Carrington, too, a clean-shaven, blue-eyed, grey-haired man, churchwarden of Saint Sepulchre's, was a representative of the straitest views, and desperately in earnest. For him the world ranged itself into the redeemed and the damned; these two companies were the pivots of life for him; and every subject of mind or desire was significant only so far as it bore relations to be immutable decrees of God. But his fierce and merciless theological insistence was disguised by a real human tenderness and a marked courtesy of manner; and Isabel found him a kindly and thoughtful host.

Yet the mechanical strictness of the household, and the overpowering sense of the weightiness of life that it conveyed, was a revelation to Isabel. Dr. Carrington at family prayers was a tremendous figure, as he kneeled upright at the head of the table in the sombre dining-room; and it seemed to Isabel in her place that the pitiless all-seeing Presence that kept such terrifying silence as the Doctor cried on Jehovah, was almost a different God to that whom she knew in the morning parlour at home, to whom her father prayed with more familiarity but no less romance, and who answered in the sunshine that lay on the carpet, and the shadows of boughs that moved across it, and the chirp of the birds under the eaves. And all day long she thought she noticed the same difference; at Great Keynes life was made up of many parts, the love of family, the country doings, the worship of God, the garden, and the company of the Hall ladies; and the Presence of God interpenetrated all like light or fragrance; but here life was lived under the glare of His eye, and absorption in any detail apart from the consciousness of that encompassing Presence had the nature of sin.

On the Saturday after her arrival, as she was walking by the Nen with Kate Carrington, one of the two girls, she asked her about the crowd of ministers she had seen in the streets that morning.

"They have been to the Prophesyings," said Kate. "My father says that there is no exercise that sanctifies a godly young minister so quickly."

Kate went on to describe them further. The ministers assembled each Saturday at nine o'clock, and one of their number gave a short Bible-reading or lecture. Then all present were invited to join in the discussion; the less instructed would ask questions, the more experienced would answer, and debate would run high. Such a method Kate explained, who herself was a zealous and well instructed Calvinist, was the surest and swiftest road to truth, for every one held the open Scriptures in his hand, and interpreted and checked the speakers by the aid of that infallible guide.

"But if a man's judgment lead him wrong?" asked Isabel, who professedly admitted authority to have some place in matters of faith.

"All must hold the Apostles' Creed first of all," said Kate, "and must set his name to a paper declaring the Pope to be antichrist, with other truths upon it."

Isabel was puzzled; for it seemed now as if Private Judgment were not supreme among its professors; but she did not care to question further. It began to dawn upon her presently, however, why the Queen was so fierce against Prophesyings; for she saw that they exercised that spirit of exclusiveness, the property of Papist and Puritan alike; which, since it was the antithesis of the tolerant comprehensiveness of the Church of England, was also the enemy of the theological peace that Elizabeth was seeking to impose upon the country; and that it was for that reason that Papist and Puritan, sundered so far in theology, were united in suffering for conscience' sake.

On the Sunday morning Isabel went with Mrs. Carrington and the two girls to the round Templars' Church of Saint Sepulchre, for the Morning Prayer at eight o'clock, and then on to St. Peter's for the sermon. It was the latter function that was important in Puritan eyes; for the word preached was considered to have an almost sacramental force in the application of truth and grace to the soul; and crowds of people, with downcast eyes and in sombre dress, were pouring down the narrow streets from all the churches round, while the great bell beat out its summons from the Norman tower. The church was filled from end to end as they came in, meeting Dr. Carrington at the door, and they all passed up together to the pew reserved for the churchwarden, close beneath the pulpit.

As Isabel looked round her, it came upon her very forcibly what she had begun to notice even at Great Keynes, that the religion preached there did not fit the church in which it was set forth; and that, though great efforts had been made to conform the building to the worship. There had been no half measures at Northampton, for the Puritans had a loathing of what they called a "mingle-mangle." Altars, footpaces, and piscinæ had been swept away and all marks of them removed, as well as the rood-loft and every image in the building; the stained windows had been replaced by plain glass painted white; the walls had been whitewashed from roof to floor, and every suspicion of colour erased except where texts of Scripture ran rigidly across the open wall spaces: "We are not under the Law, but under Grace," Isabel read opposite her, beneath the clerestory windows. And, above all, the point to which all lines and eyes converged, was occupied no longer by the Table but by the tribunal of the Lord. Yet underneath the disguise the old religion triumphed still. Beneath the great plain orderly scheme, without depth of shadows, dominated by the towering place of Proclamation where the crimson-faced herald waited to begin, the round arches and the elaborate mouldings, and the cool depths beyond the pillars, all declared that in the God for whom that temple was built, there was mystery as well as revelation, Love as well as Justice, condescension as well as Majesty, beauty as well as awfulness, invitations as well as eternal decrees.

Isabel looked up presently, as the people still streamed in, and watched the minister in his rustling Genevan gown, leaning with his elbows on the Bible that rested open on the great tasselled velvet cushion before him. Everything about him was on the grand scale; his great hands were clasped and protruded over the edge of the Book; and his heavy dark face looked menacingly round on the crowded church; he had the air of a melancholy giant about to engage in some tragic pleasure. But Isabel's instinctive dislike began to pass into positive terror so soon as he began to preach.

When the last comers had found a place, and the talking had stopped, he presently gave out his text, in a slow thunderous voice, that silenced the last whispers:

"What shall we then say to these things? If God be on our side, who can be against us?"

There were a few slow sentences, in a deep resonant voice, uttering each syllable deliberately like the explosion of a far-off gun, and in a minute or two he was in the thick of Calvin's smoky gospel. Doctrine, voice, and man were alike terrible and overpowering.

There lay the great scheme in a few minutes, seen by Isabel as though through the door of hell, illumined by the glare of the eternal embers. The huge merciless Will of God stood there before her, disclosed in all its awfulness, armed with thunders, moving on mighty wheels. The foreknowledge of God closed the question henceforth, and, if proof were needed, made predestination plain. There was man's destiny, irrevocably fixed, iron-bound, changeless and immovable as the laws of God's own being. Yet over the rigid and awful Face of God, flickered a faint light, named mercy; and this mercy vindicated its existence by demanding that some souls should escape the final and endless doom that was the due reward of every soul conceived and born in enmity against God and under the frown of His Justice.

Then, heralded too by wrath, the figure of Jesus began to glimmer through the thunderclouds; and Isabel lifted her eyes, to look in hope. But He was not as she had known him in His graciousness, and as He had revealed Himself to her in tender communion, and among the flowers and under the clear skies of Sussex. Here, in this echoing world of wrath He stood, pale and rigid, with lightning in His eyes, and the grim and crimson Cross behind him; and as powerless as His own Father Himself to save one poor timid despairing hoping soul against whom the Eternal Decree had gone forth. Jesus was stern and forbidding here, with the red glare of wrath on His Face too, instead of the rosy crown of Love upon His forehead; His mouth was closed with compressed lips which surely would only open to condemn; not that mouth, quivering and human, that had smiled and trembled and bent down from the Cross to kiss poor souls that could not hope, nor help themselves, that had smiled upon Isabel ever since she had known Him. It was appalling to this gentle maiden soul that had bloomed and rejoiced so long in the shadow of His healing, to be torn out of her retreat and set thus under the consuming noonday of the Justice of this Sun of white-hot Righteousness.

For, as she listened, it was all so miserably convincing; her own little essays of intellect and flights of hopeful imagination were caught up and whirled away in the strong rush of this man's argument; her timid expectancy that God was really Love, as she understood the word in the vision of her Saviour's Person,—this was dashed aside as a childish fancy; the vision of the Father of the Everlasting Arms receded into the realm of dreams; and instead there lowered overhead in this furious tempest of wrath a monstrous God with a stony Face and a stonier Heart, who was eternally either her torment or salvation; and Isabel thought, and trembled at the blasphemy, that if God were such as this, the one would be no less agony than the other. Was this man bearing false witness, not only against his neighbour, but far more awfully, against his God? But it was too convincing; it was built up on an iron hammered framework of a great man's intellect and made white hot with another great man's burning eloquence. But it seemed to Isabel now and again as if a thunder-voiced virile devil were proclaiming the Gospel of Everlasting shame. There he bent over the pulpit with flaming face and great compelling gestures that swayed the congregation, eliciting the emotions he desired, as the conductor's baton draws out the music (for the man was a great orator), and he stormed and roared and seemed to marshal the very powers of the world to come, compelling them by his nod, and interpreting them by his voice; and below him sat this poor child, tossed along on his eloquence, like a straw on a flood; and yet hating and resenting it and struggling to detach herself and disbelieve every word he spoke.

As the last sands were running out in his hour-glass, he came to harbour from this raging sea; and in a few deep resonant sentences, like those with which he began, he pictured the peace of the ransomed soul, that knows itself safe in the arms of God; that rejoices, even in this world, in the Light of His Face and the ecstasy of His embrace; that dwells by waters of comfort and lies down in the green pastures of the Heavenly Love; while, round this little island of salvation in an ocean of terror, the thunders of wrath sound only as the noise of surge on a far-off reef.

The effect on Isabel was very great. It was far more startling than her visit to London; there her quiet religion had received high sanction in the mystery of S. Paul's. But here it was the plainest Calvinism preached with immense power. The preacher's last words of peace were no peace to her. If it was necessary to pass those bellowing breakers of wrath to reach the Happy Country, then she had never reached it yet; she had lived so far in an illusion; her life had been spent in a fool's paradise, where the light and warmth and flowers were but artificial after all; and she knew that she had not the heart to set out again. Though she recognised dimly the compelling power of this religion, and that it was one which, if sincerely embraced, would make the smallest details of life momentous with eternal weight, yet she knew that her soul could never respond to it, and whether saved or damned that it could only cower in miserable despair under a Deity that was so sovereign as this.

So her heart was low and her eyes sad as she followed Mrs. Carrington out of church. Was this then really the Revelation of the Love of God in the Person of Jesus Christ? Had all that she knew as the Gospel melted down into this fiery lump?

The rest of the day did not alter the impression made on her mind. There was little talk, or evidence of any human fellowship, in the Carrington household on the Lord's Day; there was a word or two of grave commendation on the sermon during dinner; and in the afternoon there was the Evening Prayer to be attended in St. Sepulchre's followed by an exposition, and a public catechising on Calvin's questions and answers. Here the same awful doctrines reappeared, condensed with an icy reality, even more paralysing than the burning presentation of them in the morning's sermon. She was spared questions herself, as she was a stranger; and sat to hear girls of her own age and older men and women who looked as soft-hearted as herself, utter definitions of the method of salvation and the being and character of God that compelled the assent of her intellect, while they jarred with her spiritual experience as fiercely as brazen trumpets out of tune.

In the evening there followed further religious exercises in the dark dining-room, at the close of which Dr. Carrington read one of Mr. Calvin's Genevan discourses, from his tall chair at the head of the table. She looked at him at first, and wondered in her heart whether that man, with his clear gentle voice, and his pleasant old face crowned with iron-grey hair seen in the mellow candlelight, really believed in the terrible gospel of the morning; for she heard nothing of the academic discourse that he was reading now, and presently her eyes wandered away out of the windows to the pale night sky. There still glimmered a faint streak of light in the west across the Market Square; it seemed to her as a kind of mirror of her soul at this moment; the tender daylight had faded, though she could still discern the token of its presence far away, and as from behind the bars of a cage; but the night of God's wrath was fast blotting out the last touch of radiance from her despairing soul.

Dr. Carrington looked at her with courteous anxiety, but with approval too, as he held her hand for a moment as she said good-night to him. There were shadows of weariness and depression under her eyes, and the corners of her mouth drooped a little; and the doctor's heart stirred with hope that the Word of God had reached at last this lamb of His who had been fed too long on milk, and sheltered from the sun; but who was now coming out, driven it might be, and unhappy, but still on its way to the plain and wholesome pastures of the Word that lay in the glow of the unveiled glory of God.

Isabel in her dark room upstairs was miserable; she stood long at her window her face pressed against the glass, and looked at the sky, from which the last streak of light had now died, and longed with all her might for her own oak room at home, with her prie-dieu and the familiar things about her; and the pines rustling outside in the sweet night-wind. It seemed to her as if an irresistible hand had plucked her out from those loved things and places, and that a penetrating eye were examining every corner of her soul. In one sense she believed herself nearer to God than ever before, but it was heartbreaking to find Him like this. She went to sleep with the same sense of a burdening Presence resting on her spirit.

The next morning Dr. Carrington saw her privately and explained to her a notice that she had not understood when it had been given out in church the day before. It was to the effect that the quarterly communion would be administered on the following Sunday, having been transferred that year from the Sunday after Michaelmas Day, and that she must hold herself in readiness on the Wednesday afternoon to undergo the examination that was enforced in every household in Northampton, at the hands of the Minister and Churchwardens.

"But you need not fear it, Mistress Norris," he said kindly, seeing her alarm. "My daughter Kate will tell you all that is needful."

Kate too told her it would be little more than formal in her case.

"The minister will not ask you much," she said, "for you are a stranger, and my father will vouch for you. He will ask you of irresistible grace, and of the Sacrament." And she gave her a couple of books from which she might summarise the answers; especially directing her attention to Calvin's Catechism, telling her that that was the book with which all the servants and apprentices were obliged to be familiar.

When Wednesday afternoon came, one by one the members of the household went before the inquisition that held its court in the dining-room; and last of all Isabel's turn came. The three gentlemen who sat in the middle of the long side of the table, with their backs to the light, half rose and bowed to her as she entered; and requested her to sit opposite to them. To her relief it was the Minister of St. Sepulchre's who was to examine her—he who had read the service and discoursed on the Catechism, not the morning preacher. He was a man who seemed a little ill at ease himself; he had none of the superb confidence of the preacher; but appeared to be one to whose natural character this stern rôle was not altogether congenial. He asked a few very simple questions; as to when she had last taken the Sacrament; how she would interpret the words, "This is my Body"; and looked almost grateful when she answered quietly and without heat. He asked her too three or four of the simpler questions which Kate had indicated to her; all of which she answered satisfactorily; and then desired to know whether she was in charity with all men; and whether she looked to Jesus Christ alone as her one Saviour. Finally he turned to Dr. Carrington, and wished to know whether Mistress Norris would come to the sacrament at five or nine o'clock, and Dr. Carrington answered that she would no doubt wish to come with his own wife and daughters at nine o'clock; which was the hour for the folks who were better to do. And so the inquisition ended much to Isabel's relief.

But this was a very extraordinary experience to her; it gave her a first glimpse into the rigid discipline that the extreme Puritans wished to see enforced everywhere; and with it a sense of corporate responsibility that she had not appreciated before; the congregation meant something to her now; she was no longer alone with her Lord individually, but understood that she was part of a body with various functions, and that the care of her soul was not merely a personal matter for herself, but involved her minister and the officers of the Church as well. It astonished her to think that this process was carried out on every individual who lived in the town in preparation for the sacrament on the following Sunday.

Isabel, and indeed the whole household, spent the Friday and Saturday in rigid and severe preparation. No flesh food was eaten on either of the days; and all the members of the family were supposed to spend several hours in their own rooms in prayer and meditation. She did not find this difficult, as she was well practised in solitude and prayer, and she scarcely left her room all Saturday except for meals.

"O Lord," Isabel repeated each morning and evening at her bedside during this week, "the blind dulness of our corrupt nature will not suffer us sufficiently to weigh these thy most ample benefits, yet, nevertheless, at the commandment of Jesus Christ our Lord, we present ourselves to this His table, which He hath left to be used in remembrance of His death until His coming again, to declare and witness before the world, that by Him alone we have received liberty and life; that by Him alone dost thou acknowledge us to be thy children and heirs; that by Him alone we have entrance to the throne of thy grace; that by Him alone we are possessed in our spiritual kingdom, to eat and drink at His table, with whom we have our conversation presently in heaven, and by whom our bodies shall be raised up again from the dust, and shall be placed with Him in that endless joy, which Thou, O Father of mercy, hast prepared for thine elect, before the foundation of the world was laid."

And so she prepared herself for that tryst with her Beloved in a foreign land where all was strange and unfamiliar about her: yet He was hourly drawing nearer, and she cried to Him day by day in these words so redolent to her with associations of past communions, and of moments of great spiritual elevation. The very use of the prayer this week was like a breeze of flowers to one in a wilderness.

On the Saturday night she ceremoniously washed her feet as her father had taught her; and lay down happier than she had been for days past, for to-morrow would bring the Lover of her soul.

On the Sunday all the household was astir early at their prayers, and about half-past eight o'clock all, including the servants who had just returned from the five o'clock service, assembled in the dining-room; the noise of the feet of those returning from church had ceased on the pavement of the square outside, and all was quiet except for the solemn sound of the bells, as Dr. Carrington offered extempore prayer for all who were fulfilling the Lord's ordinance on that day. And Isabel once more felt her heart yearn to a God who seemed Love after all.

St. Sepulchre's was nearly full when they arrived. The mahogany table had been brought down from the eastern wall to beneath the cupola, and stood there with a large white cloth, descending almost to the ground on every side; and a row of silver vessels, flat plates and tall new Communion cups and flagons, shone upon it. Isabel buried her face in her hands, and tried to withdraw into the solitude of her own soul; but the noise of the feet coming and going, and the talking on all sides of her, were terribly distracting. Presently four ministers entered and Isabel was startled to see, as she raised her face at the sudden silence, that none of them wore the prescribed surplice; for she had not been accustomed to the views of the extreme Puritans to whom this was a remnant of Popery; an indifferent thing indeed in itself, as they so often maintained; but far from indifferent when it was imposed by authority. One entered the pulpit; the other three took their places at the Holy Table; and after a metrical Psalm sung in the Genevan fashion, the service began. At the proper place the minister in the pulpit delivered an hour's sermon of the type to which Isabel was being now introduced for the first time; but bearing again and again on the point that the sacrament was a confession to the world of faith in Christ; it was in no sense a sacrificial act towards God, "as the Papists vainly taught"; this part of the sermon was spoiled, to Isabel's ears at least, by a flood of disagreeable words poured out against the popish doctrine; and the end of the sermon consisted of a searching exhortation to those who contemplated sin, who bore malice, who were in any way holding aloof from God, "to cast themselves mightily upon the love of the Redeemer, bewailing their sinful lives, and purposing to amend them." This act, wrought out in the silence of the soul even now would transfer the sinner from death unto life; and turn what threatened to be poison into a "lively and healthful food." Then he turned to those who came prepared and repentant, hungering and thirsting after the Bread of Life and the Wine that the Lord had mingled; and congratulated them on their possession of grace, and on the rich access of sanctification that would be theirs by a faithful reception of this comfortable sacrament; and then in half a dozen concluding sentences he preached Christ, as "food to the hungry; a stream to the thirsty; a rest for the weary. It is He alone, our dear Redeemer, who openeth the Kingdom of Heaven, to which may He vouchsafe to bring us for His Name's sake."

Isabel was astonished to see that the preacher did not descend from the pulpit after the sermon, but that as soon as he had announced that the mayor would sit at the Town Hall with the ministers and churchwardens on the following Thursday to inquire into the cases of all who had not presented themselves for Communion, he turned and began to busy himself with the great Bible that lay on the cushion. The service went on, and the conducting of it was shared among the three ministers standing, one at the centre of the table which was placed endways, and the others at the two ends. As the Prayer of Consecration was begun, Isabel hid her face as she was accustomed to do, for she believed it to be the principal part of the service, and waited for the silence that in her experience generally followed the Amen. But a voice immediately began from the pulpit, and she looked up, startled and distracted.

"Then Jesus said unto them," pealed out the preacher's voice, "All ye shall be offended by me this night, for it is written, I will smite the shepherd and the sheep shall be scattered. But after I am risen, I will go into Galilee before you." Ah! why would not the man stop? Isabel did not want the past Saviour but the present now; not a dead record but a living experience; above all, not the minister but the great High Priest Himself.

"He began to be troubled and in great heaviness, and said unto them, My soul is very heavy, even unto the death; tarry here and watch."

The three ministers had communicated by now; and there was a rustle and clatter of feet as the empty seats in front, hung with houselling cloths, began to be filled. The murmur of the three voices below as the ministers passed along with the vessels were drowned by the tale of the Passion that rang out overhead.

"Couldest thou not watch one hour? Watch and pray, that ye enter not into temptation. The spirit indeed is ready, but the flesh is weak."

It was coming near to Isabel's turn; the Carringtons already were beginning to move; and in a moment or two she rose and followed them out. The people were pressing up the aisles; and as she stood waiting her turn to pass into the white-hung seat, she could not help noticing the disorder that prevailed; some knelt devoutly, some stood, some sat to receive the sacred elements; and all the while louder and louder, above the rustling and the loud whispering of the ministers and the shuffling of feet, the tale rose and fell on the cadences of the preacher's voice. Now it was her turn; she was kneeling with palms outstretched and closed eyes. Ah! would he not be silent for one moment? Could not the reality speak for itself, and its interpreter be still? Surely the King of Love needed no herald when Himself was here.

"And anon in the dawning, the high Priests held a Council with Elders and the Scribes and the whole Council, and bound Jesus and led Him away." ...

And so it was over presently, and she was back again in her seat, distracted and miserable; trying to pray, forcing herself to attend now to the reader, now to her Saviour with whom she believed herself in intimate union, and finding nothing but dryness and distraction everywhere. How interminable it was! She opened her eyes, and what she saw amazed and absorbed her for a few moments; some were sitting back and talking; some looking cheerfully about them as if at a public entertainment; one man especially overwhelmed her imagination; with a great red face and neck like a butcher, animal and brutal, with a heavy hanging jowl and little narrow lack-lustre eyes—how bored and depressed he was by this long obligatory ceremony! Then once more she closed her eyes in self-reproach at her distractions; here were her lips still fragrant with the Wine of God, the pressure of her Beloved's arm still about her; and these were her thoughts, settling like flies, on everything....

When she opened them again the last footsteps were passing down the aisle, the dripping Cups were being replaced by the ministers, and covered with napkins, and the tale of Easter was in telling from the pulpit like the promise of a brighter day.

"And they said one to another, Who shall roll us away the stone from the door of the sepulchre? And when they looked, they saw that the stone was rolled away (for it was a very great one)."

So read the minister and closed the book; and Our Father began.

In the evening, when all was over, and the prayers said and the expounding and catechising finished, in a kind of despair she slipped away alone, and walked a little by herself in the deepening twilight beside the river; and again she made effort after effort to catch some consciousness of grace from this Sacrament Sunday, so rare and so precious; but an oppression seemed to dwell in the very air. The low rain-clouds hung over the city, leaden and chill, the path where she walked was rank with the smell of dead leaves, and the trees and grass dripped with lifeless moisture. As she goaded and allured alternately her own fainting soul, it writhed and struggled but could not rise; there was no pungency of bitterness in her self-reproach, no thrill of joy in her aspiration; for the hand of Calvin's God lay heavy on the delicate languid thing.

She walked back at last in despair over the wet cobblestones of the empty market square; but as she came near the house, she saw that the square was not quite empty. A horse stood blowing and steaming before Dr. Carrington's door, and her own maid and Kate were standing hatless in the doorway looking up and down the street. Isabel's heart began to beat, and she walked quicker. In a moment Kate saw her, and began to beckon and call; and the maid ran to meet her.

"Mistress Isabel, Mistress Isabel," she cried, "make haste."

"What is it?" asked the girl, in sick foreboding.

"There is a man come from Great Keynes," began the maid, but Kate stopped her.

"Come in, Mistress Isabel," she said, "my father is waiting for you."

Dr. Carrington met her at the dining-room door; and his face was tender and full of emotion.

"What is it?" whispered the girl sharply. "Anthony?"

"Dear child," he said, "come in, and be brave."

There was a man standing in the room with cap and whip in hand, spurred and splashed from head to foot; Isabel recognised one of the grooms from the Hall.

"What is it?" she said again with a piteous sharpness.

Dr. Carrington laid his hands gently on her shoulders, and looked into her eyes.

"It is news of your father," he said, "from Lady Maxwell."

He paused, and the steady gleam of his eyes strengthened and quieted her, then he went on deliberately, "The Lord hath given and the Lord hath taken it."

He paused as if for an answer, but no answer came; Isabel was staring white-faced with parted lips into those strong blue eyes of his: and he finished:

"Blessed be the name of the Lord."

Chapter Twelve - A Winding-Up

The curtained windows on the ground-floor of the Dower House shone red from within as Isabel and Dr. Carrington, with three or four servants behind, rode round the curving drive in front late on the Monday evening. A face peeped from Mrs. Carroll's window as the horse's hoofs sounded on the gravel, and by the time that Isabel, pale, wet, and worn-out with her seventy miles' ride, was dismounted, Mistress Margaret herself was at the door, with Anthony's face at her shoulder, and Mrs. Carroll looking over the banisters.

Isabel was not allowed to see her father's body that night, but after she was in bed, Lady Maxwell herself, who had been sent for when he lay dying, came down from the Hall, and told her what there was to tell; while Mistress Margaret and Anthony entertained Dr. Carrington below.

"Dear child," said the old lady, leaning with her elbow on the bed, and holding the girl's hand tenderly as she talked, "it was all over in an hour or two. It was the heart, you know. Mrs. Carroll sent for me suddenly, on Saturday morning; and by the time I reached him he could not speak. They had carried him upstairs from his study, where they had found him; and laid him down on his bed, and—yes, yes—he was in pain, but he was conscious, and he was praying I think; his lips moved. And I knelt down by the bed and prayed aloud; he only spoke twice; and, my dear, it was your name the first time, and the name of His Saviour the second time. He looked at me, and I could see he was trying to speak; and then on a sudden he spoke 'Isabel.' And I think he was asking me to take care of you. And I nodded and said that I would do what I could, and he seemed satisfied and shut his eyes again. And then presently Mr. Bodder began a prayer—he had come in a moment before; they could not find him at first—and then, and then your dear father moved a little and raised his hand, and the minister stayed; and he was looking up as if he saw something; and then he said once, 'Jesus' clear and loud; and, and—that was all, dear child."

The next morning she and Anthony, with the two old ladies, one of whom was always with them during these days, went into the darkened oak room on the first floor, where he had died and now rested. The red curtains made a pleasant rosy light, and it seemed to the children impossible to believe that that serene face, scarcely more serene than in life, with its wide closed lids under the delicate eyebrows, and contented clean-cut mouth, and the scholarly hands closed on the breast, all in a wealth of autumn flowers and dark copper-coloured beech leaves, were not the face and hands of a sleeping man.

But Isabel did not utterly break down till she saw his study. She drew the curtains aside herself, and there stood his table; his chair was beside it, pushed back and sideways as if he had that moment left it; and on the table itself the books she knew so well.

In the centre of the table stood his inlaid desk, with the papers lying upon it, and his quill beside them, as if just laid down; even the ink-pot was uncovered just as he had left it, as the agony began to lay its hand upon his heart. She stooped and read the last sentence.

"This is the great fruit, that unspeakable benefit that they do eat and drink of that labour and are burden, and come—" and there it stopped; and the blinding tears rushed into the girl's eyes, as she stooped to kiss the curved knob of the chair-arm where his dear hand had last rested.

When all was over a day or two later the two went up to stay at the Hall, while the housekeeper was left in charge of the Dower House. Lady Maxwell and Mistress Margaret had been present at the parish church on the occasion of the funeral, for the first time ever since the old Marian priest had left; and had assisted too at the opening of the will, which was found, tied up and docketed in one of the inner drawers of the inlaid desk; and before its instructions were complied with, Lady Maxwell wished to have a word or two with Isabel and Anthony.

She made an opportunity on the morning of Anthony's departure for Cambridge, two days after the funeral, when Mistress Margaret was out of the room, and Hubert had ridden off as usual with Piers, on the affairs of the estate.

"My child," said she to Isabel, who was lying back passive and listless on the window-seat. "What do you think your cousin will direct to be done? He will scarcely wish you to leave home altogether, to stay with him. And yet, you understand, he is your guardian."

Isabel shook her head.

"We know nothing of him," she said, wearily, "he has never been here."

"If you have a suggestion to make to him you should decide at once," the other went on, "the courier is to go on Monday, is he not, Anthony?"

The boy nodded.

"But will he not allow us," he said, "to stay at home as usual? Surely—"

Lady Maxwell shook her head.

"And Isabel?" she asked, "who will look after her when you are away?"

"Mrs. Carroll?" he said interrogatively.

Again she shook her head.

"He would never consent," she said, "it would not be right."

Isabel looked up suddenly, and her eyes brightened a little.

"Lady Maxwell—" she began, and then stopped, embarrassed.

"Well, my dear?"

"What is it, Isabel?" asked Anthony.

"If it were possible—but, but I could not ask it."

"If you mean Margaret, my dear"; said the old lady serenely, drawing her needle carefully through, "it was what I thought myself; but I did not know if you would care for that. Is that what you meant?"

"Oh, Lady Maxwell," said the girl, her face lighting up.

Then the old lady explained that it was not possible to ask them to live permanently at the Hall, although of course Isabel must do so until an arrangement had been made; because their father would scarcely have wished them to be actually inmates of a Catholic house; but that he plainly had encouraged close relations between the two houses, and indeed, Lady Maxwell interpreted his mention of his daughter's name, and his look as he said it, in the sense that he wished those relations to continue. She thought therefore that there was no reason why their new guardian's consent should not be asked to Mistress Margaret's coming over to the Dower House to take charge of Isabel, if the girl wished it. He had no particular interest in them; he lived a couple of hundred miles away, and the arrangement would probably save him a great deal of trouble and inconvenience.

"But you, Lady Maxwell," Isabel burst out, her face kindled with hope, for she had dreaded the removal terribly, "you will be lonely here."

"Dear child," said the old lady, laying down her embroidery, "God has been gracious to me; and my husband is coming back to me; you need not fear for me." And she told them, with her old eyes full of happy tears, how she had had a private word, which they must not repeat, from a Catholic friend at Court, that all had been decided for Sir Nicholas' release, though he did not know it himself yet, and that he would be at home again for Advent. The prison fever was beginning to cause alarm, and it seemed that a good fine would meet the old knight's case better than any other execution of justice.

So then, it was decided; and as Isabel walked out to the gatehouse after dinner beside Anthony, with her hand on his horse's neck, and as she watched him at last ride down the village green and disappear round behind the church, half her sorrow at losing him was swallowed up in the practical certainty that they would meet again before Christmas in their old home, and not in a stranger's house in the bleak North country.

On the following Thursday, Sir Nicholas' weekly letter showed evidence that the good news of his release had begun to penetrate to him; his wife longed to tell him all she had heard, but so many jealous eyes were on the watch for favouritism that she had been strictly forbidden to pass on her information. However there was little need.

"I am in hopes," he wrote, "of keeping Christmas in a merrier place than prison. I do not mean heaven," he hastened to add, for fear of alarming his wife. "Good Mr. Jakes tells me that Sir John is ill to-day, and that he fears the gaol-fever; and if it is the gaol-fever, sweetheart, which pray God it may not be for Sir John's sake, it will be the fourteenth case in the Tower; and folks say that we shall all be let home again; but with another good fine, they say, to keep us poor and humble, and mindful of the Queen's Majesty her laws. However, dearest, I would gladly pay a thousand pounds, if I had them, to be home again."

But there was news at the end of the letter that caused consternation in one or two hearts, and sent Hubert across, storming and almost crying, to Isabel, who was taking a turn in the dusk at sunset. She heard his step beyond the hedge, quick and impatient, and stopped short, hesitating and wondering.

He had behaved to her with extraordinary tact and consideration, and she was very conscious of it. Since her sudden return ten days before from the visit which had been meant to separate them, he had not spoken a word to her privately, except a shy sentence or two of condolence, stammered out with downcast eyes, but which from the simplicity and shortness of the words had brought up a sob from her heart. She guessed that he knew why she had been sent to Northampton, and had determined not to take advantage in any way of her sorrow. Every morning he had disappeared before she came down, and did not come back till supper, where he sat silent and apart, and yet, when an occasion offered itself, behaved with a quick attentive deference that showed her where his thoughts had been.

Now she stood, wondering and timid, at that hurried insistent step on the other side of the hedge. As she hesitated, he came quickly through the doorway and stopped short.

"Mistress Isabel," he said, with all his reserve gone, and looking at her imploringly, but with the old familiar air that she loved, "have you heard? I am to go as soon as my father comes back. Oh! it is a shame!"

His voice was full of tears, and his eyes were bright and angry. Her heart leapt up once and then seemed to cease beating.

"Go?" she said; and even as she spoke knew from her own dismay how dear that quiet chivalrous presence was to her.

"Yes," he went on in the same voice. "Oh! I know I should not speak; and—and especially now at all times; but I could not bear it; nor that you should think it was my will to go."

She stood still looking at him.

"May I walk with you a little," he said, "but—I must not say much—I promised my father."

And then as they walked he began to pour it out.

"It is some old man in Durham," he said, "and I am to see to his estates. My father will not want me here when he comes back, and, and it is to be soon. He has had the offer for me; and has written to tell me. There is no choice."

She had turned instinctively towards the house, and the high roofs and chimneys were before them, dark against the luminous sky.

"No, no," said Hubert, laying his hand on her arm; and at the touch she thrilled so much that she knew she must not stay, and went forward resolutely up the steps of the terrace.

"Ah! let me speak," he said; "I have not troubled you much, Mistress Isabel."

She hesitated again a moment.

"In my father's room," he went on, "and I will bring the letter."

She nodded and passed into the hall without speaking, and turned to Sir Nicholas' study; while Hubert's steps dashed up the stairs to his mother's room. Isabel went in and stood on the hearth in the firelight that glowed and wavered round the room on the tapestry and the prie-dieu and the table where Hubert had been sitting and the tall shuttered windows, leaning her head against the mantelpiece, doubtful and miserable.

"Listen," said Hubert, bursting into the room a moment later with the sheet open in his hand.

"'Tell Hubert that Lord Arncliffe needs a gentleman to take charge of his estates; he is too old now himself, and has none to help him. I have had the offer for Hubert, and have accepted it; he must go as soon as I have returned. I am sorry to lose the lad, but since James—'" and Hubert broke off. "I must not read that," he said.

Isabel still stood, stretching her hands out to the fire, turned a little away from him.

"But what can I say?" went on the lad passionately, "I must go; and—and God knows for how long, five or six years maybe; and I shall come back and find you—and find you—" and a sob rose up and silenced him.

"Hubert," she said, turning and looking with a kind of wavering steadiness into his shadowed eyes, and even then noticing the clean-cut features and the smooth curve of his jaw with the firelight on it, "you ought not—"

"I know, I know; I promised my father; but there are some things I cannot bear. Of course I do not want you to promise anything; but I thought that if perhaps you could tell me that you thought—that you thought there would be no one else; and that when I came back—"

"Hubert," she said again, resolutely, "it is impossible: our religions—"

"But I would do anything, I think. Besides, in five years so much may happen. You might become a Catholic—or—or, I might come to see that the Protestant Religion was nearly the same, or as true at least—or—or—so much might happen.—Can you not tell me anything before I go?"

A keen ray of hope had pierced her heart as he spoke; and she scarcely knew what she said.

"But, Hubert, even if I were to say—"

He seized her hands and kissed them again and again.

"Oh! God bless you, Isabel! Now I can go so happily. And I will not speak of it again; you can trust me; it will not be hard for you."

She tried to draw her hands away, but he still held them tightly in his own strong hands, and looked into her face. His eyes were shining.

"Yes, yes, I know you have promised nothing. I hold you to nothing. You are as free as ever to do what you will with me. But,"—and he lifted her hands once more and kissed them, and dropped them; seized his cap and was gone.

Isabel was left alone in a tumult of thought and emotion. He had taken her by storm; she had not guessed how desperately weak she was towards him, until he had come to her like this in a whirlwind of passion and stood trembling and almost crying, with the ruddy firelight on his face, and his eyes burning out of shadow. She felt fascinated still by that mingling of a boy's weakness and sentiment and of a man's fire and purpose; and she sank down on her knees before the hearth and looked wonderingly at her hands which he had kissed so ardently, now transparent and flaming against the light as if with love. Then as she looked at the red heart of the fire the sudden leaping of her heart quieted, and there crept on her a glow of steady desire to lean on the power of this tall young lover of hers; she was so utterly alone without him it seemed as if there were no choice left; he had come and claimed her in virtue of the master-law, and she—how much had she yielded? She had not promised; but she had shown evidently her real heart in those half dozen words; and he had interpreted them for her; and she dared not in honesty repudiate his interpretation. And so she knelt there, clasping and unclasping her hands, in a whirl of delight and trembling; all the bounds of that sober inner life seemed for the moment swept away; she almost began to despise its old coldnesses and limitations. How shadowy after all was the love of God, compared with this burning tide that was bearing her along on its bosom!...

She sank lower and lower into herself among the black draperies, clasping those slender hands tightly across her breast.

Suddenly a great log fell with a crash, the red glow turned into leaping flames; the whole dark room seemed alive with shadows that fled to and fro, and she knelt upright quickly and looked round her, terrified and ashamed.— What was she doing here? Was it so soon then that she was setting aside the will of her father, who trusted and loved her so well, and who lay out there in the chancel vault? Ah! she had no right here in this room—Hubert's room now, with his cap and whip lying across the papers and the estate-book, and his knife and the broken jesses on the seat of the chair beside her. There was his step overhead again. She must be gone before he came back.

There was high excitement on the estate and in the village a week or two later when the rumour of Sir Nicholas' return was established, and the paper had been pinned up to the gatehouse stating, in Lady Maxwell's own handwriting, that he would be back sometime in the week before Advent Sunday. Reminiscences were exchanged of the glorious day when the old knight came of age, over forty years ago; of the sports on the green, of the quintain-tilting for the gentlefolks, and the archery in the meadow behind the church for the vulgar; of the high mass and the dinner that followed it. It was rumoured that Mr. Hubert and Mr. Piers had already selected the ox that was to be roasted whole, and that materials for the bonfire were in process of collection in the woodyard of the home farm.

Sir Nicholas' letters became more and more emphatically underlined and incoherent as the days went on, and Lady Maxwell less and less willing for Isabel to read them; but the girl often found the old lady hastily putting away the thin sheets which she had just taken out to read to herself once again, on which her dear lord had scrawled down his very heart itself, as if his courting of her were all to do again.

It was not until the Saturday morning that the courier rode in through the gatehouse with the news that Sir Nicholas was to be released that day, and would be down if possible before nightfall. All the men on the estate were immediately called in and sent home to dress themselves; and an escort of a dozen grooms and servants led by Hubert and Piers rode out at once on the north road, with torches ready for kindling, to meet the party and bring them home; and all other preparations were set forward at once.

Towards eight o'clock Lady Maxwell was so anxious and restless that Isabel slipped out and went down to the gatehouse to look out for herself if there were any signs of the approach of the party. She went up to one of the little octagonal towers, and looked out towards the green.

It was a clear starlight night, but towards the village all was bathed in the dancing ruddy light of the bonfire. It was burning on a little mound at the upper end of the green, just below where Isabel stood, and a heavy curtain of smoke drifted westwards. As she looked down on it she saw against it the tall black posts of the gigantic jack and the slowly revolving carcass of the ox; and round about the stirring crowd of the village folk, their figures black on this side, luminous on that. She could even make out the cassock and square cap of Mr. Bodder as he moved among his flock. The rows of houses on either side, bright and clear at this end, melted away into darkness at the lower end of the green, where on the right the church tower rose up, blotting out the stars, itself just touched with ruddy light, and on the top of which, like a large star itself, burned the torch of the watcher who was looking out towards the north road. There was a ceaseless hum of noise from the green, pierced by the shrill cries of the children round the glowing mass of the bonfire, but there was no disorder, as the barrels that had been rolled out of the Hall cellars that afternoon still stood untouched beneath the Rectory garden-wall. Isabel contrasted in her mind this pleasant human tumult with the angry roaring she had heard from these same country-folk a few months before, when she had followed Lady Maxwell out to the rescue of the woman who had injured her; and she wondered at these strange souls, who attended a Protestant service, but were so fierce and so genial in their defence and welcome of a Catholic squire.

As she thought, there was a sudden movement of the light on the church tower; it tossed violently up and down, and a moment later the jubilant clangour of the bells broke out. There was a sudden stir in the figures on the green, and a burst of cheering rose. Isabel strained her eyes northwards, but the road took a turn beyond the church and she could see nothing but darkness and low-hung stars and one glimmering window. She turned instinctively to the house behind her, and there was the door flung wide, and she could make out the figures of the two ladies against the brightly lit hall beyond, wrapped like herself, in cloak and hood, for the night was frosty and cold.

As she turned once more she heard the clear rattle of trotting hoofs on the hard road, and a glow began to be visible at the lower dark end of the village. The cheering rose higher, and the bells were all clashing together in melodious discord, as in the angle of the road a group of tossing torches appeared. Then she could make out the horsemen; three riding together, and the others as escort round them. The crowd had poured off the grass on to the road by now, and the horses were coming up between two shouting gesticulating lines which closed after them as they went. Now she could make out the white hair of Sir Nicholas, as he bowed bare-headed right and left; and Hubert's feathered cap, on one side of him, and Mr. Boyd's black hat on the other. They had passed the bonfire now, and were coming up the avenue, the crowds still streaming after them, and the church tower bellowing rough music overhead. Isabel leaned out over the battlements, and saw beneath her the two old ladies waiting just outside the gate by the horse-block; and then she drew back, her eyes full of tears, for she saw Sir Nicholas' face as he caught sight of his wife.

There was a sudden silence as the horses drew up; and the crowds ceased shouting, and when Isabel leaned over again Sir Nicholas was on the horse-block, the two ladies immediately behind him, and the people pressing forward to hear his voice. It was a very short speech; and Isabel overhead could not catch more than detached phrases of it, "for the faith"—"my wife and you all"—"home again"—"my son Hubert here"—"you and your families"—"the Catholic religion"—"the Queen's grace"—"God save her Majesty."

Then again the cheering broke out; and Isabel crossed over to see them pass up to the house and to the bright door set wide for them, and even as she watched them go up the steps, and Hubert's figure close behind, she suddenly dropped her forehead on to the cold battlement, and drew a sharp breath or two, for she remembered again what it all meant to him and to herself.

Part Two

Chapter One - Anthony in London

The development of a nation is strangely paralleled by the development of an individual. There comes in both a period of adolescence, of the stirring of new powers, of an increase of strength, of the dawn of new ideals, of the awaking of self-consciousness; contours become defined and abrupt, awkward and hasty movements succeed to the grace of childhood; and there is a curious mingling of refinement and brutality, stupidity and tenderness; the will is subject to whims; it is easily roused and not so easily quieted. Yet in spite of the attendant discomforts the whole period is undeniably one of growth.

The reign of Elizabeth coincided with this stage in the development of England. The young vigour was beginning to stir—and Hawkins and Drake taught the world that it was so, and that when England stretched herself catastrophe abroad must follow. She loved finery and feathers and velvet, and to see herself on the dramatic stage and to sing her love-songs there, as a growing maid dresses up and leans on her hand and looks into her own eyes in the mirror—and Marlowe and Greene and Shakespeare are witnesses to it. Yet she loved to hang over the arena too and watch the bear-baiting and see the blood and foam and listen to the snarl of the hounds, as a lad loves sport and things that minister death. Her policy, too, under Elizabeth as her genius, was awkward and ill-considered and capricious, and yet strong and successful in the end, as a growing lad, while he is clumsier, yet manages to leap higher than a year ago.

And once more, to carry the parallel still further, during the middle period of the reign, while the balance of parties and powers remained much the same, principles and tendencies began to assert themselves more definitely, just as muscles and sinews begin to appear through the round contour of the limbs of a growing child.

Thus, from 1571 to 1577, while there was no startling reversal of elements in the affairs of England, the entire situation became more defined. The various parties, though they scarcely changed in their mutual relations, yet continued to develop swiftly along their respective lines, growing more pronounced and less inclined to compromise; foreign enmities and expectations became more acute; plots against the Queen's life more frequent and serious, and the countermining of them under Walsingham more patient and skilful; competition and enterprise in trade more strenuous; Scottish affairs more complicated; movements of revolt and repression in Ireland more violent.

What was true of politics was also true of religious matters, for the two were inextricably mingled. The Puritans daily became more clamorous and intolerant; their "Exercises" more turbulent, and their demands more unreasonable and one-sided. The Papists became at once more numerous and more strict; and the Government measures more stern in consequence. The act of '71 made it no less a crime than High Treason to reconcile or be reconciled to the Church of Rome, to give effect to a Papal Bull, to be in possession of any muniments of superstition, or to declare the Queen a heretic or schismatic. The Church of England, too, under the wise guidance of Parker, had begun to shape her course more and more resolutely along the lines of inclusiveness and moderation; to realise herself as representing the religious voice of a nation that was widely divided on matters of faith; and to attempt to include within her fold every individual that was not an absolute fanatic in the Papist or Puritan direction.

Thus, in every department, in home and foreign politics, in art and literature, and in religious independence, England was rising and shaking herself free; the last threads that bound her to the Continent were snapped by the Reformation, and she was standing with her soul, as she thought, awake and free at last, conscious of her beauty and her strength, ready to step out at last before the world, as a dominant and imperious power.

Anthony Norris had been arrested, like so many others, by the vision of this young country of his, his mother and mistress, who stood there, waiting to be served. He had left Cambridge in '73, and for three years had led a somewhat aimless life; for his guardian allowed him a generous income out of his father's fortune. He had stayed with Hubert in the north, had yawned and stretched himself at Great Keynes, had gone to and fro among friends' houses, and had at last come to the conclusion, to which he was aided by a chorus of advisers, that he was wasting his time. He had begun then to look round him for some occupation, and in the final choice of it his early religious training had formed a large element. It had kept alive in him a certain sense of the supernatural, that his exuberance of physical life might otherwise have crushed; and now as he looked about to see how he could serve his country, he became aware that her ecclesiastical character had a certain attraction for him; he had had indeed an idea of taking Orders; but he had relinquished this by now, though he still desired if he might to serve the National Church in some other capacity. There was much in the Church of England to appeal to her sons; if there was a lack of unity in her faith and policy, yet that was largely out of sight, and her bearing was gallant and impressive. She had great wealth, great power and great dignity. The ancient buildings and revenues were hers; the civil power was at her disposal, and the Queen was eager to further her influence, and to protect her bishops from the encroaching power of Parliament, claiming only for the crown the right to be the point of union for both the secular and ecclesiastical sections of the nation, and to stamp by her royal approval or annul by her veto the acts of Parliament and Convocation alike. It seemed then to Anthony's eyes that the Church of England had a tremendous destiny before her, as the religious voice of the nation that was beginning to make itself so dominant in the council of the world, and that there was no limit to the influence she might exercise by disciplining the exuberant strength of England, and counteracting by her soberness and self-restraint the passionate fanaticism of the Latin nations. So little by little in place of the shadowy individualism that was all that he knew of religion, there rose before him the vision of a living church, who came forth terrible as an army with banners, surrounded by all the loyalty that nationalism could give her, with the Queen herself as her guardian, and great princes and prelates as her supporters, while at the wheels of her splendid car walked her hot-blooded chivalrous sons, who served her and spread her glories by land and sea, not perhaps chiefly for the sake of her spiritual claims, but because she was bone of their bone; and was no less zealous than themselves for the name and character of England.

When, therefore, towards the end of '76, Anthony received the offer of a position in the household of the Archbishop of Canterbury, through the recommendation of the father of one of his Cambridge friends, he accepted it with real gratitude and enthusiasm.

The post to which he was appointed was that of Gentleman of the Horse. His actual duties were not very arduous owing to the special circumstances of Archbishop Grindal; and he had a good deal of time to himself. Briefly, they were as follows—He had to superintend the Yeoman of the Horse, and see that he kept full accounts of all the horses in stable or at pasture, and of all the carriages and harness and the like. Every morning he had to present himself to the Archbishop and receive stable-orders for the day, and to receive from the yeoman accounts of the stables. Every month he examined the books of the yeoman before passing them on to the steward. His permission too was necessary before any guest's or stranger's horse might be cared for in the Lambeth stables.

He was responsible also for all the men and boys connected with the stable; to engage them, watch their morals and even the performance of their religious duties, and if necessary report them for dismissal to the steward of the household. In Archbishop Parker's time this had been a busy post, as the state observed at Lambeth and Croydon was very considerable; but Grindal was of a more retiring nature, disliking as was said, "lordliness"; and although still the household was an immense affair, in its elaborateness and splendour beyond almost any but royal households of the present day, still Anthony's duties were far from heavy. The Archbishop indeed at first dispensed with this office altogether, and concentrated all the supervision of the stable on the yeoman, and Anthony was the first and only Gentleman of the Horse that Archbishop Grindal employed. The disgrace and punishment under which the Archbishop fell so early in his archiepiscopate made this particular post easier than it would even otherwise have been; as fewer equipages were required when the Archbishop was confined to his house, and the establishment was yet further reduced.

Ordinarily then his duties were over by eleven o'clock, except when special arrangements were to be made. He rose early, waited upon the Archbishop by eight o'clock, and received his orders for the day; then interviewed the yeoman; sometimes visited the stables to receive complaints, and was ready by half-past ten to go to the chapel for the morning prayers with the rest of the household. At eleven he dined at the Steward's table in the great hall, with the other principal officers of the household, the chaplain, the secretaries, and the gentlemen ushers, with guests of lesser degree. This great hall with its two entrances at the lower end near the gateway, its magnificent hammer-beam roof, its daïs, its stained glass, was a worthy place of entertainment, and had been the scene of many great feasts and royal visits in the times of previous archbishops in favour with the sovereign, and of a splendid banquet at the beginning of Grindal's occupancy of the see. Now, however, things were changed. There were seldom many distinguished persons to dine with the disgraced prelate; and he himself preferred too to entertain those who could not repay him again, after the precept of the gospel; and besides the provision for the numerous less important guests who dined daily at Lambeth, a great tub was set at the lower end of the hall as it had been in Parker's time, and every day after dinner under the steward's direction was filled with food from the tables, which was afterwards distributed at the gate to poor people of the neighbourhood.

After dinner Anthony's time was often his own, until the evening prayers at six, followed by supper again spread in the hall. It was necessary for him always to sleep in the house, unless leave was obtained from the steward. This gentleman, Mr. John Scot, an Esquire, took a fancy to Anthony, and was indulgent to him in many ways; and Anthony had, as a matter of fact, little difficulty in coming and going as he pleased so soon as his morning duties were done. Lambeth House had been lately restored by Parker, and was now a very beautiful and well-kept place. Among other repairs and buildings he had re-roofed the great hall that stood just within Morton's gateway; he had built a long pier into the Thames where the barge could be entered easily even at low tide; he had rebuilt the famous summer-house of Cranmer's in the garden, besides doing many sanitary alterations and repairs; and the house was well kept up in Grindal's time.

Anthony soon added a great affection and tenderness to the awe that he felt for the Archbishop, who was almost from the first a pathetic and touching figure. When Anthony first entered on his duties in November '76, he found the Archbishop in his last days of freedom and good favour with the Queen. Elizabeth, he soon learnt from the gossip of the household, was as determined to put down the Puritan "prophesyings" as the popish services; for both alike tended to injure the peace she was resolved to maintain. Rumours were flying to and fro; the Archbishop was continually going across the water to confer with his friends and the Lords of the Council, and messengers came and went all day; and it was soon evident that the Archbishop did not mean to yield. It was said that his Grace had sent a letter to her Majesty bidding her not to meddle with what did not concern her, telling her that she, too, would one day have to render account before Christ's tribunal, and warning her of God's anger if she persisted.

Her Majesty had sworn like a trooper, a royal page said one day as he lounged over the fire in the guard-room, and had declared that if she was like Ozeas and Ahab and the rest, as Grindal had said she was, she would take care that he, at least, should be like Micaiah the son of Imlah, before she had done with him. Then it began to leak out that Elizabeth was sending her commands to the bishops direct instead of through their Metropolitan; and, as the days went by, it became more and more evident that disgrace was beginning to shadow Lambeth. The barges that drew up at the watergate were fewer as summer went on, and the long tables in hall were more and more deserted; even the Archbishop himself seemed silent and cast down. Anthony used to watch him from his window going up and down the little walled garden that looked upon the river, with his hands clasped behind him and his black habit gathered up in them, and his chin on his breast. He would be longer than ever too in chapel after the morning prayer, and the company would wait and wonder in the anteroom till his Grace came in and gave the signal for dinner. And at last the blow fell.

On one day in June, Anthony, who had been on a visit to Isabel at Great Keynes, returned to Lambeth in time for morning prayer and dinner just before the gates were shut by the porter, having ridden up early with a couple of grooms. There seemed to him to be an air of constraint abroad as the guests and members of the household gathered for dinner. There were no guests of high dignity that day, and the Archbishop sat at his own table silent and apart. Anthony, from his place at the steward's table, noticed that he ate very sparingly, and that he appeared even more preoccupied and distressed than usual. His short-sighted eyes, kind and brown, surrounded by wrinkles from his habit of peering closely at everything, seemed full of sadness and perplexity, and his hand fumbled with his bread continually. Anthony did not like to ask anything of his neighbours, as there were one or two strangers dining at the steward's table that day; and the moment dinner was over, and grace had been said and the Archbishop retired with his little procession preceded by a white wand, an usher came running back to tell Master Norris that his Grace desired to see him at once in the inner cloister.

Anthony hastened round through the court between the hall and the river, and found the Archbishop walking up and down in his black habit with the round flapped cap, that, as a Puritan, he preferred to the square head-dress of the more ecclesiastically-minded clergy, still looking troubled and cast down, continually stroking his dark forked beard, and talking to one of his secretaries. Anthony stood at a little distance at the open side of the court near the river, cap in hand, waiting till the Archbishop should beckon him. The two went up and down in the shade in the open court outside the cloisters, where the pump stood, and where the pulpit had been erected for the Queen's famous visit to his predecessor; when she had sat in a gallery over the cloister and heard the chaplain's sermon. On the north rose up the roof of the chapel. The cloisters themselves were poor buildings—little more than passages with a continuous row of square windows running along them the height of a man's head.

After a few minutes the secretary left the Archbishop with an obeisance, and hastened into the house through the cloister, and presently the Archbishop, after a turn or two more with the same grave air, peered towards Anthony and then called him.

Anthony immediately came towards him and received orders that half a dozen horses with grooms should be ready as soon as possible, who were to receive orders from Mr. Richard Frampton, the secretary; and that three or four horses more were to be kept saddled till seven o'clock that evening in case further messages were wanted.

"And I desire you, Mr. Norris," said the Archbishop, "to let the men under your charge know that their master is in trouble with the Queen's Grace; and that they can serve him best by being prompt and obedient."

Anthony bowed to the Archbishop, and was going to withdraw, but the Archbishop went on:

"I will tell you," he said, "for your private ear only at present, that I have received an order this day from my Lords of the Council, bidding me to keep to my house for six months; and telling me that I am sequestered by the Queen's desire. I know not how this will end, but the cause is that I will not do her Grace's will in the matter of the Exercises, as I wrote to tell her so; and I am determined, by God's grace, not to yield in this thing; but to govern the charge committed to me as He gives me light. That is all, Mr. Norris."

The whole household was cast into real sorrow by the blow that had fallen at last on the master; he was "loving and grateful to servants"; and was free and liberal in domestic matters, and it needed only a hint that he was in trouble, for his officers and servants to do their utmost for him.

Anthony's sympathy was further aroused by the knowledge that the Papists, too, hated the old man, and longed to injure him. There had been a great increase of Catholics this year; the Archbishop of York had reported that "a more stiff-necked, wilful, or obstinate people did he never hear of"; and from Hereford had come a lament that conformity itself was a mockery, as even the Papists that attended church were a distraction when they got there, and John Hareley was instanced as "reading so loud upon his Latin popish primer (that he understands not) that he troubles both minister and people." In November matters were so serious that the Archbishop felt himself obliged to take steps to chastise the recusants; and in December came the news of the execution of Cuthbert Maine at Launceston in Cornwall.

How much the Catholics resented this against the Archbishop was brought to Anthony's notice a day or two later. He was riding back for morning prayer after an errand in Battersea, one frosty day, and had just come in sight of Morton's Gateway, when he observed a man standing by it, who turned and ran, on hearing the horse's footsteps, past Lambeth Church and disappeared in the direction of the meadows behind Essex House. Anthony checked his horse, doubtful whether to follow or not, but decided to see what it was that the man had left pinned to the door. He rode up and detached it, and found it was a violent and scurrilous attack upon the Archbishop for his supposed share in the death of the two Papists. It denounced him as a "bloody pseudo-minister," compared him to Pilate, and bade him "look to his congregation of lewd and profane persons that he named the Church of England," for that God would avenge the blood of his saints speedily upon their murderers.

Anthony carried it into the hall, and after showing it to Mr. Scot, put it indignantly into the fire. The steward raised his eyebrows.

"Why so, Master Norris?" he asked.

"Why," said Anthony sharply, "you would not have me frame it, and show to my lord."

"I am not sure," said the other, "if you desire to injure the Papists. Such foul nonsense is their best condemnation. It is best to keep evidence against a traitor, not destroy it. Besides, we might have caught the knave, and now we cannot," he added, looking at the black shrivelling sheet half regretfully.

"It is a mystery to me," said Anthony, "how there can be Papists."

"Why, they hate England," said the steward, briefly, as the bell rang for morning prayer. As Anthony followed him along the gallery, he thought half guiltily of Sir Nicholas and his lady, and wondered whether that was true of them. But he had no doubt that it was true of Catholics as a class; they had ceased to be English; the cause of the Pope and the Queen were irreconcilable; and so the whole incident added more fuel to the hot flame of patriotism and loyalty that burnt so bright in the lad's soul.

But it was fanned yet higher by a glimpse he had of Court-life; and he owed it to Mary Corbet whom he had only seen momentarily in public once or twice, and never to speak to since her visit to Great Keynes over six years ago. He had blushed privately and bitten his lip a good many times in the interval, when he thought of his astonishing infatuation, and yet the glamour had never wholly faded; and his heart quickened perceptibly when he opened a note one day, brought by a royal groom, that asked him to come that very afternoon if he could, to Whitehall Palace, where Mistress Corbet would be delighted to see him and renew their acquaintance.

As he came, punctual to the moment, into the gallery overlooking the tilt-yard, the afternoon sun was pouring in through the oriel window, and the yard beyond seemed all a haze of golden light and dust. He heard an exclamation, as he paused, dazzled, and the servant closed the door behind him; and there came forward to him in the flood of glory, the same resplendent figure, all muslin and jewels, that he remembered so well, with the radiant face, looking scarcely older, with the same dancing eyes and scarlet lips. All the old charm seemed to envelop him in a moment as he saluted her with all the courtesy of which he was capable.

"Ah!" she cried, "how happy I am to see you again—those dear days at Great Keynes!" And she took both his hands with such ardour that poor Anthony was almost forced to think that he had never been out of her thoughts since.

"How can I serve you, Mistress Corbet?" he asked.

"Serve me? Why, by talking to me, and telling me of the country. What does the lad mean? Come and sit here," she said, and she drew him to the window seat.

Anthony looked out into the shining haze of the tilt-yard. Some one with a long pole was struggling violently on the back of a horse, jerking the reins and cursing audibly.

"Look at that fool," said Mary, "he thinks his horse as great a dolt as himself. Chris, Chris," she screamed through her hands—"you sodden ass; be quieter with the poor beast—soothe him, soothe him. He doesn't know what you want of him with your foul temper and your pole going like a windmill about his ears."

The cursing and jerking ceased, and a red furious face with thick black beard and hair looked up. But before the rider could speak, Mary went on again:

"There now, Chris, he is as quiet as a sheep again. Now take him at it."

"What does he want?" asked Anthony. "I can scarcely see for the dust."

"Why, he's practising at the quintain;—ah! ah!" she cried out again, as the quintain was missed and swung round with a hard buffet on the man's back as he tore past. "Going to market, Chris? You've got a sturdy shepherd behind you. Baa, baa, black sheep."

"Who's that?" asked Anthony, as the tall horseman, as if driven by the storm of contumely from the window, disappeared towards the stable.

"Why that's Chris Hatton—whom the Queen calls her sheep, and he's as silly as one, too, with his fool's face and his bleat and his great eyes. He trots about after her Grace, too, like a pet lamb. Bah! I'm sick of him. That's enough of the ass; tell me about Isabel."

Then they fell to talking about Isabel; and Mary eyed him as he answered her questions.

"Then she isn't a Papist, yet?" she asked.

Anthony's face showed such consternation that she burst out laughing.

"There, there, there!" she cried. "No harm's done. Then that tall lad, who was away last time I was there—well, I suppose he's not turned Protestant?"

Anthony's face was still more bewildered.

"Why, my dear lad," she said, "where are your eyes?"

"Mistress Corbet," he burst out at last, "I do not know what you mean. Hubert has been in Durham for years. There is no talk—" and he stopped.

Mary's face became sedate again.

"Well, well," she said, "I always was a tattler. It seems I am wrong again. Forgive me, Master Anthony."

Anthony was indeed astonished at her fantastic idea. Of course he knew that Hubert had once been fond of Isabel, but that was years ago, when they had been all children together. Why, he reflected, he too had been foolish once— and he blushed a little.

Then they went on to talk of Great Keynes, Sir Nicholas, and Mr. Stewart's arrest and death; and Mary asked Anthony to excuse her interest in such matters, but Papistry had always been her religion, and what could a poor girl do but believe what she was taught? Then they went on to speak of more recent affairs, and Mary made him describe to her his life at Lambeth, and everything he did from the moment he got up to the moment he went to bed again; and whether the Archbishop was a kind master, and how long they spent at prayers, and how many courses they had at dinner; and Anthony grew more and more animated and confidential—she was so friendly and interested and pretty, as she leaned towards him and questioned and listened, and the faint scent of violet from her dress awakened his old memories of her.

And then at last she approached the subject on which she had chiefly wished to see him—which was that he should speak to the steward at Lambeth on behalf of a young man who was to be dismissed, it seemed, from the Archbishop's service, because his sister had lately turned Papist and fled to a convent abroad. It was a small matter; and Anthony readily promised to do his best, and, if necessary, to approach the Archbishop himself: and Mistress Corbet was profusely grateful.

They had hardly done talking of the matter, when a trumpet blew suddenly somewhere away behind the building they were in. Mary held up a white finger and put her head on one side.

"That will be the Ambassador," she said.

Anthony looked at her interrogatively.

"Why, you country lad!" she said, "come and see."

She jumped up, and he followed her down the gallery, and along through interminable corridors and ante-chambers, and up and down the stairs of this enormous palace; and Anthony grew bewildered and astonished as he went at the doors on all sides, and the roofs that ranged themselves every way as he looked out. And at last Mary stopped at a window, and pointed out.

The courtyard beneath was alive with colour and movement. In front of the entrance opposite waited the great gilded state carriage, and another was just driving away. On one side a dozen ladies on grey horses were drawn up, to follow behind the Queen when she should come out; and a double row of liveried servants were standing bare-headed round the empty carriage. The rest of the court was filled with Spanish and English nobles, mounted, with their servants on foot; all alike in splendid costumes—the Spaniards with rich chains about their necks, and tall broad-brimmed hats decked with stones and pearls, and the Englishmen in feathered buckled caps and short cloaks thrown back. Two or three trumpeters stood on the steps of the porch. Anthony did not see much state at Lambeth, and the splendour and gaiety of this seething courtyard exhilarated him, and he stared down at it all, fascinated, while Mary Corbet poured out a caustic commentary:

"There is the fat fool Chris again, all red with his tilting. I would like to baa at him again, but I dare not with all these foreign folk. There is Leicester, that tall man with a bald forehead in the cap with the red feather, on the white horse behind the carriage—he always keeps close to the Queen. He is the enemy of your prelate, Master Anthony, you know.... That is Oxford, just behind him on the chestnut. Yes, look well at him. He is the prince of the tilt-yard; none can stand against him. You would say he was at his nine-pins, when he rides against them all.... And he can do more than tilt. These sweet-washed gloves"—and she flapped an embroidered pair before Anthony—"these he brought to England. God bless and reward him for it!" she added fervently.... "I do not see Burghley. Eh! but he is old and gouty these days; and loves a cushion and a chair and a bit of flannel better than to kneel before her Grace. You know, she allows him to sit when he confers with her. But then, she is ever prone to show mercy to bearded persons.... Ah! there is dear Sidney; that is a sweet soul. But what does he do here among the stones and mortar when he has the beeches of Penshurst to walk beneath. He is not so wise as I thought him.... But I must say I grow weary of his nymphs and his airs of Olympus. And for myself, I do not see that Flora and Phœbus and Maia and the rest are a great gain, instead of Our Lady and Saint Christopher and the court of heaven. But then I am a Papist and not a heathen, and therefore blind and superstitious. Is that not so, Master Anthony?... And there is Maitland beside him, with the black velvet cap and the white feather, and his cross eyes and mouth. Now I wish he were at Penshurst, or Bath—or better still, at Jericho, for it is further off. I cannot bear that fellow.... Why, Sussex is going on the water, too, I see. Now what brings him here? I should have thought his affairs gave him enough to think of.... There he is, with his groom behind him, on the other chestnut. I am astonished at him. He is all for this French marriage, you know. So you may figure to yourself Mendoza's love for him! They will be like two cats together on the barge; spitting and snarling softly at one another. Her Grace loves to balance folk like that; first one stretches his claws, and then the other; then one arches his back and snarls, and the other scratches his face for him; and then when all is flying fur and blasphemy, off slips her Grace and does what she will."

It was an astonishing experience for Anthony. He had stepped out from his workaday life among the grooms and officers and occasional glimpses of his lonely old master, into an enchanted region, where great personages whose very names were luminous with fame, now lived and breathed and looked cheerful or sullen before his very eyes; and one who knew them in their daily life stood by him and commented and interpreted them for him. He listened and stared, dazed with the strangeness of it all.

Mistress Corbet was proceeding to express her views upon the foreign element that formed half the pageant, when the shrill music broke out again in the palace, and the trumpeters on the steps took it up; and a stir and bustle began. Then out of the porch began to stream a procession, like a river of colour and jewels, pouring from the foot of the carved and windowed wall, and eddying in a tumbled pool about the great gilt carriage;—ushers and footmen and nobles and ladies and pages in bewildering succession. Anthony pressed his forehead to the glass as he watched, with little exclamations, and Mary watched him, amused and interested by his enthusiasm.

And last moved the great canopy bending and swaying under the doorway, and beneath it, like two gorgeous butterflies, at the sight of whom all the standing world fell on its knees, came the pale Elizabeth with her auburn hair, and the brown-faced Mendoza, side by side; and entered the carriage with the five plumes atop and the caparisoned horses that stamped and tossed their jingling heads. The yard was already emptying fast, en route for Chelsea Stairs; and as soon as the two were seated, the shrill trumpets blew again, and the halberdiers moved off with the carriage in the midst, the great nobles going before, and the ladies behind. The later comers mounted as quickly as possible, as their horses were brought in from the stable entrance, and clattered away, and in five minutes the yard was empty, except for a few sentries at their posts, and a servant or two lounging at the doorway; and as Anthony still stared at the empty pavement and the carpeted steps, far away from the direction of the Abbey came the clear call of the horns to tell the loyal folk that the Queen was coming.

It was a great inspiration for Anthony. He had seen world-powers incarnate below him in the glittering rustling figure of the Queen, and the dark-eyed courtly Ambassador in his orders and jewels at her side. There they had sat together in one carriage; the huge fiery realm of the south, whose very name was redolent with passion and adventure and boundless wealth; and the little self-contained northern kingdom, now beginning to stretch its hands, and quiver all along its tingling sinews and veins with fresh adolescent life. And Anthony knew that he was one of the cells of this young organism; and that in him as well as in Elizabeth and this sparkling creature at his side ran the fresh red blood of England. They were all one in the possession of a common life; and his heart burned as he thought of it.

After he had parted from Mary he rode back to Westminster, and crossed the river by the horse-ferry that plied there. And even as he landed and got his beast, with a deal of stamping and blowing, off the echoing boards on to the clean gravel again, there came down the reaches of the river the mellow sound of music across a mile of water, mingled with the deep rattle of oars, and sparkles of steel and colour glittered from the far-away royal barges in the autumn sunshine; and the lad thought with wonder how the two great powers so savagely at war upon the salt sea, were at peace here, sitting side by side on silken cushions and listening to the same trumpets of peace upon the flowing river.

Chapter Two - Some New Lessons

The six years that followed Sir Nicholas' return and Hubert's departure for the North had passed uneventfully at Great Keynes. The old knight had been profoundly shocked that any Catholic, especially an agent so valuable as Mr. Stewart, should have found his house a death-trap; and although he continued receiving his friends and succouring them, he did so with more real caution and less ostentation of it. His religious zeal and discretion were further increased by the secret return to the "Old Religion" of several of his villagers during the period; and a very fair congregation attended Mass so often as it was said in the cloister wing of the Hall. The new rector, like his predecessor, was content to let the squire alone; and unlike him had no wife to make trouble.

Then, suddenly, in the summer of '77, catastrophes began, headed by the unexpected return of Hubert, impatient of waiting, and with new plans in his mind.

Isabel had been out with Mistress Margaret walking in the dusk one August evening after supper, on the raised terrace beneath the yews. They had been listening to the loud snoring of the young owls in the ivy on the chimney-stack opposite, and had watched the fierce bird slide silently out of the gloom, white against the blackness, and disappear down among the meadows. Once Isabel had seen him pause, too, on one of his return journeys, suspicious of the dim figures beneath, silhouetted on a branch against the luminous green western sky, with the outline of a mouse with its hanging tail plain in his crooked claws, before he glided to his nest again. As Isabel waited she heard the bang of the garden-door, but gave it no thought, and a moment after Mistress Margaret asked her to fetch a couple of wraps from the house for them both, as the air had a touch of chill in it. She came down the lichened steps, crossed the lawn, and passed into the unlighted hall. As she entered, the door opposite opened, and for a moment she saw the silhouette of a man's figure against the bright passage beyond. Her heart suddenly leapt, and stood still.

"Anthony!" she whispered, in a hush of suspense.

There was a vibration and a step beside her.

"Isabel!" said Hubert's voice. And then his arms closed round her for the first time in her life. She struggled and panted a moment as she felt his breath on her face; and he released her. She recoiled to the door, and stood there silent and panting.

"Oh! Isabel!" he whispered; and again, "Isabel!"

She put out her hand and grasped the door-post behind her.

"Oh! Hubert! Why have you come?"

He came a step nearer and she could see the faint whiteness of his face in the western glimmer.

"I cannot wait," he said, "I have been nearly beside myself. I have left the north—and I cannot wait so long."

"Well?" she said; and he heard the note of entreaty and anxiety in her voice.

"I have my plans," he answered; "I will tell you to-morrow. Where is my aunt?"

Isabel heard a step on the gravel outside.

"She is coming," she said sharply. Hubert melted into the dark, and she saw the opposite door open and let him out.

The next day Hubert announced his plans to Sir Nicholas, and a conflict followed.

"I cannot go on, sir," he said, "I cannot wait for ever. I am treated like a servant, too; and you know how miserably I am paid, I have obeyed you for six years, sir; and now I have thrown up the post and told my lord to his face that I can bear with him no longer."

Sir Nicholas' face, as he sat in his upright chair opposite the boy, grew flushed with passion.

"It is your accursed temper, sir," he said violently. "I know you of old. Wait? For what? For the Protestant girl? I told you to put that from your mind, sir."

Hubert did not propose as yet to let his father into all his plans.

"I have not spoken her name, sir, I think. I say I cannot wait for my fortune; I may be impatient, sir—I do not deny it."

"Then how do you propose to better it?" sneered his father.

"In November," said Hubert steadily, looking his father in the eyes, "I sail with Mr. Drake."

Sir Nicholas' face grew terrific. He rose, and struck the table twice with his clenched fist.

"Then, by God, sir, Mr. Drake may have you now."

Hubert's face grew white with anger; but he had his temper under control.

"Then I wish you good-day, sir," and he left the room.

When the boy had left the house again for London, as he did the same afternoon, Lady Maxwell tried to soothe the old man. It was impossible, even for her, to approach him before.

"Sweetheart," she said tranquilly, as he sat and glowered at his plate when supper was over and the men had left the room, "sweetheart, we must have Hubert down here again. He must not sail with Mr. Drake."

The old man's face flared up again in anger.

"He may follow his own devices," he cried. "I care not what he does. He has given up the post that I asked for him; and he comes striding and ruffling home with his hat cocked and—and—"; his voice became inarticulate.

"He is only a boy, sweetheart; with a boy's hot blood—you would sooner have him like that than a milk-sop. Besides—he is our boy."

The old man growled. His wife went on:

"And now that James cannot have the estate, he must have it, as you know, and carry on the old name."

"He has disgraced it," burst out the angry old man, "and he is going now with that damned Protestant to harry Catholics. By the grace of God I love my country, and would serve her Grace with my heart's blood—but that my boy should go with Drake——!" and again his voice failed.

It was a couple of days before she could obtain her husband's leave to write a conciliatory letter, giving leave to Hubert to go with Drake, if he had made any positive engagement (because, as she represented to Sir Nicholas, there was nothing actually wrong or disloyal to the Faith in it)—but entreating him with much pathos not to leave his old parents so bitterly.

"Oh, my dear son," the end of the letter ran, "your father is old; and God, in whose hand are our days, alone knows how long he will live; and I, too, my son, am old. So come back to us and be our dear child again. You must not think too hardly of your father's words to you; he is quick and hot, as you are, too—but indeed we love you dearly. Your room here is ready for you; and Piers wants a firm hand now over him, as your father is so old. So come back, my darling, and make our old hearts glad again."

But the weeks passed by, and no answer came, and the old people's hearts grew sick with suspense; and then, at last, in September the courier brought a letter, written from Plymouth, which told the mother that it was too late; that he had in fact engaged himself to Mr. Drake in August before he had come to Great Keynes at all; and that in honour he must keep his engagement. He asked pardon of his father for his hastiness; but it seemed a cold and half-hearted sorrow; and the letter ended by announcing that the little fleet would sail in November; and that at present they were busy fitting the ships and engaging the men; and that there would be no opportunity for him to return to wish them good-bye before he sailed. It was plain that the lad was angry still.

Sir Nicholas did not say much; but a silence fell on the house. Lady Maxwell sent for Isabel, and they had a long interview. The old lady was astonished at the girl's quietness and resignation.

Yes, she said, she loved Hubert with all her heart. She had loved him for a long while. No, she was not angry, only startled. What would she do about the difference in religion? Could she marry him while one was a Catholic and the other a Protestant? No, they would never be happy like that; and she did not know what she would do. She supposed she would wait and see. Yes, she would wait and see; that was all that could be done.—And then had come a silent burst of tears, and the girl had sunk down on her knees and hidden her face in the old lady's lap, and the wrinkled jewelled old hand passed quietly over the girl's black hair; but no more had been said, and Isabel presently got up and went home to the Dower House.

The autumn went by, and November came, and there was no further word from Hubert. Then towards the end of November a report reached them from Anthony at Lambeth that the fleet had sailed; but had put back into Falmouth after a terrible storm in the Channel. And hope just raised its head.

Then one evening after supper Sir Nicholas complained of fever and restlessness, and went early to bed. In the night he was delirious. Mistress Margaret hastened up at midnight from the Dower House, and a groom galloped off to Lindfield before morning to fetch the doctor, and another to fetch Mr. Barnes, the priest, from Cuckfield. Sir Nicholas was bled to reduce the fever of the pneumonia that had attacked him. All day long he was sinking. About eleven o'clock that night he fell asleep, apparently, and Lady Maxwell, who had watched incessantly, was persuaded to lie down; but at three o'clock in the morning, on the first of December, Mistress Margaret awakened her, and together they knelt by the bedside of the old man. The priest, who had anointed him on the previous evening, knelt behind, repeating the prayers for the dying.

Sir Nicholas lay on his back, supported by pillows, under the gloom of the black old four-posted bed. A wood-fire glowed on the hearth, and the air was fragrant with the scent of the burning cedar-logs. A crucifix was in the old man's hands; but his eyes were bright with fever, and his fingers every now and then relaxed, and then tightened their hold again on the cool silver of the figure of the crucified Saviour. His lips were moving tremulously, and his ruddy old face was pale now.

The priest's voice went on steadily; the struggle was beginning.

"Proficiscere, anima christiana, de hoc mundo.—Go forth, Christian soul, from this world in the name of God the Father Almighty, who created thee; in the name of Jesus Christ, Son of the living God, Who suffered for thee; in the name of the Holy Ghost, who was shed forth upon thee; In the name of Angels and Archangels; in the name of Thrones and Dominions; in the name of Principalities and Powers—"

Suddenly the old man, whose head had been slowly turning from side to side, ceased his movement, and his open mouth closed; he was looking steadily at his wife, and a look of recognition came back to his eyes.

"Sweetheart," he said; and smiled, and died.

Isabel did not see much of Mistress Margaret for the next few days; she was constantly with her sister, and when she came to the Dower House now and then, said little to the girl. There were curious rumours in the village; strangers came and went continually, and there was a vast congregation at the funeral, when the body of the old knight was laid to rest in the Maxwell chapel. The following day the air of mystery deepened; and young Mrs. Melton whispered to Isabel, with many glances and becks, that she and her man had seen lights through the chapel windows at three o'clock that morning. Isabel went into the chapel presently to visit the grave, and there was a new smear of black on the east wall as if a taper had been set too near.

The courier who had been despatched to announce to Hubert that his father had died and left him master of the Hall and estate, with certain conditions, returned at the end of the month with the news that the fleet had sailed again on the thirteenth, and that Hubert was gone with it; so Lady Maxwell, now more silent and retired than ever, for the present retained her old position and Mr. Piers took charge of the estate.

Although Isabel outwardly was very little changed in the last six years, great movements had been taking place in her soul, and if Hubert had only known the state of the case, possibly he would not have gone so hastily with Mr. Drake.

The close companionship of such an one as Mistress Margaret was doing its almost inevitable work; and the girl had been learning that behind the brilliant and even crude surface of the Catholic practice, there lay still and beautiful depths of devotion which she had scarcely dreamed of. The old nun's life was a revelation to Isabel; she heard from her bed in the black winter mornings her footsteps in the next room, and soon learnt that Mistress Margaret spent at least two hours in prayer before she appeared at all. Two or three times in the day she knew that she retired again for the same purpose, and again an hour after she was in bed, there were the same gentle movements next door. She began to discover, too, that for the Catholic, as well as for the Puritan, the Person of the Saviour was the very heart of religion; that her own devotion to Christ was a very languid flame by the side of the ardent inarticulate passion of this soul who believed herself His wedded spouse; and that the worship of the saints and the Blessed Mother instead of distracting the love of the Christian soul rather seemed to augment it. The King of Love stood, as she fancied sometimes, to Catholic eyes, in a glow of ineffable splendour; and the faces of His adoring Court reflected the ruddy glory on all sides; thus refracting the light of their central Sun, instead of, as she had thought, obscuring it.

Other difficulties, too, began to seem oddly unreal and intangible, when she had looked at them in the light of Mistress Margaret's clear old eyes and candid face. It was a real event in her inner life when she first began to understand what the rosary meant to Catholics. Mistress Corbet had told her what was the actual use of the beads; and how the mysteries of Christ's life and death were to be pondered over as the various prayers were said; but it had hitherto seemed to Isabel as if this method were an elaborate and superstitious substitute for reading the inspired record of the New Testament.

She had been sitting out in the little walled garden in front of the Dower House one morning on an early summer day after her father's death, and Mistress Margaret had come out in her black dress and stood for a moment looking at her irresolutely, framed in the dark doorway. Then she had come slowly across the grass, and Isabel had seen for the first time in her fingers a string of ivory beads. Mistress Margaret sat down on a garden chair a little way from her, and let her hands sink into her lap, still holding the beads. Isabel said nothing, but went on reading. Presently she looked up again, and the old lady's eyes were half-closed, and her lips just moving; and the beads passing slowly through her fingers. She looked almost like a child dreaming, in spite of her wrinkles and her snowy hair; the pale light of a serene soul lay on her face. This did not look like the mechanical performance that Isabel had always associated with the idea of beads. So the minutes passed away; every time that Isabel looked up there was the little white face with the long lashes lying on the cheek, and the crown of snowy hair and lace, and the luminous look of a soul in conscious communion with the unseen.

When the old lady had finished, she twisted the beads about her fingers and opened her eyes. Isabel had an impulse to speak.

"Mistress Margaret," she said, "may I ask you something?"

71

"Of course, my darling," the old lady said.

"I have never seen you use those before—I cannot understand them."

"What is it," asked the old lady, "that you don't understand?"

"How can prayers said over and over again like that be any good?"

Mistress Margaret was silent for a moment.

"I saw young Mrs. Martin last week," she said, "with her little girl in her lap. Amy had her arms round her mother's neck, and was being rocked to and fro; and every time she rocked she said 'Oh, mother.'"

"But then," said Isabel, after a moment's silence, "she was only a child."

"'Except ye become like little children—'" quoted Mistress Margaret softly—"you see, my Isabel, we are nothing more than children with God and His Blessed Mother. To say 'Hail Mary, Hail Mary,' is the best way of telling her how much we love her. And then this string of beads is like Our Lady's girdle, and her children love to finger it, and whisper to her. And then we say our paternosters, too; and all the while we are talking she is shewing us pictures of her dear Child, and we look at all the great things He did for us, one by one; and then we turn the page and begin again."

"I see," said Isabel; and after a moment or two's silence Mistress Margaret got up and went into the house.

The girl sat still with her hands clasped round her knee. How strange and different this religion was to the fiery gospel she had heard last year at Northampton from the harsh stern preacher, at whose voice a veil seemed to rend and show a red-hot heaven behind! How tender and simple this was—like a blue summer's sky with drifting clouds! If only it was true! If only there were a great Mother whose girdle was of beads strung together, which dangled into every Christian's hands; whose face bent down over every Christian's bed; and whose mighty and tender arms that had held her Son and God were still stretched out beneath her other children. And Isabel, whose soul yearned for a mother, sighed as she reminded herself that there was but "one Mediator between God and man—the man, Christ Jesus."

And so the time went by, like an outgoing tide, silent and steady. The old nun did not talk much to the girl about dogmatic religion, for she was in a difficult position. She was timid certainly of betraying her faith by silence, but she was also timid of betraying her trust by speech. Sometimes she felt she had gone too far, sometimes not far enough; but on the whole her practice was never to suggest questions, but only to answer them when Isabel asked; and to occupy herself with affirmative rather than with destructive criticism. More than this she hesitated to do out of honour for the dead; less than this she dared not do out of love for God and Isabel. But there were three or four conversations that she felt were worth waiting for; and the look on Isabel's face afterwards, and the sudden questions she would ask sometimes after a fit of silence, made her friend's heart quicken towards her, and her prayers more fervent.

The two were sitting together one December day in Isabel's upstairs room and the girl, who had just come in from a solitary walk, was half kneeling on the window-seat and drumming her fingers softly on the panes as she looked out at the red western sky.

"I used to think," she said, "that Catholics had no spiritual life; but now it seems to me that in comparison we Puritans have none. You know so much about the soul, as to what is from God and what from the Evil One; and we have to grope for ourselves. And yet our Saviour said that His sheep should know His voice. I do not understand it." And she turned towards Mistress Margaret who had laid down her work and was listening.

"Dear child," she said, "if you mean our priests and spiritual writers, it is because they study it. We believe in the science of the soul; and we consult our spiritual guides for our soul's health, as the leech for our body's health."

"But why must you ask the priest, if the Lord speaks to all alike?"

"He speaks through the priest, my dear, as He does through the physician."

"But why should the priest know better than the people?" pursued Isabel, intent on her point.

"Because he tells us what the Church says," said the other smiling, "it is his business. He need not be any better or cleverer in other respects. The baker may be a thief or a foolish fellow; but his bread is good."

"But how do you know," went on Isabel, who thought Mistress Margaret a little slow to see her point—"how do you know that the Church is right?"

The old nun considered a moment, and then lifted her embroidery again.

"Why do you think," she asked, beginning to sew, "that each single soul that asks God's guidance is right?"

"Because the Holy Ghost is promised to such," said Isabel wondering.

"Then is it not likely," went on the other still stitching, "that the millions of souls who form Holy Church are right, when they all agree together?" Isabel moved a little impatiently.

"You see," went on Mistress Margaret, "that is what we Catholics believe our Saviour meant when He said that the gates of hell should not prevail against His Church."

But Isabel was not content. She broke in:

"But why are not the Scriptures sufficient? They are God's Word."

The other put down her embroidery again, and smiled up into the girl's puzzled eyes.

"Well, my child," she said, "do they seem sufficient, when you look at Christendom now? If they are so clear, how is it that you have the Lutherans, and the Anabaptists, and the Family of Love, and the Calvinists, and the Church of England, all saying they hold to the Scriptures alone. Nay, nay; the Scriptures are the grammar, and the Church is the dame that teaches out of it, and she knows so well much that is not in the grammar, and we name that tradition. But where there is no dame to teach, the children soon fall a-fighting about the book and the meaning of it."

Isabel looked at Mistress Margaret a moment, and then turned back again to the window in silence.

At another time they had a word or two about Peter's prerogatives.

"Surely," said Isabel suddenly, as they walked together in the garden, "Christ is the one Foundation of the Church, St. Paul tells us so expressly."

"Yes, my dear," said the nun, "but then Christ our Lord said: 'Thou art Peter, and on this rock I will build my Church.' So he who is the only Good Shepherd, said to Peter, 'Feed My sheep'; and He that is Clavis David and that openeth and none shutteth said to him, 'I will give thee the keys, and whatsoever thou shalt bind on earth shall be bound in heaven.' That is why we call Peter the Vicar of Christ."

Isabel raised her eyebrows.

"Surely, surely—" she began.

"Yes, my child," said Mistress Margaret, "I know it is new and strange to you; but it was not to your grandfather or his forbears: to them, as to me, it is the plain meaning of the words. We Catholics are a simple folk. We hold that what our Saviour said simply He meant simply: as we do in the sacred mystery of His Body and Blood. To us, you know," she went on, smiling, with a hand on the girl's arm, "it seems as if you Protestants twisted the Word of God against all justice."

Isabel smiled back at her; but she was puzzled. The point of view was new to her. And yet again in the garden, a few months later, as they sat out together on the lawn, the girl opened the same subject.

"Mistress Margaret," she said, "I have been thinking a great deal; and it seems very plain when you talk. But you know our great divines could answer you, though I cannot. My father was no Papist; and Dr. Grindal and the Bishops are all wise men. How do you answer that?"

The nun looked silently down at the grass a moment or two.

"It is the old tale," she said at last, looking up; "we cannot believe that the babes and sucklings are as likely to be right in such matters as the wise and prudent—even more likely, if our Saviour's words are to be believed. Dear child, do you not see that our Lord came to save all men, and call all men into His Church; and that therefore He must have marked His Church in such a manner that the most ignorant may perceive it as easily as the most learned? Learning is very well, and it is the gift of God; but salvation and grace cannot depend upon it. It needs an architect to understand why Paul's Church is strong and beautiful, and what makes it so; but any child or foolish fellow can see that it is so."

"I do not understand," said Isabel, wrinkling her forehead.

"Why this—that you are as likely to know the Catholic Church when you see it, as Dr. Grindal or Dr. Freake, or your dear father himself. Only a divine can explain about it and understand it, but you and I are as fit to see it and walk into it, as any of them."

"But then why are they not all Catholics?" asked Isabel, still bewildered.

"Ah!" said the nun, softly, "God alone knows, who reads hearts and calls whom He will. But learning, at least, has nought to do with it."

Conversations of this kind that took place now and then between the two were sufficient to show Mistress Margaret, like tiny bubbles on the surface of a clear stream, the swift movement of this limpid soul that she loved so well. But on the other hand, all the girl's past life, and most sacred and dear associations, were in conflict with this movement; the memory of her quiet, wise father rose and reproached her sometimes; Anthony's enthusiastic talk, when he came down from Lambeth, on the glorious destinies of the Church of England, of her gallant protest against the corruptions of the West, and of her future unique position in Christendom as the National Church of the most progressive country—all this caused her to shrink back terrified from the bourne to which she was drifting, and from the breach that must follow with her brother. But above all else that caused her pain was the shocking suspicion that her love for Hubert perhaps was influencing her, and that she was living in gross self-deception as to the sincerity of her motives.

This culminated at last in a scene that seriously startled the old nun; it took place one summer night after Hubert's departure in Mr. Drake's expedition. Mistress Margaret had seen Isabel to her room, and an hour later had finished her night-office and was thinking of preparing herself to bed, when there was a hurried tap at the door, and Isabel came quickly in, her face pale and miserable, her great grey eyes full of trouble and distraction, and her hair on her shoulders.

"My dear child," said the nun, "what is it?"

Isabel closed the door and stood looking at her, with her lips parted.

"How can I know, Mistress Margaret," she said, in the voice of a sleep-walker, "whether this is the voice of God or of my own wicked self? No, no," she went on, as the other came towards her, frightened, "let me tell you. I must speak."

"Yes, my child, you shall; but come and sit down first," and she drew her to a chair and set her in it, and threw a wrap over her knees and feet; and sat down beside her, and took one of her hands, and held it between her own.

"Now then, Isabel, what is it?"

"I have been thinking over it all so long," began the girl, in the same tremulous voice, with her eyes fixed on the nun's face, "and to-night in bed I could not bear it any longer. You see, I love Hubert, and I used to think I loved our Saviour too; but now I do not know. It seems as if He was leading me to the Catholic Church; all is so much more plain and easy there—it seems—it seems—to make sense in the Catholic Church; and all the rest of us are wandering in the dark. But if I become a Catholic, you see, I can marry Hubert then; and I cannot help thinking of that; and wanting to marry him. But then perhaps that is the reason that I think I see it all so plainly; just because I want to see it plainly. And what am I to do? Why will not our Lord shew me my own heart and what is His Will?"

Mistress Margaret shook her head gently.

"Dear child," she said, "our Saviour loves you and wishes to make you happy. Do you not think that perhaps He is helping you and making it easy in this way, by drawing you to His Church through Hubert. Why should not both be His Will? that you should become a Catholic and marry Hubert as well?"

"Yes," said Isabel, "but how can I tell?"

"There is only one thing to be done," went on the old lady, "be quite simple and quiet. Whenever your soul begins to be disturbed and anxious, put yourself in His Hands, and refuse to decide for yourself. It is so easy, so easy."

"But why should I be so anxious and disturbed, if it were not our Lord speaking and warning me?"

"In the Catholic Church," said Mistress Margaret, "we know well about all those movements of the soul; and we call them scruples. You must resist them, dear child, like temptations. We are told that if a soul is in grace and desires to serve God, then whenever our Lord speaks it is to bring sweetness with Him; and when it is the evil one, he brings disturbance. And that is why I am sure that these questionings are not from God. You feel stifled, is it not so, when you try to pray? and all seems empty of God; the waves and storms are going over you. But lie still and be content; and refuse to be disturbed; and you will soon be at peace again and see the light clearly."

Mistress Margaret found herself speaking simply in short words and sentences as to a child. She had seen that for a long while past the clouds had been gathering over Isabel, and that her soul was at present completely overcast and unable to perceive or decide anything clearly; and so she gave her this simple advice, and did her utmost to soothe her, knowing that such a clean soul would not be kept long in the dark.

She knelt down with Isabel presently and prayed aloud with her, in a quiet even voice; a patch of moonlight lay on the floor, and something of its white serenity seemed to be in the old nun's tones as she entreated the merciful Lord to bid peace again to this anxious soul, and let her see light again through the dark.

And when she had taken Isabel back again to her own room at last, and had seen her safely into bed, and kissed her good-night, already the girl's face was quieter as it lay on the pillow, and the lines were smoothed out of her forehead.

"God bless you!" said Mistress Margaret.

Chapter Three - Hubert's Return

After the sailing of Mr. Drake's expedition, the friends of the adventurers had to wait in patience for several months before news arrived. Then the Elizabeth, under the command of Mr. Winter, which had been separated from Mr. Drake's Pelican in a gale off the south-west coast of America, returned to England, bringing the news of Mr. Doughty's execution for desertion; but of the Pelican herself there was no further news until complaints arrived from the Viceroy of New Spain of Mr. Drake's ravages up the west coast. Then silence again fell for eighteen months. Anthony had followed the fortunes of the Pelican, in which Hubert had sailed, with a great deal of interest: and it was with real relief that after the burst of joy in London at the news of her safe return to Plymouth with an incalculable amount of plunder, he had word from Lady Maxwell that she hoped he would come down at once to Great Keynes, and help to welcome Hubert home. He was not able to go at once, for his duties detained him; but a couple of days after the Hall had welcomed its new master, Anthony was at the Dower House again with Isabel. He found her extraordinarily bright and vivacious, and was delighted at the change, for he had been troubled the last time he had seen her a few months before, at her silence and listlessness; but her face was radiant now, as she threw herself into his arms at the door, and told him that they were all to go to supper that night at the Hall; and that Hubert had been keeping his best stories on purpose for his return. She showed him, when they got up to his room at last, little things Hubert had given her—carved nuts, a Spanish coin or two, and an ingot of gold—but of which she would say nothing, but only laugh and nod her head.

Hubert, too, when he saw him that evening seemed full of the same sort of half-suppressed happiness that shone out now and again suddenly. There he sat, for hours after supper that night, broader and more sunburnt than ever, with his brilliant eyes glancing round as he talked, and his sinewy man's hand, in the delicate creamy ruff, making little explanatory movements, and drawing a map once or twice in spilled wine on the polished oak; the three ladies sat forward and watched him breathlessly, or leaned back and sighed as each tale ended, and Anthony found himself, too, carried away with enthusiasm again and again, as he looked at this gallant sea-dog in his gold chain and satin and jewels, and listened to his stories.

"It was bitter cold," said Hubert in his strong voice, telling them of Mr. Doughty's death, "on the morning itself: and snow lay on the decks when we rose. Mr. Fletcher had prepared a table in the poop-cabin, with a white cloth and bread and wine; and at nine of the clock we were all assembled where we might see into the cabin: and Mr. Fletcher said the Communion service, and Mr. Drake and Mr. Doughty received the sacrament there at his hands. Some of Mr. Doughty's men had all they could do to keep back their tears; for you know, mother, they were good friends. And then when it was done, we made two lines down the deck to where the block stood by the main-mast; and the two came down together; and they kissed one another there. And Mr. Doughty spoke to the men, and bade them pray for the Queen's Grace with him; and they did. And then he and Mr. Drake put off their doublets, and Mr. Doughty knelt at the block, and said another prayer or two, and then laid his head down, and he was shivering a little with cold, and then, when he gave the sign, Mr. Drake—" and Hubert brought the edge of his hand down sharply, and the glasses rang, and the ladies drew quick hissing breaths; and Lady Maxwell put her hand on her son's arm, as he looked round on all their faces.

Then he told them of the expedition up the west coast, and of the towns they sacked; and the opulent names rolled oddly off his tongue, and seemed to bring a whiff of southern scent into this panelled English room,—Valparaiso, Tarapaca, and Arica—; and of the capture of the Cacafuego off Quibdo; and of the enormous treasure they took, the great golden crucifix with emeralds of the size of pigeon's eggs, and the chests of pearls, and the twenty-six tons of silver, and the wedges of pure gold from the Peruvian galleon, and of the golden falcon from the Chinese trader that they captured south of Guatulco. And he described the search up the coast for the passage eastwards that never existed; and of Drake's superb resolve to return westwards instead, by the Moluccas; and how they stayed at Ternate, south of Celebes, and coasted along Java seeking a passage, and found it in the Sunda straits, and broke out from the treacherous islands into the open sea; crossed to Africa, rounded the Cape of Good Hope; came up the west coast, touching at Sierra Leone, and so home again along the Spanish and French coasts, to Plymouth Sound and the pealing of Plymouth bells.

And he broke out into something very like eloquence when he spoke of Drake.

"Never was such a captain," he cried, "with his little stiff beard and his obstinate eyes. I have seen him stand on the poop, when the arrows were like hail on the deck, with one finger in the ring round his neck,—so": and Hubert thrust a tanned finger into a link of his chain, and lifted his chin, "just making little signs to the steersman, with his hand behind his back, to bring the ship nearer to the Spaniard; as cool, I tell you, as cool as if he were playing merelles. Oh! and then when we boarded, out came his finger from his ring; and there was none that struck so true and fierce; and all in silence too, without an oath or a cry or a word; except maybe to give an order. But he was very sharp with all that angered him. When we sighted the Madre di Dios, I ran into his cabin to tell him of it, without saluting, so full was my head of the chase. And he looked at me like ice; and then roared at me to know where my manners were, and bade me go out and enter again properly, before he would hear my news; and then I heard him rating the man that stood at his door for letting me pass in that state. At his dinner, too, which he took alone, there were always trumpets to blow, as when her Grace dines. When he laughed it seemed as if he did it with a grave face. There was a piece of grand fooling when we got out from among those weary Indian islands; where the great crabs be, and flies that burn in the dark, as I told you. Mr. Fletcher, the minister, played the coward one night when we ran aground; and bade us think of our sins and our immortal souls, instead of urging us to be smart about the ship; and he did it, too, not as Mr. Drake might do, but in such a melancholy voice as if we were all at our last hour; so when we were free of our trouble, and out on the main again, we were all called by the drum to the forecastle, and there Mr. Drake sat on a sea-chest as solemn as a judge, so that not a man durst laugh, with a pair of pantoufles in his hand; and Mr. Fletcher was brought before him, trying to smile as if 'twas a jest for him too, between two guards; and there he was arraigned; and the witnesses were called; and Tom Moore said how he was tapped on the shoulder by Mr. Fletcher as he was getting a pick from the hold; and how he was as white as a ghost and bade him think on Mr. Doughty, how there was no mercy for him when he needed it, and so there would be none for us—and then other witnesses came, and then Mr. Fletcher tried to make his defence, saying how it was the part of a minister to bid men think on their souls; but 'twas no good. Mr. Drake declared him guilty; and sentenced him to be kept in irons till he repented of that his cowardice; and then, which was the cream of the joke, since the prisoner was a minister, Mr. Drake declared him excommunicate, and cut off from the Church of God, and given over to the devil. And he was put in irons, too, for a while; so 'twas not all a joke."

"And what is Mr. Drake doing now?" asked Lady Maxwell.

"Oh! Drake is in London," said Hubert. "Ah! yes, and you must all come to Deptford when her Grace is going to be there. Anthony, lad, you'll come?"

Anthony said he would certainly do his best; and Isabel put out her hand to her brother, and beamed at him; and then turned to look at Hubert again.

"And what are you to do next?" asked Mistress Margaret.

"Well," he said, "I am to go to Plymouth again presently, to help to get the treasure out of the ships; and I must be there, too, for the spring and summer, for Drake wants me to help him with his new expedition."

"But you are not going with him again, my son?" said his mother quickly.

Hubert put out his hand to her.

"No, no," he said, "I have written to tell him I cannot. I must take my father's place here. He will understand"; and he gave one swift glance at Isabel, and her eyes fell.

Anthony was obliged to return to Lambeth after a day or two, and he carried with him a heart full of admiration and enthusiasm for his friend. He had wondered once or twice, too, as his eyes fell on Isabel, whether there was anything in what Mistress Corbet had said; but he dared not speak to her, and still less to Hubert, unless his confidence was first sought.

The visit to Deptford, which took place a week or two later, gave an additional spurt to Anthony's nationalism. London was all on fire at the return of the buccaneers, and as Anthony rode down the south bank of the river from Lambeth to join the others at the inn, the three miles of river beyond London Bridge were an inspiriting sight in the bright winter sunshine, crowded with craft of all kinds, bright with bunting, that were making their way down to the naval triumph. The road, too, was thick with vehicles and pedestrians.

It was still early when he met his party at the inn, and Hubert took them immediately to see the Pelican that was drawn up in a little creek on the south bank. Mistress Margaret had not come, so the four went together all over the ship that had been for these years the perilous home of this sunburnt lad they all loved so well. Hubert pointed out Drake's own cabin at the poop, with its stern-windows, where the last sacrament of the two friends had been celebrated; and where Drake himself had eaten in royal fashion to the sound of trumpets and slept with all-night sentries at his door. He showed them too his own cabin, where he had lived with three more officers, and the upper poop-deck where Drake would sit hour after hour with his spy-glass, ranging the horizons for treasure-ships. And he showed them, too, the high forecastle, and the men's quarters; and Isabel fingered delicately the touch-holes of the very guns that had roared and snapped so fiercely at the Dons; and they peered down into the dark empty hold where the treasure-chests had lain, and up at the three masts and the rigging that had borne so long the swift wings of the Pelican. And they heard the hiss and rattle of the ropes as Hubert ordered a man to run up a flag to show them how it was done; and they smelled the strange tarry briny smell of a sea-going ship.

"You are not tired?" Anthony said to his sister, as they walked back to the inn from which they were to see the spectacle. She shook her head happily; and Anthony, looking at her, once more questioned himself whether Mistress Corbet were right or not.

When they had settled down at last to their window, the crowds were gathering thicker every moment about the entrance to the ship, which lay in the creek perhaps a hundred yards from the inn, and on the road along which the Queen was to come from Greenwich. Anthony felt his whole heart go out in sympathy to these joyous shouting folk beneath, who were here to celebrate the gallant pluck of a little bearded man and his followers, who for the moment stood for England, and in whose presence just now the Queen herself must take second place. Even the quacks and salesmen who were busy in their booths all round used patriotism to push their bargains.

"Spanish ointment, Spanish ointment!" bellowed a red-faced herbalist in a doctor's gown, just below the window. "The Dons know what's best for wounds and knocks after Frankie Drake's visit"; and the crowd laughed and bought up his boxes. And another drove a roaring business in green glass beads, reported to be the exact size of the emeralds taken from the Cacafuego; and others sold little models of the Pelican, warranted to frighten away Dons and all other kinds of devils from the house that possessed one. Isabel laughed with pleasure, and sent Anthony down to buy one for her.

But perhaps more than all else the sight of the seamen themselves stirred his heart. Most of them, officers as well as men, were dressed with absurd extravagance, for the prize-money, even after the deduction of the Queen's lion-share, had been immense, but beneath their plumed and jewel-buckled caps, brown faces looked out, alert and capable, with tight lips and bright, puckered eyes, with something of the terrier in their expression. There they swaggered along with a slight roll in their walk, by ones or twos, through the crowd that formed lanes to let them pass, and surged along in their wake, shouting after them and clapping them on the back. Anthony watched them eagerly as they made their way from all directions to where the Pelican lay; for it was close on noon. Then from far away came the boom of the Tower guns, and then the nearer crash of those that guarded the dockyard; and last the deafening roar of the Pelican broadside; and then the smoke rose and drifted in a heavy veil in the keen frosty air over the cheering crowds. When it lifted again, there was the flash of gold and colour from the Greenwich road, and the high braying of the trumpets pierced the roaring welcome of the people. But the watchers at the windows could see no more over the heads of the crowd than the plumes of the royal carriage, as the Queen dismounted, and a momentary glimpse of her figure and the group round her as she passed on to the deck of the Pelican and went immediately below to the banquet, while the parish church bells pealed a welcome.

Lady Maxwell insisted that Isabel should now dine, as there would be no more to be seen till the Queen should come up on deck again.

Of the actual ceremony of the knighting of Mr. Drake they had a very fair view, though the figures were little and far away. The first intimation they had that the banquet was over was the sight of the scarlet-clad yeomen emerging one by one up the little hatchway that led below. The halberdiers lined the decks already, with their weapons flashing in long curved lines; and by the time that the trumpets began to sound to show that the Queen was on her way from below, the decks were one dense mass of colour and steel, with a lane left to the foot of the poop-stairs by which she would ascend. Then at last the two figures appeared, the Queen radiant in cloth of gold, and Mr. Drake, alert and brisk, in his Court suit and sword. There was silence from the crowd as the adventurer knelt before the Queen, and Anthony held his breath with excitement as he caught the flash of the slender sword that an officer had put into the Queen's hand; and then an inconceivable noise broke out as Sir Francis Drake stood up. The crowd was one open mouth, shouting, the church bells burst into peals overhead, answered by the roll of drums from the deck and the blare of trumpets; and then the whole din sank into nothingness for a moment under the heart-shaking crash of the ship's broadside, echoed instantly by the deeper roar of the dockyard guns, and answered after a moment or two from far away by the dull boom from the Tower. And Anthony leaned yet further from the window and added his voice to the tumult.

As he rode back alone to Lambeth, after parting with the others at London Bridge, for they intended to go down home again that night, he was glowing with national zeal. He had seen not only royalty and magnificence but an apotheosis of character that day. There in the little trim figure with the curly hair kneeling before the Queen was England at its best—England that sent two ships against an empire; and it was the Church that claimed Sir Francis Drake as a son, and indeed a devoted one, in a sense, that Anthony himself was serving here at Lambeth, and for which he felt a real and fervent enthusiasm.

He was surprised a couple of days later to receive a note in Lady Maxwell's handwriting, brought up by a special messenger from the Hall.

"There is a friend of mine," she wrote, "to come to Lambeth House presently, he tells me, to be kept a day or two in ward before he is sent to Wisbeach. He is a Catholic, named Mr. Henry Buxton, who showed me great love during the sorrow of my dear husband's death; and I write to you to show kindness to him, and to get him a good bed, and all that may comfort him: for I know not whether Lambeth Prison is easy or hard; but I hope perhaps that since my Lord Archbishop is a prisoner himself he has pity on such as are so too; and so my pains be in vain. However, if you will see Mr. Buxton at least, and have some talk with him, and show him this letter, it will cheer him perhaps to see a friend's face."

Anthony of course made inquiries at once, and found that Mr. Buxton was to arrive on the following afternoon. It was the custom to send prisoners occasionally to Lambeth, more particularly those more distinguished, or who, it was hoped, could be persuaded to friendly conference. Mr. Buxton, however, was thought to be incorrigible, and was only sent there because there was some delay in the preparations for his reception at Wisbeach, which since the previous year had been used as an overflow prison for Papists.

On the evening of the next day, which was Friday, Anthony went straight out from the Hall after supper to the gateway prison, and found Mr. Buxton at a fish supper in the little prison in the outer part of the eastern tower. He introduced himself, but found it necessary to show Lady Maxwell's letter before the prisoner was satisfied as to his identity.

"You must pardon me, Mr. Norris," he said, when he had read the letter and asked a question or two, "but we poor Papists are bound to be shy. Why, in this very room," he went on, pointing to the inner corner away from the door, and smiling, "for aught I know a man sits now to hear us."

Anthony was considerably astonished to see this stranger point so confidently to the hiding-hole, where indeed the warder used to sit sometimes behind a brick partition, to listen to the talk of the prisoners; and showed his surprise.

"Ah, Mr. Norris," the other said, "we Papists are bound to be well informed; or else where were our lives? But come, sir, let us sit down."

Anthony apologised for interrupting him at his supper, and offered to come again, but Mr. Buxton begged him not to leave, as he had nearly finished. So Anthony sat down, and observed the prison and the prisoner. It was fairly well provided with necessaries: a good straw bed lay in one corner on trestles; and washing utensils stood at the further wall; and there was an oil lamp that hung high up from an iron pin. The prisoner's luggage lay still half unpacked on the floor, and a row of pegs held a hat and a cloak. Mr. Buxton himself was a dark-haired man with a short beard and merry bright eyes; and was dressed soberly as a gentleman; and behaved himself with courtesy and assurance. But it was a queer place with this flickering lamp, thought Anthony, for a gentleman to be eating his supper in. When Mr. Buxton had finished his dish of roach and a tankard of ale, he looked up at Anthony, smiling.

"My lord knows the ways of Catholics, then," he said, pointing to the bones on his plate.

Anthony explained that the Protestants observed the Friday abstinence, too.

"Ah yes," said the other, "I was forgetting the Queen's late injunctions. Let us see; how did it run? 'The same is not required for any liking of Papish Superstitions or Ceremonies (is it?) hitherto used, which utterly are to be detested of all Christian folk'; (no, the last word or two is a gloss), 'but only to maintain the mariners in this land, and to set men a-fishing.' That is the sense of it, is it not, sir? You fast, that is, not for heavenly reasons, which were a foolish and Papish thing to do; but for earthly reasons, which is a reasonable and Protestant thing to do."

Anthony might have taken this assault a little amiss, if he had not seen a laughing light in his companion's eyes; and remembered, too, that imprisonment is apt to breed a little bitterness. So he smiled back at him. Then soon they fell to talking of Lady Maxwell and Great Keynes, where it seemed that Mr. Buxton had stayed more than once.

"I knew Sir Nicholas well," he said, "God rest his soul. It seems to me he is one of those whose life continually gave the lie to men who say that a Catholic can be no true Englishman. There never beat a more loyal heart than his."

Anthony agreed; but asked if it were not true that Catholics were in difficulties sometimes as to the proper authority to be obeyed—the Pope or the Prince.

"It is true," said the other, "or it might be. Yet the principle is clear, Date Cæsari quae sunt Cæsaris. The difficulty lies but in the application of the maxim."

"But with us," said Anthony—"Church of England folk,—there hardly can be ever any such difficulty; for the Prince of the State is the Governor of the Church as well."

"I take your point," said Mr. Buxton. "You mean that a National Church is better, for that spiritual and temporal authorities are then at one."

"Just so," said Anthony, beginning to warm to his favourite theme. "The Church is the nation regarded as religious. When England wars on land it is through her army, which is herself under arms; when on sea she embarks in the navy; and in the warfare with spiritual powers, it is through her Church. And surely in this way the Church must always be the Church of the people. The Englishman and the Spaniard are like cat and dog; they like not the same food nor the same kind of coat; I hear that their buildings are not like ours; their language, nay, their faces and minds, are not like ours. Then why should be their prayers and their religion? I quarrel with no foreigner's faith; it is God who made us so."

Anthony stopped, breathless with his unusual eloquence; but it was the subject that lay nearest to his heart at present, and he found no lack of words. The prisoner had watched him with twinkling eyes, nodding his head as if in agreement; and when he had finished his little speech, nodded again in meditative silence.

"It is complete," he answered, "complete. And as a theory would be convincing; and I envy you, Master Norris, for you stand on the top of the wave. That is what England holds. But, my dear sir, Christ our Lord refused such a kingdom as that. My kingdom, He said, is not of this world—is not, that is, ruled by the world's divisions and systems. You have described Babel,—every nation with its own language. But it was to undo Babel and to build one spiritual city that our Saviour came down, and sent the Holy Ghost to make the Church at Pentecost out of Arabians and Medes and Elamites—to break down the partition-walls, as the apostle tells us,—that there be neither Jew nor Greek, barbarian nor Scythian—and to establish one vast kingdom (which for that very reason we name Catholic), to destroy differences between nation and nation, by lifting each to be of the People of God—to pull down Babel, the City of Confusion, and build Jerusalem the City of Peace. Dear God!" cried Mr. Buxton, rising in his excitement, and standing over Anthony, who looked at him astonished and bewildered. "You and your England would parcel out the Kingdom of heaven into national Churches, as you name them—among all the kingdoms of the world; and yet you call yourselves the servants of Him who came to do just the opposite—yes, and who will do it, in spite of you, and make the kingdoms of this world, instead, the Kingdom of our Lord and of His Christ. Why, if each nation is to have her Church, why not each county and each town—yes, and each separate soul, too; for all are different! Nay, nay, Master Norris, you are blinded by the Prince of this world. He is shewing you even now from an high mountain the kingdoms of this world and the glory of them: lift your eyes, dear lad, to the hills from whence cometh your help;

those hills higher than the mountain where you stand; and see the new Jerusalem, and the glory of her, coming down from God to dwell with men."

Mr. Buxton stood, his eyes blazing, plainly carried away wholly by enthusiasm; and Anthony, in spite of himself, could not be angry. He moistened his lips once or twice.

"Well, sir; of course I hold with what you say, in one sense; but it is not come yet; and never will, till our Lord comes back to make all plain."

"Not come yet?" cried the other, "Not come yet! Why, what is the one Holy Catholic and Apostolic Church but that? There you have one visible kingdom, gathered out of every nation and tongue and people, as the apostle said. I have a little estate in France, Master Norris, where I go sometimes; and there are folk in their wooden shoes, talking a different human tongue to me, but, thank God! the same divine one—of contrition and adoration and prayer. There we have the same mass, the same priesthood, the same blessed sacrament and the same Faith, as in my own little oratory at Stanfield. Go to Spain, Africa, Rome, India; wherever Christ is preached; there is the Church as it is here—the City of Peace. And as for you and your Church! with whom do you hold communion?"

This stung Anthony, and he answered impulsively.

"In Geneva and Frankfort, at least, there are folk who speak the same divine tongue, as you call it, as we do; they and we are agreed in matters of faith."

"Indeed," said Mr. Burton sharply, "then what becomes of your Nationalism, and the varied temperaments that you told me God had made?"

Anthony bit his lip; he had overshot his mark. But the other swept on; and as he talked began to step up and down the little room, in a kind of rhapsody.

"Is it possible?" he cried, "that men should be so blind as to prefer the little divided companies they name National Churches—all confusion and denial—to that glorious kingdom that Christ bought with his own dear blood, and has built upon Peter, against which the gates of hell shall not prevail. Yes, I know it is a flattering and a pleasant thought that this little nation should have her own Church; and it is humbling and bitter that England should be called to submit to a foreign potentate in the affairs of faith—Nay, cry they like the Jews of old, not Christ but Barabbas—we will not have this Man to reign over us. And yet this is God's will and not that. Mark me, Mr. Norris, what you hope will never come to be—the Liar will not keep his word—you shall not have that National Church that you desire: as you have dealt, so will it be dealt to you: as you have rejected, so will you be rejected. England herself will cast you off: your religious folk will break into a hundred divisions. Even now your Puritans mock at your prelates—so soon! And if they do thus now, what will they do hereafter? You have cast away Authority, and authority shall forsake you. Behold your house is left unto you desolate."

"Forgive me, Mr. Norris," he added after a pause, "if I have been discourteous, and have forgotten my manners; but—but I would, as the apostle said, that you were altogether as I am, except these bonds."

Chapter Four - A Counter-March

Isabel was sitting out alone in the Italian garden at the Hall, one afternoon in the summer following the visit to Deptford. Hubert was down at Plymouth, assisting in the preparations for the expedition that Drake hoped to conduct against Spain. The two countries were technically at peace, but the object with which he was going out, with the moral and financial support of the Queen, was a corporate demonstration against Spain, of French, Portuguese, and English ships under the main command of Don Antonio, the Portuguese pretender; it was proposed to occupy Terceira in the Azores; and Drake and Hawkins entertained the highest hopes of laying their hands on further plunder. She was leaning back in her seat, with her hands behind her head, thinking over her relations with Hubert. When he had been at home at the end of the previous year, he had apparently taken it for granted that the marriage would be celebrated; he had given her the gold nugget, that she had showed Anthony, telling her he had brought it home for the wedding-ring; and she understood that he was to come for his final answer as soon as his work at Plymouth was over. But not a word of explanation had passed between them on the religious difficulty. He had silenced her emphatically and kindly once when she had approached it; and she gathered from his manner that he suspected the direction in which her mind was turning and was generously unwilling for her to commit herself an inch further than she saw. Else whence came his assurance? And, for herself, things were indeed becoming plain: she wondered why she had hesitated so long, why she was still hesitating; the cup was brimming above the edge; it needed but a faint touch of stimulus to precipitate all.

And so Isabel lay back and pondered, with a touch of happy impatience at the workings of her own soul; for she dared not act without the final touch of conviction. Mistress Margaret had taught her that the swiftest flight of the soul was when there was least movement, when the soul knew how to throw itself with that supreme effort of cessation into the Hands of God, that He might bear it along: when, after informing the intellect and seeking by prayer for God's bounty, the humble client of Heaven waited with uplifted eyes and ready heart until God should answer. And so she waited, knowing that the gift was at hand, yet not daring to snatch it. But, in the meanwhile, her imagination at least might act without restraint; so she sent it out, like a bird from the Ark, to bring her the earnest of peace. There, in the cloister-wing, somewhere, lay the chapel, where she and Hubert would kneel together;—somewhere beneath that grey roof. That was the terrace where she would walk one day as one who has a right there. Which of these windows would be hers? Not Lady Maxwell's, of course; she must keep that.... Ah! how good God was!

The tall door on to the terrace opened, and Mistress Margaret peered out with a letter in her hand. Isabel called to her; and the old nun came down the steps into the garden. Why did she walk so falteringly, the girl wondered, as if she could not see? What was it? What was it?

Isabel rose to her feet, startled, as the nun with bent head came up the path. "What is it, Mistress Margaret?"

The other tried to smile at her, but her lips were trembling too much; and the girl saw that her eyes were brimming with tears. She put the letter into her hand.

Isabel lifted it in an agony of suspense; and saw her name, in Hubert's handwriting.

"What is it?" she said again, white to the lips.

The old lady as she turned away glanced at her; and Isabel saw that her face was all twitching with the effort to keep back her tears. The girl had never seen her like that before, even at Sir Nicholas' death. Was there anything, she wondered as she looked, worse than death? But she was too dazed by the sight to speak, and Mistress Margaret went slowly back to the house unquestioned.

Isabel turned the letter over once or twice; and then sat down and opened it. It was all in Hubert's sprawling handwriting, and was dated from Plymouth.

It gave her news first about the squadron; saying how Don Antonio had left London for Plymouth, and was expected daily; and then followed this paragraph:

"And now, dearest Isabel, I have such good news to give you. I have turned Protestant; and there is no reason why we should not be married as soon as I return. I know this will make you happy to think that our religions are no longer different. I have thought of this so long; but would not tell you before for fear of disappointing you. Sir Francis Drake's religion seems to me the best; it is the religion of all the 'sea-dogs' as they name us; and of the Queen's Grace, and it will be soon of all England; and more than all it is the religion of my dearest mistress and love. I do not, of course, know very much of it as yet; but good Mr. Collins here has shown me the superstitions of Popery; and I hope now to be justified by faith without works as the gospel teaches. I fear that my mother and aunt will be much distressed by this news; I have written, too, to tell them of it. You must comfort them, dear love; and perhaps some day they, too, will see as we do." Then followed a few messages, and loving phrases, and the letter ended.

Isabel laid it down beside her on the low stone wall; and looked round her with eyes that saw nothing. There was the grey old house before her, and the terrace, and the cloister-wing to the left, and the hot sunshine lay on it all, and drew out scents and colours from the flower-beds, and joy from the insects that danced in the trembling air; and it all meant nothing to her; like a picture when the page is turned over it. Five minutes ago she was regarding her life and seeing how the Grace of God was slowly sorting out its elements from chaos to order—the road was unwinding itself before her eyes as she trod on it day by day—now a hand had swept all back into disorder, and the path was hidden by the ruins.

Then gradually one thought detached itself, and burned before her, vivid and startling; and in all its terrible reality slipped between her and the visible world on which she was staring. It was this: to embrace the Catholic Faith meant the renouncing of Hubert. As a Protestant she might conceivably have married a Catholic; as a Catholic it was inconceivable that she should marry an apostate.

Then she read the letter through again carefully and slowly; and was astonished at the unreality of Hubert's words about Romish superstition and gospel simplicity. She tried hard to silence her thoughts; but two reasons for Hubert's change of religion rose up and insisted on making themselves felt; it was that he might be more in unity with the buccaneers whom he admired; second, that there might be no obstacle to their marriage. And what then, she asked, was the quality of the heart he had given her?

Then, in a flash of intuition, she perceived that a struggle lay before her, compared with which all her previous spiritual conflicts were as child's play; and that there was no avoiding it. The vision passed, and she rose and went indoors to find the desolate mother whose boy had lost the Faith.

A month or two of misery went by. For Lady Maxwell they passed with recurring gusts of heart-broken sorrow and of agonies of prayer for her apostate son. Mistress Margaret was at the Hall all day, soothing, encouraging, even distracting her sister by all the means in her power. The mother wrote one passionate wail to her son, appealing to all that she thought he held dear, even yet to return to the Faith for which his father had suffered and in which he had died; but a short answer only returned, saying it was impossible to make his defence in a letter, and expressing pious hopes that she, too, one day would be as he was; the same courier brought a letter to Isabel, in which he expressed his wonder that she had not answered his former one.

And as for Isabel, she had to pass through this valley of darkness alone. Anthony was in London; and even if he had been with her could not have helped her under these circumstances; her father was dead—she thanked God for that now—and Mistress Margaret seemed absorbed in her sister's grief. And so the girl fought with devils alone. The arguments for Catholicism burned pitilessly clear now; every line and feature in them stood out distinct and hard. Catholicism, it appeared to her, alone had the marks of the Bride, visible unity, visible Catholicity, visible Apostolicity, visible Sanctity;—there they were, the seals of the most High God. She flung herself back furiously into the Protestantism from which she had been emerging; there burned in the dark before her the marks of the Beast, visible disunion, visible nationalism, visible Erastianism, visible gulfs where holiness should be: that system in which now she could never find rest again glared at her in all its unconvincing incoherence, its lack of spirituality, its adulterous union with the civil power instead of the pure wedlock of the Spouse of Christ. She wondered once more how she dared to have hesitated so long; or dared to hesitate still.

On the theological side intellectual arguments of this kind started out, strong and irrefutable; her emotional drawings towards Catholicism for the present retired. Feelings might have been disregarded or discredited by a strong effort of the will; these apparently cold phenomena that presented themselves to her intellect, could not be thus dealt with. Yet, strangely enough, even now she would not throw herself resolutely into Catholicism: the fierce stimulus instead of precipitating the crisis, petrified it. More than once she started up from her knees in her own dark room, resolved to awaken the nun and tell her she would wait no longer, but would turn Catholic at once and have finished with the misery of suspense: and even as she moved to the door her will found itself against an impenetrable wall.

And then on the other side all her human nature cried out for Hubert—Hubert—Hubert. There he stood by her in fancy, day and night, that chivalrous, courteous lad, who had been loyal to her so long; had waited so patiently; had run to her with such dear impatience; who was so wholesome, so strong, so humble to her; so quick to understand her wants, so eager to fulfil them; so bound to her by associations; so fit a mate for the very differences between them. And now these two claims were no longer compatible; in his very love for her he had ended that possibility. All those old dreams; the little scenes she had rehearsed, of their first mass, their first communion together; their walks in the twilight; their rides over the hills; the new ties that were to draw the old ladies at the Hall and herself so close together—all this was changed; some of those dreams were now for ever impossible, others only possible on terms that she trembled even to think of. Perhaps it was worst of all to reflect that she was in some measure responsible for his change of religion; she fancied that it was through her slowness to respond to light, her delaying to confide in him, that he had been driven through impatience to take this step. And so week after week went by and she dared not answer his letter.

The old ladies, too, were sorely puzzled at her. It was impossible for them to know how far her religion was changing. She had kept up the same reserve towards them lately as towards Hubert, chiefly because she feared to disappoint them; and so after an attempt to tell each other a little of their mutual sympathy, the three women were silent on the subject of the lad who was so much to them all.

She began to show her state a little in her movements and appearance. She was languid, soon tired and dispirited; she would go for short, lonely walks, and fall asleep in her chair worn out when she came in. Her grey eyes looked longer and darker; her eyelids and the corners of her mouth began to droop a little.

Then in October he came home.

Isabel had been out a long afternoon walk by herself through the reddening woods. They had never, since the first awakening of the consciousness of beauty in her, meant so little to her as now. It appeared as if that keen unity of a life common to her and all living things had been broken or obscured; and that she walked in an isolation all the more terrible in that she was surrounded by the dumb presence of what she loved. Last year the quick chattering cry of the blackbird, the evening mists over the meadows, the stir of the fading life of the woods, the rustling scamper of the rabbit over the dead leaves, the solemn call of the homing rooks—all this, only last year, went to make up the sweet natural atmosphere in which her spirit moved and breathed at ease. Now she was excommunicate from that pleasant friendship, banned by nature and forgotten by the God who made it and was immanent within it. Her relations to the Saviour, who only such a short time ago had been the Person round whom all the joys of life had centred, from whom they radiated, and to whom she referred them all—these relations had begun to be obscured by her love for Hubert, and now had vanished altogether. She had regarded her earthly and her heavenly lover as two persons, each of whom had certain claims upon her heart, and each of whom she had hoped to satisfy in different ways; instead of identifying the two, and serving each not apart from, but in the other. And it now seemed to her that she was making experience of a Divine jealousy that would suffer her to be satisfied neither with God nor man. Her soul was exhausted by internal conflict, by the swift alternations of attraction and repulsion between the poles of her super-natural and natural life; so that when it turned wearily from self to what lay outside, it was not even capable, as before, of making that supreme effort of cessation of effort which was necessary to its peace. It seemed to her that she was self-poised in emptiness, and could neither touch heaven or earth—crucified so high that she could not rest on earth, so low that she could not reach to heaven.

She came in weary and dispirited as the candles were being lighted in her sitting-room upstairs; but she saw the gleam of them from the garden with no sense of a welcoming brightness. She passed from the garden into the door of the hall which was still dark, as the fire had nearly burned itself out. As she entered the door opposite opened, and once more she saw the silhouette of a man's figure against the lighted passage beyond; and again she stopped frightened, and whispered "Anthony."

There was a momentary pause as the door closed and all was dark again; and then she heard Hubert's voice say her name; and felt herself wrapped once more in his arms. For a moment she clung to him with furious longing. Ah! this is a tangible thing, she felt, this clasp; the faint cleanly smell of his rough frieze dress refreshed her like wine, and she kissed his sleeve passionately. And the wide gulf between them yawned again; and her spirit sickened at the sight of it.

"Oh! Hubert, Hubert!" she said.

She felt herself half carried to a high chair beside the fire-place and set down there; then he re-arranged the logs on the hearth, so that the flames began to leap again, showing his strong hands and keen clear-cut face; then he turned on his knees, seized her two hands in his own, and lifted them to his lips; then laid them down again on her knee, still holding them; and so remained.

"Oh! Isabel," he said, "why did you not write?"

She was silent as one who stares fascinated down a precipice.

"It is all over," he went on in a moment, "with the expedition. The Queen's Grace has finally refused us leave to go—and I have come back to you, Isabel."

How strong and pleasant he looked in this leaping fire-light! how real! and she was hesitating between this warm human reality and the chilly possibilities of an invisible truth. Her hands tightened instinctively within his, and then relaxed.

"I have been so wretched," she said piteously.

"Ah! my dear," and he threw an arm round her neck and drew her face down to his, "but that is over now." She sat back again; and then an access of purpose poured into her and braced her will to an effort.

"No, no," she began, "I must tell you. I was afraid to write. Hubert, I must wait a little longer. I—I do not know what I believe."

He looked at her, puzzled.

"What do you mean, dearest?"

"I have been so much puzzled lately—thinking so much—and—and—I am sorry you have become a Protestant. It makes all so hard."

"My dear, this is—I do not understand."

"I have been thinking," went on Isabel bravely, "whether perhaps the Catholic Church is not right after all."

Hubert loosed her hands and stood up. She crouched into the shadow of the interior of the high chair, and looked up at him, terrified. His cheek twitched a little.

"Isabel, this is foolishness. I know what the Catholic faith is. It is not true; I have been through it all."

He was speaking nervously and abruptly. She said nothing. Then he suddenly dropped on his knees himself.

"My dearest, I understand. You were doing this for me. I quite understand. It is what I too—" and then he stopped.

"I know, I know," she cried piteously. "It is just what I have feared so terribly—that—that our love has been blinding us both. And yet, what are we to do, what are we to do? Oh! God—Hubert, help me."

Then he began to speak in a low emphatic voice, holding her hands, delicately stroking one of them now and again, and playing with her fingers. She watched his curly head in the firelight as he talked, and his keen face as he looked up.

"It is all plain to me," he said, caressingly. "You have been living here with my aunt, a dear old saint; and she has been talking and telling you all about the Catholic religion, and making it seem all true and good. And you, my dear child, have been thinking of me sometimes, and loving me a little, is it not so? and longing that religion should not separate us; and so you began to wish it was true; and then to hope it was; and at last you have begun to think it is. But it is not your true sweet self that believes it. Ah! you know in your heart of hearts, as I have known so long, that it is not true; that it is made up by priests and nuns; and it is very beautiful, I know, my dearest, but it is only a lovely tale; and you must not spoil all for the sake of a tale. And I have been gradually led to the light; it was your—" and his voice faltered—"your prayers that helped me to it. I have longed to understand what it was that made you so sweet and so happy; and now I know; it is your own simple pure religion; and—and—it is so much more sensible, so much more likely to be true than the Catholic religion. It is all in the Bible you see; so plain, as Mr. Collins has showed me. And so, my dear love, I have come to believe it too; and you must put all these fancies out of your head, these dreams; though I love you, I love you," and he kissed her hand again, "for wishing to believe them for my sake—and—and we will be married before Christmas; and we will have our own fairy-tale, but it shall be a true one."

This was terrible to Isabel. It seemed as if her own haunting thought that she was sacrificing a dream to reality had become incarnate in her lover and was speaking through his lips. And yet in its very incarnation, it seemed to reveal its weakness rather than its strength. As a dark suggestion the thought was mighty; embodied in actual language it seemed to shrink a little. But then, on the other hand—and so the interior conflict began to rage again.

She made a movement as if to stand up; but he pressed her back into the chair.

"No, my dearest, you shall be a prisoner until you give your parole."

Twice Isabel made an effort to speak; but no sound came. It seemed as if the raging strife of thoughts deafened and paralysed her.

"Now, Isabel," said Hubert.

"I cannot, I cannot," she cried desperately, "you must give me time. It is too sudden, your returning like this. You must give me time. I do not know what I believe. Oh, dear God, help me."

"Isabel, promise! promise! Before Christmas! I thought it was all to be so happy, when I came in through the garden just now. My mother will hardly speak to me; and I came to you, Isabel, as I always did; I felt so sure you would be good to me; and tell me that you would always love me, now that I had given up my religion for love of you. And now—" and Hubert's voice ended in a sob.

Her heart seemed rent across, and she drew a sobbing sigh. Hubert heard it, and caught at her hands again as he knelt.

"Isabel, promise, promise."

Then there came that gust of purpose into her heart again; she made a determined effort and stood up; and Hubert rose and stood opposite her.

"You must not ask me," she said, bravely. "It would be wicked to decide yet. I cannot see anything clearly. I do not know what I believe, nor where I stand. You must give me time."

There was a dead silence. His face was so much in shadow that she could not tell what he was thinking. He was standing perfectly still.

"Then that is all the answer you will give me?" he said, in a perfectly even voice.

Isabel bowed her head.

"Then—then I wish you good-night, Mistress Norris," and he bowed to her, caught up his cap and went out.

She could not believe it for a moment, and caught her breath to cry out after him as the door closed; but she heard his step on the stone pavement outside, the crunch of the gravel, and he was gone. Then she went and leaned her head against the curved mantelshelf and stared into the logs that his hands had piled together.

This, then, she thought, was the work of religion; the end of all her aspirations and efforts, that God should mock them by bringing love into their life, and then when they caught at it and thanked him for it, it was whisked away again, and left their hands empty. Was this the Father of Love in whom she had been taught to believe, who treated His children like this? And so the bitter thoughts went on; and yet she knew in her heart that she was powerless; that she could not go to the door and call Hubert and promise what he asked. A great Force had laid hold of her, it might be benevolent or not—at this moment she thought not—but it was irresistible; and she must bow her head and obey.

And even as she thought that, the door opened again, and there was Hubert. He came in two quick steps across the room to her, and then stopped suddenly.

"Mistress Isabel," he asked, "can you forgive me? I was a brute just now. I do not ask for your promise. I leave it all in your hands. Do with me what you will. But—but, if you could tell me how long you think it will be before you know—"

He had touched the right note. Isabel's heart gave a leap of sorrow and sympathy. "Oh, Hubert," she said brokenly, "I am so sorry; but I promise I will tell you—by Easter?" and her tone was interrogative.

"Yes, yes," said Hubert. He looked at her in silence, and she saw strange lines quivering at the corners of his mouth, and his eyes large and brilliant in the firelight. Then the two drew together, and he took her in his arms strongly and passionately.

There was a scene that night between the mother and son. Mistress Margaret had gone back to the Dower House for supper; and Lady Maxwell and Hubert were supping in Sir Nicholas' old study that would soon be arranged for Hubert now that he had returned for good. They had been very silent during the meal, while the servants were in the room, talking only of little village affairs and of the estate, and of the cancelling of the proposed expedition. Hubert had explained to his mother that it was generally believed that Elizabeth had never seriously intended the English ships to sail, but that she only wished to draw Spain's attention off herself by setting up complications between that country and France; and when she had succeeded in this by managing to get the French squadron safe at Terceira, she then withdrew her permission to Drake and Hawkins, and thus escaped from the quarrel altogether. But it was a poor makeshift for conversation.

When the servants had withdrawn, a silence fell. Presently Hubert looked across the table between the silver branched candlesticks.

"Mother," he said, "of course I know what you are thinking. But I cannot consent to go through all the arguments; I am weary of them. Neither will I see Mr. Barnes to-morrow at Cuckfield or here. I am satisfied with my position."

"My son," said Lady Maxwell with dignity, "I do not think I have spoken that priest's name; or indeed any."

"Well," said Hubert, impatiently, "at any rate I will not see him. But I wish to say a few words about this house. We must have our positions clear. My father left to your use, did he not, the whole of the cloister-wing? I am delighted, dear mother, that he did so. You will be happy there I know; and of course I need not say that I hope you will keep your old room overhead as well; and, indeed, use the whole house as you have always done. I shall be grateful if you will superintend it all, as before—at least, until a new mistress comes."

"Thank you, my son."

"I will speak of that in a moment," he went on, looking steadily at the table-cloth; "but there was a word I wished to say first. I am now a loyal subject of her Grace in all things; in religion as in all else. And—and I fear I cannot continue to entertain seminary priests as my father used to do. My—my conscience will not allow that. But of course, mother, I need not say that you are at perfect liberty to do what you will in the cloister-wing; I shall ask no questions; and I shall set no traps or spies. But I must ask that the priests do not come into this part of the house, nor walk in the garden. Fortunately you have a lawn in the cloister; so that they need not lack fresh air or exercise."

"You need not fear, Hubert," said his mother, "I will not embarrass you. You shall be in no danger."

"I think you need not have said that, mother; I am not usually thought a coward."

Lady Maxwell flushed a little, and began to finger her silver knife.

"However," Hubert went on, "I thought it best to say that. The chapel, you see, is in that wing; and you have that lawn; and—and I do not think I am treating you hardly."

"And is your brother James not to come?" asked his mother.

"I have thought much over that," said Hubert; "and although it is hard to say it, I think he had better not come to my part of the house—at least not when I am here; I must know nothing of it. You must do what you think well when I am away, about him and others too. It is very difficult for me, mother; please do not add to the difficulty."

"You need not fear," said Lady Maxwell steadily; "you shall not be troubled with any Catholics besides ourselves."

"Then that is arranged," said the lad. "And now there is a word more. What have you been doing to Isabel?" And he looked sharply across the table. His mother's eyes met his fearlessly.

"I do not understand you," she said.

"Mother, you must know what I mean. You have seen her continually."

"I have told you, my son, that I do not know."

"Why," burst out Hubert, "she is half a Catholic."

"Thank God," said his mother.

"Ah! yes; you thank God, I know; but whom am I to thank for it?"

"I would that you could thank Him too."

Hubert made a sharp sound of disgust.

"Ah! yes," he said scornfully, "I knew it; Non nobis Domine, and the rest."

"Hubert," said Lady Maxwell, "I do not think you mean to insult me in this house; but either that is an insult, or else I misunderstood you wholly, and must ask your pardon for it."

"Well," he said, in a harsh voice, "I will make myself plain. I believe that it is through the influence of you and Aunt Margaret that this has been brought about."

At the moment he spoke the door opened.

"Come in, Margaret," said her sister, "this concerns you."

The old nun came across to Hubert with her anxious sweet face; and put her old hand tenderly on his black satin sleeve as he sat and wrenched at a nut between his fingers.

"Hubert, dear boy," she said, "what is all this? Will you tell me?"

Hubert rose, a little ashamed of himself, and went to the door and closed it; and then drew out a chair for his aunt, and put a wine-glass for her.

"Sit down, aunt," he said, and pushed the decanter towards her.

"I have just left Isabel," she said, "she is very unhappy about something. You saw her this evening, dear lad?"

"Yes," said Hubert, heavily, looking down at the table and taking up another nut, "and it is of that that I have been speaking. Who has made her unhappy?"

"I had hoped you would tell us that," said Mistress Margaret; "I came up to ask you."

"My son has done us—me—the honour—" began Lady Maxwell; but Hubert broke in:

"I left Isabel here last Christmas happy and a Protestant. I have come back here now to find her unhappy and half a Catholic, if not more—and—"

"Oh! are you sure?" asked Mistress Margaret, her eyes shining. "Thank God, if it be so!"

"Sure?" said Hubert, "why she will not marry me; at least not yet."

"Oh, poor lad," she said tenderly, "to have lost both God and Isabel."

Hubert turned on her savagely. But the old nun's eyes were steady and serene.

"Poor lad!" she said again.

Hubert looked down again; his lip wrinkled up in a little sneer.

"As far as I am concerned," he said, "I can understand your not caring, but I am astonished at this response of yours to her father's confidence!"

Lady Maxwell grew white to the lips.

"I have told you," she began—"but you do not seem to believe it—that I have had nothing to do, so far as I know, with her conversion, which"—and she raised her voice bravely—"I pray God to accomplish. She has, of course, asked me questions now and then; and I have answered them—that is all."

"And I," said Mistress Margaret, "plead guilty to the same charge, and to no other. You are not yourself, dear boy, at present; and indeed I do not wonder at it; and I pray God to help you; but you are not yourself, or you would not speak like this to your mother."

Hubert rose to his feet; his face was white under the tan, and the ruffle round his wrist trembled as he leaned heavily with his fingers on the table.

"I am only a plain Protestant now," he said bitterly, "and I have been with Protestants so long that I have forgotten Catholic ways; but—"

"Stay, Hubert," said his mother, "do not finish that. You will be sorry for it presently, if you do. Come, Margaret." And she moved towards the door; her son went quickly past and opened it.

"Nay, nay," said the nun. "Do you be going, Mary. Let me stay with the lad, and we will come to you presently." Lady Maxwell bowed her head and passed out, and Hubert closed the door.

Mistress Margaret looked down on the table.

"You have given me a glass, dear boy; but no wine in it."

Hubert took a couple of quick steps back, and faced her.

"It is no use, it is no use," he burst out, and his voice was broken with emotion, "you cannot turn me like that. Oh, what have you done with my Isabel?" He put out his hand and seized her arm. "Give her back to me, Aunt Margaret; give her back to me."

He dropped into his seat and hid his face on his arm; and there was a sob or two.

"Sit up and be a man, Hubert," broke in Mistress Margaret's voice, clear and cool.

He looked up in amazement with wet indignant eyes. She was looking at him, smiling tenderly.

"And now, for the second time, give me half a glass of wine, dear boy."

He poured it out, bewildered at her self-control.

"For a man that has been round the world," she said, "you are but a foolish child."

"What do you mean?"

"Have you never thought of a way of yet winning Isabel," she asked.

"What do you mean?" he repeated.

"Why, come back to the Church, dear lad; and make your mother and me happy again, and marry Isabel, and save your own soul."

"Aunt Margaret," he cried, "it is impossible. I have truly lost my faith in the Catholic religion; and—and—you would not have me a hypocrite."

"Ah! ah!" said the nun, "you cannot tell yet. Please God it may come back. Oh! dear boy, in your heart you know it is true."

"Before God, in my heart I know that it is not true."

"No, no, no," she said; but the light died out of her eyes, and she stretched a tremulous hand.

"Yes, Aunt Margaret, it is so. For years and years I have been doubting; but I kept on just because it seemed to me the best religion; and—and I would not be driven out of it by her Grace's laws against my will, like a dog stoned from his kennel."

"But you are only a lad still," she said piteously. He laughed a little.

"But I have had the gift of reason and discretion nearly twenty years, a priest would tell me. Besides, Aunt Margaret, I could not be such a—a cur—as to come back without believing. I could never look Isabel in the eyes again."

"Well, well," said the old lady, "let us wait and see. Do you intend to be here now for a while?"

"Not while Isabel is like this," he said. "I could not. I must go away for a while, and then come back and ask her again."

"When will she decide?"

"She told me by next Easter," said Hubert. "Oh, Aunt Margaret, pray for us both."

The light began to glimmer again in her eyes.

"There, dear boy," she said, "you see you believe in prayer still."

"But, aunt," said Hubert, "why should I not? Protestants pray."

"Well, well," said the old nun again. "Now you must come to your mother; and—and be good to her."

Chapter Five - The Coming of The Jesuits

The effect on Anthony of Mr. Buxton's conversation was very considerable. He had managed to keep his temper very well during the actual interview; but he broke out alone afterwards, at first with an angry contempt. The absurd arrogance of the man made him furious—the arrogance that had puffed away England and its ambitions and its vigour—palpable evidences of life and reality, and further of God's blessing—in favour of a miserable Latin nation which had the presumption to claim the possession of Peter's Chair and of the person of the Vicar of Christ! Test it, said the young man to himself, by the ancient Fathers and Councils that Dr. Jewel quoted so learnedly, and the preposterous claim crumbled to dust. Test it, yet again, by the finger of Providence; and God Himself proclaimed that the pretensions of the spiritual kingdom, of which the prisoner in the cell had bragged, are but a blasphemous fable. And Anthony reminded himself of the events of the previous year.

Three great assaults had been made by the Papists to win back England to the old Religion. Dr. William Allen, the founder of Douai College, had already for the last seven or eight years been pouring seminary priests into England, and over a hundred and twenty were at work among their countrymen, preparing the grand attack. This was made in three quarters at once.

In Scotland it was chiefly political, and Anthony thought, with a bitter contempt, of the Count d'Aubigny, Esmé Stuart, who was supposed to be an emissary of the Jesuits; how he had plotted with ecclesiastics and nobles, and professed Protestantism to further his ends; and of all the stories of his duplicity and evil-living, told round the guardroom fire.

In Ireland the attempt was little else than ludicrous. Anthony laughed fiercely to himself as he pictured the landing of the treacherous fools at Dingle, of Sir James FitzMaurice and his lady, very wretched and giddy after their voyage, and the barefooted friars, and Dr. Sanders, and the banner so solemnly consecrated; and of the sands of Smerwick, when all was over a year later, and the six hundred bodies, men and women who had preferred Mr. Buxton's spiritual kingdom to Elizabeth's kindly rule, stripped and laid out in rows, like dead game, for Lord Grey de Wilton to reckon them by.

But his heart sank a little as he remembered the third method of attack, and of the coming of the Jesuits. By last July all London knew that they were here, and men's hearts were shaken with apprehension. They reminded one another of the April earthquake that had tolled the great Westminster bell, and thrown down stones from the churches. One of the Lambeth guards, a native of Blunsdon, in Wiltshire, had told Anthony himself that a pack of hell-hounds had been heard there, in full cry after a ghostly quarry. Phantom ships had been seen from Bodmin attacking a phantom castle that rode over the waves off the Cornish coast. An old woman of Blasedon had given birth to a huge-headed monster with the mouth of a mouse, eight legs, and a tail; and, worse than all, it was whispered in the Somersetshire inns that three companies of black-robed men, sixty in number, had been seen, coming and going overhead in the gloom. These two strange emissaries, Fathers Persons and Campion—how they appealed to the imagination, lurking under a hundred disguises, now of servants, now of gentlemen of means and position! It was known that they were still in England, going about doing good, their friends said who knew them; stirring up the people, their enemies said who were searching for them. Anthony had seen with his own eyes some of the papers connected with their presence—that containing a statement of their objects in coming, namely, that they were spiritual not political agents, seeking recruits for Christ and for none else; Campion's "Challenge and Brag," offering to meet any English Divine on equal terms in a public disputation; besides one or two of the controversial pamphlets, purporting to be printed at Douai, but really emanating from a private printing-press in England, as the Government experts had discovered from an examination of the water-marks of the paper employed.

Yet as the weeks went by, and his first resentment cooled, Mr. Buxton's arguments more and more sank home, for they had touched the very point where Anthony had reckoned that his own strength lay. He had never before heard Nationalism and Catholicism placed in such flat antithesis. In fact, he had never before really heard the statement of the Catholic position; and his fierce contempt gradually melted into respect. Both theories had a concrete air of reality about them; his own imaged itself under the symbols of England's power; the National Church appealed to him so far as it represented the spiritual side of the English people; and Mr. Buxton's conception appealed to him from its very audacity. This great spiritual kingdom, striding on its way, trampling down the barriers of temperament and nationality, disregarding all earthly limitations and artificial restraints, imperiously dominating the world in spite of the world's struggles and resentment—this, after all, as he thought over it, was—well—was a new aspect of affairs. The coming of the Jesuits, too, emphasised the appeal: here were two men, as the world itself confessed, of exceptional ability—for Campion had been a famous Oxford orator, and Persons a Fellow of Balliol—choosing, under a free-will obedience, first a life of exile, and then one of daily peril and apprehension, the very thought of which burdened the imagination with horror; hunted like vermin, sleeping and faring hard, their very names detested by the majority of their countrymen, with the shadow of the gallows moving with them, and the reek of the hangman's cauldron continually in their nostrils—and for what? For Mr. Buxton's spiritual kingdom! Well, Anthony thought to himself as the weeks went by and his new thoughts sank deeper, if it is all a superstitious dream, at least it is a noble one!

What, too, was the answer, he asked himself, that England gave to Father Campion's challenge, and the defence that the Government was preparing against the spiritual weapons of the Jesuits? New prisons at Framingham and Battersea; new penalties enacted by Parliament; and, above all, the unanswerable argument of the rack, and the gallows finally to close the discussion. And what of the army that was being set in array against the priests, and that was even now beginning to scour the country round Berkshire, Oxfordshire, and London? Anthony had to confess to himself that they were queer allies for the servants of Christ; for traitors, liars, and informers were among the most trusted Government agents.

In short, as the spring drew on, Anthony was not wholly happy. Again and again in his own room he studied a little manuscript translation of Father Campion's "Ten Reasons," that had been taken from a popish prisoner, and that a friend had given him; and as he read its exultant rhetoric, he wondered whether the writer was indeed as insincere and treacherous as Mr. Scot declared. There seemed in the paper a reckless outspokenness, calculated rather to irritate than deceive.

"I turn to the Sacraments," he read, "none, none, not two, not one, O holy Christ, have they left. Their very bread is poison. Their baptism, though it be true, yet in their judgment is nothing. It is not the saving water! It is not the channel of Grace! It brings not Christ's merits to us! It is but a sign of salvation!" And again the writer cried to Elizabeth to return to the ancient Religion, and to be in truth what she was in name, the Defender of the Faith.

"'Kings shall be thy nursing fathers,' thus Isaiah sang, 'and Queens thy nursing mothers.' Listen, Elizabeth, most Mighty Queen! To thee the great Prophet sings! He teaches thee thy part. Join then thyself to these princes!... O Elizabeth, a day, a day shall come that shall show thee clearly which have loved thee the better, the Society of Jesus or Luther's brood!"

What arrogance, thought Anthony to himself, and what assurance too!

Meanwhile in the outer world things were not reassuring to the friends of the Government: it was true that half a dozen priests had been captured and examined by torture, and that Sir George Peckham himself, who was known to have harboured Campion, had been committed to the Marshalsea; but yet the Jesuits' influence was steadily on the increase. More and more severe penalties had been lately enacted; it was now declared to be high treason to reconcile or be reconciled to the Church of Rome; overwhelming losses in fortune as well as liberty were threatened against all who said or heard Mass or refused to attend the services of the Establishment; but, as was discovered from papers that fell from time to time into the hands of the Government agents, the only answer of the priests was to inveigh more strenuously against even occasional conformity, declaring it to be the mortal sin of schism, if not of apostasy, to put in an appearance under any circumstances, except those of actual physical compulsion, at the worship in the parish churches. Worse than all, too, was the fact that this severe gospel began to prevail; recusancy was reported to be on the increase in all parts of the country; and many of the old aristocracy began to return to the faith of their fathers: Lords Arundel, Oxford, Vaux, Henry Howard, and Sir Francis Southwell were all beginning to fall under the suspicion of the shrewdest Government spies.

The excitement at Lambeth ran higher day by day as the summer drew on; the net was being gradually contracted in the home counties; spies were reported to be everywhere, in inns, in the servants' quarters of gentlemen's houses, lounging at cross roads and on village greens. Campion's name was in every mouth. Now they were on his footsteps, it was said; now he was taken; now he was gone back to France; now he was in London; now in Lancashire; and each rumour in turn corrected its predecessor.

Anthony shared to the full in the excitement; the figure of the quarry, after which so many hawks were abroad, appealed to his imagination. He dreamed of him at night, once as a crafty-looking man with narrow eyes and stooping shoulders, that skulked and ran from shadow to shadow across a moonlit country; once as a ruddy-faced middle-aged gentleman riding down a crowded street; and several times as a kind of double of Mr. Stewart, whom he had never forgotten, since he had watched him in the little room of Maxwell Hall, gallant and alert among his enemies. At last one day in July, as it drew on towards evening, and as Anthony was looking over the stable-accounts in his little office beyond the Presence Chamber, a buzz of talk and footsteps broke out in the court below; and a moment later the Archbishop's body-servant ran in to say that his Grace wished to see Mr. Norris at once in the gallery that opened out of the guard-room.

"And I think it is about the Jesuits, sir," added the man, evidently excited.

Anthony ran down at once and found his master pacing up and down, with a courier waiting near the steps at the lower end that led to Chichele's tower. The Archbishop stopped by a window, emblazoned with Cardinal Pole's emblem, and beckoned to him.

"See here, Master Norris," he said, "I have received news that Campion is at last taken: it may well be false, as so often before; but take horse, if you please, and ride into the city and find the truth for me. I will not send a groom; they believe the maddest tales. You are at liberty?" he added courteously.

"Yes, your Grace, I will ride immediately."

As he rode down the river-bank towards London Bridge ten minutes later, he could not help feeling some dismay as well as excitement at the news he was to verify. And yet what other end was possible? But what a doom for the brilliant Oxford orator, even though he had counted the cost!

Streams of excited people were pouring across the bridge into the city; Campion's name was on every tongue; and Anthony, as he passed under the high gate, noticed a man point up at the grim spiked heads above it, and laugh to his companion. There seemed little doubt, from the unanimity of those whom he questioned, that the rumour was true; and some even said that the Jesuit was actually passing down Cheapside on his way to the Tower. When at last Anthony came to the thoroughfare the crowd was as dense as for a royal progress. He checked his horse at the door of an inn-yard, and asked an ostler that stood there what it was all about.

"It is Campion, the Jesuit, sir," said the man. "He has been taken at Lyford, and is passing here presently."

The man had hardly finished speaking when a yell came from the end of the street, and groans and hoots ran down the crowd. Anthony turned in his saddle, and saw a great stir and movement, and then horses' and men's heads moving slowly down over the seething surface of the crowd, as if swimming in a rough sea. He could make little out, as the company came towards him, but the faces of the officers and pursuivants who rode in the front rank, four or five abreast; then followed the faces of three or four others, also riding between guards, and Anthony looked eagerly at them; but they were simple faces enough, a little pale and quiet; one was like a farmer's, ruddy and bearded;—surely Campion could not be among those! Then more and more, riding two and two, with a couple of armed guards with each pair; some looked like country-men or servants, some like gentlemen, and one or two might be priests; but the crowd seemed to pay them no attention beyond a glance or two. Ah! what was this coming behind?

There was a space behind the last row of guards, and then came a separate troop riding all together, of half a dozen men at least, and one in the centre, with something white in his hat. The ferment round this group was tremendous; men were leaping up and yelling, like hounds round a carted stag; clubs shot up menacingly, and a storm of ceaseless execration raged outside the compact square of guards who sat alert and ready to beat off an attack. Once a horse kicked fiercely as a man sprang to his hind-quarters, and there was a scream of pain and a burst of laughing.

Anthony sat trembling with excitement as the first group had passed, and this second began to come opposite the entrance where he sat. This then was the man!

The rider in the centre sat his horse somewhat stiffly, and Anthony saw that his elbows were bound behind his back, and his hands in front; the reins were drawn over his horse's head and a pursuivant held them on either side. The man was dressed as a layman, in a plumed hat and a buff jerkin, such as soldiers or plain country-gentlemen might use; and in the hat was a great paper with an inscription. Anthony spelt it out.

"Campion, the Seditious Jesuit."

Then he looked at the man's face.

It was a comely refined face, a little pale but perfectly serene: his pointed dark brown beard and moustache were carefully trimmed; and his large passionate eyes looked cheerfully about him. Anthony stared at him, wholly fascinated; for above the romance that hung about the hunted priest and the glamour of the dreaded Society which he represented, there was a chivalrous fearless look in his face that drew the heart of the young man almost irresistibly. At least he did not look like the skulking knave at whom all the world was sneering, and of whom Anthony had dreamt so vividly a few nights before.

The storm of execration from the faces below, and the faces crowding at the windows, seemed to affect him not at all; and he looked from side to side as if they were cheering him rather than crying against him. Once his eyes met Anthony's and rested on them for a moment; and a strange thrill ran through him and he shivered sharply.

And yet he felt, too, a distinct and irresistible movement of attraction towards this felon who was riding towards his agony and passion; and he was conscious at the same time of that curious touch of wonder that he had felt years before towards the man whipped at the cart's tail, as to whether the solitary criminal were not in the right, and the clamorous accusers in the wrong. Campion in a moment had passed on and turned his head.

In that moment, too, Anthony caught a sudden clear instantaneous impression of a group of faces in the window opposite. There were a couple of men in front, stout city personages no doubt, with crimson faces and open mouths cursing the traitorous Papist and the crafty vagrant fox trapped at last; but between them, looking over their shoulders, was a woman's face in which Anthony saw the most intense struggle of emotions. The face was quite white, the lips parted, the eyes straining, and sorrow and compassion were in every line, as she watched the cheerful priest among his warders; and yet there rested on it, too, a strange light as of triumph. It was the face of one who sees victory even at the hour of supremest failure. In an instant more the face had withdrawn itself into the darkness of the room.

When the crowds had surged down the street in the direction of the Tower, yelling in derision as Campion saluted the lately defaced Cheapside Cross, Anthony guided his horse out through the dispersing groups, realising as he did so, with a touch of astonishment at the coincidence, that he had been standing almost immediately under the window whence he and Isabel had leaned out so many years before.

The sun was going down behind the Abbey as he rode up towards Lambeth, and the sky above and the river beneath were as molten gold. The Abbey itself, with Westminster Hall and the Houses of Parliament below, stood up like mystical palaces against the sunset; and it seemed to Anthony as he rode, as if God Himself were illustrating in glorious illumination the closing pages of that human life of which a glimpse had opened to him in Cheapside. It did not appear to him as it had done in the days of his boyish love as if heaven and earth were a stage for himself to walk and pose upon; but he felt intensely now the dominating power of the personality of the priest; and that he himself was no more than a spectator of this act of a tragedy of which the priest was both hero and victim, and for which this evening glory formed so radiant a scene. The old intellectual arguments against the cause that the priest represented for the moment were drowned in this flood of splendour. When he arrived at Lambeth and had reached the Archbishop's presence, he told him the news briefly, and went to his room full of thought and perplexity.

In a few days the story of Campion's arrest was known far and wide. It had been made possible by the folly of one Catholic and the treachery of another; and when Anthony heard it, he was stirred still more by the contrast between the Jesuit and his pursuers. The priest had returned to the moated grange at Lyford, after having already paid as long a visit there as was prudent, owing to the solicitations of a number of gentlemen who had ridden after him and his companion, and who wished to hear his eloquence. He had returned there again, said mass on the Sunday morning, and preached afterwards, from a chair set before the altar, a sermon on the tears of the Saviour over apostate Jerusalem. But a false disciple had been present who had come in search of one Payne; and this man, known afterwards by the Catholics as Judas Eliot or Eliot Iscariot, had gathered a number of constables and placed them about the manor-house; and before the sermon was over he went out quickly from the table of the Lord, the house was immediately surrounded, and the alarm was raised by a watcher placed in one of the turrets after Eliot's suspicious departure. The three priests present, Campion and two others, were hurried into a hiding-hole over the stairs. The officers entered, searched, and found nothing; and were actually retiring, when Eliot succeeded in persuading them to try again; they searched again till dark, and still found nothing. Mrs. Yate encouraged them to stay the night in the house, and entertained them with ale; and then when all was quiet, insisted on hearing some parting words from her eloquent guest. He came out into the room where she had chosen to spend the night until the officers were gone; and the rest of the Catholics, some Brigittine nuns and others, met there through private passages and listened to him for the last time. As the company was dispersing one of the priests stumbled and fell, making a noise that roused the sentry outside. Again the house was searched, and again with no success. In despair they were leaving it, when Jenkins, Eliot's companion, who was coming downstairs with a servant of the house, beat with his stick on the wall, saying that they had not searched there. It was noticed that the servant showed signs of agitation; and men were fetched to the spot; the wall was beaten in and the three priests were found together, having mutually shriven one another, and made themselves ready for death.

Campion was taken out and sent first to the Sheriff of Berkshire, and then on towards London on the following day. The summer days went by, and every day brought its fresh rumour about Campion. Sir Owen Hopton, Governor of the Tower, who at first had committed his prisoner to Little-Ease, now began to treat him with more honour; he talked, too, mysteriously, of secret interviews and promises and understandings; and gradually it began to get about that Campion was yielding to kindness; that he had seen the Queen; that he was to recant at Paul's Cross; and even that he was to have the See of Canterbury. This last rumour caused great indignation at Lambeth, and Anthony was more pressed than ever to get what authentic news he could of the Jesuit. Then at the beginning of August came a burst of new tales; he had been racked, it was said, and had given up a number of names; and as the month went by more and more details, authentic and otherwise, were published. Those favourably inclined to the Catholics were divided in opinion; some feared that he had indeed yielded to an excess of agony; others, and these proved to be in the right when the truth came out, that he had only given up names which were already known to the authorities; though even for this he asked public pardon on the scaffold.

Towards the end of August the Archbishop again sent expressly for Anthony and bade him accompany his chaplain on the following day to the Tower, to be present at the public disputation that was to take place between English divines and the Jesuit.

"Now he will have the chance he craved for," said Grindal. "He hath bragged that he would meet any and all in dispute, and now the Queen's clemency hath granted it him."

On the following day in the early morning sunshine the minister and Anthony rode down together to the Tower, where they arrived a few minutes before eight o'clock, and were passed through up the stairs into St. John's chapel to the seats reserved for them.

It was indeed true that the authorities had determined to give Campion his chance, but they had also determined to make it as small as possible. He was not even told that the discussion was to take place until the morning of its occasion, and he was allowed no opportunity for developing his own theological position; the entire conduct of the debate was in the hands of his adversaries; he might only parry, seldom riposte, and never attack.

When Anthony found himself in his seat he looked round the chapel. Almost immediately opposite him, on a raised platform against a pillar, stood two high seats occupied by Deans Nowell and Day, who were to conduct the disputation, and who were now talking with their heads together while a secretary was arranging a great heap of books on the table before them. On either side, east and west, stretched chairs for the divines that were to support them in debate, should they need it; and the platform on which Anthony himself had a chair was filled with a crowd of clergy and courtiers laughing and chatting together. A little table, also heaped with books, with seats for the notaries, stood in the centre of the nave, and not far from it were a number of little wooden stools which the prisoners were to occupy. Plainly they were to be allowed no advisers and no books; even the physical support of table and chairs was denied to them in spite of their weary racked bodies. The chapel, bright with the morning sunlight that streamed in through the east windows of the bare Norman sanctuary, hummed with the talk and laughter of those who had come to see the priest-baiting and the vindication of the Protestant Religion; though, as Anthony looked round, he saw here and there an anxious or a downcast face of some unknown friend of the Papists.

He himself was far from easy in his mind. He had been studying Campion's "Ten Reasons" more earnestly than ever, and was amazed to find that the very authorities to which Dr. Jewel deferred, namely, the Scriptures interpreted by Fathers and Councils and illustrated by History, were exactly Campion's authorities, too; and that the Jesuit's appeal to them was no less confident than the Protestant's. That fact had, of course, suggested the thought that if there were no further living authority in existence to decide between these two scholars, Christendom was in a poor position. When doctors differed, where was the layman to turn? To his own private judgment, said the Protestant. But then Campion's private judgment led him to submit to the Catholic claim! This then at present weighed heavily on Anthony's mind. Was there or was there not an authority on earth capable of declaring to him the Revelation of God? For the first time he was beginning to feel a logical and spiritual necessity for an infallible external Judge in matters of faith; and that the Catholic Church was the only system that professed to supply it. The question of the existence of such an authority was, with the doctrine of justification, one of those subjects continually in men's minds and conversations, and to Anthony, unlike others, it appeared more fundamental even than its companion. All else seemed secondary. Indulgences, the Mass, Absolution, the Worship of Mary and the Saints—all these must stand or fall on God's authority made known to man. The one question for him was, Where was that authority to be certainly found?

There came the ringing tramp of footsteps; the buzz of talk ceased and then broke out again, as the prisoners, with all eyes bent upon them, surrounded by a strong guard of pikemen, were seen advancing up the chapel from the north-west door towards the stools set ready for them. Anthony had no eyes but for Campion who limped in front, supported on either side by a warder. He could scarcely believe at first that this was the same priest who had ridden so bravely down Cheapside. Now he was bent, and walked like an old broken man; his face was deathly pale, with shadows and lines about his eyes, and his head trembled a little. There were one or two exclamations of pity, for all knew what had caused the change; and Anthony heard an undertone moan of sorrow and anger from some one in a seat behind him.

The prisoners sat down; and the guards went to their places. Campion took his seat in front, and turned immediately from side to side, running his dark eyes along the faces to see where were his adversaries; and once more Anthony met his eyes, and thrilled at it. Through the pallor and pain of his face, the same chivalrous spirit looked out and called for homage and love, that years ago at Oxford had made young men, mockingly nicknamed after their leader, to desire his praise more passionately than anything on earth, and even to imitate his manners and dress and gait, for very loyalty and devotion. Anthony could not take his eyes off him; he watched the clear-cut profile of his face thrown fearlessly forward, waited in tense expectation to hear him speak, and paid no attention to the whisperings of the chaplain beside him.

Presently the debate began. It was opened by Dean Nowell from his high seat, who assured Father Campion of the disinterested motives of himself and his reverend friends in holding this disputation. It was, after all, only what the priest had demanded; and they trusted by God's grace that they would do him good and help him to see the truth. There was no unfairness, said the Dean, who seemed to think that some apology was needed, in taking him thus unprepared, since the subject of debate would be none other than Campion's own book. The Jesuit looked up, nodded his head, and smiled.

"I thank you, Mr. Dean," he said, in his deep resonant voice, and there fell a dead hush as he spoke. "I thank you for desiring to do me good, and to take up my challenge; but I must say that I would I had understood of your coming, that I might have made myself ready."

Campion's voice thrilled strangely through Anthony, as the glance from his eyes had done. It was so assured, so strong and delicate an instrument, and so supremely at its owner's command, that it was hardly less persuasive than his personality and his learning that made themselves apparent during the day. And Anthony was not alone in his impressions of the Jesuit. Lord Arundel afterwards attributed his conversion to Campion's share in the discussions. Again and again during the day a murmur of applause followed some of the priest's clean-cut speeches and arguments, and a murmur of disapproval the fierce thrusts and taunts of his opponents; and by the end of the day's debate, so marked was the change of attitude of the crowd that had come to triumph over the Papist, and so manifest their sympathy with the prisoners, that it was thought advisable to exclude the public from the subsequent discussions.

On this first day, all manner of subjects were touched upon, such as the comparative leniency of Catholic and Protestant governments, the position of Luther with regard to the Epistle of St. James, and other matters comparatively unimportant, in the discussion of which a great deal of time was wasted. Campion entreated his opponents to leave such minor questions alone, and to come to doctrinal matters; but they preferred to keep to details rather than to principles, and the priest had scarcely any opportunity to state his positive position at all. The only doctrinal matter seriously touched upon was that of Justification by Faith; and texts were flung to and fro without any great result. "We are justified by faith," cried one side. "Though I have all faith and have not charity, I am nothing," cried the other.

The effect on Anthony of this day's debate arose rather from the victorious personality of the priest than from his arguments. His gaiety, too, was in strange contrast to the solemn Puritanism of his enemies. For instance, he was on the point that Councils might err in matters of fact, but that the Scriptures could not.

"As for example," he said, his eyes twinkling out of his drawn face, "I am bound under pain of damnation to believe that Toby's dog had a tail, because it is written, he wagged it."

The Deans looked sternly at him, as the audience laughed.

"Now, now," said one of them, "it becomes not to deal so triflingly with matters of weight."

Campion dropped his eyes, demurely, as if reproved.

"Why, then," he said, "if this example like you not, take another. I must believe that Saint Paul had a cloak, because he willeth Timothy to bring it with him."

Again the crowd laughed; and Anthony laughed, too, with a strange sob in his throat at the gallant foolery, which, after all, was as much to the point as a deal that the Deans were saying.

But the second day's debate, held in Hopton's Hall, was on more vital matters; and Anthony again and again found himself leaning forward breathlessly, as Drs. Goode and Fulke on the one side, and Campion on the other, respectively attacked and defended the Doctrine of the Visible Church; for this, for Anthony, was one of the crucial points of the dispute between Catholicism and Protestantism. Anthony believed already that the Church was one; and if it was visible, surely, he thought to himself, it must be visibly one; and in that case, it is evident where that Church is to be found. But if it is invisible, it may be invisibly one, and then as far as that matter is concerned, he may rest in the Church of England. If not—and then he recoiled from the gulf that opened.

"It must be an essential mark of the Church," said Campion, "and such a quality as is inseparable. It must be visible, as fire is hot, and water moist."

Goode answered that when Christ was taken and the Apostles fled, then at least the Church was invisible; and if then, why not always?

"It was a Church inchoate," answered the priest, "beginning, not perfect."

But Goode continued to insist that the true Church is known only to God, and therefore invisible.

"There are many wolves within," he said, "and many sheep without."

"I know not who is elect," retorted Campion, "but I know who is a Catholic."

"Only the elect are of the Church," said Goode.

"I say that both good and evil are of the visible Church," answered the other.

"To be elect or true members of Christ is one thing," went on Goode, "and to be in the visible Church is another."

As the talk went on, Anthony began to see where the confusion lay. The Protestants were anxious to prove that membership in a visible body did not ensure salvation but then the Catholics never claimed that it did; the question was: Did or did not Christ intend there to be a visible Church, membership in which should be the normal though not the infallible means of salvation?

They presently got on to the a priori point as to whether a visible Church would seem to be a necessity.

"There is a perpetual commandment," said the priest, "in Matthew eighteen—'Tell the Church'; but that cannot be unless the Church is visible; ergo, the visibility of the Church is continual."

"When there is an established Church," said Goode, "this remedy is to be sought for. But this cannot be always had."

"The disease is continual," answered Campion; "ergo the remedy must be continual." Then he left the a priori ground and entered theirs. "To whom should I have gone," he cried, "before Luther's time? What prelates should I have made my complaint unto in those days? Where was your Church nine hundred years ago? Whose were John Huss, Jerome of Prague, the Waldenses? Were they yours?" Then he turned scornfully to Fulke, "Help him, Master Doctor."

And Fulke repeated Goode's assertion, that valuable as the remedy is, it cannot always be had.

Anthony sat back, puzzled. Both sides seemed right. Persecution must often hinder the full privileges of Church membership and the exercise of discipline. Yet the question was, What was Christ's intention? Was it that the Church should be visible? It seemed that even the ministers allowed that, now. And if so, why then the Catholic's claim that Christ's intention had never been wholly frustrated, but that a visible unity was to be found amongst themselves—surely this was easier to believe than the Protestant theory that the Church which had been visible for fifteen centuries was not really the Church at all; but that the true Church had been invisible—in spite of Christ's intention—during all that period, and was now to be found only in small separated bodies scattered here and there. How of the prevailing of the gates of hell, if that were allowed to be true?

At two o'clock they reassembled for the afternoon conference; and now they got even closer to the heart of the matter, for the subject was to be, whether the Church could err?

Fulke asserted that it could, and did; and made a syllogism:

"Whatsoever error is incident to every member, is incident to the whole. But it is incident to every member to err; ergo, to the whole."

"I deny both major and minor," said Campion quietly. "Every man may err, but not the whole gathered together; for the whole hath a promise, but so hath not every particular man."

Fulke denied this stoutly, and beat on the table.

"Every member hath the spirit of Christ," he said, "which is the spirit of truth; and therefore hath the same promise that the whole hath."

"Why, then," said Campion, smiling, "there should be no heretics."

"Yes," answered Fulke, "heretics may be within the Church, but not of the Church."

And so they found themselves back again where they started from.

Anthony sat back on the oak bench and sighed, and glanced round at the interested faces of the theologians and the yawns of the amateurs, as the debate rolled on over the old ground, and touched on free will, and grace, and infant baptism; until the Lieutenant interposed:

"Master Doctors," he said, with a judicial air, "the question that was appointed before dinner was, whether the visible Church may err"—to which Goode retorted that the digressions were all Campion's fault.

Then the debate took the form of contradictions.

"Whatsoever congregation doth err in matters of faith," said Goode, "is not the true Church; but the Church of Rome erreth in matters of faith; ergo, it is not the true Church."

"I deny your minor," said Campion, "the Church of Rome hath not erred." Then the same process was repeated over the Council of Trent; and the debate whirled off once more into details and irrelevancies about imputed righteousness, and the denial of the Cup to the laity.

Again the audience grew restless. They had not come there, most of them, to listen to theological minutiæ, but to see sport; and this interminable chopping of words that resulted in nothing bored them profoundly. A murmur of conversation began to buzz on all sides.

Campion was in despair.

"Thus shall we run into all questions," he cried hopelessly, "and then we shall have done this time twelve months."

But Fulke would not let him be; but pressed on a question about the Council of Nice.

"Now we shall have the matter of images," sighed Campion.

"You are nimis acutus," retorted Fulke, "you will leap over the stile or ever you come to it. I mean not to speak of images."

And so with a few more irrelevancies the debate ended.

The third debate in September (on the twenty-third), at which Anthony was again present, was on the subject of the Real Presence in the Blessed Sacrament.

Fulke was in an evil temper, since it was common talk that Campion had had the best of the argument on the eighteenth.

"The other day," he said, "when we had some hope of your conversion, we forbare you much, and suffered you to discourse; but now that we see you are an obstinate heretic, and seek to cover the light of the truth with multitude of words, we mean not to allow you such large discourses as we did."

"You are very imperious to-day," answered Campion serenely, "whatsoever the matter is. I am the Queen's prisoner, and none of yours."

"Not a whit imperious," said Fulke angrily,—"though I will exact of you to keep the right order of disputation."

Then the argument began. It soon became plain to Anthony that it was possible to take the Scripture in two senses, literally and metaphorically. The sacrament either was literally Christ's body, or it was not. Who then was to decide? Father Campion said it meant the one; Dr. Fulke the other. Could it be possible that Christ should leave His people in doubt as to such a thing? Surely not, thought Anthony. Well, then, where is the arbiter? Father Campion says, The Church; Dr. Fulke says, The Scripture. But that is a circular argument, for the question to be decided is: What does the Scripture mean? for it may mean at least two things, at least so it would seem. Here then he found himself face to face with the claims of the Church of Rome to be that arbiter; and his heart began to grow sick with apprehension as he saw how that Church supplied exactly what was demanded by the circumstances of the case—that is, an infallible living guide as to the meaning of God's Revelation. The simplicity of her claim appalled him.

He did not follow the argument closely, since it seemed to him but a secondary question now; though he heard one or two sentences. At one point Campion was explaining what the Church meant by substance. It was that which transcended the senses.

"Are you not Dr. Fulke?" he said. "And yet I see nothing but your colour and exterior form. The substance of Dr. Fulke cannot be seen."

"I will not vouchsafe to reply upon this answer," snarled Fulke, whose temper had not been improved by the debate—"too childish for a sophister!"

Then followed interminable syllogisms, of which Campion would not accept the premises; and no real progress was made. The Jesuit tried to explain the doctrine that the wicked may be said not to eat the Body in the Sacrament, because they receive not the virtue of It, though they receive the Thing; but Fulke would not hear him. The distinction was new to Anthony, with his puritan training, and he sat pondering it while the debate passed on.

The afternoon discussion, too, was to little purpose. More and more Anthony, and others with him, began to see that the heart of the matter was the authority of the Church; and that unless that was settled, all other debate was beside the point; and the importance of this was brought out for him more clearly than ever on the 27th of the month, when the fourth and last debate took place, and on the subject of the sufficiency of the Scriptures unto salvation.

Mr. Charke, who had now succeeded as disputant, began with extempore prayer, in which as usual the priest refused to join, praying and crossing himself apart.

Mr. Walker then opened the disputation with a pompous and insolent speech about "one Campion," an "unnatural man to his country, degenerate from an Englishman, an apostate in religion, a fugitive from this realm, unloyal to his prince." Campion sat with his eyes cast down, until the minister had done.

Then the discussion began. The priest pointed out that Protestants were not even decided as to what were Scriptures and what were not, since Luther rejected three epistles in the New Testament; therefore, he argued, the Church is necessary as a guide, first of all, to tell men what is Scripture. Walker evaded by saying he was not a Lutheran but a Christian; and then the talk turned on to apocryphal books. But it was not possible to evade long, and the Jesuit soon touched his opponent.

"To leave a door to traditions," he said, "which the Holy Ghost may deliver to the true Church, is both manifest and seen: as in the Baptism of infants, the Holy Ghost proceeding from Father to Son, and such other things mentioned, which are delivered by tradition. Prove these directly by the Scripture if you can!"

Charke answered by the analogy of circumcision which infants received, and by quoting Christ's words as to "sending" of the Comforter; and they were soon deep in detailed argument; but once more Anthony saw that it was all a question of the interpretation of Scripture; and, therefore, that it would seem that an authoritative interpreter was necessary—and where could such be found save in an infallible living Voice? And once more a question of Campion's drove the point home.

"Was all Scripture written when the Apostles first taught?" And Charke dared not answer yes.

The afternoon's debate concerned justification by faith, and this, more than ever, seemed to Anthony a secondary matter, now that he was realising what the claim of a living authority meant; and he sat back, only interested in watching the priest's face, so controlled yet so transparent in its simplicity and steadfastness, as he listened to the ministers' brutal taunts and insolence, and dealt his quiet skilful parries and ripostes to their incessant assaults. At last the Lieutenant struck the table with his hand, and intimated that the time was past, and after a long prayer by Mr. Walker, the prisoners were led back to their cells.

As Anthony rode back alone in the evening sunlight, he was as one who was seeing a vision. There was indeed a vision before him, that had been taking shape gradually, detail by detail, during these last months, and ousting the old one; and which now, terribly emphasised by Campion's arguments and illuminated by the fire of his personality, towered up imperious, consistent, dominating—and across her brow her title, The Catholic Church. Far above all the melting cloudland of theory she moved, a stupendous fact; living, in contrast with the dead past to which her enemies cried in vain; eloquent when other systems were dumb; authoritative when they hesitated; steady when they reeled and fell. About her throne dwelt her children, from every race and age, secure in her protection, and wise with her knowledge, when other men faltered and questioned and doubted: and as Anthony looked up and saw her for the first time, he recognised her as the Mistress and Mother of his soul; and although the blinding clouds of argument and theory and self-distrust rushed down on him again and filled his eyes with dust, yet he knew he had seen her face in very truth, and that the memory of that vision could never again wholly leave him.

Chapter Six - Some Contrasts

In the Lambeth household the autumn passed by uneventfully. The rigour of the Archbishop's confinement had been mitigated, and he had been allowed now and again to visit his palace at Croydon; but his inactivity still continued as the sequestration was not removed; Elizabeth had refused to listen to the petition of Convocation in '80 for his reinstatement. Anthony went down to the old palace once or twice with him; and was brought closer to him in many ways; and his affection and tenderness towards his master continually increased. Grindal was a pathetic figure at this time, with few friends, in poor health, out of favour with the Queen, who had disregarded his existence; and now his afflictions were rendered more heavy than ever by the blindness that was creeping over him. The Archbishop, too, in his loneliness and sorrow, was drawn closer to his young officer than ever before; and gradually got to rely upon him in many little ways. He would often walk with Anthony in the gardens at Lambeth, leaning upon his arm, talking to him of his beloved flowers and herbs which he was now almost too blind to see; telling him queer facts about the properties of plants; and even attempting to teach him a little irrelevant botany now and then.

They were walking up and down together, soon after Campion's arrest, one August morning before prayers in a little walled garden on the river that Grindal had laid out with great care in earlier years.

"Ah," said the old man, "I am too blind to see my flowers now, Mr. Norris; but I love them none the less; and I know their places. Now there," he went on, pointing with his stick, "there I think grows my mastick or marum; perhaps I smell it, however. What is that flower like, Mr. Norris?"

Anthony looked at it, and described its little white flower and its leaves.

"That is it," said the Archbishop, "I thought my memory served me. It is a kind of marjoram, and it has many virtues, against cramps, convulsions and venomous bites—so Galen tells us." Then he went on to talk of the simple old plants that he loved best; of the two kinds of basil that he always had in his garden; and how good it was mixed in sack against the headache; and the male penny-royal, and how well it had served him once when he had great internal trouble.

"Mr. Gerrard was here a week or two ago, Mr. Norris, when you were down at Croydon for me. He is my Lord Burghley's man; he oversees his gardens at Wimbledon House, and in the country. He was telling me of a rascal he had seen at a fair, who burned henbane and made folks with the toothache breathe in the fumes; and then feigned to draw a worm forth from the aching tooth; but it was no worm at all, but a lute string that he held ready in his hand. There are sad rascals abroad, Mr. Norris."

The old man waxed eloquent when they came to the iris bed.

"Ah! Mr. Norris, the flowers-de-luce are over by now, I fear; but what wonderful creatures of God they are, with their great handsome heads and their cool flags. I love to hear a bed of them rustle all together and shake their spears and nod their banners like an army in array. And then they are not only for show. Apuleius says that they are good against the gout. I asked Mr. Gerrard whether my lord had tried them; but he said no, he would not."

At the violet bed he was yet more emphatic.

"I think, Mr. Norris, I love these the best of all. They are lowly creatures; but how sweet! and like other lowly creatures exalted by their Maker to do great things as his handmaidens. The leaves are good against inflammations, and the flowers against ague and hoarseness as well. And then there is oil-of-violets, as you know; and violet-syrup and sugar-violet; then they are good for blisters; garlands of them were an ancient cure for the headache, as I think Dioscorides tells us. And they are the best of all cures for some children's ailments."

And so they walked up and down together; the Archbishop talking quietly on and on; and helping quite unknown to himself by his tender irrelevant old man's talk to soothe the fever of unrest and anxiety that was beginning to torment Anthony so much now. His conversation, like the very flowers he loved to speak of, was "good against inflammations."

Anthony came to him one morning, thinking to please him, and brought him a root that he had bought from a travelling pedlar just outside the gateway.

"This is a mandrake root, your Grace; I heard you speak of it the other day."

The Archbishop took it, smiling, felt it carefully, peered at it a minute or two. "No, my son," he said, "I fear you have met a knave. This is briony-root carved like a mandrake into the shape of a man's legs. It is worthless, I fear; but I thank you for the kind thought, Mr. Norris," and he gave the root back to him. "And the stories we hear of the mandrake, I fear, are fables, too. Some say that they only grow beneath gallows from that which falls there; that the male grows from the corruption of a man's body; and the female from that of a woman's; but that is surely a lie, and a foul one, too. And then folks say that to draw it up means death; and that the mandrake screams terribly as it comes up; and so they bid us tie a dog to it, and then drive the dog from it so as to draw it up so. I asked Mr. Baker, the chirurgeon in the household of my Lord Oxford, the other day, about that; and he said that such tales be but doltish dreams and old wives' fables. But the true mandrake is a clean and wholesome plant. The true ointment Populeon should have the juice of the leaves in it; and the root boiled and strained causes drowsiness. It hath a predominate cold faculty, Galen saith; but its true home is not in England at all. It comes from Mount Garganus in Apulia."

It was pathetic, Anthony thought sometimes, that this old prelate should be living so far from the movements of the time, owing to no fault of his own. During these months the great tragedy of Campion's passion was proceeding a couple of miles away; but the Archbishop thought less of it than of the death of an old tree. The only thing from the outside world that seemed to ruffle him was the behaviour of the Puritans. Anthony was passing through "le velvet-room" one afternoon when he heard voices in the Presence Chamber beyond; and almost immediately heard the Archbishop, who had recognised his step, call his name. He went in and found him with a stranger in a dark sober dress.

"Take this gentleman to Mr. Scot," he said, "and ask him to give him some refreshment; for that he must be gone directly."

When Anthony had taken the gentleman to the steward, he returned to the Archbishop for any further instructions about him.

"No, Mr. Norris, my business is done with him. He comes from my lord of Norwich, and must be returning this evening. If you are not occupied, Mr. Norris, will you give me your arm into the garden?"

They went out by the vestry-door into the little cloisters, and skirting the end of the creek that ran up by Chichele's water-tower began to pace up and down the part of the garden that looked over the river.

"My lord has sent to know if I know aught of one Robert Browne, with whom he is having trouble. This Mr. Browne has lately come from Cambridge, and so my lord thought I might know something of him; but I do not. This gentleman has been saying some wild and foolish things, I fear; and desires that every church should be free of all others; and should appoint its own minister, and rule its own affairs without interference, and that prophesyings should be without restraint. Now, you know, Mr. Norris, I have always tried to serve that party, and support them in their gospel religion; but this goes too far. Where were any governance at all, if all this were to come about? where were the Rule of Faith? the power of discipline? Nay, where were the unity for which our Saviour prayed? It liketh me not. Good Dr. Freake, as his messenger tells me, feels as I do about this; and desires to restrain Mr. Browne, but he is so hot he will not be restrained; and besides, he is some kin to my Lord Burghley, so I fear his mouth will be hard to stop."

Anthony could not help thinking of Mr. Buxton's prediction that the Church of England had so repudiated authority, that in turn her own would one day be repudiated.

"A Papist prisoner, your Grace," he said, "said to me the other day that this would be sure to come: that the whole principle of Church authority had been destroyed in England; and that the Church of England would more and more be deserted by her children; for that there was no necessary centre of unity left, now that Peter was denied."

"It is what a Papist is bound to say," replied the Archbishop; "but it is easy to prophesy, when fulfilment may be far away. Indeed, I think we shall have trouble with some of these zealous men; and the Queen's Grace was surely right in desiring some restraint to be put upon the Exercises. But it is mere angry raving to say that the Church of England will lose the allegiance of her children."

Anthony could not feel convinced that events bore out the Archbishop's assertion. Everywhere the Puritans were becoming more outrageously disloyal. There were everywhere signs of disaffection and revolt against the authorities of the Establishment, even on the part of the most sincere and earnest men, many of whom were looking forward to the day when the last rags of popery should be cast away, and formal Presbyterianism inaugurated in the Church of England. Episcopal Ordination was more and more being regarded as a merely civil requirement, but conveying no ministerial commission; recognition by the congregation with the laying on of the hands of the presbyterate was the only ordination they allowed as apostolic.

Anthony said a word to the Archbishop about this.

"You must not be too strict," said the old man. "Both views can be supported by the Scriptures; and although the Church of England at present recognises only Episcopal Ordination within her own borders, she does not dare to deny, as the Papists fondly do, that other rites may not be as efficacious as her own. That, surely, Master Norris, is in accordance with the mind of Christ that hath the spirit of liberty."

Much as Anthony loved the old man and his gentle charity, this doctrinal position as stated by the chief pastor of the Church of England scarcely served to establish his troubled allegiance.

During these autumn months, too, both between and after the disputations in the Tower, the image of Campion had been much in his thoughts. Everywhere, except among the irreconcilables, the Jesuit was being well spoken of: his eloquence, his humour, and his apparent sincerity were being greatly commented on in London and elsewhere. Anthony, as has been seen, was being deeply affected on both sides of his nature; the shrewd wit of the other was in conflict with his own intellectual convictions, and this magnetic personality was laying siege to his heart. And now the last scene of the tragedy, more affecting than all, was close at hand.

Anthony was present first at the trial in Westminster Hall, which took place during November, and was more than ever moved by what he saw and heard there. The priest, as even his opponents confessed, had by now "won a marvellously good report, to be such a man as his like was not to be found, either for life, learning, or any other quality which might beautify a man." And now here he stood at the bar, paler than ever, so numbed with racking that he could not lift his hand to plead—that supple musician's hand of his, once so skilful on the lute—so that Mr. Sherwin had to lift it for him out of the furred cuff in which he had wrapped it, kissing it tenderly as he did so, in reverence for its sufferings; and he saw, too, the sleek face of Eliot, in his red yeoman's coat, as he stood chatting at the back, like another Barabbas whom the people preferred to the servant of the Crucified. And, above all, he heard Campion's stirring defence, spoken in that same resonant sweet voice, though it broke now and then through weakness, in spite of the unconquerable purpose and cheerfulness that showed in his great brown eyes, and round his delicate humorous mouth. It was indeed an astonishing combination of sincerity and eloquence, and even humour, that was brought to bear on the jury, and all in vain, during those days.

"If you want to dispute as though you were in the schools," cried one of the court, when he found himself out of his depth, "you are only proving yourself a fool."

"I pray God," said Campion, while his eyes twinkled, "I pray God make us both sages." And, in spite of the tragedy of the day, a little hum of laughter ran round the audience.

"If a sheep were stolen," he argued again, in answer to the presupposition that since some Catholics were traitors, therefore these were—"and a whole family called in question for the same, were it good manner of proceeding for the accusers to say 'Your great grandfathers and fathers and sisters and kinsfolk all loved mutton; ergo, you have stolen the sheep'?"

Again, in answer to the charge that he and his companions had conspired abroad, he said,

"As for the accusation that we plotted treason at Rheims, reflect, my lords, how just this charge is! For see! First we never met there at all; then, many of us have never been at Rheims at all; finally, we were never in our lives all together, except at this hour and in prison."

Anthony heard, too, Campion expose the attempt that was made to shift the charge from religion to treason.

"There was offer made to us," he cried indignantly, "that if we would come to the church to hear sermons and the word preached, we should be set at large and at liberty; so Pascall and Nicholls"—(two apostates) "otherwise as culpable in all offences as we, upon coming to church were received to grace and had their pardon granted; whereas, if they had been so happy as to have persevered to the end, they had been partakers of our calamities. So that our religion was cause of our imprisonment, and ex consequenti, of our condemnation."

The Queen's Counsel tried to make out that certain secrets that Campion, in an intercepted letter, had sworn not to reveal, must be treasonable or he would not so greatly fear their publication. To this the priest made a stately defence of his office, and declaration of his staunchness. He showed how by his calling as a priest he was bound to secrecy in matters heard in confession, and that these secret matters were of this nature.

"These were the hidden matters," he said, "these were the secrets, to the revealing whereof I cannot nor will not be brought, come rack, come rope!"

And again, when Sergeant Anderson interpreted a phrase of Campion's referring to the great day to which he looked forward, as meaning the day of a foreign papal invasion, the prisoner cried in a loud voice:

"O Judas, Judas! No other day was in my mind, I protest, than that wherein it should please God to make a restitution of faith and religion. Whereupon, as in every pulpit every Protestant doth, I pronounced a great day, not wherein any temporal potentate should minister, but wherein the terrible Judge should reveal all men's consciences, and try every man of each kind of religion. This is the day of change, this is the great day which I threatened; comfortable to the well-behaving, and terrible to all heretics. Any other day but this, God knows I meant not."

Then, after the other prisoners had pleaded, Campion delivered a final defence to the jury, with a solemnity that seemed to belong to a judge rather than a criminal. The babble of tongues that had continued most of the day was hushed to a profound silence in court as he stood and spoke, for the sincerity and simplicity of the priest were evident to all, and combined with his eloquence and his strange attractive personality, dominated all but those whose minds were already made up before entering the court.

"What charge this day you sustain," began the priest, in a steady low voice, with his searching eyes bent on the faces before him, "and what account you are to render at the dreadful Day of Judgment, whereof I could wish this also were a mirror, I trust there is not one of you but knoweth. I doubt not but in like manner you forecast how dear the innocent is to God, and at what price He holdeth man's blood. Here we are accused and impleaded to the death,"—he began to raise his voice a little—"here you do receive our lives into your custody; here must be your device, either to restore them or condemn them. We have no whither to appeal but to your consciences; we have no friends to make there but your heeds and discretions." Then he touched briefly on the evidence, showing how faulty and circumstantial it was, and urged them to remember that a man's life by the very constitution of the realm must not be sacrificed to mere probabilities or presumptions; then he showed the untrustworthiness of his accusers, how one had confessed himself a murderer, and how another was an atheist. Then he ended with a word or two of appeal.

"God give you grace," he cried, "to weigh our causes aright, and have respect to your own consciences; and so I will keep the jury no longer. I commit the rest to God, and our convictions to your good discretions."

When the jury had retired, and all the judges but one had left the bench until the jury should return, Anthony sat back in his place, his heart beating and his eyes looking restlessly now on the prisoners, now on the door where the jury had gone out, and now on Judge Ayloff, whom he knew a little, and who sat only a few feet away from him on one side. He could hear the lawyers sitting below the judge talking among themselves; and presently one of them leaned over to him.

"Good-day, Mr. Norris," he said, "you have come to see an acquittal, I doubt not. No man can be in two minds after what we have heard; at least concerning Mr. Campion. We all think so, here, at any rate."

The lawyer was going on to say a word or two more as to the priest's eloquence, when there was a sharp exclamation from the judge. Anthony looked up and saw Judge Ayloff staring at his hand, turning it over while he held his glove in the other; and Anthony saw to his surprise that the fingers were all blood-stained. One or two gentlemen near him turned and looked, too, as the judge, still staring and growing a little pale, wiped the blood quickly away with the glove; but the fingers grew crimson again immediately.

"'S'Body!" said Ayloff, half to himself; "'tis strange, there is no wound." A moment later, looking up, he saw many of his neighbours glancing curiously at his hand and his pale face, and hastily thrust on his glove again; and immediately after the jury returned, and the judges filed in to take their places. Anthony's attention was drawn off again, and the buzz of talk in the court was followed again by a deep silence.

The verdict of Guilty was uttered, as had been pre-arranged, and the Queen's Counsel demanded sentence.

"Campion and the rest," said Chief Justice Wray, "What can you say why you should not die?"

Then Campion, still steady and resolute, made his last useless appeal.

"It was not our death that ever we feared. But we knew that we were not lords of our own lives, and therefore for want of answer would not be guilty of our own deaths. The only thing that we have now to say is, that if our religion do make us traitors, we are worthy to be condemned; but otherwise are and have been true subjects as ever the Queen had. In condemning us, you condemn all your own ancestors," and as he said this, his voice began to rise, and he glanced steadily and mournfully round at the staring faces about him, "all the ancient priests, bishops, and kings—all that was once the glory of England, the island of saints, and the most devoted child of the See of Peter."

Then, as he went on, he flung out his wrenched hands, and his voice rang with indignant defiance. "For what have we taught," he cried, "however you may qualify it with the odious name of treason, that they did not uniformly teach? To be condemned with these old lights—not of England only, but of the world—by their degenerate descendants, is both gladness and glory to us." Then, with a superb gesture, he sent his voice pealing through the hall: "God lives, posterity will live; their judgment is not so liable to corruption as that of those who are now about to sentence us to death."

There was a burst of murmurous applause as he ended, which stilled immediately, as the Chief Justice began to deliver sentence. But when the horrible details of his execution had been enumerated, and the formula had ended, it was the prisoner's turn to applaud:—

"Te Deum laudamus!" cried Campion; "Te Dominum confitemur."

"Haec est dies," shouted Sherwin, "quam fecit Dominus; exultemus et laetemur in illâ": and so with the thanksgiving and joy of the condemned criminals, the mock-trial ended.

When Anthony rode down silently and alone in the rain that December morning a few days later, to see the end, he found a vast silent crowd assembled on Tower Hill and round the gateway, where the four horses were waiting, each pair harnessed to a hurdle laid flat on the ground. He would not go in, for he could scarcely trust himself to speak, so great was his horror of the crime that was to be committed; so he backed his horse against the wall, and waited over an hour in silence, scarcely hearing the murmurs of impatience that rolled round the great crowd from time to time, absorbed in his own thoughts. Here was the climax of these days of misery and self-questioning that had passed since the trial in Westminster Hall. It was no use, he argued to himself, to pretend otherwise. These three men of God were to die for their religion—and a religion too which was gradually detaching itself to his view from the mists and clouds that hid it, as the one great reality and truth of God's Revelation to man. He had come, he knew, to see not an execution but a martyrdom.

There was a trampling from within, the bolts creaked, and the gate rolled back; a company of halberdiers emerged, and in their midst the three priests in laymen's dress; behind followed a few men on horseback, with a little company of ministers, bible in hand; and then a rabble of officers and pursuivants. Anthony edged his horse in among the others, as the crowd fell back, and took up his place in the second rank of riders between a gentleman of his acquaintance who made room for him on the one side, and Sir Francis Knowles on the other, and behind the Tower officials.

Then, once more he heard that ringing bass voice whose first sound silenced the murmurs of the surging excited crowd.

"God save you all, gentlemen! God bless you and make you all good Catholics."

Then, as the priest turned to kneel towards the east, he saw his face paler than ever now, after his long fast in preparation for death. The rain was still falling as Campion in his frieze gown knelt in the mud. There was silence as he prayed, and as he ended aloud by commending his soul to God.

"In manus tuas, Domine, commendo spiritum meum."

The three were secured to the hurdles, Briant and Sherwin on the one, Campion on the other, all lying on their backs, with their feet towards the horse's heels. The word to start was given by Sir Owen Hopton who rode with Charke, the preacher of Gray's Inn, in the front rank; the lashed horses plunged forward, with the jolting hurdles spattering mud behind them; and the dismal pageant began to move forward through the crowd on that way of sorrows. There was a ceaseless roar and babble of voices as they went. Charke, in his minister's dress, able now to declaim without fear of reply, was hardly silent for a moment from mocking and rebuking the prisoners, and making pompous speeches to the people.

"See here," he cried, "these rogueing popish priests, laid by the heels—aye, by the heels—at last; in spite of their tricks and turns. See this fellow in his frieze gown, dead to the world as he brags; and know how he skulked and hid in his disguises till her Majesty's servants plucked him forth! We will disguise him, we will disguise him, ere we have done with him, that his own mother should not know him. Ha, now! Campion, do you hear me?"

And so the harsh voice rang out over the crowd that tramped alongside, and up to the faces that filled every window; while the ministers below kept up a ceaseless murmur of adjuration and entreaty and threatening, with a turning of leaves of their bibles, and bursts of prayer, over the three heads that jolted and rocked at their feet over the cobblestones and through the mud. The friends of the prisoners walked as near to them as they dared, and their lips moved continually in prayer.

Every now and then as Anthony craned his head, he could see Campion's face, with closed eyes and moving lips that smiled again and again, all spattered and dripping with filth; and once he saw a gentleman walking beside him fearlessly stoop down and wipe the priest's face with a handkerchief. Presently they had passed up Cheapside and reached Newgate; in a niche in the archway itself stood a figure of the Mother of God looking compassionately down; and as Campion's hurdle passed beneath it, her servant wrenched himself a few inches up in his bonds and bowed to his glorious Queen; and then laid himself down quietly again, as a chorus of lament rose from the ministers over his superstition and obstinate idolatry that seemed as if it would last even to death; and Charke too, who had become somewhat more silent, broke out again into revilings.

The crowd at Tyburn was vast beyond all reckoning. Outside the gate it stretched on every side, under the elms, a few were even in the branches, along the sides of the stream; everywhere was a sea of heads, out of which, on a little eminence like another Calvary, rose up the tall posts of the three-cornered gallows, on which the martyrs were to suffer. As the hurdles came slowly under the gate, the sun broke out for the first time; and as the horses that drew the hurdles came round towards the carts that stood near the gallows and the platform on which the quartering block stood, a murmur began that ran through the crowd from those nearest the martyrs.—"But they are laughing, they are laughing!"

The crowd gave a surge to and fro as the horses drew up, and Anthony reined his own beast back among the people, so that he was just opposite the beam on which the three new ropes were already hanging, and beneath which was standing a cart with the back taken out. In the cart waited a dreadful figure in a tight-fitting dress, sinewy arms bare to the shoulder, and a butcher's knife at his leather girdle. A little distance away stood the hateful cauldron, bubbling fiercely, with black smoke pouring from under it: the platform with the block and quartering-axe stood beneath the gallows; and round this now stood the officers, with Norton the rack-master, and Sir Owen Hopton and the rest, and the three priests, with the soldiers forming a circle to keep the crowd back.

The hangman stooped as Anthony looked, and a moment later Campion stood beside him on the cart, pale, mud-splashed, but with the same serene smile; his great brown eyes shone as they looked out over the wide heaving sea of heads, from which a deep heart-shaking murmur rose as the famous priest appeared. Anthony could see every detail of what went on; the hangman took the noose that hung from above, and slipped it over the prisoner's head, and drew it close round his neck; and then himself slipped down from the cart, and stood with the others, still well above the heads of the crowd, but leaving the priest standing higher yet on the cart, silhouetted, rope and all, framed in the posts and cross-beam, from which two more ropes hung dangling against the driving clouds and blue sky over London city.

Campion waited perfectly motionless for the murmur of innumerable voices to die down; and Anthony, fascinated and afraid beneath that overpowering serenity, watched him turn his head slowly from side to side with a "majesti-cal countenance," as his enemies confessed, as if he were on the point of speaking. Silence seemed to radiate out from him, spreading like a ripple, outwards, until the furthest outskirts of that huge crowd was motionless and quiet; and then without apparent effort, his voice began to peal out.

"'Spectaculum facti sumus Deo, angelis et hominibus.' These are the words of Saint Paul, Englished thus, 'We are made a spectacle or sight unto God, unto His angels, and unto men';—verified this day in me, who am here a specta-cle unto my Lord God, a spectacle unto His angels, and unto you men, satisfying myself to die as becometh a true Christian and Catholic man."

He was interrupted by cries from the gentlemen beneath, and turned a little, looking down to see what they wished. "You are not here to preach to the people," said Sir Francis Knowles, angrily, "but to confess yourself a traitor." Campion smiled and shook his head.

"No, no," he said: and then looking up and raising his voice,—"as to the treasons which have been laid to my charge, and for which I am come here to suffer, I desire you all to bear witness with me, that I am thereof altogether inno-cent."

There was a chorus of anger from the gentlemen, and one of them called up something that Anthony could not hear. Campion raised his eyebrows.

"Well, my lord," he cried aloud, and his voice instantly silenced again the noisy buzz of talk, "I am a Catholic man and a priest: in that faith have I lived, and in that faith do I intend to die. If you esteem my religion treason, then am I guilty; as for other treason, I never committed any, God is my judge. But you have now what you desire. I beseech you to have patience, and suffer me to speak a word or two for discharge of my conscience."

There was a furious burst of refusals from the officers.

"Well," said Campion, at last, looking straight out over the crowd, "it seems I may not speak; but this only will I say; that I am wholly innocent of all treason and conspiracy, as God is my judge; and I beseech you to credit me, for it is my last answer upon my death and soul. As for the jury I do not blame them, for they were ignorant men and easily deceived. I forgive all who have compassed my death or wronged me in any whit, as I hope to be forgiven; and I ask the forgiveness of all those whose names I spoke upon the rack."

Then he said a word or two more of explanation, such as he had said during his trial, for the sake of those Catholics whom this a concession of his had scandalised, telling them that he had had the promise of the Council that no harm should come to those whose names he revealed; and then was silent again, closing his eyes; and Anthony, as he watched him, saw his lips moving once more in prayer.

Then a harsh loud voice from behind the cart began to proclaim that the Queen punished no man for religion but only for treason. A fierce murmur of disagreement and protest began to rise from the crowd; and Anthony turning saw the faces of many near him frowning and pursing their lips, and there was a shout or two of denial here and there. The harsh voice ceased, and another began:

"Now, Mr. Campion," it cried, "tell us, What of the Pope? Do you renounce him?"

Campion opened his eyes and looked round.

"I am a Catholic," he said simply; and closed his eyes again for prayer, as the voice cried brutally:

"In your Catholicism all treason is contained."

Again a murmur from the crowd.

Then a new voice from the black group of ministers called out:

"Mr. Campion, Mr. Campion, leave that popish stuff, and say, 'Christ have mercy on me.'"

Again the priest opened his eyes.

"You and I are not one in religion, sir, wherefore I pray you content yourself. I bar none of prayer, but I only desire them of the household of faith to pray with me; and in mine agony to say one creed."

Again he closed his eyes.

"Pater noster qui es in cælis."...

"Pray in English, pray in English!" shouted a voice from the minister's group.

Once more the priest opened his eyes; and, in spite of the badgering, his eyes shone with humour and his mouth broke into smiles, so that a great sob of pity and love broke from Anthony.

"I will pray to God in a language that both He and I well understand."

"Ask her Grace's forgiveness, Mr. Campion, and pray for her, if you be her true subject."

"Wherein have I offended her? In this I am innocent. This is my last speech; in this give me credit—I have and do pray for her."

"Aha! but which queen?—for Elizabeth?"

"Ay, for Elizabeth, your queen and my queen, unto whom I wish a long quiet reign with all prosperity."

There was the crack of a whip, the scuffle of a horse's feet, a rippling movement over the crowd, and a great murmured roar, like the roar of the waves on a pebbly beach, as the horse's head began to move forward; and the priest's figure to sway and stagger on the jolting cart. Anthony shut his eyes, and the murmur and cries of the crowd grew louder and louder. Once more the deep sweet voice rang out, loud and penetrating:

"I die a true Catholic...."

Anthony kept his eyes closed, and his head bent, as great sobs began to break up out of his heart....

Ah! he was in his agony now! that sudden cry and silence from the crowd showed it. What was it he had asked? one creed?—

"I believe in God the Father Almighty." ...

The soft heavy murmur of the crowd rose and fell. Catholics were praying all round him, reckless with love and pity:

"Jesu, Jesu, save him! Be to him a Jesus!"...

"Mary pray! Mary pray!"...

"Credo in Deum Patrem omnipotentem."...

"Passus sub Pontio Pilato."...

"Crucified dead and buried."...

"The forgiveness of sins."...

"And the Life Everlasting."...

Anthony dropped his face forward on to his horse's mane.

Chapter Seven - A Message From The City

Sir Francis Walsingham sat in his private room a month after Father Campion's death.

He had settled down again now to his work which had been so grievously interrupted by his mission to France in connection with a new treaty between that country and England in the previous year. The secret detective service that he had inaugurated in England chiefly for the protection of the Queen's person was a vast and complicated business, and the superintendence of this, in addition to the other affairs of his office, made him an exceedingly busy man. England was honeycombed with mines and countermines both in the political and the religious world, and it needed all this man's brilliant and trained faculties to keep abreast with them. His spies and agents were everywhere; and not only in England: they circled round Mary of Scotland like flies round a wounded creature, seeking to settle and penetrate wherever an opening showed itself. These Scottish troubles would have been enough for any ordinary man; but Walsingham was indefatigable, and his agents were in every prison, lurking round corridors in private houses, found alike in thieves' kitchens and at gentlemen's tables.

Just at present Walsingham was anxious to give all the attention he could to Scottish affairs; and on this wet dreary Thursday morning in January as he sat before his bureau, he was meditating how to deal with an affair that had come to him from the heart of London, and how if possible to shift the conduct of it on to other shoulders.

He sat and drummed his fingers on the desk, and stared meditatively at the pigeon-holes before him. His was an interesting face, with large, melancholy, and almost fanatical eyes, and a poet's mouth and forehead; but it was probably exactly his imaginative faculties that enabled him to picture public affairs from the points of view of the very various persons concerned in them; and thereby to cope with the complications arising out of these conflicting interests.

He stroked his pointed beard once or twice, and then struck a hand-bell at his side; and a servant entered.

"If Mr. Lackington is below," he said, "show him here immediately," and the servant went out.

Lackington, sometime servant to Sir Nicholas Maxwell, had entered Sir Francis' service instead, at the same time that he had exchanged the Catholic for the Protestant religion; and he was now one of his most trusted agents. But he had been in so many matters connected with recusancy, that a large number of the papists in London were beginning to know him by sight; and the affairs were becoming more and more scarce in which he could be employed among Catholics with any hope of success. It was his custom to call morning by morning at Sir Francis' office and receive his instructions; and just now he had returned from business in the country. Presently he entered, closing the door behind him, and bowed profoundly to his master.

"I have a matter on hand, Lackington," said Sir Francis, without looking at him, and without any salutation beyond a glance and a nod as he entered,—"a matter which I have not leisure to look into, as it is not, I think, anything more than mere religion; but which might, I think, repay you for your trouble, if you can manage it in any way. But it is a troublesome business. These are the facts.

"No. 3 Newman's Court, in the City, has been a suspected house for some while. I have had it watched, and there is no doubt that the papists use it. I thought at first that the Scots were mixed up with it; but that is not so. Yesterday, a boy of twelve years old, left the house in the afternoon, and was followed to a number of houses, of which I will give you the list presently; and was finally arrested in Paul's Churchyard and brought here. I frightened him with talk of the rack; and I think I have the truth out of him now; I have tested him in the usual ways—and all that I can find is that the house is used for mass now and then; and that he was going to the papists' houses yesterday to bid them come for next Sunday morning. But he was stopped too soon: he had not yet told the priest to come. Now unless the priest is told to-night by one whom he trusts, there will be no mass on Sunday, and the nest of papists will escape us. It is of no use to send the boy; as he will betray all by his behaviour, even if we frighten him into saying what we wish to the priest. I suppose it is of no use your going to the priest and feigning to be a Catholic messenger; and I cannot at this moment see what is to be done. If there were anything beyond mere religion in this, I would spare no pains to hunt them out; but it is not worth my while. Yet there is the reward; and if you think that you can do anything, you can have it for your pains. I can spare you till Monday, and of course you shall have what men you will to surround the house and take them at mass, if you can but get the priest there."

"Thank you, sir," said Lackington deferentially. "Have I your honour's leave to see the boy in your presence?"

Walsingham struck the bell again.

"Bring the lad that is locked in the steward's parlour," he said, when the servant appeared.—"Sit down, Lackington, and examine him when he comes."

And Sir Francis took down some papers from a pigeon-hole, sorted out one or two, and saying, "Here are his statements," handed them to the agent; who began to glance through them at once. Walsingham then turned to his table again and began to go on with his letters.

In a moment or two the door opened, and a little lad of twelve years old, came in, followed by the servant.

"That will do," said Walsingham, without looking up; "You can leave him here," and the servant went out. The boy stood back against the wall by the door, his face was white and his eyes full of horror, and he looked in a dazed way at the two men.

"What is your name, boy?" began Lackington in a sharp, judicial tone.

"John Belton," said the lad in a tremulous voice.

"And you are a little papist?" asked the agent.

"No sir; a Protestant."

"Then how is it that you go on errands for papists?"

"I am a servant, sir," said the boy imploringly.

Lackington turned the papers over for a moment or two.

"Now you know," he began again in a threatening voice, "that this gentleman has power to put you on the rack; you know what that is?"

The boy nodded in mute white-faced terror.

"Well, now, he will hear all you say; and will know whether you say the truth or not. Now tell me if you still hold to what you said yesterday."

And then Lackington with the aid of the papers ran quickly over the story that Sir Francis had related. "Now do you mean to tell me, John Belton," he added, "that you, a Protestant, and a lad of twelve, are employed on this work by papists, to gather them for mass?"

The boy looked at him with the same earnest horror.

"Yes, sir, yes, sir," he said, and there was a piteous sob in his voice. "Indeed it is all true: but I do not often go on these messages for my master. Mr. Roger generally goes: but he is sick."

"Oho!" said Lackington, "you did not say that yesterday."

The boy was terrified.

"No, sir," he cried out miserably, "the gentleman did not ask me."

"Well, who is Mr. Roger? What is he like?"

"He is my master's servant, sir; and he wears a patch over his eye; and stutters a little in his speech."

These kinds of details were plainly beyond a frightened lad's power of invention, and Lackington was more satisfied.

"And what was the message that you were to give to the folk and the priest?"

"Please, sir, 'Come, for all things are now ready.'"

This was such a queer answer that Lackington gave an incredulous exclamation.

"It is probably true," said Sir Francis, without looking up from his letters; "I have come across the same kind of cypher, at least once before."

"Thank you, sir," said the agent. "And now, my boy, tell me this. How did you know what it meant?"

"Please, sir," said the lad, a little encouraged by the kinder tone, "I have noticed that twice before when Mr. Roger could not go, and I was sent with the same message, all the folks and the priest came on the next Sunday; and I think that it means that all is safe, and that they can come."

"You are a sharp lad," said the spy approvingly. "I am satisfied with you."

"Then, sir, may I go home?" asked the boy with hopeful entreaty in his voice.

"Nay, nay," said the other, "I have not done with you yet. Answer me some more questions. Why did you not go to the priest first?"

"Because I was bidden to go to him last," said the boy. "If I had been to all the other houses by five o'clock last night, then I was to meet the priest at Papists' Corner in Paul's Church. But if I had not done them—as I had not,—then I was to see the priest to-night at the same place."

Lackington mused a moment.

"What is the priest's name?" he asked.

"Please, sir, Mr. Arthur Oldham."

The agent gave a sudden start and a keen glance at the boy, and then smiled to himself; then he meditated, and bit his nails once or twice.

"And when was Mr. Roger taken ill?"

"He slipped down at the door of his lodging and hurt his foot, at dinner-time yesterday; and he could not walk."

"His lodging? Then he does not sleep in the house?"

"No sir; he sleeps in Stafford Alley, round the corner."

"And where do you live?"

"Please, sir, I go home to my mother nearly every night; but not always."

"And where does your mother live?"

"Please, sir, at 4 Bell's Lane."

Lackington remained deep in thought, and looked at the boy steadily for a minute or two.

"Now, sir; may I go?" he asked eagerly.

Lackington paid no attention, and he repeated his question. The agent still did not seem to hear him, but turned to Sir Francis, who was still at his letters.

"That is all, sir, for the present," he said. "May the boy be kept here till Monday?"

The lad broke out into wailing; but Lackington turned on him a face so savage that his whimpers died away into horror-stricken silence.

"As you will," said Sir Francis, pausing for a moment in his writing, and striking the bell again; and, on the servant's appearance, gave orders that John Belton should be taken again to the steward's parlour until further directions were received. The boy went sobbing out and down the passage again under the servant's charge, and the door closed.

"And the mother?" asked Walsingham abruptly, pausing with pen upraised.

"With your permission, sir, I will tell her that her boy is in trouble, and that if his master sends to inquire for him, she is to say he is sick upstairs."

"And you will report to me on Monday?"

"Yes, sir; by then I shall hope to have taken the crew."

Sir Francis nodded his head sharply, and the pen began to fly over the paper again; as Lackington slipped out.

Anthony Norris was passing through the court of Lambeth House in the afternoon of the same day, when the porter came to him and said there was a child waiting in the Lodge with a note for him; and would Master Norris kindly come to see her. He found a little girl on the bench by the gate, who stood up and curtseyed as the grand gentleman came striding in; and handed him a note which he opened at once and read.

"For the love of God," the note ran, "come and aid one who can be of service to a friend: follow the little maid Master Norris, and she will bring you to me. If you have any friends at Great Keynes, for the love you bear to them, come quickly."

Anthony turned the note over; it was unsigned, and undated. On his inquiry further from the little girl, she said she knew nothing about the writer; but that a gentleman had given her the note and told her to bring it to Master Anthony Norris at Lambeth House; and that she was to take him to a house that she knew in the city; she did not know the name of the house, she said.

It was all very strange, thought Anthony, but evidently here was some one who knew about him; the reference to Great Keynes made him think uneasily of Isabel and wonder whether any harm had happened to her, or whether any danger threatened. He stood musing with the note between his fingers, and then told the child to go straight down to Paul's Cross and await him there, and he would follow immediately. The child ran off, and Anthony went round to the stables to get his horse. He rode straight down to the city and put up his horse in the Bishop's stables, and then went round with his riding-whip in his hand to Paul's Cross.

It was a dull miserable afternoon, beginning to close in with a fine rain falling, and very few people were about; and he found the child crouched up against the pulpit in an attempt to keep dry.

"Come," he said kindly, "I am ready; show me the way."

The child led him along by the Cathedral through the churchyard, and then by winding passages, where Anthony kept a good look-out at the corners; for a stab in the back was no uncommon thing for a well-dressed gentleman off his guard. The houses overhead leaned so nearly together that the darkening sky disappeared altogether now and then; at one spot Anthony caught a glimpse high up of Bow Church spire; and after a corner or two the child stopped before a doorway in a little flagged court.

"It is here," she said; and before Anthony could stop her she had slipped away and disappeared through a passage.

He looked at the house. It was a tumble-down place; the door was heavily studded with nails, and gave a most respectable air to the house: the leaded windows were just over his head, and tightly closed. There was an air of mute discretion and silence about the place that roused a vague discomfort in Anthony's mind; he slipped his right hand into his belt and satisfied himself that the hilt of his knife was within reach. Overhead the hanging windows and eaves bulged out on all sides; but there was no one to be seen; it seemed a place that had slipped into a backwater of the humming stream of the city. The fine rain still falling added to the dismal aspect of the little court. He looked round once more; and then rapped sharply at the door to which the child had pointed.

There was silence for at least a minute; then as he was about to knock again there was a faint sound overhead, and he looked up in time to see a face swiftly withdrawn from one of the windows. Evidently an occupant of the house had been examining the visitor. Then shuffling footsteps came along a passage within, and a light shone under the door. There was a noise of bolts being withdrawn, and the rattle of a chain; and then the handle turned and the door opened slowly inwards, and an old woman stood there holding an oil lamp over her head. This was not very formidable at any rate.

"I have been bidden to come here," he said, "by a letter delivered to me an hour ago."

"Ah," said the old woman, and looked at him peeringly, "then you are for Mr. Roger?"

"I daresay," said Anthony, a little sharply. He was not accustomed to be treated like this. The old woman still looked at him suspiciously; and then, as Anthony made a movement of impatience, she stepped back.

"Come in, sir," she said.

He stepped in, and she closed and fastened the door again behind him; and then, holding the oil-lamp high over her head, she advanced in her slippers towards the staircase, and Anthony followed. On the stairs she turned once to see if he was coming, and beckoned him on with a movement of her head. Anthony looked about him as he went up: there was nothing remarkable or suspicious about the house in any way. It was cleaner than he had been led to expect by its outside aspect; wainscoted to the ceiling with oak; and the stairs were strong and well made. It was plainly a very tolerably respectable place; and Anthony began to think from its appearance that he had been admitted at the back door of some well-to-do house off Cheapside. The banisters were carved with some distinction; and there were the rudimentary elements of linen-pattern design on the panels that lined the opposite walls up to the height of the banisters. The woman went up and up, slowly, panting a little; at each landing she turned and glanced back to see that her companion was following: all the doors that they passed were discreetly shut; and the house was perfectly dark except for the flickering light of the woman's lamp, and silent except for the noise of the footsteps and the rush of a mouse now and then behind the woodwork.

At the third landing she stopped, and came close up to Anthony.

"That is the door," she whispered hoarsely; and pointed with her thumb towards a doorway that was opposite the staircase. "Ask for Master Roger."

And then without saying any more, she set the lamp down on the flat head of the top banister and herself began to shuffle downstairs again into the dark house.

Anthony stood still a moment, his heart beating a little. What was this strange errand? and Isabel! what had she to do with this house buried away in the courts of the great city? As he waited he heard a door close somewhere behind him, and the shuffling footsteps had ceased. He touched the hilt of his knife once again to give himself courage; and then walked slowly across and rapped on the door. Instantly a voice full of trembling expectancy, cried to him to come in; he turned the handle and stepped into the fire-lit room.

It was extremely poorly furnished; a rickety table stood in the centre with a book or two and a basin with a plate, a saucepan hissed and bubbled on the fire; in the corner near the window stood a poor bed; and to this Anthony's attention was immediately directed by a voice that called out hoarsely:

"Thank God, sir, thank God, sir, you have come! I feared you would not."

Anthony stepped towards it wondering and expectant, but reassured. Lying in the bed, with clothes drawn up to the chin was the figure of a man. There was no light in the room, save that given by the leaping flames on the hearth; and Anthony could only make out the face of a man with a patch over one eye; the man stretched a hand over the bed clothes as he came near, and Anthony took it, a little astonished, and received a strong trembling grip of apparent excitement and relief: "Thank God, sir!" the man said again, "but there is not too much time."

"How can I serve you?" said Anthony, sitting on a chair near the bedside. "Your letter spoke of friends at Great Keynes. What did you mean by that?"

"Is the d-door closed, sir?" asked the man anxiously; stuttering a little as he spoke.

Anthony stepped up and closed it firmly; and then came back and sat down again.

"Well then, sir; I believe you are a friend of the priest Mr. M-Maxwell's."

Anthony shook his head.

"There is no priest of that name that I know."

"Ah," cried the man, and his voice shook, "have I said too much? You are Mr. Anthony Norris of the Dower House, and of the Archbishop's household?"...

"I am," said Anthony, "but yet—"

"Well, well," said the man, "I must go forward now. He whom you know as Mr. James Maxwell is a Catholic p-priest, known to many under the name of Mr. Arthur Oldham. He is in sore d-danger."

Anthony was silent through sheer astonishment. This then was the secret of the mystery that had hung round Mr. James so long. The few times he had met him in town since his return, it had been on the tip of his tongue to ask what he did there, and why Hubert was to be master of the Hall; but there was something in Mr. James' manner that made the asking of such a question appear an impossible liberty; and it had remained unasked.

"Well," said the man in bed, in anxious terror, "there is no mistake, is there?"

"I said nothing," said Anthony, "for astonishment; I had no idea that he was a priest. And how can I serve him?"

"He is in sore danger," said the man, and again and again there came the stutter. "Now I am a Catholic: you see how much I t-trust you sir. I am the only one in this house. I was entrusted with a m-message to Mr. Maxwell to put him on his guard against a danger that threatens him. I was to meet him this very evening at five of the clock; and this afternoon as I left my room, I slipped and so hurt my foot that I cannot put it to the ground. I dared not send a l-letter to Mr. Maxwell, for fear the child should be followed; I dared not send to another Catholic; nor indeed did I know where to find one whom Mr. M-Maxwell would know and trust, as he is new to us here; but I had heard him speak of his friend Mr. Anthony Norris, who was at Lambeth House; and I determined, sir, to send the child to you; and ask you to do this service for your friend; for an officer of the Archbishop's household is beyond suspicion. N-now, sir, will you do this service? If you do it not, I know not where to turn for help."

Anthony was silent. He felt a little uneasy. Supposing that there was sedition mixed up in this! How could he trust the man's story? How could he be certain in fact that he was a Catholic at all? He looked at him keenly in the fire-light.

The man's one eye shone in deep anxiety, and his forehead was wrinkled; and he passed his hand nervously over his mouth again and again.

"How can I tell," said Anthony, "that all this is true?"

The man with an impatient movement unfastened his shirt at the neck and drew up on a string that was round his neck a little leather case.

"Th-there, sir," he stammered, drawing the string over his head. "T-take that to the fire and see what it is."

Anthony took it curiously, and holding it close to the fire drew off the little case; there was the wax medal stamped with the lamb, called Agnus Dei.

"Th-there," cried the man from the bed, "now I have p-put myself in your hands—and if more is w-wanted—" and as Anthony came back holding the medal, the man fumbled beneath the pillow and drew out a rosary.

"N-now, sir, do you believe me?"

It was felony to possess these things and Anthony had no more doubts.

"Yes," he said, "and I ask your pardon." And he gave back the Agnus Dei. "But there is no sedition in this?"

"N-none, sir, I give you my word," said the man, apparently greatly relieved, and sinking back on his pillow. "I will tell you all, and you can judge for yourself; but you will promise to be secret." And when Anthony had given his word, he went on.

"M-Mass was to have been said in Newman's Court on Sunday, at number 3, but that c-cursed spy Walsingham, hath had wind of it. His men have been lurking round there; and it is not safe. However, there is no need to say that to Mr. Maxwell; he will understand enough if you will give him a message of half a dozen words from me,—Mr. Roger. You can tell him that you saw me, if you wish to. But ah! sir, you give me your word to say no more to any one, not even to Mr. Maxwell himself, for it is in a public place. And then I will tell you the p-place and the m-message; but we must be swift, because the time is near; it is at five of the clock that he will look for a messenger."

"I give you my word," said Anthony.

"Well, sir, the place is Papists' Corner in the Cathedral, and the words are these, 'Come, for all things are now ready.' You know sir, that we Catholics go in fear of our lives, and like the poor hares have to double and turn if we would escape. If any overhears that message, he will never know it to be a warning. And it was for that that I asked your word to say no more than your message, with just the word that you had seen me yourself. You may tell him, of course sir, that Mr. Roger had a patch over his eye and st-stuttered a little in his speech; and he will know it is from me then. Now, sir, will you tell me what the message is, and the place, to be sure that you know them; and then, sir, it will be time to go; and God bless you, sir. God bless you for your kindness to us poor papists!"

The man seized Anthony's gloved hand and kissed it fervently once or twice.

Anthony repeated his instructions carefully. He was more touched than he cared to show by the evident gratitude and relief of this poor terrified Catholic.

"Th-that is right, sir; that is right; and now, sir, if you please, be gone at once; or the Father will have left the Cathedral. The child will be in the court below to show you the way out to the churchyard. God bless you, sir; and reward you for your kindness!"

And as Anthony went out of the room he heard benedictions mingled with sobs following him. The woman was nowhere to be seen; so he took the oil-lamp from the landing, and found his way downstairs again, unfastened the front door, and went out, leaving the lamp on the floor. The child was leaning against the wall opposite; he could just see the glimmer of her face in the heavy dusk.

"Come, my child," he said, "show me the way to the churchyard."

She came forward, and he began to follow her out of the little flagged court. He turned round as he left the court and saw high up against the blackness overhead a square of window lighted with a glow from within; and simultaneously there came the sound of bolts being shut in the door that he had just left. Evidently the old woman had been on the watch, and was now barring the door behind him.

It wanted courage to do as Anthony was doing, but he was not lacking in that; it was not a small matter to go to Papists' Corner and give a warning to a Catholic priest: but firstly, James Maxwell was his friend, and in danger: secondly, Anthony had no sympathy with religious persecution; and thirdly, as has been seen, the last year had made a really deep impression upon him: he was more favourably inclined to the Catholic cause than he had ever imagined to be possible.

As he followed the child through the labyrinth of passages, passing every now and then the lighted front of a house, or a little group of idlers (for the rain had now ceased) who stared to see this gentleman in such company, his head was whirling with questions and conjectures. Was it not after all a dishonourable act to the Archbishop in whose service he was, thus to take the side of the Papists? But that it was too late to consider now.—How strange that James Maxwell was a priest! That of course accounted at once for his long absence, no doubt in the seminary abroad, and his ultimate return, and for Hubert's inheriting the estates. And then he passed on to reflect as he had done a hundred times before on this wonderful Religion that allured men from home and wealth and friends, and sent them rejoicing to penury, suspicion, hatred, peril, and death itself, for the kingdom of heaven's sake.

Suddenly he found himself in the open space opposite the Cathedral—the child had again disappeared.

It was less dark here; the leaden sky overhead still glimmered with a pale sunset light; and many house-windows shone out from within. He passed round the south side of the Cathedral, and entered the western door. The building was full of deep gloom only pricked here and there by an oil-lamp or two that would presently be extinguished when the Cathedral was closed. The air was full of a faint sound, made up from echoes of the outside world and the foot-steps of a few people who still lingered in groups here and there in the aisles, and talked among themselves. The col-umns rose up in slender bundles and faded into the pale gloom overhead; as he crossed the nave on the way to Pa-pists' Corner far away to the east rose the dark carving of the stalls against the glimmering stone beyond. It was like some vast hall of the dead; the noise of the footsteps seemed like an insolent intrusion on this temple of silence; and the religious stillness had an active and sombre character of its own more eloquent and impressive than all the tu-mult that man could make.

As Anthony came to Papists' Corner he saw a very tall solitary figure passing slowly from east to west; it was too dark to distinguish faces; so he went towards it, so that at the next turn they would meet face to face. When he was within two or three steps the man before him turned abruptly; and Anthony immediately put out his hand smiling.

"Mr. Arthur Oldham," he said.

The man started and peered curiously through the gloom at him.

"Why Anthony!" he exclaimed, and took his hand, "what is your business here?" And they began slowly to walk westwards together.

"I am come to meet Mr. Oldham," he said, "and to give him a message; and this is it, 'Come, for all things are now ready!'"

"My dear boy," said James, stopping short, "you must forgive me; but what in the world do you mean by that?"

"I come from Mr. Roger," said Anthony, "you need not be afraid. He has had an accident and sent for me."

"Mr. Roger?" said James interrogatively.

"Yes," said Anthony, "he hath a patch over one eye; and stutters somewhat."

James gave a sigh of relief.

"My dear boy," he said, "I cannot thank you enough. You know what it means then?"

"Why, yes," said Anthony.

"And you a Protestant, and in the Archbishop's household?"

"Why, yes," said Anthony, "and a Christian and your friend."

"God bless you, Anthony," said the priest; and took his hand and pressed it.

They were passing out now under the west door, and stood together for a moment looking at the lights down Ludgate Hill. The houses about Amen Court stood up against the sky to their right.

"I must not stay," said Anthony, "I must fetch my horse and be back at Lambeth for evening prayers at six. He is sta-bled at the Palace here."

"Well, well," said the priest, "I thank God that there are true hearts like yours. God bless you again my dear boy—and—and make you one of us some day!"

Anthony smiled at him a little tremulously, for the gratitude and the blessing of this man was dear to him; and after another hand grasp, he turned away to the right, leaving the priest still half under the shadow of the door looking after him.

He had done his errand promptly and discreetly.

Chapter Eight - The Massing-House

Newman's Court lay dark and silent under the stars on Sunday morning a little after four o'clock. The gloomy weather of the last three or four days had passed off in heavy battalions of sullen sunset clouds on the preceding evening, and the air was full of frost. By midnight thin ice was lying everywhere; pendants of it were beginning to form on the overhanging eaves; and streaks of it between the cobble-stones that paved the court. The great city lay in a frosty stillness as of death.

The patrol passed along Cheapside forty yards away from the entrance of the court, a little after three o'clock; and a watchman had cried out half an hour later, that it was a clear night; and then he too had gone his way. The court it-self was a little rectangular enclosure with two entrances, one to the north beneath the arch of a stable that gave on to Newman's Passage, which in its turn opened on to St. Giles' Lane that led to Cheapside; the other, at the further

106

end of the long right-hand side, led by a labyrinth of passages down in the direction of the wharfs to the west of London Bridge. There were three houses to the left of the entrance from Newman's Passage; the back of a ware-house faced them on the other long side with the door beyond; and the other two sides were respectively formed by the archway of the stable with a loft over it, and a blank high wall at the opposite end.

A few minutes after four o'clock the figure of a woman suddenly appeared soundlessly in the arch under the stables; and after standing there a moment advanced along the front of the houses till she reached the third door. She stood here a moment in silence, listening and looking towards the doorway opposite, and then rapped gently with her finger-nail eleven or twelve times. Almost immediately the door opened, showing only darkness within; she stepped in, and it closed silently behind her. Then the minutes slipped away again in undisturbed silence. At about twenty minutes to five the figure of a very tall man dressed as a layman slipped in through the door that led towards the river, and advanced to the door where he tapped in the same manner as the woman before him, and was admitted at once. After that people began to come more frequently, some hesitating and looking about them as they entered the court, some slipping straight through without a pause, and going to the door, which opened and shut noiselessly as each tapped and was admitted. Sometimes two or three would come together, sometimes singly; but by five o'clock about twenty or thirty persons had come and been engulfed by the blackness that showed each time the door opened; while no glimmer of light from any of the windows betrayed the presence of any living soul within. At five o'clock the stream stopped. The little court lay as silent under the stars again as an hour before. It was a night of breathless stillness; there was no dripping from the eaves; no sound of wheels or hoofs from the city; only once or twice came the long howl of a dog across the roofs.

Ten minutes passed away.

Then without a sound a face appeared like a pale floating patch in the dark door that opened on to the court. It remained hung like a mask in the darkness for at least a minute; and then a man stepped through on to the cobble-stones. Something on his head glimmered sharply in the starlight; and there was the same sparkle at the end of a pole that he carried in his hand; he turned and nodded; and three or four men appeared behind him.

Then out of the darkness of the archway at the other end of the court appeared a similar group. Once a man slipped on the frozen stones and cursed under his breath, and the leader turned on him with a fierce indrawing of his breath; but no word was spoken.

Then through both entrances streamed dark figures, each with a steely glitter on head and breast, and with something that shone in their hands; till the little court seemed half full of armed men; but the silence was still formidable in its depth.

The two leaders came together to the door of the third house, and their heads were together; and a few sibilant consonants escaped them. The breath of the men that stood out under the starlight went up like smoke in the air. It was now a quarter-past five.

Three notes of a hand-bell sounded behind the house; and then, without any further attempt at silence, the man who had entered the court first advanced to the door and struck three or four thundering blows on it with a mace, and shouted in a resonant voice:

"Open in the Queen's Name."

The men relaxed their cautious attitudes, and some grounded their weapons; others began to talk in low voices; a small party advanced nearer their leaders with weapons, axes and halberds, uplifted.

By now the blows were thundering on the door; and the same shattering voice cried again and again:

"Open in the Queen's name; open in the Queen's name!"

The middle house of the three was unoccupied; but the windows of the house next the stable, and the windows in the loft over the archway, where the stable-boys slept, suddenly were illuminated; latches were lifted, the windows thrust open and heads out of them.

Then one or two more pursuivants came up the dark passage bearing flaming torches with them. A figure appeared on the top of the blank wall at the end, and pointed and shouted. The stable-boys in a moment more appeared in their archway, and one or two persons came out of the house next the stable, queerly habited in cloaks and hats over their night-attire.

The din was now tremendous; the questions and answers shouted to and fro were scarcely audible under the thunder that pealed from the battered door; a party had advanced to it and were raining blows upon the lock and hinges. The court was full of a ruddy glare that blazed on the half-armour and pikes of the men, and the bellowing and the crashes and the smoke together went up into the night air as from the infernal pit. It was a hellish transformation from the deathly stillness of a few minutes—a massacre of the sweet night silence. And yet the house where the little silent stream of dark figures had been swallowed up rose up high above the smoky cauldron, black, dark, and irre-sponsive.

There rose a shrill howling from behind the house, and the figure on the top of the wall capered and gesticulated again. Then footsteps came running up the passage, and a pursuivant thrust his way through to the leaders; and, in a moment or two, above the din a sharp word was given, and three or four men hurried out through the doorway by which the man had come. Almost at the same moment the hinges of the door gave way, the whole crashed inwards, and the attacking party poured into the dark entrance hall beyond. By this time the noise had wakened many in the houses round, and lights were beginning to shine from the high windows invisible before, and a concourse of people to press in from all sides. The approaches had all been guarded, but at the crash of the door some of the sentries round the nearer corners hurried into the court, and the crowd poured after them; and by the time that the officers and men had disappeared into the house, their places had been filled by the spectators, and the little court was again full of a swaying, seething, shouting mass of men, with a few women with hoods and cloaks among them—inquiries and information were yelled to and fro.

"It was a nest of papists—a wasp's nest was being smoked out—what harm had they done?—It was a murder; two women had had their throats cut.—No, no; it was a papists' den—a massing-house.—Well, God save her Grace and rid her of her enemies. With these damned Spaniards everywhere, England was going to ruin.—They had escaped at the back. No; they tried that way, but it was guarded.—There were over fifty papists, some said, in that house.—It was a plot. Mary was mixed up in it. The Queen was to be blown up with powder, like poor Darnley. The barrels were all stored there.—No, no, no! it was nothing but a massing-house.—Who was the priest?—Well, they would see him at Tyburn on a hurdle; and serve him right with his treasonable mummery.—No, no! they had had enough of blood.—Campion had died like a man; and an Englishman too—praying for his Queen."—The incessant battle and roar went up.

Meanwhile lights were beginning to shine everywhere in the dark house. A man with a torch was standing in a smoky glare half way up the stairs seen through the door, and the interior of the plain hall was illuminated. Then the leaded panes overhead were beginning to shine out. Steel caps moved to and fro; gigantic shadows wavered; the shadow of a halberd head went across a curtain at one of the lower windows.

A crimson-faced man threw open a window and shouted instructions to the sentry left at the door, who in answer shook his head and pointed to the bellowing crowd; the man at the window made a furious gesture and disappeared. The illumination began to climb higher and higher as the searchers mounted from floor to floor; thin smoke began to go up from one or two of the chimneys in the frosty air;—they were lighting straw to bring down any fugitives concealed in the chimneys. Then the sound of heavy blows began to ring out; they were testing the walls everywhere for hiding-holes; there was a sound of rending wood as the flooring was torn up. Then over the parapet against the stairs looked a steel-crowned face of a pursuivant. The crowd below yelled and pointed at first, thinking he was a fugitive; but he grinned down at them and disappeared.

Then at last came an exultant shout; then a breathless silence; then the crowd began to question and answer again. "They had caught the priest!—No, the priest had escaped,—damn him!—It was half a dozen women. No, no! they had had the women ten minutes ago in a room at the back.—What fools these pursuivants were!—They had found the chapel and the altar.—What a show it would all make at the trial!—Ah! ah! it was the priest after all."

Those nearest the door saw the man with the torch on the stairs stand back a little; and then a dismal little procession began to appear round the turn.

First came a couple of armed men, looking behind them every now and then; then a group of half a dozen women, whom they had found almost immediately, but had been keeping for the last few minutes in a room upstairs; then a couple more men. Then there was a little space; and then more constables and more prisoners. Each male prisoner was guarded by two men; the women were in groups. All these came out to the court. The crowd began to sway back against the walls, pointing and crying out; and a lane with living walls was formed towards the archway that opened into Newman's Passage.

When the last pursuivants who brought up the rear had reached the door, an officer, who had been leaning from a first-floor window with the pale face of Lackington peering over his shoulder, gave a sharp order; and the procession halted. The women, numbering fourteen or fifteen, were placed in a group with some eight men in hollow square round them; then came a dozen men, each with a pursuivant on either side. But plainly they were not all come; they were still waiting for something; the officer and Lackington disappeared from the window; and for a moment too, the crowd was quiet.

A murmur of excitement began to rise again, as another group was seen descending the stairs within. The officer came first, looking back and talking as he came; then followed two pursuivants with halberds, and immediately behind them, followed by yet two men, walked James Maxwell in crimson vestments all disordered, with his hands behind him, and his comely head towering above the heads of the guard. The crowd surged forward, yelling; and the men at the door grounded their halberds sharply on the feet of the front row of spectators. As the priest reached the door, a shrill cry either from a boy or a woman pierced the roaring of the mob. "God bless you, father," and as he heard it he turned and smiled serenely. His face was white, and there was a little trickle of blood run down across it from some wound in his head. The rest of the prisoners turned towards him as he came out; and again he smiled and nodded at them. And so the Catholics with their priest stood a moment in that deafening tumult of revilings, before the officer gave the word to advance.

Then the procession set forward through the archway; the crowd pressing back before them, like the recoil of a wave, and surging after them again in the wake. High over the heads of all moved the steel halberds, shining like grim emblems of power; the torches tossed up and down and threw monstrous stalking shadows on the walls as they passed; the steel caps edged the procession like an impenetrable hedge; and last moved the crimson-clad priest, as if in some church function, but with a bristling barrier about him; then came the mob, pouring along the narrow passages, jostling, cursing, reviling, swelled every moment by new arrivals dashing down the alleys and courts that gave on the thoroughfare; and so with tramp and ring of steel the pageant went forward on its way of sorrows.

Before six o'clock Newman's Court was empty again, except for one armed figure that stood before the shattered door of No. 3 to guard it. Inside the house was dark again except in one room high up where the altar had stood. Here the thick curtains against the glass had been torn down, and the window was illuminated; every now and again the shadows on the ceiling stirred a little as if the candle was being moved; and once the window opened and a pale smooth face looked out for a moment, and then withdrew again. Then the light disappeared altogether; and presently shone out in another room on the same floor; then again after an half an hour or so it was darkened; and again reappeared on the floor below. And so it went on from room to room; until the noises of the waking city began, and the stars paled and expired. Over the smokeless town the sky began to glow clear and brilliant. The crowing of cocks awoke here and there; a church bell or two began to sound far away over the roofs. The pale blue overhead grew more and more luminous; the candle went out on the first floor; the steel-clad man stretched himself and looked at the growing dawn.

A step was heard on the stairs, and Lackington came down, carrying a small valise apparently full to bursting. He looked paler than usual; and a little hollow-eyed for want of sleep. He came out and stood by the soldier, and looked about him. Everywhere the court showed signs of the night's tumult. Crumbled ice from broken icicles and trampled frozen pools lay powdered on the stones. Here and there on the walls were great smears of black from the torches, and even one or two torn bits of stuff and a crushed hat marked where the pressure had been fiercest. Most eloquent of all was the splintered door behind him, still held fast by one stout bolt, but leaning crookedly against the dinted wall of the interior.

"A good night's work, friend," said Lackington to the man. "Another hive taken, and here"—and he tapped his valise—"here I bear the best of the honey."

The soldier looked heavily at the bag. He was tired too; and he did not care for this kind of work.

"Well," said Lackington again, "I must be getting home safe. Keep the door; you shall be relieved in one hour."

The soldier nodded at him; but still said nothing; and Lackington lifted the valise and went off too under the archway.

That same morning Lady Maxwell in her room in the Hall at Great Keynes awoke early before dawn with a start. She had had a dream but could not remember what it was, except that her son James was in it, and seemed to be in trouble. He was calling on her to save him, she thought, and awoke at the sound of his voice. She often dreamt of him at this time; for the life of a seminary priest was laid with snares and dangers. But this dream seemed worse than all. She struck a light, and looked timidly round the room; it seemed still ringing with his voice. A great tapestry in a frame hung over the mantelpiece, Actæon followed by his hounds; the hunter panted as he ran, and was looking back over his shoulder; and the long-jawed dogs streamed behind him down a little hill.

So strong was the dream upon the old lady that she felt restless, and presently got up and went to the window and opened a shutter to look out. A white statue or two beyond the terrace glimmered in the dusk, and the stars were bright in the clear frosty night overhead. She closed the shutter and went back again to bed; but could not sleep.

Again and again as she was dozing off, something would startle her wide awake again: sometimes it was a glimpse of James' face; sometimes he seemed to be hurrying away from her down an endless passage with closed doors; he was dressed in something crimson. She tried to cry out, her voice would not rise above a whisper. Sometimes it was the dream of his voice; and once she started up crying out, "I am coming, my son." Then at last she awoke again at the sound of footsteps coming along the corridor outside; and stared fearfully at the door to see what would enter. But it was only the maid come to call her mistress. Lady Maxwell watched her as she opened the shutters that now glimmered through their cracks, and let a great flood of light into the room from the clear shining morning outside.

"It is a frosty morning, my lady," said the maid.

"Send one of the men down to Mistress Torridon," said Lady Maxwell, "and ask her to come here as soon as it is convenient. Say I am well; but would like to see her when she can come."

There was no priest in the house that Sunday, so there could be no mass; and on these occasions Mistress Margaret usually stayed at the Dower House until after dinner; but this morning she came up within half an hour of receiving the message.

She did not pretend to despise her sister's terror, or call it superstitious.

"Mary," she said, taking her sister's jewelled old fingers into her own two hands, "we must leave all this to the good God. It may mean much, or little, or nothing. He only knows; but at least we may pray. Let me tell Isabel; a child's prayers are mighty with Him; and she has the soul of a little child still."

So Isabel was told; and after church she came up to dine at the Hall and spend the day there; for Lady Maxwell was thoroughly nervous and upset: she trembled at the sound of footsteps, and cried out when one of the men came into the room suddenly.

Isabel went again to evening prayer at three o'clock; but could not keep her thoughts off the strange nervous horror at the Hall, though it seemed to rest on no better foundation than the waking dreams of an old lady—and her mind strayed away continually from the darkening chapel in which she sat, so near where Sir Nicholas himself lay, to the upstairs parlour where the widow sat shaken and trembling at her own curious fancies about her dear son.

Mr. Bodder's sermon came to an end at last; and Isabel was able to get away, and hurry back to the Hall. She found the old ladies as she had left them in the little drawing-room, Lady Maxwell sitting on the window-seat near the harp, preoccupied and apparently listening for something she knew not what. Mistress Margaret was sitting in a tall padded porter's chair reading aloud from an old English mystic, but her sister was paying no attention, and looked strangely at the girl as she came in. Isabel sat down near the fire and listened; and as she listened the memory of that other day, years ago, came to her when she sat once before with these two ladies in the same room, and Mistress Margaret read to them, and the letter came from Sir Nicholas; and then the sudden clamour from the village. So now she sat with terror darkening over her, glancing now and again at that white expectant face, and herself listening for the first far-away rumour of the dreadful interruption that she now knew must come.

"The Goodness of God," read the old nun, "is the highest prayer, and it cometh down to the lowest part of our need. It quickeneth our soul and bringeth it on life, and maketh it for to waxen in grace and virtue. It is nearest in nature; and readiest in grace: for it is the same grace that the soul seeketh, and ever shall seek till we know verily that He hath us all in Himself enclosed. For he hath no despite of that He hath made, nor hath He any disdain to serve us at the simplest office that to our body belongeth in nature, for love of the soul that He hath made to His own likeness. For as the body is clad in the clothes, and the flesh in the skin, and the bones in the flesh, and the heart in the whole, so are we, soul and body, clad in the Goodness of God, and enclosed. Yea, and more homely; for all these may waste and wear away, but the Goodness of God is ever whole; and more near to us without any likeness; for truly our Lover desireth that our soul cleave to Him with all its might, and that we be evermore cleaving to His goodness. For of all things that heart may think, this most pleaseth God, and soonest speedeth us. For our soul is so specially loved of Him that is highest, that it overpasseth the knowing of all creatures—"

"Hush," said Lady Maxwell suddenly, on her feet, with a lifted hand.

There was a breathless silence in the room; Isabel's heart beat thick and heavy and her eyes grew large with expectancy; it was a windless frosty night again, and the ivy outside on the wall, and the laurels in the garden seemed to be silently listening too.

"Mary, Mary," began her sister, "you——;" but the old lady lifted her hand a little higher; and silence fell again.

Then far away in the direction of the London road came the clear beat of the hoofs of a galloping horse.

Lady Maxwell bowed her head, and her hand slowly sank to her side. The other two stood up and remained still while the beat of the hoofs grew and grew in intensity on the frozen road.

"The front door," said Lady Maxwell.

Mistress Margaret slipped from the room and went downstairs; Isabel took a step or two forward, but was checked by the old lady's uplifted hand again. And again there was a breathless silence, save for the beat of the hoofs now close and imminent.

A moment later the front door was opened, and a great flood of cold air swept up the passages; the portrait of Sir Nicholas in the hall downstairs, lifted and rattled against the wall. Then came the clatter on the paved court; and the sound of a horse suddenly checked with the slipping up of hoofs and the jingle and rattle of chains and stirrups.

There were voices in the hall below, and a man's deep tones; then came steps ascending.

Lady Maxwell still stood perfectly rigid by the window, waiting, and Isabel stared with white face and great open eyes at the door; outside, the flame of a lamp on the wall was blowing about furiously in the draught.

Then a stranger stepped into the room; evidently a gentleman; he bowed to the two ladies, and stood, with the rime on his boots and a whip in his hand, a little exhausted and disordered by hard riding.

"Lady Maxwell?" he said.

Lady Maxwell bowed a little.

"I come with news of your son, madam, the priest; he is alive and well; but he is in trouble. He was taken this morning in his mass-vestments; and is in the Marshalsea."

Lady Maxwell's lips moved a little; but no sound came.

"He was betrayed, madam, by a friend. He and thirty other Catholics were taken all together at mass."

Then Lady Maxwell spoke; and her voice was dead and hard.

"The friend, sir! What was his name?"

"The traitor's name, madam, is Anthony Norris."

The room turned suddenly dark to Isabel's eyes; and she put up her hand and tore at the collar round her throat.

"Oh no, no, no, no!" she cried, and tottered a step or two forward and stood swaying.

Lady Maxwell looked from one to another with eyes that seemed to see nothing; and her lips stirred again.

Mistress Margaret who had followed the stranger up, and who stood now behind him at the door, came forward to Isabel with a little cry, with her hands trembling before her. But before she could reach her, Lady Maxwell herself came swiftly forward, her head thrown back, and her arms stretched out towards the girl, who still stood dazed and swaying more and more.

"My poor, poor child!" said Lady Maxwell; and caught her as she fell.

Chapter Nine - From Fulham to Greenwich

Anthony in London, strangely enough, heard nothing of the arrest on the Sunday, except a rumour at supper that some Papists had been taken. It had sufficient effect on his mind to make him congratulate himself that he had been able to warn his friend last week.

At dinner on Monday there were a few guests; and among them, one Sir Richard Barkley, afterwards Lieutenant of the Tower. He sat at the Archbishop's table, but Anthony's place, on the steward's left hand, brought him very close to the end of the first table where Sir Richard sat. Dinner was half way through, when Mr. Scot who was talking to Anthony, was suddenly silent and lifted his hand as if to check the conversation a moment.

"I saw them myself," said Sir Richard's voice just behind.

"What is it?" whispered Anthony.

"The Catholics," answered the steward.

"They were taken in Newman's Court, off Cheapside," went on the voice, "nearly thirty, with one of their priests, at mass, in his trinkets too—Oldham his name is."

There was a sudden crash of a chair fallen backwards, and Anthony was standing by the officer.

"I beg your pardon, Sir Richard Barkley," he said;—and a dead silence fell in the hall.—"But is that the name of the priest that was taken yesterday?"

Sir Richard looked astonished at the apparent insolence of this young official.

"Yes, sir," he said shortly.

"Then, then,——" began Anthony; but stopped; bowed low to the Archbishop and went straight out of the hall.

Mr. Scot was waiting for him in the hall when he returned late that night. Anthony's face was white and distracted; he came in and stood by the fire, and stared at him with a dazed air.

"You are to come to his Grace," said the steward, looking at him in silence.

Anthony nodded without speaking, and turned away.

"Then you cannot tell me anything?" said Mr. Scot. The other shook his head impatiently, and walked towards the inner door.

The Archbishop was sincerely shocked at the sight of his young officer, as he came in and stood before the table, staring with bewildered eyes, with his dress splashed and disordered, and his hands still holding the whip and gloves. He made him sit down at once, and after Anthony had drunk a glass of wine, he made him tell his story and what he had done that day.

He had been to the Marshalsea; it was true Mr. Oldham was there, and had been examined. Mr. Young had conducted it.—The house at Newman's Court was guarded: the house behind Bow Church was barred and shut up, and the people seemed gone away.—He could not get a word through to Mr. Oldham, though he had tried heavy bribery.—And that was all.

Anthony spoke with the same dazed air, in short broken sentences; but became more himself as the wine and the fire warmed him; and by the time he had finished he had recovered himself enough to entreat the Archbishop to help him.

"It is useless," said the old man. "What can I do? I have no power. And—and he is a popish priest! How can I interfere?"

"My lord," cried Anthony desperately, flushed and entreating, "all has been done through treachery. Do you not see it? I have been a brainless fool. That man behind Bow Church was a spy. For Christ's sake help us, my lord!"

Grindal looked into the lad's great bright eyes; sighed; and threw out his hands despairingly.

"It is useless; indeed it is useless, Mr. Norris. But I will tell you all that I can do. I will give you to-morrow a letter to Sir Francis Walsingham. I was with him abroad as you know, in the popish times of Mary: and he is still in some sort a friend of mine—but you must remember that he is a strong Protestant; and I do not suppose that he will help you. Now go to bed, dear lad; you are worn out."

Anthony knelt for the old man's blessing, and left the room.

The interview next day was more formidable than he had expected. He was at the Secretary's house by ten o'clock, and waited below while the Archbishop's letter was taken up. The servant came back in a few minutes, and asked him to follow; and in an agony of anxiety, but with a clear head again this morning, and every faculty tense, he went upstairs after him, and was ushered into the room where Walsingham sat at a table.

There was silence as the two bowed, but Sir Francis did not offer to rise, but sat with the Archbishop's letter in his hand, glancing through it again, as the other stood and waited.

"I understand," said the Secretary at last, and his voice was dry and unsympathetic,—"I understand, from his Grace's letter, that you desire to aid a popish priest called Oldham or Maxwell, arrested at mass on Sunday morning in Newman's Court. If you will be so good as to tell me in what way you desire to aid him, I can be more plain in my answer. You do not desire, I hope, Mr. Norris, anything but justice and a fair trial for your friend?"

Anthony cleared his throat before answering.

"I—he is my friend, as you say, Sir Francis; and—and he hath been caught by foul means. I myself was used, as I have little doubt, in his capture. Surely there is no justice, sir, in betraying a man by means of his friend." And Anthony described the ruse that had brought it all about.

Sir Francis listened to him coldly; but there came the faintest spark of amusement into his large sad eyes.

"Surely, Mr. Norris," he said, "it was somewhat simple; and I have no doubt at all that it all is as you say; and that the poor stuttering cripple with a patch was as sound and had as good sight and power of speech as you and I; but the plan was, it seems, if you will forgive me, not so simple as yourself. It would be passing strange, surely that the man, if a friend of the priest's, could find no Catholic to take his message; but not at all strange if he were his enemy. I do not think sincerely, sir, that it would have deceived me. But that is not now the point. He is taken now, fairly or foully, and—what was it you wished me to do?"

"I hoped," said Anthony, in rising indignation at this insolence, "that you would help me in some way to undo this foul unjustice. Surely, sir, it cannot be right to take advantage of such knavish tricks."

"Good Mr. Norris," said the Secretary, "we are not playing a game, with rules that must not be broken, but we are trying to serve justice"—his voice rose a little in sincere enthusiasm—"and to put down all false practices, whether in religion or state, against God or the prince. Surely the point for you and me is not, ought this gentleman to have been taken in the manner he was; but being taken, is he innocent or guilty?"

"Then you will not help me?"

"I will certainly not help you to defeat justice," said the other. "Mr. Norris, you are a young man; and while your friendship does your heart credit, your manner of forwarding its claims does not equally commend your head. I counsel you to be wary in your speech and actions; or they may bring you into trouble some day yourself. After all, as no doubt your friends have told you, you played what, as a minister of the Crown, I must call a knave's part in attempting to save this popish traitor, although by God's Providence, you were frustrated. But it is indeed going too far to beg me to assist you. I have never heard of such audacity!"

Anthony left the house in a fury. It was true, as the Archbishop had said, that Sir Francis Walsingham was a convinced Protestant; but he had expected to find in him some indignation at the methods by which the priest had been captured; and some desire to make compensation for it.

He went again to the Marshalsea; and now heard that James had been removed to the Tower, with one or two of the Catholics who had been in trouble before. This was serious news; for to be transferred to the Tower was often but the prelude to torture or death. He went on there, however, and tried again to gain admittance, but it was refused, and the doorkeeper would not even consent to take a message in. Mr. Oldham, he said, was being straitly kept, and it would be as much as his place was worth to admit any communication to him without an order from the Council.

When Anthony got back to Lambeth after this fruitless day, he found an imploring note from Isabel awaiting him; and one of the grooms from the Hall to take his answer back.

"Write back at once, dear Anthony," she wrote, "and explain this terrible thing, for I know well that you could not do what has been told us of you. But tell us what has happened, that we may know what to think. Poor Lady Maxwell is in the distress you may imagine; not knowing what will come to Mr. James. She will come to London, I think, this week. Write at once now, my Anthony, and tell us all."

Anthony scribbled a few lines, saying how he had been deceived; and asking her to explain the circumstances to Lady Maxwell, who no doubt would communicate them to her son as soon as was possible; he added that he had so far failed to get a message through the gaoler. He gave the note himself to the groom; telling him to deliver it straight into Isabel's hands, and then went to bed.

In the morning he reported to the Archbishop what had taken place.

"I feared it would be so," Grindal said. "There is nothing to be done but to commit your friend into God's hands, and leave him there."

"My Lord," said Anthony, "I cannot leave it like that. I will go and see my lord bishop to-day; and then, if he can do nothing to help, I will even see the Queen's Grace herself."

Grindal threw up his hands with a gesture of dismay.

"That will ruin all," he said. "An officer of mine could do nothing but anger her Grace."

"I must do my best," said Anthony; "it was through my folly he is in prison, and I could never rest if I left one single thing undone."

Just as Anthony was leaving the house, a servant in the royal livery dashed up to the gate; and the porter ran out after Anthony to call him back. The man delivered to him a letter which he opened then and there. It was from Mistress Corbet.

"What can be done," the letter ran, "for poor Mr. James? I have heard a tale of you from a Catholic, which I know is a black lie. I am sure that even now you will be doing all you can to save your friend. I told the man that told me, that he lied and that I knew you for an honest gentleman. But come, dear Mr. Anthony; and we will do what we can between us. Her Grace noticed this morning that I had been weeping; I put her off with excuses that she knows to be excuses; and she is so curious that she will not rest till she knows the cause. Come after dinner to-day; we are at Greenwich now; and we will see what may be done. It may even be needful for you to see her Grace yourself, and tell her the story. Your loving friend, Mary Corbet."

Anthony gave a message to the royal groom, to tell Mistress Corbet that he would do as she said, and then rode off immediately to the city. There was another disappointing delay as the Bishop was at Fulham; and thither he rode directly through the frosty streets under the keen morning sunshine, fretting at the further delay.

He had often had occasion to see the Bishop before, and Aylmer had taken something of a liking to this staunch young churchman; and now as the young man came hurrying across the grass under the elms, the Bishop, who was walking in his garden in his furs and flapped cap, noticed his anxious eyes and troubled face, and smiled at him kindly, wondering what he had come about. The two began to walk up and down together. The sunshine was beginning to melt the surface of the ground, and the birds were busy with breakfast-hunting.

"Look at that little fellow!" cried the Bishop, pointing to a thrush on the lawn, "he knows his craft."

The thrush had just rapped several times with his beak at a worm's earth, and was waiting with his head sideways watching.

"Aha!" cried the Bishop again, "he has him." The thrush had seized the worm who had come up to investigate the noise, and was now staggering backwards, bracing himself, and tugging at the poor worm, who, in a moment more was dragged out and swallowed.

"My lord," said Anthony, "I came to ask your pity for one who was betrayed by like treachery."

The Bishop looked astonished, and asked for the story; but when he heard who it was that had been taken, and under what circumstances, the kindliness died out of his eyes. He shook his head severely when Anthony had done.

"It is useless coming to me, sir," he said. "You know what I think. To be ordained beyond the seas and to exercise priestly functions in England is now a crime. It is useless to pretend anything else. It is revolt against the Queen's Grace and the peace of the realm. And I must confess I am astonished at you, Mr. Norris, thinking that anything ought to be done to shield a criminal, and still more astonished that you should think I would aid you in that. I tell you plainly that I am glad that the fellow is caught, for that I think there will be presently one less fire-brand in England. I know it is easy to cry out against persecution and injustice; that is ever the shallow cry of the mob; but this is not a religious persecution, as you yourself very well know. It is because the Roman Church interferes with the peace of the realm and the Queen's authority that its ordinances are forbidden; we do not seek to touch a man's private opinions. However, you know all that as well as I."

Anthony was raging now with anger.

"I am not so sure, my lord, as I was," he said. "I had hoped from your lordship at any rate to find sympathy for the base trick whereby my friend was snared; and I find it now hard to trust the judgment of any who do not feel as I do about it."

"That is insolence, Mr. Norris," said Aylmer, stopping in his walk and turning upon him his cold half-shut eyes, "and I will not suffer it."

"Then, my lord, I had better begone to her Grace at once."

"To her Grace!" exclaimed the Bishop.

"Appello Cæsarem," said Anthony, and was gone again.

As Anthony came into the courtyard of Greenwich Palace an hour or two later he found it humming with movement and noise. Cooks were going to and fro with dishes, as dinner was only just ending; servants in the royal livery were dashing across with messages; a few great hounds for the afternoon's baiting were in a group near one of the gateways, snuffing the smell of cookery, and howling hungrily now and again.

Anthony stopped one of the men, and sent him with a message to Mistress Corbet; and the servant presently returned, saying that the Court was just rising from dinner, and Mistress Corbet would see him in a parlour directly, if the gentleman would kindly follow him. A groom took his horse off to the stable, and Anthony himself followed the servant to a little oak-parlour looking on to a lawn with a yew hedge and a dial. He felt as one moving in a dream, bewildered by the rush of interviews, and oppressed by the awful burden that he bore at his heart. Nothing any longer seemed strange; and he scarcely gave a thought to what it meant when he heard the sound of trumpets in the court, as the Queen left the Hall. In five minutes more Mistress Corbet burst into the room; and her anxious look broke into tenderness at the sight of the misery in the lad's face.

"Oh, Master Anthony," she cried, seizing his hand, "thank God you are here. And now what is to be done for him?"

They sat down together in the window-seat. Mary was dressed in an elaborate rose-coloured costume; but her pretty lips were pale, and her eyes looked distressed and heavy.

"I have hardly slept," she said, "since Saturday night. Tell me all that you know."

Anthony told her the whole story, mechanically and miserably.

"Ah," she said, "that was how it was. I understand it now. And what can we do? You know, of course, that he has been questioned in the Tower."

Anthony turned suddenly white and sick.

"Not the—not the—" he began, falteringly.

She nodded at him mutely with large eyes and compressed lips.

"Oh, my God," said Anthony; and then again, "O God."

She took up one of his brown young hands and pressed it gently between her white slender ones.

"I know," she said, "I know; he is a gallant gentleman."

Anthony stood up shaking; and sat down again. The horror had goaded him into clearer consciousness.

"Ah! what can we do?" he said brokenly. "Let me see the Queen. She will be merciful."

"You must trust to me in this," said Mary, "I know her; and I know that to go to her now would be madness. She is in a fury with Pinart to-day at something that has passed about the Duke. You know Monsieur is here; she kissed him the other day, and the Lord only knows whether she will marry him or not. You must wait a day or two; and be ready when I tell you."

"But," stammered Anthony, "every hour we wait, he suffers."

"Oh, you cannot tell that," said Mary, "they give them a long rest sometimes; and it was only yesterday that he was questioned."

Anthony sat silently staring out on the fresh lawn; there was still a patch of frost under the shadow of the hedge he noticed.

"Wait here a moment," said Mary, looking at him; and she got up and went out.

Anthony still sat staring and thinking of the horror. Presently Mary was at his side again with a tall venetian wine-glass brimming with white wine.

"Here," she said, "drink this,"—and then—"have you dined to-day?"

"There was not time," said Anthony.

She frowned at him almost fiercely.

"And you come here fasting," she said, "to face the Queen! You foolish boy; you know nothing. Wait here," she added imperiously, and again she left the room.

Anthony still stared out of doors, twisting the empty glass in his hand; until again came her step and the rustle of her dress. She took the glass from him and put it down. A servant had followed her back into the room in a minute or two with a dish of meat and some bread; he set it on the table, and went out.

"Now," said Mary, "sit down and eat before you speak another word." And Anthony obeyed. The servant presently returned with some fruit, and again left them. All the while Anthony was eating, Mary sat by him and told him how she had heard the whole story from another Catholic at court; and how the Queen had questioned her closely the night before, as to what the marks of tears meant on her cheeks.

"It was when I heard of the racking," explained Mary, "I could not help it. I went up to my room and cried and cried. But I would not tell her Grace that: it would have been of no use; so I said I had a headache; but I said it in such a way as to prepare her for more. She has not questioned me again to-day; she is too full of anger and of the bear-baiting; but she will—she will. She never forgets; and then Mr. Anthony, it must be you to tell her. You are a pleasant-faced young man, sir, and she likes such as that. And you must be both forward and modest with her. She loves boldness, but hates rudeness. That is why Chris is so beloved by her. He is a fool, but he is a handsome fool, and a forward fool, and withal a tender fool; and sighs and cries, and calls her his Goddess; and says how he takes to his bed when she is not there, which of course is true. The other day he came to her, white-faced, sobbing like a frightened child, about the ring she had given Monsieur le petit grenouille. And oh, she was so tender with him. And so, Mr. Anthony, you must not be just forward with her, and frown at her and call her Jezebel and tyrant, as you would like to do; but you must call her Cleopatra, and Diana as well. Forward and backward all in one; that is the way she loves to be wooed. She is a woman, remember that."

"I must just let my heart speak," said Anthony, "I cannot twist and turn."

"Yes, yes," said Mary, "that is what I mean; but mind that it is your heart."

They went on talking a little longer; when suddenly the trumpets pealed out again. Mary rose with a look of consternation.

"I must fly," she said, "her Grace will be starting for the pit directly; and I must be there. Do you follow, Mr. Anthony; I will speak to a servant in the court about you." And in a moment she was gone.

When Anthony had finished the fruit and wine, he felt considerably refreshed; and after waiting a few minutes, went out into the court again, which he found almost deserted, except for a servant or two. One of these came up to him, and said respectfully that Mistress Corbet had left instructions that Mr. Norris was to be taken to the bear-pit; so Anthony followed him through the palace to the back.

It was a startlingly beautiful sight that his eyes fell upon when he came up the wooden stairs on to the stage that ran round the arena where the sport was just beginning. It was an amphitheatre, perhaps forty yards across; and the seats round it were filled with the most brilliant costumes, many of which blazed with jewels. Hanging over the top of the palisade were rich stuffs and tapestries. The Queen herself no doubt with Alençon was seated somewhere to the right, as Anthony could see by the canopy, with the arms of England and France embroidered upon its front; but he was too near to her to be able to catch even a glimpse of her face or figure. The awning overhead was furled, as the day was so fine, and the winter sunshine poured down on the dresses and jewels. All the Court was there; and Anthony recognised many great nobles here and there in the specially reserved seats. A ceaseless clangour of trumpets and cymbals filled the air, and drowned not only the conversation but the terrific noise from the arena where half a dozen great dogs, furious with hunger and excited as much by the crowds and the brazen music overhead as by the presence of their fierce adversary, were baiting a huge bear chained to a ring in the centre of the sand.

Anthony's heart sank a little as he noticed the ladies of the Court applauding and laughing at the abominable scene below, no doubt in imitation of their mistress who loved this fierce sport; and as he thought of the kind of heart to which he would have to appeal presently.

So through the winter afternoon the bouts went on; the band answered with harsh chords the death of the dogs one by one, and welcomed the collapse of the bear with a strident bellowing passage on the great horns and drums; and by the time it was over and the spectators rose to their feet, Anthony's hopes were lower than ever. Can there be any compassion left, he wondered, in a woman to whom such an afternoon was nothing more than a charming entertainment?

By the time he was able to get out of his seat and return to the courtyard, the procession had again disappeared, but he was escorted by the same servant to the parlour again, where Mistress Corbet presently rustled in.

"You must stay to-night," she said, "as late as possible. I wish you could sleep here; but we are so crowded with these Frenchmen and Hollanders that there is not a bed empty. The Queen is in better humour, and if the play goes well, it may be that a word said even to-night might reach her heart. I will tell you when it is over. You must be present. I will send you supper here directly."

Anthony inquired as to his dress.

"Nay, nay," said Mistress Corbet, "that will do very well; it is sober and quiet, and a little splashed: it will appear that you came in such haste that you could not change it. Her Grace likes to see a man hot and in a hurry sometimes; and not always like a peacock in the shade.—And, Master Anthony, it suits you very well."

He asked what time the play would be over, and that his horse might be saddled ready for him when he should want it; and Mary promised to see to it.

He felt much more himself as he supped alone in the parlour. The bewilderment had passed; the courage and spirit of Mary had infected his own, and the stirring strange life of the palace had distracted him from that dreadful brooding into which he had at first sunk.

When he had finished supper he sat in the window seat, pondering and praying too that the fierce heart of the Queen might be melted, and that God would give him words to say.

There was much else too that he thought over, as he sat and watched the illuminated windows round the little lawn on which his own looked, and heard the distant clash of music from the Hall where the Queen was supping in state. He thought of Mary and of her gay and tender nature; and of his own boyish love for her. That indeed had gone, or rather had been transfigured into a brotherly honour and respect. Both she and he, he was beginning to feel, had a more majestic task before them than marrying and giving in marriage. The religion which made this woman what she was, pure and upright in a luxurious and treacherous Court, tender among hard hearts, sympathetic in the midst of selfish lives—this Religion was beginning to draw this young man with almost irresistible power. Mary herself was doing her part bravely, witnessing in a Protestant Court to the power of the Catholic Faith in her own life; and he, what was he doing? These last three days were working miracles in him. The way he had been received by Walsingham and Aylmer, their apparent inability to see his point of view on this foul bit of treachery, the whole method of the Government of the day;—and above all the picture that was floating now before his eyes over the dark lawn, of the little cell in the Tower and the silent wrenched figure lying upon the straw—the "gallant gentleman" as Mary had called him, who had reckoned all this price up before he embarked on the life of a priest, and was even now paying it gladly and thankfully, no doubt—all this deepened the previous impressions that Anthony's mind had received; and as he sat here amid the stir of the royal palace, again and again a vision moved before him, of himself as a Catholic, and perhaps—But Isabel! What of Isabel? And at the thought of her he rose and walked to and fro.

Presently the servant came again to take Anthony to the Presence Chamber, where the play was to take place.

"I understand, sir, from Mistress Corbet," said the man, closing the door of the parlour a moment, "that you are come about Mr. Maxwell. I am a Catholic, too, sir, and may I say, sir, God bless and prosper you in this.—I—I beg your pardon, sir, will you follow me?"

The room was full at the lower end where Anthony had to stand, as he was not in Court dress; and he could see really nothing of the play, and hear very little either. The children of Paul's were acting some classical play which he did not know: all he could do was to catch a glimpse now and again of the protruding stage, with the curtains at the back, and the glitter of the armour that the boys wore; and hear the songs that were accompanied by a little string band, and the clash of the brass at the more martial moments. The Queen and the Duke, he could see, sat together immediately opposite the stage, on raised seats under a canopy; a group of halberdiers guarded them, and another small company of them was ranged at the sides of the stage. Anthony could see little more than this, and could hear only isolated sentences here and there, so broken was the piece by the talking and laughing around him. But he did not like to move as Mistress Corbet had told him to be present, so he stood there listening to the undertone talk about him, and watching the faces. What he did see of the play did not rouse him to any great enthusiasm. His heart was too heavy with his errand, and it seemed to him that the occasional glimpses he caught of the stage showed him a very tiresome hero, dressed in velvet doubled and hose and steel cap, strangely unconvincing, who spoke his lines pompously, and was as unsatisfactory as the slender shrill-voiced boy who, representing a woman of marvellous beauty and allurement, was supposed to fire the conqueror's blood with passion.

At last it ended; and an "orator" in apparel of cloth of gold, spoke a kind of special epilogue in rhyming metre in praise of the Virgin Queen, and then retired bowing.

Immediately there was a general movement; the brass instruments began to blare out, and an usher at the door desired those who were blocking the way to step aside to make way for the Queen's procession, which would shortly pass out. Anthony himself went outside with one or two more, and then stood aside waiting.

There was a pause and then a hush; and the sound of a high rating woman's voice, followed by a murmur of laughter. In a moment more the door was flung open again, and to Anthony's surprise Mistress Corbet came rustling out, as the people stepped back to make room. Her eyes fell on Anthony near the door, and she beckoned him to follow, and he went down the corridor after her, followed her silently along a passage or two, wondering why she did not speak, and then came after her into the same little oak parlour where he had supped. A servant followed them immediately with lighted candles which he set down and retired.

Anthony looked at Mistress Corbet, and saw all across her pale cheek the fiery mark of the five fingers of a hand, and saw too that her eyes were full of tears, and that her breath came unevenly.

"It is no use to-night," she said, with a sob in her voice; "her Grace is angry with me."

"And, and—" began Anthony in amazement.

"And she struck me," said Mary, struggling bravely to smile. "It was all my fault,"—and a bright tear or two ran down on to her delicate lace. "I was sitting near her Grace, and I could not keep my mind off poor James Maxwell; and I suppose I looked grave, because when the play was over, she beckoned me up, and—and asked how I liked it, and why I looked so solemn—for she would know—was it for Scipio Africanus, or some other man? And—and I was silent; and Alençon, that little frog-man burst out laughing and said to her Grace something—something shameful—in

116

French—but I understood, and gave him a look; and her Grace saw it, and, and struck me here, before all the Court, and bade me begone."

"Oh! it is shameful," said Anthony, furiously, his own eyes bright too, at the sight of this gallant girl and her humiliation.

"You cannot stay here, Mistress Corbet. This is the second time at least, is it not?"

"Ah! but I must stay," she said, "or who will speak for the Catholics? But now it is useless to think of seeing her Grace to-night. Yet to-morrow, maybe, she will be sorry,—she often is—and will want to make amends; and then will be our time, so you must be here to-morrow by dinner-time at least."

"Oh, Mistress Corbet," said the boy, "I wish I could do something."

"You dear lad!" said Mary, and then indeed the tears ran down.

Anthony rode back to Lambeth under the stars, anxious and dispirited, and all night long dreamed of pageants and progresses that blocked the street down which he must ride to rescue James. The brazen trumpets rang out whenever he called for help or tried to explain his errand; and Elizabeth rode by, bowing and smiling to all save him.

The next day he was at Greenwich again by dinner-time, and again dined by himself in the oak parlour, waited upon by the Catholic servant. He was just finishing his meal when in sailed Mary, beaming.

"I told you so," she said delightedly, "the Queen is sorry. She pinched my ear just now, and smiled at me, and bade me come to her in her private parlour in half an hour; and I shall put my petition then; so be ready, Master Anthony, be ready and of a good courage; for, please God, we shall save him yet."

Anthony looked at her, white and scared.

"What shall I say?" he said.

"Speak from your heart, sir, as you did to me yesterday. Be bold, yet not overbold. Tell her plainly that he is your friend; and that it was through your action he was betrayed. Say that you love the man. She likes loyalty.—Say he is a fine upstanding fellow, over six feet in height, with a good leg. She likes a good leg.—Say that he has not a wife, and will never have one. Wives and husbands like her not—in spite of le petit grenouille.—And look straight in her face, Master Anthony, as you looked in mine yesterday when I was a cry-baby. She likes men to do that.—And then look away as if dazzled by her radiancy. She likes that even more."

Anthony looked so bewildered by these instructions that Mary laughed in his face.

"Here then, poor lad," she said, "I will tell you in a word. Tell the truth and be a man;—a man! She likes that best of all; though she likes sheep too, such as Chris Hatton, and frogs like the Duke, and apes like the little Spaniard, and chattering dancing monkeys like the Frenchman—and—and devils, like Walshingham. But do you be a man and risk it. I know you can manage that." And Mary smiled at him so cheerfully, that Anthony felt heartened.

"There," she said, "now you look like one. But you must have some more wine first, I will send it in as I go. And now I must go. Wait here for the message." She gave him her hand, and he kissed it, and she went out, nodding and smiling over her shoulder.

Anthony sat miserably on the window-seat.

Ah! so much depended on him now. The Queen was in a good humour, and such a chance might never occur again;—and meantime James Maxwell waited in the Tower.

The minutes passed; steps came and went in the passage outside; and Anthony's heart leaped into his mouth at each sound. Once the door opened, and Anthony sprang to his feet trembling. But it was only the servant with the wine. Anthony took it—a fiery Italian wine, and drew a long draught that sent his blood coursing through his veins, and set his heart a-beating strongly again. And even as he set the cup down, the door was open again, and a bowing page was there.

"May it please you, sir, the Queen's Grace has sent me for you."

Anthony got up, swallowed in his throat once or twice, and motioned to go; the boy went out and Anthony followed. They went down a corridor or two, passing a sentry who let the well-known page and the gentleman pass without challenging; ascended a twisted oak staircase, went along a gallery, with stained glass of heraldic emblems in the windows, and paused before a door. The page, before knocking, turned and looked meaningly at Anthony, who stood with every pulse in his body racing; then the boy knocked, opened the door; Anthony entered, and the door closed behind him.

Chapter Ten - The Appeal to Caesar

The room was full of sunshine that poured in through two tall windows opposite, upon a motionless figure that sat in a high carved chair by the table, and watched the door. This figure dominated the whole room: the lad as he dropped on his knees, was conscious of eyes watching him from behind the chair, of tapestried walls, and a lute that lay on the table, but all those things were but trifling accessories to that scarlet central figure with a burnished halo of auburn hair round a shadowed face.

There was complete silence for a moment or two; a hound bayed in the court outside, and there came a far-away bang of a door somewhere in the palace. There was a rustle of silk that set every nerve of his body thrilling, and then a clear hard penetrating voice spoke two words.

"Well, sir?"

Anthony drew a breath, and swallowed in his throat.

"Your Grace," he said, and lifted his eyes for a moment, and dropped them again. But in the glimpse every detail stamped itself clear on his imagination. There she sat in vivid scarlet and cloth of gold, radiating light; with high puffed sleeves; an immense ruff fringed with lace. The narrow eyes were fixed on him, and as he now waited again, he knew that they were running up and down his figure, his dark splashed hose and his tumbled doublet and ruff.

"You come strangely dressed."

Anthony drew a quick breath again.

"My heart is sick," he said.

There was another slight movement.

"Well, sir," the voice said again, "you have not told us why you are here."

"For justice from my queen," he said, and stopped. "And for mercy from a woman," he added, scarcely knowing what he said.

Again Elizabeth stirred in her chair.

"You taught him that, you wicked girl," she said.

"No, madam," came Mary's voice from behind, subdued and entreating, "it is his heart that speaks."

"Enough, sir," said Elizabeth; "now tell us plainly what you want of us."

Then Anthony thought it time to be bold. He made a great effort, and the sense of constraint relaxed a little.

"I have been, your Grace, to Sir Francis Walsingham, and my lord Bishop of London, and I can get neither justice nor mercy from either; and so I come to your Grace, who are their mistress, to teach them manners."

"Stay," said Elizabeth, "that is insolence to my ministers."

"So my lord said," answered Anthony frankly, looking into that hard clear face that was beginning to be lined with age. And he saw that Elizabeth smiled, and that the face behind the chair nodded at him encouragingly.

"Well, insolence, go on."

"It is on behalf of one who has been pronounced a felon and a traitor by your Grace's laws, that I am pleading; but one who is a very gallant Christian gentleman as well."

"Your friend lacks not courage," interrupted Elizabeth to Mary.

"No, your Grace," said the other, "that has never been considered his failing."

Anthony waited, and then the voice spoke again harshly.

"Go on with the tale, sir. I cannot be here all day."

"He is a popish priest, your Majesty; and he was taken at mass in his vestments, and is now in the Tower; and he hath been questioned on the rack. And, madam, it is piteous to think of it. He is but a young man still, but passing strong and tall."

"What has this to do with me, sir?" interrupted the Queen harshly. "I cannot pardon every proper young priest in the kingdom. What else is there to be said for him?"

"He was taken through the foul treachery of a spy, who imposed upon me, his friend, and caused me all unknowing to say the very words that brought him into the net."

And then, more and more, Anthony began to lose his self-consciousness, and poured out the story from the beginning; telling how he had been brought up in the same village with James Maxwell; and what a loyal gentleman he was; and then the story of the trick by which he had been deceived. As he spoke his whole appearance seemed to change; instead of the shy and rather clumsy manner with which he had begun, he was now natural and free; he moved his hands in slight gestures; his blue eyes looked the Queen fairly in the face; he moved a little forward on his knees as he pleaded, and he spoke with a passion that astonished both Mary and himself afterwards when he thought of it, in spite of his short and broken sentences. He was conscious all the while of an intense external strain and pressure, as if he were pleading for his life, and the time was short. Elizabeth relaxed her rigid attitude, and leaned her chin on her hand and her elbow on the table and watched him, her thin lips parted, the pearl rope and crown on her head, and the pearl pendants in her ears moving slightly as she nodded at points in his story.

"Ah! your Grace," he cried, lifting his open hands towards her a little, "you have a woman's heart; all your people say so. You cannot allow this man to be so trapped to his death! Treachery never helped a cause yet. If your men cannot catch these priests fairly, then a-God's name, let them not catch them at all! But to use a friend, and make a Judas of

118

him; to make the very lips that have spoken friendly, speak traitorously; to bait the trap like that—it is devilish. Let him go, let him go, madam! One priest more or less cannot overthrow the realm; but one more foul crime done in the name of justice can bring God's wrath down on the nation. I hold that a trick like that is far worse than all the diso- bedience in the world; nay—how can we cry out against the Jesuits and the plotters, if we do worse ourselves? Mad- am, madam, let him go! Oh! I know I cannot speak as well in this good cause, as some can in a bad cause, but let the cause speak for itself. I cannot speak, I know."

"Nay, nay," said Elizabeth softly, "you wrong yourself. You have an honest face, sir; and that is the best recommenda- tion to me.

"And so, Minnie," she went on, turning to Mary, "this was your petition, was it; and this your advocate? Well, you have not chosen badly. Now, you speak yourself."

Mary stood a moment silent, and then with a swift movement came round the arm of the Queen's chair, and threw herself on her knees, with her hands upon the Queen's left hand as it lay upon the carved boss, and her voice was as Anthony had never yet heard it, vibrant and full of tears.

"Oh! madam, madam; this poor lad cannot speak, as he says; and yet his sad honest face, as your Grace said, is more eloquent than all words. And think of the silence of the little cell upstairs in the Tower; where a gallant gentleman lies, all rent and torn with the rack; and,—and how he listens for the footsteps outside of the tormentors who come to drag him down again, all aching and heavy with pain, down to that fierce engine in the dark. And think of his gal- lant heart, your Grace, how brave it is; and how he will not yield nor let one name escape him. Ah! not because he loves not your Grace nor desires to serve you; but because he serves your Grace best by serving and loving his God first of all.—And think how he cannot help a sob now and again; and whispers the name of his Saviour, as the pulleys begin to wrench and twist.—And,—and,—do not forget his mother, your Grace, down in the country; how she sits and listens and prays for her dear son; and cannot sleep, and dreams of him when at last she sleeps, and wakes screaming and crying at the thought of the boy she bore and nursed in the hands of those harsh devils. And—and, you can stop it all, your Grace, with one little word; and make that mother's heart bless your name and pray for you night and morning till she dies;—and let that gallant son go free, and save his racked body before it be torn asun- der;—and you can make this honest lad's heart happy again with the thought that he has saved his friend instead of slaying him. Look you, madam, he has come confessing his fault; saying bravely to your Grace that he did try to do his friend a service in spite of the laws, for that he held love to be the highest law. Ah! how many happy souls you can make with a word; because you are a Queen.—What is it to be a Queen!—to be able to do all that!—Oh! madam, be pitiful then, and show mercy as one day you hope to find it."

Mary spoke with an intense feeling; her voice was one long straining sob of appeal; and as she ended her tears were beginning to rain down on the hand she held between her own; she lifted it to her streaming face and kissed it again and again; and then dropped her forehead upon it, and so rested in dead silence.

Elizabeth swallowed in her throat once or twice; and then spoke, and her voice was a little choked.

"Well, well, you silly girl.—You plead too well."

Anthony irresistibly threw his hands out as he knelt.

"Oh! God bless your Grace!" he said; and then gave a sob or two himself.

"There, there, you are a pair of children," she said; for Mary was kissing her hand again and again. "And you are a pretty pair, too," she added. "Now, now, that is enough, stand up."

Anthony rose to his feet again and stood there; and Mary went round again behind the chair.

"Now, now, you have put me in a sore strait," said Elizabeth; "between you I scarcely know how to keep my word. They call me fickle enough already. But Frank Walsingham shall do it for me. He is certainly at the back of it all, and he shall manage it. It shall be done at once. Call a page, Minnie."

Mary Corbet went to the back of the room into the shadow, opened a door that Anthony had not noticed, and beck- oned sharply; in a moment or two a page was bowing before Elizabeth.

"Is Sir Francis Walsingham in the palace?" she asked,—"then bring him here," she ended, as the boy bowed again.

"And you too," she went on, "shall hear that I keep my word,"—she pointed towards the door whence the page had come.—"Stand there," she said, "and leave the door ajar."

Mary gave Anthony her hand and a radiant smile as they went together.

"Aha!" said Elizabeth, "not in my presence."

Anthony flushed with fury in spite of his joy.

They went in through the door, and found themselves in a tiny panelled room with a little slit of a window; it was used to place a sentry or a page within it. There were a couple of chairs, and the two sat down to wait.

"Oh, thank God!" whispered Anthony.

Again the harsh voice rang out from the open door.

"Now, now, no love-making within there!"

Mary smiled and laid her finger on her lips. Then there came the ripple of a lute from the outer room, played not unskilfully. Mary smiled again and nodded at Anthony. Then, a metallic voice, but clear enough and tuneful, began to sing a verse of the little love-song of Harrington's, Whence comes my love?

It suddenly ceased in the middle of the line, and the voice cried to some one to come in.

Anthony could hear the door open and close again, and a movement or two, which doubtless represented Walsingham's obeisance. Then the Queen's voice began again, low, thin, and distinct. The two in the inner room listened breathlessly.

"I wish a prisoner in the Tower to be released, Sir Francis; without any talk or to-do. And I desire you to do it for me."

There was silence, and then Walsingham's deep tones.

"Your Grace has but to command."

"His name is James Maxwell, and he is a popish priest."

A longer silence followed.

"I do not know if your Grace knows all the circumstances."

"I do, sir, or I should not interfere."

"The feeling of the people was very strong."

"Well, and what of that?"

"It will be a risk of your Grace's favour with them."

"Have I not said that my name was not to appear in the matter? And do you think I fear my people's wrath?"

There was silence again.

"Well, Sir Francis, why do you not speak?"

"I have nothing to say, your Grace."

"Then it will be done?"

"I do not see at present how it can be done, but doubtless there is a way."

"Then you will find it, sir, immediately," rang out the Queen's metallic tones.

(Mary turned and nodded solemnly at Anthony, with pursed lips.)

"He was questioned on the rack two days ago, your Grace."

"Have I not said I know all the circumstances? Do you wish me to say it again?"

The Queen was plainly getting angry.

"I ask your pardon, madam; but I only meant that he could not travel probably, yet awhile. He was on the rack for four hours, I understand."

(Anthony felt that strange sickness rise again; but Mary laid her cool hand on his and smiled at him.)

"Well, well," rasped out Elizabeth, "I do not ask impossibilities."

"They would cease to be so, madam, if you did."

(Mary within the little room put her lips to Anthony's ear:

"Butter!" she whispered.)

"Well, sir," went on the Queen, "you shall see that he has a physician, and leave to travel as soon as he will."

"It shall be done, your Grace."

"Very well, see to it."

"I beg your Grace's pardon; but what—"

"Well, what is it now?"

"I would wish to know your Grace's pleasure as to the future for Mr. Maxwell. Is no pledge of good behaviour to be exacted from him?"

"Of course he says mass again at his peril. Either he must take the oath at once, or he shall be allowed forty-eight hours' safe-conduct with his papers for the Continent."

"Your Grace, indeed I must remonstrate—"

Then the Queen's wrath burst out; they heard a swift movement, and the rap of her high heels as she sprang to her feet.

"By God's Son," she screamed, "am I Queen or not? I have had enough of your counsel. You presume, sir—" her ringed hand came heavily down on the table and they heard the lute leap and fall again.—"You presume on your position, sir. I made you, and I can unmake you, and by God I will, if I have another word of your counselling. Be gone, and see that it be done; I will not bid twice."

There was silence again; and they heard the outer door open and close.

Anthony's heart was beating wildly. He had sprung to his feet in a trembling excitement as the Queen had sprung to hers. The mere ring of that furious royal voice, even without the sight of her pale wrathful face and blazing eyes that Walsingham looked upon as he backed out from the presence, was enough to make this lad's whole frame shiver.

Mary apparently was accustomed to this; for she looked up at Anthony, laughing silently, and shrugged her shoulders.

Then they heard the Queen's silk draperies rustle and her pearls chink together as she sank down again and took up her lute and struck the strings. Then the metallic voice began again, with a little tremor in it, like the ground-swell after a storm; and she sang the verse through in which she had been interrupted:

"Why thus, my love, so kind bespeak
Sweet eye, sweet lip, sweet blushing cheek—
Yet not a heart to save my pain;
O Venus, take thy gifts again!
Make not so fair to cause our moan,
Or make a heart that's like your own."
The lute rippled away into silence.

Mary rose quietly to her feet and nodded to Anthony.

"Come back, you two!" cried the Queen.

Mary stepped straight through, the lad behind her.

"Well," said the Queen, turning to them and showing her black teeth in a smile. "Have I kept my word?"

"Ah! your Grace," said Mary, curtseying to the ground, "you have made some simple loving hearts very happy to-day—I do not mean Sir Francis'."

The Queen laughed.

"Come here, child," she said, holding out her glittering hand, "down here," and Mary sank down on the Queen's footstool, and leaned against her knee like a child, smiling up into her face; while Elizabeth put her hand under her chin and kissed her twice on the forehead.

"There, there," she said caressingly, "have I made amends? Am I a hard mistress?"

And she threw her left hand round the girl's neck and began to play with the diamond pendant in her ear, and to stroke the smooth curve of her cheek with her flashing fingers.

Anthony, a little on one side, stood watching and wondering at this silky tigress who raged so fiercely just now. Elizabeth looked up in a moment and saw him.

"Why, here is the tall lad here still," she said, "eyeing us as if we were monsters. Have you never yet seen two maidens loving one another, that you stare so with your great eyes? Aha! Minnie; he would like to be sitting where I am—is it not so, sir?"

"I would sooner stand where I am, madam," said Anthony, by a sudden inspiration, "and look upon your Grace."

"Why, he is a courtier already," said the Queen. "You have been giving him lessons, Minnie, you sly girl."

"A loyal heart makes the best courtier, madam," said Mary, taking the Queen's hand delicately in her own.

"And next to looking upon my Grace, Mr. Norris," said Elizabeth, "what do you best love?"

"Listening to your Grace," said Anthony, promptly.

Mary turned and flashed all her teeth upon him in a smile, and her eyes danced in her head.

Elizabeth laughed outright.

"He is an apt pupil," she said to Mary.

"—You mean the lute, sir?" she added.

"I mean your Grace's voice, madam. I had forgotten the lute."

"Ah, a little clumsy!" said the Queen; "not so true a thrust as the others."

"It was not for lack of good-will," said poor Anthony blushing a little. He felt in a kind of dream, fencing in language with this strange mighty creature in scarlet and pearls, who sat up in her chair and darted remarks at him, as with a rapier.

"Aha!" said the Queen, "he is blushing! Look, Minnie!" Mary looked at him deliberately. Anthony became scarlet at once; and tried a desperate escape.

"It is your livery, madam," he said.

Mary clapped her hands, and glanced at the Queen.

"Yes, Minnie; he does his mistress credit."

"Yes, your Grace; but he can do other things besides talk," explained Mary.

Anthony felt like a horse being shown off by a skilful dealer, but he was more at his ease too after his blush.

"Extend your mercy, madam," he said, "and bid Mistress Corbet hold her tongue and spare my shame."

"Silence, sir!" said the Queen. "Go on, Minnie; what else can he do?"

"Ah! your Grace, he can hawk. Oh! you should see his peregrine;—named after your Majesty. That shows his loyal heart."

"I am not sure of the compliment," said the Queen; "hawks are fierce creatures."

"It was not for her fierceness," put in Anthony, "that I named her after your Grace."

"Why, then, Mr. Norris?"

"For that she soars so high above all other creatures," said the lad, "and—and that she never stoops but to conquer."

Mary gave a sudden triumphant laugh, and glanced up, and Elizabeth tapped her on the cheek sharply.

"Be still, bad girl," she said. "You must not prompt during the lesson."

And so the talk went on. Anthony really acquitted himself with great credit, considering the extreme strangeness of his position; but such an intense weight had been lifted off his mind by the Queen's pardon of James Maxwell, that his nature was alight with a kind of intoxication.

All his sharpness, such as it was, rose to the surface; and Mary too was amazed at some of his replies. Elizabeth took it as a matter of course; she was accustomed to this kind of word-fencing; she did not do it very well herself: her royalty gave her many advantages which she often availed herself of; and her address was not to be compared for a moment with that of some of her courtiers and ladies. But still she was amused by this slender honest lad who stood there before her in his graceful splashed dress, and blushed and laughed and parried, and delivered his point with force, even if not with any extraordinary skill.

But at last she began to show signs of weariness; and Mary managed to convey to Anthony that it was time to be off. So he began to make his adieux.

"Well," said Elizabeth, "let us see you at supper to-night; and in the parlours afterwards.—Ah!" she cried, suddenly, "neither of you must say a word as to how your friend was released. It must remain the act of the Council. My name must not appear; Walsingham will see to that, and you must see to it too."

They both promised sincerely.

"Well, then, lad," said Elizabeth, and stretched out her hand; and Mary rose and stood by her. Anthony came up and knelt on the cushion and received the slender scented ringed hand on his own, and kissed it ardently in his gratitude. As he released it, it cuffed him gently on the cheek.

"There, there!" said Elizabeth, "Minnie has taught you too much, it seems."

Anthony backed out of the presence, smiling; and his last glimpse was once more of the great scarlet-clad figure with the slender waist, and the priceless pearls, and the haze of muslin behind that crowned auburn head, and the pale oval face smiling at him with narrow eyes—and all in a glory of sunshine.

He did not see Mary Corbet again until evening as she was with the Queen all the afternoon. Anthony would have wished to return to Lambeth; but it was impossible, after the command to remain to supper; so he wandered down along the river bank, rejoicing in the success of his petition; and wondering whether James had heard of his release yet.

Of course it was just a fly in the ointment that his own agency in the matter could never be known. It would have been at least some sort of compensation for his innocent share in the whole matter of the arrest. However, he was too happy to feel the sting of it. He felt, of course, greatly drawn to the Queen for her ready clemency; and yet there was something repellent about her too in spite of it. He felt in his heart that it was just a caprice, like her blows and caresses; and then the assumption of youth sat very ill upon this lean middle-aged woman. He would have preferred less lute-playing and sprightly innuendo, and more tenderness and gravity.

Mary had arranged that a proper Court-suit should be at his disposal for supper, and a room to himself; so after he had returned at sunset, he changed his clothes. The white silk suit with the high hosen, the embroidered doublet with great puffed and slashed sleeves, the short green-lined cloak, the white cap and feather, and the slender sword with the jewelled hilt, all became him very well; and he found too that Mary had provided him with two great emerald brooches of her own, that he pinned on, one at the fastening of the crisp ruff and the other on his cap.

He went to the private chapel for the evening prayer at half-past six; which was read by one of the chaplains; but there were very few persons present, and none of any distinction. Religion, except as a department of politics, was no integral part of Court life. The Queen only occasionally attended evening-prayer on week days; and just now she was too busy with the affair of the Duke of Alençon to spend unnecessary time in that manner.

When the evening prayer was over he followed the little company into the long gallery that led towards the hall, through which the Queen's procession would pass to supper; and there he attached himself to a group of gentlemen, some of whom he had met at Lambeth. While they were talking, the clang of trumpets suddenly broke out from the direction of the Queen's apartments; and all threw themselves on their knees and remained there. The doors were flung open by servants stationed behind them; and the wands advanced leading the procession; then came the trumpeters blowing mightily, with a drum or two beating the step; and then in endless profusion, servants and guards; gentlemen pensioners magnificently habited, for they were continually about the Queen's person; and at last, after an official or two bearing swords, came the Queen and Alençon together; she in a superb purple toilet with brocaded underskirt and high-heeled twinkling shoes, and breathing out essences as she swept by smiling; and he, a pathetic little brown man, pockmarked, with an ill-shapen nose and a head too large for his undersized body, in a rich velvet suit sparkling all over with diamonds.

As they passed Anthony he heard the Duke making some French compliment in his croaking harsh voice. Behind came the crowd of ladies, nodding, chattering, rustling; and Anthony had a swift glance of pleasure from Mistress Corbet as she went by, talking at the top of her voice.

The company followed on to the hall, behind the distant trumpets, and Anthony found himself still with his friends somewhere at the lower end—away from the Queen's table, who sat with Alençon at her side on a daïs, with the great folks about her. All through supper the most astonishing noise went on. Everyone was talking loudly; the servants ran to and fro over the paved floor; there was the loud clatter over the plates of four hundred persons; and, to crown all, a band in the musicians' gallery overhead made brazen music all supper-time. Anthony had enough entertainment himself in looking about the great banqueting-hall, so magnificently adorned with tapestries and armour and antlers from the park; and above all by the blaze of gold and silver plate both on the tables and on the sideboards; and by watching the army of liveried servants running to and fro incessantly; and the glowing colours of the dresses of the guests.

Supper was over at last; and a Latin grace was exquisitely sung in four parts by boys and men stationed in the musicians' gallery; and then the Queen's procession went out with the same ceremony as that with which it had entered. Anthony followed behind, as he had been bidden by the Queen to the private parlours afterwards; but he presently found his way barred by a page at the foot of the stairs leading to the Queen's apartments.

It was in vain that he pleaded his invitation; it was useless, as the young gentleman had not been informed of it. Anthony asked if he might see Mistress Corbet. No, that too was impossible; she was gone upstairs with the Queen's Grace and might not be disturbed. Anthony, in despair, not however unmixed with relief at escaping a further ordeal, was about to turn away, leaving the officious young gentleman swaggering on the stairs like a peacock, when down came Mistress Corbet herself, sailing down in her splendour, to see what was become of the gentleman of the Archbishop's house.

"Why, here you are!" she cried from the landing as she came down, "and why have you not obeyed the Queen's command?"

"This young gentleman," said Anthony, indicating the astonished page, "would not let me proceed."

"It is unusual, Mistress Corbet," said the boy, "for her Grace's guests to come without my having received instructions, unless they are great folk."

Mistress Corbet came down the last six steps like a stooping hawk, her wings bulged behind her; and she caught the boy one clean light cuff on the side of the head.

"You imp!" she said, "daring to doubt the word of this gentleman. And the Queen's Grace's own special guest!"

The boy tried still to stand on his dignity and bar the way, but it was difficult to be dignified with a ringing head and a scarlet ear.

"Stand aside," said Mary, stamping her little buckled foot, "this instant; unless you would be dragged by your red ear before the Queen's Grace. Come, Master Anthony."

So the two went upstairs together, and the lad called up after them bitterly:

"I beg your pardon, Mistress; I did not recognise he was your gallant."

"You shall pay for that," hissed Mary over the banisters.

They went along a passage or two, and the sound of a voice singing to a virginal began to ring nearer as they went, followed by a burst of applause.

"Lady Leicester," whispered Mary; and then she opened the door and they went in.

There were three rooms opening on one another with wide entrances, so that really one long room was the result. They were all three fairly full; that into which they entered, the first in the row, was occupied by some gentlemen-pensioners and ladies talking and laughing; some playing shove-groat, and some of them still applauding the song that had just ended. The middle room was much the same; and the third, which was a step higher than the others, was that in which was the Queen, with Lady Leicester and a few more. Lady Leicester had just finished a song, and was laying her virginal down. There was a great fire burning in the middle room, with seats about it, and here Mary Corbet brought Anthony. Those near him eyed him a little; but his companion was sufficient warrant of his respectability; and they soon got into talk, which was suddenly interrupted by the Queen's voice from the next room.

"Minnie, Minnie, if you can spare a moment from your lad, come and help us at a dance."

The Queen was plainly in high good-humour; and Mary got up and went into the Queen's room. Those round the fire stood up and pushed the seats back, and the games ceased in the third room; as her Grace needed spectators and applause.

Then there arose the rippling of lutes from the ladies in the next room, in slow swaying measure, with the gentle tap of a drum now and again; and the pavane began—a stately dignified dance; and among all the ladies moved the great Queen herself, swaying and bending with much grace and dignity. It was the strangest thing for Anthony to find himself here, a raven among all these peacocks, and birds of paradise; and he wondered at himself and at the strange humour of Providence, as he watched the shimmer of the dresses and the sparkle of the shoes and jewels, and the soft clouds of muslin and lace that shivered and rustled as the ladies stepped; the firelight shone through the wide doorway on this glowing movement, and groups of candles in sconces within the room increased and steadied the soft intensity of the light. The soft tingling instruments, with the slow tap-tap marking the measure like a step, seemed a translation into chord and melody of this stately tender exercise. And so this glorious flower-bed, loaded too with a wealth of essences in the dresses and the sweet-washed gloves, swayed under the wind of the music, bending and rising together in slow waves and ripples. Then it ceased; and the silence was broken by a quick storm of applause; while the dancers waited for the lutes. Then all the instruments broke out together in quick triple time; the stringed instruments supplying a hasty throbbing accompaniment, while the shrill flutes began to whistle and the drums to gallop;—there was yet a pause in the dance, till the Queen made the first movement;—and then the whole whirled off on the wings of a coranto.

It was bewildering to Anthony, who had never even dreamed of such a dance before. He watched first the lower line of the shoes; and the whole floor, in reality above, and in the mirror of the polished boards below, seemed scintillating in lines of diamond light; the heavy underskirts of brocade, puffed satin, and cloth of gold, with glimpses of foamy lace beneath, whirled and tossed above these flashing vibrations. Then he looked at the higher strata, and there was a tossing sea of faces and white throats, borne up as it seemed—now revealed, now hidden—on clouds of undulating muslin and lace, with sparkles of precious stones set in ruff and wings and on high piled hair.

He watched, fascinated, the faces as they appeared and vanished; there was every imaginable expression; the serious looks of one who took dancing as a solemn task, and marked her position and considered her steps; the wild gaiety of another, all white teeth and dimples and eyes, intoxicated by movement and music and colour, as men are by wine, and guided and sustained by the furious genius of the dance, rather than by intention of any kind. There was the courtly self-restraint of one tall beauty, who danced as a pleasant duty and loved it, but never lost control of her own bending, slender grace; ah! and there was the oval face crowned with auburn hair and pearls, the lower lip drawn up under the black teeth with an effort, till it appeared to snarl, and the ropes of pearls leaping wildly on her lean purple stomacher. And over all the grave oak walls and the bright sconces and the taper flames blown about by the eddying gusts from the whirlpool beneath.

As Anthony went down the square winding staircase, an hour later when the evening was over, and the keen winter air poured up to meet him, his brain was throbbing with the madness of dance and music and whirling colour. Here, it seemed to him, lay the secret of life. For a few minutes his old day-dreams came back but in more intoxicating dress. The figure of Mary Corbet in her rose-coloured silk and her clouds of black hair, and her jewels and her laughing eyes and scarlet mouth, and her violet fragrance and her fire—this dominated the boy. As he walked towards the stables across the starlit court, she seemed to move before him, to hold out her hands to him, to call him her own dear lad; to invite him out of the drab-coloured life that lay on all sides, behind and before, up into a mystic region of jewelled romance, where she and he would live and be one in the endless music of rippling strings and shrill flutes and the maddening tap of a little hidden drum.

But the familiar touch of his own sober suit and the creaking saddle as he rode home to Lambeth, and the icy wind that sang in the river sedges, and the wholesome smell of the horse and the touch of the coarse hair at the shoulder, talked and breathed the old Puritan common sense back to him again. That warm-painted, melodious world he had left was gaudy nonsense; and dancing was not the same as living; and Mary Corbet was not just a rainbow on the foam that would die when the sun went in; but both she and he together were human souls, redeemed by the death of the Saviour, with His work to do and no time or energy for folly; and James Maxwell in the Tower—(thank God, however, not for long!)—James Maxwell with his wrenched joints and forehead and lips wet with agony, was in the right; and that lean bitter furious woman in the purple and pearls, who supped to the blare of trumpets, and danced to the ripple of lutes, wholly and utterly and eternally in the wrong.

Chapter Eleven - A Station of the Cross

Philosophers tell us that the value of existence lies not in the objects perceived, but in the powers of perception. The tragedy of a child over a broken doll is not less poignant than the anguish of a worshipper over a broken idol, or of a king over a ruined realm. Thus the conflict of Isabel during those past autumn and winter months was no less august than the pain of the priest on the rack, or the struggle of his innocent betrayer to rescue him, or the misery of Lady Maxwell over the sorrows that came to her in such different ways through her two sons.

Isabel's soul was tender above most souls; and the powers of feeling pain and of sustaining it were also respectively both acute and strong. The sense of pressure, or rather of disruption, became intolerable. She was indeed a soul on the rack; if she had been less conscientious she would have silenced the voice of Divine Love that seemed to call to her from the Catholic Church; if she had been less natural and feminine she would have trampled out of her soul the appeal of the human love of Hubert. As it was, she was wrenched both ways. Now the cords at one end or the other would relax a little, and the corresponding relief was almost a shock; but when she tried to stir and taste the freedom of decision that now seemed in her reach, they would tighten again with a snap; and she would find herself back on the torture. To herself she seemed powerless; it appeared to her, when she reflected on it consciously, that it was merely a question as to which part of her soul would tear first, as to which ultimately retained her. She began to be terrified at solitude; the thought of the coming night, with its long hours of questioning and torment until the dawn, haunted her during the day. She would read in her room, or remain at her prayers, in the hopes of distracting herself from the struggle, until sleep seemed the supreme necessity: then, when she lay down, sleep would flap its wings in mockery and flit away, leaving her wide-awake staring at the darkness of the room or of her own eyelids, until the windows began to glimmer and the cocks to crow from farm buildings.

In spite of her first resolve to fight the battle alone, she soon found herself obliged to tell Mistress Margaret all that was possible; but she felt that to express her sheer need of Hubert, as she thought it, was beyond her altogether. How could a nun understand?

"My darling," said the old lady, "it would not be Calvary without the darkness; and you cannot have Christ without Calvary. Remember that the Light of the World makes darkness His secret place; and so you see that if you were able to feel that any human soul really understood, it would mean that the darkness was over. I have suffered that Night twice myself; the third time I think, will be in the valley of death."

Isabel only half understood her; but it was something to know that others had tasted the cup too; and that what was so bitter was not necessarily poisonous.

At another time as the two were walking together under the pines one evening, and the girl had again tried to show to the nun the burning desolation of her soul, Mistress Margaret had suddenly turned.

"Listen, dear child," she said, "I will tell you a secret. Over there," and she pointed out to where the sunset glowed behind the tree trunks and the slope beyond, "over there, in West Grinsted, rests our dear Lord in the blessed sacrament. His Body lies lonely, neglected and forgotten by all but half a dozen souls; while twenty years ago all England reverenced It. Behold and see if there be any sorrow—" and then the nun stopped, as she saw Isabel's amazed eyes staring at her.

But it haunted the girl and comforted her now and then. Yet in the fierceness of her pain she asked herself again and again, was it true—was it true? Was she sacrificing her life for a dream, a fairy-story? or was it true that there the body, that had hung on the cross fifteen hundred years ago, now rested alone, hidden in a silver pyx, within locked doors for fear of the Jews.—Oh! dear Lord, was it true?

Hubert had kept his word, and left the place almost immediately after his last interview; and was to return at Easter for his final answer. Christmas had come and gone; and it seemed to her as if even the tenderest mysteries of the Christian Religion had no touch with her now. She walked once more in the realm of grace, as in the realm of nature, an exile from its spirit. All her sensitive powers seemed so absorbed in interior pain that there was nothing in her to respond to or appreciate the most keen external impressions. As she awoke and looked up on Christmas morning early, and saw the frosted panes and the snow lying like wool on the cross-bars, and heard the Christmas bells peal out in the listening air; as she came downstairs and the old pleasant acrid smell of the evergreens met her, and she saw the red berries over each picture, and the red heart of the wood-fire; nay, as she knelt at the chancel rails, and tried in her heart to adore the rosy Child in the manger, and received the sacred symbols of His Flesh and Blood, and entreated Him to remember His loving-kindness that brought Him down from heaven—yet the whole was far less real, less intimate to her, than the sound of Hubert's voice as he had said good-bye two months ago; less real than one of those darting pangs of thought that fell on her heart all day like a shower of arrows.

And then, when the sensitive strings of her soul were stretched to anguish, a hand dashed across them, striking a wailing discord, and they did not break. The news of Anthony's treachery, and still more his silence, performed the incredible, and doubled her pain without breaking her heart.

On the Tuesday morning early Lady Maxwell had sent her note by a courier; bidding him return at once with the answer. The evening had come, and he had not appeared. The night passed and the morning came; and it was not till noon that the man at last arrived, saying he had seen Mr. Norris on the previous evening, and that he had read the note through there and then, and had said there was no answer. Surely there could be but one explanation of that— that no answer was possible.

It could not be said that Isabel actively considered the question and chose to doubt Anthony rather than to trust him. She was so nearly passive now, with the struggle she had gone through, that this blow came on her with the overwhelming effect of an hypnotic suggestion. Her will did not really accept it, any more than her intellect really weighed it; but she succumbed to it; and did not even write again, nor question the man further. Had she done this she might perhaps have found out the truth, that the man, a stupid rustic with enough shrewdness to lie, but not enough to lie cleverly, had had his foolish head turned by the buzz of London town and the splendour of Lambeth stables and the friendliness of the grooms there, and had got heavily drunk on leaving Anthony; that the answer which he had put into his hat had very naturally fallen out and been lost; and that when at last he returned to the country already eight hours after his time, and found the note was missing, he had stalwartly lied, hoping that the note was unimportant and that things would adjust themselves or be forgotten before a day of reckoning should arrive.

And so Isabel's power of resistance collapsed under this last blow; and her soul lay still at last, almost too much tormented to feel. Her last hope was gone; Anthony had betrayed his friend.

The week crept by, and Saturday came. She went out soon after dinner to see a sick body or two in an outlying hamlet; for she had never forgotten Mrs. Dent's charge, and, with the present minister's approval, still visited the sick one or two days a week at least. Then towards sunset she came homewards over some high ground on the outskirts of Ashdown Forest. The snow that had fallen before Christmas, had melted a week or two ago; and the frost had broken up; it was a heavy leaden evening, with an angry glow shining, as through chinks of a wall, from the west towards which she was going. The village lay before her in the gloom; and lights were beginning to glimmer here and there. She contrasted in a lifeless way that pleasant group of warm houses with their suggestions of love and homeliness with her own desolate self. She passed up through the village towards the Hall, whither she was going to report on the invalids to Lady Maxwell; and in the appearance of the houses on either side she thought there was an unaccustomed air. Several doors stood wide open with the brightness shining out into the twilight, as if the inhabitants had suddenly deserted their homes. Others were still dark and cold, although the evening was drawing on. There was not a moving creature to be seen. She passed up, wondering a little, through the gatehouse, and turned into the gravel sweep; and there stopped short at the sight of a great crowd of men and women and children, assembled in dead silence. Some one was standing at the entrance-steps, with his head bent as if he were talking to those nearest him in a low voice.

As she came up there ran a whisper of her name; the people drew back to let her through, and she passed, sick with suspense, to the man on the steps, whom she now recognised as Mr. James' body-servant. His face looked odd and drawn, she thought.

"What is it?" she asked in a sharp whisper.

"Mr. James is here, madam; he is with Lady Maxwell in the cloister-wing. Will you please to go up?"

"Mr. James! It is no news about Mr. Anthony—or—or Mr. Hubert!"

"No, madam." The man hesitated. "Mr. James has been racked, madam."

The man's voice broke in a great sob as he ended.

"Ah!"

She reeled against the post; a man behind caught her and steadied her; and there was a quick breath of pity from the crowd.

"Ah, poor thing!" said a woman's voice behind her.

"I beg your pardon, madam," said the servant. "I should not have—"

"And—and he is upstairs?"

"He and my lady are together, madam."

She looked at him a moment, dazed with the horror of it; and then going past him, pushed open the door and went through into the inner hall. Here again she stopped suddenly: it was half full of people, silent and expectant—the men, the grooms, the maid-servants, and even two or three farm-men. She heard the rustle of her name from the white faces that looked at her from the gloom; but none moved; and she crossed the hall alone, and turned down the lower corridor that led to the cloister-wing.

At the foot of the staircase she stopped again; her heart drummed in her ears, as she listened intently with parted lips. There was a profound silence; the lamp on the stairs had not been lighted, and the terrace window only let in a pale glimmer.

It was horrible to her! this secret presence of incarnate pain that brooded somewhere in the house, this silence of living anguish, worse than death a thousand times!

Where was he? What would it look like? Even a scream somewhere would have relieved her, and snapped the tension of the listening stillness that lay on her like a shocking nightmare. This lobby with its well-known doors—the banister on which her fingers rested—the well of the staircase up which she stared with dilated eyes—all was familiar; and yet, somewhere in the shadows overhead lurked this formidable Presence of pain, mute, anguished, terrifying....

She longed to run back, to shriek for help; but she dared not: and stood panting. She went up a couple of steps—stopped, listened to the sick thumping of her heart—took another step and stopped again; and so, listening, peering, hesitating, came to the head of the stairs.

Ah! there was the door, with a line of light beneath it. It was there that the horror dwelt. She stared at the thin bright line; waited and listened again for even a moan or a sigh from within, but none came.

Then with a great effort she stepped forward and tapped.

There was no answer; but as she listened she heard from within the gentle tinkle of some liquid running into a bowl, rhythmically, and with pauses. Then again she tapped, nervously and rapidly, and there was a murmur from the room; she opened the door softly, pushed it, and took a step into the room, half closing it behind her.

There were two candles burning on a table in the middle of the room, and on the near side of it was a group of three persons....

Isabel had seen in one of Mistress Margaret's prayer-books an engraving of an old Flemish Pietà—a group of the Blessed Mother holding in her arms the body of her Crucified Son, with the Magdalen on one side, supporting one of the dead Saviour's hands. Isabel now caught her breath in a sudden gasp; for here was the scene reproduced before her.

Lady Maxwell was on a low seat bending forwards; the white cap and ruff seemed like a veil thrown all about her head and beneath her chin; she was holding in her arms the body of her son, who seemed to have fainted as he sat beside her; his head had fallen back against her breast, and his pointed beard and dark hair and her black dress beyond emphasised the deathly whiteness of his face on which the candlelight fell; his mouth was open, like a dead man's. Mistress Margaret was kneeling by his left hand, holding it over a basin and delicately sponging it; and the whole air was fragrant and aromatic with some ointment in the water; a long bandage or two lay on the ground beside the basin. The evening light over the opposite roofs through the window beyond mingled with the light of the tapers, throwing a strange radiance over the group. The table on which the tapers stood looked to Isabel like a stripped altar.

She stood by the door, her lips parted, motionless; looking with great eyes from face to face. It was as if the door had given access to another world where the passion of Christ was being re-enacted.

Then she sank on her knees, still watching. There was no sound but the faint ripple of the water into the basin and the quiet breathing of the three. Lady Maxwell now and then lifted a handkerchief in silence and passed it across her son's face. Isabel, still staring with great wide eyes, began to sigh gently to herself.

"Anthony, Anthony, Anthony!" she whispered.

"Oh, no, no, no!" she whispered again under her breath. "No, Anthony! you could not, you could not!"

Then from the man there came one or two long sighs, ending in a moan that quavered into silence; he stirred slightly in his mother's arms; and then in a piteous high voice came the words "Jesu ... Jesu ... esto mihi ... Jesus."

Consciousness was coming back. He fancied himself still on the rack.

Lady Maxwell said nothing, but gathered him a little closer, and bent her face lower over him.

Then again came a long sobbing indrawn breath; James struggled for a moment; then opened his eyes and saw his mother's face.

Mistress Margaret had finished with the water; and was now swiftly manipulating a long strip of white linen. Isabel still sunk on her knees watched the bandage winding in and out round his wrist, and between his thumb and forefinger.

Then he turned his head sharply towards her with a gasp as if in pain; and his eyes fell on Isabel.

"Mistress Isabel," he said; and his voice was broken and untuneful.

Mistress Margaret turned; and smiled at her; and at the sight the intolerable compression on the girl's heart relaxed. "Come, child," she said, "come and help me with his hand. No, no, lie still," she added; for James was making a movement as if to rise.

James smiled at her as she came forward; and she saw that his face had a strange look as if after a long illness.

"You see, Mistress Isabel," he said, in the same cracked voice, and with an infinitely pathetic courtesy, "I may not rise."

Isabel's eyes filled with sudden tears, his attempt at his old manner was more touching than all else; and she came and knelt beside the old nun.

"Hold the fingers," she said; and the familiar old voice brought the girl a stage nearer her normal consciousness again.

Isabel took the priest's fingers and saw that they were limp and swollen. The sleeve fell back a little as Mistress Margaret manipulated the bandage; and the girl saw that the forearm looked shapeless and discoloured.

127

She glanced up in swift terror at his face, but he was looking at his mother, whose eyes were bent on his; Isabel looked quickly down again.

"There," said Mistress Margaret, tying the last knot, "it is done."

Mr. James looked his thanks over his shoulder at her, as she nodded and smiled before turning to leave the room. Isabel sat slowly down and watched them.

"This is but a flying visit, Mistress Isabel," said James. "I must leave to-morrow again."

He had sat up now, and settled himself in his seat, though his mother's arm was still round him. The voice and the pitiful attempt were terrible to Isabel. Slowly the consciousness was filtering into her mind of what all this implied; what it must have been that had turned this tall self-contained man into this weak creature who lay in his mother's arms, and fainted at a touch and sobbed. She could say nothing; but could only look, and breathe, and look.

Then it suddenly came to her mind that Lady Maxwell had not spoken a word. She looked at her; that old wrinkled face with its white crown of hair and lace had a new and tremendous dignity. There was no anxiety in it; scarcely even grief; but only a still and awful anguish, towering above ordinary griefs like a mountain above the world; and there was the supreme peace too that can only accompany a supreme emotion—she seemed conscious of nothing but her son.

Isabel could not answer James; and he seemed not to expect it; he had turned back to his mother again, and they were looking at one another. Then in a moment Mistress Margaret came back with a glass that she put to James' lips; and he drank it without a word. She stood looking at the group an instant or two, and then turned to Isabel.

"Come downstairs with me, my darling; there is nothing more that we can do."

They went out of the room together; the mother and son had not stirred again; and Mistress Margaret slipped her arm quickly round the girl's waist, as they went downstairs.

In the cloister beneath was a pleasant little oak parlour looking out on to the garden and the long south side of the house. Mistress Margaret took the little hand-lamp that burned in the cloister itself as they passed along silently together, and guided the girl through into the parlour on the left-hand side. There was a tall chair standing before the hearth, and as Mistress Margaret sat down, drawing the girl with her, Isabel sank down on the footstool at her feet, and hid her face on the old nun's knees.

There was silence for a minute or two. Mistress Margaret set down the lamp on the table beside her, and passed her hands caressingly over the girl's hands and hair; but said nothing, until Isabel's whole body heaved up convulsively once or twice, before she burst into a torrent of weeping.

"My darling," said the old lady in a quiet steady voice, "we should thank God instead of grieving. To think that this house should have given two confessors to the Church, father and son! Yes, yes, dear child, I know what you are thinking of, the two dear lads we both love; well, well, we do not know, we must trust them both to God. It may not be true of Anthony; and even if it be true—well, he must have thought he was serving his Queen. And for Hubert—"

Isabel lifted her face and looked with a dreadful questioning stare.

"Dear child," said the nun, "do not look like that. Nothing is so bad as not trusting God."

"Anthony, Anthony!"... whispered the girl.

"James told us the same story as the gentleman on Sunday," went on the nun. "But he said no hard word, and he does not condemn. I know his heart. He does not know why he is released, nor by whose order: but an order came to let him go, and his papers with it: and he must be out of England by Monday morning: so he leaves here to-morrow in the litter in which he came. He is to say mass to-morrow, if he is able."

"Mass? Here?" said the girl, in the same sharp whisper; and her sobbing ceased abruptly.

"Yes, dear; if he is able to stand and use his hands enough. They have settled it upstairs."

Isabel continued to look up in her face wildly.

"Ah!" said the old nun again. "You must not look like that. Remember that he thinks those wounds the most precious things in the world—yes—and his mother too!"

"I must be at mass," said Isabel; "God means it."

"Now, now," said Mistress Margaret soothingly, "you do not know what you are saying."

"I mean it," said Isabel, with sharp emphasis; "God means it."

Mistress Margaret took the girl's face between her hands, and looked steadily down into her wet eyes. Isabel returned the look as steadily.

"Yes, yes," she said, "as God sees us."

Then she broke into talk, at first broken and incoherent in language, but definite and orderly in ideas, and in her interpretations of these last months.

Kneeling beside her with her hands clasped on the nun's knee, Isabel told her all her struggles; disentangling at last in a way that she had never been able to do before, all the complicated strands of self-will and guidance and blindness that had so knotted and twisted themselves into her life. The nun was amazed at the spiritual instinct of this

128

Puritan child, who ranged her motives so unerringly; dismissing this as of self, marking this as of God's inspiration, accepting this and rejecting that element of the circumstances of her life; steering confidently between the shoals of scrupulous judgment and conscience on the one side, and the hidden rocks of presumption and despair on the other—these very dangers that had baffled and perplexed her so long—and tracing out through them all the clear deep safe channel of God's intention, who had allowed her to emerge at last from the tortuous and baffling intricacies of character and circumstance into the wide open sea of His own sovereign Will.

It seemed to the nun, as Isabel talked, as if it needed just a final touch of supreme tragedy to loosen and resolve all the complications; and that this had been supplied by the vision upstairs. There she had seen a triumphant trophy of another's sorrow and conquest. There was hardly an element in her own troubles that was not present in that human Pietà upstairs—treachery—loneliness—sympathy—bereavement—and above all the supreme sacrificial act of human love subordinated to divine—human love, purified and transfigured and rendered invincible and immortal by the very immolation of it at the feet of God—all this that the son and mother in their welcome of pain had accomplished in the crucifixion of one and the heart-piercing of the other—this was light opened to the perplexed, tormented soul of the girl—a radiance poured out of the darkness of their sorrow and made her way plain before her face.

"My Isabel," said the old nun, when the girl had finished and was hiding her face again, "this is of God. Glory to His Name! I must ask James' leave; and then you must sleep here to-night, for the mass to-morrow."

The chapel at Maxwell Hall was in the cloister wing; but a stranger visiting the house would never have suspected it. Opening out of Lady Maxwell's new sitting-room was a little lobby or landing, about four yards square, lighted from above; at the further end of it was the door into her bedroom. This lobby was scarcely more than a broad passage; and would attract no attention from any passing through it. The only piece of furniture in it was a great tall old chest as high as a table, that stood against the inner wall beyond which was the long gallery that looked down upon the cloister garden. The lobby appeared to be practically as broad as the two rooms on either side of it; but this was effected by the outer wall being made to bulge a little; and the inner wall being thinner than inside the two living-rooms. The deception was further increased by the two living-rooms being first wainscoted and then hung with thick tapestry; while the lobby was bare. A curious person who should look in the chest would find there only an old dress and a few pieces of stuff. This lobby, however, was the chapel; and through the chest was the entrance to one of the priest's hiding holes, where also the altar-stone and the ornaments and the vestments were kept. The bottom of the chest was in reality hinged in such a way that it would fall, on the proper pressure being applied in two places at once, sufficiently to allow the side of the chest against the wall to be pushed aside, which in turn gave entrance to a little space some two yards long by a yard wide; and here were kept all the necessaries for divine worship; with room besides for a couple of men at least to be hidden away. There was also a way from this hole on to the roof, but it was a difficult and dangerous way; and was only to be used in case of extreme necessity.

It was in this lobby that Isabel found herself the next morning kneeling and waiting for mass. She had been awakened by Mistress Margaret shortly before four o'clock and told in a whisper to dress herself in the dark; for it was impossible under the circumstances to tell whether the house was not watched; and a light seen from outside might conceivably cause trouble and disturbance. So she had dressed herself and come down from her room along the passages, so familiar during the day, so sombre and suggestive now in the black morning with but one shaded light placed at the angles. Other figures were stealing along too; but she could not tell who they were in the gloom. Then she had come through the little sitting-room where the scene of last night had taken place and into the lobby beyond. But the whole place was transformed.

Over the old chest now hung a picture, that usually was in Lady Maxwell's room, of the Blessed Mother and her holy Child, in a great carved frame of some black wood. The chest had become an altar: Isabel could see the slight elevation in the middle of the long white linen cloth where the altar-stone lay, and upon that again, at the left corner, a pile of linen and silk. Upon the altar at the back stood two slender silver candlesticks with burning tapers in them; and a silver crucifix between them. The carved wooden panels, representing the sacrifice of Isaac on the one half and the offering of Melchisedech on the other, served instead of an embroidered altar-frontal. Against the side wall stood a little white-covered folding table with the cruets and other necessaries upon it.

There were two or three benches across the rest of the lobby; and at these were kneeling a dozen or more persons, motionless, their faces downcast. There was a little wind such as blows before the dawn moaning gently outside; and within was a slight draught that made the taper flames lean over now and then.

Isabel took her place beside Mistress Margaret at the front bench; and as she knelt forward she noticed a space left beyond her for Lady Maxwell. A moment later there came slow and painful steps through the sitting-room, and Lady Maxwell came in very slowly with her son leaning on her arm and on a stick. There was a silence so profound that it seemed to Isabel as if all had stopped breathing. She could only hear the slow plunging pulse of her own heart.

James took his mother across the altar to her place, and left her there, bowing to her; and then went up to the altar to vest. As he reached it and paused, a servant slipped out and received the stick from him. The priest made the sign of the cross, and took up the amice from the vestments that lay folded on the altar. He was already in his cassock. Isabel watched each movement with a deep agonising interest; he was so frail and broken, so bent in his figure, so slow and feeble in his movements. He made an attempt to raise the amice but could not, and turned slightly; and the man from behind stepped up again and lifted it for him. Then he helped him with each of the vestments, lifted the alb over his head and tenderly drew the bandaged hands through the sleeves; knit the girdle round him; gave him the stole to kiss and then placed it over his neck and crossed the ends beneath the girdle and adjusted the amice; then he placed the maniple on his left arm, but so tenderly! and lastly, lifted the great red chasuble and dropped it over his head and straightened it—and there stood the priest as he had stood last Sunday, in crimson vestments again; but bowed and thin-faced now.

Then he began the preparation with the servant who knelt beside him in his ordinary livery, as server; and Isabel heard the murmur of the Latin words for the first time. Then he stepped up to the altar, bent slowly and kissed it and the mass began.

Isabel had a missal, lent to her by Mistress Margaret; but she hardly looked at it; so intent was she on that crimson figure and his strange movements and his low broken voice. It was unlike anything that she had ever imagined worship to be. Public worship to her had meant hitherto one of two things—either sitting under a minister and having the word applied to her soul in the sacrament of the pulpit; or else the saying of prayers by the minister aloud and distinctly and with expression, so that the intellect could follow the words, and assent with a hearty Amen. The minister was a minister to man of the Word of God, an interpreter of His gospel to man.

But here was a worship unlike all this in almost every detail. The priest was addressing God, not man; therefore he did so in a low voice, and in a tongue as Campion had said on the scaffold "that they both understood." It was comparatively unimportant whether man followed it word for word, for (and here the second radical difference lay) the point of the worship for the people lay, not in an intellectual apprehension of the words, but in a voluntary assent to and participation in the supreme act to which the words were indeed necessary but subordinate. It was the thing that was done; not the words that were said, that was mighty with God. Here, as these Catholics round Isabel at any rate understood it, and as she too began to perceive it too, though dimly and obscurely, was the sublime mystery of the Cross presented to God. As He looked down well pleased into the silence and darkness of Calvary, and saw there the act accomplished by which the world was redeemed, so here (this handful of disciples believed), He looked down into the silence and twilight of this little lobby, and saw that same mystery accomplished at the hands of one who in virtue of his participation in the priesthood of the Son of God was empowered to pronounce these heart-shaking words by which the Body that hung on Calvary, and the Blood that dripped from it there, were again spread before His eyes, under the forms of bread and wine.

Much of this faith of course was still dark to Isabel; but yet she understood enough; and when the murmur of the priest died to a throbbing silence, and the worshippers sank in yet more profound adoration, and then with terrible effort and a quick gasp or two of pain, those wrenched bandaged hands rose trembling in the air with Something that glimmered white between them; the Puritan girl too drooped her head, and lifted up her heart, and entreated the Most High and most Merciful to look down on the Mystery of Redemption accomplished on earth; and for the sake of the Well-Beloved to send down His Grace on the Catholic Church; to strengthen and save the living; to give rest and peace to the dead; and especially to remember her dear brother Anthony, and Hubert whom she loved; and Mistress Margaret and Lady Maxwell, and this faithful household: and the poor battered man before her, who, not only as a priest was made like to the Eternal Priest, but as a victim too had hung upon a prostrate cross, fastened by hands and feet; thus bearing on his body for all to see the marks of the Lord Jesus.

Lady Maxwell and Mistress Margaret both rose and stepped forward after the Priest's Communion, and received from those wounded hands the Broken Body of the Lord.

And then the mass was presently over; and the server stepped forward again to assist the priest to unvest, himself lifting each vestment off, for Father Maxwell was terribly exhausted by now, and laying it on the altar. Then he helped him to a little footstool in front of him, for him to kneel and make his thanksgiving. Isabel looked with an odd wonder at the server; he was the man that she knew so well, who opened the door for her, and waited at table; but now a strange dignity rested on him as he moved confidently and reverently about the awful altar, and touched the vestments that even to her Puritan eyes shone with new sanctity. It startled her to think of the hidden Catholic life of this house—of these servants who loved and were familiar with mysteries that she had been taught to dread and distrust, but before which she too now was to bow her being in faith and adoration.

After a minute or two, Mistress Margaret touched Isabel on the arm and beckoned to her to come up to the altar, which she began immediately to strip of its ornaments and cloth, having first lit another candle on one of the benches. Isabel helped her in this with a trembling dread, as all the others except Lady Maxwell and her son were now gone out silently; and presently the picture was down, and leaning against the wall; the ornaments and sacred vessels packed away in their box, with the vestments and linen in another. Then together they lifted off the heavy altar stone. Mistress Margaret next laid back the lid of the chest; and put her hands within, and presently Isabel saw the back of the chest fall back, apparently into the wall. Mistress Margaret then beckoned to Isabel to climb into the chest and go through; she did so without much difficulty, and found herself in the little room behind. There was a stool or two and some shelves against the wall, with a plate or two upon them and one or two tools. She received the boxes handed through, and followed Mistress Margaret's instructions as to where to place them; and when all was done, she slipped back again through the chest into the lobby.

The priest and his mother were still in their places, motionless. Mistress Margaret closed the chest inside and out, beckoned Isabel into the sitting-room and closed the door behind them. Then she threw her arms round the girl and kissed her again and again.

"My own darling," said the nun, with tears in her eyes. "God bless you—your first mass. Oh! I have prayed for this. And you know all our secrets now. Now go to your room, and to bed again. It is only a little after five. You shall see him—James—before he goes. God bless you, my dear!"

She watched Isabel down the passage; and then turned back again to where the other two were still kneeling, to make her own thanksgiving.

Isabel went to her room as one in a dream. She was soon in bed again, but could not sleep; the vision of that strange worship she had assisted at; the pictorial details of it, the glow of the two candles on the shoulders of the crimson chasuble as the priest bent to kiss the altar or to adore; the bowed head of the server at his side; the picture overhead with the Mother and her downcast eyes, and the radiant Child stepping from her knees to bless the world—all this burned on the darkness. With the least effort of imagination too she could recall the steady murmur of the unfamiliar words; hear the rustle of the silken vestment; the stirrings and breathings of the worshippers in the little room.

Then in endless course the intellectual side of it all began to present itself. She had assisted at what the Government called a crime; it was for that—that collection of strange but surely at least innocent things—actions, words, material objects—that men and women of the same flesh and blood as herself were ready to die; and for which others equally of one nature with herself were ready to put them to death. It was the mass—the mass—she had seen—she repeated the word to herself, so sinister, so suggestive, so mighty. Then she began to think again—if indeed it is possible to say that she had ever ceased to think of him—of Anthony, who would be so much horrified if he knew; of Hubert, who had renounced this wonderful worship, and all, she feared, for love of her—and above all of her father, who had regarded it with such repugnance:—yes, thought Isabel, but he knows all now. Then she thought of Mistress Margaret again. After all, the nun had a spiritual life which in intensity and purity surpassed any she had ever experienced or even imagined; and yet the heart of it all was the mass. She thought of the old wrinkled quiet face when she came back to breakfast at the Dower House: she had soon learnt to read from that face whether mass had been said that morning or not at the Hall. And Mistress Margaret was only one of thousands to whom this little set of actions half seen and words half heard, wrought and said by a man in a curious dress, were more precious than all meditation and prayer put together. Could the vast superstructure of prayer and effort and aspiration rest upon a piece of empty folly such as children or savages might invent?

Then very naturally, as she began now to get quieter and less excited, she passed on to the spiritual side of it.

Had that indeed happened that Mistress Margaret believed—that the very Body and Blood of her own dear Saviour, Jesus Christ, had in virtue of His own clear promise—His own clear promise!—become present there under the hands of His priest? Was it, indeed,—this half-hour action,—the most august mystery of time, the Lamb eternally slain, presenting Himself and His Death before the Throne in a tremendous and bloodless Sacrifice—so august that the very angels can only worship it afar off and cannot perform it; or was it all a merely childish piece of blasphemous mummery, as she had been brought up to believe? And then this Puritan girl, who was beginning to taste the joys of release from her misery now that she had taken this step, and united a whole-hearted offering of herself to the perfect Offering of her Lord—now her soul made its first trembling movement towards a real external authority.

"I believe," she rehearsed to herself, "not because my spiritual experience tells me that the Mass is true, for it does not; not because the Bible says so, because it is possible to interpret that in more than one way; but because that Society which I now propose to treat as Divine—the Representative of the Incarnate Word—nay, His very mystical Body—tells me so: and I rely upon that, and rest in her arms, which are the Arms of the Everlasting, and hang upon her lips, through which the Infallible Word speaks."

And so Isabel, in a timid peace at last, from her first act of Catholic faith, fell asleep.

She awoke to find the winter sun streaming into her room, and Mistress Margaret by her bedside.

"Dear child," said the old lady, "I would not wake you earlier; you have had such a short night; but James leaves in an hour's time; and it is just nine o'clock, and I know you wish to see him."

When she came down half an hour later she found Mistress Margaret waiting for her outside Lady Maxwell's room. "He is in there," she said. "I will tell Mary"; and she slipped in. Isabel outside heard the murmur of voices, and in a moment more was beckoned in by the nun.

James Maxwell was sitting back in a great chair, looking exhausted and white. His mother, with something of the same look of supreme suffering and triumph, was standing behind his chair. She smiled gravely and sweetly at Isabel, as if to encourage her; and went out at the further door, followed by her sister.

"Mistress Isabel," said the priest, without any introductory words, in his broken voice, and motioning her to a seat, "I cannot tell you what joy it was to see you at mass. Is it too much to hope that you will seek admission presently to the Catholic Church?"

Isabel sat with downcast eyes. His tone was a little startling to her. It was as courteous as ever, but less courtly: there was just the faintest ring in it, in spite of its weakness, as of one who spoke with authority.

"I—I thank you, Mr. James," she said. "I wish to hear more at any rate."

"Yes, Mistress Isabel; and I thank God for it. Mr. Barnes will be the proper person. My mother will let him know; and I have no doubt that he will receive you by Easter, and that you can make your First Communion on that day."

She bowed her head, wondering a little at his assurance.

"You will forgive me, I know, if I seem discourteous," went on the priest, "but I trust you understand the terms on which you come. You come as a little child, to learn; is it not so? Simply that?"

She bowed her head again.

"Then I need not keep you. If you will kneel, I will give you my blessing."

She knelt down at once before him, and he blessed her, lifting his wrenched hand with difficulty and letting it sink quickly down again.

By an impulse she could not resist she leaned forward on her knees and took it gently into her two soft hands and kissed it.

"Oh! forgive him, Mr. Maxwell; I am sure he did not know." And then her tears poured down.

"My child," said his voice tenderly, "in any case I not only forgive him, but I thank him. How could I not? He has brought me love-tokens from my Lord."

She kissed his hand again, and stood up; her eyes were blinded with tears; but they were not all for grief.

Then Mistress Margaret came in from the inner room, and led the girl out; and the mother came in once more to her son for the ten minutes before he was to leave her.

Chapter Twelve - A Strife of Tongues

Anthony now settled down rather drearily to the study of religious controversy. The continual contrasts that seemed forced upon him by the rival systems of England and Rome (so far as England might be said to have a coherent system at this time), all tended to show him that there were these two sharply-divided schemes, each claiming to represent Christ's Institution, and each exclusive of the other. Was it of Christ's institution that His Church should be a department of the National Life; and that the civil prince should be its final arbiter and ruler, however little he might interfere in its ordinary administration? This was Elizabeth's idea. Or was the Church, as Mr. Buxton had explained it, a huge unnational Society, dependent, it must of course be, to some extent on local circumstances, but essentially unrestricted by limit of nationality or of racial tendencies? This was the claim of Rome. Of course an immense number of other arguments circled round this—in fact, most of the arguments that are familiar to controversialists at the present day; but the centre of all, to Anthony's mind, as indeed it was to the mind of the civil and religious authorities of the time, was the question of supremacy—Elizabeth or Gregory?

He read a certain number of books; and it will be remembered that he had followed, with a good deal of intelligence, Campion's arguments. Anthony was no theologian, and therefore missed perhaps the deep, subtle arguments; but he had a normal mind, and was able to appreciate and remember some salient points.

For example, he was impressed greatly by the negative character of Protestantism in such books as Nicholl's "Pilgrimage." In this work a man was held up as a type to be imitated whose whole religion to all appearances consisted of holding the Pope to be Antichrist, and his Church the synagogue of Satan, of disliking the doctrines of merit and of justification by works, of denying the Real Presence, and of holding nothing but what could be proved to his own satisfaction by the Scriptures.

Then he read as much as he could of the great Jewell controversy. This Bishop of Salisbury, who had, however, recanted his Protestant opinions under Mary, and resumed them under Elizabeth, had published in 1562 his "Apology of the Church of England," a work of vast research and learning. Mr. Harding, who had also had the advantage of having been on both sides, had answered it; and then the battle was arrayed. It was of course mostly above Anthony's head; but he gained from what he was able to read of it a very fair estimate of the conflicting theses, though he probably could not have stated them intelligibly. He also made acquaintance with another writer against Jewell,—Rastall; and with one or two of Mr. Willet's books, the author of "Synopsis Papismi" and "Tretrastylon Papisticum."

Even more than by paper controversy, however, he was influenced by history that was so rapidly forming before his eyes. The fact and the significance of the supremacy of the Queen in religion was impressed upon him more vividly by her suspension of Grindal than by all the books he ever read: here was the first ecclesiastic of the realm, a devout, humble and earnest man, restrained from exercising his great qualities as ruler and shepherd of his people, by a woman whose religious character certainly commanded no one's respect, even if her moral life were free from scandal; and that, not because the Archbishop had been guilty of any crime or heresy, or was obviously unfitted for his post, but because his conscientious judgment on a point of Church discipline and liberty differed from hers; and this state of things was made possible not by an usurpation of power, but by the deliberately ordered system of the Church of England. Anthony had at least sufficient penetration to see that this, as a fundamental principle of religion, however obscured it might be by subsequent developments, was yet fraught with dangers compared with which those of papal interference were comparatively trifling—dangers that is, not so much to earthly peace and prosperity, as to the whole spiritual nature of the nation's Christianity.

Yet another argument had begun to suggest itself, bearing upon the same point, of the relative advantages and dangers of Nationalism. When he had first entered the Archbishop's service he had been inspired by the thought that the Church would share in the rising splendour of England; now he began to wonder whether she could have strength to resist the rising worldliness that was bound to accompany it. It is scarcely likely that men on fire with success, whether military or commercial, will be patient of the restraints of religion. If the Church is independent of the nation, she can protest and denounce freely; if she is knit closely to the nation, such rebuke is almost impossible.

A conversation that Anthony had on this subject at the beginning of February helped somewhat to clear up this point.

He was astonished after dinner one day to hear that Mr. Henry Buxton was at the porter's lodge desiring to see him, and on going out he found that it was indeed his old acquaintance, the prisoner.

"Good-day, Master Norris," said the gentleman, with his eyes twinkling; "you see the mouse has escaped, and is come to call upon the cat."

Anthony inquired further as to the details of his release.

"Well, you see," said Mr. Buxton, "they grew a-weary of me. I talked so loud at them all for one thing; and then you see I was neither priest nor agent nor conspirator, but only a plain country gentleman: so they took some hundred or two pounds off me, to make me still plainer; and let me go. Now, Mr. Norris, will you come and dine with me, and resume our conversation that was so rudely interrupted by my journey last time? But then you see her Majesty would take no denial."

"I have just dined," said Anthony, "but—"

"Well, I will not ask you to see me dine again, as you did last time; but will you then sup with me? I am at the 'Running Horse,' Fleet Street, until to-morrow."

Anthony accepted gladly; for he had been greatly taken with Mr. Buxton; and at six o'clock that evening presented himself at the "Running Horse," and was shown up to a private parlour.

He found Mr. Buxton in the highest good-humour; he was even now on his way from Wisbeach, home again to Tonbridge, and was only staying in London to finish a little business he had.

Before supper was over, Anthony had laid his difficulties before him.

"My dear friend," said the other, and his manner became at once sober and tender, "I thank you deeply for your confidence. After being thought midway between a knave and a fool for over a year, it is a comfort to be treated as an honest gentleman again. I hold very strongly with what you say; it is that, under God, that has kept me steady. As I said to you last time, Christ's Kingdom is not of this world. Can you imagine, for example, Saint Peter preaching religious obedience to Nero to be a Christian's duty? I do not say (God forbid) that her Grace is a Nero, or even a Poppæa; but there is no particular reason why some successor of hers should not be. However, Nero or not, the principle is the same. I do not deny that a National Church may be immensely powerful, may convert thousands, may number zealous and holy men among her ministers and adherents—but yet her foundation is insecure. What when the tempest of God's searching judgments begins to blow?

"Or, to put it plainer, in a parable, you have seen, I doubt not, a gallant and his mistress together. So long as she is being wooed by him, she can command; he sighs and yearns and runs on errands—in short, she rules him. But when they are wedded—ah me! It is she—if he turns out a brute, that is—she that stands while my lord plucks off his boots—she who runs to fetch the tobacco-pipe and lights it and kneels by him. Now I hold that to wed the body spiritual to the body civil, is to wed a delicate dame to a brute. He may dress her well, give her jewels, clap her kindly on the head—but she is under him and no free woman. Ah!"—and then Mr. Buxton's eyes began to shine as Anthony remembered they had done before, and his voice to grow solemn,—"and when the spouse is the Bride of Christ, purchased by His death, what then would be the sin to wed her to a carnal nation, who shall favour her, it may be, while she looks young and fair; but when his mood changes, or her appearance, then she is his slave and his drudge! His will and his whims are her laws; as he changes, so must she. She has to do his foul work; as she had to do for King Henry, as she is doing it now for Queen Bess; and as she will always have to do, God help her, so long as she is wedded to the nation, instead of being free as the handmaiden and spouse of Christ alone. My faith would be lost, Mr. Norris, and my heart broken quite, if I were forced to think the Church of England to be the Church of Christ."

They talked late that evening in the private baize-curtained parlour on the third floor. Anthony produced his difficulties one by one, and Mr. Buxton did his best to deal with them. For example, Anthony remarked on the fact that there had been no breach of succession as to the edifices and endowments of the Church; that the sees had been canonically filled, and even the benefices; and that therefore, like it or not, the Church of England now was identical with the Pre-Reformation Church.

"Distinguo," said his friend. "Of course she is the successor in one sense: what you say is very true. It is impossible to put your finger all along the line of separation. It is a serrated line. The affairs of a Church and a nation are so vast that that is sure to be so; although if you insist, I will point to the Supremacy Act of 1559 and the Uniformity Act of the same year as very clear evidences of a breach with the ancient order; in the former the governance is shifted from its original owner, the Vicar of Christ, and placed on Elizabeth; it was that that the Carthusian Fathers and Sir Thomas More and many others died sooner than allow: and the latter Act sweeps away all the ancient forms of worship in favour of a modern one. But I am not careful to insist upon those points; if you deny or disprove them,—though I do not envy any who attempts that—yet even then my principle remains, that all that to which the Church of England has succeeded is the edifices and the endowments; but that her spirit is wholly new. If a highwayman knocks me down to-morrow, strips me, clothes himself with my clothes, and rides my horse, he is certainly my successor in one sense; yet he will be rash if he presents himself to my wife and sons—though I have none, by the way—as the proper owner of my house and name."

"But there is no knocking down in the question," said Anthony. "The bishops and clergy, or the greater part of them, consented to the change."

Mr. Buxton smiled.

"Very well," he said; "yet the case is not greatly different if the gentleman threatens me with torture instead, if I do not voluntarily give him my clothes and my horse. If I were weak and yielded to him, yes, and made promises of all kinds in my cowardice—yet he would be no nearer being the true successor of my name and fortune. And if you read her Grace's Acts, and King Henry's too, you will find that that was precisely what took place. My dear sir," Mr. Buxton went on, "if you will pardon my saying it, I am astounded at the effrontery of your authorities who claim that there was no breach. Your Puritans are wiser; they at least frankly say that the old was Anti-Christian; that His Holiness (God forgive me for saying it!), was an usurper: and that the new Genevan theology is the old gospel brought to light again. That I can understand; and indeed most of your churchmen think so too; and that there was a new beginning made with Protestantism. But when her Grace calls herself a Catholic, and tells the poor Frenchmen that it is the old religion here still: and your bishops, or one or two of them rather, like Cheyney, I suppose, say so too—then I am rendered dumb—(if that were possible). If it is the same, then why, a-God's name, were the altars dragged down, and the screens burned, and the vestments and the images and the stoups and the pictures and the ornaments, all swept out? Why, a-God's name, was the old mass blotted out and this new mingle-mangle brought in, if it be all one? And for the last time, a-God's name, why is it death to say mass now, if it be all one? Go, go: Such talk is foolishness, and worse."

Mr. Buxton was silent for a moment as Anthony eyed him; and then burst out again.

"Ah! but worse than all are the folks that stand with one leg on either stool. We are the old Church, say they;—standing with the Protestant leg in the air,—therefore let us have the money and the buildings: they are our right. And then when a poor Catholic says, Then let us have the old mass, and the old penance and the old images: Nay, nay, nay, they say, lifting up the Catholic leg and standing on the other, those are Popery; and we are Protestants; we have made away with all such mummery and muniments of superstition. And so they go see-sawing to and fro. When you run at one leg they rest them on the other, and you know not where to take them."

And so the talk went on. When the evening was over, and Anthony was rising to return to Lambeth, Mr. Buxton put his hand on his arm.

"Good Mr. Norris," he said, "you have been very patient with me. I have clacked this night like an old wife, and you have borne with me: and now I ask your pardon again. But I do pray God that He may show you light and bring you to the true Church; for there is no rest elsewhere."

Anthony thanked him for his good wishes.

"Indeed," he said, too, "I am grateful for all that you have said. You have shown me light, I think, on some things, and I ask your prayers."

"I go to Stanfield to-morrow," said Mr. Buxton; "it is a pleasant house, though its master says so, not far from Sir Philip Sidney's: if you would but come and see me there!"

"I am getting greatly perplexed," said Anthony, "and I think that in good faith I cannot stay long with the Archbishop; and if I leave him how gladly will I come to you for a few days; but it must not be till then."

"Ah! if you would but make the Spiritual Exercises in my house; I will provide a conductor; and there is nothing that would resolve your doubts so quickly."

Anthony was interested in this; and asked further details as to what these were.

"It is too late," said Mr. Buxton, "to tell you to-night. I will write from Stanfield."

Mr. Buxton came downstairs with Anthony to see him on to his horse, and they parted with much good-will; and Anthony rode home with a heavy and perplexed heart to Lambeth.

He spent a few days more pondering; and then determined to lay his difficulties before the Archbishop; and resign his position if Grindal thought it well.

He asked for an interview, and the Archbishop appointed an hour in the afternoon at which he would see him in Cranmer's parlour, the room above the vestry which formed part of the tower that Archbishop Cranmer had added to Lambeth House.

Anthony, walking up and down in the little tiled cloisters by the creek, a few minutes before the hour fixed, heard organ-music rolling out of the chapel windows; and went in to see who was playing. He came in through the vestry, and looking to the west end gallery saw there the back of old Dr. Tallis, seated at the little positive organ that the late Archbishop had left in his chapel, and which the present Archbishop had gladly retained, for he was a great patron of music, and befriended many musicians when they needed help—Dr. Tallis, as well as Byrd, Morley and Tye. There were a few persons in the chapel listening, the Reverend Mr. Wilson, one of the chaplains, being among them; and Anthony thought that he could not do better than sit here a little and quiet his thoughts, which were nervous and distracted at the prospect of his coming interview. He heard voices from overhead, which showed that the Archbishop was engaged; so he spoke to an usher stationed in the vestry, telling him that he was ready as soon as the Archbishop could receive him, and that he would wait in the chapel; and then made his way down to one of the return stalls at the west end, against the screen, and took his seat there.

This February afternoon was growing dark, and the only lights in the chapel were those in the organ loft; but there was still enough daylight outside to make the windows visible—those famous windows of Morton's, which, like those in King's Chapel, Cambridge, combined and interpreted the Old and New Testaments by an ingenious system of types and antitypes, in the manner of the "Biblia Pauperum." There was then only a single subject in each light; and Anthony let his eyes wander musingly to and fro in the east window from the central figure of the Crucified to the types on either side, especially to a touching group of the unconscious Isaac carrying the wood for his own death, as Christ His Cross. Beneath, instead of the old stately altar glowing with stuffs and precious metals and jewels which had once been the heart of this beautiful shrine, there stood now a plain solid wooden table that the Archbishop used for the Communion. Anthony looked at it, and sighed a little to himself. Did the altar and the table then mean the same thing?

Meanwhile the glorious music was rolling overhead in the high vaulted roof. The old man was extemporising; but his manner was evident even in that; there was a simple solemn phrase that formed his theme, and round this adorning and enriching it moved the grave chords. On and on travelled the melody, like the flow of a broad river; now sliding steadily through a smiling land of simple harmonies, where dwelt a people of plain tastes and solid virtues; now passing over shallows where the sun glanced and played in the brown water among the stones, as light arpeggio chords rippled up and vanished round about the melody; now entering a land of mighty stones and caverns where the echoes rang hollow and resonant, as the counterpoint began to rumble and trip like boulders far down out of sight, in subaqueous gloom; now rolling out again and widening, fuller and deeper as it went, moving in great masses towards the edge of the cataract that lies like a line across the landscape: it is inevitable now, the crash must come;—a chord or two pausing,—pausing;—and then the crash, stupendous and sonorous.

Then on again through elaborate cities where the wits and courtiers dwell, and stately palaces slide past upon the banks, and barges move upon its breast, on to the sea—that final full close that embraces and engulfs all music, all effort, all doubts and questionings, whether in art or theology, all life of intellect, heart or will—that fathomless eternal deep from which all comes and to which all returns, that men call the Love of God.

Anthony stirred in his seat; he had been here ten minutes, proposing to take his restless thoughts in hand and quiet them; and, lo! it had been done for him by the master who sat overhead. Here he, for the moment, remained, ready for anything—glad to take up the wood and bear it to the Mount of Sacrifice—content to be carried on in that river of God's Will to the repose of God's Heart—content to dwell meantime in the echoing caverns of doubt—in the glancing shadows and lights of an active life—in his own simple sunlit life in the country—or even to plunge over the cataract down into the fierce tormented pools in the dark—for after all the sea lay beyond; and he who commits himself to the river is bound to reach it.

He heard a step, and the usher stood by him.

"His Grace is ready, Master Norris."

Anthony rose and followed him.

The Archbishop received him with the greatest kindness. As Anthony came in he half rose, peering with his half-blind eyes, and smiling and holding out his hands.

"Come, Master Norris," he said, "you are always welcome. Sit down;" and he placed him in a chair at the table close by his own.

"Now, what is it?" he said kindly; for the old man's heart was a little anxious at this formal interview that had been requested by this favourite young officer of his.

Then Anthony, without any reserve, told him all; tracing out the long tale of doubt by landmarks that he remembered; mentioning the effect produced on his mind by the Queen's suspension of the Archbishop, especially dwelling on the arrest, the examination and the death of Campion, that had made such a profound impression upon him; upon his own reading and trains of thought, and the conversations with Mr. Buxton, though of course he did not mention his name; he ended by saying that he had little doubt that sooner or later he would be compelled to leave the communion of the Church of England for that of Rome; and by placing his resignation in the Archbishop's hands, with many expressions of gratitude for the unceasing kindness and consideration that he had always received at his hands.

There was silence when he had finished. A sliding panel in the wall near the chapel had been pushed back, and the mellow music of Dr. Tallis pealed softly in, giving a sweet and melodious background, scarcely perceived consciously by either of them, and yet probably mellowing and softening their modes of expression during the whole of the interview.

"Mr. Norris," said the Archbishop at last, "I first thank you for the generous confidence you have shown towards me: and I shall put myself under a further obligation to you by accepting your resignation: and this I do for both our sakes. For yours, because, as you confess, this action of the Queen's—(I neither condemn nor excuse it myself)—this action has influenced your thoughts: therefore you had best be removed from it to a place where you can judge more quietly. And I accept it for my own sake too; for several reasons that I need not trouble you with. But in doing this, I desire you, Mr. Norris, to continue to draw your salary until Midsummer:—nay, nay, you must let me have my say. You are at liberty to withdraw as soon as you have wound up your arrangements with Mr. Somerdine; he will now, as Yeoman of the Horse, have your duties as well as his own; for I do not intend to have another Gentleman of the Horse. As regards an increase of salary for him, that can wait until I see him myself. In any case, Mr. Norris, I think you had better withdraw before Mid-Lent Sunday.

"And now for your trouble. I know very well that I cannot be of much service to you. I am no controversialist. But I must bear my witness. This Papist with whom you have had talk seems a very plausible fellow. His arguments sound very plain and good; and yet I think you could prove anything by them. They seem to me like that openwork embroidery such as you see on Communion linen sometimes, in which the pattern is formed by withdrawing certain threads. He has cleverly omitted just those points that would ruin his argument; and he has made a pretty design. But any skilful advocate could make any other design by the same methods. He has not thought fit to deal with such words of our Saviour as what He says on Tradition; with what the Scriptures say against the worshipping of angels; with what St. Paul says in his Epistle to the Colossians, in the second chapter, concerning all those carnal ordinances which were done away by Christ, but which have been restored by the Pope in his despite; he does not deal with those terrible words concerning the man of sin and the mystery of iniquity. In fact, he takes just one word that Christ let fall about His Kingdom, and builds this great edifice upon it. You might retort to him in a thousand ways such as these. Bishop Jewell, in his book, as you know, deals with these questions and many more; far more fully than it is possible for you and me even to dream of doing. Nay, Mr. Norris; the only argument I can lay before you is this. There are difficulties and troubles everywhere; that there are such in the Church of England, who would care to deny? that there are equally such, aye, and far more, in the Church of Rome, who would care to deny, either? Meanwhile, the Providence of God has set you here and not there. Whatever your difficulties are here, are not of your choosing; but if you fly there (and I pray God you will not) there they will be. Be content, Master Norris; indeed you have a goodly heritage; be content with it; lest losing that you lose all."

Anthony was greatly touched by this moderate and courteous line that the Archbishop was taking. He knew well in his heart that the Church of Rome was, in the eyes of this old man, a false and deceitful body, for whom there was really nothing to be said. Grindal, in his travels abroad during the Marian troubles, had been deeply attracted by the Genevan theology, with whose professors he had never wholly lost touch; and Anthony guessed what an effort it was costing him, and what a strain it was on his conscience, thus to combine courtesy with faithfulness to what he believed to be true.

Grindal apparently feared he had sacrificed his convictions, for he presently added: "You know, Mr. Norris, that I think very much worse of Papistry than I have expressed; but I have refrained because I think that would not help you; and I desire to do that more than to relieve myself."

Anthony thanked him for his gentleness; saying that he quite understood his motives in speaking as he had done, and was deeply obliged to him for it.

The Archbishop, however, as indeed were most of the English Divines of the time, was far more deeply versed in destructive than constructive theology; and, to Anthony's regret, was presently beginning in that direction.

"It is beyond my imagination. Mr. Norris," he said, "that any who have known the simple Gospel should return to the darkness. See here," he went on, rising, and fumbling among his books, "I have somewhere here what they call an Indulgence."

He searched for a few minutes, and presently shook out of the leaves of Jewell's book a paper which he peered at, and then pushed over to Anthony.

It was a little rectangular paper, some four or five inches long; bearing a figure of Christ, wounded, with His hands bound together before Him, and the Cross with the superscription rising behind. In compartments on either side were instruments of the Passion, the spear, and the reed with the sponge, with other figures and emblems. Anthony spelt out the inscription.

"Read it aloud, Mr. Norris," said the Archbishop.

"'To them,'" read Anthony, "'that before this image of pity devoutly say five paternosters, five aves and a credo, piteously beholding these arms of Christ's Passion, are granted thirty-two thousand seven hundred and fifty-five years of pardon.'"

"Now, Mr. Norris," said the Archbishop, "have you considered that it is to that kind of religion that you are attracted? I will not comment on it; there is no need."

"Your Grace," said Anthony slowly, laying the paper down, "I need not say, I think, that this kind of thing is deeply distasteful to me too. Your Grace cannot dislike it more than I do. But then I do not understand it; I do not know what indulgences mean; I only know that were they as mad and foolish as we Protestants think them, no truthful or good man could remain a Papist for a day; but then there are many thoughtful and good men Papists; and I conclude from that that what we think the indulgences to be, cannot be what they really are. There must be some other explanation.

"And again, my lord, may I add this? If I were a Turk I should find many things in the Christian religion quite as repellent to me; for example, how can it be just, I should ask, that the death of an innocent man, such as Christ was, should be my salvation? How, again, is it just that faith should save? Surely one who has sinned greatly ought to do something towards his forgiveness, and not merely trust to another. But you, my lord, would tell me that there are explanations of these difficulties, and of many more too, of which I should gradually understand more and more after I was a Christian. Or again, it appears to me even now, Christian as I am, judging as a plain man, that predestination contradicts free-will; and no explanation can make them both reasonable. Yet, by the grace of God, I believe all these doctrines and many more, not because I understand them, for I do not; but because I believe that they are part of the Revelation of God. It is just so, too, with the Roman Catholic Church. I must not take this or that doctrine by itself; but I must make up my mind whether or no it is the one only Catholic Church, and then I shall believe all that she teaches, because she teaches it, and not because I understand it. You must forgive my dulness, my lord; but I am but a layman, and can only say what I think in simple words."

"But we must judge of a Christian body by what that body teaches," said the Archbishop. "On what other grounds are you drawn to the Papists, except by what they teach?"

"Yes, your Grace," said Anthony, "I do judge of the general body of doctrine, and of the effect upon the soul as a whole; but that is not the same as taking each small part, and making all hang upon that."

"Well, Mr. Norris," said the Archbishop, "I do not think we can talk much more now. It is new to me that these difficulties are upon you. But I entreat you to talk to me again as often as you will; and to others also—Dr. Redmayn, Mr. Chambers and others will be happy if they can be of any service to you in these matters: for few things indeed would grieve me more than that you should turn Papist."

Anthony thanked the Archbishop very cordially for his kindness, and, after receiving his blessing, left his presence. He had two or three more talks with him before he left, but his difficulties were in no way resolved. The Archbishop had an essentially Puritan mind, and could not enter into Anthony's point of view at all. It may be roughly said that from Grindal's standpoint all turned on the position and responsibility of the individual towards the body to which he belonged: and that Anthony rather looked at the corporate side first and the individual second. Grindal considered, for example, the details of the Catholic religion in reference to the individual, asking whether he could accept this or that: Anthony's tendency was rather to consider the general question first, and to take the difficulties in his stride afterwards. Anthony also had interviews with the Archdeacon and chaplain whom Grindal had recommended; but these were of even less service to him, as Dr. Redmayn was so frankly contemptuous, and Mr. Chambers so ignorant, of the Romish religion that Anthony felt he could not trust their judgment at all.

In the meanwhile, during this last fortnight of Anthony's Lambeth life, he received a letter from Mr. Buxton, explaining what were the Spiritual Exercises to which he had referred, and entreating Anthony to come and stay with him at Stanfield.

"Now come, dear Mr. Norris," he wrote, "as soon as you leave the Archbishop's service; I will place three or four rooms at your disposal, if you wish for quiet; for I have more rooms than I know what to do with; and you shall make the Exercises if you will with some good priest. They are a wonderful method of meditation and prayer, designed by Ignatius Loyola (one day doubtless to be declared saint), for the bringing about a resolution of all doubts and scruples, and so clearing the eye of the soul that she discerns God's Will, and so strengthening her that she gladly embraces it. And that surely is what you need just now in your perplexity."

The letter went on to describe briefly the method followed, and ended by entreating him again to come and see him. Anthony answered this by telling him of his resignation of his post at Lambeth, and accepting his invitation; and he arranged to spend the last three weeks before Easter at Stanfield, and to go down there immediately upon leaving Lambeth. He determined not to go to Great Keynes first, or to see Isabel, lest his resolution should be weakened. Already, he thought, his motives were sufficiently mixed and perverted without his further aggravating their earthly constituents.

He wrote to his sister, however, telling her of his decision to leave Lambeth; and adding that he was going to stay with a friend until Easter, when he hoped to return to the Dower House, and take up his abode there for the present. He received what he thought a very strange letter in return, written apparently under excitement strongly restrained. He read in it a very real affection for himself, but a certain reserve in it too, and even something of compassion; and there was a sentence in it that above all others astonished him.

"J. M. has been here, and is now gone to Douai. Oh! dear brother, some time no doubt you will tell us all. I feel so certain that there is much to explain."

Had she then guessed his part in the priest's release? Anthony wondered; but at any rate he knew, after his promise to the Queen, that he must not give her any clue. He was also surprised to hear that James had been to Great Keynes. He had inquired for him at the Tower on the Monday after his visit to Greenwich, and had heard that Mr. Maxwell was already gone out of England. He had not then troubled to write again, as he had no doubt but that his message to Lady Maxwell, which he had sent in his note to Isabel, had reached her; and that certainly she, and probably James too, now knew that he had been an entirely unconscious and innocent instrument in the priest's arrest. But that note, as has been seen, never reached its destination. Lady Maxwell did not care to write to the betrayer of her son; and Isabel on the one hand hoped and believed now that there was some explanation, but on the other did not wish to ask for it again, since her first request had been met by silence.

As the last days of his life at Lambeth were coming to an end, Anthony began to send off his belongings on packhorses to Great Keynes; and by the time that the Saturday before Mid-Lent Sunday arrived, on which he was to leave, all had gone except his own couple of horses and the bags containing his personal luggage.

His last interview with the Archbishop affected him very greatly.

He found the old man waiting for him, walking up and down Cranmer's parlour in an empty part of the room, where there was no danger of his falling. He peered anxiously at Anthony as he entered.

"Mr. Norris," he said, "you are greatly on my mind. I fear I have not done my duty to you. My God has taken away the great charge he called me to years ago, to see if I were fit or not for the smaller charge of mine own household, and not even that have I ruled well."

Anthony was deeply moved.

"My lord," he said, "if I may speak plainly to you, I would say that to my mind the strongest argument for the Church of England is that she brings forth piety and goodness such as I have seen here. If it were not for that, I should no longer be perplexed."

Grindal held up a deprecating hand.

"Do not speak so, Mr. Norris. That grieves me. However, I beseech you to forgive me for all my remissness towards you, and I wish to tell you that, whatever happens, you shall never cease to have an old man's prayers. You have been a good and courteous servant to me always—more than that, you have been my loving friend—I might almost say my son: and that, in a world that has cast me off and forgotten me, I shall not easily forget. God bless you, my dear son, and give you His light and grace."

When Anthony rode out of the gateway half an hour later, with his servant and luggage behind him, it was only with the greatest difficulty that he could keep from tears as he thought of the blind old man, living in loneliness and undeserved disgrace, whom he was leaving behind him.

Chapter Thirteen - The Spiritual Exercises

Anthony found that Mr. Buxton had seriously underestimated himself in describing his position as that of a plain country gentleman. Stanfield was one of the most beautiful houses that he had ever seen. On the day after his arrival, his host took him all over the house, at his earnest request, and told him its story; and as they passed from room to room, again and again Anthony found himself involuntarily exclaiming at the new and extraordinary beauties of architecture and furniture that revealed themselves.

The house itself had been all built in the present reign, before its owner had got into trouble; and had been fitted throughout on the most lavish scale, with furniture of German as well as of English manufacture. Mr. Buxton was a collector of pictures and other objects of art; and his house contained some of the very finest specimens of painting, bronzes, enamels, plate and woodwork procurable from the Continent.

The house was divided into two sections; the chief living rooms were in a long suite looking to the south on to the gardens, with a corridor on the north side running the whole length of the house on the ground-floor, from which a staircase rose to a similar corridor or gallery on the first floor. The second section of the house was a block of some half-dozen smallish rooms, with a private staircase of their own, and a private entrance and little walled garden as well in front. The house was mostly panelled throughout, and here and there hung pieces of magnificent tapestry and cloth of arras. All was kept, too, with a care that was unusual in those days—the finest woodwork was brought to a high polish, as well as all the brass utensils and steel fire-plates and dogs and such things. No two rooms were alike; each possessed some marked characteristic of its own—one bedroom, for example, was distinguished by its fourpost bed with its paintings on the canopy and head—another, by its little two-light high window with Adam and Eve in stained glass; another with a little square-window containing a crucifix, which was generally concealed by a sliding panel; another by two secret cupboards over the fire-place, and its recess fitted as an oratory; another by a magnificent piece of tapestry representing Saint Clara and Saint Thomas of Aquin, each holding a monstrance, with a third great monstrance in the centre, supported by angels.

Downstairs the rooms were on the same scale of magnificence. The drawing-room had an exquisite wooden ceiling with great pendants elaborately carved; the dining-room was distinguished by its glass, containing a collection of coats-of-arms of many of Mr. Buxton's friends who had paid him visits; the hall by its vast fire-place and the tapestries that hung round it.

The exterior premises were scarcely less remarkable; a fine row of stables, and kennels where greyhounds were kept, stood to the north and the east of the house; but the wonder of the country was the gardens to the south. Anthony hardly knew what to say for admiration as he went slowly through these with his host, on the bright spring morning, after visiting the house. These were elaborately laid out, and under Mr. Buxton's personal direction, for he was one of the few people in England at this time who really understood or cared for the art. His avenue of small clipped limes running down the main walk of the garden, his yew-hedges fashioned with battlements and towers; his great garden house with its vane; his fantastic dial in the fashion of a tall striped pole surmounted by a dragon;— these were the astonishment of visitors; and it was freely said that had not Mr. Buxton been exceedingly adroit he would have paid the penalty of his magnificence and originality by being forced to receive a royal visit—a favour that would have gone far to impoverish, if not to ruin him. The chancel of the parish-church overlooked the west end of his lime-avenue, while the east end of the garden terminated in a great gateway, of stone posts and wrought iron gates that looked out to the meadows and farm buildings of the estate, and up to which some day no doubt a broad carriage drive would be laid down. But at present the sweep of the meadows was unbroken.

It was to this beautiful place that Anthony found himself welcomed. His host took him at once on the evening of his arrival to the west block, and showed him his bedroom—that with the little cupboards and the oratory recess; and then, taking him downstairs again, showed him a charming little oak parlour, which he told him would be altogether at his private service.

"And you see," added Mr. Buxton, "in this walled garden in front you can have complete privacy, and thus can take the air without ever coming to the rest of the house; to which there is this one entrance on the ground floor." And then he showed him how the lower end of the long corridor communicated with the block.

"The only partners of this west block," he added, "will be the two priests—Mr. Blake, my chaplain, and Mr. Robert, who is staying with me a week or two; and who, I hope, will conduct you through the Exercises, as he is very familiar with them. You will meet them both at supper: of course they will be both dressed as laymen. The Protestants blamed poor Campion for that, you know; but had he not gone in disguise, they would only have hanged him all the sooner. I like not hypocrisy."

Anthony was greatly impressed by Father Robert when he met him at supper. He was a tall and big man, who seemed about forty years of age, with a long square-jawed face, a pointed beard and moustache, and shrewd penetrating eyes. He seemed to be a man in advance of his time; he was full of reforms and schemes that seemed to Anthony remarkably to the point; and they were reforms too quite apart from ecclesiasticism, but rather such as would be classed in our days under the title of Christian Socialism.

For example, he showed a great sympathy for the condition of the poor and outcast and criminals; and had a number of very practical schemes for their benefit.

"Two things," he said, in answer to a question of Anthony's, "I would do to-morrow if I had the power. First I would allow of long leases for fifty and a hundred years. Everywhere the soil is becoming impoverished; each man squeezes out of it as much as he can, and troubles not to feed the land or to care for it beyond his time. Long leases, I hold, would remedy this. It would encourage the farmer to look before him and think of his sons and his sons' sons. And second, I would establish banks for poor men. There is many a man now a-begging who would be living still in his own house, if there had been some honest man whom he could have trusted to keep his money for him, and, maybe, give him something for the loan of it: for in these days, when there is so much enterprise, money has become, as it were, a living thing that grows; or at the least a tool that can be used; and therefore, when it is lent, it is right that the borrower should pay a little for it. This is not the same as the usury that Holy Church so rightly condemns: at least, I hold not, though some, I know, differ from me."

After supper the talk turned on education: here, too, the priest had his views.

"But you are weary of hearing me!" he said, in smiling apology. "You will think me a schoolmaster."

"And I pray you to consider me your pupil," said Mr. Buxton. The priest made a little deprecating gesture.

"First, then," he said, "I would have a great increase of grammar schools. It is grievous to think of England as she will be when this generation grows up: the schooling was not much before; but now she has lost first the schools that were kept by Religious, and now the teaching that the chantry-priests used to give. But this perhaps may turn to advantage; for when the Catholic Religion is re-established in these realms, she will find how sad her condition is; and, I hope, will remedy it by a better state of things than before—first, by a great number of grammar schools where the lads can be well taught for small fees, and where many scholarships will be endowed; and then, so great will be the increase of learning, as I hope, that we shall need to have a third university, to which I should join a third Archbishoprick, for the greater dignity of both; and all this I should set in the north somewhere, Durham or Newcastle, maybe."

He spoke, too, with a good deal of shrewdness of the increase of highway robbery, and the remedies for it; remarking that, although in other respects the laws were too severe, in this matter their administration was too lax; since robbers of gentle birth could generally rely on pardon. He spoke of the Holy Brotherhood in Spain (with which country he seemed familiar), and its good results in the putting down of violence.

Anthony grew more and more impressed by this man's practical sense and ability; but less drawn to him in consequence as his spiritual guide. He fancied that true spirituality could scarcely exist in this intensely practical nature. When supper was over, and the priests had gone back to their rooms, and his host and he were seated before a wide blazing hearth in Mr. Buxton's own little room downstairs, he hinted something of the sort. Mr. Buxton laughed outright.

"My dear friend," he said, "you do not know these Jesuits (for of course you have guessed that he is one); their training and efficiency is beyond all imagining. In a week from now you will be considering how ever Father Robert can have the heart to eat his dinner or say 'good-day' with such a spiritual vision and insight as he has. You need not fear. Like the angel in the Revelation, he will call you up to heaven, hale you to the abyss and show you things to come. And, though you may not believe it, it is the man's intense and simple piety that makes him so clear-sighted and practical; he lives so close to God that God's works and methods, so perplexing to you and me, are plain to him."

They went on talking together for a while. Mr. Buxton said that Father Robert had thought it best for Anthony not to enter Retreat until the Monday evening; by which time he could have sufficiently familiarised himself with his new surroundings, so as not to find them a distraction during his spiritual treatment. Anthony agreed to this. Then they talked of all kinds of things. His host told him of his neighbours; and explained how it was that he enjoyed such liberty as he did.

"You noticed the church, Mr. Norris, did you not, at your arrival, overlooking the garden? It is a great advantage to me to have it so close. I can sit in my own garden and hear the Genevan thunders from within. He preaches so loud that I might, if I wished, hear sermons, and thus satisfy the law and his Reverence; and at the same time not go inside an heretical meeting-house, and thus satisfy my own conscience and His Holiness. But I fear that would not have saved me, had I not the ear of his Reverence. I will tell you how it was. When the laws began to be enforced hereabouts, his Reverence came to see me; and sat in that very chair that you now occupy.

"'I hear,' said he, cocking his eye at me, 'that her Grace is becoming strict, and more careful for the souls of her subjects.'

"I agreed with him, and said I had heard as much.

"'The fine is twenty pounds a month,' says he, 'for recusancy,' and then he looks at me again."

"At first I did not catch his meaning; for, as you have noticed, Mr. Norris, I am but a dull man in dealing with these sharp and subtle Protestants: and then all at once it flashed across me.

"'Yes, your Reverence,' I said, 'and it will be the end of poor gentlemen like me, unless some kind friend has pity on them. How happy I am in having you!' I said, 'I have never yet shown my appreciation as I should: and I propose now to give you, to be applied to what purposes you will, whether the sustenance of the minister or anything else, the sum of ten pounds a month; so long as I am not troubled by the Council. Of course, if I should be fined by the Council, I shall have to drop my appreciation for six months or so.'

"Well, Mr. Norris, you will hardly believe it, but the old doctor opened his mouth and gulped and rolled his eyes, like a trout taking a fly; and I was never troubled until fifteen months ago, when they got at me in spite of him. But he has lost, you see, a matter of one hundred and fifty pounds while I have been at Wisbeach; and I shall not begin to appreciate him again for another six months; so I do not think I shall be troubled again."

Anthony was amazed, and said so.

"Well," said the other, "I was astonished too; and should never have dreamt of appreciating him in such a manner unless he had proposed it. I had a little difficulty with Mr. Blake, who told me that it was a libellum, and that I should be ashamed to pay hush money. But I told him that he might call it what he pleased, but that I would sooner pay ten pounds a month and be in peace, than twenty pounds a month and be perpetually harassed: and Father Robert agrees with me, and so the other is content now."

The next day, which was Sunday, passed quietly. Mass was no doubt said somewhere in the house; though Anthony saw no signs of it. He himself attended the reverend doctor's ministrations in the morning; and found him to be what he had been led to expect.

In the afternoon he walked up and down the lime avenue with Father Robert, while the evening prayer and sermon rumbled forth through the broken chancel window; and they talked of the Retreat and the arrangements.

"You no doubt think, Mr. Norris," said the priest, "that I shall preach at you in this Retreat, and endeavour to force you into the Catholic Church; but I shall do nothing of the kind. The whole object of the Exercises is to clear away the false motives that darken the soul; to place the Figure of our Redeemer before the soul as her dear and adorable Lover and King; and then to kindle and inspire the soul to choose her course through the grace of God, for the only true final motive of all perfect action,—that is, the pure Love of God. Of course I believe, with the consent of my whole being, that the Catholic Church is in the right; but I shall not for a moment attempt to compel you to accept her. The final choice, as indeed the Retreat too, must be your free action, not mine."

They arranged too the details of the Retreat; and Anthony was shown the little room beyond Father Robert's bed-room, where the Exercises would be given; and informed that another gentleman who lived in the neighbourhood would come in every day for them too, but that he would have his meals separately, and that Anthony himself would have his own room and the room beneath entirely at his private disposal, as well as the little walled garden to walk in.

The next day Mr. Buxton took Anthony a long ride, to invigorate him for the Retreat that would begin after supper. Anthony learned to his astonishment and delight that Mary Corbet was a great friend of Mr. Buxton's.

"Why, of course I know her," he said. "I have known her since she was a tiny girl, and threw her mass-book at the minister's face the first time he read the morning prayer. God only knows why she was so wroth with the man for differing from herself on a point that has perplexed the wisest heads: but at any rate, wroth she was, and bang went her book. I had to take her out, and she was spitting like a kitten all down the aisle when the dog puts his head into the basket.

"'What's that man doing here?' she screamed out; 'where's the altar and the priest?' And then at the door, as luck would have had it, she saw that Saint Christopher was gone; and she began bewailing and bemoaning him until you'd have thought he'd have been bound to come down from heaven, as he did once across the dark river, and see what in the world the crying child wanted with him."

They came about half-way in their ride through the village of Penshurst; and on reaching the Park turned off under the beeches towards the house.

"We have not time to go in," said Mr. Buxton, "but I hope you will see the house sometime; it is a pattern of what a house should be; and has a pattern master."

As they came up to the Edwardine Gate-house, a pleasant-faced, quietly-dressed gentleman came riding out alone.

"Why, here he is!" said Mr. Buxton, and greeted him with great warmth, and made Anthony known to him.

"I am delighted to know Mr. Norris," said Sidney, with that keen friendly look that was so characteristic of him. "I have heard of him from many quarters."

He entreated them to come in; but Mr. Buxton said they had not time; but would if they might just glance into the great court. So Sidney took them through the gate-house and pointed out one or two things of interest from the entrance, the roof of the Great Hall built by Sir John de Pulteney, the rare tracery in its windows and the fine living-rooms at one side.

"I thank God for it every day," said Sidney gravely. "I cannot imagine why He should have given it me. I hope I am not fool enough to disparage His gifts, and pretend they are nothing: indeed, I love it with all my heart. I would as soon think of calling my wife ugly or a shrew."

"That is a good man and a gentleman," said Mr. Buxton, as they rode away at last in the direction of Leigh after leaving Sidney to branch off towards Charket, "and I do not know why he is not a Catholic. And he is a critic and a poet, men say, too."

"Have you read anything of his?" asked Anthony.

"Well," said the other, "to tell the truth, I have tried to read some sheets of his that he wrote for his sister, Lady Pembroke. He calls it 'Arcadia'; I do not know whether it is finished or ever will be. But it seemed to me wondrous dull. It was full of shepherds and swains and nymphs, who are perpetually eating collations which Phœbus or sunburnt Autumn, and the like, provides of his bounty; or any one but God Almighty; or else they are bathing and surprising one another all day long. It is all very sweet and exquisite, I know; and the Greece, where they all live and love one another, must be a very delightful country, as unlike this world as it is possible to imagine; but it wearies me. I like plain England and plain folk and plain religion and plain fare; but then I am a plain man, as I tell you so often."

As the afternoon sun drew near setting, they came through Tonbridge.

"Now, what can a man ask more," said Mr. Buxton, as they rode through it, "than a good town like this? It is not a great place, I know, with solemn buildings and wide streets; neither is it a glade or a dell; but it is a good clean English town; and I would not exchange it for Arcadia or Athens either."

Stanfield lay about two miles to the west; and on their way out, Mr. Buxton talked on about the country and its joys and its usefulness.

"Over there," he said, pointing towards Eridge, "was the first cannon made in England. I do not know if that is altogether to its credit, but it at least shows that we are not quite idle and loutish in the country. Then all about here is the iron; the very stirrups you ride in, Mr. Norris, most likely came from the ground beneath your feet; but it is sad to see all the woods cut down for the smelting of it. All these places for miles about here, and about Great Keynes too, are all named after the things of forestry and hunting. Buckhurst, Hartfield, Sevenoaks, Forest Row, and the like, all tell of the country, and will do so long after we are dead and gone."

They reached Stanfield, rode past the green and the large piece of water there, and up the long village street, and turned into the iron gates beyond the church, just as the dusk fell.

That evening after supper the Retreat began. The conduct of the Spiritual Exercises had not reached the elaboration to which they have been perfected since; nor, in Anthony's case, a layman and a young man, did Father Robert think fit to apply it even in all the details in which it would be used for a priest or for one far advanced in the spiritual life; but it was severe enough.

Every evening Father Robert indicated the subject of the following day's meditation; and then after private prayer Anthony retired to his room. He rose about seven o'clock in the morning, and took a little food at eight; then shortly before nine the first meditation was given elaborately. The first examination of conscience was made at eleven; followed by dinner at half-past. From half-past twelve to half-past one Anthony rested in his room; then until three he was encouraged to walk in the garden; at three the meditation was to be recalled point by point in the chapel, followed by spiritual reading; at five o'clock supper was served; and at half-past six the meditation was repeated with tremendous emphasis and fervent acts of devotion; at half-past eight a slight collation was laid in his room; and at half-past nine the meditation for the following day was given. Father Robert in his previous talks with Anthony had given him instructions as to how to occupy his own time, to keep his thoughts fixed and so forth. He had thought it wise too not to extend the Retreat for longer than a fortnight; so that it was proposed to end it on Palm Sunday. Two or three times in the week Anthony rode out by himself; and Father Robert was always at his service, besides himself coming sometimes to talk to him when he thought the strain or the monotony was getting too heavy.

As for the Exercises themselves, the effect of them on Anthony was beyond all description. First the circumstances under which they were given were of the greatest assistance to their effectiveness. There was every aid that romance and mystery could give. Then it was in a strange and beautiful house where everything tended to caress the mind out of all self-consciousness. The little panelled room in which the exercises were given looked out over the quiet garden, and no sound penetrated there but the far-off muffled noises of the peaceful village life, the rustle of the wind in the evergreens, and the occasional coo or soft flapping flight of a pigeon from the cote in the garden. The room itself was furnished with two or three faldstools and upright wooden arm-chairs of tolerable comfort; a table was placed at the further end, on which stood a realistic Spanish crucifix with two tapers always burning before it; and a little jar of fragrant herbs. Then there was the continual sense of slight personal danger that is such a spur to refined natures; here was a Catholic house, of which every member was strictly subject to penalties, and above all one of that mysterious Society of Jesus, the very vanguard of the Catholic army, and of which every member was a picked and trained champion. Then there was the amazing enthusiasm, experience, and skill of Father Robert, as he called himself; who knew human nature as an anatomist knows the structure of the human body; to whom the bewildering tangle of motives, good, bad and indifferent, in the soul, was as plain as paths in a garden; who knew what human nature needed, what it could dispense with, what was its power of resistance; and who had at his disposal for the storming of the soul an armoury of weapons and engines, every specimen of which he had tested and wielded over and over again. Little as Anthony knew it, Father Robert, during the first two days after his arrival, had occupied himself with sounding and probing the lad's soul, trying his intellect by questions that scarcely seemed to be so, taking the temperature of his emotional nature by tales and adroit remarks, and watching the effect of them; in short, with studying the soul who had come for his treatment as a careful doctor examines the health of a new patient before he issues his prescription. And then, lastly, there were the Exercises themselves, a mighty weapon in any hands; and all but irresistible when directed by the skill, and inspired by the enthusiasm and sincere piety of such a man as Father Robert.

The Exercises fell into three parts, each averaging in Anthony's case about five days. First came the Purgative Exercises: the object of these was to cleanse and search out the very recesses of the soul; as fire separates gold from alloy.

As Anthony knelt in the little room before the Crucifix day by day, it seemed to him as if the old conventional limitations and motives of action and control were rolling back, revealing the realities of the spiritual world. The Exercises began with an elaborate exposition of the End of man—which may be roughly defined as the Glory of God attained through the saving and sanctifying of the individual. Every creature of God, then, that the soul encounters must be tested by this rule, How far does the use of it serve for the final end? For it must be used so far, and no farther. Here then was a diagram of the Exercises, given in miniature at the beginning.

Then the great facts that practically all men acknowledge, and upon which so few act, were brought into play. Hell, Judgment and Death in turn began to work upon the lad's soul—these monstrous elemental Truths that underlie all things. As Father Robert's deep vibrating voice spoke, it appeared to Anthony as if the room, the walls, the house, the world, all shrank to filmy nothingness before the appalling realities of these things. In that strange and profound "Exercise of the senses" he heard the moaning and the blasphemies of the damned, of those rebellious free wills that have enslaved themselves into eternal bondage by a deliberate rejection of God—he put out his finger and tasted the bitterness of their furious tears—the very reek of sin came to his nostrils, of that corruption that is in existence through sin; nay, he saw the very flaming hells red with man's wrath against his Maker.

Then he traced back, under the priest's direction, the Judgment through which every soul must pass; he saw the dead, great and small, stand before God; the books, black with blotted shame, were borne forth by the recording angels and spread before the tribunal. His ears tingled with that condemning silence of the Judge beyond Whom there is no appeal, from whose sentence there is no respite, and from whose prison there is no discharge; and rang with that pealing death-sentence at which the angels hide their faces, but to which the conscience of the criminal assents that it is just. His soul looked out at those whirling hosts on either side, that black cloud going down to despair, that radiant company hastening to rise to the Uncreated Light in whom there is no darkness at all—and cried in piteous suspense to know on which side she herself one day would be.

Then he came yet one step further back still, and told himself the story of his death. He saw the little room where he would lie, his bed in one corner; he saw Isabel beside the bed; he saw himself, white, gasping, convulsed, upon it—the shadows of the doctor and the priest were upon the wall—he heard his own quick sobbing breath, he put out his finger and touched his own forehead wet with the death-dew—he tasted and smelt the faint sickly atmosphere that hangs about a death chamber; and he watched the grey shadow of Azrael's wing creep across his face. Then he saw the sheet and the stiff form beneath it; and knew that they were his features that were hidden; and that they were his feet that stood up stark below the covering. Then he visited his own grave, and saw the month-old grass blowing upon it, and the little cross at the head; then he dug down through the soil, swept away the earth from his coffin-plate; drew the screws and lifted the lid....

Then he placed sin beneath the white light; dissected it, analysed it, weighed it and calculated its worth, watched its development in the congenial surroundings of an innocent soul, that is rich in grace and leisure and gifts, and saw the astonishing reversal of God's primal law illustrated in the process of corruption—the fair, sweet, fragrant creature passing into foulness. He looked carefully at the stages and modes of sin—venial sins, those tiny ulcers that weaken, poison and spoil the soul, even if they do not slay it—lukewarmness, that deathly slumber that engulfs the living thing into gradual death—and, finally, mortal sin, that one and only wholly hideous thing. He saw the indescribable sight of a naked soul in mortal sin; he saw how the earth shrank from it, how nature grew silent at it, how the sun darkened at it, how hell yelled at it, and the Love of God sickened at it.

And so, as the purgative days went by, these tempests poured over his soul, sifted through it, as the sea through a hanging weed, till all that was not organically part of his life was swept away, and he was left a simple soul alone with God. Then the second process began.

To change the metaphor, the canvas was now prepared, scoured, bleached and stretched. What is the image to be painted upon it? It is the image of Christ.

Now Father Robert laid aside his knives and his hammer, and took up his soft brushes, and began stroke by stroke, with colours beyond imagining, to lay upon the eager canvas the likeness of an adorable Lover and King. Anthony watched the portrait grow day by day with increasing wonder. Was this indeed the Jesus of Nazareth of whom he had read in the Gospels? he rubbed his eyes and looked; and yet there was no possibility of mistake,—line for line it was the same.

But this portrait grew and breathed and moved, and passed through all the stages of man's life. First it was the Eternal Word in the bosom of the Father, the Beloved Son who looked in compassion upon the warring world beneath; and offered Himself to the Father who gave Him through the Energy of the Blessed Spirit.

Then it was a silent Maid that he saw waiting upon God, offering herself with her lily beside her; and in answer on a sudden came the lightning of Gabriel's appearing, and, lo! the Eternal Word stole upon her down a ray of glory. And then at last he saw the dear Child born; and as he looked he was invited to enter the stable; and again he put out his hand and touched the coarse straw that lay in the manger, and fingered the rough brown cord that hung from Mary's waist, and smelled the sweet breath of the cattle, and the burning oil of Joseph's lantern hung against the wall, and shivered as the night wind shrilled under the ill-fitting door and awoke the tender Child.

Then he watched Him grow to boyhood, increasing in wisdom and stature, Him who was uncreated Wisdom, and in whose Hands are the worlds—followed Him, loving Him more at every step, to and from the well at Nazareth with the pitcher on His head: saw Him with blistered hands and aching back in the carpenter's shop; then at last went south with Him to Jordan; listened with Him, hungering, to the jackals in the wilderness; rocked with Him on the high Temple spire; stared with Him at the Empires of all time, and refused them as a gift. Then he went with Him from miracle to miracle, laughed with joy at the leper's new skin; wept in sorrow and joy with the mother at Nain, and the two sisters at Bethany; knelt with Mary and kissed His feet; went home with Matthew and Zaccheus, and sat at meat with the merry sinners; and at last began to follow silent and amazed with face set towards Jerusalem, up the long lonely road from Jericho.

Then, with love that almost burned his heart, he crouched at the moonlit door outside and watched the Supper begin. Judas pushed by him, muttering, and vanished in the shadows of the street. He heard the hush fall as the Bread was broken and the Red Wine uplifted; and he hid his face, for he dared not yet look with John upon a glory whose veils were so thin. Then he followed the silent company through the overhung streets to the Temple Courts, and down across the white bridge to the garden door. Then, bolder, he drew near, left the eight and the three and knelt close to the single Figure, who sobbed and trembled and sweated blood. Then he heard the clash of weapons and saw the glare of the torches, and longed to warn Him but could not; saw the bitter shame of the kiss and the arrest and the flight; and followed to Caiaphas' house; heard the stinging slap; ran to Pilate's house; saw that polished gentleman yawn and sneer; saw the clinging thongs and the splashed floor when the scourging was over; followed on to Calvary; saw the great Cross rise up at last over the heads of the crowd, and heard the storm of hoots and laughter and the dry sobs of the few women. Then over his head the sun grew dull, and the earth rocked and split, as the crosses reeled with their swinging burdens. Then, as the light came back, and the earth ended her long shudder, he saw in the evening glow that his Lord was dead. Then he followed to the tomb; saw the stone set and sealed and the watch appointed; and went home with Mary and John, and waited.

Then on Easter morning, wherever his Lord was, he was there too; with Mary in that unrecorded visit; with the women, with the Apostles; on the road to Emmaus; on the lake of Galilee; and his heart burned with Christ at his side, on lake and road and mountain.

Then at last he stood with the Twelve and saw that end that was so glorious a beginning; saw that tender sky overhead generate its strange cloud that was the door of heaven; heard far away the trumpets cry, and the harps begin to ripple for the new song that the harpers had learned at last; and then followed with his eyes the Lord whom he had now learned to know and love as never before, as He passed smiling and blessing into the heaven from which one day He will return....

There, then, as Anthony looked on the canvas, was that living, moving face and figure. What more could He have done that He did not do? What perfection could be dreamed of that was not already a thousand times His?

And when the likeness was finished, and Father Robert stepped aside from the portrait that he had painted with such tender skill and love, it is little wonder that this lad threw himself down before that eloquent vision and cried with Thomas, My Lord and my God!

Then, very gently, Father Robert led him through those last steps; up from the Illuminative to the Unitive; from the Incarnate Life with its warm human interests to that Ineffable Light that seems so chill and unreal to those who only see it through the clouds of earth, into that keen icy stillness, where only favoured and long-trained souls can breathe, up the piercing air of the slopes that lead to the Throne, and there in the listening silence of heaven, where the voice of adoration itself is silent through sheer intensity, where all colours return to whiteness and all sounds to stillness, all forms to essence and all creation to the Creator, there he let him fall in self-forgetting love and wonder, breathe out his soul in one ardent all-containing act, and make his choice.

Chapter Fourteen - Easter Day

Holy Week passed for Anthony like one of those strange dreams in which the sleeper awakes to find tears on his face, and does not know whether they are for joy or sorrow. At the end of the Retreat that closed on Palm Sunday evening, Anthony had made his choice, and told Father Robert.

It was not the Exercises themselves that were the direct agent, any more than were the books he had read: the books had cleared away intellectual difficulties, and the Retreat moral obstacles, and left his soul desiring the highest, keen to see it, and free to embrace it. The thought that he would have to tell Isabel appeared to him of course painful and difficult; but it was swallowed up in the joy of his conversion. He made an arrangement with Father Robert to be received at Cuckfield on Easter Eve; so that he might have an opportunity of telling Isabel before he took the actual step. The priest told him he would give him a letter to Mr. Barnes, so that he might be received immediately upon his arrival.

Holy Week, then, was occupied for Anthony in receiving instruction each morning in the little oak parlour from Father Robert; and in attending the devotions in the evening with the rest of the household. He also heard mass each day.

It was impossible, of course, to carry out the special devotions of the season with the splendour and elaboration that belonged to them; but Anthony was greatly impressed by what he saw. The tender reverence with which the Catholics loved to linger over the details of the Passion, and to set them like precious jewels in magnificent liturgical settings, and then to perform these stately heart-broken approaches to God with all the dignity and solemnity possible, appealed to him in strong contrast to the cold and loveless services, as he now thought them, of the Established Church that he had left.

On the Good Friday evening he was long in the parlour with Father Robert.

"I am deeply thankful, my son," he said kindly, "that you have been able to come to a decision. Of course I could have wished you to enter the Society; but God has not given you a vocation to that apparently. However, you can do great work for Him as a seminary priest; and I am exceedingly glad that you will be going to Douai so soon."

"I must just put my affairs in order at home," he said, "and see what arrangements my sister will wish to make; and by Midsummer at the latest I shall hope to be gone."

"I must be off early to-morrow," said the priest. "I have to be far from here by to-morrow night, in a house where I shall hope to stay until I, too, go abroad again. Possibly we may meet at Douai in the autumn. Well, my son, pray for me."

Anthony knelt for his blessing, and the priest was gone.

Presently Mr. Buxton came in and sat down. He was full of delight at the result of his scheme; and said so again and again.

"Who could have predicted it?" he cried. "To think that you were visiting me in prison fifteen months ago; and now this has come about in my house! Truly the Gospel blessing on your action has not been long on the way! And that you will be a priest, too! You must come and be my chaplain some day; if we are both alive and escape the gallows so long. Old Mr. Blake is sore displeased with me. I am a trial to him, I know. He will hardly speak to me in my own house; I declare I tremble when I meet him in the gallery; for fear he will rate me before my servants. I forget what his last grievance is; but I think it is something to do with a saint that he wishes me to be devout to; and I do not like her. Of course I do not doubt her sanctity; but Mr. Blake always confuses veneration and liking. I yield to none in my veneration for Saint What's-her-name; but I do not like her; and that is an end of the matter."

After a little more talk, Mr. Buxton looked at Anthony curiously a moment or two; and then said:

"I wonder you have not guessed yet who Father Robert is; for I am sure you know that that cannot be his real name." Anthony looked at him wonderingly.

"Well, he is in bed now; and will be off early to-morrow; and I have his leave to tell you. He is Father Persons, of whom you may have heard."

Anthony stared.

"Yes," said his host, "the companion of Campion. All the world supposes him to be in Rome; and I think that not half-a-dozen persons besides ourselves know where he is; but at this moment, I assure you, Father Robert Persons, of the Society of Jesus, is asleep (or awake, as the case may be) in the little tapestry chamber overhead."

"Now," went on Mr. Buxton, "that you are one of us, I will tell you quite plainly that Father Robert, as we will continue to call him, is in my opinion one of the most devout priests that ever said mass; and also one of the most shrewd men that ever drew breath; but I cannot follow him everywhere. You will find, Mr. Anthony, that the Catholics in England are of two kinds: those who seem to have as their motto the text I quoted to you in Lambeth prison; and who count their duty to Cæsar as scarcely less important than their direct duty to God. I am one of these: I sincerely desire above all things to serve her Grace, and I would not, for all the world, join in any confederacy to dethrone her, for I hold she is my lawful and true Prince. Then there is another party who would not hesitate for a moment to take part against their Prince, though I do not say to the slaying of her, if thereby the Catholic Religion could be established again in these realms. It is an exceedingly difficult point; and I understand well how honest and good men can hold that view: for they say, and rightly, that the Kingdom of God is the first thing in the world, and while they may not commit sin of course to further it, yet in things indifferent they must sacrifice all for it; and, they add, it is indifferent as to who sits on the throne of England; therefore one Prince may be pushed off it, so long as no crime is committed in the doing of it, and another seated there; if thereby the Religion may be so established again. You see the point, Mr. Anthony, no doubt; and how fine and delicate it is. Well, Father Robert is, I think, of that party; and so are many of the authorities abroad. Now I tell you all this, and on this sacred day too, because I may have no other opportunity; and I do not wish you to be startled or offended after you have become a Catholic. And I entreat you to be warm and kindly to those who take other views than your own; for I fear that many troubles lie in front of us of our own causing: for there are divisions amongst us already: although not at all of course (for which I thank God) on any of the saving truths of the Faith."

Anthony's excitement on hearing Father Robert's real name was very great. As he lay in bed that night the thought of it all would hardly let him sleep. He turned to and fro, trying to realise that there, within a dozen yards of him, lay the famous Jesuit for whose blood all Protestant England was clamouring. The name of Persons was still sinister and terrible even to this convert; and he could scarcely associate in his thoughts all its suggestiveness with that kindly fervent lover of Jesus Christ who had led him with such skill and tenderness along the way of the Gospel. Others in England were similarly astonished in later years to learn that a famous Puritan book of devotions was scarcely other than a reprint of Father Persons' "Christian Directory."

The following day about noon, after an affectionate good-bye to his host and Mr. Blake, Anthony rode out of the iron-wrought gates and down the village street in the direction of Great Keynes.

It was a perfect spring-day. Overhead there was a soft blue sky with translucent clouds floating in it; underfoot and on all sides the mystery of life was beginning to stir and manifest itself. The last touch of bitterness had passed from the breeze, and all living growth was making haste out into the air. The hedges were green with open buds, and bubbling with the laughter and ecstasy of the birds; the high sloping overhung Sussex lanes were sweet with violets and primroses; and here and there under the boughs Anthony saw the blue carpet of bell-flowers spread. Rabbits whisked in and out of the roots, superintending and provisioning the crowded nurseries underground; and as Anthony came out, now and again on the higher and open spaces larks vanished up their airy spirals of song into the illimitable blue; or hung, visible musical specks against a fleecy cloud, pouring down their thin cataract of melody. And as he rode, for every note of music and every glimpse of colour round him, his own heart poured out pulse after pulse of that spiritual essence that lies beneath all beauty, and from which all beauty is formed, to the Maker of all this and the Saviour of himself. There were set wide before him now the gates of a kingdom, compared to which this realm of material life round about was but a cramped and wintry prison after all.

How long he had lived in the cold and the dark! he thought; kept alive by the refracted light that stole down the steps to where he sat in the shadow of death; saved from freezing by the warmth of grace that managed to survive the chill about him; and all the while the Catholic Church was glowing and pulsating with grace, close to him and yet unseen; that great realm full of heavenly sunlight, that was the life of all its members—that sunlight that had poured down so steadily ever since the winter had rolled away on Calvary; and that ever since then had been elaborating and developing into a thousand intricate forms all that was capable of absorbing it. One by one the great arts had been drawn into that Kingdom, transformed and immortalised by the vital and miraculous sap of grace; philosophies, languages, sciences, all in turn were taken up and sanctified; and now this Puritan soul, thirsty for knowledge and grace, and so long starved and imprisoned, was entering at last into her heritage.

All this was of course but dimly felt in the direct perceptions of Anthony; but Father Robert had said enough to open something of the vision, and he himself had sufficient apprehension to make him feel that the old meagre life was passing away, and a new life of unfathomed possibilities beginning. As he rode the wilderness appeared to rejoice and blossom like the rose, as the spring of nature and grace stirred about and within him; and only an hour or two's ride away lay the very hills and streams of the Promised Land.

About half-past three he crossed the London road, and before four o'clock he rode round to the door of the Dower House, dismounted, telling the groom to keep his horse saddled.

He went straight through the hall, calling Isabel as he went, and into the garden, carrying his flat cap and whip and gloves: and as he came out beneath the holly tree, there she stood before him on the top of the old stone garden steps, that rose up between earthen flower-jars to the yew-walk on the north of the house. He went across the grass smiling, and as he came saw her face grow whiter and whiter. She was in a dark serge dress with a plain ruff, and a hood behind it, and her hair was coiled in great masses on her head. She stood trembling, and he came up and took her in his arms tenderly and kissed her, for his news would be heavy presently.

"Why, Isabel," he said, "you look astonished to see me. But I could not well send a man, as I had only Geoffrey with me."

She tried to speak, but could not; and looked so overwhelmed and terrified that Anthony grew frightened; he saw he must be very gentle.

"Sit down," he said, drawing her to a seat beside the path at the head of the steps: "and tell me the news."

By a great effort she regained her self-control.

"I did not know when you were coming," she said tremulously. "I was startled."

He talked of his journey for a few minutes; and of the kindness of the friend with whom he had been staying, and the beauty of the house and grounds, and so on; until she seemed herself again; and the piteous startled look had died out of her eyes: and then he forced himself to approach his point; for the horse was waiting saddled; and he must get to Cuckfield and back by supper if possible.

He took her hand and played with it gently as he spoke, turning over her rings.

"Isabel," he said, "I have news to tell you. It is not bad news—at least I think not—it is the best thing that has ever come to me yet, by the grace of God, and so you need not be anxious or frightened. But I am afraid you may think it bad news. It—it is about religion, Isabel."

He glanced at her, and saw that terrified look again in her face: she was staring at him, and her hand in his began to twitch and tremble.

"Nay, nay," he said, "there is no need to look like that. I have not lost my faith in God. Rather, I have gained it. Isabel, I am going to be a Catholic."

A curious sound broke from her lips; and a look so strange came into her face that he threw his arm round her, thinking she was going to faint: and he spoke sharply.

"Isabel, Isabel, what is there to fear? Look at me!"

Then a cry broke from her white lips, and she struggled to stand up.

"No, no, no! you are mocking me. Oh! Anthony, what have I done, that you should treat me like this?"

"Mocking!" he said, "before God I am not. My horse is waiting to take me to the priest."

"But—but—" she began again. "Oh! then what have you done to James Maxwell?"

"James Maxwell! Why? What do you mean? You got my note!"

"No—no. There was no answer, he said."

Anthony stared.

"Why, I wrote—and then Lady Maxwell! Does she not know, and James himself?"

Isabel shook her head and looked at him wildly.

"Well, well, that must wait; one thing at a time," he said. "I cannot wait now. I must go to Cuckfield. Ah! Isabel, say you understand."

Once or twice she began to speak, but failed; and sat panting and staring at him.

"My darling," he said, "do not look like that: we are both Christians still: we at least serve the same God. Surely you will not cast me off for this?"

"Cast you off?" she said; and she laughed piteously and sharply; and then was grave again. Then she suddenly cried, "Oh, Anthony, swear to me you are not mocking me."

"My darling," he said, "why should I mock you? I have made the Exercises, and have been instructed; and I have here a letter to Mr. Barnes from the priest who has taught me; so that I may be received to-night, and make my Easter duties: and Geoffrey is still at the door holding Roland to take me to Cuckfield to-night."

"To Cuckfield!" she said. "You will not find Mr. Barnes there."

"Not there! why not? Where shall I find him? How do you know?"

"Because he is here," she went on in the same strange voice, "at the Hall."

"Well," said Anthony, "that saves me a journey. Why is he here?"

"He is here to say mass to-morrow."

"Ah!"

"And—and—"

"What is it, Isabel?"

"And—to receive me into the Church to-night."

The brother and sister walked up and down that soft spring evening after supper, on the yew-walk; with the whispers and caresses of the scented breeze about them, the shy dewy eyes of the stars looking down at them between the tall spires of the evergreens overhead; and in their hearts the joy of lovers on a wedding-night.

Anthony had soon told the tale of James Maxwell and Isabel had nearly knelt to ask her brother's pardon for having ever allowed even the shadow of a suspicion to darken her heart. Lady Maxwell, too, who had come down with her sister to see Isabel about some small arrangement, was told; and she too had been nearly overwhelmed with the joy of knowing that the lad was innocent, and the grief of having dreamed he could be otherwise, and at the wholly unexpected news of his conversion; but she had gone at last back to the Hall to make all ready for the double ceremony of that night, and the Paschal Feast on the next day. Mistress Margaret was in Isabel's room, moving about with a candle, and every time that the two reached the turn at the top of the steps they saw her light glimmering.

Then Anthony, as they walked under the stars, told Isabel of his great hope that he, too, one day would be a priest, and serve God and his countrymen that way.

"Oh, Anthony," she whispered, and clung to that dear arm that held her own; terrified for the moment at the memory of what had been the price of priesthood to James Maxwell.

"And where shall you be trained for it?" she asked.

"At Douai: and—Isabel—I think I must go this summer."

"This summer!" she said. "Why—" and she was silent.

"Anthony," she went on, "I would like to tell you about Hubert."

And then the story of the past months came out; she turned away her face as she talked; and at last she told him how Hubert had come for his answer, a week before his time.

"It was on Monday," she said. "I heard him on the stairs, and stood up as he came in; and he stopped at the door in silence, and I could not bear to look at him. I could hear him breathing quickly; and then I could not bear to—think of it all; and I dropped down into my chair again, and hid my face in my arm and burst into crying. And still he said nothing, but I felt him come close up to me and kneel down by me; and he put his hand over mine, and held them tight; and then he whispered in a kind of quick way:

"'I will be what you please; Catholic or Protestant, or what you will'; and I lifted my head and looked at him, because it was dreadful to hear him—Hubert—say that: and he was whiter than I had ever seen him; and then—then he began to wrinkle his mouth—you know the way he does when his horse is pulling or kicking: and then he began to say all kinds of things: and oh! I was so sorry; because he had behaved so well till then."

"What did he say?" asked Anthony quickly.

"Ah! I have tried to forget," said Isabel. "I do not want to think of him as he was when he was angry and disappointed. At last he flung out of the room and down the stairs, and I have not seen him since. But Lady Maxwell sent for me the same evening an hour later; and told me that she could not live there any longer. She said that Hubert had ridden off to London; and would not be down again till Whitsuntide; but that she must be gone before then. So I am afraid that he said things he ought not; but of course she did not tell me one word. And she asked me to go with her. And, and—Anthony, I did not know what to say; because I did not know what you would do when you heard that I was a Catholic; I was waiting to tell you when you came home—but now—but now—Oh, Anthony, my darling!"

At last the two came indoors. Mistress Margaret met them in the hall. She looked for a moment at the two; at Anthony in his satin and lace and his smiling face over his ruff and his steady brown eyes; and Isabel on his arm, with her clear pale face and bosom and black high-piled hair, and her velvet and lace, and a rope of pearls.

"Why," said the old nun, smiling, "you look a pair of lovers."

Then presently the three went together up to the Hall.

An hour or two passed away; the Paschal moon was rising high over the tall yew hedge behind the Italian garden; and the Hall lay beneath it with silver roofs and vane; and black shadows under the eaves and in the angles. The tall oriel window of the Hall looking on to the terrace shone out with candlelight; and the armorial coats of the Maxwells and the families they had married with glimmered in the upper panes. From the cloister wing there shone out above the curtains lines of light in Lady Maxwell's suite of rooms, and the little oak parlour beneath, as well as from one or two other rooms; but the rest of the house, with the exception of the great hall and the servants' quarters, was all dark. It was as if the interior life had shifted westwards, leaving the remainder desolate. The gardens to the south were silent, for the night breeze had dropped; and the faint ripple of the fountain within the cloister-court was the only sound that broke the stillness. And once or twice the sleepy chirp of a bird nestling by his mate in the deep shrubberies showed that the life of the spring was beating out of sight.

And then at last the door in the west angle of the terrace, between the cloister wing and the front of the house, opened, and a flood of mellow light poured out on to the flat pavement. A group stood within the little oaken red-tiled lobby; Lady Maxwell and her sister, slender and dignified in their dark evening dresses and ruffs; Anthony holding his cap, and Isabel with a lace shawl over her head, and at the back the white hair and ruddy face of old Mr. Barnes in his cassock at the bottom of the stairs.

As Mistress Margaret opened the door and looked out, Lady Maxwell took Isabel in her arms and kissed her again and again. Then Anthony took the old lady's hand and kissed it, but she threw her other hand round him and kissed him too on the forehead. Then without another word the brother and sister came out into the moonlight, passed down the side of the cloister wing, and turning once to salute the group who waited, framed and bathed in golden light, they turned the corner to the Dower House. Then the door closed; the oriel window suddenly darkened, and an hour after the lights in the wing went out, and Maxwell Hall lay silver and grey again in the moonlight.

The night passed on. Once Isabel awoke, and saw her windows blue and mystical and her room full of a dim radiance from the bright night outside. It was irresistible, and she sprang out of bed and went to the window across the cool polished oak floor, and leaned with her elbows on the sill, looking out at the square of lawn and the low ivied wall beneath, and the tall trees rising beyond ashen-grey and olive-black in the brilliant glory that poured down from almost directly overhead, for the Paschal moon was at its height above the house.

And then suddenly the breathing silence was broken by a ripple of melody, and another joined and another; and Isabel looked and wondered and listened, for she had never heard before the music of the mysterious night-flight of the larks all soaring and singing together when the rest of the world is asleep. And she listened and wondered as the stream of song poured down from the wonderful spaces of the sky, rising to far-off ecstasies as the wheeling world sank yet further with its sleeping meadows and woods beneath the whirling singers; and then the earth for a moment turned in its sleep as Isabel listened, and the trees stirred as one deep breath came across the woods, and a thrush murmured a note or two beside the drive, and a rabbit suddenly awoke in the field and ran on to the lawn and sat up and looked at the white figure at the window; and far away from the direction of Lindfield a stag brayed.

"So longeth my soul," whispered Isabel to herself.

Then all grew still again; the trees hushed; the torrent of music, more tumultuous as it neared the earth, suddenly ceased; and Isabel at the window leaned further out and held her hands in the bath of light; and spoke softly into the night:

"Oh, Lord Jesus, how kind Thou art to me!"

Then at last the morning came, and Christ was risen beyond a doubt.

Just before the sun came up, when all the sky was luminous to meet him, the two again passed up and round the corner, and into the little door in the angle. There was the same shaded candle or two, for the house was yet dark within; and they passed up and on together through the sitting-room into the chapel where each had made a First Confession the night before, and had together been received into the Catholic Church. Now it was all fragrant with flowers and herbs; a pair of tall lilies leaned their delicate heads towards the altar, as if to listen for the soundless Coming in the Name of the Lord; underfoot all about the altar lay sprigs of sweet herbs, rosemary, thyme, lavender, bay-leaves; with white blossoms scattered over them—a soft carpet for the Pierced Feet; not like those rustling palm-swords over which He rode to death last week. The black oak chest that supported the altar-stone was glorious in its vesture of cloth-of-gold; and against the white-hung wall at the back, behind the silver candlesticks, leaned the gold plate of the house, to do honour to the King. And presently there stood there the radiant rustling figure of the Priest, his personality sheathed and obliterated beneath the splendid symbolism of his vestments, stiff and chinking with jewels as he moved.

The glorious Mass of Easter Day began.

"Immolatus est Christus. Itaque epulemur," Saint Paul cried from the south corner of the altar to the two converts. "Christ our Passover is sacrificed for us; therefore let us keep the feast, but not with the old leaven."

"Quis revolvet nobis lapidem?" wailed the women. "Who shall roll us away the stone from the door of the sepulchre?"

"And when they looked," cried the triumphant Evangelist, "they saw that the stone was rolled away; for it was very great"—"erat quippe magnus valde."

Here then they knelt at last, these two come home together, these who had followed their several paths so resolutely in the dark, not knowing that the other was near, yet each seeking a hidden Lord, and finding both Him and one another now in the full and visible glory of His Face—orto jam sole—for the Sun of Righteousness had dawned, and there was healing for all sorrows in His Wings.

"Et credo in unam sanctam Catholicam et Apostolicam Ecclesiam"—their hearts cried all together. "I believe at last in a Catholic Church; one, for it is built on one and its faith is one; holy, for it is the Daughter of God and the Mother of Saints; Apostolic, for it is guided by the Prince of Apostles and very Vicar of Christ."

"Et exspecto vitam venturi saeculi." "I look for the life of the world to come; and I count all things but loss, houses and brethren and sisters and father and mother and wife and children and lands, when I look to that everlasting life, and Him Who is the Way to it. Amen."

So from step to step the liturgy moved on with its sonorous and exultant tramp, and the crowding thoughts forgot themselves, and watched as the splendid heralds went by; the triumphant trumpets of Gloria in excelsis had long died away; the proclamation of the names and titles of the Prince had been made. Unum Dominum Jesum Christum; Filium Dei Unigenitum; Ex Patre natum ante omnia saecula; Deum de Deo; Lumen de Lumine; Deum Verum de Deo Vero; Genitum non factum; Consubstantialem Patri.

Then His first achievement had been declared; "Per quem omnia facta sunt."

Then his great and later triumphs; how He had ridden out alone from the Palace and come down the steep of heaven in quest of His Love; how He had disguised Himself for her sake; and by the crowning miracle of love, the mightiest work that Almighty God has ever wrought, He was made man; and the herald hushed his voice in awe as he declared it, and the people threw themselves prostrate in honour of this high and lowly Prince; then was recounted the tale of those victories that looked so bitterly like failures, and the people held their breath and whispered it too; then in rising step after step His last conquests were told; how the Black Knight was overthrown, his castle stormed and his prison burst; and the story of the triumph of the return and of the Coronation and the Enthronement at the Father's Right Hand on high.

The heralds passed on; and mysterious figures came next, bearing Melchisedech's gifts; shadowing the tremendous event that follows on behind.

After a space or two came the first lines of the bodyguard, the heavenly creatures dimly seen moving through clouds of glory, Angels, Dominations, Powers, Heavens, Virtues, and blessed Seraphim, all crying out together to heaven and earth to welcome Him Who comes after in the bright shadow of the Name of the Lord; and the trumpets peal out for the last time, "Hosanna in the highest."

Then a hush fell, and presently in the stillness came riding the great Personages who stand in heaven about the Throne; first, the Queen Mother herself, glorious within and without, moving in clothing of wrought gold, high above all others; then, the great Princes of the Blood Royal, who are admitted to drink of the King's own Cup, and sit beside Him on their thrones, Peter and Paul and the rest, with rugged faces and scarred hands; and with them great mitred figures, Linus, Cletus and Clement, with their companions.

And then another space and a tingling silence; the crowds bow down like corn before the wind, the far-off trumpets are silent; and He comes—He comes!

On He moves, treading under foot the laws He has made, yet borne up by them as on the Sea of Galilee; He Who inhabits eternity at an instant is made present; He Who transcends space is immanent in material kind; He Who never leaves the Father's side rests on His white linen carpet, held yet unconfined; in the midst of the little gold things and embroidery and candle-flames and lilies, while the fragrance of the herbs rises about Him. There rests the gracious King, before this bending group; the rest of the pageant dies into silence and nothingness outside the radiant circle of His Presence. There is His immediate priest-herald, who has marked out this halting-place for the Prince, bowing before Him, striving by gestures to interpret and fulfil the silence that words must always leave empty; here behind are the adoring human hearts, each looking with closed eyes into the Face of the Fairest of the children of men, each crying silently words of adoration, welcome and utter love.

The moments pass; the court ceremonies are performed. The Virgins that follow the Lamb, Felicitas, Perpetua, Agatha and the rest step forward smiling, and take their part; the Eternal Father is invoked again in the Son's own words; and at length the King, descending yet one further step of infinite humility, flings back the last vesture of His outward Royalty and casts Himself in a passion of haste and desire into the still and invisible depths of these two quivering hearts, made in His own Image, that lift themselves in an agony of love to meet Him....

Meanwhile the Easter morning is deepening outside; the sun is rising above the yew hedge, and the dew flashes drop by drop into a diamond and vanishes; the thrush that stirred and murmured last night is pouring out his song; and the larks that rose into the moonlight are running to and fro in the long meadow grass. The tall slender lilies that have not been chosen to grace the sacramental Presence-Chamber, are at least in the King's own garden, where He walks morning and evening in the cool of the day; and waiting for those who will have seen Him face to face....

And presently they come, the tall lad and his sister, silent and together, out into the radiant sunlight; and the joy of the morning and the singing thrush and the jewels of dew and the sweet swaying lilies are shamed and put to silence by the joy upon their faces and in their hearts.

Part Three

Chapter One - The Coming of Spain

The conflict between the Old Faith and the lusty young Nation went steadily forward after the Jesuit invasion; more and more priests poured into England; more and more were banished, imprisoned and put to death. The advent of Father Holt, the Jesuit, to Scotland in 1583 was a signal for a new outburst of Catholic feeling, which manifested itself not only in greater devotion to Religion, but, among the ill-instructed and impatient, in very questionable proceedings. In fact, from this time onward the Catholic cause suffered greatly from the division of its supporters into two groups; the religious and the political, as they may be named. The former entirely repudiated any desire or willingness to meddle with civil matters; its members desired to be both Catholics and Englishmen; serving the Pope in matters of Faith and Elizabeth in matters of civil life; but they suffered greatly from the indiscretions and fanaticism of the political group. The members of that party frankly regarded themselves as at war with an usurper and an heretic; and used warlike methods to gain their ends; plots against the Queen's life were set on foot; and their promoters were willing enough to die in defence of the cause. But the civil Government made the fatal mistake of not distinguishing between the two groups; again and again loyal Englishmen were tortured and hanged as traitors, because they shared their faith with conspirators.

There was one question, however, that was indeed on the borderline, exceedingly difficult to answer in words, especially for scrupulous consciences; and that was whether they believed in the Pope's deposing power; and this question was adroitly and deliberately used by the Government in doubtful cases to ensure a conviction. But whether or not it was possible to frame a satisfactory answer in words, yet the accused were plain enough in their deeds; and when the Armada at length was launched in '88, there were no more loyal defenders of England than the persecuted Catholics. Even before this, however, there had appeared signs of reaction among the Protestants, especially against the torture and death of Campion and his fellows; and Lord Burghley in '83 attempted to quiet the people's resentment by his anonymous pamphlet, "Execution of Justice in England," to which Cardinal Allen presently replied.

Ireland, which had been profoundly stirred by the military expedition from the continent in '80, at length was beaten and slashed into submission again; and the torture and execution of Hurley by martial law, which Elizabeth directed on account of his appointment to the See of Cashel, when the judges had pronounced there to be no case against him; and a massacre on the banks of the Moy in '86 of Scots who had come across as reinforcements to the Irish;—these were incidents in the black list of barbarities by which at last a sort of temporary quiet was brought to Ireland.

In Scottish affairs, the tangle, unravelled even still, of which Mary Stuart was the centre, led at last to her death. Walsingham, with extraordinary skill, managed to tempt her into a dangerous correspondence, all of which he tapped on the way: he supplied to her in fact the very instrument—an ingeniously made beer-barrel—through which the correspondence was made possible, and, after reading all the letters, forwarded them to their several destinations. When all was ripe he brought his hand down on a group of zealots, to whose designs Mary was supposed to be privy; and after their execution, finally succeeded, in '87, in obtaining Elizabeth's signature to her cousin's death-warrant. The storm already raging against Elizabeth on the Continent, but fanned to fury by this execution, ultimately broke in the Spanish Armada in the following year.

Meanwhile, at home, the affairs of the Church of England were far from prosperous. Puritanism was rampant; and a wail of dismay was evoked by the new demands of a Commission under Whitgift's guidance, in '82, whereby the Puritan divines were now called upon to assent to the Queen's Supremacy, the Thirty-nine Articles and the Prayer Book. In spite of the opposition, however, of Burghley and the Commons, Whitgift, who had by this time succeeded to Canterbury upon Grindal's death, remained firm; and a long and dreary dispute began, embittered further by the execution of Mr. Copping and Mr. Thacker in '83 for issuing seditious books in the Puritan cause. A characteristic action in this campaign was the issuing of a Puritan manifesto in '84, consisting of a brief, well-written pamphlet of a hundred and fifty pages under the title "A Learned Discourse of Ecclesiastical Government," making the inconsistent claim of desiring a return to the Primitive and Scriptural model, and at the same time of advocating an original scheme, "one not yet handled." It was practically a demand for the Presbyterian system of pastorate and government. To this Dr. Bridges replies with a tremendous tome of over fourteen hundred pages, discharged after three years of laborious toil; and dealing, as the custom then was, line by line, with the Puritan attack. To this in the following year an anonymous Puritan, under the name of Martin Marprelate, retorts with a brilliant and sparkling riposte addressed to "The right puissant and terrible priests, my clergy-masters of the Convocation-house," in which he mocks bitterly at the prelates, accusing them of Sabbath-breaking, time-serving, and popery,—calling one "dumb and duncetical," another "the veriest coxcomb that ever wore velvet cap," and summing them up generally as "wainscot-faced bishops," "proud, popish, presumptuous, profane paltry, pestilent, and pernicious prelates."

The Archbishop had indeed a difficult team to drive; especially as his coadjutors were not wholly proof against Martin's jibes. In '84 his brother of York had been mixed up in a shocking scandal; in '85 the Bishop of Lichfield was accused of simony; Bishop Aylmer was continually under suspicion of avarice, dishonesty, vanity and swearing; and the Bench as a whole was universally reprobated as covetous, stingy and weak.

In civil matters, England's relation with Spain was her most important concern. Bitter feeling had been growing steadily between the two countries ever since Drake's piracies in the Spanish dominions in America; and a gradually increasing fleet at Cadiz was the outward sign of it. Now the bitterness was deepened by the arrest of English ships in the Spanish ports in the early summer of '85, and the swift reprisals of Drake in the autumn; who intimidated and robbed important towns on the coast, such as Vigo, where his men behaved with revolting irreverence in the churches, and Santiago; and then proceeded to visit and spoil S. Domingo and Carthagena in the Indies.

Again in '87 Drake obtained the leave of the Queen to harass Spain once more, and after robbing and burning all the vessels in Cadiz harbour, he stormed the forts at Faro, destroyed Armada stores at Corunna, and captured the great treasure-ship San Felipe.

Elizabeth was no doubt encouraged in her apparent recklessness by the belief that with the Netherlands, which she had been compelled at last to assist, in a state of revolt, Spain would have little energy for reprisals upon England; but she grew more and more uneasy when news continued to arrive in England of the growing preparations for the Armada; France, too, was now so much involved with internal struggles, as the Protestant Henry of Navarre was now the heir to her Catholic throne, that efficacious intervention could no longer be looked for from that quarter, and it seemed at last as if the gigantic Southern power was about to inflict punishment upon the little northern kingdom which had insulted her with impunity so long.

In the October of '87 certain news arrived in England of the gigantic preparations being made in Spain and elsewhere: and hearts began to beat, and tongues to clack, and couriers to gallop. Then as the months went by, and tidings sifted in, there was something very like consternation in the country. Men told one another of the huge armament that was on its way, the vast ships and guns—all bearing down on tiny England, like a bull on a terrier. They spoke of the religious fervour, like that of a crusade, that inspired the invasion, and was bringing the flower of the Spanish nobility against them: the superstitious contrasted their own Lion, Revenge, and Elizabeth Jonas with the Spanish San Felipe, San Matteo, and Our Lady of the Rosary: the more practical thought with even deeper gloom of the dismal parsimony of the Queen, who dribbled out stores and powder so reluctantly, and dismissed her seamen at the least hint of delay.

Yet, little by little, as midsummer came and went, beacons were gathering on every hill, ships were approaching efficiency, and troops assembling at Tilbury under the supremely incompetent command of Lord Leicester.

Among the smaller seaports on the south coast, Rye was one of the most active and enthusiastic; the broad shallow bay was alive with fishing-boats, and the steep cobbled streets of the town were filled all day with a chattering exultant crowd, cheering every group of seamen that passed, and that spent long hours at the quay watching the busy life of the ships, and predicting the great things that should fall when the Spaniards encountered the townsfolk, should the Armada survive Drake's onslaught further west.

About July the twentieth more definite news began to arrive. At least once a day a courier dashed in through the south-west gate, with news that all must hold themselves ready to meet the enemy by the end of the month; labour grew more incessant and excitement more feverish.

About six o'clock on the evening of the twenty-ninth, as a long row of powder barrels was in process of shipping down on the quay, the men who were rolling them suddenly stopped and listened; the line of onlookers paused in their comments, and turned round. From the town above came an outburst of cries, followed by the crash of the alarm from the church-tower. In two minutes the quay was empty. Out of every passage that gave on to the main street poured excited men and women, some hysterically laughing, some swearing, some silent and white as they ran. For across the bay westwards, on a point beyond Winchelsea, in the still evening air rose up a stream of smoke shaped like a pine-tree, with a red smouldering root; and immediately afterwards in answer the Ypres tower behind the town was pouring out a thick drifting cloud that told to the watchers on Folkestone cliffs that the dreaded and longed-for foe was in sight of England.

Then the solemn hours of waiting began to pass. Every day and night there were watchers, straining their eyes westwards in case the Armada should attempt to coast along England to force a landing anywhere, and southwards in case they should pass nearer the French coast on their way to join the Prince of Parma; but there was little to be seen over that wide ring of blue sea except single vessels, or now and again half-a-dozen in company, appearing and fading again on some unknown quest. The couriers that came in daily could not tell them much; only that there had been indecisive engagements; that the Spaniards had not yet attempted a landing anywhere; and that it was supposed that they would not do so until a union with the force in Flanders had been effected.

And so four days of the following week passed; then on Thursday, August the fourth, within an hour or two after sunrise, the solemn booming of guns began far away to the south-west; but the hours passed; and before nightfall all was silent again.

The suspense was terrible; all night long there were groups parading the streets, anxiously conjecturing, now despondently, now cheerfully.

Then once again on the Friday morning a sudden clamour broke out in the town, and almost simultaneously a pinnace slipped out, spreading her wings and making for the open sea. A squadron of English ships had been sighted flying eastwards; and the pinnace was gone to get news. The ships were watched anxiously by thousands of eyes, and boats put out all along the coast to inquire; and within two or three hours the pinnace was back again in Rye harbour, with news that set bells ringing and men shouting. On Wednesday, the skipper reported, there had been an indecisive engagement during the dead calm that had prevailed in the Channel; a couple of Spanish store-vessels had been taken on the following morning, and a general action had followed, which again had been indecisive; but in which the English had hardly suffered at all, while it was supposed that great havoc had been wrought upon the enemy.

But the best of the news was that the Rye contingent was to set sail at once, and unite with the English fleet westward of Calais by mid-day on Saturday. The squadron that had passed was under the command of the Admiral himself, who was going to Dover for provisions and ammunition, and would return to his fleet before evening.

Before many hours were passed, Rye harbour was almost empty, and hundreds of eyes were watching the ships that carried their husbands and sons and lovers out into the pale summer haze that hung over the coast of France; while a few sharp-eyed old mariners on points of vantage muttered to one another that in the haze there was a patch of white specks to be seen which betokened the presence of some vast fleet.

That night the sun set yellow and stormy, and by morning the cobble-stones of Rye were wet and dripping with storm-showers, and a swell was beginning to lap and sob against the harbour walls.

Chapter Two - Men of War and Peace

The following days passed in terrible suspense for all left behind at Rye. Every morning all the points of vantage were crowded; the Ypres tower itself was never deserted day or night; and all the sharpest eyes in the town were bent continually out over that leaden rolling sea that faded into haze and storm-cloud in the direction of the French coast. But there was nothing to be seen on that waste of waters but the single boats that flew up channel or laboured down it against the squally west wind, far out at sea. Once or twice fishing-boats put in at Rye; but their reports were so contradictory and uncertain that they increased rather than allayed the suspense and misery. Now it was a French boat that reported the destruction of the Triumph; now an Englishman that swore to having seen Drake kill Medina-Sidonia with his own hand on his poop; but whatever the news might be, the unrest and excitement ran higher and higher. St. Clare's chapel in the old parish church of St. Nicholas was crowded every morning at five o'clock by an excited congregation of women, who came to beg God's protection on their dear ones struggling out there somewhere towards the dawn with those cruel Southern monsters. Especially great was the crowd on the Tuesday morning following the departure of the ships; for all day on Monday from time to time came a far-off rolling noise from the direction of Calais; which many declared to be thunder, with an angry emphasis that betrayed their real opinion.

When they came out of church that morning, and were streaming down to the quay as usual to see if any news had come in during the night, a seaman called to them from a window that a French vessel was just entering the harbour. When the women arrived at the water's edge they found a good crowd already assembled on the quay, watching the ship beat in against the north-west wind, which had now set in; but she aroused no particular comment as she was a well-known boat plying between Boulogne and Rye; and by seven o'clock she was made fast to the quay.

There were the usual formalities, stricter than usual during war, to be gone through before the few passengers were allowed to land: but all was in order; the officers left the boat, and the passengers came up the plank, the crowd pressing forward as they came, and questioning them eagerly. No, there was no certain news, said an Englishman at last, who looked like a lawyer; it was said at Boulogne the night before that there had been an engagement further up beyond the Straits; they had all heard guns; and it was reported by the last cruiser who came in before the boat left that a Spanish galleasse had run aground and had been claimed by M. Gourdain, the governor of Calais; but probably, added the shrewd-eyed man, that was just a piece of their dirty French pride. The crowd smiled ruefully; and a French officer of the boat who was standing by the gangway scowled savagely, as the lawyer passed on with a demure face.

Then there was a pause in the little stream of passengers; and then, out of the tiny door that led below decks, walking swiftly, and carrying a long cloak over her arm, came Isabel Norris, in a grey travelling dress, followed by Anthony and a couple of servants. The crowd fell back for the lady, who passed straight up through them; but one or two of the men called out for news to Anthony. He shook his head cheerfully at them.

"I know no more than that gentleman," he said, nodding towards the lawyer; and then followed Isabel; and together they made their way up to the inn.

Anthony was a good deal changed in the last six years; his beard and moustache were well grown; and he had a new look of gravity in his brown eyes; when he had smiled and shaken his head at the eager crowd just now, showing his white regular teeth, he looked as young as ever; but the serious look fell on his face again, as he followed Isabel up the steep little cobbled slope in his buff dress and plumed hat.

There was not so much apparent change in Isabel; she was a shade graver too, her walk a little slower and more dignified, and her lips, a little thinner, had a line of strength in them that was new; and even now as she was treading English ground again for the first time for six years, the look of slight abstraction in her eyes that is often the sign of a strong inner life, was just a touch deeper than it used to be.

They went up together with scarcely a word; and asked for a private room and dinner in two hours' time; and a carriage and horses for the servants to be ready at noon. The landlord, who had met them at the door, shook his head.

"The private room, sir, and the dinner—yes, sir—but the horses—" and he spread his hands out deprecatingly. "There is not one in the stall," he added.

Anthony considered a moment.

"Well, what do you propose? We are willing to stay a day or two, if you think that by then—"

"Ah," said the landlord, "to-morrow is another matter. I expect two of my carriages home to-night, sir, from London; but the horses will not be able to travel till noon to-morrow."

"That will do," said Anthony; and he followed Isabel upstairs.

It was very strange to them both to be back in England after so long. They had settled down at Douai with the Maxwells; but, almost immediately on their arrival, Mistress Margaret was sent for by her Superior to the house of her Order at Brussels; and Lady Maxwell was left alone with Isabel in a house in the town; for Anthony was in the seminary.

Then, in '86 Lady Maxwell had died, quite suddenly. Isabel herself had found her at her prie-dieu in the morning, still in her evening dress; she was leaning partly against the wall; her wrinkled old hands were clasped tightly together on a little ivory crucifix, on the top of the desk; and her snow-white head, with the lace drooping from it like a bridal veil, was bowed below them. Isabel, who had not dared to move her, had sent instantly for a little French doctor, who had thrown up his hands in a kind of devout ecstasy at that wonderful old figure, rigid in an eternal prayer. The two tall tapers she had lighted eight hours before were still just alight beside her, and looked strange in the morning sunshine.

"Pendant ses oraisons! pendant ses oraisons!" he murmured over and over again; and then had fallen on his knees and kissed the drooping lace of her sleeve.

"Priez pour moi, madame," he whispered to the motionless figure.

And so the old Catholic who had suffered so much had gone to her rest. The fact that her son James had been living in the College during her four years' stay at Douai had been perhaps the greatest possible consolation to her for being obliged to be out of England; for she saw him almost daily; and it was he who sang her Requiem. Isabel had then gone to live with other friends in Douai, until Anthony had been ordained priest in the June of '88, and was ready to take her to England; and now the two were bound for Stanfield, where Anthony was to act as chaplain for the present, as Mr. Buxton had predicted so long before. Old Mr. Blake had died in the spring of the year, still disapproving of his patron's liberal notions, and Mr. Buxton had immediately sent a special messenger all the way to Douai to secure Anthony's services; and had insisted moreover that Isabel should accompany her brother. They intended however to call at the Dower House on the way, which had been left under the charge of old Mrs. Carroll; and renew the memories of their own dear home.

They talked little at dinner; and only of general matters, their journey, the Armada, their joy at getting home again; for they had been expressly warned by their friends abroad against any indiscreet talk even when they thought themselves alone, and especially in the seaports, where so constant a watch was kept for seminary priests. The presence of Isabel, however, was the greatest protection to Anthony; as it was almost unknown that a priest should travel with any but male companions.

Then suddenly, as they were ending dinner, a great clamour broke out in the town below them; a gun was fired somewhere; and footsteps began to rush along the narrow street outside. Anthony ran to the window and called to know what was the matter; but no one paid any attention to him; and he presently sat down again in despair, and with one or two wistful looks.

"I will go immediately," he said to Isabel, "and bring you word."

A moment after a servant burst into the room.

"It is a Spanish ship, sir," he said, "a prize—rounding Dungeness."

In the afternoon, when the first fierce excitement was over, Anthony went down to the quay. He did not particularly wish to attract attention, and so he kept himself in the background somewhat; but he had a good view of her as she lay moored just off the quay, especially when one of the town guard who had charge of the ropes that kept the crowd back, seeing a gentleman in the crowd, beckoned him through.

"Your honour will wish to see the prize?" he said, in hopes of a trifle for himself; "make way there for the gentleman."

Anthony thought it better under these circumstances to accept the invitation, so he gave the man something, and slipped through. On the quay was a pile of plunder from the ship: a dozen chests carved and steel-clamped stood together; half-a-dozen barrels of powder; the ship's bell rested amid a heap of rich clothes and hangings; a silver crucifix and a couple of lamps with their chains lay tumbled on one side; and a parson was examining a finely carved mahogany table that stood near.

He looked up at Anthony.

"For the church, sir," he said cheerfully. "I shall make application to her Grace."

Anthony smiled at him.

"A holy revenge, sir," he said.

The ship herself had once been a merchantman brig; so much Anthony could tell, though he knew little of seamanship; but she had been armed heavily with deep bulwarks of timber, pierced for a dozen guns on each broadside. Now, however, she was in a terrible condition. The solid bulwarks were rent and shattered, as indeed was her whole hull; near the waterline were nailed sheets of lead, plainly in order to keep the water from entering the shot-holes; she had only one mast; and that was splintered in more than one place; a spar had been rigged up on to the stump of the bowsprit. The high poop such as distinguished the Spanish vessels was in the same deplorable condition; as well as the figure-head, which represented a beardless man with a halo behind his head, and which bore the marks of fierce hacks as well as of shot.

Anthony read the name,—the San Juan da Cabellas.

From the high quay too he could see down on to the middle decks, and there was the most shocking sight of all, for the boards and the mast-stumps and the bulwarks and the ship's furniture were all alike splashed with blood, some of the deeper pools not even yet dry. It was evident that the San Juan had not yielded easily.

Presently Anthony saw an officer approaching, and not wishing to be led into conversation slipped away again through the crowd to take Isabel the news.

The two remained quietly upstairs the rest of the afternoon, listening to the singing and the shouting in the streets, and watching from their window the groups that swung and danced to and fro in joy at Rye's contribution to the defeat of the invaders. When the dusk fell the noise was louder than ever as the men began to drink more deep, and torches were continually tossing up and down the steep cobbled streets; the din reached its climax about half-past nine, when the main body of the revellers passed up towards the inn, and, as Anthony saw from the window, finally entered through the archway below; and then all grew tolerably quiet. Presently Isabel said that she would go to bed, but just before she left the room, the servant again came in.

"If you please, sir, Lieutenant Raxham, of the Seahorse, is telling the tale of the capture of the Spanish ship; and the landlord bid me come and tell you."

Anthony glanced at Isabel, who nodded at him.

"Yes; go," she said, "and come up and tell me the news afterwards, if it is not very late."

When Anthony came downstairs he found to his annoyance that the place of honour had been reserved for him in a tall chair next to the landlord's at the head of the table. The landlord rose to meet his guest.

"Sit here, sir," he said. "I am glad you have come. And now, Mr. Raxham—"

Anthony looked about him with some dismay at this extreme publicity. The room was full from end to end. They were chiefly soldiers who sat at the table—heavy-looking rustics from Hawkhurst, Cranbrook and Appledore, in brigantines and steel caps, who had been sent in by the magistrates to the nearest seaport to assist in the defence of the coast—a few of them wore corselets with almain rivets and carried swords, while the pike-heads of the others rose up here and there above the crowd. The rest of the room was filled with the townsmen of Rye—those who had been retained for the defence of the coast, as well as others who for any physical reason could not serve by sea or land. There was an air of extraordinary excitement in the room. The faces of the most stolid were transfigured, for they were gathered to hear of the struggle their own dear England was making; the sickening pause of those months of waiting had ended at last; the huge southern monster had risen up over the edge of the sea, and the panting little country had flown at his throat and grappled him; and now they were hearing the tale of how deep her fangs had sunk.

The crowd laughed and applauded and drew its breath sharply, as one man; and the silence now and then was startling as the young officer told his story; although he had few gifts of rhetoric, except a certain vivid vocabulary. He himself was a lad of eighteen or so, with a pleasant reckless face, now flushed with drink and excitement, and sparkling eyes; he was seated in a chair upon the further end of the table, so that all could hear his story; and he had a cup of huff-cup in his left hand as he talked, leaving his right hand free to emphasise his points and slap his leg in a clumsy sort of oratory. His tale was full of little similes, at which his audience nodded their heads now and then, approvingly. He had apparently already begun his story, for when Anthony had taken his seat and silence had been obtained, he went straight on without any further introduction.

The landlord leaned over to Anthony. "The San Juan," he whispered behind his hot hairy hand, and nodded at him with meaning eyes.

"And every time they fired over us," went on the lieutenant, "and we fired into them; and the only damage they did us was their muskets in the tops. They killed Tom Dane like that"—there was a swift hiss of breath from the room; but the officer went straight on—"shot him through the back as he bent over his gun; and wounded old Harry and a score more; but all the while, lads, we were a-pounding at them with the broadsides as we came round, and raking them with the demi-cannon in the poop, until—well; go you and see the craft as she lies at the quay if you would know what we did. I tell you, as we came at her once towards the end, I saw that she was bleeding through her scuppers like a pig, from the middle deck. They were all packed up there together—sailors and soldiers and a priest or two; and scarce a ball could pass between the poop and the forecastle without touching flesh."

The lad stopped a moment and took a pull at his cup, and a murmur of talk broke out in the room. Anthony was surprised at his accent and manner of speaking, and heard afterwards that he was the son of the parson at one of the inland villages, and had had an education. In a moment he went on.

"Well—it would be about noon, just before the Admiral came up from Calais, that the old Seahorse was lost. We came at the dons again as we had done before, only closer than ever; and just as the captain gave the word to put her about, a ball from one of their guns which they had trained down on us, cut old Dick Kemp in half at the helm, and broke the tiller to splinters."

"Old Dick?" said a man's voice out of the reeking crowd, "Old Dick?"

There was a murmur round him, bidding him hold his tongue; and the lad went on.

"Well, we drifted nearer and nearer. There was nought to do but to bang at them; and that we did, by God—and to board her if we touched. Well, I worked my saker, and saw little else—for the smoke was like a black sea-fog; and the noise fit to crack your ears. Mine sing yet with it; the captain was bawling from the poop, and there were a dozen pikemen ready below; and then on a sudden came the crash; and I looked up and there was the Spaniards' decks above us, and the poop like a tower, with a grinning don or two looking down; and there was I looking up the muzzle of a culverin. I skipped towards the poop, shouting to the men; and the dons fired their broadside as I went.—God save us from that din! But I knew the old Seahorse was done this time—the old ship lurched and shook as the balls tore through her and broke her back; and there was such a yell as you'll never hear this side of hell. Well—I was on the poop by now, and the men after me; for you see the poop of the Seahorse was as high as the middle deck of the Spaniard, and we must board from there or not at all. Well, lads, there was the captain before me. He had fought cool till then, as cool as a parson among his roses, with never an oath from his mouth—but now he was as scarlet as a poppy, and his eyes were like blue fire, and his mouth jabbered and foamed; he was so hot, you see, at the loss of his ship. He was dancing to and fro waiting while the poop swung round on the tide; and the old craft plunged deeper in every wave that lifted her, but he cared no more for that nor for the musket-balls from the tops, nor for the brown grinning devils who shook their pikes at him from the decks, than—than a mad dog cares for a shower of leaves; but he stamped there and cursed them and damned them as they laughed at him; and then in a moment the poop touched.

"Well, lads—" and the lieutenant set his cup down on the table, clapped his hands on his knees, laughed shortly and nervously once or twice, and looked round. "Well, lads, I have never seen the like. The captain went for them like a wild cat; one step on the rail and the next among them; and was gone like a stone into water"—and the lad clapped his hand on his thigh. "I saw one face slit up from chin to eye; and another split across like an apple; and then we were after him. The men were mad, too—what was left of us; and we poured up on to the decks and left the old Seahorse to die. Well, we had our work before us—but it was no good. The dons could do nothing; I was after the captain as he went through the pack and came out just behind him; there were half a dozen of them down now; and the noise and the foreign oaths went up like smoke; and the captain himself was bleeding down one side of his face and grunting as he cut and stabbed; and I had had a knife through the arm; but he went up on to the poop; and as I followed, the Spaniards broke and threw down their arms—they saw 'twas no use, you see. When we reached the poop-stairs an officer in a blue coat came forward jabbering some jargon; but the captain would have no parley with him, but flung his dag clean into the man's face, and over he went backwards—with his damned high heels in the air."

There was a sudden murmur of laughter from the room; Anthony glanced off the lieutenant's grinning ruddy face for a moment, and saw the rows of listening faces all wrinkled with mirth.

"Well," went on the lad, "up went the captain, and I after him. Then there came across the deck, very slow and stately, the Spanish captain himself, in a fine laced coat and a plumed hat, and he was holding out his sword by the blade and bowed as we ran towards him, and began some damned foreign nonsense, with his Señor—but the captain would have none o' that, I tell you he was like Tom o' Bedlam now—so as the Señor grinned at him with his monkey face and bowed and wagged, the captain fetched him a slash across the cheek with his sword that cut up into his head; and that don went spinning across the poop like a morris-man and brought up against the rail, and then down he came," and the lad dashed his hand on his thigh again—"as dead as mutton."

Again came a louder gust of laughter from the room. Anthony half rose in his chair, and then sat down again.

"Well," said the lad, "and that was not all. Down he raged again to the decks and I behind him—I tell you, it was like a butcher's shop—but it was quieter now—the fighting was over—and the Spaniards were all run below, except half-a-dozen in the tops; looking down like young rooks at an archer. There had been a popish priest too with his crucifix in one hand and his god-almighty in the other, over a dying man as we came up; but as we came down there he lay in his black gown with a hole through his heart and his crucifix gone. One of the lads had got it no doubt. Well, the captain brought up at the main mast. 'God's blood,' he bawled, 'where are the brown devils got to?' Some one told him, and pointed down the hatch. Well, then I turned sick with my wound and the smell of the place and all; and I knew nothing more till I found myself sitting on a dead don, with the captain holding me up and pouring a cordial down my throat."

Then talk and laughter broke out in the audience; but the landlord held up his hand for silence.

"And what of the others?" he shouted.

"Dead meat too," said the lad—"the captain went down with a dozen or more and hunted them out and finished them. There was one, Dick told me afterwards," and the lieutenant gave a cackle of mirth, "that they hunted twice round the ship before he jumped over yelling to some popish saint to help him; but it seems he was deaf, like the old Baal that parson tells of o' Sundays. The dirty swine to run like that! Well, he's got his bellyful now of the salt water that he came so far to see. And then the captain with his own hands trained a robinet that was on the poop on to the tops; and down the birds came, one by one; for their powder up there was all shot off."

"And the Seahorse?" said the landlord again.

There fell a dead silence: all in the room knew that the ship was lost, but it was terrible to hear it again. The lad's face broke into lines of grief, and he spoke huskily.

"Gone down with the dead and wounded; and the rest of the fleet a mile away."

Then the lieutenant went on to describe how he himself had been deputed to bring the San Juan into port with the wounded on board, while the captain and the rest of the crew by Drake's orders attached themselves to various vessels that were short-handed, and how the English fleet had followed what was left of the Spaniards when the fight ended at sunset, up towards the North Sea.

When he finished his story there was a tremendous outburst of cheering and hammering upon the table, and the feet and the pike-butts thundered on the floor, and a name was cried again and again as the cups were emptied.

"God save her Grace and old England!" yelled a slim smooth-faced archer from Appledore.

"God send the dons and all her foes to hell!" roared a burly pikeman with his cup in the air. Then the room shook again as the toasts were drunk with applauding feet and hands.

Anthony turned to the landlord, who had just ceased thumping with his great red fists on the table.

"What was the captain's name?" he asked, when a slight lull came.

"Maxwell," said the crimson-faced man. "Hubert Maxwell—one of Drake's own men."

When Anthony came upstairs he heard his name called through the door, and went in to Isabel's room to find her sitting up in bed in the gloom of the summer night; the party below had broken up, and all was quiet except for the far-off shouts and hoots of cheerful laughter from the dispersing groups down among the narrow streets.

"Well?" she said, as he came in and stood in the doorway.

"It is just the story of the prize," he said, "and it seems that Hubert had the taking of it."

There was silence a moment. Anthony could see her face, a motionless pale outline, and her arms clasped round her knees as she sat up in bed.

"Hubert?" she asked in an even voice.

"Yes, Hubert."

There was silence a moment.

"Well?" she said again.

"He is safe," said Anthony, "and fought gallantly. I will tell you more to-morrow."

"Ah!" said Isabel softly; and then lay down again.

"Good-night, Anthony."

"Good-night."

But Anthony dared not tell her the details next day, after all.

There was still a difficulty about the horses; they had not arrived until the Wednesday morning, and were greatly exhausted by a long and troublesome journey; so the travellers consented to postpone their journey for yet one more day. The weather, which had been thickening, grew heavier still in the afternoon, and great banks of clouds were rising out of the west. Anthony started out about four o'clock for a walk along the coast; and, making a long round in the direction of Lydd, did not finally return until about seven. As he came in at the north-east of the town he noticed how empty the streets were, and passed on down in the direction of the quay. As he turned down the steep street into the harbour groups began to pour up past him, laughing and exclaiming; and in a moment more came Isabel walking alone. He looked at her anxiously, for he saw something had happened. Her quiet face was lit up with some interior emotion, and her mouth was trembling.

"The Armada is routed," she said; "and I have seen Hubert."

The two turned back together and walked silently up to the inn. There she told him the story. She had been told that Captain Maxwell was come in the Elizabeth, for provisions for Lord Howard Seymour's squadron, to which his new command was attached; and that he was even now in harbour. At that she had gone straight down alone.

"Oh, Anthony!" she cried, "you know how it is with me. I could not help it. I am not ashamed of it. God Almighty knows all, and is not wrath with me. So I went down and was in the crowd as he came down again with the mayor, Mr. Hamon; we all made way for them, and the men cheered themselves scarlet; but he came down cool and quiet; you know his way—with his eyes half shut; and—and—he was so brown; and he looks sad—and he had a great plaister on the left temple. And then he saw me."

Isabel sprang up, and came up to Anthony and took his hands. "Oh! Anthony; I was very happy then; because he took off his cap and bowed; and his face was all lighted; and he took my hand and kissed it—and then made Mr. Hamon known to me. The crowd laughed and said things—but I did not care; and he soon silenced them, he looked round so fiercely; and then I went on board with him—he would have it so—and he showed us everything—and we sat a little in the cabin; and he told me of his wife and child. She is the daughter of a Plymouth minister; he knew her when he was with Drake; and he told me all about her, so you see—" Isabel broke off; and sat down in the high window seat. "And then he asked me about you; and I said you were here; and that we were going to stay a little while with Mr. Buxton of Stanfield—you see I knew we could trust him; and Mr. Hamon was in the passage just then looking at the guns; and then a sailor came in to say that all was ready; and so we came away. But it was so good to see him again; and to know that he was so happy."

Anthony looked at his sister in astonishment; her quiet manner was gone, and she was talking again almost like an excited child; and so happily. It was very strange, he thought. He sat down beside her.

"Oh, Anthony!" she said, "do you understand? I love him dearly still; and his wife and child too. God bless them all and keep them!"

The mystery was still deep to him; and he feared to say what he should not; so he kissed Isabel silently; and the two sat there together and looked out over the crowding red roofs to the glowing western sky across the bay below them.

Chapter Three - Home-Coming

It was a stormy summer evening as the brother and sister rode up between the last long hills that led to Great Keynes. A south-west wind had been rising all day, that same wind that was now driving the ruined Armada up into the fierce North Sea, with the fiercer men behind to bar the return. But here, twenty miles inland, with the high south-downs to break the gale, the riders were in comparative quiet, though the great trees overhead tossed their heavy rustling heads as the gusts struck them now and again.

The party had turned off, as the dusk was falling, from the main-road into bridle-paths that they knew well, and were now approaching the village through the water meadows on the south-east side along a ride that would bring them, round the village, direct to the Dower House. In the gloom Anthony could make out the tall reeds, and the loosestrife and willowherb against them, that marked the course of the stream where he had caught trout, as a boy; and against the western sky, as he turned in his saddle, rose up the high windy hills where he had hawked with Hubert so many years before. It was a strange thought to him as he rode along that his very presence here in his own country was an act of high treason by the law lately passed, and that every day he lived here must be a day of danger.

For Isabel, too, it was strange to be riding up again towards the battlefield of her desires—that battlefield where she had lived for years in such childish faith and peace without a suspicion of the forces that were lurking beneath her own quiet nature. But to both of them the sense of home-coming was stronger than all else—that strange passion for a particular set of inanimate things—or, at the most, for an association of ideas—that has no parallel in human emotions; and as they rode up the darkening valley and the lights of the high windows of the Hall began to show over the trees on their right, Anthony forgot his treason and Isabel her conflicts, and both felt a lump rise in the throat, and their hearts begin to beat quicker with a strange pleasurable pulse, and to Isabel's eyes at least there rose up great tears of happiness and content; neither dared speak, but both looked eagerly about at the pool where the Mayflies used to dance, at the knoll where the pigeons nested, at the little low bridge beneath which their inch-long boats used to slide sideways into darkness, and the broad marshy flats where the gorgeous irises grew.

"How the trees have grown!" said Anthony at last, with an effort; "I cannot see the lights from the house."

"Mrs. Carroll will have made ready the first-floor rooms then, on the south."

"I am sorry they are not our own," said Anthony.

"Ah, look! there is the dovecote," cried Isabel.

They were passing up now behind the farm buildings; and directly afterwards came round in front of the little walled garden to the west of the house.

There was a sudden exclamation from Anthony; and Isabel stared in silent dismay. The old house rose up before them with its rows of square windows against the night sky, dark. There was not a glimmer anywhere; even Mrs. Carroll's own room on the south was dark. They reined their horses in and stood a moment.

"Oh, Anthony, Anthony!" cried Isabel suddenly, "what is it? Is there no one there?"

Anthony shook his head; and then put his tired beast to a shambling trot with Isabel silent again with weariness and disappointment behind him. They passed along outside the low wall, turned the corner of the house and drew up at the odd little doorway in the angle at the back of the house. The servants had drawn up behind them, and now pressed up to hold their horses; and the brother and sister slipped off and went towards the door. Anthony passed under the little open porch and put his hand out to the door; it was quite dark underneath the porch, and he felt further and further, and yet there was no door; his foot struck the step. He felt his way to the doorposts and groped for the door; but still there was none; he could feel the panelling of the lobby inside the doorway, and that was all. He drew back, as one would draw back from a dead face on which one had laid a hand in the dark.

"Oh, Anthony!" said Isabel again, "what is it?" She was still outside.

"Have you a light?" said Anthony hoarsely to the servants.

The man nearest him bent and fumbled in the saddle-bags, and after what seemed an interminable while kindled a little bent taper and handed it to him. As he went towards the porch shading it with his hand, Isabel sprang past him and went before; and then, as the light fell through the doorway, stopped in dead and bewildered silence.

The door was lying on the floor within, shattered and splintered.

Anthony stepped beside her, and she turned and clung to his arm, and a sob or two made itself heard. Then they looked about them. The banisters above them were smashed, and like a cataract, down the stairs lay a confused heap of crockery, torn embroidery and clothes, books, and broken furniture.

Anthony's hand shook so much that the shadows of the broken banisters waved on the wall above like thin exulting dancers.

Suddenly Anthony started.

"Mrs. Carroll," he exclaimed, and he darted upstairs past the ruins into her two rooms halfway up the flight; and in a minute or two was back with Isabel.

"She has escaped," he said in a low voice; and then the two stood looking about them silently again. The door leading to the cellars on the left was broken too; and fragments of casks and bottles lay about the steps; the white wall was splashed with drink, and there was a smell of spirits in the air. Evidently the stormers had thought themselves worthy of their hire.

"Come," he said again; and leaving the entrance lobby, the two passed to the hall-door and pushed that open and looked. There was the same furious confusion there; the tapestry was lying tumbled and rent on the floor—the high oak mantelpiece was shattered, and doleful cracks and splinters in the panelling all round showed how mad the attack had been; one of the pillars of the further archway was broken clean off, and the brickwork showed behind; the pictures had been smashed and added to the heap of wrecked furniture and broken glass in the middle.

"Come," he said once more; and the two passed silently through the broken archway, and going up the other flight of stairs, gradually made the round of the house. Everywhere it was the same, except in the servants' attics, where, apparently, the mob had not thought it worth while to go.

Isabel's own room was the most pitiable of all; the windows had only the leaden frames left, and those bent and battered; the delicate panelling was scarred and split by the shower of stones that had poured in through the window and that now lay in all parts of the room. A painting of her mother that had hung over her bed was now lying face downwards on the floor. Isabel turned it over silently; a stone had gone through the face; and it had been apparently slit too by some sharp instrument. Even the slender oak bed was smashed in the centre, as if half a dozen men had jumped upon it at once; and the little prie-dieu near the window had been deliberately hacked in half. Isabel looked at it all with wide startled eyes and parted lips; and then suddenly sank down on the wrecked bed where she had hoped to sleep that night, and began to sob like a child.

"Ah! I did think—I did think—" she began.

Anthony stooped and tried to lift her.

"Come, my darling," he said, "is not this a high honour? Qui relinquit domos!"

"Oh! why have they done it?" sobbed Isabel. "What harm have we done them?" and she began to wail. She was thoroughly over-tired and over-wrought; and Anthony could not find it in his heart to blame her; but he spoke again bravely.

"We are Catholics," he said; "that is why they have done it. Do not throw away this grace that our Lord has given us; embrace it and make it yours."

It was the priest that was speaking now; and Isabel turned her face and looked at him; and then got up and hid her face on his shoulder.

"Oh, Anthony, help me!" she said; and so stood there, quiet.

He came down presently to the servants, while Isabel went upstairs to prepare the rooms in the attics; for it was impossible for them to ride further that night; so they settled to sleep there, and stable the horses; and to ride on early the next day, and be out of the village before the folks were about. Anthony gave directions to the servants, who were Catholics too, and explained in a word or two what had happened; and bade them come up to the house as soon as they had fed and watered the beasts; meanwhile he took the saddle-bags indoors and spread out their remaining provisions in one of the downstairs rooms; and soon Isabel joined him.

"I have made up five beds," she said, and her voice and lips were steady, and her eyes grave and serene again.

The five supped together in the wrecked kitchen, a fine room on the east of the house, supported by a great oak pillar to which the horses of guests were sometimes attached when the stable was full.

Isabel managed to make a fire and to boil some soup; but they hung thick curtains across the shattered windows, and quenched the fire as soon as the soup was made, for fear that either the light or the smoke from the chimney should arouse attention.

When supper was over, and the two men-servants and Isabel's French maid were washing up in the scullery, Isabel suddenly turned to Anthony as they sat together near the fireplace.

"I had forgotten," she said, "what we arranged as we rode up. I must go and tell her still."

Anthony looked at her steadily a moment.

"God keep you," he said.

She kissed him and took her riding-cloak, drew the hood over her head, and went out into the dark.

It was with the keenest relief that, half an hour later, Anthony heard her footstep again in the red-tiled hall outside. The servants were gone upstairs by now, and the house was quiet. She came in, and sat by him again and took his hand.

"Thank God I went," she said. "I have left her so happy."

"Tell me all," said Anthony.

"I went through the garden," said Isabel, "but came round to the front of the house so that they might not think I came from here. When the servant came to the door—he was a stranger, and a Protestant no doubt—I said at once that I brought news of Mr. Maxwell from Rye; and he took me straight in and asked me to come in while he fetched her woman. Then her woman came out and took me upstairs, up into Lady Maxwell's old room; and there she was lying in bed under the great canopy. Oh, Anthony, she is so pretty! her golden hair was lying out all over the pillow, and her face is so sweet. She cried out when I came in, and lifted herself on her elbow; so I just said at once, 'He is safe and well'; and then she went off into sobs and laughter; so that I had to go and soothe her—her woman was so foolish and helpless; and very soon she was quiet: and then she called me her darling, and she kissed me again and again; and told the woman to go and leave us together; and then she lifted the sheet; and showed me the face of a little child. Oh Anthony; Hubert's child and hers, the second, born on Tuesday—only think of that. 'Mercy, I was going to call her,' she said, 'if I had not heard by to-morrow, but now I shall call her Victory.'"

Anthony looked quickly at his sister, with a faint smile in his eyes.

"And what did you say?" he asked.

Isabel smiled outright; but her eyes were bright with tears too.

"'You have guessed,' she said. 'Yes,' I said, 'call her Mercy all the same,' and she kissed me again, and cried, and said that she would. And then I told her all about Hubert; and about his little wound; and how well he looked; and how all the fighting was most likely over; and what his cabin looked like. And then she suddenly guessed who I was, and asked me; and I could not deny it, you know; but she promised not to tell. Then she told me all about the house here; and how she was afraid Hubert had said something impatient about people who go to foreign parts and leave their country to be attacked, 'But you know he did not really mean it,' she said; and of course he did not. Well, the people had remembered that, and it spread and spread; and when the news of the Armada came last week, a mob came over from East Grinsted, and they sat drinking and drinking in the village; and of course Grace could not go out to them; and all the old people are gone, and the Catholics on the estate—and so at last they all came out roaring and shouting down the drive, and Mrs. Carroll was warned and slipped out to the Hall; and she is now gone to Stanfield to wait for us—and then the crowd broke into the house—but, oh Anthony, Grace was so sorry, and cried sore to think of us here; and asked us to come and stay there; but of course I told her we could not: and then I said a prayer for her; and we kissed one another again; and then I came away."

Anthony looked at his sister, and there was honour and pride of her in his eyes.

The ride to Stanfield next day was a long affair, at a foot's-pace all the way: the horses were thoroughly tired with their journey, and they were obliged to start soon after three o'clock in the morning after a very insufficient rest; they did not reach Groombridge till nearly ten o'clock, when they dined, and then rode on towards Tonbridge about noon. There were heavy hearts to be carried as well. The attempt to welcome the misery of their home-coming was a bitter effort; all the more bitter for that it was an entirely unexpected call upon them. During those six years abroad probably not a day had passed without visions of Great Keynes, and the pleasant and familiar rooms and garden of their own house, and mental rehearsals of their return. The shock of the night before too had been emphasised by the horror of the cold morning light creeping through the empty windows on to the cruel heaps within. The garden too, seen in the dim morning, with its trampled lawns and wrecked flower-beds heaped with withered sunflowers, bell-blossoms and all the rich August growth, with the earthen flower-bowls smashed, the stone balls on the gate overturned, and the laurels at the corner uprooted—all this was a horrible pain to Isabel, to whom the garden was very near as dear and familiar as her own room. So it was a silent and sorrowful ride; and Anthony's heart rose in relief as at last up the grey village-street he saw the crowded roofs of Stanfield Place rise over the churchyard wall. Their welcome from Mr. Buxton went far to compensate for all.

"My dear boy," he said, "or, my dear father, as I should call you in private, you do not know what happiness is mine to-day. It is a great thing to have a priest again; but, if you will allow me to say so, it is a greater to have my friend—and what a sister you have upstairs!"

They were in Mr. Buxton's own little room on the ground-floor, and Isabel had gone to rest until supper.

Anthony told him of the grim surprise that had awaited them at Great Keynes. "So you must forgive my sister if she is a little sad."

"Yes, yes," said Mr. Buxton, "I had heard from Mrs. Carroll last night when she arrived here. But there was no time to warn you. I had expected you to-day, though Mrs. Carroll did not."

(Anthony had sent a man straight from Rye to Stanfield.)

"But Mistress Isabel, as I shall venture to call her, must do what she can with this house and garden. I need not say how wholly it is hers. And I shall call you Anthony," he added—"in public, at least. And, for strangers, you are just here as my guest; and you shall be called Capell—a sound name; and you shall be Catholics too; though you are no priest, of course, in public—and you have returned from the Continent. I hold it is no use to lie when you can be found out. I do not know what your conscience is, Father Anthony; but, for myself, I count us Catholics to be in statu belli now; and therefore I shall lie frankly and fully when there is need; and you may do as you please. Old Mr. Blake used to bid me prevaricate instead; but that always seemed to me two lies instead of one—one to the questioning party and the other to myself; and so I always said to him, but he would not have it so. I wondered he did not tell me that two negatives made an affirmative; but he was not clever enough, the good father. So my own custom is to tell one plain lie when needed, and shame the devil."

It was pleasant to Anthony to hear his friend talk again, and he said so. His host's face softened into a great tenderness.

"Dear lad, I know what you mean. Please God you may find this a happy home."

A couple of hours later, when Anthony and Isabel came down together from their rooms in the old wing, they found Mr. Buxton in his black satin and lace in the beautiful withdrawing-room on the ground-floor. It was already past the supper-hour, but their host showed no signs of going into the hall. At last he apologised.

"I ask your pardon, Mistress Isabel; but I have a guest come to stay with me, who only arrived an hour ago; and she is a great lady and must have her time. Ah! here she is."

The door was flung open and a radiant vision appeared. The door was a little way off, and there were no candles near it; but there swelled and rustled into the room a figure all in blue and gold, with a white delicate ruff; and diamond buckles shone beneath the rich brocaded petticoat. Above rose a white bosom and throat scintillating with diamonds, and a flushed face with scarlet lips, all crowned by piles of black hair, with black dancing eyes beneath. Still a little in the shadow this splendid figure swept down with a great curtsey, which Isabel met by another, while the two gentlemen bowed low; and then, as the stranger swayed up again into the full light of the sconces, Anthony recognised Mary Corbet.

He stood irresolute with happy hesitation; and she came up smiling brilliantly; and before he could stay her dropped down on one knee and took his hand and kissed it; just as the man left the room.

"God bless you, Father Anthony!" she said; and as he looked at her, as she glanced up, he could not tell whether her eyes shone with tears or laughter.

"This is very charming and proper, Mistress Corbet, and like a true daughter of the Church," put in Mr. Buxton, "but I shall be obliged to you if you will not in future kiss priests' hands nor call them Father in the presence of the servants—at least not in my house."

"Ah!" she said, "you were always prudent. Have you seen his secret doors?" she went on to Anthony. "The entire Catholic Church might play hare and hounds with the Holy Father as huntsman and the Cardinals as the whips, through Mr. Buxton's secret labyrinths."

"Wait until you are hare, and it is other than Holy Church that is a-hunting," said Mr. Buxton, "and you will thank God for my labyrinths, as you call them."

Then she greeted Isabel with great warmth.

"Why, my dear," she said, "you are not the little Puritan maiden any longer. We must have a long talk to-night; and you shall tell me everything."

"Mistress Mary is not so greatly changed," said Isabel, smiling. "She always would be told everything."

It was strange to Anthony to meet Mary again after so long, and to find her so little changed, as Isabel had said truly. He himself had passed through so much since they had last met at Greenwich over six years ago—his conversion, his foreign sojourn, and, above all, the bewildering and intoxicating sweetness of his ordination and priestly life. And yet he felt as close to Mary as ever, knit in a bond of wonderful good fellowship and brotherhood such as he had never felt to any other in just that kind and degree. He watched her, warm and content, as she talked across the polished oak and beneath the gleam of the candles; and listened, charmed by her air and her talk.

"There is not so much news of her Grace," she said, "save that she is turning soldier in her old age. She rode out to Tilbury, you know, the other day, in steel cuirass and scarlet; out to see her dear Robin and the army; and her royal face was all smiles and becks, and lord! how the soldiers cheered! But if you had seen her as I did, in her room when she first buckled on her armour, and the joints did not fit—yes, and heard her! there were no smiles to spare then. She lodged at Mr. Rich's, you know, two nights; but he would be Mr. Poor, I should suppose, by the time her Grace left him; for he will not see the worth of a shoelace again of all that he expended on her."

"You see," remarked Mr. Buxton to Isabel, "how fortunate we are in having such a friend of her Grace's with us. We hear all the cream of the news, even though it be a trifle sour sometimes."

"A lover of her Grace," said Mary, "loves the truth about her, however bitter. But then I have no secret passages where I may hide from my sovereign!"

"The cream can scarce be but sour," said Anthony, "near her Grace: there is so much thunder in the air."

"Yes, but the sun came out when you were there, Anthony," put in Isabel, smiling.

"But even the light of her glorious countenance is trying," said Mary. "She is overpowering in thunder and sunshine alike."

"We have had enough of that metaphor," observed Mr. Buxton.

Then Anthony had to talk, and tell all the foreign news of Douai and Rome and Cardinal Allen; and of Father Persons' scheme for a college at Valladolid.

"Father Robert is a superb beggar—as he is superb in all things," said Mr. Buxton. "I dare not think how much he got from me for his college; and then I do not even approve of his college. His principles are too logical for me. I have ever had a weakness for the non sequitur."

This led on to the Armada; Anthony told his experience of it; how he had seen at least the sails of Lord Howard's squadron far away against the dawn; and this led on again to a sharp discussion when the servants had left the room.

"I do not know," said Mary at last; "it is difficult—is not the choice between God and Elizabeth? If I were a man, why should I not take up arms to defend my religion? Since I am a woman, why should I not pray for Philip's success? It is a bitter hard choice, I know; but why need I prefer my country to my faith? Tell me that, Father Anthony."

"I can only tell you my private opinion," said Anthony, "and that is, that both duties may be done. As Mr. Buxton here used to tell me, the duty to Cæsar is as real as the duty to God. A man is bound to both; for each has its proper bounds. When either oversteps them it must be resisted. When Elizabeth bids me deny my faith, I tell her I would sooner die. When a priest bids me deny my country, I tell him I would sooner be damned."

Mary clapped her hands.

"I like to hear a man talk like that," she cried. "But what of the Holy Father and his excommunication of her Grace?"

Anthony looked up at her sharply, and then smiled; Isabel watched him with a troubled face.

"Aquinas holds," he said, "that an excommunication of sovereign and people in a lump is invalid. And until the Holy Father tells me himself that Aquinas is wrong, I shall continue to think he is right."

"God-a-mercy!" burst in Mr. Buxton, "what a to-do! Leave it alone until the choice must be made; and meanwhile say your prayers for Pope and Queen too, and hear mass and tell your beads and hold your tongue: that is what I say to myself. Mistress Mary, I will not have my chaplain heckled; here is his lady sister all a-tremble between heresy and treason."

They sat long over the supper-table, talking over the last six years and the times generally. More than once Mary showed a strange bitterness against the Queen. At last Mr. Buxton showed his astonishment plainly.

"I do not understand you," he said. "I know that at heart you are loyal; and yet one might say you meditated her murder."

Mary's face grew white with passion and her eyes blazed.

"Ah!" she hissed, "you do not understand, you say? Then where is your heart? But then you did not see Mary Stuart die."

Anthony looked at her, amazed.

"And you did, Mistress Mary?" he asked.

Mary bowed, with her lips set tight to check their trembling.

"I will tell you," she said, "if our host permits"; and she glanced at him.

"Then come this way," he said, and they rose from table.

They went back again to the withdrawing-room; a little cedar-fire had been kindled under the wide chimney; and the room was full of dancing shadows. The great plaster-pendants, the roses, the crowns, and the portcullises on the ceiling seemed to waver in the firelight, for Mr. Buxton at a sign from Mary blew out the four tapers that were burning in the sconces. They all sat down in the chairs that were set round the fire, Mary in a tall porter's chair with flaps that threw a shadow on her face when she leaned back; and she took a fan in her hand to keep the fire, or her friends' eyes, from her face should she need it.

She first told them very briefly of the last months of Mary's life, of the web that was spun round her by Walsingham's tactics, and her own friends' efforts, until it was difficult for her to stir hand or foot without treason, real or pretended, being set in motion somewhere. Then she described how at Christmas '86 Elizabeth had sent her—Mary Corbet—as a Catholic, up to the Queen of the Scots at Fotheringay, on a private mission to attempt to win the prisoner's confidence, and to persuade her to confess to having been privy to Babington's conspiracy; and how the Scottish Queen had utterly denied it, even in the most intimate conversations. Sentence had been already passed, but the warrant had not been signed; and it never would have been signed, said Mistress Corbet, if Mary had owned to the crime of which she was accused.

"Ah! how they insulted her!" cried Mary Corbet indignantly. "She showed me one day the room where her throne had stood. Now the cloth of state had been torn down by Sir Amyas Paulet's men, and he himself dared to sit with his hat on his head in the sovereign's presence! The insolence of the hound! But the Queen showed me how she had hung a crucifix where her royal arms used to hang. 'J'appelle,' she said to me, 'de la reine au roi des rois.'"

Mistress Corbet went on to tell of the arrival of Walsingham's brother-in-law, Mr. Beale, with the death-warrant on that February Sunday evening.

"I saw his foxy face look sideways up at the windows as he got off his horse in the courtyard; and I knew that our foes had triumphed. Then the other bloodhounds began to arrive; my lord of Kent on the Monday and Shrewsbury on the Tuesday. Then they came in to us after dinner; and they told her Grace it was to be for next day. I was behind her chair and saw her hand on the boss of the arm, and it did not stir nor clench; she said it could not be. She could not believe it of Elizabeth.

"When she did at last believe it, there was no wild weeping or crying for mercy; but she set her affairs in order, queenly, and yet sedately too. She first thought of her soul, and desired that M. de Preau might come to her and hear her confession; but they would not permit it. They offered her Dr. Fletcher instead, 'a godly man,' as my lord of Kent called him. 'Je ne m'en doute pas,' she said, smiling. But it was hard not to have a priest.

"Then she set her earthly affairs in order when she had examined her soul and made confession to God without the Dean's assistance. We all supped together when it was growing late; and I thought, Father Anthony—indeed I did—of another Supper long ago. Then M. Gorion was sent for to arrange some messages and gifts; and until two of the clock in the morning we watched with her or served her as she wrote and gave orders. The court outside was full of comings and goings. As I passed down the passage I saw the torches of the visitors that were come to see the end; and once I heard a hammering from the great hall. Then she went to her bed; and I think few lay as quiet as she in the castle that night. I was with her ladies when they waked her before dawn; and it was hard to see that sweet face on the pillow open its eyes again to what was before her.

"Then when she was dressed I went in again, and we all went to the oratory, where she received our Saviour from the golden pyx which the Holy Father had sent her; for, you see, they would allow no priest to come near her....

"Presently the gentlemen knocked. When we tried to follow we were prevented; they wished her to die alone among her enemies; but at last two of the ladies were allowed to go with her.

"I ran out another way, and sent a message to my Lord Shrewsbury, who knew me at court. As I waited in the court-yard, the musicians there were playing 'The Witches' Dirge,' as is done at the burnings—and all to mock at my queen! At last a halberdier was sent to bring me in."

Mary Corbet was silent a moment or two and leaned back in her chair; and the others dared not speak. The strange emotion of her voice and the stillness of that sparkling figure in the porter's chair affected them profoundly. Her face was now completely shaded by a fan.

"It was in the hall, where a great fire was burning on the hearth. The stage stood at the upper end; all was black. The crowd of gentlemen filled the hall and all were still and reverent except—except a devil who laughed as my queen came in, all in black. She was smiling and brave, and went up the steps and sat on her black throne and looked about her. The—the things were just in front of her.

"Then the warrant was read by Beale, and I saw the lords glance at her as it ended; but there was nought but joyous hope in her face. She looked now and again gently on the ivory crucifix in her hand, as she listened; and her lips moved to—to—Him who was delivered to death for her."

Mary Corbet gave one quick sob, and was silent again for an instant. Then she went on in a yet lower voice.

"Dr. Fletcher tried to address her, but he stammered and paused three or four times; and the queen smiled on him and bade him not trouble himself, for that she lived and died a Catholic. But they would not let her be; so she looked on her crucifix and was silent; and even then my lord of Kent badgered her and told her Christ crucified in her hand would not save her, except He was engraved on her heart.

"Then she knelt at her chair and tried to pray softly to herself; but Fletcher would not have that, and prayed himself, aloud, and all the gentlemen in the hall began to pray aloud with him. But Mary prayed on in Latin and English aloud, and prevailed, for all were silent at the end but she.

"And at last she kissed the crucifix and cried in a sweet piercing voice, 'As thine arms, O Jesus, were spread upon the Cross, so receive me into Thy mercy and forgive me my sins!'"

Again Mistress Corbet was silent; and Anthony drew a long sobbing breath of pure pity, and Isabel was crying quietly to herself.

"When the headsmen offered to assist her," went on the low voice, "the queen smiled at the gentlemen and said that she had never had such grooms before; and then they let the ladies come up. When they began to help her with her dress I covered my face—I could not help it. There was such a stillness now that I could hear her beads chink at her girdle. When I looked again, she was ready, with her sweet neck uncovered: all round her was black but the heads-man, who wore a white apron over his velvet, and she, in her beauty, and oh! her face was so fair and delicate and her eyes so tender and joyous. And as her ladies looked at her, they sobbed piteously. 'Ne criez vous,' said she.

"Then she knelt down, and Mistress Mowbray bound her eyes. She smiled again under the handkerchief. 'Adieu,' she said, and then, 'Au revoir.'

"Then she said once more a Latin psalm, and then laid her head down, as on a pillow.

"'In manus tuas, Domine,' she said."

Mary Corbet stopped, and leaned forward a little, putting her hand into her bosom; Anthony looked at her as she drew up a thin silk cord with a ruby ring attached to it.

"This was hers," she said simply, and held it out. Each of the Catholics took it and kissed it reverently, and Mary replaced it.

"When they lifted her," she added, "a little dog sprang out from her clothes and yelped. And at that the man near me, who had laughed as she came in, wept."

Then the four sat silent in the firelight.

Chapter Four - Stanfield Place

Life at Stanfield Place was wonderfully sweet to Anthony and Isabel after their exile abroad, for both of them had an intense love of England and of English ways. The very sight of fair-faced children, and the noise of their shrill familiar voices from the village street, the depths of the August woods round them, the English manners of living—all this was alive with a full deliberate joy to these two. Besides, there was the unfailing tenderness and gaiety of Mr. Buxton; and at first there was the pleasant company of Mary Corbet as well.

There was little or no anxiety resting on any of them. "God was served," as the celebration of mass was called, each morning in the little room where Anthony had made the exercises, and the three others were always present. It was seldom that the room was not filled to over-flowing on Sundays and holy-days with the household and the neighbouring Catholics.

Everything was, of course, perfection in the little chapel when it was furnished; as was all that Mr. Buxton possessed. There was a wonderful golden crucifix by an unknown artist, that he had picked up in his travels, that stood upon the altar, with the bird-types of the Saviour at each of the four ends; a pelican at the top, an eagle on the right supporting its young which were raising their wings for a flight, on the left a phœnix amid flames, and at the foot a hen gathering her chickens under her wings—all the birds had tiny emerald eyes; the figure on the cross was beautifully wrought, and had rubies in hands and feet and side. There were also two silver altar-candlesticks designed by Marrina for the Piccolomini chapel in the church of St. Francis in Siena; and two more, plainer, for the Elevation. The vestments were exquisite; those for high festivals were cloth of gold; and the other white ones were beautifully worked with seed pearls, and jewelled crosses on the stole and maniple. The other colours, too, were well represented, and were the work of a famous convent in the south of France. All the other articles, too, were of silver: the lavabo basin, the bell, the thurible, the boat and spoon, and the cruets. It was a joy to all the Catholics who came to see the worship of God carried on with such splendour, when in so many places even necessaries were scarcely forthcoming.

There was a little hiding-hole between the chapel and the priest's room, just of a size to hold the altar furniture and the priests in case of a sudden alarm; and there were several others in the house too, which Mr. Buxton had showed to Anthony with a good deal of satisfaction, on the morning after his arrival.

"I dared not show them to you the last time you were here," he said, "and there was no need; but now there must be no delay. I have lately made some more, too. Now here is one," he said, stopping before the great carved mantelpiece in the hall.

He looked round to see that no servant was in the room, and then, standing on a settee before the fire, touched something above, and a circular hole large enough for a man to clamber through appeared in the midst of the tracery.

"There," he said, "and you will find some cured ham and a candle, with a few dates within, should you ever have need to step up there—which, pray God, you may not."

"What is the secret?" asked Anthony, as the tracery swung back into place, and his host stepped down.

"Pull the third roebuck's ears in the coat of arms, or rather push them. It closes with a spring, and is provided with a bolt. But I do not recommend that refuge unless it is necessary. In winter it is too hot, for the chimney passes behind it; and in summer it is too oppressive, for there is not too much air."

At the end of the corridor that led in the direction of the little old rooms where Anthony had slept in his visit, Mr. Buxton stopped before the portrait of a kindly-looking old gentleman that hung on the wall.

"Now there is an upright old man you would say; and indeed he was, for he was my own uncle, and made a godly end of it last year. But now see what a liar I have made of him!"

Mr. Buxton put his hand behind the frame, and the whole picture opened like a door showing a space within where three or four could stand. Anthony stepped inside and his friend followed him, and after showing him some clothes hanging against the wall closed the picture after them, leaving them in the dark.

"Now see what a sharp-eyed old fellow he is too," whispered his host. Anthony looked where he was guided, and perceived two pinholes through which he could see the whole length of the corridor.

"Through the centre of each eye," whispered his friend. "Is he not shrewd and secret? And now turn this way."

Anthony turned round and saw the opposite wall slowly opening; and in a moment more he stepped out and found himself in the lobby outside the little room where he had made the exercises six years ago. He heard a door close softly as he looked about him in astonishment, and on turning round saw only an innocent-looking set of shelves with a couple of books and a little pile of paper and packet of quills upon them.

"There," said Mr. Buxton, "who would suspect Tacitus his history and Juvenal his satires of guarding the passage of a Christian ecclesiastic fleeing for his life?"

Then he showed him the secret, how one shelf had to be drawn out steadily, and the nail in another pressed simultaneously, and how then the entire set of shelves swung open.

Then they went back and he showed him the spring behind the frame of the picture.

"You see the advantage of this," he went on: "on the one side you may flee upstairs, a treasonable skulking cassocked jack-priest with the lords and the commons and the Queen's Majesty barking at your heels; and on the other side you may saunter down the gallery without your beard and in a murrey doublet, a friend of Mr. Buxton's, taking the air and wondering what the devil all the clamouring be about."

Then he took him downstairs again and showed him finally the escape of which he was most proud—the entrance, designed in the cellar-staircase, to an underground passage from the cellars, which led, he told him, across to the garden-house beyond the lime-avenue.

"That is the pride of my heart," he said, "and maybe will be useful some day; though I pray not. Ah! her Grace and her honest Council are right. We Papists are a crafty and deceitful folk, Father Anthony."

The four grew very intimate during those few weeks; they had many memories and associations in common on which to build up friendship, and the aid of a common faith and a common peril with which to cement it. The gracious beauty of the house and the life at Stanfield, too, gilded it all with a very charming romance. They were all astonished at the easy intimacy with which they behaved, one to another.

Mary Corbet was obliged to return to her duties at Court at the beginning of September; and she had something of an ache at her heart as the time drew on; for she had fallen once more seriously in love with Isabel. She said a word of it to Mr. Buxton. They were walking in the lime-avenue together after dinner on the last day of Mary's visit.

"You have a good chaplain," she said; "what an honest lad he is! and how serious and recollected! Please God he at least may escape their claws!"

"It is often so," said Mr. Buxton, "with those wholesome out-of-door boys; they grow up into such simple men of God."

"And Isabel!" said Mary, rustling round upon him as she walked. "What a great dame she is become! I used to lie on her bed and kick my heels and laugh at her; but now I would like to say my prayers to her. She is somewhat like our Lady herself, so grave and serious, and yet so warm and tender."

Mr. Buxton nodded sharply.

"I felt sure you would feel it," he said.

"Ah! but I knew her when she was just a child; so simple that I loved to startle her. But now—but now—those two ladies have done wonders with her. She has all the splendour of Mary Maxwell, and all the softness of Margaret."

"Yes," said the other meditatively; "the two ladies have done it—or, the grace of God."

Mary looked at him sideways and her lips twitched a little.

"Yes—or the grace of God, as you say."

The two laughed into each other's eyes, for they understood one another well. Presently Mary went on:

"When you and I fence together at table, she does not turn frigid like so many holy folk—or peevish and bewildered like stupid folk—but she just looks at us, and laughs far down in those deep grey eyes of hers. Oh! I love her!" ended Mary.

They walked in silence a minute or two.

"And I think I do," said Mr. Buxton softly.

"Eh?" exclaimed Mary, "you do what?" She had quite forgotten her last sentence.

"It is no matter," he said yet more softly; and would say no more.

Presently the talk fell on the Maxwells; and came round to Hubert.

"They say he would be a favourite at Court," said Mary, "had he not a wife. But her Grace likes not married men. She looked kindly upon him at Deptford, I know; and I have seen him at Greenwich. You know, of course, about Isabel?"

Mr. Buxton shook his head.

"Why, it was common talk that they would have been man and wife years ago, had not the fool apostatised."

Her companion questioned her further, and soon had the whole story out of her. "But I am thankful," ended Mary, "that it has so ended."

The next day she went back to Court; and it was with real grief that the three watched her wonderful plumed riding-hat trot along behind the top of the churchyard wall, with her woman beside her, and her little liveried troop of men following at a distance.

The days passed by, bringing strange tidings to Stanfield. News continued to reach the Catholics of the good confessions witnessed here and there in England by priests and laity. At the end of July, three priests, Garlick, Ludlam and Sympson, had been executed at Derby, and at the end of August the defeat of the Armada seemed to encourage Elizabeth yet further, and Mr. Leigh, a priest, with four laymen and Mistress Margaret Ward, died for their religion at Tyburn.

By the end of September the news of the hopeless defeat and disappearance of the Armada had by now been certified over and over again. Terrible stories had come in during August of that northward flight of all that was left of the fleet over the plunging North Sea up into the stormy coast of Scotland; then rumours began of the miseries that were falling on the Spaniards off Ireland—Catholic Ireland from which they had hoped so much. There was scarcely a bay or a cape along the west coast where some ship had not put in, with piteous entreaties for water and aid—and scarcely a bay or a cape that was not blood-guilty. Along the straight coast from Sligo Bay westwards, down the west coast, Clew Bay, Connemara, and haunted Dingle itself, where the Catholic religion under arms had been so grievously chastened eight years ago—everywhere half-drowned or half-starved Spaniards, piteously entreating, were stripped and put to the sword either by the Irish savages or the English gentlemen. The church-bells were rung in Stanfield and in every English village, and the flame of national pride and loyalty burned fiercer and higher than ever.

On the last day of September Isabel, just before dinner in her room, heard the trot of a couple of horses coming up the short drive, and on going downstairs almost ran against Hubert as he came from the corridor into the hall, as the servant ushered him in.

The two stopped and looked at one another in silence.

Hubert was flushed with hard riding and looked excited; Isabel's face showed nothing but pleasure and surprise. The servant too stopped, hesitating.

Then Isabel put out her hand, smiling; and her voice was natural and controlled.

"Why, Mr. Hubert," she said, "it is you! Come through this way"; and she nodded to the servant, who went forward and opened the door of the little parlour and stood back, as Isabel swept by him.

When the door was closed, and the servant's footsteps had died away, Hubert, as he stood facing Isabel, spoke at last.

"Mistress Isabel," he said almost imploringly, "what can I say to you? Your home has been wrecked; and partly through those wild and foolish words of mine; and you repay it by that act of kindness to my wife! I am come to ask your pardon, and to thank you. I only reached home last night."

"Ah! that was nothing," said Isabel gently; "and as for the house—"

"As for the house," he said, "I was not master of myself when I said those words that Grace told you of; and I entreat you to let me repair the damage."

"No, no," she said, "Anthony has given orders; that will all be done."

"But what can I do then?" he cried passionately; "if you but knew my sorrow—and—and—more than that, my—"

Isabel had raised her grave eyes and was looking him full in the face now; and he stopped abashed.

"How is Grace, and Mercy?" she asked in perfectly even tones.

"Oh! Isabel—" he began; and again she looked at him, and then went to the door.

"I hear Mr. Buxton," she said; and steps came along through the hall; she opened the door as he came up. Mr. Buxton stopped abruptly, and the two men drew themselves up and seemed to stiffen, ever so slightly. A shade of aggressive contempt came on Hubert's keen brown face that towered up so near the low oak ceiling; while Mr. Buxton's eyelids just drooped, and his features seemed to sharpen. There was an unpleasant silence: Isabel broke it.

"You remember Master Hubert Maxwell?" she said almost entreatingly. He smiled kindly at her, but his face hardened again as he turned once more to Hubert.

"I remember the gentleman perfectly," he said, "and he no doubt knows me, and why I cannot ask him to remain and dine with us."

Hubert smiled brutally.

"It is the old story of course, the Faith! I must ask your pardon, sir, for intruding. The difficulty never came into my mind. The truth is that I have lived so long now among Protestants that I had quite forgotten what Catholic charity is like!"

He said this with such extreme bitterness and fury that Isabel put out her hand instinctively to Mr. Buxton, who smiled at her once more, and pressed it in his own. Hubert laughed again sharply; his face grew white under the tan, and his lips wrinkled back once or twice.

"So, if you can spare me room to pass," he went on in the same tone, "I will begone to the inn."

167

Mr. Buxton stepped aside from the door, and Hubert bowed to Isabel so low that it was almost an insult in itself, and strode out, his spurs ringing on the oak boards.

When he half turned outside the front door to beckon to his groom to bring up the horses, he became aware that Isabel was beside him.

"Hubert," she said, "Hubert, I cannot bear this."

There were tears in her voice, and he could not help turning and looking at her. Her face, more grave and transparent than ever, was raised to his; her red down-turned lips were trembling, and her eyes were full of a great emotion. He turned away again sharply.

"Hubert," she said again, "I was not born a Catholic, and I do not feel like Mr. Buxton. And—and I do thank you for coming; and for your desire to repair the house; and—and will you give my love to Grace?"

Then he suddenly turned to her with such passion in his eyes that she shrank back. At the same moment the groom brought up the horses; he turned and mounted without a word, but his eyes were dim with love and anger and jealousy. Then he drove his spurs into his great grey mare, and Isabel watched him dash between the iron gates, with his groom only half mounted holding back his own plunging horse. Then she went within doors again.

Chapter Five - Joseph Lackington

It was a bitter ride back to Great Keynes for Hubert. He had just returned from watching the fifty vessels, which were all that were left of the Great Armada, pass the Blaskets, still under the nominal command of Medina Sidonia, on their miserable return to Spain; and he had come back as fast as sails could carry him, round the stormy Land's-End up along the south coast to Rye, where on his arrival he had been almost worshipped by the rejoicing townsfolk. Yet all through his voyage and adventures, at any rate since his interview with her at Rye, it had been the face of Isabel there, and not of Grace, that had glimmered to him in the dark, and led him from peril to peril. Then, at last, on his arrival at home, he had heard of the disaster to the Dower House, and his own unintended share in it; and of Isabel's generous visit to his wife; and at that he had ordered his horse abruptly over-night and ridden off without a word of explanation to Grace on the following morning. And he had been met by a sneering man who would not sit at table with him, and who was the protector and friend of Isabel.

He rode up through the village just after dark and in through the gatehouse up to the steps. A man ran to open the door, and as Hubert came through told him that a stranger had ridden down from London and had arrived at mid-day, and that he had been waiting ever since.

"I gave the gentleman dinner in the cloister parlour, sir; and he is at supper now," added the man.

Hubert nodded and pushed through the hall. He heard his name called timidly from upstairs, and looking up saw his wife's golden head over the banisters.

"Well!" he said.

"Ah, it is you. I am so glad."

"Who else should it be?" said Hubert, and passed through towards the cloister wing, and opened the door of the little parlour where Isabel and Mistress Margaret had sat together years before, the night of Mr. James' return, and of the girl's decision.

A stranger rose up hastily as he came in, and bowed with great deference. Hubert knew his face, but could not remember his name.

"I ask your pardon, Mr. Maxwell; but your man would take no denial," and he indicated the supper-table with a steaming dish and a glass jug of wine ruddy in the candlelight. Hubert looked at him curiously.

"I know you, sir," he said, "but I cannot put a name to your face."

"Lackington," said the man with a half smile; "Joseph Lackington."

Hubert still stared; and then suddenly burst into a short laugh.

"Why, yes," he said; "I know now. My father's servant."

The man bowed.

"Formerly, sir; and now agent to Sir Francis Walsingham," he said, with something of dignity in his manner.

Hubert saw the hint, but could not resist a small sneer.

"Why, I am pleased to see you," he said. "You have come to see your old—home?" and he threw himself into a chair and stretched his legs to the blaze, for he was stiff with riding. Lackington instantly sat down too, for his pride was touched.

"It was not for that, Mr. Maxwell," he said almost in the tone of an equal, "but on a mission for Sir Francis."

Hubert looked at him a moment as he sat there in the candlelight, with his arm resting easily on the table. He was plainly prosperous, and was even dressed with some distinction; his reddish beard was trimmed to a point; his high forehead was respectably white and bald; and his seals hung from his belt beside his dagger with an air of ease and solidity. Perhaps he was of some importance; at any rate, Sir Francis Walsingham was. Hubert sat up a little.

"A mission to me?" he said.

Lackington nodded.

"A few questions on a matter of state."

He drew from his pouch a paper signed by Sir Francis authorising him as an agent, for one month, and dated three days back; and handed it to Hubert.

"I obtained that from Sir Francis on Monday, as you will see. You can trust me implicitly."

"Will the business take long?" asked Hubert, handing the paper back.

"No, Mr. Maxwell; and I must be gone in an hour in any case. I have to be at Rye at noon to-morrow; and I must sleep at Mayfield to-night."

"At Rye," said Hubert, "why I came from there yesterday."

Lackington bowed again, as if he were quite aware of this; but said nothing.

"Then I will sup here," went on Hubert, "and we will talk meantime."

When a place had been laid for him, he drew his chair round to the table and began to eat.

"May I begin at once?" asked Lackington, who had finished.

Hubert nodded.

"Then first I believe it to be a fact that you spoke with Mistress Isabel Morris on board the Elizabeth at Rye on the tenth of August last."

Hubert had started violently at her name; but did his utmost to gain outward command of himself again immediately.

"Well?" he said.

"And with Master Anthony Norris, lately made a priest beyond the seas."

"That is a lie," said Hubert.

Lackington politely lifted his eyebrows.

"Indeed?" he said. "That he was made a priest, or that you spoke with him?"

"That I know aught of him," said Hubert. His heart was beating furiously.

Lackington made a note rather ostentatiously; he could see that Hubert was frightened, and thought that it was because of a possible accusation of having dealings with a traitor.

"And as regards Mistress Norris," he said judicially, with his pencil raised, "you deny having spoken with her?"

Hubert was thinking furiously. Then he saw that Lackington knew too much for its being worth his own while to deny it.

"No, I never denied that," he said, lifting his fork to his mouth; and he went on eating with a deliberate ease as Lackington again made a note.

The next question was a home-thrust.

"Where are they both now?" asked Lackington, looking at him. Hubert's mind laboured like a mill.

"I do not know," he said.

"You swear it?"

"I swear it."

"Then Mistress Norris has changed her plans?" said Lackington swiftly.

"What do you mean by that?"

"Why she told you where they were going when you met?" said the other in a remonstrating tone.

Hubert suddenly saw the game. If the authorities really knew that, it would have been a useless question. He stared at Lackington with an admirable vacancy.

"Indeed she did not," he said. "For aught I know, they—she is in France again."

"They?" said Lackington shrewdly. "Then you do know somewhat of the priest?"

But Hubert was again too sharp.

"Only what you told me just now, when you said he was at Rye. I supposed you were telling the truth."

Lackington passed his hand smoothly over his mouth and beard, and smiled. Either Hubert was very sharp or else he had told everything; and he did not believe him sharp.

"Thank you, Mr. Maxwell," he said, with a complete dropping of his judicial manner. "I will not pretend not to be disappointed; but I believe what you say about France is true; and that it is no use looking for him further."

Hubert experienced an extraordinary relief. He had saved Isabel. He drank off a glass of claret. "Tell me everything," he said.

"Well," said Lackington, "Mr. Thomas Hamon is my informant. He sent up to Sir Francis the message that a lady of the name of Norris had been introduced to him at Rye; because he thought he remembered some stir in the county several years ago about some reconciliations to Rome connected with that name. Of course we knew everything about that: and we have our agents at the seminaries too; so we concluded that she was one of our birds; the rest, of course, was guesswork. Mr. Norris has certainly left Douai for England; and he may possibly even now be in England; but from your information and others', I now believe that Mistress Isabel came across first, and that she found the country too hot, what with the Spaniards and all; and that she returned to France at once. Of course during that dreadful week, Mr. Maxwell, we could not be certain of all vessels that came and went; so I think she just slipped across again; and that they are both waiting in France. We shall keep good watch now at the ports, I can promise you."

Hubert's emotions were varied during this speech. First shame at having entirely forgotten the mayor of Rye and his own introduction of Isabel to him; then astonishment at the methods of Walsingham's agents; and lastly intense triumph and relief at having put them off Isabel's track. For Anthony, too, he had nothing but kindly feelings; so, on the whole, he thought he had done well for his friends.

The two talked a little longer; Lackington was a stimulating companion from both his personality and his position; and Hubert found himself almost sorry when his companion said he must be riding on to Mayfield. As he walked out with him to the front door, he suddenly thought of Mr. Buxton again and his reception in the afternoon. They had wandered in their conversation so far from the Norrises by now that he felt sure he could speak of him without doing them any harm. So, as they stood on the steps together, waiting for Lackington's horse to come round, he suddenly said:

"Do you know aught of one Buxton, who lives somewhere near Tonbridge, I think?"

"Buxton, Buxton?" said the other.

"I met him in town once," went on Hubert smoothly; "a little man, dark, with large eyes, and looks somewhat like a Frenchman."

"Buxton, Buxton?" said the other again. "A Papist, is he not?"

"Yes," said Hubert, hoping to get some information against him.

"A friend?" asked Lackington.

"No," said Hubert with such vehemence that Lackington looked at him.

"I remember him," he said in a moment; "he was imprisoned at Wisbeach six or seven years ago. But I do not think he has been in trouble since. You wish, you wish——?" he went on interrogatively.

"Nothing," said Hubert; but Lackington saw the hatred in his eyes.

The horses came round at this moment; and Lackington said good-bye to Hubert with a touch of the old deference again, and mounted. Hubert watched him out under the gatehouse-lamp into the night beyond, and then he went in again, pondering.

His wife was waiting for him in the hall now—a delicate golden-haired figure, with pathetic blue eyes turned up to him. She ran to him and took his arm timidly in her two hands.

"Oh! I am glad that man has gone, Hubert."

He looked down at her almost contemptuously.

"Why, you know nothing of him!" he said.

"Not much," she said, "but he asked me so many questions."

Hubert started and looked suddenly at her, in terror.

"Oh, Hubert!" she said, shrinking back frightened.

"Questions!" he said, seizing her hands. "Questions of whom?"

"Of—of—Mistress Isabel Norris," she said, almost crying.

"And—and—what did you say? Did you tell him?"

"Oh, Hubert!—I am so sorry—ah! do not look like that."

"What did you say? What did you say?" he said between his teeth.

"I—I—told a lie, Hubert; I said I had never seen her."

Hubert took his wife suddenly in his two arms and kissed her three or four times.

"You darling, you darling!" he said; and then stooped and picked her up, and carried her upstairs, with her head against his cheek, and her tears running down because he was pleased with her, instead of angry.

They went upstairs and he set her down softly outside the nursery door.

"Hush," she said, smiling up at him; and then softly opened the door and listened, her finger on her lip; there was no sound from within; then she pushed the door open gently, and the wife and husband went in.

There was a shaded taper still burning in a high bracket where an image of the Mother of God had stood in the Catholic days of the house. Hubert glanced up at it and remembered it, with just a touch at his heart. Beneath it was a little oak cot, where his four-year-old boy lay sleeping; the mother went across and bent over it, and Hubert leaned his brown sinewy hands on the end of the cot and watched him. There his son lay, with tangled curls on the pillow; his finger was on his lips as if he bade silence even to thought. Hubert looked up, and just above the bed, where the crucifix used to hang when he himself had slept in this nursery, probably on the very same nail, he thought to himself, was a rusty Spanish spur that he himself had found in a sea-chest of the San Juan. The boy had hung up with a tarry bit of string this emblem of his father's victory, as a protection while he slept.

The child stirred in his sleep and murmured as the two watched him.

"Father's home again," whispered the mother. "It is all well. Go to sleep again."

When she looked up again to her husband, he was gone.

It was not often that Hubert had regrets for the Faith he had lost; but to-night things had conspired to prick him. There was his rebuff from Mr. Buxton; there was the sight of Isabel in the dignified grace that he had noticed so plainly before; there had been the interview with the ex-Catholic servant, now a spy of the Government, and a remorseless enemy of all Catholics; and lastly there were the two little external reminders of the niche and the nail over his son's bed.

He sat long before the fire in Sir Nicholas' old room, now his own study. As he lay back and looked about him, how different this all was, too! The mantelpiece was almost unaltered; the Maxwell devices, two-headed eagles, hurcheons and saltires, on crowded shields, interlaced with the motto Reviresco, all newly gilded since his own accession to the estate, rose up in deep shadow and relief; but over it, instead of the little old picture of the Vernacle that he remembered as a child, hung his own sword. Was that a sign of progress? he wondered. The tapestry on the east wall was the same, a hawking scene with herons and ladies in immense headdresses that he had marvelled at as a boy. But then the books on the shelves to the right of the door, they were different; there had been old devotional books in his father's time, mingled strangely with small works on country life and sports; now the latter only remained, and the nearest to a devotional book was a volume of a mystical herbalist who identified plants with virtues, strangely and ingeniously. Then the prie-dieu, where the beads had hung and the little wooden shield with the Five Wounds painted upon it—that was gone; and in its place hung a cupboard where he kept a crossbow and a few tools for it; and old hawk-lures and jesses and the like.

Then he lay back again, and thought.

Had he then behaved unworthily? This old Faith that had been handed down from father and son for generations; that had been handed to him too as the most precious heirloom of all—for which his father had so gladly suffered fines and imprisonment, and risked death—he had thrown it over, and for what? For Isabel, he confessed to himself; and then the—the Power that stands behind the visible had cheated him and withdrawn that for which he had paid over that great price. Was that a reckless and brutal bargain on his side—to throw over this strange delicate thing called the Faith for which so many millions had lived and died, all for a woman's love? A curious kind of family pride in the Faith began to prick him. After all, was not honour in a manner bound up with it too; and most of all when such heavy penalties attached themselves to the profession of it? Was that the moment when he should be the first of his line to abandon it?

Reviresco—"I renew my springtide." But was not this a strange grafting—a spur for a crucifix, a crossbow for a place of prayer? Reviresco—There was sap indeed in the old tree; but from what soil did it draw its strength?

His heart began to burn with something like shame, as it had burned now and again at intervals during these past years. Here he lay back in his father's chair, in his father's room, the first Protestant of the Maxwells. Then he passed on to a memory.

As he closed his eyes, he could see even now the chapel upstairs, with the tapers alight and the stiff figure of the priest in the midst of the glow; he could smell the flowers on the altar, the June roses strewn on the floor in the old manner, and their fresh dewy scent mingled with the fragrance of the rich incense in an intoxicating chord; he could hear the rustle that emphasised the silence, as his mother rose from his side and went up for communion, and the breathing of the servants behind him.

Then for contrast he remembered the whitewashed church where he attended now with his wife, Sunday by Sunday, the pulpit occupied by the black figure of the virtuous Mr. Bodder pronouncing his discourse, the great texts that stood out in their new paint from the walls, the table that stood out unashamed and sideways in the midst of the chancel. And which of the two worships was most like God?...

Then he compared the worshippers in either mode. Well, Drake, his hero, was a convinced Protestant; the bravest man he had ever met or dreamed of—fiery, pertinacious, gloriously insolent. He thought of his sailors, on whom a portion of Drake's spirit fell, their gallantry, their fearlessness of death and of all that comes after; of Mr. Bodder, who was now growing middle-aged in the Vicarage—yes, indeed, they were all admirable in various ways, but were they like Christ?

On the other hand, his father, in spite of his quick temper, his mother, brother, aunt, the priests who came and went by night, Isabel—and at that he stopped: and like a deep voice in his ear rose up the last tremendous question, What if the Catholic Religion be true after all? And at that the supernatural began to assert itself. It seemed as if the empty air were full of this question, rising in intensity and emphasis. What if it is true? What if it is true? What if it is true? He sat bolt upright and looked sharply round the room; the candles burned steadily in the sconce near the door. The tapestry lifted and dropped noiselessly in the draught; the dark corners beyond the press and in the window recesses suggested presences that waited; the wide chimney sighed suddenly once.

Was that a voice in his ear just now, or only in his heart? But in either case—

He made an effort to command himself, and looked again steadily round the room; but there seemed no one there. But what if the old tale be true? In that case he is not alone in this little oak room, for there is no such thing as loneliness. In that case he is sitting in full sight of Almighty God, whom he has insulted; and of the saints whose power he has repudiated; and of the angels good and bad who have—Ah! what was that? There had seemed to come a long sigh somewhere behind him; on his left surely.—What was it? Some wandering soul? Was it, could it be the soul of one who had loved him and desired to warn him before it was too late? Could it have been—and then it came again; and the hair prickled on his head.

How deathly still it is, and how cold! Ah! was that a rustle outside; a tap?... In God's name, who can that be?...

And then Hubert licked his dry lips and brought them together and smiled at Grace, who had come down, opening the doors as she came, to see why he had not come to bed.

Bah! what a superstitious fool he was, after all!

Chapter Six - A Departure

The months went by happily at Stanfield; and, however ill went the fortunes of the Church elsewhere, here at least were peace and prosperity. Most discouraging news indeed did reach them from time to time. The severe penalties now enacted against the practice of the Catholic Religion were being enforced with great vigour, and the weak members of the body began to fail. Two priests had apostatised at Chichester earlier in the year, one of them actually at the scaffold on Broyle Heath; and then in December there were two more recantations at Paul's Cross. Those Catholics too who threw up the Faith generally became the most aggressive among the persecutors, to testify to their own consciences, as well to the Protestants, of the sincerity of their conversion.

But in Stanfield the Church flourished, and Anthony had the great happiness of receiving his first convert in the person of Mr. Rowe, the young owner of a house called East Maskells, separated from Stanfield Place by a field-path of under a mile in length, though the road round was over two; and the comings and goings were frequent now between the two houses. Mr. Rowe was at present unmarried, and had his aunt to keep house for him, a tolerant old maiden lady who had conformed placidly to the Reformed Religion thirty years before, and was now grown content with it. Several "schismatics" too—as those Catholics were called who attended their parish church—had waxed bolder, and given up their conformity to the Establishment; so it was a happy and courageous flock that gathered Sunday by Sunday at Stanfield Place.

Just before Christmas, Anthony received a long and affectionate letter from James Maxwell, who was still at Douai. "The Rector will still have me here," he wrote, "and shows me to the young men as if I were a kind of warrior; which is bad for pride; but then he humbles me again by telling me I am of more use here as an example, than I should be in England; and that humbles me again. So I am content to stay. It is a humbling thing, too, to find young men who can tell me the history of my arms and legs better than I know it myself. But the truth is, I can never walk well again—yet laudetur Jesus Christus."

Then James Maxwell wrote a little about his grief for Hubert; gave a little news of foreign movements among the Catholics; and finally ended as follows:

"At last I understand who your friend was behind Bow Church, who stuttered and played the Catholic so well. It was our old servant Lackington; who turned Protestant and entered Walsingham's service. I hear all this from one P. lately in the same affairs, but now turned to Christ his service instead; and who has entered here as a student. So beware of him; he has a pointed beard now, and a bald forehead. I hear, too, from the same source that he was on your track when you landed, but now thinks you to be in France. However, he knows of you; so I counsel you not to abide over long in one place. Perhaps you may go to Lancashire; that is like heaven itself for Catholics. Their zeal and piety there are beyond praise; but I hear they somewhat lack priests. God keep you always, my dear Brother; and may the Queen of Heaven intercede for you. Pray for me."

Soon after the New Year, Mary Corbet was able to get away from Court and come down again to her friends for a month or two at Stanfield.

During her stay they all had an adventure together at East Maskells. They had been out a long expedition into the woods one clear frosty day and rode in just at sunset for an early supper with Mr. Rowe and his aunt.

They had left their horses at the stable and come in round the back of the house; so that they missed the servant Miss Rowe had placed at the front door to warn them, and came straight into the winter-parlour, where they found Miss Rowe in conversation with an ecclesiastic. There was no time to retreat; and Anthony in a moment more found himself being introduced to a minister he had met at Lambeth more than once—the Reverend Robert Carr, who had held the odd title of "Archbishop's Curate" and the position of minister in charge of the once collegiate church of All Saints', Maidstone, ever since the year '59. He had ridden up from Maidstone for supper and lodging, and was on his way to town.

Anthony managed to interrupt Miss Rowe before she came to his assumed name Capell, and remarked rather loudly that he had met Mr. Carr before; who recognised him too, and greeted him by his real name.

It was an uncomfortable situation, as Mr. Carr was quite unaware of the religion of five out of six of those present, and very soon began to give voice to his views on Papistry. He was an oldish man by now, and of some importance in Maidstone, where he had been appointed Jurat by the Corporation, and was a very popular and influential man.

"The voice of the people," he said in the midst of a conversation on the national feeling towards Spain, "that is what we must hearken to. Even sovereigns themselves must come to that some day. They must rule by obeying; as man does with God's laws in nature."

"Would you say that, sir, of her Grace?" asked Mary Corbet meekly.

"I should, madam; though I fear she has injured her power by her behaviour this year. It was her people who saved her.—Hawkins, who is now ruined as he says; my lord Howard, who has paid from his own purse for the meat and drink of her Grace's soldiers, and those who fought with them; and not her Grace, who saved them; or Leicester, now gone to his account, who sat at Tilbury and did the bowing and the prancing and the talking while Hawkins and the rest did the fighting. No, madam, it is the voice of the people to which we must hearken."

This was rather confused and dangerous talking too; but here was plainly a man to be humoured; he looked round him with a suffused face and the eye of a cock, and a little white plume on his forehead increased his appearance of pugnacity.

"It is the same in religion," he said, when all preserved a deferential silence; "it is that that lies at the root of papist errors. As you know very well," he went on, turning suddenly on Anthony, "our bishops do nothing to guide men's minds; they only seem to: they ride atop like the figure on a cock-horse, but it is the legs beneath that do the work and the guiding too: now that is right and good; and the Church of England will prosper so long as she goes like that. But if the bishops try to rule they will find their mistake. Now the Popish Church is not like that; she holds that power comes from above, that the Pope guides the bishops, the bishops the priests, and the priests the people."

"And the Holy Ghost the Pope; is it not so, sir?" asked Mr. Buxton.

Mr. Carr turned an eye on him.

"So they hold, sir," he said after a pause.

"They think then, sir, that the shepherds guide the sheep?" asked Anthony humbly.

Mary Corbet gave a yelp of laughter; but when Mr. Carr looked at her she was grave and deferential again. Miss Rowe looked entreatingly from face to face. The minister did not notice Anthony's remark; but swept on again on what was plainly his favourite theme,—the infallibility of the people. It was a doctrine that was hardly held yet by any; but the next century was to see its gradual rise until it reached its climax in the Puritanism of the Stuart times. It was true, as Mr. Carr said, that Elizabeth had ruled by obeying; and that the people of England, encouraged by success in resisting foreign domination, were about to pass on to the second position of resisting any domination at all.

Presently he pulled out of his pocket a small printed sheet, and was soon declaiming from it. It was not very much to the point, except as illustrating the national spirit which he believed so divine. It was a ballad describing the tortures which the Spaniards had intended to inflict upon the heretic English, and began:

"All you that list to look and see
What profit comes from Spain,
And what the Pope and Spaniards both
Prepared for our gain.
Then turn your eyes and lend your ears
And you shall hear and see
What courteous minds, what gentle hearts,
They bear to thee and me!

And it ended in the same spirit:
"Be these the men that are so mild
Whom some so holy call!
The Lord defend our noble Queen
And country from them all!"

"There!" the minister cried when he had done, "that is what the Papists are like! Trust me; I know them. I should know one in a moment if he ventured into this room, by his crafty face. But the Lord will defend His own Englishmen; nay! He has done so. 'God blew and they were scattered,'" he ended, quoting from the Armada medal.

As the four rode home by pairs across the field-path in the frosty moonlight Mr. Buxton lamented to Anthony the effect of the Armada.

"The national spirit is higher than ever," he said, "and it will be the death of Catholicism here for the present. Our country squires, I fear, faithful Catholics to this time, are beginning to wonder and question. When will our Catholic kings learn that Christ His Kingdom is not of this world? Philip has smitten the Faith in England with the weapon which he drew in its defence, as he thought."

"I was once of that national spirit myself," said Anthony.

"I remember you were," said Mr. Buxton, smiling; "and what grace has done to you it may do to others."

The spring went by, and in the week after Easter, James' news about Lancashire was verified by a letter from a friend of Mr. Buxton's, a Mr. Norreys, the owner of one of the staunch Catholic houses, Speke Hall, on the bank of the Mersey.

"Here," he wrote, "by the mercy of God there is no lack of priests, though there be none to spare; my own chaplain says mass by dispensation thrice on Sunday; but on the moors the sheep look up and are not fed; and such patient sheep! I heard but last week of a church where the folk resort, priest or no, each Sunday to the number of two hundred, and are led by a lector in devotion, ending with an act of spiritual communion made all together. These damnable heresies of which the apostle wrote have not poisoned the springs of sound doctrine; some of us here know naught yet of Elizabeth and her supremacy, or even of seven-wived Harry his reformation. Send us then, dear friend, a priest, or at least the promise of one; lest we perish quite."

Mr. Buxton had a sore struggle with himself over this letter; but at last he carried it to Anthony.

"Read that," he said; and stood waiting.

Anthony looked up when he had done.

"I am your chaplain," he said, "but I am God's priest first."

"Yes, dear lad," said his friend, "I feared you would say so; and I will say so to Norreys"; and he left the room at once.

And so at last it came to be arranged that Anthony should leave for Lancashire at the end of July; and that after his departure Stanfield should be served occasionally by the priest who lived on the outskirts of Tonbridge; but the daily mass would have to cease, and that was a sore trouble to Mr. Buxton. No definite decision could be made as to when Anthony could return; that must wait until he saw the needs of Lancashire; but he hoped to be able at least to pay a visit to Stanfield again in the spring of the following year.

It was arranged also, of course, that Isabel should accompany her brother. They were both of large independent means, and could travel in some dignity; and her presence would be under these circumstances a protection as well as a comfort to Anthony. It would need very great sharpness to detect the seminary priest under Anthony's disguise, and amid the surroundings of his cavalcade of four or five armed servants, a French maid, and a distinguished-looking lady.

Yet, in spite of this, Mr. Buxton resolved to do his utmost to prevent Isabel from going to Lancashire; partly, of course, he disliked the thought of the dangers and hardships that she was certain to encounter; but the real motive was that he had fallen very deeply in love with her. It was her exceptional serenity that seemed to him her greatest charm; her movements, her face, her grey eyes, the very folds of her dress seemed to breathe with it; and to one of Mr. Buxton's temperament such a presence was cool and sweet and strangely fascinating.

It was now April, and he resolved to devote the next month or two to preparing her for his proposal; and he wrote frankly to Mary Corbet telling her how matters stood, entreating her to come down for July and counsel him. Mary wrote back at once, rather briefly, promising to come; but not encouraging him greatly.

"I would I could cheer you more," she wrote; "of course I have not seen Isabel since January; but, unless she has changed, I do not think she will marry you. I am writing plainly you see, as you ask in your letter. But I can still say, God prosper you."

As the spring went by and the summer came on, Isabel grew yet more silent. As the evenings began to lengthen out she used to spend much time before and after supper in walking up and down the clipped lime avenue between the east end of the church and the great gates that looked over the meadows across which the stream and the field-path

174

ran towards East Maskells. Mr. Buxton would watch her sometimes from an upstairs window, himself unseen, and occasionally would go out and talk with her; but he found it harder than he used to get on to intimate relations; and he began to suspect that he had displeased her in some way, and that Mary Corbet was right. In the afternoon she and Anthony would generally ride out together, once or twice going round by Penshurst, and their host would torture himself by his own indecision as regards accompanying them; sometimes doing so, sometimes refraining, and regretting whichever he did. More and more he began to look forward to Mary's coming and the benefit of her advice; and at last, at the end of June, she came.

Their first evening together was delightful for them all. She was happy at her escape from Court; her host was happy at the prospect of her counsel; and all four were happy at being together again.

They did not meet till supper, and even that was put off an hour, because Mary had not come, and when she did arrive she was full of excitement.

"I will tell you all at supper," she said to her host, whom she met in the hall. "Oh! how late I am!" and she whirled past him and upstairs without another word.

"I will first give you the news in brief," she said, when Anthony had said grace and they were seated, all four of them as before; and the trumpet-flourish was silent that had announced the approach of the venison.

"Mutton's new chaplain, Dr. Bancroft, will be in trouble soon; he hath been saying favourable things for some of us poor papists, and hath rated the Precisians soundly. Sir Francis Knollys is wroth with him; but that is no matter.— Her Grace played at cards till two of the clock this morning, and that is why I am so desperate sleepy to-night, for I had to sit up too; and that is a great matter.—Drake and Norris, 'tis said, have whipped the dons again at Corunna; and the Queen has sworn to pull my lord Essex his ears for going with them and adventuring his precious self; and that is no matter at all, but will do him good.—George Luttrell hath put up a coat of arms in his hall at Dunster, which is a great matter to him, but to none else;—and I have robbed a highwayman this day in the beech woods this side of Groombridge."

"Dear lady," said Mr. Buxton resignedly, as the others looked up startled, "you are too swift for our dull rustic ears; we will begin at the end, if you please. Is it true you have robbed an highwayman?"

"It is perfectly true," she said, and unlatched a ruby brooch, made heart-shape, from her dress. "There is the plunder," and she held it out for inspection.

"Then tell us the tale," said Anthony.

"It would be five of the clock," said Mary, "as we came through Groombridge, and then into the woods beyond. I had bidden my knaves ride on before with my woman; I came down into a dingle where there was a stream; and, to tell the truth, I had my head down and was a-nodding, when my horse stopped; and I looked up of a sudden and there was a man on a bay mare, with a mask to his mouth, a gay green suit, a brown beard turning grey, and this ruby brooch at his throat; and he had caught my bridle. I saw him start when I lifted my head, as if he were taken aback. I said nothing, but he led my horse off the road down among the trees with a deep little thicket where none could see us. As we went I was thinking like a windmill; for I knew I had seen the little red brooch before.

"When we reached the little open space, I asked him what he wished with me.

"'Your purse, madam,' said he.

"'My woman hath it,' said I.

"'Your jewels then, madam,' said he.

"'My woman hath them,' said I, 'save this paste buckle in my hat, to which you are welcome.' It was diamonds, you know; but I knew he would not know that.

"'What a mistake,' I said, 'to stop the mistress and let the maid go free!'

"'Nay,' he said, 'I am glad of it; for at least I will have a dance with the mistress; and I could not with the maid.'

"'You are welcome to that,' I said, and I slipped off my horse, to humour him, and even as I slipped off I knew who he was, for although many have red brooches, and many brown beards turning grey, few have both together; but I said nothing. And there—will you believe it?—we danced under the beech-trees like Phyllis and Corydon, or whoever they are that Sidney is always prating of; or like two fools, I would sooner say. Then when we had done, I made him a curtsey.

"'Now you must help me up,' said I, and he mounted me without a word, for he was a stoutish gallant and somewhat out of breath. And then what did the fool do but try to kiss me, and as he lifted his arm I snatched the brooch and put spur to my horse, and as we went up the bank I screamed at him, 'Claude, you fool, go home to your wife and take shame to yourself.' And when I was near the road I looked back, and he still stood there all agape."

"And what was his name?" asked Anthony.

"Nay, nay, I have mocked him enough. And I know four Claudes, so you need not try to guess."

When supper was over, Mr. Buxton and Mary walked up and down the south path of the garden between the yews, while the other two sat just outside the hall window on a seat placed on the tiled terrace that ran round the house.

"How I have longed for you to come, Mistress Mary," he said, "and counsel me of the matter we wrote about. Tell me what to do."

Mary looked meditatively out to the strip of moon that was rising out to the east in the June sky. Then she looked tenderly at her friend.

"I hate to pain you," she said, "but cannot you see that it is impossible? I may be wrong; but I think her heart is so given to our Saviour that there is no love of that sort left."

"Ah, how can you say that?" he cried; "the love of the Saviour does not hinder earthly love; it purifies and transfigures it."

"Yes," said Mary gravely, "it is often so—but the love of the true spouse of Christ is different. That leaves no room for an earthly bridegroom."

Mr. Buxton was silent a moment or two.

"You mean it is the love of the consecrated soul?"

Mary bowed her head. "But I cannot be sure," she added.

"Then what shall I do?" he said again, almost piteously; and Mary could see even in the faint moonlight that his pleasant face was all broken up and quivering. She laid her hand gently on his arm, and her rings flashed.

"You must be very patient," she said, "very full of deference—and grave. You must not be ardent nor impetuous, but speak slowly and reverently to her, but at no great length; be plain with her; do not look in her face, and do not show anxiety or despair or hope. You need not fear that your love will not be plain to her. Indeed, I think she knows it already."

"Why, I have not—" he began.

"I know you have not spoken to her; but I saw that she only looked at you once during supper, and that was when your face was turned from her; she does not wish to look you in the eyes."

"Ah, she hates me," he sighed.

"Do not be foolish," said Mary, "she honours you, and loves you, and is grieved for your grief; but I do not think she will marry you."

"And when shall I speak?" he asked.

"You must wait; God will make the opportunity—in any case. You must not attempt to make it. That would terrify her."

"And you will speak for me."

Mary smiled at him.

"Dear friend," she said, "sometimes I think you do not know us at all. Do you not see that Isabel is greater than all that? What she knows, she knows. I could tell her nothing."

The days passed on; the days of the last month of the Norrises' stay at Stanfield. Half-way through the month came the news of the Oxford executions.

"Ah! listen to this," cried Mr. Buxton, coming out to them one evening in the garden with a letter in his hand.

"'Humphrey Prichard,'" he read, "'made a good end. He protested he was condemned for the Catholic Faith; that he willingly died for it; that he was a Catholic. One of their ministers laughed at him, saying he was a poor ignorant fellow who knew not what it was to be a Catholic. 'I know very well;' said Humphrey, 'though I cannot say it in proper divinity language.' There is the Religion for you!" went on Mr. Buxton; "all meet there, wise and simple alike. There is no difference; no scholarship is needed for faith. 'I know what it is,' cried Humphrey, 'though I cannot explain it!'"

The news came to Anthony just when he needed it; he felt he had done so little to teach his flock now he was to leave them; but if he had only done something to keep alive the fire of faith, he had not lost his time; and so he went about his spiritual affairs with new heart, encouraging the wavering, whom he was to leave, warning the over-confident, urging the hesitating, and saying good-bye to them all. Isabel went with him sometimes; or sometimes walked or rode with Mary, and was silent for the most part in public. The master of the house himself did his affairs, and carried a heavier heart each day. And at last the opportunity came which Mary had predicted.

He had come in one evening after a hot ride alone over to Tonbridge on some business with the priest there; and had dressed for supper immediately on coming in.

As there was still nearly an hour before supper, he went out to walk up and down the same yew-alley near the garden-house where he had walked with Mary. Anthony and Isabel had returned a little later from East Maskells, and they too had dressed early. Isabel threw a lace shawl over her head, and betook herself too to the alley; and there she turned a corner and almost ran into her host.

It was, as Mary had said, a God-made opportunity. Neither time nor place could have been improved. If externals were of any value to this courtship, all that could have helped was there. The setting of the picture was perfect; a tall yew-hedge ran down the northern side of the walk, cut, as Bacon recommended, not fantastically but "with some pretty pyramids"; a strip of turf separated it from the walk, giving a sense both of privacy and space; on the south side ran flower-beds in the turf, with yews and cypresses planted here and there, and an oak paling beyond; to the east lay the "fair mount," again recommended by the same authority, but not so high, and with but one ascent; to the west the path darkened under trees, and over all rose up against the sunset sky the tall grotesque towers and vanes of the garden-house. The flowers burned with that ember-like glow which may be seen on summer evenings, and poured out their scent; the air was sweet and cool, and white moths were beginning to poise and stir among the blossoms. The two actors on this scene too were not unworthy of it; his dark velvet and lace with the glimmer of diamonds here and there, and his delicate bearded clean-cut face, a little tanned, thrown into relief by the spotless crisp ruff beneath, and above all his air of strength and refinement and self-possession—all combined to make him a formidable stormer of a girl's heart. And as he looked on her—on her clear almost luminous face and great eyes, shrined in the drooping lace shawl, through which a jewel or two in her black hair glimmered, her upright slender figure in its dark sheath, and the hand, white and cool, that held her shawl together over her breast—he had a pang of hope and despair at once, at the sudden sense of need of this splendid creature of God to be one with him, and reign with him over these fair possessions; and of hopelessness at the thought that anything so perfect could be accomplished in this imperfect world.

He turned immediately and walked beside her, and they both knew, in the silence that followed, that the crisis had come.

"Mistress Isabel," he said, still looking down as he spoke, and his voice sounded odd to her ears, "I wonder if you know what I would say to you."

There came no sound from her, but the rustle of her dress.

"But I must say it," he went on, "follow what may. It is this. I love you dearly."

Her walk faltered beside him, and it seemed as if she would stand still.

"A moment," he said, and he lifted his white restrained face. "I ask you to be patient with me. Perhaps I need not say that I have never said this to any woman before; but more, I have never even thought it. I do not know how to speak, nor what I should say; beyond this, that since I first met you at the door across there, a year ago, you have taught me ever since what love means; and now I am come to you, as to my dear mistress, with my lesson learnt."

They were standing together now; he was still turned a little away from her, and dared not lift his eyes to her face again. Then of a sudden he felt her hand on his arm for a moment, and he looked up, and saw her eyes all swimming with sorrow.

"Dear friend," she said quite simply, "it is impossible—Ah! what can I say?"

"Give me a moment more," he said; and they walked on slowly. "I know what presumption this is; but I will not spin phrases about that. Nor do I ask what is impossible; but I will only ask leave to teach you in my turn what love means."

"Oh! that is the hardest of all to say," she said, "but I know already."

He did not quite understand, and glanced at her a moment.

"I once loved too," she whispered. He drew a sharp breath.

"Forgive me," he said, "I forced that from you."

"You are never anything but courteous and kind," she said, "and that makes this harder than all."

They walked in silence half a dozen steps.

"Have I distressed you?" he asked, glancing at her again.

Then she looked full in his face, and her eyes were overflowing.

"I am grieved for your sorrow," she said, "and at my own unworthiness, you know that?"

"I know that you are now and always will be my dear mistress and queen."

His voice broke altogether as he ended, and he bent and took her hand delicately in his own, as if it were royal, and kissed it. Then she gave a great sob and slipped away through the opening in the clipped hedge; and he was left alone with the dusk and his sorrow.

A week later Anthony and Isabel were saying good-bye to him in the early summer morning: the pack-horses had started on before, and there were just the two saddle-horses at the low oak door, with the servants' behind. When Mr. Buxton had put Isabel into the saddle, he held her hand for a moment; Anthony was mounting behind.

"Mistress Isabel," he whispered; "forgive me; but I find I cannot take your answer; you will remember that."

She shook her head without speaking, but dared not even look into his eyes; though she turned her head as she rode out of the gates for a last look at the peaked gables and low windows of the house where she had been so happy. There was still the dark figure motionless against the pale oak door.

"Oh, Anthony!" she whispered brokenly, "our Lord asks very much."

Chapter Seven - Northern Religion

The Northern counties were distinguished among all in England for their loyalty to the old Faith; and this was owing, no doubt, to the characters of both the country and the inhabitants;—it was difficult for the officers of justice to penetrate to the high moorland and deep ravines, and yet more difficult to prevail with the persons who lived there. Twenty-two years before the famous Lancashire League had been formed, under the encouragement of Dr. Allen, afterwards the Cardinal, whose members pledged themselves to determined recusancy; with the result that here and there church-doors were closed, and the Book of Common Prayer utterly refused. Owing partly to Bishop Downman's laxity towards the recusants, the principles of the League had retained their hold throughout the county, ever since '68, when ten obstinate Lancastrians had been haled before the Council, of whom one, the famous Sir John Southworth himself, suffered imprisonment more than once.

Anthony and Isabel then found their life in the North very different to that which they had been living at Stanfield. Near the towns, of course, precaution was as necessary as anywhere else in England, but once they had passed up on to the higher moorlands they were able to throw off all anxiety, as much as if the penal laws of England were not in force there.

It was pleasant, too, to go, as they did, from great house to great house, and find the old pre-Reformation life of England in full vigour; the whole family present at mass so often as it was said, desirous of the sacraments, and thankful for the opportunities of grace that the arrival of the priest afforded. Isabel would often stay at such houses a week or two together, while Anthony made rounds into the valleys and to the moorland villages round-about; and then the two would travel on together with their servants to the next village. Anthony's ecclesiastical outfit was very simple. Among Isabel's dresses lay a brocade vestment that might easily pass notice if the luggage was searched; and Anthony carried in his own luggage a little altar-stone, a case with the holy oils, a tiny chalice and paten, singing-cakes, and a thin vellum-bound Missal and Ritual in one volume, containing the order of mass, a few votive masses, and the usual benedictions for holy-water, rue and the like, and the occasional offices.

In this manner they first visited many of the famous old Lancashire houses, some of which still stand, Borwick Hall, Hall-i'-the-Wood, Lydiate Hall, Thurnham, Blainscow, where Campion had once been so nearly taken, and others, all of which were provided with secret hiding-places for the escape of the priest, should a sudden alarm be raised. In none of them, however, did he find the same elaboration of device as at Stanfield Place.

First, however, they went to Speke Hall, the home of Mr. Norreys, on the banks of the Mersey, a beautiful house of magpie architecture, and furnished with a remarkable underground passage to the shore of the Mersey, the scene of Richard Brittain's escape.

Here they received a very warm welcome.

"It is as I wrote to Mr. Buxton," said his host on the evening of their arrival, "in many places in this country any religion other than the Catholic is unknown. The belief of the Protestant is as strange as that of the Turk, both utterly detested. I was in Cumberland a few months back; there in more than one village the old worship goes on as it has done since Christianity first came to this island. But I hope you will go up there, now that you have come so far. You would do a great work for Christ his Church."

He told him, too, a number of stories of the zeal and constancy shown on behalf of the Religion; of small squires who were completely ruined by the fines laid upon them; of old halls that were falling to pieces through the ruin brought upon their staunch owners; and above all of the priests that Lancashire had added to the roll of the martyrs—Anderton, Marsden, and Thompson among others—and of the joy shown when the glorious news of their victory over death reached the place where they had been born or where they had ministered.

"At Preston," he said, "when the news of Mr. Greenaway's death reached them, they tolled the bells for sorrow. But his old mother ran from her house to the street when they had broken the news to her: 'Peal them, peal them!' she cried, 'for I have borne a martyr to God.'"

He talked, too, of Campion, of his sermons on "The King who went a journey," and the "Hail, Mary"; and told him of the escape at Blainscow Hall, where the servant-girl, seeing the pursuivants at hand, pushed the Jesuit, with quick wit and courage, into the duck-pond, so that he came out disguised indeed—in green mud—and was mocked at by the very officers as a clumsy suitor of maidens.

Anthony's heart warmed within him as he sat and listened to these tales of patience and gallantry.

"I would lay down my life to serve such folk," he said; and Isabel looked with deep-kindled eyes from the one to the other.

They did not stay more than a day or two at Speke Hall, for, as Mr. Norreys said, the necessaries of salvation were to be had there already; but they moved on almost at once northwards, always arriving at some central point for Saturdays and Sundays, so that the Catholics round could come in for shrift and housel. In this manner they passed up through Lancashire, and pushed still northwards, hearing that a priest was sorely needed, through the corner of Westmoreland, up the Lake country, through into Cumberland itself. At Kendal, where they stayed two nights, Anthony received a message that determined him, after consultation with Isabel, to push on as far as Skiddaw, and to make that the extreme limit of his journey. He sent the messenger, a wild-looking North-countryman, back with a verbal answer to that effect, and named a date when they would arrive.

It was already dark, two weeks later, when they arrived at the point where the guide was to meet them, as they had lost their way more than once already. Here were a couple of men with torches, waiting for them behind a rock, who had come down from the village, a mile farther on, to bring them up the difficult stony path that was the only means of access to it. The track went up a ravine, with a rock-wall rising on their left, on which the light of the torches shone, and tumbled ground, covered with heather, falling rapidly away on their right down to a gulf of darkness whence they could hear the sound of the torrent far below; the path was uneven, with great stones here and there, and sharp corners in it, and as they went it was all they could do to keep their tired horses from stumbling, for a slip would have been dangerous under the circumstances. The men who led them said little, as it was impossible for a horse and a man to walk abreast, but Anthony was astonished to see again and again, as they turned a corner, another man with a torch and some weapon, a pike, or a sword, start up and salute him, or sometimes a group, with barefooted boys, and then attach themselves to the procession either before or behind; until in a short while there was an escort of some thirty or forty accompanying the cavalcade. At last, as they turned a corner, the lighted windows of a belfry showed against the dark moor beyond, and in a moment more, as if there were a watcher set there to look out for the torches, a peal of five bells clashed out from the tower; then, as they rose yet higher, the path took a sudden turn and a dip between two towering rocks, and the whole village lay beneath them, with lights in every window to welcome the priest, the first that they had seen for eight months, when the old Marian rector, the elder brother of the squire, had died.

It was now late, so Anthony and Isabel were conducted immediately to the Hall, an old house immediately adjoining the churchyard; and here, too, the windows were blazing with welcome, and the tall squire, Mr. Brian, with his wife and children behind, was standing before the bright hall-door at the top of the steps. The men and boys that had brought them so far, and were standing in the little court with their torches uplifted, now threw themselves on their knees to receive the priest's blessing, before they went home; and Anthony blessed them and thanked them, and went indoors with his sister, strangely moved and uplifted.

The two following days were full of hard work and delight for Anthony. He was to say mass at half-past six next morning, and came out of the house a little after six o'clock; the sun was just rising to his right over a shoulder of Skiddaw, which dominated the eastern horizon; and all round him, stretched against the sky in all directions, were the high purple moors in the strange dawn-light. Immediately in front of him, not thirty yards away, stood the church, with its tower, two aisles, and a chapel on a little promontory of rock which jutted out over the bed of the torrent along which he had climbed the night before; and to his left lay the straggling street of the village. All was perfectly still except for the dash of the stream over the rocks; but from one or two houses a thin skein of smoke was rising straight into the air. Anthony stood rapt in delight, and drew long breaths of the cool morning air, laden with freshness and fragrant with the mellow scent of the heather and the autumnal smells.

He was completely taken by surprise when he entered the church, for, for the first time since he could remember, he saw an English church in its true glory. It had been built for a priory-church of Holm-Cultram, but for some reason had never been used as that, and had become simply the parish church of the village. Across the centre and the northern aisle ran an elaborate screen, painted in rich colours, and the southern chapel, which ran eastwards of the porch, was separated in a similar way from the rest of the church. Over the central screen was the great rood, with its attendant figures, exquisitely carved and painted; in every direction, as Anthony looked beyond the screens, gleamed rich windows, with figures and armorial bearings; here and there tattered banners hung on the walls; St. Christopher stood on the north wall opposite the door, to guard from violence all who looked upon him day by day; a little painting of the Baptist hung on a pillar over against the font, and a Vernacle by the pulpit; and all round the walls hung little pictures, that the poor and unlearned might read the story of redemption there. But the chief glory of all was the solemn high altar, with its riddells surmounted by taper-bearing gilded angels, with its brocade cloth, and its painted halpas behind; and above it, before the rich window which smouldered against the dawn, hung the awful pyx, covered by the white silk cloth, but empty; waiting for the priest to come and bid the Shechinah of the Lord to brood there again over this gorgeous throne beneath, against the brilliant halo of the painted glass behind. Anthony knelt a moment and thanked God for bringing him here, and then passed up into the north aisle, where the image of the Mother of God presided, as she had done for three hundred years, over her little altar against the wall. Anthony said his preparation and vested at the altar; and was astonished to find at least thirty people to hear mass: none, of course, made their communion, but Anthony, when he had ended, placed the Body of the Lord once more in the hanging pyx and lit the lamp before it.

Then all day he sat in the north chapel, with the dash and loud thunder of the mountain stream entering through the opened panes of the east window, and the stained sunlight, in gorgeous colours, creeping across the red tiles at his feet, glowing and fading as the clouds moved over the sun, while the people came and were shriven; with the exception of an hour in the middle of the day and half an hour for supper in the evening, he was incessantly occupied until nine o'clock at night. From the upland dales all round they streamed in, at news of the priest, and those who had come from far and were fasting he communicated at once from the Reserved Sacrament. At last, tired out, but intensely happy, he went back to the Hall.

But the next morning was yet more startling. Mass was at eight o'clock, and by the time Anthony entered the church he found a congregation of nearly two hundred souls; the village itself did not number above seventy, but many came in from the country round, and some had stayed all night in the church-porch. Then, too, he heard the North-country singing in the old way; all the mass music was sung in three parts, except the unchanging melody of the creed, which, like the tremendous and unchanging words themselves, at one time had united the whole of England; but what stirred Anthony more than all were the ancient hymns sung here and there during the service, some in Latin, which a few picked voices rendered, and some in English, to the old lilting tunes which were as much the growth of the north-country as the heather itself. The "Ave Verum Corpus" was sung after the Elevation, and Anthony felt that his heart would break for very joy; as he bent before the Body of his Lord, and the voices behind him rose and exulted up the aisles, the women's and children's voices soaring passionately up in the melody, the mellow men's voices establishing, as it seemed, these ecstatic pinnacles of song on mighty and immovable foundations.

Vespers were said at three o'clock, after baptisms and more confessions; and Anthony was astonished at the number of folk who could answer the priest. After vespers he made a short sermon, and told the people something of what he had seen in the South, of the martyrdoms at Tyburn, and of the constancy of the confessors.

"'Be thou faithful unto death,'" he said. "So our Saviour bids us, and He gives us a promise too: 'I will give thee a crown of life.' Beloved, some day the tide of heresy will creep up these valleys too; and it will bear many things with it, the scaffold and the gallows and the knife maybe. And then our Lord will see which are His; then will be the time that grace will triumph—that those who have used the sacraments with devotion; that have been careful and penitent with their sins, that have hungered for the Bread of Life—the Lord shall stand by them and save them, as He stood by Mr. Sherwin on the rack, and Father Campion on the scaffold, and Mistress Ward and many more, of whom I have not had time to tell you. He who bids us be faithful, Himself will be faithful; and He who wore the crown of thorns will bestow upon us the crown of life."

Then they sang a hymn to our Lady:

"Hail be thou, Mary, the mother of Christ,"

and the old swaying tune rocked like a cradle, and the people looked up towards their Mother's altar as they sang—their Mother who had ruled them so sweetly and so long—and entreated her in their hearts, who stood by her Son's Cross, to stand by theirs too should God ever call them to die upon one.

The next day Mr. Brian took Anthony a long walk as soon as dinner was over, across the moors towards the north side of Skiddaw. Anthony found the old man a delightful and garrulous companion, full of tales of the countryside, historical, religious, naturalistic, and supernatural. As they stood on a little eminence and looked back to where the church-tower pricked out of the deep crack in the moors where it stood, he told him the tale of the coming of the pursuivants.

"They first troubled us in '72," he said; "they had not thought it worth while before to disturb themselves for one old man like my brother, who was like to die soon; but in April of that year they first sent up their men. But it was only a pair of pursuivants, for they knew nothing of the people; they came up, the poor men, to take my brother down to Cockermouth to answer on his religion to some bench of ministers that sat there. Well, they met him, in his cassock and square cap, coming out of the church, where he had just replaced the Most Holy Sacrament after giving communion to a dying body. 'Heh! are you the minister?' say they.

"'Heh! I am the priest, if that is what you mean,' he answers back. (He was a large man, like myself, was my brother.)

"'Well, come, old man,' say they, 'we must help you down to Cockermouth.'

"Well, a few words passed; and the end was that he called out to Tim, who lived just against the church; and told them what was forward.

"Well, the pursuivants got back to Cockermouth with their lives, but not much else; and reported to the magistrates that the wild Irish themselves were little piminy maids compared to the folk they had visited that day.

"So there was a great to-do, and a deal of talk; and in the next month they sent up thirty pikemen with an officer and a dozen pursuivants, and all to take one old priest and his brother. I had been in Kendal in April when they first came—but they put it all down to me.

"Well, we were ready for them this time; the bells had been ringing to call in the folk since six of the clock in the morning; and by dinner-time, when the soldiers were expected, there was a matter of two hundred men, I should say, some with scythes and sickles, and some with staves or shepherds' crooks; the children had been sent down sooner to stone the men all the way up the path; and by the time that they had reached the churchyard gate there was not a man of them but had a cut or a bruise upon him. Then, when they turned the corner, black with wrath, there were the lads gathered about the church-porch each with his weapon, and each white and silent, waiting for what should fall.

"Now you wonder where we were. We were in the church, my brother and I; for our people had put us there against our will, to keep us safe, they said. Eh! but I was wroth when Olroyd and the rest pushed me through the door. However, there we were, locked in; I was up in one window, and my brother was in the belfry as I thought, each trying to see what was forward. I saw the two crowds of them, silent and wrathful, with not twenty yards between them, and a few stones still sailing among the soldiers now and again; the pikes were being set in array, and our lads were opening out to let the scythes have free play, when on a sudden I heard the tinkle of a bell round the outside of the tower, and I climbed down from my place, and up again to one of the west windows; there was a fearsome hush outside now, and I could see some of the soldiers in front were uneasy; they had their eyes off the lads and round the side of the tower. And then I saw little Dickie Olroyd in his surplice ringing a bell and bearing a candle, and behind him came my brother, in a purple cope I had never set eyes on before, with his square cap and a great book, and his eyes shining out of his head, and his lips opening and mouthing out Latin; and then he stopped, laid the book reverently on a tombstone, lifted both hands, and brought them down with the fingers out, and his eyes larger than ever. I could see the soldiers were ready to break and scatter, for some were Catholics no doubt, and many more feared the priest; and then on a sudden my brother caught the candle out of Dickie's hand, blew it out with a great puff, while Dickie rattled upon the bell, and then he dashed the smoking candle among the soldiers. The soldiers broke and fled like hares, out of the churchyard, down the street and down the path to Cockermouth; the officer tried to stay them, but 'twas no use; the fear of the Church was upon them, and her Grace herself could not have prevailed with them. Well, when they let us out, the lads were all a-trembling too; for my brother's face, they said, was like the destroying angel; and I was somewhat queer myself, and I was astonished too; for he was kind-hearted, was my brother, and would not hurt a fly's body; much less damn his soul; and, after all, the poor soldiers were not to blame; and 'twas a queer cursing, I thought too, to be done like that; but maybe 'twas a new papal method. I went round to the north chapel, and there he was taking off his cope.

"'Well,' he said to me, 'how did I do it?'

"'Do it?' I said; 'do it? Why, you've damned those poor lads' souls eternally. The hand of the Lord was with you,' I said.

"'Damned them?' said he; 'nonsense! 'Twas only your old herbal that I read at them; and the cope too, 'twas inside out.'"

Then the old man told Anthony other stories of his earlier life, how he had been educated at the university and been at Court in King Henry's reign and Queen Mary's, but that he had lost heart at Elizabeth's accession, and retired to his hills, where he could serve God according to his conscience, and study God's works too, for he was a keen naturalist. He told Anthony many stories about the deer, and the herds of wild white hornless cattle that were now practically extinct on the hills, and of a curious breed of four-horned sheep, skulls of all of which species hung in his hall, and of the odd drinking-horns that Anthony had admired the day before. There was one especially that he talked much of, a buffalo horn on three silver feet fashioned like the legs of an armed man; round the centre was a filleting inscribed, "Qui pugnat contra tres perdet duos," and there was a cross patée on the horn, and two other inscriptions, "Nolite extollere cornu in altu'" and "Qui bibat me adhuc siti'." Mr. Brian told him it had been brought from Italy by his grandfather.

They put up a quantity of grouse and several hares as they walked across the moor; one of the hares, which had a curious patch of white between his ears like a little night-cap, startled Mr. Brian so much that he exclaimed aloud, crossed himself, and stood, a little pale, watching the hare's head as it bobbed and swerved among the heather.

"I like it not," he said to Anthony, who inquired what was the matter. "Satan hath appeared under some such form to many in history. Joachimus Camerarius, who wrote de natura dæmonum, tells, I think, a story of a hare followed by a fox that ran across the path of a young man who was riding on a horse, and who started in pursuit. Up and down hills and dales they went, and soon the fox was no longer there, and the hare grew larger and blacker as it went; and the young man presently saw that he was in a country that he knew not; it was all barren and desolate round him, and the sky grew dark. Then he spurred his horse more furiously, and he drew nearer and nearer to the great hare that now skipped along like a stag before him; and then, as he put out his hand to cut the hare down, the creature sprang into the air and vanished, and the horse fell dead; and the man was found in his own meadow by his friends, in a swound, with his horse dead beside him, and trampled marks round and round the field, and the pug-marks of what seemed like a great tiger beside him, where the beast had sprung into the air."

When Mr. Brian found that Anthony was interested in such stories, he told him plenty of them; especially tales that seemed to join in a strange unity of life, demons, beasts and men. It was partly, no doubt, his studies as a naturalist that led him to insist upon points that united rather than divided the orders of creation; and he told him stories first from such writers as Michael Verdunus and Petrus Burgottus, who relate among other marvels how there are ointments by the use of which shepherds have been known to change themselves into wolves and tear the sheep that they should have protected; and he quoted to him St. Augustine's own testimony, to the belief that in Italy certain women were able to change themselves into heifers through the power of witchcraft. Finally, he told him one or two tales of his own experience.

"In the year '63," he said, "before my marriage, I was living alone in the Hall; I was a young man, and did my best to fear nought but deadly sin. I was coming back late from Threlkeld, round the south of Skiddaw that you see over there; and was going with a lantern, for it would be ten o'clock at night, and the time of year was autumn. I was still a mile or two from the house, and was saying my beads as I came, for I hold that is a great protection; when I heard a strange whistling noise, with a murmur in it, high up overhead in the night. 'It is the birds going south,' I said to myself, for you know that great flocks fly by night when the cold begins to set in; but the sound grew louder and more distinct, and at last I could hear the sound as of words gabbled in a foreign tongue; and I knew they were no birds, though maybe they had wings like them. But I knew that a Christened soul in grace has nought to fear from hell; so I crossed myself and said my beads, and kept my eyes on the ground, and presently I saw my lights burning in the house, and heard the roar of the stream, and the gabbling above me ceased, as the sound of the running water began. But that night I awoke again and again; and the night seemed hot and close each time, as if a storm was near, but there was no thunder. Each time I heard the roar of the stream below the house, and no more. At last, towards the morning, I set my window wide that looks towards the stream, and leaned out; and there beneath me, crowded against the wall of the house, as I could see in the growing light, was a great flock of sheep, with all their heads together towards the house, as close as a score of dogs could pack them, and they were all still as death, and their backs were dripping wet; for they had come down the hills and swum the stream, in order to be near a Christened man and away from what was abroad that night.

"My shepherds told me the same that day, that everywhere the sheep had come down to the houses, as if terrified near to death; and at Keswick, whither I went the next market-day, they told me the same tale, and that two men had each found a sheep that could not travel; one had a broken leg, and the other had been cast; but neither had another mark or wound or any disease upon him, but that both were lying dead upon Skiddaw; and the look in the dead eyes, they said, was fit to make a man forget his manhood."

Anthony found the old man the most interesting companion possible, and he persuaded him to accompany him on several of the expeditions that he had to make to the hamlets and outlying cottages round, in his spiritual ministrations; and both he and Isabel were sincerely sorry when two Sundays had passed away, and they had to begin to move south again in their journeyings.

And so the autumn passed and winter began, and Anthony was slowly moving down again, supplying the place of priests who had fallen sick or had died, visiting many almost inaccessible hamlets, and everywhere encouraging the waverers and seeking the wanderers, and rejoicing over the courageous, and bringing opportunities of grace to many who longed for them. He met many other well-known priests from time to time, and took counsel with them, but did not have time to become very intimate with any of them, so great were the demands upon his services. In this manner he met John Colleton, the canonist, who had returned from his banishment in '87, but found him a little dull and melancholy, though his devotion was beyond praise. He met, too, the Jesuit Fathers Edward Oldcorne and Richard Holtby, the former of whom had lately come from Hindlip.

He spent Christmas near Cartmel-in-Furness, and after the new year had opened, crossed the Ken once more near Beetham, and began to return slowly down the coast. Everywhere he was deeply touched by the devotion of the people, who, in spite of long months without a priest, had yet clung to the observance of their religion so far as was possible, and now welcomed him like an angel of God; and he had the great happiness too of reconciling some who, yielding to loneliness and pressure, had conformed to the Establishment. In these latter cases he was almost startled by the depth of Catholic convictions that had survived.

"I never believed it, father," said a young squire to him, near Garstang. "I knew that it was but a human invention, and not the Gospel that my fathers held, and that Christ our Saviour brought on earth; but I lost heart, for that no priest came near us, and I had not had the sacraments for nearly two years; and I thought that it were better to have some religion than none at all, so at last I went to church. But there is no need to talk to me, father, now I have made my confession, for I know with my whole soul that the Catholic Religion is the true one—and I have known it all the while, and I thank God and His Blessed Mother, and you, father, too, for helping me to say so again, and to come back to grace."

At last, at the beginning of March, Anthony and Isabel found themselves back again at Speke Hall, warmly welcomed by Mr. Norreys.

"You have done a good work for the Church, Mr. Capell," said his host, "and God will reward you and thank you for it Himself, for we cannot."

"And I thank God," said Anthony, "for the encouragement to faith that the sight of the faithful North has given to me; and pray Him that I may carry something of her spirit back with me to the south."

There were letters waiting for him at Speke Hall, one from Mr. Buxton, urging them to come back, at least for the present, to Stanfield Place, so soon as the winter work in the north was over; and another from the Rector of the College at Douai to the same effect. There was also one more, written from a little parish in Kent, from a Catholic lady who was altogether a stranger to him, but who plainly knew all about him, entreating him to call at her house when he was in the south again; her husband, she said, had met him once at Stanfield and had been strongly attracted by him to the Catholic Church, and she believed that if Anthony would but pay them a visit her husband's conversion would be brought about. Anthony could not remember the man's name, but Isabel thought that she did remember some such person at a small private conference that Anthony had given in Mr. Buxton's house, for the benefit of Catholics and those who were being drawn towards the Religion.

The lady, too, gave him instructions as to how he should come from London to her house, recommending him to cross the Thames at a certain spot that she described near Greenhithe, and to come on southwards along a route that she marked for him, to the parish of Stanstead, where she lived. This, then, was soon arranged, and after letters had been sent off announcing Anthony's movements, he left Speke Hall with Isabel, about a fortnight later.

Chapter Eight - In Stanstead Woods

On the first day of June, Anthony and Isabel, with their three armed servants and the French maid behind them, were riding down through Thurrock to the north bank of the Thames opposite Greenhithe. As they went Anthony pulled out and studied the letter and the little map that Mrs. Kirke had sent to guide them.

"On the right-hand side," she wrote, "when you come to the ferry, stands a little inn, the 'Sloop,' among trees, with a yard behind it. Mr. Bender, the host, is one of us; and he will get your horses on board, and do all things to forward you without attracting attention. Give him some sign that he may know you for a Catholic, and when you are alone with him tell him where you are bound."

There were one or two houses standing near the bank, as they rode down the lane that led to the river, but they had little difficulty in identifying the "Sloop," and presently they rode into the yard, and, leaving their horses with the servants, stepped round into the little smoky front room of the inn.

A man, dressed somewhat like a sailor, was sitting behind a table, who looked up with a dull kind of expectancy and whom Anthony took as the host; and, in order to identify him and show who he himself was, he took up a little cake of bread that was lying on a platter on the table, and broke it as if he would eat. This was one of Father Persons' devices, and was used among Catholics to signify their religion when they were with strangers, since it was an action that could rouse no suspicion among others. The man looked in an unintelligent way at Anthony, who turned away and rapped upon the door, and as a large heavily-built man came out, broke it again, and put a piece into his mouth. The man lifted his eyebrows slightly, and just smiled, and Anthony knew he had found his friend.

"Come this way, sir," he said, "and your good lady, too."

They followed him into the inner room of the house, a kind of little kitchen, with a fire burning and a pot over it, and one or two barrels of drink against the wall. A woman was stirring the pot, for it was near dinner-time, and turned round as the strangers came in. It was plainly an inn that was of the poorest kind, and that was used almost entirely by watermen or by travellers who were on their way to cross the ferry.

"The less said the better," said the man, when he had shut the door. "How can I serve you, sir?"

"We wish to take our horses and ourselves across to Greenhithe," said Anthony, "and Mrs. Kirke, to whom we are going, bade us make ourselves known to you."

The man nodded and smiled.

"Yes, sir, that can be managed directly. The ferry is at the other bank now, sir; and I will call it across. Shall we say in half an hour, sir; and, meanwhile, will you and your lady take something?"

Anthony accepted gladly, as the time was getting on, and ordered dinner for the servants too, in the outer room. As the landlord was going to the door, he stopped him.

"Who is that man in the other room?" he asked.

The landlord gave a glance at the door, and came back towards Anthony.

"To tell the truth, sir, I do not know. He is a sailor by appearance, and he knows the talk; but none of the watermen know him; and he seems to do nothing. However, sir, there's no harm in him that I can see."

Anthony told him that he had broken the bread before him, thinking he was the landlord. The real landlord smiled broadly.

"Thank God, I am somewhat more of a man than that," for the sailor was lean and sun-dried. Then once more Mr. Bender went to the door to call the servants in.

"Why, the man's gone," he said, and disappeared. Then they heard his voice again. "But he's left his groat behind him for his drink, so all's well"; and presently his voice was heard singing as he got the table ready for the servants.

In a little more than half an hour the party and the horses were safely on the broad bargelike ferry, and Mr. Bender was bowing on the bank and wishing them a prosperous journey, as they began to move out on to the wide river to-wards the chalk cliffs and red roofs of Greenhithe that nestled among the mass of trees on the opposite bank. In less than ten minutes they were at the pier, and after a little struggle to get the horses to land, they were mounted and riding up the straight little street that led up to the higher ground. Just before they turned the corner they heard far away across the river the horn blown to summon the ferry-boat once more.

There were two routes from Greenhithe to Stanstead, the one to the right through Longfield and Ash, the other to the left through Southfleet and Nursted. There was very little to choose between them as regards distance, and Mrs. Kirke had drawn a careful sketch-map with a few notes as to the characteristics of each route. There were besides, particularly through the thick woods about Stanstead itself, innumerable cross-paths intersecting one another in all directions. The travellers had decided at the inn to take the road through Longfield; since, in spite of other disad-vantages, it was the less frequented of the two, and they were anxious above all things to avoid attention. Their horses were tired; and as they had plenty of time before them they proposed to go at a foot's-pace all the way, and to take between two and three hours to cover the nine or ten miles between Greenhithe and Stanstead.

It was a hot afternoon as they passed through Fawkham, and it was delightful to pass from the white road in under the thick arching trees just beyond the village. There everything was cool shadow, the insects sang in the air about them, an early rabbit or two cantered across the road and disappeared into the thick undergrowth; once the song of the birds about them suddenly ceased, and through an opening in the green rustling vault overhead they saw a cruel shape with motionless wings glide steadily across.

They did not talk much, but let the reins lie loose; and enjoyed the cool shadow and the green lights and the fragrant mellow scents of the woods about them; while their horses slouched along on the turf, switching their tails and even stopping sometimes for a second in a kind of desperate greediness to snatch a green juicy mouthful at the side.

Isabel was thinking of Stanfield, and wondering how the situation would adjust itself; Mary Corbet would be there, she knew, to meet them; and it was a comfort to think she could consult her; but what, she asked herself, would be her relations with the master of the house?

Suddenly Anthony's horse stepped off the turf on the opposite side of the road and began to come towards her, and she moved her beast a little to let him come on the turf beside her.

"Isabel," said Anthony, "tell me if you hear anything."

She looked at him, suddenly startled.

"No, no," he said, "there is nothing to fear; it is probably my fancy; but listen and tell me."

She listened intently. There was the creaking of her own saddle, the soft footfalls of the horses, the hum of the sum-mer woods, and the sound of the servants' horses behind.

"No," she said, "there is nothing beyond—"

"There!" he said suddenly; "now do you hear it?"

Then she heard plainly the sound either of a man running, or of a horse walking, somewhere behind them.

"Yes," she said, "I hear something; but what of it?"

"It is the third time I have heard it," he said: "once in the woods behind Longfield, and once just before the little vil-lage with the steepled church."

The sound had ceased again.

"It is some one who has come nearly all the way from Greenhithe behind us. Perhaps they are not following—but again—"

"They?" she said; "there is only one."

"There are three," he answered; "at least; the other two are on the turf at the side—but just before the village I heard all three of them—or rather certainly more than two—when they were between those two walls where there was no turf."

Isabel was staring at him with great frightened eyes. He smiled back at her tranquilly.

"Ah, Isabel!" he said, "there is nothing really to fear, in any case."

"What shall you do?" she asked, making a great effort to control herself.

"I think we must find out first of all whether they are after us. We must certainly not ride straight to the Manor Lodge if it is so."

Then he explained his plan.

"See here," he said, holding the map before her as he rode, "we shall come to Fawkham Green in five minutes. Then our proper road leads straight on to Ash, but we will take the right instead, towards Eynsford. Meanwhile, I will leave Robert here, hidden by the side of the road, to see who these men are, and what they look like; and we will ride on slowly. When they have passed, he will come out and take the road we should have taken, and he then will turn off to the right too before he reaches Ash; and by trotting he will easily come up with us at this corner," and he pointed to it on the map—"and so he will tell us what kind of men they are; and they will never know that they have been spied upon; for, by this plan, he will not have to pass them. Is that a good plot?" and he smiled at her.

Isabel assented, feeling dazed and overwhelmed. She could hardly bring her thoughts to a focus, for the fears that had hovered about her ever since they had left Lancashire and come down to the treacherous south, had now darted upon her, tearing her heart with terror and blinding her eyes, and bewildering her with the beating of their wings. Anthony quietly called up Robert, and explained the plan. He was a lad of a Catholic family at Great Keynes, perfectly fearless and perfectly devoted to the Church and to the priest he served. He nodded his head briskly with approval as the plan was explained.

"Of course it may all be nothing," ended Anthony, "and then you will think me a poor fool?"

The lad grinned cheerfully.

"No, sir," he said.

All this while they had been riding slowly on together, and now the wood showed signs of coming to an end; so Anthony told the groom to ride fifty yards into the undergrowth at once, to bandage his horse's eyes, and to tie him to a tree; and then to creep back himself near the road, so as to see without being seen. The men who seemed to be following were at least half a mile behind, so he would have plenty of time.

Then they all rode on together again, leaving Robert to find his way into the wood. As they went, Isabel began to question her brother, and Anthony gave her his views.

"They have not come up with us, because they know we are four men to three—if, as I think, they are not more than three—that is one reason; and another is that they love to track us home before they take us; and thus take our hosts too as priests' harbourers. Now plainly these men do not know where we are bound, or they would not follow us so closely. Best of all, too, they love to catch us at mass for then they have no trouble in proving their case. I think then that they will not try to take us till we reach the Manor Lodge; and we must do our best to shake them off before that. Now the plot I have thought of is this, that—should it prove as I think it will—we should ride slower than ever, as if our horses were weary, down the road along which Robert will have come after he has joined us, and turn down as if to go to Kingsdown, and when we have gone half a mile, and are well round that sharp corner, double back to it, and hide all in the wood at the side. They will follow our tracks, and there are no houses at which they can ask, and there seem no travellers either on these by-roads, and when they have passed us we double back at the gallop, and down the next turning, which will bring us in a couple of miles to Stanstead. There is a maze of roads thereabouts, and it will be hard if we do not shake them off; for there is not a house, marked upon the map, at which they can ask after us."

Isabel did her utmost to understand, but the horror of the pursuit had overwhelmed her. The quiet woods into which they had passed again after leaving Fawkham Green now seemed full of menace; the rough road, with the deep powdery ruts and the grass and fir-needles at the side, no longer seemed a pleasant path leading home, but a treacherous device to lead them deeper into danger. The creatures round them, the rabbits, the pigeons that flapped suddenly out of all the tall trees, the tits that fluttered on and chirped and fluttered again, all seemed united against Anthony in some dreadful league. Anthony himself felt all his powers of observation and device quickened and established. He had lived so long in the expectation of a time like this, and had rehearsed and mastered the emotions of terror and suspense so often, that he was ready to meet them; and gradually his entire self-control and the unmoved tones of his voice and his serene alert face prevailed upon Isabel; and by the time that they slowly turned the last curve and saw Robert on his black horse waiting for them at the corner, her sense of terror and bewilderment had passed, her heart had ceased that sick thumping, and she, too, was tranquil and capable.

Robert wheeled his horse and rode beside Anthony round the sharp corner to the left up the road along which he had trotted just now.

"There are three of them, sir," he said in an even, businesslike voice; "one of them, sir, on a brown mare, but I couldn't see aught of him, sir; he was on the far side of the track; the second is like a groom on a grey horse, and the third is dressed like a sailor, sir, on a brown horse."

"A sailor?" said Anthony; "a lean man, and sunburnt, with a whistle?"

"I did not see the whistle, sir; but he is as you say."

This made it certain that it was the man they had seen in the inn opposite Greenhithe; and also practically certain that he was a spy; for nothing that Anthony had done could have roused his suspicions except the breaking of the bread; and that would only be known to one who was deep in the counsels of the Catholics. All this made the pursuit the more formidable.

So Anthony meditated; and presently, calling up the servants behind, explained the situation and his plan. The French maid showed signs of hysteria and Isabel had to take her aside and quiet her, while the men consulted. Then it was arranged, and the servants presently dropped behind again a few yards, though the maid still rode with Isabel. Then they came to the road on the right that would have led them to Kingsdown, and down this they turned. As they went, Anthony kept a good look-out for a place to turn aside; and a hundred yards from the turning saw what he wanted. On the left-hand side a little path led into the wood; it was overgrown with brambles, and looked as if it were now disused. Anthony gave the word and turned his horse down the entrance, and was followed in single file by the others. There were thick trees about them on every side, and, what was far more important, the road they had left at this point ran higher than usual, and was hard and dry; so the horses' hoofs as they turned off left no mark that would be noticed.

After riding thirty or forty yards, Anthony stopped, turned his horse again, and forced him through the hazels with some difficulty, and the others again followed in silence through the passage he had made. Presently Anthony stopped; the branches that had swished their faces as they rode through now seemed a little higher; and it was possible to sit here on horseback without any great discomfort.

"I must see them myself," he whispered to Isabel; and slipped off his horse, giving the bridle to Robert.

"Oh! mon Dieu!" moaned the maid; "mon Dieu! Ne partez pas!"

Anthony looked at her severely.

"You must be quiet and brave," he said sternly. "You are a Catholic too; pray, instead of crying."

Then Isabel saw him slip noiselessly towards the road, which was some fifty yards away, through the thick growth. It was now a breathless afternoon. High overhead the sun blazed in a cloudless sky, but down here all was cool, green shadow. There was not a sound to be heard from the woods, beyond the mellow hum of the flies; Anthony's faint rustlings had ceased; now and then a saddle creaked, or a horse blew out his nostrils or tossed his head. One of the men wound his handkerchief silently round a piece of his horse's head-harness that jingled a little. The maid drew a soft sobbing breath now and then, but she dared not speak after the priest's rebuke.

Then suddenly there came another sound to Isabel's ears; she could not distinguish at first what it was, but it grew nearer, and presently resolved itself into the fumbling noise of several horses' feet walking together, twice or three times a stirrup chinked, once she heard a muffled cough; but no word was spoken. Nearer and nearer it came, until she could not believe that it was not within five yards of her. Her heart began again that sick thumping; a fly that she had brushed away again and again now crawled unheeded over her face, and even on her white parted lips; but a sob of fear from the maid recalled her, and she turned a sharp look of warning on her. Then the fumbling noise began to die away: the men were passing. There was something in their silence that was more terrible than all else; it reminded her of hounds running on a hot scent.

Then at last there was silence; then gentle rustlings again over last year's leaves; and Anthony came back through the hazels. He nodded at her sharply.

"Now, quickly," he said, and took his horse by the bridle and began to lead him out again the way they had come. At the entrance he looked out first; the road was empty and silent. Then he led his horse clear, and mounted as the others came out one by one in single file.

"Now follow close; and watch my hand," he said; and he put his horse to a quick walk on the soft wayside turf. As the distance widened between them and the men who were now riding away from them, the walk became a trot, and then quickly a canter, as the danger of the sound being carried to their pursuers decreased.

It seemed to Isabel like some breathless dream as she followed Anthony's back, watching the motions of his hand as he signed in which direction he was going to turn next. What was happening, she half wondered to herself, that she should be riding like this on a spent horse, as if in some dreadful game, turning abruptly down lanes and rides, out across the high road, and down again another turn, with the breathing and creaking and jingling of others behind her? Years ago the two had played Follow-my-leader on horseback in the woods above Great Keynes. She remembered this now; and a flood of memories poured across her mind and diluted the bitterness of this shocking reality. Dear God, what a game!

Anthony steered with skill and decision. He had been studying the map with great attention, and even now carried it loose in his hand and glanced at it from time to time. Above all else he wished to avoid passing a house, for fear that the searchers might afterwards inquire at it; and he succeeded perfectly in this, though once or twice he was obliged to retrace his steps. There was little danger, he knew now, of the noise of the horses' feet being any guide to those who were searching, for the high table-land on which they rode was a labyrinth of lanes and rides, and the trees too served to echo and confuse the noise they could not altogether avoid making. Twice they passed travellers, one a farmer on an old grey horse, who stared at this strange hurrying party; and once a pedlar, laden with his pack, who trudged past, head down.

Isabel's horse was beginning to strain and pant, and she herself to grow giddy with heat and weariness, when she saw through the trees an old farmhouse with latticed windows and a great external chimney, standing in a square of cultivated ground; and in a moment more the path they were following turned a corner, and the party drew up at the back of the house.

At the noise of the horses' footsteps a door at the back had opened, and a woman's face looked out and drew back again; and presently from the front Mrs. Kirke came quickly round. She was tall and slender and middle-aged, with a somewhat anxious face; but a look of great relief came over it as she saw Anthony.

"Thank God you are come," she said; "I feared something had happened."

Anthony explained the circumstances in a few words.

"I will ride on gladly, madam, if you think right; but I will ask you in any case to take my sister in."

"Why, how can you say that?" she said; "I am a Catholic. Come in, father. But I fear there is but poor accommodation for the servants."

"And the horses?" asked Anthony.

"The barn at the back is got ready for them," she said; "perhaps it would be well to take them there at once." She called a woman, and sent her to show the men where to stable the horses, while Anthony and Isabel and the maid dismounted and came in with her to the house.

There, they talked over the situation and what was best to be done. Her husband had ridden over to Wrotham, and she expected him back for supper; nothing then could be finally settled till he came. In the meantime the Manor Lodge was probably the safest place in all the woods, Mrs. Kirke declared; the nearest house was half a mile away, and that was the Rectory; and the Rector himself was a personal friend and favourable to Catholics. The Manor Lodge, too, stood well off the road to Wrotham, and not five strangers appeared there in the year. Fifty men might hunt the woods for a month and not find it; in fact, Mr. Kirke had taken the house on account of its privacy, for he was weary, his wife said, of paying her fines for recusancy; and still more unwilling to pay his own, when that happy necessity should arrive; for he had now practically made up his mind to be a Catholic, and only needed a little instruction before being received.

"He is a good man, father," she said to Anthony, "and will make a good Catholic."

Then she explained about the accommodation. Isabel and the maid would have to sleep together in the spare room, and Anthony would have the little dressing-room opening out of it; and the men, she feared, would have to shake down as well as they could in the loft over the stable in the barn.

At seven o'clock Mr. Kirke arrived; and when the situation had been explained to him, he acquiesced in the plan. He seemed confident that there was but little danger; and he and Anthony were soon deep in theological talk.

Anthony found him excellently instructed already; he had, in fact, even prepared for his confession; his wife had taught him well; and it was the prospect of this one good opportunity of being reconciled to the Church that had precipitated matters and decided him to take the step. He was a delightful companion, too, intelligent, courageous, humorous and modest, and Anthony thought his own labour and danger well repaid when, a little after midnight, he heard his confession and received him into the Church. It was impossible for Mr. Kirke to receive communion, as he had wished, for there were wanting some of the necessaries for saying mass; so he promised to ride across to Stanfield in a week or so, stay the night and communicate in the morning.

Then early the next morning a council was held as to the best way for the party to leave for Stanfield. The men were called up, and their opinions asked; and gradually step by step a plan was evolved.

The first requirement was that, if possible, the party should not be recognisable; the second that they should keep together for mutual protection; for to separate would very possibly mean the apprehension of some one of them; the third was that they should avoid so far as was possible villages and houses and frequented roads.

Then the first practical suggestion was made by Isabel that the maid should be left behind, and that Mr. Kirke should bring her on with him to Stanfield when he came a week later. This he eagerly accepted, and further offered to keep all the luggage they could spare, take charge of the men's liveries, and lend them old garments and hats of his own—to one a cloak, and to another a doublet. In this way, he said, it would appear to be a pleasure party rather than one of travellers, and, should they be followed, this would serve to cover their traces. The travelling by unfrequented roads was more difficult; for that in itself might attract attention should they actually meet any one.

Anthony, who had been thinking in silence a moment or two, now broke in.

"Have you any hawks, Mr. Kirke?" he asked.

"Only one old peregrine," he said, "past sport."

"She will do," said Anthony; "and can you borrow another?"

"There is a merlin at the Rectory," said Mr. Kirke.

Then Anthony explained his plan, that they should pose as a hawking-party. Isabel and Robert should each carry a hawk, while he himself would carry on his wrist an empty leash and hood as if a hawk had escaped; that they should then all ride together over the open country, avoiding every road, and that, if they should see any one on the way, they should inquire whether he had seen an escaped falcon or heard the tinkle of the bells; and this would enable them to ask the way, should it be necessary, without arousing suspicion.

This plan was accepted, and the maid was informed to her great relief that she might remain behind for a week or so, and then return with Mr. Kirke after the searchers had left the woods.

It was a twenty-mile ride to Stanfield; and it was thought safer on the whole not to remain any longer where they were, as it was impossible to know whether a shrewd man might not, with the help of a little luck, stumble upon the house; so, when dinner was over, and the servants had changed into Mr. Kirke's old suits, and the merlin had been borrowed from the Rectory for a week's hawking, the horses were brought round and the party mounted.

Mr. Kirke and Anthony had spent a long morning together discussing the route, and it had been decided that it would be best to keep along the high ridge due west until they were a little beyond Kemsing, which they would be able to see below them in the valley; and then to strike across between that village and Otford, and keeping almost due south ride up through Knole Park; then straight down on the other side into the Weald, and so past Tonbridge home. Mr. Kirke himself insisted on accompanying them on his cob until he had seen them clear of the woods on the high ground. Both he and his wife were full of gratitude to Anthony for the risk and trouble he had undergone, and did their utmost to provide them with all that was necessary for their disguise. At last, about two o'clock, the five men and Isabel rode out of the little yard at the back of the Manor Lodge and plunged into the woods again.

The afternoon hush rested on the country as they followed Mr. Kirke along a narrow seldom-used path that led almost straight to the point where it was decided that they should strike south. In half a dozen places it cut across lanes, and once across the great high road from Farningham to Wrotham. As they drew near this, Mr. Kirke, who was riding in front, checked them.

"I will go first," he said, "and see if there is danger."

In a minute he returned.

"There is a man about a hundred yards up the road asleep on a bank; and there is a cart coming up from Wrotham: that is all I can see. Perhaps we had better wait till the cart is gone."

"And what is the man like?" asked Anthony.

"He is a beggar, I should say; but has his hat over his eyes."

They waited till the cart had passed. Anthony dismounted and went to the entrance of the path and peered out at the man; he was lying, as Mr. Kirke had said, with his hat over his eyes, perfectly still. Anthony examined him a minute or two; he was in tattered clothes, and a great stick and a bundle lay beside him.

"It is a vagabond," he said, "we can go on."

The whole party crossed the road, pushing on towards the edge of the high downs over Kemsing; and presently came to the Ightam road where it began to run steeply down hill; here, too, Mr. Kirke looked this way and that, but no one was in sight, and then the whole party crossed; they kept inside the edge of the wood all the way along the downs for another mile or so, with the rich sunlit valley seen in glimpses through the trees here and there, and the Pilgrim's Way lying like a white ribbon a couple of hundred feet below them, until at last Kemsing Church, with St. Edith's Chantry at the side, lay below and behind them, and they came out on to the edge of a great scoop in the hill, like a theatre, and the blue woods and hills of Surrey showed opposite beyond Otford and Brasted.

Here they stopped, a little back from the edge, and Mr. Kirke gave them their last instructions, pointing out Seal across the valley, which they must leave on their left, skirting the meadows to the west of the church, and passing up towards Knole beyond.

"Let the sun be a little on your right," he said, "all the way; and you will strike the country above Tonbridge."

Then they said good-bye to one another; Mr. Kirke kissed the priest's hand in gratitude for what he had done for him, and then turned back along the edge of the downs, riding this time outside the woods, while the party led their horses carefully down the steep slope, across the Pilgrim's Way, and then struck straight out over the meadows to Seal.

Their plan seemed supremely successful; they met a few countrymen and lads at their work, who looked a little astonished at first at this great party riding across country, but more satisfied when Anthony had inquired of them whether they had seen a falcon or heard his bells. No, they had not, they said; and went on with their curiosity satisfied. Once, as they were passing down through a wood on to the Weald, Isabel, who had turned in her saddle, and was looking back, gave a low cry of alarm.

"Ah! the man, the man!" she said.

The others turned quickly, but there was nothing to be seen but the long straight ride stretching up to against the sky-line three or four hundred yards behind them. Isabel said she thought she saw a rider pass across this little opening at the end, framed in leaves; but there were stags everywhere in the woods here, and it would have been easy to mistake one for the other at that distance, and with such a momentary glance.

Once again, nearer Tonbridge, they had a fright. They had followed up a grass ride into a copse, thinking it would bring them out somewhere, but it led only to the brink of a deep little stream, where the plank bridge had been re-moved, so they were obliged to retrace their steps. As they re-emerged into the field from the copse, a large heavily-built man on a brown mare almost rode into them. He was out of breath, and his horse seemed distressed. Anthony, as usual, immediately asked if he had seen or heard anything of a falcon.

"No, indeed, gentlemen," he said, "and have you seen aught of a bitch who bolted after a hare some half mile back. A greyhound I should be loath to lose."

They had not, and said so; and the man, still panting and mopping his head, thanked them, and asked whether he could be of any service in directing them, if they were strange to the country; but they thought it better not to give him any hint of where they were going, so he rode off presently up the slope across their route and disappeared, whistling for his dog.

And so at last, about four o'clock in the afternoon, they saw the church spire of Stanfield above them on the hill, and knew that they were near the end of their troubles. Another hundred yards, and there were the roofs of the old house, and the great iron gates, and the vanes of the garden-house seen over the clipped limes; and then Mary Cor-bet and Mr. Buxton hurrying in from the garden, as they came through the low oak door, into the dear tapestried hall.

Chapter Nine - The Alarm

A very happy party sat down to supper that evening in Stanfield Place.

Anthony had taken Mr. Buxton aside privately when the first greetings were over, and told him all that happened: the alarm at Stanstead; his device, and the entire peace they had enjoyed ever since.

"Isabel," he ended, "certainly thought she saw a man behind us once; but we were among the deer, and it was dusky in the woods; and, for myself, I think it was but a stag. But, if you think there is danger anywhere, I will gladly ride on."

Mr. Buxton clapped him on the shoulder.

"My dear friend," he said, "take care you do not offend me. I am a slow fellow, as you know; but even my coarse hide is pricked sometimes. Do not suggest again that I could permit any priest—and much less my own dear friend—to leave me when there was danger. But there is none in this case—you have shaken the rogues off, I make no doubt; and you will just stay here for the rest of the summer at the very least."

Anthony said that he agreed with him as to the complete baffling of the pursuers, but added that Isabel was still a little shaken, and would Mr. Buxton say a word to her.

"Why, I will take her round the hiding-holes myself after supper, and show her how strong and safe we are. We will all go round."

In the withdrawing-room he said a word or two of reassurance to her before the others were down.

"Anthony has told me everything, Mistress Isabel; and I warrant that the knaves are cursing their stars still on Stan-stead hills, twenty miles from here. You are as safe here as in Greenwich palace. But after supper, to satisfy you, we will look to our defences. But, believe me, there is nothing to fear."

He spoke with such confidence and cheerfulness that Isabel felt her fears melting, and before supper was over she was ashamed of them, and said so.

"Nay, nay," said Mr. Buxton, "you shall not escape. You shall see every one of them for yourself. Mistress Corbet, do you not think that just?"

"You need a little more honest worldliness, Isabel," said Mary. "I do not hesitate to say that I believe God saves the priests that have the best hiding-holes. Now that is not profane, so do not look at me like that."

"It is the plainest sense," said Anthony, smiling at them both.

They went the round of them all with candles, and Anthony refreshed his memory; they visited the little one in the chapel first, then the cupboard and portrait-door at the top of the corridor, the chamber over the fireplace in the hall, and lastly, in the wooden cellar-steps they lifted the edge of the fifth stair from the bottom, so that its front and the top of the stair below it turned on a hinge and dropped open, leaving a black space behind: this was the entrance to the passage that led beneath the garden to the garden-house on the far side of the avenue.

Mistress Corbet wrinkled her nose at the damp earthy smell that breathed out of the dark.

"I am glad I am not a priest," she said. "And I would sooner be buried dead than alive. And there is a rat there that sorely needs burying."

"My dear lady!" cried the contriver of the passage indignantly, "her Grace might sleep there herself and take no harm. There is not even the whisker of a rat."

"It is not the whisker that I mind," said Mary, "it is the rest of him."

Mr. Buxton immediately set his taper down and climbed in.

"You shall see," he said, "and I in my best satin too!"

He was inside the stairs now and lying on his back on the smooth board that backed them. He sidled himself slowly along towards the wall.

"Press the fourth brick of the fourth row," he said.

"You remember, Father Anthony?"

He had reached now what seemed to be the brick wall against which the ends of the stairs rested; and that closed that end of the cellars altogether. Anthony leaned in with a candle, and saw how that part of the wall against his friend's right side slowly turned into the dark as the fourth brick was pressed, and a little brick-lined passage appeared beyond. Mr. Buxton edged himself sideways into the passage, and then stood nearly upright. It was an excellent contrivance. Even if the searchers should find the chamber beneath the stairs, which was unlikely, they would never suspect that it was only a blind to a passage beyond. The door into the passage consisted of a strong oaken door disguised on the outside by a facing of brick-slabs; all the hinges were within.

"As sweet as a flower," said the architect, looking about him. His voice rang muffled and hollow.

"Then the friends have removed the corpse," said Mary, putting her head in, "while you were opening the door. There! come out; you will take cold. I believe you."

"Are you satisfied?" said Mr. Buxton to Isabel, as they went upstairs again.

"What are your outer defences?" asked Mary, before Isabel could answer.

"You shall see the plan in the hall," said Mr. Buxton.

He took down the frame that held the plan of the house, and showed them the outer doors. There was first the low oak front door on the north, opening on to the little court; this was immensely strong and would stand battering. Then on the same side farther east, within the stable-court, there was the servants' door, protected by chains, and an oak bolt that ran across. On the extreme east end of the house there was a door opening into the garden from the withdrawing-room, the least strong of all; there was another on the south side, opposite the front door—that gave on to the garden; and lastly there was an entrance into the priests' end of the house, at the extreme west, from the little walled garden where Anthony had meditated years ago. This walled garden had a very strong door of its own opening on to the lane between the church and the house.

"But there are only three ways out, really," said Mr. Buxton, "for the garden walls are high and strong. There is the way of the walled garden; the iron-gates across the drive; and through the stable-yard on to the field-path to East Maskells. All the other gates are kept barred; and indeed I scarcely know where the keys are."

"I am bewildered," said Mary.

"Shall we go round?" he asked.

"To-morrow," said Mary; "I am tired to-night, and so is this poor child. Come, we will go to bed."

Anthony soon went too. Both he and Isabel were tired with the journey and the strain of anxiety, and it was a keen joy to him to be back again in his own dear room, with the tapestry of St. Thomas of Aquin and St. Clare opposite the bed, and the wide curtained bow-window which looked out on the little walled garden.

Mr. Buxton was left alone in the great hall below with the two tapers burning, and the starlight with all the suffused glow of a summer night making the arms glimmer in the tall windows that looked south. Lower, the windows were open, and the mellow scents of the June roses, and of the sweet-satyrian and lavender poured in; the night was very still, but the faintest breath came from time to time across the meadows and rustled in the stiff leaves with the noise of a stealthy movement.

"I will look round," said Mr. Buxton to himself.

He stepped out immediately into the garden by the hall door, and turned to the east, passing along the lighted windows. His step sounded on the tiles, and a face looked out swiftly from Isabel's room overhead; but his figure was plain in the light from the windows as he came out round the corner; and the face drew back. He crossed the east end of the house, and went through a little door into the stable-yard, locking it after him. In the kennels in the corner came a movement, and a Danish hound came out silently into the cage before her house, and stood up, like a slender grey ghost, paws high up in the bars, and whimpered softly to her lord. He quieted her, and went to the door in the yard that opened on to the field-path to East Maskells, unbarred it and stepped through. There was a dry ditch on his left, where nettles quivered in the stirring air; and a heavy clump of bushes rose beyond, dark and impenetrable. Mr.

Buxton stared straight at these a moment or two, and then out towards East Maskells. There lay his own meadows, and the cattle and horses secure and sleeping. Then he stepped back again; barred the door and walked up through the stable-yard into the front court. There the great iron gates rose before him, diaphanous-looking and flimsy in the starlight. He went up to them and shook them; and a loose shield jangled fiercely overhead. Then he peered through, holding the bars, and saw the familiar patch of grass beyond the gravel sweep, and the dark cottages over the way. Then he made his way back to the front door, unlocked it with his private key, passed through the hall, through a parlour or two into the lower floor of the priests' quarters; unlocked softly the little door into the walled garden, and went out on tip-toe once more. Even as he went, Anthony's light overhead went out. Mr. Buxton went to the garden door, unfastened it, and stepped out into the road. Above him on his left rose up the chancel of the parish church, the roofs crowded behind; and immediately in front was the high-raised churchyard, with the tall irregular wall and the trees above all, blotting out the stars.

Then he came back the same way, fastening the doors as he passed, and reached the hall, where the tapers still burned. He blew out one and took the other.

"I suppose I am a fool," he said; "the lad is as safe as in his mother's arms." And he went upstairs to bed.

Mary Corbet rose late next morning, and when she came down at last found the others in the garden. She joined them as they walked in the little avenue.

"Have not the priest-hunters arrived?" she asked. "What are they about? And you, dear Isabel, how did you sleep?"

Isabel looked a little heavy-eyed. "I did not sleep well," she said.

"I fear I disturbed her," said Mr. Buxton. "She heard me as I went round the house."

"Why did you go round the house?" asked Anthony.

"I often do," he said shortly.

"And there was no one?" asked Mary.

"There was no one."

"And what would you have done if there had been?"

"Yes," said Anthony, "what would you have done to warn us all?"

Mr. Buxton considered.

"I should have rung the alarm, I think," he said.

"But I did not know you had one," said Mary.

Mr. Buxton pointed to a turret peeping between two high gables, above his own room.

"And what does it sound like?"

"It is deep, and has a dash of sourness or shrillness in it. I cannot describe it. Above all, it is marvellous loud."

"Then, if we hear it, we shall know the priest-hunters are on us?" asked Mary. Mr. Buxton bowed.

"Or that the house is afire," he said, "or that the French or Spanish are landed."

To tell the truth, he was just slightly uneasy. Isabel had been far more silent than he had ever known her, and her nerves were plainly at an acute tension; she started violently even now, when a servant came out between two yew-hedges to call Mr. Buxton in. Her alarm had affected him, and besides, he knew something of the extraordinary skill and patience of Walsingham's agents, and even the story of the ferry had startled him. Could it really be, he had wondered as he tossed to and fro in the hot night, that this innocent priest had thrown off his pursuers so complete-ly as had appeared? In the morning he had sent down a servant to the inn to inquire whether anything had been seen or heard of a disquieting nature; now the servant had come to tell him, as he had ordered, privately. He went with the man in through the hall-door, leaving the others to walk in the avenue, and then faced him.

"Well?" he said sharply.

"No, sir, there is nothing. There is a party there travelling on to Brighthelmstone this afternoon, and four drovers who came in last night, sir; and two gentlemen travelling across country; but they left early this morning."

"They left, you say?"

"They left at eight o'clock, sir."

Mr. Buxton's attention was attracted to these two gentlemen.

"Go and find out where they came from," he said, "and let me know after dinner."

The man bowed and left the room, and almost immediately the dinner-bell rang.

Mary was frankly happy; she loved to be down here in this superb weather with her friends; she enjoyed this beauti-ful house with its furniture and pictures, and even took a certain pleasure in the hiding-holes themselves; although in this case she was satisfied they would not be needed. She had heard the tale of the Stanstead woods, and had no shadow of doubt but that the searchers, if, indeed, they were searchers at all, were baffled. So at dinner she talked exactly as usual; and the cloud of slight discomfort that still hung over Isabel grew lighter and lighter as she listened. The windows of the hall were flung wide, and the warm summer air poured from the garden into the cool room with its polished floor, and table decked with roses in silver bowls, with its grave tapestries stirring on the walls behind the grim visors and pikes that hung against them.

The talk turned on music.

"Ah! I would I had my lute," sighed Mary, "but my woman forgot to bring it. What a garden to sing in, in the shade of the yews, with the garden-house behind to make the voice sound better than it is!"

Mr. Buxton made a complimentary murmur.

"Thank you," she said, "Master Anthony, you are wool-gathering."

"Indeed not," he said, "but I was thinking where I had seen a lute. Ah! it is in the little west parlour."

"A lute!" cried Mary. "Ah! but I have no music; and I have not the courage to sing the only song I know, over and over again."

"But there is music too," said Anthony.

Mary clapped her hands.

"When dinner is over," she said, "you and I will go to find it."

Dinner was over at last, and the four rose.

"Come," said Mary; while Isabel turned into the garden and Mr. Buxton went to his room. "We will be with you presently," she cried after Isabel.

Then the two went together to the little west parlour, oak-panelled, with a wide fireplace with the logs in their places, and the latticed windows with their bottle-end glass, looking upon the walled garden. Anthony stood on a chair and opened the top window, letting a flood of summer noises into the room.

They found the lute music, written over its six lines with the queer F's and double F's and numerals—all Hebrew to Anthony, but bursting and blossoming with delicate melodies to Mary's eyes. Then she took up the lute, and tuned it on her knee, still sitting in a deep lounging-chair, with her buckled feet before her; while Anthony sat opposite and watched her supple flashing fingers busy among the strings, and her grave abstracted look as she listened critically. Then she sounded the strings in little rippling chords.

"Ah! it is a sweet old lute," she said. "Put the music before me."

Anthony propped it on a chair.

"Is that the right side up?" he asked.

Mary smiled and nodded, still looking at the music.

"Now then," she said, and began the prelude.

Anthony threw himself back in his chair as the delicate tinkling began to pour out and overscore the soft cooing of a pigeon on the roofs somewhere and the murmur of bees through the open window. It was an old precise little love-song from Italy, with a long prelude, suggesting by its tender minor chords true and restrained love, not passionate but tender, not despairing but melancholy; it was a love that had for its symbols not the rose and the lily, but the lavender and thyme—acrid in its sweetness. The prelude had climbed up by melodious steps to the keynote, and was now rippling down again after its aspirations.

Mary stirred herself.

Ah! now the voice would come in the last chord—when all the music was first drowned and then ceased, as with crash after crash a great bell, sonorous and piercing, began to sound from overhead.

Chapter Ten - The Passage to the Garden-House

The two looked at one another with parted lips, but without a word. Then both rose simultaneously. Then the bell jangled and ceased; and a crowd of other noises began; there were shouts, tramplings of hoofs in the court; shrill voices came over the wall; then a scream or two. Mary sprang to the door and opened it, and stood there listening. Then from the interior of the house came an indescribable din, tramplings of feet and shouts of anger; then violent blows on woodwork. It came nearer in a moment of time, as a tide comes in over flat sands, remorselessly swift.

Then Mary with one movement was inside again, and had locked the door and drawn the bolt.

"Up there," she said, "it is the only way—they are outside," and she pointed to the chimney.

Anthony began to remonstrate. It was intolerable, he felt, to climb up the chimney like a hunted cat, and he began a word or two. But Mary seized his arm.

"You must not be caught," she said, "there are others"; and there came a confused battering and trampling outside. She pushed him towards the chimney. Then decision came to him, and he bent his head and stepped upon the logs laid upon the ashes, crushing them down.

"Ah! go," said Mary's voice behind him, as the door began to bulge and creak. There was plainly a tremendous struggle in the little passage outside.

Anthony threw his hands up and felt a high ledge in the darkness, gripped it with his hands and made a huge effort combined of a tug and a spring; his feet rapped sharply for a moment or two on the iron fire-plate; and then his knee reached the ledge and he was up. He straightened himself on the ledge, stood upright and looked down; two white hands with rings on them were lifting the logs and drawing them out from the ashes, shaking them and replacing them by others from the wood-basket; and all deliberately, as if laying a fire. Then her voice came up to him, hushed but distinct.

"Go up quickly. I will feign to be burning papers; there will be smoke, but no sparks. It is green wood."

Anthony again felt above him, and found two iron half-rings in the chimney, one above the other; he was in semi-darkness here, but far above there was a patch of pale smoky light; and all the chimney seemed full of a murmurous sound. He tugged at the rings and found them secure, and drew himself up steadily by the higher one, until his knee struck the lower; then with a great effort he got his knee upon it, then his left foot, and again straightened himself. Then, as he felt in the darkness once more, he found a system of rings, one above the other, up the side of the chimney, by which it was not hard to climb. As he went up he began to perceive a sharp acrid smell, his eyes smarted and he closed them, but his throat burned; he climbed fiercely; and then suddenly saw immediately below him another hearth; he was looking over the fireplate of some other room. In a moment more he thrust his head over, and drew a long breath of clear air; then he listened intently. From below still came a murmur of confusion; but in this room all was quiet. He began to think frantically. He could not remain in the chimney, it was hopeless; they would soon light fires, he knew, in all the chimneys, and bring him down. What room was this? He was bewildered and could not remember. But at least he would climb into it and try to escape. In a moment more he had lifted himself over the fireplate and dropped safely on to the hearth of his own bedroom.

The fresh air and the familiarity of the room, as he looked round, swept the confusion out of his brain like a breeze. The thundering and shouting continued below. Then he went on tip-toe to the door and opened it. Round to the right was the head of the stairs which led straight into the little passage where the struggle was going on. He could hear Robert's voice in the din; plainly there was no way down the stairs. To the left was the passage that ended in a window, with the chapel door at the left and the false shelves on the right. He hesitated a moment between the two hiding-places, and then decided for the cupboard; there was a clean doublet there; his own was one black smear of soot, and as he thought of it, he drew off his sooty shoes. His hose were fortunately dark. He stepped straight out of the door, leaving it just ajar. Even as he left it there was a thunder of footsteps on the stairs, and he was at the shelves in a moment, catching a glimpse through the window on his left of the front court crowded with men and horses. He had opened and shut the secret door three or four times the evening before, and his hands closed almost instinctively on the two springs that must be worked simultaneously. He made the necessary movement, and the shelves with the wall behind it softly slid open and he sprang in. But as he closed it he heard one of the two books drop, and an exclamation from the passage he had just left; then quick steps from the head of the stairs; the steps clattered past the door and into the chapel opposite and stopped.

Anthony felt about him in the darkness, found the doublet and lifted it off the nail; slipped off his own, tearing his ruff as he did so; and then quickly put on the other. He had no shoes; but that would not be so noticeable. He had not seriously thought of the possibility of escaping through the portrait-door, as he felt sure the house would be overrun by now; but he put his eyes to the pinholes and looked out; and to his astonishment saw that the gallery was empty. There it lay, with its Flemish furniture on the right and its row of windows on the left, and all as tranquil as if there were no fierce tragedy of terror and wrath raging below. Again decision came to him; by a process of thought so swift that it was an intuition, he remembered that the fall of the book outside would concentrate attention on that corner; it could not be long before the shelves were broken in, and if he did not escape now there would be no possibility later. Then he unslid the inside bolt, and the portrait swung open; he closed it behind, and sped on silent shoeless feet down the polished floor of the gallery.

Of course the great staircase was hopeless. The hall would be seething with men. But there was just a chance through the servants' quarters. He dashed past the head of the stairs, catching a glimpse of heads and sparkles of steel over the banisters, and through the half-opened door at the end, finding himself in the men's corridor that was a continuation of the gallery he had left. On his left rose the head of the back-stairs, that led first with a double flight to the offices, the pantry, the buttery and the kitchen, and than, lower still, a single third flight down to the cellar. He looked down the stairs; at the bottom of the first double flight were a couple of maids, screaming and white-faced, leaning and pressing against the door, immediately below the one he had just come through himself. The door was plainly barred as well, for it was now thudding and cracking with blows that were being showered upon it from the other side. The maids, it seemed to him, in a panic had locked the door; but that panic might be his salvation. He dashed down the stairs; the maids screamed louder than ever when they saw this man, whom they did not recognise, with blackened face and hands come in noiseless leaps down towards them; but Anthony put his finger on his lips as he flew past them; then he dashed open the little door that shut off the cellar-flight, closed it behind him, and was immediately in the dark.

Then he groped his way down, feeling the rough brick wall as he went, till he reached the floor of the cellar. The air was cool and damp here, and it refreshed him, for he was pouring with sweat. The noise, too, and confusion which, during his flight, had been reverberating through the house with a formidable din, now only reached him as a far-away murmur.

As he counted the four steps up, and then lifted the overhanging edge, there came upon him irresistibly the contrast between the serene party here last night, with their tapers and their delicate dresses and Mary's cool clear-clipped voice—and his own soot-stained person, his desperate energy and his quick panting and heart-beating. Then the steps dropped and he slid in; lifted them again as he lay on his back, and heard the spring catch as they closed. Then he was in silence, too, and comparative safety. But he dared not rest yet, and edged himself along as he had seen Mr. Buxton do last night. Which brick was it? "The fourth of the fourth," he murmured, and counted, and pressed it. Again the door pushed back, and with a little struggle he was first on his knees, and then on his feet. Then he swung the door to again behind him.

Then for the first time he rested; he leaned against the brick-lined side of the tunnel and passed his blackened hands over his face. Five minutes ago—yes—certainly not five minutes ago he was lounging in the west parlour, at the other end of the house, while Mary played the prelude to an Italian love-song.—What was she doing now? God bless her for her quick courage!—And Isabel and Buxton—where were they all? How deadly sick and tired he felt!—Again he passed his hands over his face in the pitch darkness.—Well, he must push on.

He turned and began to grope patiently through the blackness—step by step—feeling the roughness of the bricks beneath with his shoeless feet before he set them down; once or twice he stepped into a little icy pool, which had collected through some crack in the vaulting overhead; once, too, he slipped on a lump of something wet and shapeless; and thought even then of Mary's suspicions the night before. He pushed on, shivering now with cold and excitement, through what seemed the interminable tunnel, until at last his outstretched hands touched wood before him. He had not seen this end of the passage for nearly two years, and he wondered if he could remember the method of opening, and gave a gulp of horror at the thought that he might not. But there had been no reason to make a secret of the inside of the door, and he presently found a button and drew it; it creaked rustily, but gave, and the door with another pull opened inwards, and there was a faint glimmer of light. Then he remembered that the entrances to the tunnel at either end were exactly on the same system; and putting out his hands felt the slope of the underside of the staircase, cutting diagonally across the opening of the passage. He slid himself on to the boarding sideways, and drew the brickwork towards him till the spring snapped, and lay there to consider before he went farther.

First he ran over in his mind the construction of the garden-house.

The basement in which he was lying corresponded to the cellar under the house from which he had come, and ran the whole length of the building, about forty feet by twenty. It was a large empty chamber, where nothing of any value was kept. He remembered last time he was here seeing a heap of tiles in one corner, with a pile of disused poles; pieces of rope, and old iron in another. The stairs led up through an ordinary trap-door into what was the ground-floor of the house. This, too, was one immense room, with four latticed windows looking on to the garden, and one with opaque glass on to the lane at the back; and a great door, generally kept locked, for rather more valuable things were kept here, such as the garden-roller, flower-pots, and the targets for archery. Then a light staircase led straight up from this room to the next floor, which was divided into two, both of which, so far as Anthony remembered, were empty. Mr. Buxton had thought of letting his gardeners sleep there when he had at first built this immense useless summer-house; but he had ultimately built a little gardener's cottage adjoining it. The two fantastic towers that flanked the building held nothing but staircases, which could be entered by either of the two floors, and which ascended to tiny rooms with windows on all four sides.

When Anthony had run over these details as he lay on his back, he pushed up the stair over his face and let the front of it with the step of the next swing inwards; the light was stronger now, and poured in, though still dim, through three half-moon windows, glazed and wired, that just rose above the level of the ground outside. Then he extricated himself, closed the steps behind him, and went up the stairs.

The trap-door at the top was a little stiff, but he soon raised it, and in a moment more was standing in the ground-floor room of the garden-house. All round him was much as he remembered it; he first went to the door and found it securely fastened, as it often was for days together; he glanced at the windows to assure himself that they were bottle-glass too, and then went to them to look out. He was fortunate enough to find the corner of one pane broken away; he put his eye to this, and there lay a little lawn, with a yew-hedge beyond blotting out all of the great house opposite except the chimneys,—the house which even across the whole space of garden hummed like a hive. On the lawn was a chair, and an orange-bound book lay face down on the grass beside it. Anthony stared at it; it was the book that he had seen in Isabel's hand not half an hour ago, as she had gone out into the garden from the hall to wait until he and Mary joined her with the lute.

And at that the priest knelt down before the window, covered his face with his hands, and began to stammer and cry to God: "O God! God! God!" he said.

When Mary Corbet had seen Anthony's feet disappear, she already had the outline of a plan in her mind. To light a fire and pretend to be burning important papers would serve as an excuse for keeping the door fast; it would also suggest at least that no one was in the chimney. The ordinary wood, however, sent up sparks; but she had noticed before a little green wood in the basket, and knew that this did not do so to the same extent; so she pulled out the dry wood that Anthony had trodden into the ashes and substituted the other. Then she had looked round for pa-per;—the lute music, that was all. Meantime the door was giving; the noise outside was terrible; and it was evident that one or two of the servants were obstructing the passage of the pursuivants.

When at last the door flew in, there was a fire cracking furiously on the hearth, and a magnificently dressed lady kneeling before it, crushing paper into the flames. Half a dozen men now streamed in and more began to follow, and stood irresolute for a moment, staring at her. From the resistance they had met with they had been certain that the priest was here, and this sight perplexed them. A big ruddy man, however, who led them, sprang across the room, seized Mary Corbet by the shoulders and whisked her away against the wall, and then dashed the half-burnt paper out of the grate and began to beat out the flames.

Mary struggled violently for a moment; but the others were upon her and held her, and she presently stood quiet. Then she began upon them.

"You insolent hounds!" she cried, "do you know who I am?" Her cheeks were scarlet and her eyes blazing; she seemed in a superb fury.

"Burning treasonable papers," growled the big man from his knees on the hearth, "that is enough for me."

"Who are you, sir, that dare to speak to me like that?"

The man got up; the flames were out now, and he slipped the papers into a pocket. Mary went on immediately.

"If I may not burn my own lute music, or keep my door locked, without a riotous mob of knaves breaking upon me—Ah! how dare you?" and she stamped furiously.

The pursuivant came up close to her, insolently.

"See here, my lady—" he began.

The men had fallen back from her a little now that the papers were safe, and she lifted her ringed hand and struck his ruddy face with all her might. There was a moment of confusion and laughter as he recoiled.

"Now will you remember that her Grace's ladies are not to be trifled with?"

There was a murmur from the crowded room, and a voice near the door cried:

"She says truth, Mr. Nichol. It is Mistress Corbet."

Nichol had recovered himself, but was furiously angry.

"Very good, madam, but I have these papers now," he said, "they can still be read."

"You blind idiot," hissed Mary, "do you not know lute music when you see it?"

"I know that ladies do not burn lute music with locked doors," observed Nichol bitterly.

"The more fool you!" screamed Mary, "when you have caught one at it."

"That will be seen," sneered Mr. Nichol.

"Not by a damned blind scarlet-faced porpoise!" screamed Mary, apparently more in a passion than ever, and a burst of laughter came from the men.

This was too much for Mr. Nichol. This coarse abuse stung him cruelly.

"God's blood," he bellowed at the room; "take this vixen out and search the place." And a torrent of oaths drove the crowd about the door out into the passage again.

A couple of men took Mary by the fierce ringed hands of hers that still twitched and clenched, and led her out; she spat insults over her shoulders as she went. But she had held him in talk as she intended.

"Now then," roared Nichol again, "search, you dogs!"

He himself went outside too, and seeing the stairs stamped up them. He was just in time to see the Tacitus settle down with crumpled pages; stopped for a moment, bewildered, for it lay in the middle of the passage; and then rushed at the open door on the left, dashed it open, and found a little empty room, with a chair or two, and a table—but no sign of the priest. It was like magic.

Then out he came once more, and went into Anthony's own room. The great bed was on his right, the window oppo-site, the fireplace to the left, and in the middle lay two sooty shoes. Instinctively he bent and touched them, and found them warm; then he sprang to the door, still keeping his face to the room, and shouted for help.

"He is here, he is here!" he cried. And a thunder of footsteps on the stairs answered him.

195

Meanwhile the men that held Mary followed the others along the passage, but while the leaders went on and round into the lower corridor, the two men-at-arms with their prisoner turned aside into the parlour that served as an ante-chamber to the hall beyond, where they released her. Here, though it was empty of people, all was in confusion; the table had been overturned in the struggle that had raged along here between Lackington's men, who had entered from the front door, and the servants of the house, who had rushed in from their quarters at the first alarm and intercepted them. One chair lay on its side, with its splintered carved arm beside it. As Mary stood a moment looking about her, the door from the hall that had been closed, again opened, and Isabel came through; and a man's voice said:

"You must wait here, madam"; then the door closed behind her.

"Isabel," said Mary.

The two looked at one another a moment, but before either spoke again the door again half-opened, and a voice began to speak, as if its owner still held the handle.

"Very well, Lackington, keep him in his room. I will go through here to Nichol."

Isabel had drawn a sharp breath as the voice began, and as the door opened wider she turned and faced it. Then Hubert came in, and recoiled on the threshold. There fell a complete silence in the room.

"Hubert," said Isabel after a moment, "what are you doing here?"

Hubert shut the door abruptly and leaned against it, staring at her; his face had gone white under the tan. Isabel still looked at him steadily, and her eyes were eloquent. Then she spoke again, and something in her voice quickened the beating of Mary's heart as she listened.

"Hubert, have you forgotten us?"

Still Hubert stared; then he stood upright. The two men-at-arms were watching in astonishment.

"I will see to the ladies," he said abruptly, and waved his hand. They still hesitated a moment.

"Go," he said again sharply, and pointed to the door. He was a magistrate, and responsible; and they turned and went.

Then Hubert looked at Isabel again.

"Isabel," he said, "if I had known—"

"Stay," she interrupted, "there is no time for explanations except mine. Anthony is in the house; I do not know where. You must save him."

There was no entreaty or anxiety in her voice; nothing but a supreme dignity and an assurance that she would be obeyed.

"But—" he began. The door was opened from the hall, and a little party of searchers appeared, but halted when the magistrate turned round.

"Come with me," he said to the two women, "you must have a room kept for you upstairs," and he held back the door for them to pass.

Isabel put out her hand to Mary, and the two went out together into the hall past the men, who stood back to let them through, and Hubert followed. They turned to the left to the stairs, looking as they went upon the wild confusion. Above them rose the carved ceiling, and in the centre of the floor, untouched, by a strange chance, stood the dinner-table, still laid with silver and fruit and flowers. But all else was in disarray. The leather screen that had stood by the door into the entrance hall had been overthrown, and had carried with it a tall flowering plant that now lay trampled and broken before the hearth. A couple of chairs lay on their backs between the windows; the rug under the window was huddled in a heap, and all over the polished boards were scratches and dents; a broken sword-hilt lay on the floor with a feathered cap beside it. There were half a dozen men guarding the four doors; but the rest were gone; and from overhead came tramplings and shouts as the hunt swept to and fro in the upper floors.

At the top of the stairs was Mary's room; the two ladies, who had gone silently upstairs with Hubert behind them, stopped at the door of it.

"Here, if you please," said Mary.

Before Hubert could answer, Lackington came down the passage, hurrying with a drawn sword, and his hat on his head. Isabel did not recognise him as he stopped and tapped Hubert on the arm familiarly.

"The prisoners must not be together," he said.

Hubert drew back his arm and looked the man in the face.

"They are not prisoners; and they shall be together. Take off your hat, sir."

Then, as Lackington drew back astonished, he opened the door.

"You shall not be disturbed here," he said, and the two went in, and the door closed behind them. There was a murmur of voices outside the door, and they heard a name called once or twice, and the sound of footsteps. Then came a tap, and Hubert stepped in quietly and closed the door.

"I have placed my own man outside," he said, "and none shall trouble you—and—Mistress Isabel—I will do my best."
Then he bowed and went out.

The long miserable afternoon began. They watched through the windows the sentries going up and down the broad paths between the glowing flower-beds; and out, over the high iron fence that separated the garden from the meadows, the crowd of villagers and children watching.

But the real terror for them both lay in the sounds that came from the interior of the house. There was a continual tramp of the sentries placed in every corridor and lobby, and of the messengers that went to and fro. Then from room after room came the sounds of blows, the rending of woodwork, and once or twice the crash of glass, as the searchers went about their work; and at every shout the women shuddered or drew their breath sharply, for any one of the noises might be the sign of Anthony's arrest.

The two had soon talked out every theory in low voices, but they both agreed that he was still in the house somewhere, and on the upper floor. It was impossible, they thought, for him to have made his way down. There were four possibilities, therefore: either he might still be in the chimney—in that case it was no use hoping; or he was in the chapel-hole; or in that behind the portrait; or in one last one, in the room next to their own. The searchers had been there early in the afternoon, but perhaps had not found it; its entrance was behind the window shutter, and was contrived in the thickness of the wall. So they talked, these two, and conjectured and prayed, as the evening drew on; and the sun began to sink behind the church, and the garden to lie in cool shadow.

About eight there was a tap at the door, and Hubert came in with a tray of food in his hands, which he set down.
"All is in confusion," he said, "but this is the best I can do."—He broke off.

"Mistress Isabel," he said, coming nearer to the two as they sat together in the window-seat, "I can do little; they have found three hiding-holes; but so far he has escaped. I do what I can to draw them off, but they are too clever and zealous. If you can tell me more, perhaps I can do more."

The two were looking at him with startled eyes.

"Three?" Mary said.

"Yes, three—and indeed—" He stopped as Isabel got up and came towards him.

"Hubert," she said resolutely, "I must tell you. He must be still in the chimney of the little west parlour. Do what you can."

"The west parlour!" he said. "That was where Mistress Corbet was burning the papers?"

"Yes," said Mary.

"He is not there," said Hubert; "we have sent a boy up and down it already."

"Ah! dear God!" said Mary from the window-seat, "then he has escaped."

Isabel looked from one to the other and shook her head.

"It cannot be," she said. "The guards were all round the house before the alarm rang."

Hubert nodded, and Mary's face fell.

"Then is there no way out?" he asked.

Mary sprang up with shining eyes.

"He has done it," she said, and threw her arms round Isabel and kissed her.

"Well," said Hubert, "what can I do?"

"You must leave us," said Isabel; "come back later."

"Then when we have searched the garden-house—why, what is it?"

A look of such anguish had come into their faces that he stopped amazed.

"The garden-house!" cried Mary; "no, no, no!"

"No, no, Hubert, Hubert!" cried Isabel, "you must not go there."

"Why," he said, "it was I that proposed it; to draw them from the house."

There came from beneath the windows a sudden tramp of footsteps, and then Nichol's voice, distinctly heard through the open panes.

"We cannot wait for him. Come, men."

"They are going without me," said Hubert; and turned and ran through the door.

Chapter Eleven - The Garden-House

During that long afternoon the master of the house had sat in his own room, before his table, hearing the ceaseless footsteps and the voices overhead, and the ring of feet on the tiles outside his window, knowing that his friend and priest was somewhere in the house, crouching in some dark little space, listening to the same footsteps and voices as they came and went by his hiding-place, and that he himself was absolutely powerless to help.

He had been overpowered in the first rush as he pealed on the alarm-bell, to which he had rushed when the groom burst in from the stable-yard crying that the outer court was full of men. Lackington had then sent him under guard to his own room, where he had been locked in with an armed constable to prevent any possibility of escape. In the struggle he had received a blow on the head which had completely dazed him; all his resource left him; and he had no desire even to move from his chair.

Now he sat, with his head on his breast, and his mind going the ceaseless round of all the possible places where Anthony might be. Little scenes, too, of startling vividness moved before him, as he sat there with half-closed eyes— scenes of the imagined arrest—the scuffle as the portrait was torn away and Anthony burst out in one last desperate attempt to escape. He saw him under every kind of circumstance—dashing up stairs and being met at the top by a man with a pike—running and crouching through the withdrawing-room itself next door—gliding with burning eyes past the yew-hedges in a rush for the iron gates, only to find them barred—on horseback with his hands bound and a despairing uplifted face with pike-heads about him.—So his friend dreamed miserably on, open-eyed, but between waking and the sleep of exhaustion, until the crowning vision flashed momentarily before his eyes of the scaffold and the cauldron with the fire burning and the low gallows over the heads of the crowd, and the butcher's block and knife; and then he moaned and sat up and stared about him, and the young pursuivant looked at him half-apprehensively.

Towards evening the house grew quieter; once, about six o'clock, there were voices outside, the door from the hall was unlocked, and a heavily-built, ruddy man came in with two pikemen, locking the door behind him. They paid no attention to the prisoner, and he watched them mechanically as they went round the room, running their eyes up and down the panelling, and tapping here and there.

"The room has been searched, sir, already," said the young constable to the ruddy-faced man, who glanced at him and nodded, and then continued the scrutiny. They reached the fireplace and the officer reached up and tapped the wood over the mantelpiece half-a-dozen times.

"Here," he called, pointing to a spot.

A pikeman came up, placed the end of his pike into the oak, and leaned suddenly and heavily upon it: the steel crashed in an inch, and stopped as it met the stonework behind. The officer made a motion, the pike was withdrawn, and he stood on tip-toe and put his finger into the splintered panel. Then he was satisfied and they passed on, still tapping the walls, and went out of the other door, locking it again behind them.

An hour later there were voices and steps again, and a door was unlocked and opened, and Mr. Graves, the Tonbridge magistrate stepped in alone. He was a pale scholarly-looking man with large eyes, and a weak mouth only partly covered by his beard.

"You can go," he said nervously to the constable, "but remain outside." The young man saluted him and passed out. The magistrate looked quickly and sideways at Mr. Buxton as he sat and looked at him.

"I am come to tell you," he said, "that we cannot find the priest." He hesitated and stopped. "We have found several hiding-holes," he went on, "and they are all empty. I—I hope there is no mistake."

A little thrill ran through the man who sat in the chair; the lethargy began to clear from his brain, like a morning mist when a breeze rises; he sat a little more upright and gripped the arms of his chair; he said nothing yet, but he felt power and resource flowing back to his brain, and the pulse in his temples quieted. Why, if the lad had not been taken yet, he must surely be out of the house.

"I trust there is no mistake," said the magistrate again nervously.

"You may well trust so," said the other; "it will be a grievous thing for you, sir, otherwise."

"Indeed, Mr. Buxton, I think you know I am no bigot. I was sent for by Mr. Lackington last night. I could not refuse. It was not my wish—"

"Yet you have issued your warrant, and are here in person to execute it. May I inquire how many of my cupboards you have broken into? And I hope your men are satisfied with my plate."

"Indeed, sir," said the magistrate, "there has been nothing of that kind. And as for the cupboards, there were but three—"

Three!—then the lad is out of the house, thought the other. But where?

"And I trust you have not spared to break down my servants' rooms, and the stables as well as pierce all my panelling."

"There was no need to search the stables, Mr. Buxton; our men were round the house before we entered. They have been watching the entrances since eight o'clock last night."

Mr. Buxton felt bewildered. His instinct had been right, then, the night before.

"The party was followed from near Wrotham," went on the magistrate. "The priest was with them then; and, we suppose, entered the house."

"You suppose!" snapped the other. "What the devil do you mean by supposing? You have looked everywhere and cannot find him?"

The magistrate shrugged his shoulders deprecatingly, as he stood and stared at the angry man.

"And the roofs?" added Mr. Buxton sneeringly.

"They have been thoroughly searched."

Then there is but one possible theory, he reflected. The lad is in the garden-house. And what if they search that?

"Then may I ask what you propose to destroy next, Mr. Graves?"

He saw that this tone was having its effect on the magistrate, who was but a half-hearted persecutor, with but feeble convictions and will, as he knew of old.

"I—I entreat you not to speak to me like that, sir," he said. "I have but done my duty."

Then the other rose from his chair, and his eyes were stern and bright again and his lips tight.

"Your duty, sir, seems a strange matter, when it leads you to break into a friend's house, assault him and his servants and his guests, and destroy his furniture, in search of a supposed priest whom you have never even seen. Now, sir, if this matter comes to her Grace's ears, I will not answer for the consequences; for you know Mistress Corbet, her lady-in-waiting, is one of my guests.—And, speaking of that, where are my guests?"

"The two ladies, Mr. Buxton, are safe and sound upstairs, I assure you."

The magistrate's voice was trembling.

"Well, sir, I have one condition to offer you. Either you and your men withdraw within half an hour from my house and grounds, and leave me and my two guests to ourselves, or else I lay the whole matter, through Mistress Corbet, before her Grace." Mr. Buxton beat his hand once on the table as he ended, and looked with a contemptuous inquiry at the magistrate.

But the worm writhed up at the heel.

"How can you talk like this, sir," he burst out, "as if you had but two guests?"

"Two guests? I do not understand you. How should there be more?"

"Then for whom are the four places laid at table?" he answered indignantly.

Mr. Buxton felt a sudden desperate sinking, and he could not answer for a moment. The magistrate passed his shaking hand over his mouth and beard once or twice; but the thrust had gone home, and there was no parry or riposte. He followed it up.

"Now, sir, be reasonable. I came in here to make terms. We know the priest has been here. It is certain beyond all question. All that is uncertain is whether he is here now or escaped. We have searched thoroughly; we must search again to-morrow; but in the meanwhile, while you yourself must be under restraint, your guests shall have what liberty they wish; and you yourself shall have all reasonable comfort and ease. So—so, if we do not find the priest, I trust that you and—and—Mistress Corbet will agree to overlook any rashness on my part—and—and let her Grace remain in ignorance."

Mr. Buxton had been thinking furiously during this little speech. He saw the mistake he had made in taking the high line, and his wretched forgetfulness of the fourth place at table. He must make terms, though it tasted bitter.

"Well, Mr. Graves," he said, "I have no wish to be hard upon you. All I ask is to be out of the house when the search is made, and that the ladies shall come and go as they please."

The magistrate leapt at the lure like a trout.

"Yes, yes, Mr. Buxton, it shall be as you say. And to what house will you retire?"

Mr. Buxton appeared to reflect; he tapped on the table with a meditative finger and looked at the ceiling.

"It must not be too far away," he said slowly, "and—and the Rector would scarce like to receive me. Perhaps in—or—Why not my summer-house?" he added suddenly.

Mr. Graves' face was irradiated with smiles.

"Thank you, Mr. Buxton, certainly, it shall be as you say. And where is the summer-house?"

"It is across the garden," said the other carelessly. "I wonder you have not searched it in your zeal."

"Shall I send a man to prepare it?" asked the magistrate eagerly. "Will you go there to-night?"

"Well, shall we go across there together now? I give you my parole," he added, smiling, and standing up.

"Indeed,—as you wish. I cannot tell you, sir, how grateful I am. You have made my duty almost a pleasure, sir."

They went out together into the hall, Mr. Buxton carrying the key of the garden-house that he had taken from the drawer of his table; he glanced ruefully at the wrecked furniture and floor, and his eyes twinkled for a moment as they rested on the four places at table still undisturbed, and then met the magistrate's sidelong look. The men were still at the doors, resting now on chairs or leaning against the wall, with their weapons beside them; it was weary work this mounting sentry and losing the hunt, and their faces showed it. The two passed out together into the garden, and began to walk up the path that led straight across the avenue to where the high vanes of the garden-house stood up grotesque and towering against the evening sky, above the black yew-hedges.

All the while they went Mr. Buxton was thinking out his plan. It was still incoherent; but, at any rate, it was a step gained to be able to communicate with Anthony again; and at least the poor lad should have some supper. And then he smiled to himself with relief as he saw what an improvement there had been in the situation as it had appeared to him an hour ago. Why, they would search the house again next day; find no one, and retire apologising. His occupancy of the garden-house with the magistrate's full consent would surely secure it from search; and he was not so well satisfied with the disguised entrance to the passage at this end as with that in the cellar.

They reached the door at last. There were three steps going up to it, and Mr. Buxton went up them, making a good deal of noise as he did so, to ensure Anthony's hearing him should he be above ground. Then, as if with great difficulty, he unlocked the door, rattling it, and clicking sharply with his tongue at its stiffness.

"You see, Mr. Graves." he said, rather loud, as he opened the door a little, "my prison will not be a narrow one." He threw the door open, gave a glance round, and was satisfied. The targets leaned against one wall, and two rows of flower-pots stood in the corner near where the window opened into the lane, but there was no sign of occupation. Mr. Buxton went across, threw the window open and looked out. There was a steel cap three or four feet below, and a pike-head; and at the sound of the latch a bearded face looked up.

"I see you have a sentry there," said Mr. Buxton carelessly.

"Ah! that is one of Mr. Maxwell's men."

"Mr. Maxwell's!" said the other, startled. "Is he in this affair too?"

"Yes; have you not heard? He came from Great Keynes this morning. Mr. Lackington sent for him."

Mr. Buxton's face grew dark.

"Ah yes, I see—a pretty revenge."

The magistrate was on the point of asking an explanation, for he felt on the best of terms again now with his prisoner, when there were footsteps outside and voices; and there stood four constables, with Nichol, Hubert Maxwell and Lackington in furious debate coming up the path behind.

They looked up suddenly, and saw the door open and the magistrate and his prisoner standing in the opening. The four constables stood waiting for further orders while their three chiefs came up.

"Now, now, now!" said Mr. Graves peevishly, "what is all this?"

"We have come to search this house, sir," said Nichol cheerfully.

"See here, sir," said Hubert, "have you given orders for this?"

"Enough, enough," said Lackington coolly. "Search, men."

The pursuivants advanced to the steps. Then Mr. Buxton turned fiercely on them all.

"See here!" he cried, and his voice rang out across the garden. "You bring me here, Mr. Graves, promising me a little peace and quietness, after your violent and unwarranted attack upon my house to-day. I have been patient and submissive to all suggestions; I leave my entire house at your disposal; I promise to lay no complaints before her Grace, so long as you will let me retire here till it is over—and now your men persecute me even here. Have you no mind of your own, sir?" he shouted.

"Really, sir—" began Hubert.

"And as for you, Mr. Maxwell," went on the other fiercely, "are you not content with your triumph so far? Cannot you leave me one corner to myself, or would your revenge be not full enough for you, then?"

"You mistake me, sir," said Hubert, making a violent effort to control himself; "I am on your side in this matter."

"That is what I am beginning to think," said Lackington insolently.

"You think!" roared Mr. Buxton; "and who the devil are you?"

"See here, gentlemen," said Mr. Nichol, "what is the dispute? Here is an empty house, Mr. Buxton tells us; and Mr. Maxwell tells us the same. Well, then, let these honest fellows run through the empty house; it will not take ten minutes, and Mr. Buxton and his friend can take the air meanwhile. A-God's name, let us not dispute over a trifle."

"Then, a-God's name, let me go to my own house," bellowed Mr. Buxton, "and these gentlemen can have the empty house to disport themselves in till doomsday—or till her Grace looks into the matter"; and he made a motion to run down the steps, but his heart sank. Mr. Graves put out a deprecating hand and touched his arm; and Mr. Buxton very readily turned at once with a choleric face!

"No, no, no!" cried the magistrate. "These gentlemen are here on my warrant, and they shall not search the place. Mr. Buxton, I entreat you not to be hasty. Come back, sir."

Mr. Buxton briskly reascended.

"Well, then, Mr. Graves, I entreat you to give your orders, and let your will be known. I am getting hungry for my supper, too, sir. It is already an hour past my time."

"Sup in the house, sir," said Mr. Nichol smoothly, "and we shall have done by then."

Then Hubert blazed up; he took a step forward.

"Now, you fellow," he said to Nichol, "hold your damned tongue. Mr. Graves and I are the magistrates here, and we say that this gentleman shall sup and sleep here in peace, so you may take your pursuivants elsewhere."

Lackington looked up with a smile.

"No, Mr. Maxwell, I cannot do that. These men are under my orders, and I shall leave two of them here and send another to keep your fellow company at the back, We will not disturb Mr. Buxton further to-night; but to-morrow we shall see."

Mr. Buxton paid no sort of further attention to him, but turned to the magistrates.

"Well, gentlemen, what is your decision?"

"You shall sleep here in peace, sir," said Mr. Graves resolutely. "I can promise nothing for to-morrow."

"Then will you kindly allow one of my men to bring me supper and a couch of some kind, and I shall be obliged if the ladies may sup with me."

"That they shall," assented Mr. Graves. "Mr. Maxwell, will you escort them here?"

Hubert, who was turning away, nodded and disappeared round the yew-hedge. Lackington, who had been talking in an undertone to the pursuivants, now went up another alley with one of them and Mr. Nichol, and disappeared too in the gathering gloom of the garden. The other two pursuivants separated and each moved a few steps off and remained just out of sight. Plainly they were to remain on guard. Mr. Buxton and the magistrate sat down on a couple of garden-chairs.

"That is an obstinate fellow, sir," said Mr. Graves.

"They are certainly both of them very offensive fellows, sir. I was astonished at your indulgence towards them."

The magistrate was charmed by this view of the case, and remained talking with Mr. Buxton until footsteps again were heard, and the two ladies appeared, with Hubert with them, and a couple of men carrying each a tray and the other necessaries he had asked for.

Mr. Buxton and the magistrate rose to meet the ladies and bowed.

"I cannot tell you," began their host elaborately, "what distress all this affair has given me. I trust you will forgive any inconvenience you may have suffered."

Both Isabel and Mary looked white and strained, but they responded gallantly; and as the table was being prepared the four talked almost as if there were no bitter suspense at three of their hearts at least. Mr. Graves was nervous and uneasy, but did his utmost to propitiate Mary. At last he was on the point of withdrawing, when Mr. Buxton entreated him to sup with them.

"I must not," he said; "I am responsible for your property, Mr. Buxton."

"Then I understand that these ladies may come and go as they please?" he asked carelessly.

"Certainly, sir."

"Then may I ask too the favour that you will place one of your own men at the door who can conduct them to the house when they wish to go, and who can remain and protect me too from any disturbance from either of the two officious persons who were here just now?"

Mr. Graves, delighted at this restored confidence, promised to do so, and took an elaborate leave; and the three sat down to supper; the door was left open, and they could see through it the garden, over which veil after veil of darkness was beginning to fall. The servants had lighted two tapers, and the inside of the great room with its queer furniture of targets and flower-pots was plainly visible to any walking outside. Once or twice the figure of a man crossed the strip of light that lay across the gravel.

It was a strange supper. They said innocent things to one another in a tone loud enough for any to hear who cared to be listening, about the annoyance of it all, the useless damage that had been done, the warmth of the summer night, and the like, and spoke in low soundless sentences of what was in all their hearts.

"That red-faced fellow," said Mary, "would be the better of some manners. (He is in the passage below, I suppose.)"

"It is scarce an ennobling life—that of a manhunter," said Mr. Buxton. ("Yes. I am sure of it.")

"They have broken your little cupboard, I fear." said Mary again. ("Tell me your plan, if you have one.")

And so step by step a plan was built up. It had been maturing in Mr. Buxton's mind gradually after he had learnt the ladies might sup with him; and little by little he conveyed it to them. He managed to write down the outline of it as he sat at table, and then passed it to each to read, and commented on it and answered their questions about it, all in the same noiseless undertone, with his lips indeed scarcely moving. There were many additions and alterations made in it as the two ladies worked upon it too, but by the time supper was over it was tolerably complete. It seemed, indeed, almost desperate, but the case was desperate. It was certain that the garden-house would be searched next day; Lackington's suspicions were plainly roused, and it was too much to hope that searchers who had found three hiding-places in one afternoon would fail to find a fourth. It appeared then that it was this plan or none.

They supped slowly, in order to give time to think out and work out the scheme, and to foresee any difficulties beyond those they had already counted on; and it was fully half-past nine before the two ladies rose. Their host went with them to the door, called up Mr. Graves' man, and watched them pass down the path out of sight. He stood a minute or two longer looking across towards the house at the dusky shapes in the garden and the strip of gravel, grass, and yew that was illuminated from his open door. Then he spoke to the men that he knew were just out of sight.

"I am going to bed presently. Kindly do not disturb me." There was no answer; and he closed the two high doors and bolted them securely.

He dared not yet do what he wished, for fear of arousing suspicion, so he went to the other window and looked out into the lane. He could just make out the glimmer of steel on the opposite bank.

"Good-night, my man," he called out cheerfully.

Again there was no answer. There was something sinister in these watching presences that would not speak, and his heart sank a little as he put-to the window without closing it. He went next to the pile of rugs and pillows that his men had brought across, and arranged them in the corner, just clear of the trap-door. Then he knelt and said his evening prayers, and here at least was no acting. Then he rose again and took off his doublet and ruff and shoes so that he was dressed only in a shirt, trunks and hose. Then he went across to the supper-table, where the tapers still burned, and blew them out, leaving the room in complete darkness. Then he went back to his bed, and sat and listened.

Up to this point he had been aware that probably at least one pair of eyes had been watching him; for, although the windows were of bottle-end glass, yet it was exceedingly likely that there would be some clear glass in them; and, with the tapers burning inside, his movements would all have been visible to either of Lackington's men who cared to put his eye to the window. But now he was invisible. Yet, as he thought of it, he slipped on his doublet again to hide the possible glimmer of his white shirt. There was the silence of the summer night about him—the silence only emphasised by its faint sounds. The house was quiet across the garden, though once or twice he thought he heard a horse stamp. Once there came a little stifled cough from outside his window; there was the silky rustle of the faint breeze in the trees outside; and now and again came the snoring of a young owl in the ivy somewhere overhead.

He counted five hundred deliberately, to compel himself to wait; and meanwhile his sub-conscious self laboured at the scheme. Then he glanced this way and that with wide eyes; his ears sang with intentness of listening. Then, very softly he shifted his position, and found with his fingers the ring that lifted the trap-door above the stairs.

There was no concealment about this, and without any difficulty he lifted the door with his right hand and leaned it against the wall; then he looked round again and listened. From below came up the damp earthy breath of the basement, and he heard a rat scamper suddenly to shelter. Then he lifted his feet from the rugs and dropped them noiselessly on the stairs, and supporting himself by his hands on the floor went down a step or two. Then a stair creaked under his weight; and he stopped in an agony, hearing only the mad throbbing in his own ears. But all was silent outside. And so step by step he descended into the cool darkness. He hesitated as to whether he should close the trap-door or not, there was a risk either way; but he decided to do so, as he would be obliged to make some noise in opening the secret doors and communicating with Anthony. At last his feet touched the earth floor, and he turned as he sat and counted the steps—the fourth, the fifth, and tapped upon it. There was no answer; he put his lips to it and whispered sharply:

"Anthony, Anthony, dear lad."

Still there was no answer. Then he lifted the lid, and managed to hold the woodwork below, as he knelt on the third step, so that it descended noiselessly. He put out his other hand and felt the boards. Anthony had retired into the passage then, he told himself, as he found the space empty. He climbed into the hole, pushed himself along and counted the bricks—the fourth of the fourth—pressed it, and pushed at the door; and it was fast.

For the first time a horrible spasm of terror seized him. Had he forgotten? or was it all a mistake, and Anthony not there? He turned in his place, put his shoulders against the door and his feet against the woodwork of the stairs, and pushed steadily; there were one or two loud creaks, and the door began to yield. Then he knew Anthony was there; a rush of relief came into his heart—and he turned and whispered again.

"Anthony, dear lad, Anthony, open quickly; it is I."

The brickwork slid back and a hand touched his face out of the pitch darkness of the tunnel.

"Who is it? Is it you?" came a whisper.

"It is I, yes. Thank God you are here. I feared—"

"How could I tell?" came the whisper again. "But what is the news? Are you escaped?"

"No, I am a prisoner, and on parole. But there is no time for that. You must escape—we have a plan—but there is not much time."

"Why should I not remain here?"

"They will search to-morrow—and—and this end of the tunnel is not so well concealed as the other. They would find you. They suspect you are here, and there are guards round this place."

There was a movement in the dark.

"Then why think—" began the whisper.

"No, no, we have a plan. Mary and Isabel approve. Listen carefully. There is but one guard at the back here, in the lane. Mary has leave to come and go now as she pleases—they are afraid of her; she will leave the house in a few minutes now to ride to East Maskells, with two grooms and a maid behind one of them. She will ride her own horse. When she has passed the inn she will bid the groom who has the maid to wait for her, while she rides down the lane with the other, Robert, to speak to me through the window. The pursuivant, we suppose, will not forbid that, as he knows they have supped with me just now. As we talk, Robert will watch his chance and spring on the pursuivant. As soon as the struggle begins you will drop from the window; it is but eight feet; and help him to secure the man and gag him. However much din they make the others cannot reach the man in time to help, for they will have to come round from the house, and you will have mounted Robert's horse; and you and Mary together will gallop down the lane into the road, and then where you will. We advise East Maskells. I do not suppose there will be any pursuit. They will have no horses ready. Do you understand it?"

There was silence a moment; Mr. Buxton could hear Anthony breathing in the darkness.

"I do not like it," came the whisper at last; "it seems desperate. A hundred things may happen. And what of Isabel and you?"

"Dear friend; I know it is desperate, but not so desperate as your remaining here would be for us all."

Again there was silence.

"What of Robert? How will he escape?"

"If you escape they will have nothing against Robert; for they can prove nothing as to your priesthood. But if they catch you here—and they certainly will, if you remain here—they will probably hang him, for he fought for you gallantly in the house. And he too will have time to run. He can run through the door into the meadows. But they will not care for him if they know you are off."

Again silence.

"Well?" whispered Mr. Buxton.

"Do you wish it?"

"I think it is the only hope."

"Then I will do it."

"Thank God! And now you must come up with me. Put off your shoes."

"I have none."

"Then follow, and do not make a sound."

Very cautiously Mr. Buxton extricated himself; for he had been lying on his side while he whispered to Anthony; and presently was crouched on the stairs above, as he heard the stirrings of his friend in the dark below him. There came the click of the brickwork door; then slow shufflings; once a thump on the hollow boards that made his heart leap; then after what seemed an interminable while, came the sound of latching the fifth stair into its place; and he felt his foot grasped. Then he turned and ascended slowly on hands and knees, feeling now and again for the trap-door over him—touched it—raised it, and crawled out on to the rugs. The room seemed to him comparatively light after the heavy darkness of the basement, and passage below, and he could make out the supper-table and the outline of the targets on the opposite wall. Then he saw a head follow him; then shoulders and body; and Anthony crept out and sat on the rugs beside him. Their hands met in a trembling grip.

"Supper, dear lad?" whispered Mr. Buxton, with his mouth to the other's ear.

"Yes, I am hungry," came the faintest whisper back.

Mr. Buxton rose and went on tip-toe to the table, took off some food and a glass of wine that he had left purposely filled and came back with them.

There the two friends sat; Mr. Buxton could just hear the movement of Anthony's mouth as he ate. The four windows glimmered palely before them, and once or twice the tall doors rattled faintly as the breeze stirred them.

Then suddenly came a sound that made Anthony's hand pause on the way to his mouth; Mr. Buxton drew a sharp breath; it was the noise of three or four horses on the road beyond the church. Then they both stood up without a word, and Mr. Buxton went noiselessly across to the window that looked on to the lane and remained there, listening. The horses were now passing down the street, and the noise of their hoofs grew fainter behind the houses. Anthony saw his friend in the twilight beckon, and he went across and stood by him. Suddenly the hoofs sounded loud and near; and they heard the pursuivant below stand up from the bank opposite. Then Mary's voice came distinct and cheerful.

"How dark it is!"

The horses were coming down the lane.

Chapter Twelve - The Night-Ride

The sound of hoofs came nearer; Anthony's heart, as he crouched below the window, ready to spring up and over when the signal was given, beat in sick thumpings at the base of his throat, but with a fierce excitement and no fear. His hands clenched and unclenched. Mr. Buxton stood back a little, waiting; he must feign to be asleep at first. Then came suddenly a sharp challenge from the sentry.

"It is Mistress Corbet," came Mary's cool high tones, "and I desire to speak with Mr. Buxton."

The man hesitated.

"You cannot," he said.

"Cannot!" she cried; "why, fellow, do you know who I am? And I have just supped with him."

There came a sudden sound from the other side of the summer-house, and both men in the room knew that the guards in the garden were listening.

"I am sorry, madam, but I have no orders."

"Then do not presume, you hound," came Mary's voice again, with a ring of anger. "Ho, there, Mr. Buxton, come to the window."

"Be ready," he whispered to Anthony.

"Stand back, madam," said the pursuivant, "or I shall call for help."

Then Mr. Buxton threw back the window.

"Who is there?" he asked coolly. ("Stand up Anthony.")

"It is I, Mr. Buxton, but this insolent dog—"

"Stand back, madam, I say," cried the voice of the guard. Then from the garden behind came running footsteps and voices; and a red light shone through the windows behind.

"Now," whispered the voice over Anthony's head sharply.

There came a loud shout from the guard, "Help there, help!"

Anthony put his hands on to the sill and lifted himself easily. The groom had slipped from his horse while Mary held the bridle, and was advancing at the guard, and there was something in his hand. The sentry, who was standing immediately under the window, now dropped his pike point forward; and as a furious rattling began at the doors on the garden side, Anthony dropped, and came down astride of the man's neck, who crashed to the ground. Then the groom was on him too.

"Leave him to me, sir. Mount."

The groom's hands were busy with something about the struggling man's neck: the shouts choked and ceased.

"You will strangle the man," said Anthony sharply.

"Nonsense," said Mary; "mount, mount. They are coming."

Anthony ran to the horse, that was beginning to scurry and plunge; threw himself across the saddle and caught the reins.

"Up?" said Mary.

"Up"; and he slung his right leg over the flank and sat up, as Mary released the bridle, and dashed off, scattering gravel.

From the direction of the church came cries and the quick rattle of a galloping horse. Anthony dashed his shoeless heels into the horse's sides and leaned forward, and in a moment more was flying down the lane after Mary. From in front came a shout of warning, with one or two screams, and then Anthony turned the corner, checking his horse slightly at the angle, saw a torch somewhere to his right, a group of scared faces, a groom and woman clinging to him on a plunging horse, and the white road; and then found himself with loose reins, and flying stirrups, thundering down the village street, with Mary on her horse not two lengths in front. The roar of the hoofs behind, and of the little shouting crowd, with the screaming woman on the horse, died behind him as the wind began to boom in his ears. Mary was looking round now, and slightly checking her horse as they neared the bottom of the long village street. In half a dozen strides Anthony came up on her right. Then the pool gleamed before them just beyond the fork of the road.

"Left!" screamed Mary through the roar of the racing air, and turned her horse off up the road that led round in a wide sweep of two miles to East Maskells and the woods beyond, and Anthony followed. He had settled down in the saddle now, and had brought his maddened horse under control; his feet were in the stirrups, but there was no lessening of the speed. They had left the last house now, and on either side the black bushes and heatherland streamed past, with the sudden gleam of water here and there under the starlight that showed the ditches and holes with which the ground on either side of the road was honeycombed.

Then Mary turned her head again, and the words came detached and sharp.

"They are after us—could not help—horses saddled."

Anthony turned his head to release one ear from the roar of the air, and heard the thundering rattle of hoofs in the distance, but even as he listened it grew fainter.

"We are gaining!" he shouted.

Mary nodded, and her teeth gleamed white in a smile.

"Ours are fresh," she screamed.

Then there was silence between them again; they had reached a little hill and eased their horses up it; a heavy fringe of trees crowned it on their right, black against the stars, and a gleam of light showed the presence of a house among them. Farther and farther behind them sounded the hoofs; then they were swaying and rocking again down the slope that led to the long flat piece of road that ended in the slope up to East Maskells. It was softer going now and darker too, as there were trees overhead; pollared willows streamed past them as they went; and twice there was a snort and a hollow thunder of hoofs as a young sleeping horse awoke and raced them a few yards in the meadows at the side. Once Anthony's horse shied at a white post, and drew in front a yard or two; and he heard for a moment under the rattle the cool gush of the stream that flowed beneath the road and the scream of a water-fowl as she burst from the reeds.

A great exultation began to fill Anthony's heart. What a ride this was, in the glorious summer night—reckless and intoxicating! What a contrast, this sweet night air streaming past him, this dear world of living things, his throbbing horse beneath him, the birds and beasts round him, and this gallant girl swaying and rejoicing too beside him! What a contrast was all this to that terrible afternoon, only a few hours away—of suspense and skulking like a rat in a sewer; in a dark, close passage underground breathing death and silence round him! An escape with the fresh air in the face and the glorious galloping music of hoofs is another matter to an escape contrived by holding the breath and fearing to move in a mean hiding-hole. And as all this flooded in upon him, incoherently but overpoweringly, he turned and laughed loud with joy.

They had nearly come to an end of the flat by now. In front of them rose the high black mass of trees where safety lay; somewhere to the right, not a quarter of a mile in front, just off the road, lay East Maskells. They would draw rein, he reflected, when they reached the outer gates, and listen; and if all was quiet behind them, Mary at least should ask for shelter. For himself, perhaps it would be safer to ride on into the woods for the present. He began to move his head as he rode to see if there were any light in the house before him; it seemed dark; but perhaps he could not see the house from here. Gradually his horse slackened a little, as the rise in the ground began, and he tossed the reins once or twice.

Then there was a sharp hiss and blow behind him; his horse snorted and leapt forward, almost unseating him, and then, still snorting with head raised and jerking, dashed at the slope. There was a cry and a loud report; he tugged at the reins, but the horse was beside himself, and he rode fifty yards before he could stop him. Even as he wrenched him into submission another horse with head up and flying stirrup and reins thundered past him and disappeared into the woods beyond the house.

Then, trembling so that he could hardly hold the reins, he urged his horse back again at a stumbling trot towards what he knew lay at the foot of the slope, and to meet the tumult that grew in nearness and intensity up the road along which he had just galloped.

There was a dark group on the pale road in front of him, twenty yards this side of the field-path that led from Stanfield Place; he took his feet from the stirrups as he got near, and in a moment more threw his right leg forward over the saddle and slipped to the ground.

He said no word but pushed away the two men, and knelt by Mary, taking her head on his knee. The men rose and stood looking down at them.

"Mary," he said, "can you hear me?"

He bent close over the white face; her hand rose to her breast, and came away dark. She was shot through the body. Then she pushed him sharply.

"Go," she whispered, "go."

"Mary," he said again, "make your confession—quickly. Stand back, you men."

They obeyed him; and he bent his ear towards the mouth he could so dimly see. There was a sob or two—a long moaning breath—and then the murmur of words, very faint and broken by gulps for breath. He noticed nothing of the hoofs that dashed up the road and stopped abruptly, and of the murmur of voices that grew round him; he only heard the gasping whisper, the words that rose one by one, with pauses and sighs, into his ear....

"Is that all?" he said, and a silence fell on all who stood round, now a complete circle about the priest and the penitent. The pale face moved slightly in assent; he could see the lips were open, and the breath was coming short and agonised.

"... In nomine Patris—his hand rose above her and moved cross-ways in the air—et Filii et Spiritus Sancti. Amen."

Then he bent low again and looked; the bosom was still rising and falling, the shut eyes lifted once and looked at him. Then the lids fell again.

"Benedictio Dei omnipotentis, Patris et Filii et Spiritus sancti, descendat super te et maneat semper. Amen."

Then there fell a silence. A horse blew out its nostrils somewhere behind and stamped; then a man's voice cried brutally:

"Now then, is that popish mummery done yet?"

There was a murmur and stir in the group. But Anthony had risen.

"That is all," he said.

Chapter Thirteen - In Prison

Anthony found several friends in the Clink prison in Southwark, whither he was brought up from Stanfield Place after his arrest.

Life there was very strange, a combination of suffering and extraordinary relaxation. He had a tiny cell, nine feet by five, with one little window high up, and for the first month of his imprisonment wore irons; at the same time his gaoler was so much open to bribery that he always found his door open on Sunday morning, and was able to shuffle upstairs and say mass in the cell of Ralph Emerson, once the companion of Campion, and a lay-brother of the Society of Jesus. There he met a large number of Catholics—some of whom he had come across in his travels—and he even ministered the sacraments to others who managed to come in from the outside. His chief sorrow was that his friend and host had been taken to the Counter in Wood Street.

It was a month before he heard all that had happened on the night of his arrest, and on the previous days: he had been separated at once from his friends; and although he had heard his guards talking both in the hall where he had been kept the rest of the night, and during the long hot ride to London the next day, yet at first he was so bewildered by Mary's death that what they said made little impression on him. But after he had been examined both by magistrates and the Commissioners, and very little evidence was forthcoming, his irons were struck off and he was allowed much more liberty than before; and at last, to his great joy, Isabel was admitted to see him. She herself had come straight up to the Marretts' house, both of whom still lived on in Wharf Street, though old and infirm; and day by day she attempted to get access to her brother; until at last, by dint of bribery, she was successful.

Then she told him the whole story.

"When we left the garden-house," she said, "we went straight back, and Mary found Mr. Graves in the parlour off the hall. Oh, Anthony, how she ordered him about! And how frightened he was of her! The end was that he sent a message to the stables for her horses to be got ready, as she said. I went up with her to help her to make ready, and we kissed one another up there, for, you know, we dared not make as if we said good-bye downstairs. Then we came down for her to mount; and then we saw what we had not known before, that all the stable-yard was filled with the men's horses saddled and bridled. However, we said nothing, except that Mary asked a man what—what the devil he was looking at, when he stared up at her as she stood on the block drawing on her gloves before she mounted. There were one or two torches burning in cressets, and I saw her so plainly turn the corner down towards the church.

"Then I went upstairs again, but I could not go to my room, but stood at the gallery window outside looking down at the court, for I knew that if there was any danger it would come from there.

"Then presently I heard a noise, and a shouting, and a man ran in through the gates to the stable-yard; and, almost directly it seemed, three or four rode out, at full gallop across the court and down by the church. The window was open and I could hear the noise down towards the village. Then more and more came pouring out, and all turned the corner and galloped; all but one, whose horse slipped and came down with a crash. Oh, Anthony! how I prayed!

"Then I saw Mr. Lackington"—Isabel stopped a moment at the name, and then went on again—"and he was on horseback too in the court; but he was shouting to two or three more who were just mounting. 'Across the field—across the field—cut them off!' I could hear it so plainly; and I saw the stable-gate was open, and they went through, and I could hear them galloping on the grass. And then I knew what was happening; and I went back to my room and shut the door."

Isabel stopped again; and Anthony took her hand softly in his own and stroked it. Then she went on.

"Well, I saw them bring you back, from the gallery window—and ran to the top of the stairs and saw you go through into the hall where the magistrates were waiting, and the door was shut; and then I went back to my place at the window—and then presently they brought in Mary. I reached the bottom of the stairs just as they set her down. And I told them to bring her upstairs; and they did, and laid her on the bed where we had sat together all the afternoon.... And I would let no one in: I did it all myself; and then I set the tapers round her, and put the crucifix that was round my neck into her fingers, which I had laid on her breast ... and there she lay on the great bed ... and her face was like a child's, fast asleep—smiling: and then I kissed her again, and whispered, 'Thank you, Mary'; for, though I did not know all, I knew enough, and that it was for you."

Anthony had thrown his arms on the table and his face was buried in them. Isabel put out her hand and stroked his curly head gently as she went on, and told him in the same quiet voice of how Mary had tried to save him by lashing his horse, as she caught sight of the man waiting at the entrance of the field-path, and riding in between him and Anthony. The man had declared in his panic of fear before the magistrates that he had never dreamt of doing Mistress Corbet an injury, but that she had ridden across just as he drew the trigger to shoot the priest's horse and stop him that way.

When Isabel had finished Anthony still lay with his head on his arms.

"Why, Anthony, my darling," she said, "what could be more perfect? How proud I am of you both!"

She told him, too, how they had been tracked to Stanfield—Lackington had let it out in his exultation.

The sailor at Greenhithe was one of his agents—an apostate, like his master. He had recognised that the party consisted of Catholics by Anthony's breaking of the bread. He had been placed there to watch the ferry; and had sent messages at once to Nichol and Lackington. Then the party had been followed, but had been lost sight of, thanks to Anthony's ruse. Nichol had then flung out a cordon along the principal roads that bounded Stanstead Woods on the south; and Lackington, when he arrived a few hours later, had kept them there all night. The cordon consisted of idlers and children picked up at Wrotham; and the tramp who feigned to be asleep had been one of them. When they had passed, he had given the signal to his nearest neighbour, and had followed them up. Nichol was soon at the place, and after them; and had followed to Stanfield with Lackington behind. Then watchers had been set round the house; the magistrates communicated with; and as soon as Hubert and Mr. Graves had arrived the assault had been made. Hubert had not been told who the priest was; but he had leapt at an opportunity to harass Mr. Buxton: he had been given to understand that Anthony and Isabel were still in the north.

"He did not know; indeed he did not," cried Isabel piteously.

At another time, when she had gained admittance to him, she gave him messages from the Marretts, who had kept a great affection for the lad, who had told them tales of College that Christmas time; and she told him too of the coming of an old friend to see her there.

"It was poor Mr. Dent," she said; "he looks so old now. His wife died three years ago; you know he has a city-living and does chaplain's work at the Tower sometimes; and he is coming to see you, Anthony, and talk to you."

Three or four days later he came.

Anthony was greatly touched at his kindness in coming. He looked considerably older than his age; his hair had grown thin and grey about his temples, and the sharp birdlike outline of his face and features seemed blurred and indeterminate. His creed too, and his whole manner of looking at things of faith, seemed to have undergone a similar process. The two had a long talk.

"I am not going to argue with you, Mr. Norris," he said, "though I still think your religion wrong. But I have learnt this at least, that the greatest of all is charity, and if we love the same God, and His Blessed Son, and one another, I think that is best of all. I have learnt that from my wife—my dear wife," he added softly. "I used to hold much with doctrine at one time, and loved to chop arguments; but our Saviour did not, and so I will not."

Anthony was delighted that he took this line, for he knew there are some minds that apparently cannot be loyal to both charity and truth at the same time, and Mr. Dent's seemed to be one of them; so the two talked of old times at Great Keynes, and of the folks there, and at last of Hubert.

"I saw him in the City last week," said Mr. Dent, "and he is a changed man. He looks ten years older than this time last year; I scarcely know what has come to him. I know he has thrown up his magistracy, and the Lindfield parson tells me that the talk is that Mr. Maxwell is going on another voyage, and leaving his wife and children behind him again."

Anthony told him gently of Hubert's share in the events at Stanfield, adding what real and earnest attempts he had made to repair the injury he had done as soon as he had learnt that it was his friend that was in hiding.

"There was no treachery against me, Mr. Dent, you see," he added.

Mr. Dent pecked a little in the air with pursed lips and eyes fixed on the ground; and a vision of the pulpit at Great Keynes moved before Anthony's eyes.

"Yes, yes, yes," he said; "I understand—I quite understand."

Before Mr. Dent took his leave he unburdened himself of what he had really come to say.

"Master Anthony," he said, standing up and fingering his hat round and round, "I said I talked no doctrine now; but I must unsay that; and—you will not think me impertinent if I ask you something?"

"My dear Mr. Dent—" began the other, standing and smiling too.

"Thank you, thank you—I felt sure—then it is this: I do not know much about the Popish religion, though I used to once, and I may be very mistaken; but I would like you to satisfy me before I go on one point"; and he fixed his anxious peering eyes on Anthony's face. "Can you say, Master Anthony, from a full heart, that you fix all your hope and confidence for salvation in Christ's merits alone?"

Anthony smiled frankly in his face.

"Indeed, in none other," he said, "and from a full heart."

"Ah well," and the birdlike face began to beam and twitch, "and—and there is nothing of confidence in yourself and your works—and—and there is no talk of Holy Mary in the matter?"

Anthony smiled again. He wished to avoid useless controversy.

"Briefly," he said, "my belief is that I am a very great sinner, that I deserve eternal hell; but I humbly place all my trust in the Precious Blood of my Saviour, and in that alone. Does that satisfy you?"

Mr. Dent's face was breaking into smiles, and at the end he took the priest's face in his hands and kissed him gently twice on the cheeks.

"Then, my dear boy, I fear nothing for you. May that salvation you hope for be yours." And then without a word he was gone.

Anthony's conscience reproached him a little that he had said nothing of the Church to the minister; but Mr. Dent had been so peremptory about doctrine that it was hard for the younger man to say what he would have wished. He told him, however, plainly on his next visit that he held whole-heartedly too that the Catholic Church was the treasury of Grace that Christ had instituted, and added a little speech about his longing to see his old friend a Catholic too; but Mr. Dent shook his head. The corners of his eyes wrinkled a little, and a shade of his old fretfulness passed over his face.

"Nay, if you talk like that," he said, "I must be gone. I am no theologian. You must let me alone."

He gave him news this time of Mr. Buxton.

"He is in the Counter, as you know," he said, "and is a very bright and cheerful person, it seems to me. Mistress Isabel asked me to see him and give her news of him, for she cannot get admittance. He is in a cell, little and nasty; but he said to me that a Protestant prison was a Papist's pleasaunce—in fact he said it twice. And he asked very eagerly after you and Mistress Isabel. He tried, too, to inveigle me into talk of Peter his prerogative, but I would not have it. It was Lammas Day when I saw him, and he spoke much of it."

Anthony asked whether there was anything said of what punishment Mr. Buxton would suffer.

"Well," said Mr. Dent, "the Lieutenant of the Tower told me that her Grace was so sad at the death of Mistress Corbet that she was determined that no more blood should be shed than was obliged over this matter; and that Mr. Buxton, he thought, would be but deprived of his estates and banished; but I know not how that may be. But we shall soon know."

These weeks of waiting were full of consolation and refreshment to Anthony: the nervous stress of the life of the seminary priest in England, full of apprehension and suspense, crowned, as it had been in his case, by the fierce excitement of the last days of his liberty—all this had strained and distracted his soul, and the peace of the prison life, with the certainty that no efforts of his own could help him now, quieted and strengthened him for the ordeal he foresaw. At this time, too, he used to spend two or three hours a day in meditation, and found the greatest benefit in following the tranquil method of prayer prescribed by Louis de Blois, with whose writings he had made acquaintance at Douai. Each morning, too, he said a "dry mass," and during the whole of his imprisonment at the Clink managed to make his confession at least once a week, and besides his communion at mass on Sundays, communicated occasionally from the Reserved Sacrament, which he was able to keep in a neighbouring cell, unknown to his gaoler. And so the days went by, as orderly as in a Religious House; he rose at a fixed hour, observed the greatest exactness in his devotions, and did his utmost to prevent any visitors being admitted to see him, or any from another cell coming into his own, until he had finished his first meditation and said his office. And there began to fall upon him a kind of mellow peace that rose at times of communion and prayer to a point so ravishing, that he began to understand that it would not be a light cross for which such preparatory graces were necessary.

Towards the middle of September he received intelligence that evidence had been gathering against him, and that one or two were come from Lancashire under guard; and that he would be brought before the Commissioners again immediately.

Within two days this came about. He was sent for across the water to the Tower, and after waiting an hour or two with his gaoler downstairs in the basement of the White Tower, was taken up into the great Hall where the Council sat. There was a table at the farther end where they were sitting, and as Anthony looked round he saw through openings all round in the inner wall the little passage where the sentries walked, and heard their footfalls.

The preliminaries of identification and the like had been disposed of at previous examinations before Mr. Young—a name full of sinister suggestiveness to the Catholics; and so, after he had been given a seat at a little distance from the table behind which the Commissioners sat, he was questioned minutely as to his journey in the North of England.

"What were you there for, Mr. Norris?" inquired the Secretary of the Council.

"I went to see friends, and to do my business."

"Then that resolves itself into two heads: One, Who are your friends. Two, What was your business?"

Now it had been established beyond a doubt at previous examinations that he was a priest; a student of Douai who had apostatised had positively identified him; so Anthony answered boldly:

"My friends were Catholics; and my business was the reconciling of souls to their Creator."

"And to the Pope of Rome," put in Wade.

"Who is Christ's Vicar," continued Anthony.

"And a pestilent knave," concluded a fiery-faced man whom Anthony did not know.

But the Commissioners wanted more than that; it was true that Anthony was already convicted of high treason in having been ordained beyond the seas and in exercising his priestly functions in England; but the exacting of the penalty for religion alone was apt to raise popular resentment; and it was far preferable in the eyes of the authorities to entangle a priest in the political net before killing him. So they passed over for the present his priestly functions and first demanded a list of all the places where he had stayed in the north.

"You ask what is impossible," said Anthony, with his eyes on the ground and his heart beating sharply, for he knew that now peril was near.

"Well," said Wade, "let us put it another way. We know that you were at Speke Hall, Blainscow, and other places. I have a list here," and he tapped the table, "but we want your name to it."

"Let me see the paper," said Anthony.

"Nay, nay, tell us first."

"I cannot sign the paper except I see it," said Anthony, smiling.

"Give it him," said a voice from the end of the table.

"Here then," said Wade unwillingly.

Anthony got up and took the paper from him, and saw one or two places named where he had not been, and saw that it had been drawn up at any rate partly on guesswork.

He put the paper down and went back to his chair and sat down.

"It is not true," he said, looking steadily at the Secretary; "I cannot sign it."

"Do you deny that you have been to any of these places?" inquired Wade indignantly.

"The paper is not true," said Anthony again.

"Well, then, show us what is not true upon it."

"I cannot."

"We will find means to persuade you," said the Secretary.

"If God permits," said Anthony.

Wade glanced round inquiringly and shrugged his shoulders; one or two shook their heads.

"Well, then, we will turn to another point. There are known to have been certain Jesuit priests in Lancashire in November of last year—do you deny that, sir?"

"You ask too much," said Anthony, smiling again; "they may have been there for aught I know, for I certainly did not see them elsewhere at the time you mention."

Wade frowned, but the one at the end laughed loud.

"He has you there, Wade," he said.

"This is foolery," said the Secretary. "Well, these two, Father Edward Oldcorne and Father Holtby were in Lancashire in November; and you, Mr. Norris, spoke with them then. We wish to know where they are now, and you must tell us."

"You have yet to prove that I spoke with them," said Anthony, for the trap was too transparent.

"But we know that."

"That may or may not be; but it is for you to prove it."

"Nay, for you to tell us."

"For you to prove it."

Wade lost his temper.

"Well, then," he cried, "take this paper and see which of us is in the right."

Anthony rose again, wondering what the paper could be, and came towards the table. He saw it bore a name at the end, and as he advanced saw that it had an official appearance. Wade still held it; but Anthony took it in his hand too to steady it, and began to read; but as he read a mist rose before his eyes, and the paper shook violently. It was a warrant to put him to the torture.

Wade laughed a little.

"Why, see, Mr. Norris, how you tremble at the warrant; what will it be when you—"

But a voice murmured "Shame!" and he stopped and stared.

Anthony passed his hand over his eyes and went back to his chair and sat down; he saw his knees trembling as he sat, and hated himself for it; but he cried bravely:

"The flesh is weak, but, please God, the spirit is willing."

"Well, then," said Wade again, "must we execute this warrant, or will you tell us what we would know?"

"You must do what God permits," said Anthony.

Wade sat down, throwing the warrant on the table, and began to talk in a low voice to those who sat next him. Anthony fixed his eyes on the ground, and did his utmost to keep his thoughts steady.

Now he realised where he was, and what it all meant. The little door to the left, behind him, that he had noticed as he came in, was the door of which he had heard other Catholics speak, that led down to the great crypt, where so many before him had screamed and fainted and called on God, from the rack that stood at the foot of the stairs, or from the pillar with the fixed ring at its summit.

He had faced all this in his mind again and again, but it was a different thing to have the horror within arm's length; old phrases he had heard of the torture rang in his mind—a boast of Norton's, the rackmaster, who had racked Brian, and which had been repeated from mouth to mouth—that he had "made Brian a foot longer than God made him"; words of James Maxwell's that he had let drop at Douai; the remembrance of his limp; and of Campion's powerlessness to raise his hand when called upon to swear—all these things crowded on him now; and there seemed to rest on him a crushing swarm of fearful images and words. He made a great effort, and closed his eyes, and repeated the holy name of Jesus over and over again; but the struggle was still fierce when Wade's voice, harsh and dry, broke in and scattered the confusion of mind that bewildered him.

"Take the prisoner to a cell; he is not to go back to the Clink."

Anthony felt a hand on his arm, and the gaoler was looking at him with compassion.

"Come, sir," he said.

Anthony rose feeling heavy and exhausted; but remembered to bow to the Commissioners, one or two of whom returned it. Then he followed the gaoler out into the ante-room, who handed him over to one of the Tower officials.

"I must leave you here, sir," he said; "but keep a good heart; it will not be for to-day."

When Anthony got to his new cell, which was in the Salt Tower, he was bitterly angry and disappointed with himself. Why, he had turned white and sick like a child, not at the pain of the rack, not even at the sight of it, but at the mere warrant! He threw himself on his knees, and bowed down till his head beat against the boards.

"O Lord Jesus," he prayed, "give me of Thy Manhood."

He found that this prison was more rigorous than the Clink; no liberty to leave the cell could possibly be obtained, and no furniture was provided. The gaoler, when he had brought up his dinner, asked whether he could send any message for him for a bed. Anthony gave Isabel's address, knowing that the authorities were already aware that she was a Catholic, and indeed she had given bail to come up for trial if called upon, and that his information could injure neither her nor the Marretts, who were sound Church of England people; and in the afternoon a mattress and some clothes arrived for him.

Anthony noticed at dinner that the knife provided was of a very inconvenient shape, having a round blunt point, and being sharp only at a lower part of the blade; and when the keeper came up with his supper he asked him to bring him another kind. The man looked at him with a queer expression.

"What is the matter?" asked Anthony; "cannot you oblige me?"

The man shook his head.

"They are the knives that are always given to prisoners under warrant for torture."

Anthony did not understand him, and looked at him, puzzled.

"For fear they should do themselves an injury," added the gaoler.

Then the same shudder ran over his body again.

"You mean—you mean...." he began. The gaoler nodded, still looking at him oddly, and went out; and Anthony sat, with his supper untasted, staring before him.

By a kind of violent reaction he had a long happy dream that night. The fierce emotions of that day had swept over his imagination and scoured it as with fire, and now the underlying peace rose up and flooded it with sweetness.

He thought he was in the north again, high up on a moor, walking with one who was quite familiar to him, but whose person he could not remember when he woke; he did not even know whether it was man or woman. It was a perfect autumn day, he thought, like one of those he had spent there last year; the heather and the gorse were in flower, and the air was redolent from their blossoms; he commented on this to the person at his side, who told him it was always so there. Mile after mile the moor rose and dipped, and, although Skiddaw was on his right, purple and grey, yet to his left there was a long curved horizon of sparkling blue sea. It was a cloudless day overhead, and the air seemed kindling and fresh round him as it blew across the stretches of heather from the western sea. He himself felt full of an extraordinary vitality, and the mere movement of his limbs gave him joy as he went swiftly and easily forward over the heather. There was the sound of the wind in his ears, and again and again there came the gush of water from somewhere out of sight—as he had heard it in the church by Skiddaw. There was no house or building of any kind within sight, and he felt a great relief in these miles of heath and the sense of holiday that they gave him. But all the joy round him and in his heart found their point for him in the person that went with him; this presence was their centre, as a diamond in a gold ring, or as a throned figure in a Court circle. All else existed for the sake of this person;—the heather blossomed and the gorse incensed the air, and the sea sparkled, and the sky was blue, and the air kindled, and his own heart warmed and throbbed, for that only. When he tried to see who it was, there was nothing to see; the presence existed there as a centre in a sphere, immeasurable and indiscernible; sometimes he thought it was Mary, sometimes he thought it Henry Buxton, sometimes Isabel—once even he assured himself it was Mistress Margaret, and once James Maxwell—and with the very act of identification came indecision again. This uncertainty waxed into a torment, and yet a sweet torment, as of a lover who watches his mistress' shuttered house; and this torment swelled yet higher and deeper until it was so great that it had absorbed the whole radiant fragrant circle of the hills where he walked; and then came the blinding knowledge that the Presence was all these persons so dear to him, and far more; that every tenderness and grace that he had loved in them—Mary's gallantry and Isabel's serene silence and his friend's fellowship, and the rest—floated in the translucent depths of it, stained and irradiated by it, as motes in a sunbeam.

And then he woke, and it was through tears of pure joy that he saw the rafters overhead, and the great barred door, and the discoloured wall above his bed.

When his gaoler brought him dinner that day it was half an hour earlier than usual; and when Anthony asked him the reason he said that he did not know, but that the orders had run so; but that Mr. Norris might take heart; it was not for the torture, for Mr. Topcliffe, who superintended it, had told the keeper of the rack-house that nothing would be wanted that day.

He had hardly finished dinner when the gaoler came up again and said that the Lieutenant was waiting for him below, and that he must bring his hat and cloak.

Since his arrest he had worn his priest's habit every day, so he now threw the cloak over his arm and took his hat, and followed the gaoler down.

In passing through the court he went by a group of men that were talking together, and he noticed very especially a tall old man with a grey head, in a Court suit with a sword, and very lean about the throat, who looked at him hard as he passed. As he reached the archway where the Lieutenant was waiting, he turned again and saw the sunken eyes of the old man still looking after him; when he turned to the gaoler he saw the same odd look in his face that he had noticed before.

"Why do you look like that?" he asked. "Who is that old man?"

"That is Mr. Topcliffe," said the keeper.

The Lieutenant of the Tower, Sir Richard Barkley, saluted him kindly at the gate, and begged him to follow him; the keeper still came after and another stepped out and joined them, and the group of four together passed out through the Lion's Tower and across the moat to a little doorway where a closed carriage was waiting. The Lieutenant and Anthony stepped inside; the two keepers mounted outside; and the carriage set off.

Then the Lieutenant turned to the priest.

"Do you know where you are going, Mr. Norris?"

"No, sir."

"You are going to Whitehall to see the Queen's Grace."

Chapter Fourteen - An Open Door

When the carriage reached the palace they were told that the Queen was not yet come from Greenwich; and they were shown into a little ante-room next the gallery where the interview was to take place. The Queen, the Lieutenant told Anthony, was to come up that afternoon passing through London, and that she had desired to see him on her way through to Nonsuch; he could not tell him why he was sent for, though he conjectured it was because of Mistress Corbet's death, and that her Grace wished to know the details.

"However," said the Lieutenant, "you now have your opportunity to speak for yourself, and I think you a very fortunate man, Mr. Norris. Few have had such a privilege, though I remember that Mr. Campion had it too, though he made poor use of it."

Anthony said nothing. His mind was throbbing with memories and associations. The air of state and luxury in the corridors through which he had just come, the discreet guarded doors, the servants in the royal liveries standing here and there, the sense of expectancy that mingled with the solemn hush of the palace—all served to bring up the figure of Mary Corbet, whom he had seen so often in these circumstances; and the thought of her made the peril in which he stood and the hope of escape from it seem very secondary matters. He walked to the window presently and looked out upon the little court below, one of the innumerable yards of that vast palace, and stood staring down on the hound that was chained there near one of the entrances, and that yawned and blinked in the autumn sunshine. Even as he looked the dog paused in the middle of his stretch and stood expectant with his ears cocked, a servant dashed bareheaded down a couple of steps and out through the low archway; and simultaneously Anthony heard once more the sweet shrill trumpets that told of the Queen's approach; then there came the roll of drums and the thunder of horses' feet and the noise of wheels; the trumpets sang out again nearer, and the rumbling waxed louder as the Queen's cavalcade, out of sight, passed the entrance of the archway down upon which Anthony looked; and then stilled, and the palace itself began to hum and stir; a door or two banged in the distance, feet ran past the door of the ante-room, and the strain of the trumpets sounded once in the house itself. Then all grew quiet once more, and Anthony turned from the window and sat down again by the Lieutenant.

There was silence for a few minutes. The Lieutenant stroked his beard gently and said a word or two under his breath now and again to Anthony; once or twice there came the swift rustle of a dress outside as a lady hurried past; then the sound of a door opening and shutting; then more silence; then the sound of low talking, and at last the sound of footsteps going slowly up and down the gallery which adjoined the ante-room.

Still the minutes passed, but no summons came. Anthony rose and went to the window again, for, in spite of himself, this waiting told upon him. The dog had gone back to his kennel and was lying with his nose just outside the opening. Anthony wondered vacantly to himself what door it was that he was guarding, and who lived in the rooms that looked out beside it. Then suddenly the door from the gallery opened and a page appeared.

"The Queen's Grace will see Mr. Norris alone."

Anthony went towards him, and the page opened the door wide for him to go through, and then closed it noiselessly behind him, and Anthony was in the presence.

It was with a sudden bewilderment that he recognised he was in the same gallery as that in which he had talked and sat with Mary Corbet. There were the long tapestries hanging opposite him, with the tall three windows dividing them, and the suits of steel armour that he remembered. He even recalled the pattern of the carpet across which Mary Corbet had come forward to meet him, and that still lay before the tall window at the end that looked on to the Tilt-yard. The sun was passing round to the west now, and shone again across the golden haze of the yard through this great window, with the fragments of stained glass at the top. The memory leapt into life even as he stepped out and stood for a moment, dazed in the sunshine, at the door that opened from the ante-room.

But the figure that turned from the window and faced him was not like Mary's. It was the figure of an old woman, who looked tall with her towering head-dress and nodding plume; she was dressed in a great dark red mantle thrown back on her shoulders, and beneath it was a pale yellow dress sown all over with queer devices; on the puffed sleeve of the arm that held the stick was embroidered a great curling snake that shone with gold thread and jewels in the sunlight, and powdered over the skirt were representations of human eyes and other devices, embroidered with dark thread that showed up plainly on the pale ground. So much he saw down one side of the figure on which the light shone; the rest was to his dazzled eyes in dark shadow. He went down on his knees at once before this tremendous figure, seeing the buckled feet that twinkled below the skirt cut short in front, and remained there. There was complete silence for a moment, while he felt the Queen looking at him, and then the voice he remembered, only older and harsher, now said:

"What is all this, Mr. Norris?"

Anthony looked for a moment and saw the Queen's eyes fixed on him; but he said nothing, and looked down again.

"Stand up," said the Queen, not unkindly, "and walk with me."

Anthony stood up at once, and heard the stiff rustle of her dress and the tap of her heels and stick on the polished boards as she came towards him. Then he turned with her down the long gallery.

Until this moment, ever since he had heard that he was to see the Queen, he had felt nervous and miserable; but now this had left him, and he felt at his ease. To be received in this way, in privacy, and to accompany her up and down the gallery as she took her afternoon exercise was less embarrassing than the formal interview he had expected. The two walked the whole length of the gallery without a word, and it was not until they turned and faced the end that looked on to the Tilt-yard that the Queen spoke; and her voice was almost tender.

"I understand that you were with Minnie Corbet when she died," she said.

"She died for me, your Grace," said Anthony.

The Queen looked at him sharply.

"Tell me the tale," she said.

And Anthony told her the whole story of the escape and the ride; speaking too for his friend, Mr. Buxton, and of Mary's affection for him.

"Your Grace," he ended, "it sounds a poor tale of a man that a woman should die for him so; but I can say with truth that with God's grace I would have died a hundred deaths to save her."

The Queen was silent for a good while when the story was over, and Anthony thought that perhaps she could not speak; but he dared not look at her.

Then she spoke very harshly:

"And you, Mr. Norris, why did you not escape?"

"Your Grace would not have done so."

"When I saw that she was dying, I would."

"Not if you had been a priest, your Grace."

"What is that?" asked the Queen, suddenly facing him.

"I am a priest, madam, and she was a Catholic, and my duty was beside her."

"Eh?"

"I shrived her, your Grace, before she died."

"Why! they did not tell me that."

Anthony was silent.

They walked on a few steps, and the Queen stood silent too, looking down upon the Tilt-yard. Then she turned abruptly, and Anthony turned with her, and they began to go up and down again.

"It was gallant of you both," she said shortly. "I love that my people should be of that sort." Then she paused. "Tell me," she went on, "did Mary love me?"

Anthony was silent for a moment.

"The truth, Mr. Norris," she said.

"Mistress Corbet was loyalty itself," he answered.

"Nay, nay, nay, not loyalty but love I asked you of. How did she speak of me?"

"Well, your Grace, Mistress Corbet had a shrewd wit, and she used it freely on friend and foe, but her very sharpness on your Grace, sometimes, showed her love; for she hated to think you otherwise than what she deemed the best."

The Queen stopped full in her walk.

"That is very pleasantly put," she said; "I told Minnie you were a courtier."

Again the two walked on.

"Then she used her tongue on me?"

"Your Grace, I have never met one on whom she did not: but her heart was true."

"I know that, I know that, Mr. Norris. Tell me something she said."

Anthony racked his brains for something not too severe.

"Mistress Corbet once said that the Queen's most disobedient subject was herself."

"Eh?" said Elizabeth, stopping in her walk.

"'Because,' said Mistress Corbet, 'she can never command herself,'" finished Anthony.

The Queen looked at Anthony, puzzled a moment; and then chuckled loudly in her throat.

"The impertinent minx!" she said, "that was when I had clouted her, no doubt."

Again they walked up and down in silence a little while. Anthony began to wonder whether this was all for which the Queen had sent for him. He was astonished at his own self-possession; all the trembling awe with which he had faced the Queen at Greenwich was gone; he had forgotten for the moment even his own peril; and he felt instead even something of pity for this passionate old woman, who had aged so quickly, whose favourites one by one were dropping off, or at the best giving her only an exaggerated and ridiculous devotion, at the absurdity of which all the world laughed. Here was this old creature at his side, surrounded by flatterers and adventurers, advancing through the world in splendid and jewelled raiment, with trumpets blowing before her, and poets singing her praises, and crowds applauding in the streets, and sneering in their own houses at the withered old virgin-Queen who still thought herself a Diana—and all the while this triumphal progress was at the expense of God's Church, her car rolled over the bodies of His servants, and her shrunken, gemmed fingers were red in their blood;—so she advanced, thought Anthony, day by day towards the black truth and the eternal loneliness of the darkness that lies outside the realm where Christ only is King.

Elizabeth broke in suddenly on his thoughts.

"Now," she said, "and what of you, Mr. Norris?"

"I am your Grace's servant," he said.

"I am not so sure of that," said Elizabeth. "If you are my servant, why are you a priest, contrary to my laws?"

"Because I am Christ's servant too, your Grace."

"But Christ's apostle said, 'Obey them that have the rule over you.'"

"In indifferent matters, madam."

The Queen frowned and made a little angry sound.

"I cannot understand you Papists," said the Queen. "What a-God's name do you want? You have liberty of thought and faith; I desire to inquire into no man's private opinions. You may worship Ashtaroth if it please you, in your own hearts; and God looks to the heart, and not to the outer man. There is a Church with bishops like your own, and ministers; there are the old churches to worship in—nay, you may find the old ornaments still in use. We have sacraments as you have; you may seek shrift if you will; nay, in some manner we have the mass—though we do not call it so—but we follow Christ's ordinance in the matter, and you can do no more. We have the Word of God as you have, and we use the same creeds. What more can the rankest Papist ask? Tell me that, Mr. Norris; for I am a-weary of your folk."

The Queen turned and faced him again a moment, and her eyes were peevish and resentful.

Presently she went on again.

"Mr. Campion told me it was the oath that troubled him. He could not take it, he said. I told the fool that I was not Head of the Church as Christ was, but only the supreme governor, as the Act declares, in all spiritual and ecclesiastical things:—I forget how it runs,—but I showed it him, and asked him whether it were not true; and I asked him too how it was that Margaret Roper could take the oath, and so many thousands of persons as full Christian as himself—and he could not answer me."

The Queen was silent again. Then once more she went on indignantly:

"It is yourselves that have brought all this trouble on your heads. See what the Papists have done against me; they have excommunicated me, deposed me—though in spite of it I still sit on the throne; they have sent an Armada against me; they have plotted against me, I know not how many times; and then, when I defend myself and hang a few of the wolves, lo! they are Christ's flock at once for whom he shed His precious blood, and His persecuted lambs, and I am Jezebel straightway and Athaliah and Beelzebub's wife—and I know not what."

The Queen stopped, out of breath, and looked fiercely at Anthony, who said nothing.

"Tell me how you answer that, Mr. Norris?" said the Queen.

"I dare not deal with such great matters," said Anthony, "for your Grace knows well that I am but a poor priest that knows nought of state-craft; but I would like to ask your Highness two questions only. The first is: whether your Grace had aught to complain of in the conduct of your Catholic subjects when the Armada was here; and the second, whether there hath been one actual attempt upon your Grace's life by private persons?"

"That is not to the purpose," said the Queen peevishly.

"It was Catholics who fought against me in the Armada, and it was Catholics who plotted against me at Court."

"Then there is a difference in Catholics, your Grace," said Anthony.

"Ah! I see what you would be at."

"Yes, your Highness; I would rather say, Although they be Catholics they do these things."

There was silence again, which Anthony did not dare to break; and the two walked up the whole length of the gallery without speaking.

"Well, well," said Elizabeth at last, "but this was not why I sent for you. We will speak of yourself now, Mr. Norris. I hope you are not an obstinate fellow. Eh?"

Anthony said nothing, and the Queen went on.

"Now, as I have told you, I judge no man's private opinions. You may believe what you will. Remember that. You may believe what you will; nay, you may practise your religion so long as it is private and unknown to me."

214

Anthony began to wonder what was coming; but he still said nothing as the Queen paused. She stood a moment looking down into the empty Tilt-yard again, and then turned and sat suddenly in a chair that stood beside the window, and put up a jewelled hand to shield her face, with her elbow on the arm, while Anthony stood before her.

"I remember you, Mr. Norris, very well at Greenwich; you spoke up sharply enough, and you looked me in the eyes now and then as I like a man to do; and then Minnie loved you, too. I wish to show you kindness for her sake."

Anthony's heart began to fail him, for he guessed now what was coming and the bitter struggle that lay before him.

"Now, I know well that the Commissioners have had you before them; they are tiresome busybodies. Walsingham started all that and set them a-spying and a-defending of my person and the rest of it; but they are loyal folk, and I suppose they asked you where you had been and with whom you had stayed, and so on?"

"They did, your Grace."

"And you would not tell them, I suppose?"

"I could not, madam; it would have been against justice and charity to do so."

"Well, well, there is no need now, for I mean to take you out of their hands."

A great leap of hope made itself felt in Anthony's heart; he did not know how heavy the apprehension lay on him till this light shone through.

"They will be wrath with me, I know, and will tell me that they cannot defend me if I will not help them; but, when all is said, I am Queen. Now I do not ask you to be a minister of my Church, for that, I think, you would never be; but I think you would like to be near me—is it not so? And I wish you to have some post about the Court; I must see what it is to be."

Anthony's heart began to sink again as he watched the Queen's face as she sat tapping a foot softly and looking on the floor as she talked. Those lines of self-will about the eyes and mouth surely meant something.

Then she looked up, still with her cheek on her right hand.

"You do not thank me, Mr. Norris."

Anthony made a great effort; but he heard his own voice quiver a little.

"I thank your Grace for your kindly intentions toward me, with all my heart."

The Queen seemed satisfied, and looked down again.

"As to the oath, I will not ask you to take it formally, if you will give me an assurance of your loyalty."

"That, your Grace, I give most gladly."

His heart was beating again in great irregular thumps in his throat; he had the sensation of swaying to and fro on the edge of a precipice, now towards safety and now towards death; it was the cruellest pain he had suffered yet. But how was it possible to have some post at Court without relinquishing the exercise of his priesthood? He must think it out; what did the Queen mean?

"And, of course, you will not be able to say mass again; but I shall not hinder your hearing it at the Ambassador's whenever you please."

Ah! it had come; his heart gave a leap and seemed to cease.

"Your Grace must forgive me, but I cannot consent."

There was a dead silence; when Anthony looked up, she was staring at him with the frankest astonishment.

"Did you think, Mr. Norris, you could be at Court and say mass too whenever you wished?" Her voice rang harsh and shrill; her anger was rising.

"I was not sure what your Grace intended for me."

"The fellow is mad," she said, still staring at him. "Oh! take care, take care!"

"Your Grace knows I intend no insolence."

"You mean to say, Mr. Norris, that you will not take a pardon and a post at Court on those terms?"

Anthony bowed; he could not trust himself to speak, so bitter was the reaction.

"But, see man, you fool; if you die as a traitor you will never say mass again either."

"But that will not be with my consent, your Grace."

"And you refuse the pardon?"

"On those terms, your Grace, I must."

"Well—" and she was silent a moment, "you are a fool, sir."

Anthony bowed again.

"But I like courage.—Well, then, you will not be my servant?"

"I have ever been that, your Grace; and ever will be."

"Well, well,—but not at Court?"

"Ah! your Grace knows I cannot," cried Anthony, and his voice rang sorrowfully.

Again there was silence.

"You must have your way, sir, for poor Minnie's sake; but it passes my understanding what you mean by it. And let me tell you that not many have their way with me, rather than mine."

Again hope leapt up in his heart. The Queen then was not so ungracious.

He looked up and smiled—and down again.

"Why, the man's lips are all a-quiver. What ails him?"

"It is your Grace's kindness."

"I must say I marvel at it myself," observed Elizabeth. "You near angered me just now; take care you do not so quite."

"I would not willingly, as your Grace knows."

"Then we will end this matter. You give me your assurance of loyalty to my person."

"With all my heart, madam," said Anthony eagerly.

"Then you must get to France within the week. The other too—Buxton—he loses his estate, but has his life. I am doing much for Minnie's sake."

"How can I thank your Grace?"

"And I will cause Sir Richard to give it out that you have taken the oath. Call him in."

There was a quick gasp from the priest; and then he cried with agony in his voice:

"I cannot, your Grace, I cannot."

"Cannot call Sir Richard! Why, you are mad, sir!"

"Cannot consent; I have taken no oath."

"I know you have not. I do not ask it."

Elizabeth's voice came short and harsh; her patience was vanishing, and Anthony knew it and looked at her. She had dropped her hand, and it was clenching and unclenching on her knee. Her stick slipped on the polished boards and fell; but she paid it no attention. She was looking straight at the priest; her high eyebrows were coming down; her mouth was beginning to mumble a little; he could see in the clear sunlight that fell on her sideways through the tall window a thousand little wrinkles, and all seemed alive; the lines at the corners of her eyes and mouth deepened as he watched.

"What a-Christ's name do you want, sir?"

It was like the first mutter of a storm on the horizon; but Anthony knew it must break. He did not answer.

"Tell me, sir; what is it now?"

Anthony drew a long breath and braced his will, but even as he spoke he knew he was pronouncing his own sentence.

"I cannot consent to leave the country and let it be given out that I had taken the oath, your Grace. It would be an apostasy from my faith."

Elizabeth sprang to her feet without her stick, took one step forward, and gave Anthony a fierce blow on the cheek with her ringed hand. He recoiled a step at the shock of it, and stood waiting with his eyes on the ground. Then the Queen's anger poured out in words. Her eyes burned with passion out of an ivory-coloured face, and her voice rang high and harsh, and her hands continually clenched and unclenched as she screamed at him.

"God's Body! you are the ungratefullest hound that ever drew breath. I send for you to my presence, and talk and walk with you like a friend. I offer you a pardon and you fling it in my face. I offer you a post at Court and you mock it; you flaunt you in your treasonable livery in my very face, and laugh at my clemency. You think I am no Queen, but a weak woman whom you can turn and rule at your will. God's Son! I will show you which is sovereign. Call Sir Richard in, sir; I will have him in this instant. Sir Richard, Sir Richard!" she screamed, stamping with fury.

The door into the ante-room behind opened, and Sir Richard Barkley appeared, with a face full of apprehension. He knelt at once.

"Stand up, Sir Richard," she cried, "and look at this man. You know him, do you not? and I know him now, the insolent dog! But his own mother shall not in a week. Look at him shaking there, the knave; he will shake more before I have done with him. Take him back with you, Sir Richard, and let them have their will of him. His damned pride and insolence shall be broken. S' Body, I have never been so treated! Take him out, Sir Richard, take him out, I tell you!"

Chapter Fifteen - The Rolling of the Stone

It was a week later, and a little before dawn, that Isabel was kneeling by Anthony's bed in his room in the Tower.

The Lieutenant had sent for her to his lodging the evening before, and she had spent the whole night with her brother. He had been racked four times in one week, and was dying.

The city and the prison were very quiet now; the carts had not yet begun to roll over the cobble-stones and the last night-wanderers had gone home. He lay, on the mattress that she had sent in to him, in the corner of his cell under the window, on his back and very still, covered from chin to feet with her own fur-lined cloak that she had thrown over him; his head was on a low pillow, for he could not bear to lie high; his feet made a little mound under the coverlet, and his arms lay straight at his side; but all that could be seen of him was his face, pinched and white now with hollows in his cheeks and dark patches and lines beneath his closed eyes, and his soft pointed brown beard that just rested on the fur edging of Isabel's cloak; his lips were drawn tight, but slightly parted, showing the rim of his white teeth, as if he snarled with pain.

The only furniture in the room was a single table and chair; the table was drawn up not far from the bed, and a book or two, with a flask of cordial and some fragments of food on a plate lay upon it; his cloak and doublet and ruff lay across the chair and his shoes below it, and a little linen lay in a pile in another corner; but the clothes in which he had been tortured the evening before, his shirt and hose, could not be taken off him and he lay in them still. They had been so soaked with sweat, that Isabel had found him shivering, and laid her cloak over him, and now he lay quiet and warm.

Earlier in the night she had been reading to him, and a taper still burned in a candlestick on the table; but for the last two hours he had lain either in a sleep or a swoon, and she had laid the book down and was watching him.

He was so motionless that he would have seemed dead except for the steady rise and fall of a fold in the mantle, and for a sudden muscular twitch every few minutes. Isabel herself was scarcely less motionless; her face was clear and pale as it always was, but perfectly serene, and even her lips did not quiver. She was kneeling and leaning back now, and her hands were clasped in her lap. There was a proud content in her face; her dear brother had not uttered one name on the rack except those of the Saviour and of the Blessed Mother. So the Lieutenant had told her.

Suddenly his eyes opened and there was nothing but peace in them; and his lips moved. Isabel leaned forward on her hands and bent her ear to his mouth till his breath was warm on it, and she could hear the whisper....

Then she opened the book that lay face down on the table and began to read on, from the point at which she had laid it down two hours before.

"'Erat autem hora tertia: et crucifixerunt eum. And it was the third hour and they crucified him ... And with him they crucify two thieves, the one on his right hand, and the other on his left. And the scripture was fulfilled which saith, And he was numbered with the transgressors.'"

Her voice was slow and steady as she read the unfamiliar Latin, still kneeling, with the book a little raised to catch the candlelight, and her grave tranquil eyes bent upon it. Only once did her voice falter, and then she commanded it again immediately; and that, as she read "Erant autem et mulieres de longe aspicientes." "There were also women looking on afar off."

And so the tale crept on, minute by minute, and the priest lay with closed eyes to hear it; until the mocking was complete, and the darkness of the sixth hour had come and gone, and the Saviour had cried aloud on His Father, and given up the ghost; and the centurion that stood by had borne witness. And the great Criminal slept in the garden, in the sepulchre "wherein was never man yet laid."

There was a listening silence as the voice ceased without another falter. Isabel laid the book down and looked at him again; and his eyes opened languidly.

He had not yet said more than single words, and even now his voice was so faint that she had to put her ear close to his mouth. It seemed to her that his soul had gone into some inner secret chamber of profound peace, so deep that it was a long and difficult task to send a thought to the surface through his lips.

She could just hear him, and she answered clearly and slowly as to a dazed child, pausing between every word.

"I cannot get a priest; it is not allowed."

Still his eyes bent on her; what was it he said? what was it?...

Then she heard, and began to repeat short acts of contrition clearly and distinctly, pausing between the phrases, in English, and his eyes closed as she began:

"O my Jesus—I am heartily sorry—that I have—crucified thee—by my sins—Wash my soul—in Thy Precious Blood. O my God—I am sorry—that I have—displeased Thee—because thou art All-good. I hate all the sins—that I have done—against Thy Divine Majesty."

And so phrase after phrase she went on, giving him time to hear and to make an inner assent of the will; and repeating also other short vocal prayers that she knew by heart. And so the delicate skein of prayer rose from the altar where this morning sacrifice lay before God, waiting the consummation of His acceptance.

Presently she ended, and he lay again with closed eyes and mute face. Then again they opened, and she bent down to listen....

"It will all be well with me," she answered, raising her head again. "Mistress Margaret has written from Brussels. I shall go there for a while.... Yes, Mr. Buxton will take me; next week: he goes to Normandy, to his estate."

Again his lips moved and she listened....

A faint flush came over her face. She shook her head.

"I do not know; I think not. I hope to enter Religion.... No, I have not yet determined.... The Dower House?... Yes, I will sell it.... Yes, to Hubert, if he wishes it."

Every word he whispered was such an effort that she had to pause again and again before he could make her understand; and often she judged more by the movement of his lips than by any sound that came from him. Now and then too she lifted her handkerchief, soaked in a strong violet scent, and passed it over his forehead and lips. She motioned with the flask of cordial once or twice, but his eyes closed for a negative.

As she knelt and watched him, her thoughts circled continually in little flights; to the walled garden of the Dower House in sunshine, and Anthony running across it in his brown suit, with the wallflowers behind him against the old red bricks and ivy, and the tall chestnut rising behind; to the wind-swept hills, with the thistles and the golden-rod, and the hazel thickets, and Anthony on his pony, sunburnt and voluble, hawk on wrist, with a light in his eyes; to the warm panelled hall in winter, with the tapers on the round table, and Anthony flat on his face, with his feet in the air before the hearth, that glowed and roared up the wide chimney behind, and his chin on his hands, and a book open before him; or, farther back even still, to Anthony's little room at the top of the house, his clothes on a chair, and the boy himself sitting up in bed with his arms round his knees as she came in to wish him good-night and talk to him a minute or two. And every time the circling thought came home and settled again on the sight of that still straight figure lying on the mattress, against the discoloured bricks, with the light of the taper glimmering on his thin face and brown hair and beard; and every time her heart consented that this was the best of all.

A bird chirped suddenly from some hole in the Tower, once, and then three or four times; she glanced up at the window and the light of dawn was beginning. Then, as the minutes went by, the city began to stir itself from sleep. There came a hollow whine from the Lion-gate fifty yards away; up from the river came the shout of a waterman; two or three times a late cock crew; and still the light crept on and broadened. But Anthony still lay with his eyes closed.

At last over the cobbles outside a cart rattled, turned a corner and was silent. Anthony had opened his eyes now and was looking at her again; and again she bent down to listen; ... and then opened and read again.

"'Et cum transisset sabbatum Maria Magdalene et Maria Jacobi et Salome emerunt aromata, ut venientes ungerent Jesum.'

"'And when the Sabbath was past, Mary Magdalene and Mary the mother of James and Salome, had bought sweet spices that they might come and anoint him.'"

A slight sound made her look up. Anthony's eyes were kindling and his lips moved; she bent again and listened.... What was it he said?...

Yes, it was so, and she smiled and nodded at him: she was reading the Gospel for Easter Day, the Gospel of the first mass that they had heard together on that spring morning at Great Keynes, when their Lord had led them so far round by separate paths to meet one another at His altar. And now they were met again here. She read on:

"'Et valde mane una sabbatorum, veniunt ad monumentum, orto jam sole.'

"'Very early they came unto the sepulchre at the rising of the sun; and they said among themselves, Who shall roll us away the stone from the door of the sepulchre? And when they looked, they saw that the stone was rolled away, for it was very great.'...

"'... magnus valde,'" read Isabel; and looked up again;—and then closed the book. There was no need to read more.

She walked across the court half an hour later, just as the sun came up; and passed out through the Lieutenant's lodging, and out by the narrow bridge on to the Tower wharf.

To the left and behind her, as she looked eastwards down the river, lay the heavy masses of the prison she had left, and the high walls and turrets were gilded with glory. The broad river itself was one rolling glory too; the tide was coming in swift and strong and a barge or two moved upwards, only half seen in the bewildering path of the sun. The air was cool and keen, and a breeze from the water stirred Isabel's hair as she stood looking, with the light on her face. It was a cloudless October morning overhead. Even as she stood a flock of pigeons streamed across from the south side, swift-flying and bathed in light; and her eyes followed them a moment or two.

As she stood there silent, a step came up the wharf from the direction of St. Katharine's street, and a man came walking quickly towards her. He did not see who she was until he was close, and then he started and took off his hat; it was Lackington on his way to some business at the Tower; but she did not seem to see him. She turned almost immediately and began to walk westwards, and the glory in her eyes was supreme. And as she went the day deepened above her.